Suffer The Children

Suffer The Children

Dave Gleason

DL Gleason

Foreword

My father, David Monroe Gleason was the greatest man I have ever known. The love and guidance he provided to me and my four siblings shaped our lives and, in my mind, we could not have had a better role model as a father. Unfortunately, not every child experiences love like this. This principle is what I believe was the impetus for my father when he began to write this book.

Our childhood was full of laughter. Dad had a way with humor and everyone that knew him adored him. He loved the outdoors and taught us how to fish, which was my first love. I still love to fish. He taught us about music and how to play the guitar, drums and encouraged us to play other instruments he didn't know how to play. He made us watch educational T.V. for an hour a week with him and took us to Civil War battlefields on vacations. Almost every summer we went on a family vacation: Florida, the Badlands, Washington D.C., Colorado, North Carolina, New York City, Winter Park, CO and Niagara Falls are a few places we went. He lived for his family and his children. He never missed a chance to spend time with us. He coached our sports, attended every game or wrestling match we had and by the way, filmed it all. We have hundreds of hours of film that he took of us over the years and before he died, he archived it all to DVD. He read the Great Illustrated Classics to us like Moby Dick, Tom Sawyer and The Hunchback of Notre Dame and recorded them so we could listen to them at night. He helped us with our projects and challenged us. We played chess for fun at night. He was a safety Nazi and came down hard on us when we were unsafe. He was firm, but loving. He understood the preciousness of life and tried to squeeze every ounce of love and joy out of it.

He was taken way too early from us. David Monroe Gleason, Dave, was born January 5, 1952 and died on May 9th, 2005 in a tragic school bus accident in Liberty, MO while stopped at a stoplight. He was an attorney who owned his own firm and was on his way to a court proceeding that had actually been cancelled. Someone failed to get him the message. Over 50 kids were on that bus that hit him and another man. We sat through 8 weeks of court after 8 years had passed and expert witnesses claimed those two vehicles saved the lives of those children. The bus essentially rode the vehicles over an embankment and took the brunt of the force. Sadly, a few children were still seriously injured, but without those two men, the death toll would have been catastrophic. In a way, they gave their lives for these children. This book, eerily and ironically, deals with individuals faced with the peril of children in danger and the moral dilemma of whether or not they should put their lives on the line for them.

We will never know what happened on that day in May in 2005 and the court system shockingly surmised that the bus driver, who had a squeaky clean record, just forgot which pedal was the break and which one was the gas, even though there was substantial evidence that the brake components on the bus were carelessly maintained through ill-advised instructions from the manufacturers and a slew of evidence that I will spare you, (8 weeks' worth). So, two children, a quadriplegic and another with serious brain damage, and my family, (the other man's case was not a part of this trial), were left without any compensation for our losses from the manufacturers and distributors of the bus. I can't whine or complain. That's the court system, but the injustice done is part of the reason why I was so propelled to finish this book. I wanted his name, his legacy, his death to have more meaning than just a senseless, random act of nothingness that took his life.

I often think of the events that morning that led up to him sitting in that exact spot. He could have slept in one minute later, changed lanes back in Gladstone, sped through a red light or stopped at a yellow, put his pants on differently, forgot his keys in the house, answered or not answered a phone call that rang in his office, but where do you stop? All the events that happened in his life led him to that spot. Going to law school, getting married, having children… but he wouldn't have changed any of that. Sometimes I wish I had kept him up later the night before. In another eerie and ironic twist, we watched the movie "Finding Neverland". Okay, alone that may just be a coincidence, but together with all the other components, it begs the question: *Did Dave know, consciously or subconsciously, his fate? If so, did he willingly lead himself to that point?* Another thing that happened was that in my room, before he hugged me and told me he loved me for the last time, I asked him for some good guitar blues songs and he wrote: "Going Home" by Ten Years After. I mean that could have possibly been the very last thing he wrote! Was he telling me a message? The other song was "Catfish" by Taste, which is a song about a man singing about how he wishes he was a catfish, swimming in the deep blue sea. Again, a stretch, but could easily fit into the reincarnation theme.

And then there was the photo he posted in his office of me in my state finals match in on a shot. I lost that match by one point at the very end, but in that moment, it looked like I was going to win. He wrote, "One-minute left" on the picture. What was he motivating himself to do? I know he was proud of me and how I handled that loss, but why post that in his office? Did the "one minute" symbolize the short amount of time he had left on the planet? Was he reminding himself of this? And if so, why? To make sure he left everything in good order? Like the massive video archives that he preserved? Or the book he was creating? Or to remind himself to enjoy the time he had left? Or how about how one of the main characters in his book was named Lana? That was the name of the wife of the other man who was involved in the bus accident. Oh, and by the way, that man's advertising literature was found on my Dad's desk even though they had never met and didn't know of each other as far as anyone knew.

Why I am I doing this? Why am I telling you these details? It's because it is a part of the story. This book is way more than a book. The whole story is unbelievable. It takes two incidents that almost everyone I've ever talked to in Kansas City knows about and ties them together. Most people remember Precious Doe and the "Bus accident". The philosophical implications regarding life and death are mind-boggling. Do I think my dad was psychic? No, honestly, I don't. I think he was a normal man who loved his family. But some of the things previously mentioned are just straight up weird, especially in the light of the plot of the book, which revolves around psychic connections between children and their subjects.

One other thing I will mention is the picture collage Dad made that he had in his dashboard when he died that I now carry in my truck. It was pictures of me throughout my life and one big picture of him standing in front of a whiteboard at one of our Gleason Video Productions meetings. I stayed home and went to William Jewell College so we could do the video production business together, in fact I had finished my last day of my freshman year the Friday before the Monday accident when I woke up to see the horrid images of a mangled black truck on the side of the road from the view of a helicopter. On the whiteboard was a pyramid and on the pyramid was the building blocks of projects we would complete, (i.e. sports videos, weddings, commercials, documentaries) so we could make it to the very top: Hollywood movies. He had this collage in his truck to motivate him I'm guessing. He knew I stayed close to home for this reason and I could have gone somewhere and played sports, but I didn't. He wanted the business to be successful. He had pictures of his other children in the vehicle as well and just for the record, I have to say this, he loved us all equally. But this specific collage of me and the Hollywood movie at the top, gave me even more of a deep conviction to finish his work. Maybe in doing so, I could complete his dream. Our dream. Maybe this book could be made into a movie one day. It's going to take the help of the readers to spread the word though, so I deeply thank you for reading our story.

Now that I've given you some background on Dave, here is some background on what motivated Dad to write the book. I see it only fitting to explain the back-story. In April of 2001, a little girl was found in the woods off Kensington Street in Kansas City, MO. Her body was found in a trash bag and a few days later, her head was found in another trash bag. The little girl's identity was unknown and she affectionately became known as "Precious Doe". The way in which her body was treated and the fact that no one came forward to claim her shocked the city and sent ripples throughout the nation. The little girl's identity finally became known in May of 2005, (another ironic twist as it was four days before my father's accident) and it became clear why she was unknown for so long. If you don't know, I won't tell as it becomes a part of the plot of the book, but how such evil could exist shocked my father and inspired him to write this novel.

We had so much time left to spend with Dad. He never will get to know my three beautiful children, my wife or his other grandchildren. He wasn't there for my wedding and he won't be there when I become a Grandpa, but his legacy lives on through all of us. I had conversations with him regarding this book before he died, but the dots weren't connected. He had given me bits and pieces and written chapters all over the place, but I had to connect the hard dots and try to give the readers an experience that was unpredictable, yet believable. Hopefully I was able to do that and give my father's work the justice it is due. I spent thousands of hours over more than a decade to complete it, building it slowly as things happened to me in my life that helped shape the writing I contributed. I sincerely hope you enjoy reading it.

Chapter 1

On a Sunday morning in August 2002, it was stormy. As the clouds declared war on the sky and thunder blasted through the atmosphere, Lynn and Dusty lay cozily under the covers. While the dark clouds dominated the sky, another dark and ominous fog rolled into the subconscious activities of Lynn's mind. It was 8:05 am. They were sleeping in because, well, it was Sunday. Suddenly without warning, Lynn shot up from her slumber sobbing uncontrollably.

"No! No! Please God tell me this isn't real," she shouted as she covered her head with the sheets. Dusty arose immediately, disturbed by the commotion. He struggled to open his eyes as the sun shone through the window, but his hands searched for Lynn's body to comfort her.

"What's the matter? Are you okay? Jesus you scared the crap out of me!" Dusty's eyes were finally open wide enough to read the clock. He thought to himself, "Is it really past 8?" He never slept in. His attention quickly returned to the horrified screams of Lynn. "Lynn, are you okay babe? What happened?"

Lynn's voice was trembling, but she was able to finally spit out, "I think I'm seeing another child, Dusty!" She temporarily lost control and thrashed her pillow about. Dusty's stomach dropped. He began to feel as if he were falling off a cliff. His senses were overwhelmed with grief, fear, confusion—he was terrified of losing her. She had recently become convinced that dying was the only way to catch the killers. Dusty thought this might be a possibility himself, but he never told this to Lynn. He kept

1

telling her there was another way. In either scenario, he knew that seeing another child might push her over the proverbial edge of a suicidal cliff.

Dusty could not think of anything to say. Images of a dying Lynn flooded his mind: slit wrists, blood covering the walls, a gunshot to the head, a bottle of pills, a running car in a garage... he didn't want to but he couldn't stop thinking about losing her. His whole life, he never cared for anything as much as he did for Lynn and he was afraid it was too good to be true. He knew how frail she was already—how sensitive she was to the lives of those little children. She had 7 nieces and nephews and loved every one of them like they were her own. Kids were her soft spot.

"Was it a boy? A girl? What did he look like?"

"Dusty! What in the hell am I going to do? I can't live like this... I have seven nieces and nephews! These kids are someone else's nieces and nephews," tears were still flooding from her red-rimmed eyes. There weren't many times in Dusty's life when he didn't know how to handle a situation. He had a silver tongue. He talked his way out of trouble, swooned females, comforted friends, persuaded juries and astounded judges his whole life. But right here, in this moment, amidst the near mental breakdown of what could be the love of his life, he was speechless. "I have to do it!"

Dusty, in shock of what she could have meant, incredulously asked, "Do what?"

"Kill myself. I have to. I can't just sit on standby while more kids die!"

"Lynn, no. You can't. That's not... no! There has to be another way. Don't even talk like that, please."

"How Dusty? Wait for the murderer to turn himself in while I see more and more children? Yeah that sounds like a good plan."

"You are strong Lynn! I need you. I need you to help me solve this riddle because everyone killing themselves off isn't the answer! Because there is an answer Lynn."

"Well maybe it is. If I do it and the killer is caught, there is no denying it works. You know that."

"And so, what, you think by committing suicide and proving it works, everyone else will follow suit?"

"Yeah. I do actually. I think the people in our group would do anything to save the lives of children and put the souls of their dreamers to rest. Wouldn't you, Dusty?"

This question hit him like a ton of bricks, "I, of course I would, but…"

"But what? You aren't seeing multiple kids?" Dusty felt entrapped.

"No, that's not what I meant." She guessed right. That was the thought that entered his brain, but he didn't want to say it. It would only validate her reason for wanting to kill herself, and that's the last thing he wanted to do. "I just meant that I'm not ready to give up. I have you. I want to spend a long life together with you babe. That's all I want. I don't want to give up."

Well that's sweet Dusty, it really is, but this is above even love. If we are soul mates, then we'll find each other again on some plane of existence."

"Lynn! Please, fucking stop! You are not killing yourself and neither am I! You are just upset. I know how bad this hurts you. I do, but please, I'm begging you, don't give up yet. Just give me a little more time. Please! I'm begging you." Dusty wasn't crying, but he was very visibly emotional and distraught.

"How long? How long Dusty? Until I see another kid? Is that enough? Wait until another kid dies to the hands of some sadistic, sick, mental bastard?"

"I… I don't know. No. Of course I don't want that. I mean, you just started seeing a second one, that doesn't mean it just happened. Maybe it happened a long time ago and she just couldn't come to you yet, kind of like Bruce. It wasn't like another kid died and BAM, he started seeing it. Those kids had been dead before he started seeing any of them."

"Well, maybe, but…" Lynn's voice trailed off. She put her hands in her face. She moped for a moment, and then threw her arms around Dusty. "Dusty…" she continued to sob. "I don't know what to do." Dusty stroked the back of her head. A tear rolled down his cheek.

"Lynn, trust me. Please trust me. Give me some more time. Please."

"I can't. I just, I just can't let this go."

"What if I make a deal? What if…" Dusty's mind was racing, trying to find something that might work, "what if we do it together? If one of us sees another child, doesn't matter who, we do it together?" Dusty started to feel like a sick, demented, cult driven, desperate person, but he had to stretch it to have a chance to live a life with her.

3

Now Lynn started to actually *think* about Dusty dying, which made the idea of her dying more real, which made her sick. To seriously consider ending this life, the one she was living, created a sort of existential crisis within her. When it was just her dying in this picture, she was somewhat okay, but now to think about Dusty, that really upset her. "We can't both do it together. What if it doesn't work?"

"I don't care. If you do it, I'm doing it. I'm not living without you." He had hit her soft spot.

"Dusty! That's not fair! You can't take that from me."

"I'm sorry. That's the deal."

Lynn thought on this proposal a moment. She pictured her and Dusty's children running around in a field, laughing, singing and playing with Dusty. Her heart melted and started to transform from darkness to light for a brief instant. She didn't want to die. She really didn't. She wanted to live a life with Dusty too. "Okay."

"Please promise me you won't kill yourself," he pleaded pitifully with his eyes.

"Okay. I promise."

Dusty breathed a deep sigh of relief. He had dodged the bullet momentarily.

Now I have to find my little girl's killer. It's not an option. I will find him. Then I will know how to help Lynn. I gotta get going, like now!

They both were motionless on the bed. Lynn buried her head into the pillow as Dusty stared off into space, caressing her back. He stared into the black hole on the bedroom wall that was attempting to suck all the positive thoughts from his brain and deprive him of any capacity to comfort Lynn. He knew though, deep down, that there was nothing he could do to take her pain away. Nothing.

There wasn't a thing in the world that could have happened that day to help the case for the suffering children—past, future, or present—more than Lynn seeing another child. Dusty was now motivated by love and nothing was going to stop him.

Chapter 2

Two years prior

The little black girl was back. She had first appeared to Dusty in a dream last night. It was so disturbing that he thought about it all the next day. He didn't think he had ever seen her before, but he racked his brain to try and think of a reason why he would be dreaming of a little black girl. He didn't even know any black children. She seemed to be about six years old. Her frame was frail and her hair was in tiny corn rows braided to her shoulders. Her eyes were big and round, dominating her face and full of fear. They pled for help.

Tonight, the dream was the same as the night before. Everything was pitch-black, except for the little girl. She wore pink overalls. She looked impoverished. Her arms and legs were skinny and she didn't look well fed. Her skin was tight around her face, but she was a beautiful child . . . angelic and innocent looking. He saw no blemishes or scars, yet he sensed that this precious, tiny urchin had come to him from a place of terror, trauma and suffering. Her eyes were crying, but there were no tears, only a mist in her dark, doe shaped eyes. Her lips were moving frantically. Her arms reached out desperately to grasp him, yet she was just beyond his fingertips. This dream was the most vivid dream Dusty had ever had.

It was not an exact replay of the night before, but she had definitely come to him again, dressed the same and beckoning the same. It terrified him. It ripped at his guts. This little black girl was trying to tell him something. She needed him. She was frantically trying to make him understand something, but there was an invisible, impenetrable veil that kept them from touching or hearing each other.

He cried out, "Who are you? What can I do?" His voice was muffled and echoed like he was in a deep, dark cave. She could see him . . . he knew it, but all she could do was reach for him. Her mouth was moving, but he could not read her lips. All she seemed to be doing was moaning. It reminded him of a horrifying painting he saw as a child, *The Silent Scream*. Her mouth opened wide for a few seconds and then shut, repeating this motion over and over again.

The dream would not end, no matter how hard he tried. She was drowning in a pool of some indiscernible terror . . . "Can you say something . . . tell me what I can do! Let me read your lips," he pleaded. "Can you use your hands? Make letters . . . show me some kind of sign. Are you in trouble? Are you a real person? If you can hear me, close your eyes. Can you see me? Can you clap your hands? Is there anything you can do to let me know you hear me?" It seemed to last for hours. He watched, helpless, as she reached for him and wailed silently.

His eyes popped open. He was awake . . . bathed in sweat, heart pounding. The dream was over . . . she was gone. He snapped his head to his left to look at the alarm clock—6:00 a.m. A second later, the alarm went off, just like the night before.

Chapter 3

T he courtroom was full of people, mostly lawyers. It was what they call a motion docket. The morning is set aside for the judge to review motions filed by attorneys for various reasons: to make the other side turn over evidence, keep the other side from getting evidence, get trial dates set, get a trial date changed, etc. The judge would allow 15 minutes for each matter. In some cases, the attorneys would present statutes or prior legal decisions to the judge to persuade the judge to decide in their favor.

Judge Ralston presided in Division I of the Cook County Illinois Circuit Court. He got all the big civil cases - personal injuries, employment discrimination and corporate litigation - just about anything in which one party was suing another party for millions of dollars. The Honorable James D. Ralston was 64, had rugged chiseled features, was clean-shaven and had a head full of thick, silver hair. He was a big man. He'd played tackle on the Harvard football team in the late 1940's. He wore no glasses; his eyesight was still as sharp as his intellect. His thick, gravelly voice filled the courtroom.

"Perez v. Hilliard."

The first case was called and two attorneys approached the bench to discuss a motion filed for one attorney to give him additional time to turn evidence over to the other attorney. The judge's clerk sat to the judge's left. She had a stack of about 20 files in front of her. She handed "Perez v. Hilliard" to the Judge. To the right of his Honor sat a court reporter typing every word that was spoken at the bench. A waist high rail with a swinging door separated the attorneys from the spectators. There were about 25 to 30 attorneys seated inside the rail, some were seated in the jury box, waiting silently. No talking was allowed. There were six rows of church pews divided by a wide center aisle for the spectators. The pews were about half full.

A middle aged, portly lady in a wheelchair sat in an area reserved at the back of the courtroom for the handicapped. Somewhere in that stack was Johnston v. Hampton—Dusty's biggest case to date. Dusty represented Hampton, a landlord who was being sued by a tenant who had fallen on the front steps due to rotting wood. The woman, an elementary school cook, suffered a spinal injury, which left her paralyzed from the waist down. Florence Johnston was the lady in the wheelchair at the back of the courtroom. She was accompanied by her only child, a daughter, who taught 4th grade at the elementary school where her mother worked. Florence had lost her husband to liver cancer four years earlier.

Technically, Dusty represented All American Insurance Company. They carried the liability policy for the landlord, but the insurance company was never named in the lawsuit. The fact that the landlord has insurance can't even be mentioned to the jury. This was one of the rules of law that had been passed down through the ages to prevent "undue prejudice" to the defendant, the person being sued. The law assumes that if a jury knows the defendant has insurance, the jury would likely give the plaintiff a verdict every time. If the word "insurance" is even mentioned, a mistrial is called. Dusty didn't mind the rule because he usually defended the insurance companies, but it did seem to show a lack of faith in the jury system: *The mighty lawmakers patronizing the lowly commoners who are not smart enough to handle something so complex as the truth.*

What's ironic about the situation is that most jurors know that an insurance company is involved in one way or another. Most people, even in the lower class, carry at least liability insurance to protect their assets in case something drastic happens and they are sued. Despite of this, juries still often find in favor of the defendant, even though in the backs of their minds they know that if a judgment is awarded the insurance company will be paying the bill. Doctors win their lawsuits 70 percent of the time and they have the most insurance of all.

But none of this mattered to Dusty today; he was going to win this case before it even got to a jury. He had filed a Motion for Summary Judgment against the plaintiff, Mrs. Johnston. It is an attempt to get a case dismissed by the Judge on the spot. An MSJ is actually filed by an attorney in most cases, even if the attorney doesn't have strong relevant basis. It is one of the many tactics attorneys have available to them to try to leverage the law to reach a favorable outcome for their client. It simply says: *Even if the other side proves everything they say, we win anyway because there is no remedy that is provided by law.* In other words, if you and your neighbor stayed out by the pool all day and you got sunburned real bad and had to go to the hospital and ended up getting an infection and missing six months of work, you couldn't sue your neighbor for not offering you sun block because, no matter how much you suffered, there is no law that says someone has to offer you sun block. Even though MSJs are filed frequently, they rarely pan out because in most situations a law exists that pertains to it. This was not the case for Dusty today though and he knew it was going to work.

"Hey, Dusty, make a little room," Chandler C. Gray, III plopped on the bench beside Dusty. Chad's office was down the hall from Dusty's. They had also gone to law school together.

Chad was blond with surfer boy looks and attitude. He got into Chicago Law School because his dad and grandfather had gone there. He partied all the time, bragged about his sexual conquests and just barely passed, but his family connections got him a job at SC&R, (Stanley, Clifford and Ruth). Chad's grandfather had retired as a federal judge many years ago and his dad sat on the Illinois Court of Appeals. Chad was a self-centered, two-faced, rich boy prick, a back stabber and brown-noser. Dusty had little use for him.

In all honesty, Dusty thought that he didn't like Chad because he saw things in Chad that reminded him of himself. Sometimes *Dusty* was a self-centered prick, but at least he felt guilty about it. He was working on it. On top of that, he worked hard to get where he was without back stabbing or brown-nosing. Dusty and Chad had always played the roles of friends and comrades, but there was always an underlying tension...an unspoken rivalry. Dusty didn't really feel threatened by Chad… he was too sure of himself. He just went about his job and endured Chad with a smile.

Sometimes he actually enjoyed Chad's company, but Chad really was threatened by Dusty. Dusty was everything Chad wished he were, but he was too small and devious to allow himself to admire Dusty openly. Dusty knew that Chad ached inwardly at each of Dusty's successes. But Dusty had always been able to tolerate Chad pretty well, until recently.

One of the partners, Joshua Clifford, had recently died in a scuba diving accident off the Cayman Islands. Dusty had heard through the grapevine that Chad was going behind his back, even going as far as starting rumors, to get the promotion that Dusty was vying for. Clifford had recruited Dusty into the firm at the same time Charles Ruth brought Chad into the firm, but Clifford took a special liking to Dusty. Dusty had in fact impressed all of the partners in a short time. Now that Clifford was gone, everyone in the firm expected Dusty to get the call up. Everyone except Chad.

Chad wanted the empty office Clifford left on the 26th floor. His daddy had already made overtures to Ruth and Clinton Stanley. Ruth and Daddy Gray were drinking buddies at the Country Club and had been for 20 years. To Chad, this should have been enough on its own to guarantee him the job. When he found out it wasn't, he thought of anything he could to secretly tarnish Dusty's name. He was just arrogant enough to think Dusty wouldn't find out, but he had.

"Were you up all night preparing? Chad relished the thought that Dusty could lose today's motion.

"No, I've been prepared for quite a while. You're late. You're lucky Ralston didn't pull your case first." Dusty chided his associate. Ralston had no tolerance for tardiness or unpreparedness in his courtroom.

"I called Rhonda in the clerk's office and told her to put my file at the bottom of the stack. I railed her, you know."

"Rhonda?"

"Oh, yeah several times, she's one of those who like to . . ."

"Hey, man, what've you got on the docket?" Dusty cut Chad off. That was another thing he didn't like about Chad - talking about the girls he slept with. Dusty knew Rhonda. She was cute, single, nice - somewhat naive. She probably thought Chad had really been interested in her. It bothered Dusty that every guy in the county would eventually be told all the intimate details and features of the hot little file clerk in Division I.

"I filed a Motion for Continuance on the Everly case. I've got a witness that won't be available. You think Ralston will do it?"

"I don't know, maybe." Dusty knew that Chad probably needed a continuance because he was never ready for trial. When Chad actually went to trial, he spent the week before yelling at his secretary, berating the paralegals and threatening everyone's jobs if they didn't stay late and make extraordinary sacrifices to get him ready in time. If he won, he took all the glory and never praised them. If he lost, he degraded and criticized the staff for weeks.

"Hey, Dusty, how'd you like to taste some of that brown sugar?" Chad was nodding towards the back of the courtroom at the striking black woman standing behind Mrs. Johnston.

"That's the daughter of the plaintiff in my case. I don't think that's likely to happen."

Chad kept staring back at her, hungry, like a predator, like if he could just make eye contact with her, she would succumb to his evident charms.

Dusty felt sorry for her and her mom. Imprisoned by a wheelchair the rest of her life, yet she would never collect a dime from Dusty's client. That wasn't Dusty's fault. The law did not allow for it. She may as well have been struck by lightning. People get hurt all the time in circumstances that don't offer financial recovery under the law. Dusty had done the research. He would stop this claim today. It was his job. If she had been hit by a city dump truck and sustained the same injuries, she would have recovered millions by now, possibly without even filing a lawsuit. But Dusty knew that his remarks to the judge would kill her claim and save his client millions of dollars. Hell, she probably has some kind of health insurance to pay for her bills. If nothing else, a good bankruptcy attorney could get them discharged. She would certainly be getting social security disability payments by now. Life's tough. It's tougher on some than others. Dusty had to keep telling himself these little poetic justifications to keep his mind in the right place.

 Mrs. Johnston was the kind of person Dusty's dad represented, the injured plaintiff. But even he would not be able to beat Dusty today. It had nothing to do with Dusty's character or ethics or honesty. Dusty would merely recite the law to the Judge. It was one of the biggest cases in SC&R at this time and THE Clinton V. Stanley had given it to Dusty. All eyes were on him. The office upstairs was vacant and Dusty was going for a slam-dunk.

Chad was still leering at Mrs. Johnston's daughter. To him, she may as well have been one of those super sexed girls used as props for nearly every male hip hop video. Good for nothing but male sexual gratification. Dusty had never slept with a black girl. Not because he saw them inferior or unattractive, it just hadn't happened. He really didn't know very many black people beyond a casual friendship. The last few days however, Dusty found himself thinking more about black people...black girls...black fathers of little black girls... his little black girl.

Dusty's mind went adrift momentarily: *What does she mean? Does she have anything to do with Mrs. Johnston? Is she Mrs. Johnston as a child? Why is she crying? Is she Mrs. Johnston's daughter as a child? Is there a connection? Am I about to do something to this family that affects this little black girl?* Whatever it was, she had a message, a need, maybe a warning.

Dusty looked back at the Johnstons. They did not resemble the girl in his dreams—it was something about the shape of her face that didn't match—but that's hardly enough evidence to rule out a connection. She could be Mrs. Johnston's granddaughter for all he knew. As Dusty observed them from afar, they looked straight ahead, solemn, serious, pained at the circumstance life had brought them. Their attorney, a savvy plaintiff's attorney by the name of Leonard Dreyfuss, was sitting in the jury box chatting to another attorney. This case to him merely represented a hefty percentage of any settlement or judgment in their favor. To the Johnstons, it offered some hope to recover some of the quality of life, however insufficient, however lacking, for Mrs. Johnston.

After moments of considering the possibility that his little girl was somehow connected to Mrs. Johnston, Dusty decided he didn't feel the connection. As serious and painful as Mrs. Johnston's suffering had been, and would continue to be, the little black girl was trying to convey something more horrible, more shocking, more disturbing.

Chad leaned into Dusty, "Hey, Dusty, you ever had any black p . . ."

"Johnston V Hampton," the Judge's voice filled the courtroom.

Dusty stood and walked to the bench. His opponent, Leonard Dreyfuss, worked his way out of the jury box full of attorneys and their briefcases and came before the judge. Judge Ralston thumbed through the file for a few moments before addressing the attorneys.

"Counsel, I've read Mr. Burch's MSJ as well as the response filed by Mr. Dreyfuss. I am fully aware of the facts of the case and had read the research and case histories you provided. I will allow each of you five minutes of oral argument before I rule. Mr. Burch, you filed the motion, you may proceed."

Dusty held the file in his hands but it was closed. He never used notes; he didn't have to. He always knew his case inside and out, even when giving opening and closing arguments to a jury. Dusty never even glanced at a legal pad. He was always able to speak from the heart, spontaneously and with conviction. Most attorneys were prisoners to the little outlines and scribbling jotted down on legal pads and 3 x 5 cards the night before.

Dusty began, "Your honor is aware that the plaintiff claims she fell through the steps on her front porch because of a rotten board. The plaintiff sustained severe injuries, which left her paralyzed from the waist down. The plaintiff is a tenant on the property and claims that the landlord had a duty to keep the property in good repair and failed that duty and is therefore liable for her medical bills, pain and suffering." Dusty knew that Mrs. Johnston and her lovely daughter would be staring daggers from the back of the court. The judge glanced briefly over Dusty's shoulders. Ralston must've figured out who the lady in the wheelchair was.

Dusty continued, relaxed and with a rhythm of confidence, "Your honor, the tragedy that has befallen Mrs. Johnston is unfortunate. We all sympathize with her. From all indications she is a fine woman and certainly did not deserve such misfortune. Your honor is aware the legal status between landlord and tenants of residential homes has been somewhat ambiguous over the years, however, the Appellate Court in Holmes V Lockwood just a few weeks ago, finally settled the question of what duty the landlord owes the tenant. The court said that the landlord has no duty to repair property on the premises, no matter what degree of decay there may be, unless the landlord has consented to it in writing or it is stated in the lease. Your honor will see that I have attached a copy of the original lease to my motion. Nowhere in the lease did the landlord agree to repair the premises. As a matter of fact, the lease states that the tenant takes the premises *'as is.'*" The judge was skimming over the lease as Dusty

13

presented. "Our sadness over what happened to Mrs. Johnston, and our desire for a happy ending, cannot corrupt the clear and decisive ruling by the Appellate Court in Holmes V Lockwood. I respectfully submit, your Honor, that even if the whole porch was rotten, no matter how serious Mrs. Johnston's injuries, Illinois law does not allow her to sue her landlord. I ask the Court to dismiss the plaintiff's case," Dusty stepped back.

Leonard Dreyfuss began his arguments, citing the perilous injuries to his client and the unfairness of it all. The landlord had a moral duty to fix the porch. If the landlord didn't compensate her, who would? Dreyfuss referenced several cases in which the landlord was found liable to a tenant, however, Dusty knew that they had all become obsolete as a result of Holmes v Lockwood, the case Dusty had cited. Dreyfuss finished, "And for those reasons, your Honor, I believe Mr. Burch's motion should be dismissed and let a jury decide Mrs. Johnston's fate."

The judge waited until Dreyfuss stopped and gave his decision. "It is tragic, the injuries and suffering endured by the plaintiff. Many people suffer without any recourse other than the grace provided to them by the Almighty, who I might add, allowed the suffering in the first place. My job is to determine whether or not our laws entitle the sufferer to hold another accountable. In some cases, the sufferer is fortunate enough to benefit from a law that holds another liable. In some cases, the injured party is lucky enough to find a liable party with substantial financial resources from which to compensate for such negligence. However, it is a matter of law as to whether the criteria exist that would allow an injured party to seek compensation from an alleged wrongdoer. There is no absolute or moral principle that exists to allow recourse outside of the law. I have no choice but to follow the law that has been handed down by those cloaked with more authority than me. Counselor Burch has presented me with a recent case that represents the current state of the law regarding a landlord's duty to the tenant. Holmes v Lockwood is the current and binding precedent. I address issues nearly identical to the case before us today. Mrs. Johnston and her family have my sincere condolences and best wishes; however, I am dismissing their lawsuit. Of course, they can appeal my decision, but I'm sure counsel will advise them that I'm dismissing their case based on an appellate decision that was rendered only a few weeks ago."

There was an audible sigh from the back of the courtroom. Dusty could hear muffled sobs. Was it the mother, or the daughter, or both? The judge closed the file unceremoniously and reached for another file. Dreyfuss attempted to rebut, but Judge Ralston shot him down and very casually asked that the next case be called to the docket. Just like that, Mrs. Johnston's fate had been decided. Dusty thanked the judge and turned to leave. As he walked down the aisle of the courtroom, he saw his colleague Chad Grey grinning with phony camaraderie. Chad handed Dusty his briefcase, "Do you want me to go ahead and carry this up to the top floor for you, your majesty?"

Dusty knew that Chad's gestures were thinly veiled envy disguised as sarcasm. Chad just had the good sense to feign congratulations. This ruling meant that Dusty was now more of a threat to Chad's run at the 26th floor, and they both knew it. There were a lot of big shots in the courtroom from big firms, many of them good friends of Stanley and Ruth that would no doubt convey Dusty's commanding performance to them. Stanley's heralded protégé had been impressive. He had delivered the goods. He was on the fast track for the "Good Ole' Boy Club" where the life is privileged, powerful and rich. Several attorneys extended their hands to Dusty as he made his way out. Some of his law school buddies were in the room and offered genuine grins and thumbs up and a few subtle "low" fives as he walked past. They were proud and enthusiastic for Dusty. It was apparent to every defense attorney in the courtroom that it would definitely benefit them to be a friend of Dusty Burch, rather than a foe. As for the Plaintiff's attorneys… the hoped they never had to try a case against him.

Dusty's good feeling evaporated as he got to the back of the courtroom. It had been the daughter crying. Now she was openly weeping, tears dripping onto her mother's back as she maneuvered the wheelchair into the aisle. Mrs. Johnston just stared ahead - no emotion - eyes unblinking. Her face registered the kind of passivity and resignation that Dusty had often seen on older black faces in similar circumstances. Even *with* favorable terms, he commonly observed that they never expected anything good to come from the system. Even 150 years after the Emancipation Proclamation, blacks seemed to question the level of justice they received from a predominantly Caucasian court system. Dusty figured it was understandably the evil residual of slavery and its progeny… racism. Of

15

course, most of the time judgments have nothing to do with racism—just coincidence or bad luck or some impartial serendipity that brings good or bad to all of us unexpectedly—but many blacks, for what used to be a very relevant reason, could not disassociate misfortune from racism. Dusty felt that racism in court had overall become obsolete, but all it takes is one racist juror or one racist judge and the whole system is tainted.

The daughter eased her mother into the aisle. Her tears were streaming now, but they were not for effect. There was no false drama. Dusty could see that she was actually trying to fight back the tears. It had probably never occurred to her that her mother would have the rug pulled out from under her. Only the most studious of attorneys would have been aware of the case Dusty had just leveraged to shatter the expectations of this family. The daughter's tears drained into the corners of her lips, off of her chin, like tiny rivulets overflowing from a great reservoir of disappointment and grief. The daughter's hands were on the wheelchair. She had no Kleenex or any way to stop the flow. Dusty had a handkerchief in his pockets. His expensive suits always sported an expensive handkerchief, which never, ever got used. That's not what they were for. Should he offer it to her? Would that only mock her? Before he could decide the proper thing, the daughter turned and stared directly, fiercely into Dusty's eyes. The tears still rolled out, forming several salt-water deltas on her cheeks before making their way across her face. She never even let go of her mother's chair to wipe the tears. The daughter was not intimidated by Dusty. She was poised, beautiful and he had never been looked at with such seething hatred. The daughter said nothing. Those beautiful, dark, tear rimmed eyes said it all. They didn't even scream. They just scolded; they communicated the daughter's feelings as forcefully, succinctly and eloquently as those beautiful lips could have ever done. But she would not part those lips for even one syllable. What she had to say was for Dusty alone. Those eyes burned a hole right on Dusty's soul like an ant smoking under a magnifying glass on a bright sunny day. Those remarkable eyes lasered right through Dusty's eyes, out the retina and through his brain, cauterizing their message on the back of his skull forever:

I know this was not racism but nor was it justice. He took her rent every month but wouldn't spend twenty dollars to replace that rotten board, even though he kept telling her he would. I know it's your job and you do it well.

But you represent scum. You will leave here and be richer and with more prestige. There will be accolades and celebrations waiting for you at your office. I have a job, too. I'm a schoolteacher. It doesn't pay as much as yours, but at least I aim to HELP people. I love people. I do not spend my life and energy helping the amoral avoid the consequences of their irresponsible actions. You have saved some insurance corporation hundreds of thousands of dollars, but even that money would not have given my mother back the use of her legs and arms. It could not hold her grandchildren. It could not plant her flower garden, but it could have provided the best treatment and services available to a quadriplegic. And, by the way, I now have a second job and I will love that job, too, and do it well. That job will be taking care of my mother, easing her discomfort and serving her needs until she eventually succumbs to her injuries and dies.

She broke eye contact and wheeled her mother out into the hall. They didn't even wait for their attorney. Dusty watched them as they made their way down the hall and into the elevator. The daughter stroking her mother's head, alternately with one hand and then the other displaying more poise and grace than Dusty had ever seen exhibited in any courtroom by an attorney. He reflected over the look she had given him. It had lasted only a few seconds, but in those few seconds it had been electrifying and disturbing enough to make an impression on Dusty for a lifetime.

Dusty's heart was troubled. The glow of conquest was gone. The daughter's eyes had riveted him; they had spoken to him. In truth, it was Dusty's own soul that had spoken to him, chastising him:

The landlord should have spent the twenty dollars to fix Mrs. Johnston's front porch and the insurance company should have had to dip into their billions to pay for the landlord's negligence. Just because you found some case that set some standard of law doesn't make you, or anyone else, God. In fact, it probably disappoints God that a piece of paper, signed by the loyal and trusting tenant, can reign supreme over the Golden Rule. You rotten piece of shit...

Dusty's dad had always refused to defend insurance companies for these reasons. He always told Dusty that "right and wrong are not determined by fine print, loopholes and legal maneuvering." Dusty tried to repress these thoughts. He had been in numerous, endless discussions about the ethics of law with his father. An attorney's primary duty is to the client, period.

Right? At least that's what they teach in law school. Every Bar Association and legal group in the country constantly hammers it into each attorney's psyche. The higher morality embraces logic whose goal is not necessarily justice, but winning, at any cost. If you represent a murderer or child molester and get him off because the police failed to read him his rights, you should be proud. You are a hero. You have forced law enforcement to do a better job. You have made our legal system better. By God, you have protected the Constitution. It's no matter that a criminal goes free and a victim further victimized. It's a small sacrifice to pay for the betterment of our legal system, ergo, our free society as a whole.

Dusty could just hear his dad:

Bullshit. Law professors, attorneys and judges have to create some new morality to keep them from being ashamed of what they really feel. It's all about winning. No attorney ever felt heroic or patriotic for getting a killer off. No. It's "I won. I put together a masterful defense. I blocked the prosecutor from getting DNA evidence to the jury. I kept the jury from finding out that my client had a long history of violent crime. Goddamn, I'm good! I beat them. I will be in the news. And when the cameras roll, I'll tell them I think this was a victory for the constitutional rights of every citizen. This sends a message to law enforcement that the rights of the poor and downtrodden will be championed as long as I am allowed to practice law."

The truth is, most attorneys don't give a shit about their clients. They may as well stuff their client's head and mount it on the wall as a trophy to the lawyer's skill, but attorneys have too much of their lives and school loans at stake to question whose side they were on. In some cases, you might represent the good guy. In the others, you have to bend your values and come up with some honorable rationale to advocate the "rights" of your client. That's why I don't do defense work, because you just never know what scum you might have to represent or the job you might have to do to see to it that he is treated 'justly' in the eyes of the law.

Right now, Dusty didn't feel proud or even happy. That "look" had punctured the celebration balloon. That "look" had carried more truth in the courtroom this morning. It struck deep and was purifying. Dusty's father had not made as much money as a lawyer as he could have, but

Dusty knew he never had to feel like this. Suddenly Dusty just wanted to go back home and see his mom and dad.

That night, Dusty found himself deep in the clutches of a little girl's silent agony. The first couple extremely vivid dreams he had were normal dreams. This dream state was lucid.

Normally when he dreamt of anything, he didn't know he was dreaming. He would wake up in the morning, carry on through his morning routine, and then something would eventually trigger a memory from a dream he dreamt the night before. Only then would he realize that the memory was dreamt. At the time the memory was created, it was nearly impossible for his brain to create the perceptions, perceive them, and realize none of it was real. This is true for most people. Tonight, however, Dusty recognized—as he was dreaming—that he was asleep, yet he could do nothing about it.

Throughout the next few weeks, Dusty encountered her every night. It became like a jail... a slumbering jail that he could not escape from. He would recognize after a few minutes that he was dreaming. Eventually, it took him only a few seconds. He began experimenting. He tried sign language, mouthing words, closing his eyes and attempting ESP, clapping his hands, whistling, running as fast as he could toward her... nothing worked.

When he was awake, Dusty was always thinking about the little black girl. He did not give her a name because names have connotations, personalities. Whatever this girl meant to him, he did not want it distorted or sentimentalized. Until he knew who she was, or if she was even real, she would remain, affectionately, *the little black girl.*

Although the dreams were extremely disturbing, they did not rob Dusty of sleep. She left him feeling physically revived from the night's sleep, but mentally and emotionally he was drained. She never left his thoughts. No matter where he was, no matter what he was doing, she was with him.

When Dusty was in trial, cross-examining a stubborn witness, he would resort to his friends the five "W's" and their cousin "H" (who, what, when, where, why, how). If you had an answer to all of those, you knew it all. Sometimes just having an answer to just one of them, you could figure out the rest of it. She didn't give him any answers though, just questions. It was a desperate riddle that imposed its will on Dusty constantly. It never let up. It demanded that Dusty figure it out, because somehow it was important. It was as if his soul knew that this was the most necessary and meaningful task that he, or anyone for that matter, could be given. Every other endeavor, his job, his social life, even his own life, paled in comparison.

If only she could just give him one of the W's, or the H. *Who* was she? Why did she come to Dusty? What was she doing or what was he supposed to do? Where is she? Obviously, she was in his dreams, but were they really dreams? Dreams aren't real. She exists somewhere, but where? It May not be on earth in a geographic location, but maybe it was in some psychic plain, some metaphysical dimension. He wasn't sure, but he could feel that she was a being and that she has a soul.

Where does she go when he works? Where is she now? Is she with him? How does she come to him? How does she work her way into his mind? When? Dusty wasn't sure when she first came. He had the vague recollection that she has been coming to him for a while. It just wasn't vivid. He sort of remembered having dreams of her for a couple months. For some reason, she wasn't real at first. Those early dreams had been vague, out of focus, sporadic. They weren't very remarkable, just odd dreams now and then that a person usually forgets within a few minutes of waking up. But she had been seeping into his consciousness like a developing Polaroid. She is crystal clear now in his sleep. He could see her as clear as a fully developed photograph, or movie. He just couldn't communicate with her or enter her world, any more than a person can communicate with a subject in a photo or one projected onto a movie screen.

But when? Maybe that was the one W that Dusty had to figure out. If he knew exactly when she first came, the who, why, what, where and how would reveal themselves.

Maybe she didn't know how to come to him at first. Maybe she had to learn how to come to him. Maybe that's why Dusty can't be sure when she first visited him. Like footprints in the sand, those first impressions on his mind are, murky, distorted perceptions that have been dissipated and can no longer be conjured up. But when were the footprints first left? There must be a connection. She had been coming to him a long time, but only recently was he aware that she wanted him to understand something... to figure something out. She was not some demon pranking him in the night. This little black girl was sweet. Precious. She was not playing a cosmic joke on him. Dusty had no idea how he would figure it out, but he was determined to discover why his little girl was coming to him.

Chapter 4

Three months had passed since he started vividly remembering the dreams of his little girl. At first, it was just a freaky feeling he felt when he woke up, but eventually it faded throughout the day and he was able to work without distraction. After a couple of weeks though, he began carrying it with him wherever he went. There were moments where he could concentrate on his work, but they were sporadic. After two months, he felt like he was on the verge of going crazy. He didn't go out. He neglected the girl he was dating that he actually really liked, Karlee, and she dumped him. He was starting to fall asleep at his desk at work and forgot several meetings with clients. His professional career was blossoming and he had just been given his biggest case. His little girl could not have come at a worse time.

"You look terrible," she said as she peered over the rims of her reading glasses. Dusty grinned at his secretary, Marilyn, as he headed down the long hallway to his corner office on the 25th floor of the 26-story downtown Chicago building. He never had to guess what she was thinking.

The firm they worked for, Stanley, Clifford & Ruth P.C. represented the biggest companies in the Midwest that were in need of personal injury defense work. The firm was 280 attorneys strong—all bluebloods. Among them were some of the oldest and most powerful attorneys in the city, reinforced by the youngest and the brightest minds fresh out of law school. Dusty was one of the golden boys. He graduated summa cum laude from Purdue and finished third in his class at Chicago Law School, (he could've been first, but hey, you gotta have some fun along the way). At twenty-seven-years-old, Dusty had never lost a jury trial. Great job, great friends, extremely eligible and pursued… most rock stars didn't have it better.

Dusty checked his appearance in the mirror on his office wall. "Yes, you need a shave," teased Marilyn, now coming in with an armload of files and several messages.

Marilyn had been with him since he started and she loved him like a son. No one bothered Dusty without going through her, not even the big guys on the 26th floor. She was the best legal assistant any attorney could ever ask for and Dusty knew it. She was his disciple, the only woman in the building, (and that included a lot of attorneys), who could force his undivided attention. Other workers, including attorneys, resented her and wanted to put her in her place, but no one said a bad word about Marilyn around Dusty.

She lost her husband, eleven-year-old daughter and sixteen-year-old son to a drunk driver eleven years ago. Marilyn was devastated. Her family had been her life and they were gone. Marilyn lost her mind, her friends and her home. She filed bankruptcy eight years ago. She had no skills and was hired out as a temp. She'd been working as a floating secretary at SCR until Dusty came and she was assigned to him. From the beginning, Dusty took to her and gave her purpose. He could see her frailty and insecurity. He gave her encouragement and praise at every opportunity. She learned to love life again and now she came on like a drill sergeant. As far as she had come since her trauma, there were still frequently moments when Dusty looked into her eyes and could feel her sadness and all he wanted to do was hug her. He didn't mind being her newfound pride and joy.

Dusty gazed trance-like into the mirror. He was thinking of her, the little black girl…the sad little night visitor that was no more an illusion than the reflection of his face in the mirror. His reflection breathed and moved and gazed back, but his fingers could not go beyond the rigid, impenetrable barrier… the glass. She was real, but like his reflection, she too was beyond the glass. He couldn't prove it, but somewhere, somehow, in some cosmic dimension, he knew she existed and was reaching out to him. She was so real that he couldn't even make up a name for her. He could call her Becky, or Sally, or Amy for convenience sake, but that's what you do to fictional characters to give them identity and make them more real. She did not need any such device to help burn herself into his psyche. She had a name and he would eventually know it.

He began to wonder if he should stop thinking of her as "the little black girl". What relevance was the color of her skin? Were her torment and her cries of anguish somehow less disturbing because she was a little black girl? No. He decided to make a conscious effort to refer to her as she, or her, or "my little girl", until she could—or would—tell him her name and inevitably her horrible story.

"Are you OK?" Marilyn was still there with his files and messages for the day. Dusty snapped back to the here-and-now.

"I'm sorry. I haven't had a good night's sleep for several weeks.

Marilyn immediately became maternal, "Why don't you go home for the morning. I can reschedule your AM appointments. You've got the Draper mediation this afternoon. I don't think we can get around that. Dusty fixed on Marilyn's kind face. His big blue eyes were tired, bloodshot and sad— his countenance weary and depressed. She had seen him hung-over and disheveled from all-nighters and one-night stands. She had come in to work to find him still at his desk after working on a trial all night. Dusty *never* let his fun detract him from his work, but she had never seen him depressed. He was the most fun, positive-minded, charming, "up" young man she had ever met, other than her own son. He moshed at Marilyn Manson concerts on one extreme, and on the other listened to Nightingale-Conant self-improvement tapes in his car. He was the loveable brat that all coaches, teachers, bosses and girlfriends hated to love. But they all did. *He* was never depressed! So, she knew something deep inside of him had to be eating him up.

"Can I help you Hun?" She didn't call him "Honey." It sounded too sexual. She sometimes called him "Hun", like an experienced nurturer instinctively calls out to a distressed child.

"Nah, I'm okay. You do enough for me already." Dusty trusted Marilyn's wisdom and advice, certainly, but he just wasn't ready to let her in on his…paranormal activity. He tried to play it off, but life had made her a genius at distilling the phony and superficial from what was real and substantial. Once you know hurt, once your heart is ground to pulp, other people's pain can't hide behind smiles and poses. It seeps from every pore.

Dusty knew that Marilyn had this gift of discernment, yet he tried to push past it. As with the young Buddha, he had been privileged and sheltered as a young man and suffering was alien to him. Human tragedy had never touched him. Dusty was a loving and empathetic human because it had been taught to him as a child, but he had never experienced anything even close to Marilyn's tragedy. So far, Dusty's sojourn into life had been blessed in that his suffering was confined to a light intermittence of teen angst and a broken heart or two from college. The God's had fed broken glass to Marilyn, which made her much more adept at hiding sadness. Dusty was just pure lousy at it, so Marilyn pushed on.

"Do you want to talk? Is your family OK?" Marilyn wasn't the type to be nosey or intrusive, she just hated seeing Dusty in distress. She wasn't used to it. "You sit down. I'm taking these files back to my desk. I'll get you some coffee."

"No," Dusty protested. He had never let Marilyn get his coffee for him. "Marilyn…" he gestured towards the door as if to push it shut. Marilyn understood. This was a common signal between them. She shut the door and sat down attentively in one of the two chairs in front of his expensive desk. Dusty sat in his chair and turned to the credenza behind him. He pushed the busy button on the phone and turned back to Marilyn. There was a short, uncomfortable silence. He knew he couldn't tell her about the little girl. Dusty wasn't ready to get into that, but he needed to confide something and Marilyn was too loyal and deserving to be left speculating about his recent behavior.

"I've been having bad dreams…" Marilyn's soft, brown eyes dilated. She didn't blink. Her eyebrows tightened ever so slightly with concern. Dusty knew that nothing would leave this office with her, but it was still too confusing, too mysterious to disclose everything. He wasn't ready to try and dissect it with another person yet, no matter how close. He needed to discuss it with a stranger, someone who didn't matter who he had no risk of scaring off first. He didn't care if this person thought he was crazy, but he had to hear someone try and explain it back to him; someone who would keep it a secret; someone whose friendship wasn't important to him; someone who he could talk to until he got it all resolved, or out of his system at least. And after Dusty convinced this person that he was demented, psychotic, or whatever, he could walk away and never have to face this person again. It would have to be a "him", because maybe it could only be understood through the male psychological filters. *Or could it?* Dusty knew he wasn't going insane, but he *knew* others would be convinced he was. In any case, he had to talk, to get it out, to hear the response, to debate his sanity with someone, just not Marilyn. Maybe this person was a shrink and could make the dreams—and "her"—go away, but that proposition was unsettling to Dusty. What would that mean? What if she really did need him and he just blocked her out? Neither scenario sounded appealing to Dusty.

"The nightmares keep me up all night. I don't want to talk about them. They're not perverted or demented or anything like that. They're just disturbing. They come every night. I can't make them stop."

Marilyn stared silently, compassionately. He knew she wouldn't interrupt. She would take on Dusty's hurt if he would let her. He couldn't allow that... there might come a time when he would have to tell her, but not now. He needed the indifference of a professional listener.

"What was the name of that psychiatrist we used in the Arney case... the guy who committed suicide after purchasing a big insurance policy?"

Marilyn frowned, "you mean the father of three who was hit by the semi head-on?"

"I know you didn't like that verdict, Marilyn, but the guy was depressed, psycho... our shrink had him pegged."

Marilyn plucked a piece of lint from her sweater subconsciously, "His name was Zimmer. Ronald Zimmer. I didn't like him. He was vain and opinionated. He took personal pleasure in the fact that his testimony swayed, or I should say confused, the jury into returning a defendant's verdict."

"Now Marilyn, we are a defense firm..."

"I know you didn't feel good about that case either. I could tell. You beat 'em even when you're not trying very hard."

Dusty smiled—the first time today. "Someday Marilyn you may talk me into a job at my Dad's firm."

"He'd make you a partner—50/50—in a heartbeat." Dusty opened his mouth to rebuttal, but she kept going, "I know what you're going to say. You don't want people to think you couldn't make it without your dad.

Well, I say, maybe your bad dreams have something to do with the fact you represent scum."

Dusty was grinning. *She is great!* Only Marilyn could talk to him this way. She might be right, or wrong, but she loved him.

"Thank you, Marilyn, for mapping out my life," she was back to picking lint from her sweater. "But do you know how many attorneys would kill for this job? I mean, how many judges have practiced in these halls . . . What about the lowlifes that get in a fender bender and then want to retire at the insurance company's expense? Somebody stubs their toe in a church parking lot, shows up at choir practice in a neck brace and wheelchair." Dusty realized he was starting to sound like an insurance loss prevention seminar. Marilyn was looking straight through his eyes at the gentle little boy that lived in his brain. Dusty saw she wasn't buying. After a brief silence Dusty broke a smile and went another direction, "Marilyn, whether my dad would make me partner or not, you know I could never leave you anyway!"

Marilyn smiled and shook her head with mock exasperation. She had just been charmed, even though she tried her hardest not to let Dusty see it. "I'll get Dr. Zimmer's number, but just don't turn into a prick like him." That was the closest thing to a four-letter word Dusty had ever heard her use. She turned to Dusty just before walking out, "Do you want me to try and get you out of the meeting with Reston for the Draper case this afternoon?" Dusty was pulling an electric razor from his desk.

"No. Would you please bring me that file? Bring the whole thing, pictures and all."

Dusty leaned his head back against the chair and closed his eyes. Another child, this one living and breathing in the real world, had begun to haunt Dusty. When Brian Draper was a toddler, he had curly blond hair, rosy cheeks and beautiful blue eyes. He looked like a child in a toy commercial. He still has his blue eyes. Brian was now 11 years old. The upper half of his body had been badly burned when he was three years old. He was getting ready to enter puberty with all its angst and sexual mystery and the top half of Brian resembled a cheese pizza.

Brian had been playing in his living room with his six-year-old brother while his father slept, intoxicated, in the bedroom. Brian's brother, Dennis, found a small toy pistol under one of the couch cushions. The pistol was, in reality, a cigarette lighter that had fallen out of his dad's pocket. Dennis pulled the tiny trigger and a flame shot out the barrel two or three inches. The two boys were immediately fascinated by the novelty and began to grapple with each other for possession of the toy. The trigger got pulled and the flame ignited Brian's long sleeve wool sweater. He went up in a flash, screaming and running around the house, setting spot fires on everything he bounced off of. Dennis ran out the front door as soon as the fire started.

A neighbor, who had been washing his car half a block away, heard Brian's screams and ran to the flaming house. He found Brian laying on the front porch unconscious, covered in flames. Smoke was belching out of the door. The interior of the house was in flames. The neighbor picked up Brian and then threw him out into the yard. A garden hose lying in the flower bed finally extinguished the tiny torch wearing tattered blue Velcro tennis shoes that had burned a hole in the yard, revealing a sight so horrible that the neighbor collapsed to his knees amid tears and vomit. Dennis watched silently, still holding the prized toy gun. The father was already dead inside the house.

Brian had undergone nine surgeries and 22 skin grafts in the last seven years. As his body grew, skin had to be taken from his unblemished lower half to cover the scar tissue that cracked from the expansion. He was constantly fighting infection of some sort. Brian's mother had become so repulsed by his appearance that she finally abandoned him to her parents. However, she continued to raise Dennis in her custody somewhere in California. Brian's life was defined by one word: *pain*, physical and emotional.

But lest anyone feel too sorry for him, there was one reprieve. His genitals had not been damaged. Brian would still be able to have sex with any girl who had a fetish for molten skin.

Dusty represented the tobacco company who manufactured the lighter.

. . . .

Marilyn dropped two thick files on Dusty's desk. "Is our client still denying liability?"

"Don't start on me," Dusty warned with feigned conviction, eyes still shut.

"They need to give that little boy some money . . ." Dusty pulled the pictures out of one of the files. They had been taken with a Polaroid, probably by his grandfather. The quality was poor. Still, Marilyn turned away. She'd seen them before. "All I know is, if I was on the jury . . ." Marilyn was leaving, and then stopped. "Oh, here's Dr. Zimmer's number." She handed him a post-it note and left, closing the door.

Dusty called Dr. Zimmer's office to make an appointment with the secretary. It would be six weeks before they could get him in. Dusty pleaded with her and reminded her that they had paid the good doctor well for his testimony about a year ago. The appointment was scheduled in two weeks. The doctor would surely explain his nightmares and teach him mental exercises to get rid of them or, if nothing else, prescribe some pills to restore his sleep. Until then, Dusty knew his little girl would stalk him every night into slumber land.

Dusty was tired from restless sleep, but he knew he had to perform if he wanted a shot at promotion to the 26th floor. The representatives of Reston Tobacco were coming this afternoon to discuss the Brian Draper case. SC&R did all of Reston's legal representation and was one of the firm's three biggest clients. They had successfully defended several lung cancer claims. This was the only Reston case that had been assigned to Dusty. The 26th floor was watching him. He may have made it up the first 25 floors relatively easily, but the Sears Tower couldn't fit in the ladder between the 25th and 26th floors.

Dusty began to nod off in his chair again. A little power nap would be great. She didn't come to him in his daytime naps. She also let him sleep a couple hours during the middle of the night. Every morning she would leave just as he woke, always at one minute before 6 a.m. Actually, Dusty had experimented somewhat by setting his alarm at 6:30 or 7:15. Whatever he set it at she always let him wake seconds before the alarm went off. It never failed. The problem was that no matter what time Dusty went to bed at night, he couldn't rest knowing that she was there, waiting for him. The anticipation was often more frightening and unsettling than the actual

29

dream. His encounters with "her" occurred somewhere between the hallucinogenic, surrealistic, amorphous terrain of dreamland and the tangible, logical state of awake.

If she was a proverbial figment of his imagination, then there must be something horrible and unresolved buried deep in his subconscious. That was even more reason to discuss it with a stranger. Who knows what validity lies in claims of repressed memories and recalled events that somehow make their way into television movies "based on true events?" That was one thing Dusty had observed in his brief encounters with Dr. Zimmer. He had a serious, academic approach to psychology, although somewhat cynical. Dusty didn't go in for new age psychobabble. He knew Dr. Zimmer wouldn't bullshit him. He also knew Dr. Zimmer wouldn't try to draw him in as a long-term paying client by placating his visions of a fictional child. No, she *was* real, suspended somewhere in the actual metaphysical universe. Dusty just knew she wasn't a dream, illusion or repressed memory. He could feel it, but he still felt he needed to address a professional to eradicate any possibility that he might be slightly insane.

Whether insane or not, Dusty needed a power nap before his meeting with the Reston suits this afternoon. The Draper case represented the golden rung on the ladder up to where the air is thin but celestial. They wanted to discuss "strategy" regarding the upcoming mediation. Dusty already had his strategy mapped out and he thought the meeting was a waste of time. He saw it as a platform for Reston's CEO, Ron Davis, to bitch more about the lawsuit and the huge inconvenience it was to him. This "inconvenience" he typically bitched about is with complete and utter disregard to the nothing but inconvenient lifestyle of the little boy whose life Reston Tobacco had so dreadfully affected, but Dusty knew Reston had a hand on the red phone that rang in Stanley's corner penthouse suite on the 26th floor, so he was willing to absorb a little more bitching than usual.

Dusty was dreaming up a normal, relaxing setting on a lake…clouds, fishing (his second favorite pastime), a beautiful girl, (his favorite pastime), whose appearance kept morphing into one beautiful girl after another. It was one of the few times he had dreamt normally in weeks, maybe months, and he was enjoying it thoroughly. The woman was wearing a provocative swimsuit and began walking through the shallows towards the deeper water. She began untying her top, reaching back behind her shoulder blades with her hand, tantalizing Dusty. He stopped reeling his line and stared, waiting for the moment she would expose herself. The knot came untied and she began to pull the pink top away from herself. Just a little, bit, more…

"Hey, Sleeping Beauty, they're here." Dusty flinched. Marilyn was at the door smiling. Dusty glanced at the clock on his desk phone, still trying to surface from his slumber. "What time is it?"

"You've got 15 minutes before the meeting. They're in the conference room with coffee and snacks. I've got your files all organized on the conference table. All you need to do is straighten your tie and wipe the sleep out of your eyes. Do you want me to sit in on the conference with you?"

"No, Marilyn, thanks. Thanks for getting everyone situated. Tell them I'll be in in a few minutes. How many are there?"

"There are three of them." Dusty pictured them around the table in the conference room in their $1,200 suits and Rolex watches. They were probably going over their strategy to make an impact on the case, which ultimately revolved around how to control and manipulate Dusty.

"Okay." Marilyn stood at the door for a second before turning around to leave, "Marilyn…"

She turned back to the entryway, "Yes?"

"I'm sorry for falling asleep like that. Thanks for covering for me. Seriously."

"Don't mention it. A person doesn't sleep that hard unless they really need it. Just get yourself together and be ready for whatever they throw at you."

"Yes ma'am!" Dusty saluted her playfully.

The "they" Marilyn referred to comprised of: Ron Davis, CEO of Reston Tobacco, a ruthless bottom feeder with no conscience; James Standers, VP of Unity Insurance, the liability carrier for Reston—they paid the law firm's fees at $600 per hour and would be writing the check for any settlement or verdict; and Vincent Leverette, counsel for Unity. He would be assisting Dusty in the case, primarily as liaison for Unity Insurance.

Dusty grabbed his suit coat from the coat rack in the corner. He glanced at the picture on the wall of him winning the Illinois High School State Wrestling Championship at 171 pounds. His hand was held high by the referee at center mat, a huge pad wrapped around his right elbow. His opponent was on his knees behind him, his forehead pressed against the mat in defeat. The inscription read: "Beating the Bully". Everyone thought the "Bully" represented the opponent on the mat— it didn't.

Dusty missed the one-on-one, mano y mano of wrestling. Wrestling had been Dusty's proving ground, forging his self-discipline, self-confidence and refining Dusty's natural competitive nature. There had been setbacks, though. Dusty won first in state at 152 pounds in the 8th grade. He made high school varsity as a freshman and his lackadaisical attitude and mediocre performance sent him down to junior varsity midway through the season. The humiliation ripped at Dusty's ego. He kicked ass back to varsity but had lost too much ground to go to state.

Dusty was finally realizing in his junior year what a gifted athlete he was. He went undefeated until the state championship and lost to a senior from Gross Point who went on to make the Olympic team. Senior year, Dusty was the pre-season favorite, rated number one in all the state preseason polls. He was in the best shape of his life. Focused, confident, unbeatable but as John Lennon once said, "Life is what happens when you're making other plans." Dusty blew out his right elbow in his third match, the result of an illegal throw from an inferior wrestler. His season was over they said.

Dusty went through the therapy, the weights, the push-ups and gave twice as much as was requested. He was angry. He fought the depression. He cried from the pain. It was exhausting. He didn't listen to anyone who told him he couldn't fight his way back. The only voice he listened to was his own inner demon that taunted him daily with the obsession:

You will win the last match of your wrestling career, but first I will drag your broken, bleeding, swollen, sobbing body to the clutches of the angriest and hungriest combatants in the 171-pound class, who all remember your preseason rating. And just in case they're a little slow witted, every coach will point out the brace on your elbow that serves as a big banner, "This is the part of Dusty you work on."

Dusty was back on the mat with one month left in the regular season, nine matches before Districts. After Districts was Sectionals, then State. He placed fourth at districts and third at sectionals. Every wrestler had treated

Dusty's right elbow like a jungle gym. In the match to go to state, Dusty was returned to the mat violently, injuring his elbow further. Finally, Doc Raney used a hypodermic needle at mat side to inject painkiller and anti-inflammatory drugs into his elbow. Dusty won the match. Throughout the comeback that season, Dusty was never pinned.

Dusty went to state as the underdog. Two or three guys in his bracket were expected to battle it out for the top; he wasn't one of them. He pinned his first opponent and beat his second and third by points. Before the third match, the semi-finals, they had to inject his elbow again because he was in so much pain. He had to fight through a double over-time, excruciatingly painful bout where his opponent took multiple blood time-outs due to Dusty's legal physicality. That win put him in the finals, but it was against Jeremy Cody, an undefeated senior who had already been given a full ride to Iowa. Dusty was tailing 5 to 2 in the third period. He got a one-point escape to make it 5-3 and tied it up with a two-point takedown in the last 5 seconds. The match went into overtime, again.

In overtime, Jeremy went to work on Dusty's arm. Dusty had never felt so much pain in his life. Halfway through the one-minute overtime, Jeremy caught Dusty off-balance and threw him to the mat by his arm. With catlike reflexes, Dusty reacted and literally bounced off the mat, circling hard enough to keep Jeremy from getting behind him and scoring. In the scuffle, Dusty grabbed Jeremy's leg. Without wasting anytime, Dusty sucked in the leg and summoned all the strength in his entire body to lift Jeremy off the mat and return him, scoring the takedown that would give him the state championship he had dreamed of.

As a child, Dusty's grandma had read all the Bible stories to him. His favorite was the story of Jacob wrestling the angel. The angel wrestled Jacob all night and couldn't beat him, so the angel, exhausted and frustrated, used his magic and broke Jacob's hip. This allowed him to beat Jacob by an illegal move. Dusty always played the game in his head that it was the shadow always boxing with Dusty. It was the angel who was willing to cheat to beat him. It always bothered Dusty that the angel got pissed and in a cowardly rage, broke Jacob's hip. He thought of the angel as a heavenly bully, one of the lesser spirits. He enjoyed imagining that it was the angel who had actually busted his elbow that season. Jeremy just happened to be the unfortunate soul to experience the repercussions.

That picture served as a sort of mantra for Dusty: *NEVER, never, quit.* He reflected upon it all the time. That's why it hung on the wall by the door to his office. Nothing out there would ever be as impossible as that season. That year, he learned a lot about adversity and the power of the will. It forever changed him.

Chapter 5

Dusty entered the expansive conference room. Ron Davis, Vincent Leverette and James Standers were seated on one side of the large burnished walnut table. Dusty took one of the six empty chairs on the other side of the table. The three accordion files of Brian Draper were in the middle of the desk. The three men stopped their small talk.

Ron Davis didn't bother standing, "I've got a meeting downtown in an hour. We want to go over the strategy for the upcoming mediation—make sure we're all together on this."

Dusty sensed from the very beginning that Davis would have preferred Clinton Stanley to be the leading charge, rather than serving in an advisory capacity to Dusty. Davis never hesitated to second-guess Dusty's comments or legal maneuvers.

Leverette, the attorney for Unity Insurance spoke, "We're not offering them any money. You ought to be able to get this dismissed by Summary Judgment."

Davis looked annoyed, "Speak English, please."

Leverette stuttered defiantly, "Well, uh, it's a motion we file before the trial in which we ask the judge to dismiss the case because either the facts or the law are so overwhelmingly in our favor that it shouldn't even go to a jury. We get cases dismissed all the time on Summary Judgment."

Davis glared at Dusty, "I know they don't have facts. What kind of law do they have?"

"They do have some facts on their side," retorted Dusty, expressionless, with unblinking eyes.

Davis predictably objected, "Bullshit, the kid's dad wasn't watching him. Furthermore, he shouldn't have left his lighter laying around for little kids to play with. They don't sue matchmakers every time a kid burns himself."

Standers, Unity's VP, broke in, "The kid's attorney has never even tried a jury case. It's way over her head. She can't afford to take us on anyway. They don't even have one of those lighters to show the jury."

Dusty asked, "Where's the lighter they took from the scene. Wasn't the brother still holding it?"

Leverette answered, "The fire marshal took it for his report and lost it."

Dusty wasn't buying it yet, "There must be other lighters out there she can show the jury."

"No. They were all taken off the shelf after six weeks. That was 8 years ago. No one can find one," Davis replied. "No one has one because they weren't selling."

Standers chimed in, "She'll cave. She was the court appointed guardian for the boy. That's how she got the case, for God's sake."

Dusty realized they were underestimating their competition, "I went to law school with her. She's not in it for the money. She's a loner, idealistic zealot. She's out to make a difference. Those are the hardest to . . ." Dusty started to say 'buy off' but paused, "manipulate."

Davis again demanded, "So What *facts* do they have?"

Dusty maintained his poise, "The lighter looked like a toy. It was designed to shoot a flame out four inches. The law calls that an attractive hazard. The boy was injured in one of the most agonizing ways imaginable. His mother disowned him, his medical bills have been one million dollars and he looks like melted wax."

Davis, "Medicare paid his bills."

"The jury will never know that."

"We took all those lighters off the market six weeks after they hit the stores."

"Which makes us look like we were aware of the danger."

"They weren't selling. Look, if you can't make this thing go away, I'll have Stanley put someone on who has got balls. What are we paying $600 an hour for anyway?"

The not so veiled threat was clear to everyone at the table. They would all enjoy watching the meltdown of this cocky young protégé.

Dusty didn't blink or sweat, "I'm not going to tell you what you want to hear to win your approval. We won't win a Summary Judgment. She will only be fortified by our loss. We should offer some money, enough to make her worry about the odds of losing it all if she lost Summary Judgment. After we lose Summary Judgment, we'll have to offer her more. We can't let a jury see this boy, or hear his story!"

Davis and Leverette exchanged glances. Davis, "Offer her $100,000. She'll get a third of that. It'll pay off her student loans. I'm not giving her a fuckin' dime more. That's the facts, and the law, Mr. Burch."

He got up without any courtesies and left. The others followed him out, leaving Dusty alone with both middle fingers extended to the closed door. The door opened and Dusty snapped them back, but not before Marilyn observed the greeting. "Well, I guess I won't ask you if you need anything." Marilyn walked in with a Coke for him and looked at his melancholy expression, "Why do you always have to represent people you don't like?"

It made Dusty smile, "What are you talking about? I love those..." Dusty paused, looking respectfully at Marilyn.

"Bastard ass cocksuckers?" Marilyn finished the sentence, unable to hide her blush.

Dusty laughed out loud for the first time in a long time, "Right, bastard ass cocksuckers." He continued giggling for 15 or 20 seconds as he tried getting it together, but he was not used to such vernacular from Marilyn.

"Well, I know you are upset, but try not to concentrate on that right now. You have that mediation for Draper in a couple hours. Right now, that's all that matters. Are you prepared?"

"As always," Dusty responded with a sly smile. He was always prepared.

Chapter 6

Dusty sipped a glass of water and studied the downtown Chicago skyline. The parties were all gathered around a monolithic glass table in a corner conference room on the thirty-fourth floor of the Illinois Bank Building. Dusty opened his brief case and pulled a legal pad and pen out and set them on the large glass table in front of him. Next to him was Chad, Davis, Leverette and a team of assistants. Across the table sat Brian's attorney Karee Andrews. She was nervously shuffling through her file. She wasn't looking for anything in particular, rather just trying keeping her hands and eyes busy in the uncomfortable silence. She sported a black dress suit and a white blouse that fit her athletic body tastefully, yet provocative. Her blonde hair was straight, flowing down well passed her shoulders and her red lipstick contrasted against her dark brown eyes in a professional, yet extremely sexy manner. Brian sat next to Karee, wearing a black turtleneck sweatshirt and Chicago Bears ball cap. His facial expressions were almost impossible to read, but Dusty thought he looked terrified and self-conscious to be in a room with so many strangers, knowing that each of them were stealing glances at him out of the corners of their eyes whenever they felt he wasn't looking. Next to Brian sat a middle-aged couple, casually dressed, Wal-Mart style, looking nervous and very unsophisticated surrounded by expensive walnut furniture, $2,000 Armani suits and two corner walls of floor to ceiling windows. Dusty had never met them, but he assumed they were Brian's legal guardians.

The court had ordered the parties in Draper v. Reston Tobacco to mediation. The judge appointed Vance Pullman to be the mediator. Vance was a retired judge of twenty-two years who discovered that golf and bass fishing would not sustain him intellectually or financially through his golden retirement years. Vance had outlived his first wife who died after a long bout with brain cancer. Faithful to his wife for thirty-two years, he now was living the life of a rich, distinguished, fun-loving bachelor, playing the fields of thirtyish fun-loving women. Though in his seventies, he had a red Corvette, handlebar mustache, a small earring and a tattoo in a location only his girlfriends could see. Vance had made his reputation as a young defense lawyer in one of the city's biggest firms. He remained loyal to defense sentiments after taking the bench. Vance Pullman had a ninety five percent success rate in mediation cases to a settlement. However, most experienced attorneys knew that his success rate was due to Vance's understating that it is easier to get Plaintiffs to lose faith in their case, pressured by cost of litigation, than to get defense firms who are paid $300 per hour to an early resolution of the case.

Dusty's paralegal, Jennifer, sat to his immediate right. She is two years out of college, moderately attractive with brunette hair and green eyes and just trying to get a feel for the law field before diving into law school and taking on a tremendous amount of debt, plus she had heard law school was the worst three years any human could put themselves through. Her father urged her to get a job before she betrothed herself to a life she may hate. She listened and as of this moment, she was still undecided. Today she was there to assist Dusty with the three boxes of documents that served as his toolbox for the mediation. They rested on the floor against the wall behind her.

"We want to see the boy's injuries," were the first words out of Davis' mouth.

Pullman raised his eyebrows and glanced at Karee. Dusty was somewhat confused. They had dozens of pictures of the boy's burns. The attorney had provided them with the initial claim. Karee seemed confused also. "You already have the pictures. I gave you all I have."

"We're not pleased with the quality. We want to take our own." Davis had not said anything to Dusty about pictures. Dusty resented the way Davis kept referring to "we". The pictures were graphic and spoke for themselves. "We" didn't need any more.

Everyone in the room shifted around uncomfortably except Davis and his assistant Michael. Both were glancing at Karee with challenging and menacing faces. Karee stared back, barely concealing her anger. "What were they trying to pull?" she thought.

Pullman broke the silence, "Did you bring a camera, Ron?" Michael was already pulling an expensive Nikon 35 mm and a palm video camera from his briefcase. Dusty observed that Pullman did not seem at all surprised when the camera appeared from the briefcase.

Pullman turned to Karee, "How about it, I've got a vacant office down the hall with good lighting. It would be more private." Karee looked at Pullman. She never blinked. She knew she was being ambushed. Brian sat, passive. He would do whatever his attorney told him. Karee looked at Dusty. Her face remained frozen, however, her large, brown eyes changed expressions slightly from anger to hurt. Clearly, she didn't expect this from Dusty. For the first time, Dusty didn't see her as the enemy. She was hurting for her young client, alone and afraid to make the wrong move.

Davis was sending a message: "We are prepared to degrade an innocent, mutilated child, if that's what it takes."

Dusty turned to Davis, "Have you seen all the pictures, Ron? We have quite a few." Davis wasn't buying because the pictures weren't the issue. He was going to make that boy take his clothes off for his own voyeuristic cameras.

Davis smiled, "We may as well get it over with because he's going to have to do it in the courtroom." It was pure intimidation. Dusty knew that no judge would allow that to be done to a child. Karee blinked for the first time. She wasn't sure. Pullman knew what Davis was doing and played into the drama.

"Under the rules of discovery, a party is entitled to examine all evidence. We could reschedule the mediation and you could force Mr. Davis' attorney to get a court order for physical examination of the boy." Pullman was trying to appear neutral, helpful, but he was bullshitting. The pictures were more than sufficient and everyone on the defense knew it. Pullman knew it, too.

Karee knew she was being bullied. "He's not going to take his clothes off for you." Her compassion for the boy was unmistakable.

Dusty felt a pit in his stomach. His team was playing dirty, with an enabling referee. "Then we're out of here," Ron started to stand.

"I don't mind," the small, angelic voice had a conciliatory ring to it, as if he were the mediator intervening to stop the adults from arguing.

Dusty had never heard Brian speak. He was stunned by the sweet, melodic sound that came from a form that appeared more beastly than human and resembled something from "The Night of the Living Dead."

They all went down the hall to a small vacant office with a large outside window. Dusty could see people working in the office across the street. Karee went to close the blinds. "We'll need the blinds open for light," Ron protested.

"I think the camera will do the job with interior light," Dusty grabbed one of the blinds and closed it as Karee was closing the others. Dusty never looked at Davis. He had contradicted the emperor and the emperor would not forget.

"I think these lights will work. We can bring in some lamps if you want, Ron." Pullman was still trying to give the facade of neutrality. They were all standing. There were no chairs.

"Let's see the burns," Ron snapped.

Michael held the video camera and motioned Brian over to a vacant wall. Brian walked slowly to the wall and turned his back to everyone. He began pulling his long sleeve turtleneck sweatshirt off over the top of his barren head. Jennifer gasped as the first glimpse of molten flesh was revealed on Brian's back above the belt line. She had been sorting through documents and pictures for weeks assisting Dusty, but nothing prepared her for the site before her. It looked like anything but flesh; there wasn't even the color of flesh. The purple, red, pink and gray lumps of mutilated skin appeared more like an aerial photo of a rugged Martian terrain or a surrealistic painting than human skin.

Brian continued to pull the sweatshirt over his head. There was not one centimeter of normal human skin on his entire back. Jennifer's eyes welled with tears. She turned and left the room without saying a word. Ann, Leverette's notoriously bitchy secretary, whispered, "Jennifer," and took the opportunity to follow her out the door.

The countenances of those who remained in the room turned grim and serious, except for Ron Davis and his assistant Michael. They remained expressionless. They might as well have been watching a butterfly flutter through a pasture on a warm spring day. Michael had been clicking his camera from the first glimpse of Brian's wounds.

Over the years, Dusty had become immune to the images on TV of horrible injuries, mutations, gunshot wounds, people burning alive, disease, disfigurements... they no longer made him feel anything. But this was real, tangible, unavoidable and only a few feet in front of him. The sight was repugnant to all of his senses. The sound of the sweatshirt scraped over Brian's skin at a different, sickening frequency than the somewhat sensual sound of clothing pulled across normal flesh. Even the odor was overwhelming. The damaged perspiration glands emitted a distinct, putrid smell that resembled human sweat, but was abnormal enough to be sickening and nauseating. They may as well have been in a small, enclosed room with a dead, decaying body. They were all horrified and repulsed, except for Davis and the camera-clicking idiot. They were enjoying this.

Brian bent forward to pull the shirt off of his arms and head. Deep fissures on Brian's back widened, gaped open, creating a sickening sound as if inner tubes were being squeezed. Brian did not have arms. The fire had devoured much of the muscle of his upper and lower arms. His limbs resembled long, skinny sirloin strips, cooked rare and cut close to the bone, laced with gristle and fat. Chad Gray left the room. Pullman looked at his shoes, horrified; he was affected. Brian's parent's acted nonchalant. They had learned to love this child when he was young. Dusty glanced at them and realized they only saw their beautiful child being exploited like a circus freak.

Dusty observed Karee, who never looked away from Brian. She would not leave the room. She would not let Brian see her even grimace. Brian began to turn and face them. Michael was still clicking his camera furiously, like he might miss the perfect shot. Ron was unmoved. Dusty didn't know if he would keep his composure and look Brian in the face. Yes, he would, and he gave Brian a warm, friendly smile as Brian came around and looked straight at Dusty. Pullman was still looking at his feet, as if checking for scuff marks.

"Son, can you take the pants off?" Ron instructed impatiently.

Before Karee could weather a protest, Brian said "Sure" and began lowering his sweat pants and revealed Fruit of the Loom white undershorts and legs that were as scarred and corrugated as his arms. Brian tossed the sweats aside. All his life when Dusty and his friends had talked about dying and the worst way to die, they usually deduced that burning would be the worst death. But this boy had not been so blessed. Here stood a boy, a human sacrifice that lived, and embodied as much horror, suffering and repugnance that could be galvanized into the body and soul of a living creature. Dusty thought to himself, 'How could a loving God, or even a vengeful demon, design such a tragic life… this boy's one and only trip through the universe? How could this boy not hate every waking moment? Every being he came into contact with? Every form of human expression? Every manifestation of God's wonderful creation? Could there be a more perfect way to make a human being despise life?

Brian stood there with a twisted, tortured smile on his face, daring them to make him feel any shame or embarrassment. Brian had slain those dragons years ago. Dusty noticed that Brian resembled any young boy from about mid-calf down to the floor. He wore white socks with the famous black swoosh pulled up to mid-calf. He wore new Michael Jordan tennis shoes. Something about those shoes, that attempt to adorn this wretched body with a popular fashion statement, broke Dusty's heart.

"I think we need to see him with his underwear off." Ron looked at Karee. "You know, were his genitals damaged? Is he claiming sterility or loss of future consortium?"

Brian reached for the rubber waistband of his Fruit of the Looms.

"No!" exclaimed Karee, eyes enraged at Ron, holding her hand toward Brian like a traffic cop. Michael was still rapidly clicking. Dusty was furious with Davis. What did it matter? This poor boy would never have sex with anyone even if he were fully intact.

"We are not making such a claim. He was wearing short pants and a diaper when he was burned. It's the only part of his body that didn't burn. He's not taking them off."

In a way, Dusty felt even worse for Brian. It would have been better for the Almighty to show a little mercy and at least make him a eunuch. There was no possibility that any girl would be desperate enough to overcome her revulsion of Brian to consider touching him, let alone have sex with him.

Finally, Vance Pullman made a belated attempt to salvage his integrity. "The boy's not going to take his underwear off in my mediation, unless there's a claim of genital disfigurement. Let him put his clothes on and let's get back to the table."

"We haven't videoed yet," Michael reminded Vance. The tide had shifted for Vance. He had no more stomach for Davis' little side show. Vance looked at his watch. He still couldn't look at Brian.

"He's got thirty seconds and let's get back to business." Michael instructed Brian to turn around slowly. Brian obeyed. Dusty could hear the motor of the camera zooming in and out for the close-up effect. Dusty watched Brian yield for the camera with all the poise of a supermodel. Ironically, this child—standing proud in his Air Jordan's—had more inner, genuine courage and strength than all of them, standing there with their good looks, expensive clothes, $600 shoes and law degrees, combined. But lest anyone feel too sorry for him, there was one reprieve. His genitals had not been damaged. They were developing and raging as the fire that consumed his head and torso. Brian would still be able to have sex with any girl who had a fetish for molten skin.

....

Everyone had resumed their places back in the mediation room. The smugness and air of condescension had left the faces of all on the defense side, except of course for Davis and his assistant. Even Vance had shed his veneer of congeniality and authority. Leverette's secretary, Ann, was visibly shaken. Though she never looked at Brian, Dusty sensed her tough, bitchy attitude had withered away in that room and that she felt genuine pity and compassion, maybe for the first time in her life.

Davis spoke, "We'll pay $100,000 to settle any and all claims your client may have against any and all defendants. That about equals the medical bills that haven't already been paid by Medicaid." Karee looked at Vance, as if he honestly brought reason and compromise to the table. Davis, looking at his watch, "Now you have thirty seconds. You have no lighter. Brian's mother and brother now claim that Brian was playing with matches and there were never any other incidents of a person being injured by the lighter. You have fifteen seconds to guarantee that your client gets at least something, and I'm sure the court will give you at least a third of it."

Karee kept looking at Vance, expecting him to assert some influence over the proceeding. But she knew it had all been a farce. Karee was crumbling inside, but for Brian's sake, her exterior remained tough, resolved. She turned to Ron, but not before making the slightest eye contact with Dusty. Dusty felt sorry and conflicted. He knew Karee was a decent person. There had been several times that their eyes had met briefly, but the communication had been precise and inescapable. Karee's eyes had pled, "Dusty, I know you are not one of them. When are you going to find the goodness within you?"

In a soft, poised feminine voice, Karee said, "No.

"We're done." Davis stood, shoved his chair back and exited the room. His staff immediately scrambled for their notes and briefcases and purses and marched out to catch up with their leader. Leverette and his staff followed. Only Dusty and Jennifer remained at the defense side of the table. Karee, Brian and his parents sat still across from them.

Vance stood and broke the awkward silence, "I think I could call Davis this afternoon and get him to hold open the offer of $100,000." He knew it would never happen. He was just hoping for a segue out of the room. "Thanks for coming. Don't hesitate to call. It was nice to meet you Brian."

They were alone. Karee couldn't help but ask, "You have a statement from Brian's mother and brother?"

Dusty, compelled to be honest with her, "That was the first I'd heard about it."

Karee looked incredulous. A small part of her was scared that she had just squandered her best opportunity at recovering any damages for Brian, but she knew he deserved way more than a measly $100,000. It wasn't about how much she would get paid. Dusty even knew that. Realizing that Davis threw Dusty under the bus and appreciative of his candor, she said, "I'll look into it."

Dusty was starting to believe he was on the wrong side. But in law school they taught in *Legal Responsibility and Ethics* that "there is no wrong side". You have a moral duty to argue, defend and promote the cause of the client who retained you. Dusty wanted to say something nice to Karee, maybe even consoling or encouraging, but he was afraid he might say something he might regret, something that betrayed his client… something unethical.

He came around the table and extended his hand to Karee. "I will be in touch." She didn't stand but took his hand without smiling. Dusty moved beside Brian's chair. He gently placed his left hand on Brian's shoulder and extended his hand, "Thank you for coming Brian." Brian clinched Dusty's hand with the shriveled claw of fried skin and bone. It felt a little moist. Dusty could feel the slightest squeeze of muscle in Brian's grip. This was the first time he had ever touched a burn victim. The sensation of Brian's skin pressed against his sent a shock of revulsion through Dusty's nervous system. Dusty was nearly overcome by nausea. "You take care, Brian." Dusty was careful not to withdraw his hand first. Brian continued to grip and looked into Dusty's eyes. His face resembled some barren, crater pocked moonscape with a slit for a mouth and two wormholes for a nose and jagged ridges that sheltered two large blue eyes, that were as clear and beautiful as the day he'd been born. Brian let go and Dusty shook the parents' hands and left the room, puzzling over who had taken the statements of Brian's mother and brother.

Chapter 7

It was after midnight and Dusty was just now leaving his office. He couldn't stop thinking about how ashamed he was to represent a scumbag like Ron Davis. He wanted to get this case moving as quickly as he could, so he put in a few extra hours. He was no stranger to working late hours at the office anyway—it's when he gets his best work done. The sooner he could be done working for Ron, the better. Never before had he represented someone whom he actually despised. The whole situation made him sick.

On the drive home, "Rock N Roll All Night" came on the radio. He liked Kiss. His dad had taken him to see Kiss twice. His dad had also taken him to see Ozzie, Megadeath, Korn, as well as Tim McGraw, George Strait, Madame Butterfly and Wayne Newton. Dusty could listen to any kind of music, as long as it was "good." He got that trait from his dad. He loved his dad dearly. Even with all of his strange viewpoints and conservative demeanor, he was still cool. Although it hurt him to admit it, his dad was also somewhat racist, though he denied it. Dusty was glad that part didn't rub off on him.

He continued to punch the preset buttons on the radio. ""Stayin' Alive," the Bee Gees, yuck, disco. "Close to You" by the Carpenters, nope. Car commercial, beer commercial . . . "Lyin' Eyes" by The Eagles, *not tonight*.

"If you've been arrested for DUI, call the Law Offices of Brandon Cardello . . ." Dusty hated those attorneys that infested the air waves, the bottom of the attorney food chain soliciting the bottom of the client food chain.

It didn't matter what came on, Dusty really wasn't in the mood for music. He just didn't want to be alone in the car. He needed something to keep his mind occupied… something to keep from thinking about his little girl. She would be back tonight, scaring him, troubling him, robbing his sleep. It almost felt like some kind of curse. She wasn't some "racial guilt metaphor." He wasn't going crazy. She was tangible and so real he could do everything but touch her. Nothing had ever made him panic and sweat the way this little girl did.

"Let's try A.M, sports talk is on," he said out loud to himself. His thoughts continued to race, reflecting his negative disposition; *Some loser is having a bad day because the coach waited too long to send the relief pitcher in tonight's game,* the *kind of moron whose life ebbs and flows with the fortunes of the local sports teams, whose million-dollar prima donnas are temporarily holding court here. My team has lost. I can't cope. I must call the guy at the radio station. He understands. He cares. I must vent because the team has let me down. If only I was in charge. Here' what I think the team needs to do.* Dusty was letting his mind go negative, something he tried not to let happen very often, but tonight he had no tenacity to stop it.

Dusty hit the button, a man's voice "My 401k has dropped" . . . click . . . commercial . . . click . . . commercial . . . a woman's nasally voice, "I'm calling from Seattle . . ." *I know, your lover is married and he really loves you but he can't leave his wife because of the children. What can you do to convince him to leave her?*

Dusty started to click, "I have bad dreams." Dusty stopped. *You and me both, lady.* He decided to give her a few more seconds to interest him before he punched her out with his finger.

The doctor, "Go on."

The lady responded, "A child comes to me every night. He's trying to tell me something but I can't hear him. I can't touch him or read his lips. He's in some kind of trouble."

"Do you recognize him?"

"No, no. He's . . ."

"How long has this child been appearing in your dreams?"

"Every night for about four months."

"Every night?"

"Yes, but I think the child first came to me about a year ago. I seem to remember having dreams about this child. They have become more vivid recently though."

"Well, dreams can represent a number of things."

Let her finish!

"They can represent repressed fears or desires. They're often sexual metaphors."

Let her talk, you idiot!

"I just want them to stop. I've tried sleeping pills. I've changed my diet."

"Do you have children?"

"Yes, three adult children, all grown up and married. My husband and I have been married for 37 years. We still love each other. There are no deep dark secrets. This little boy is in some kind of trouble or pain or something. It's like he has specifically chosen me to help him. It is so real, I can't . . ."

"Were you an abused child? Many times we suppress . . ."

"No! It's not like that at all. It's like I was really with this child all night. I wake up exhausted and crying. My husband thinks I'm crazy. He wants me to go to a shrink. I can't talk to people about it without breaking out in tears. They really are ready to put me away."

"What about your husband? Have you suspected him of abusing a child? Did you ever have a miscarriage?"

"No. I know you think this dream has some hidden meaning and we've just got to uncover it. But it doesn't have the normal qualities of a dream. Things don't drift in and out and change shape or color."

"Are there other images in the dream? How is he dressed?"

"It's just him. He's always dressed the same. We're always in a dark place and he always lets me wake up just before my alarm goes off at 6:15 am." An eerie chill shot up Dusty's spine as this comment rang between his ears.

"Well, Lana, your nightmare is probably the result of some forgotten trauma. You should talk to a licensed psychiatrist in your area. There is a chapter in my new book devoted to dreams and what they mean. If you will stay on the line, my staff can tell you how to order a signed copy of my book. Let's take a commercial break and then we'll talk to Paul in Jacksonville, Florida.

Dusty pulled the car over and grabbed his cell phone. *What's that Doctor's name? What station? Was her name Lana? Seattle? Holy Shit!*

Chapter 8

"Thank you for calling KKCR Talk Radio. May I help you?" The woman's voice sounded bored and mechanical. Dusty's heart was racing. He had pulled his car over to the side of the road. His hand trembled around the wafer sized cell phone. For the first time in over a year, he felt a glimmer of hope. He wasn't crazy. Whatever had visited him in the form of his little girl had clearly afflicted the lady in Seattle... and maybe more.

"The lady from Seattle, Lana, she just called in. I need to talk to her. Is there any way I can have her number?"

"I'm sorry sir, we don't give out that information." the robotic response. Dusty expected as much.

"Listen, I understand you can't give me any information but this is very urgent! I know it sounds dramatic but it could be a matter of life or death."

"I wish I could help you but we could lose our license . . ." the voice was unmoved, unwavering. Dusty knew he was a part of something big, something significant, and something that might redefine him forever. The only thing between him and some long-awaited answer was this minimum wage telephone clerk.

"Please . . . I know you think I'm just one of the nuts that call in. I know you would lose your job if you broke the rules. This is very important. Can I ask your first name?" If he could keep her on the phone and make small talk, maybe he could develop a small bond between them. There was silence on the other end.

Dusty continued, "My name is Dustin Burch. I'm an attorney in Chicago. One of your callers made reference to a situation that may involve a small child I know . . ." Silence. "Are you still there?"

"Yes, Mr. Burch."

Dusty continued, "Thank you for staying on the line. I don't want you to lose your job or get anyone in trouble. I'd like to ask a favor. I will give you my phone number and address. If you ever need any legal advice, or anything for that matter, I will forever be indebted to you."

"My name is Mary . . . I'll try to help you but I can't give out any names or phone numbers, I'm sorry."

Dusty detected a slight tone of compassion, "Mary, would it be possible for you to call the lady, Lana, who just called from Seattle? Give her my name and number. Tell her I have the same problem she does. Give her my name and number and tell her I would love to talk to her. Can you do that? I won't bug you anymore. I'll hang up and if she doesn't call me, I will leave you alone. You can't imagine how important it is."

A short pause on the other end, "Mr. Burch . . . my name is Mary Ann. Let me put you on hold for a second."

The phone went dead. Did she hang up? Was she talking to her supervisor? Dusty's stomach was doing flip flops, like he'd just asked Mary Ann to the prom and she was thinking about it.

Please God. He wasn't religious but he was beginning to believe that there is so much more out there than he could ever comprehend. Call it God, The Force, Allah, whatever... it lay just beyond his earthly bearing. But it was real and it had summoned him for some cosmic purpose.

"Mr. Burch, I talked to Dr. Lewis. He says under no circumstances can we get involved. There are too many liability issues."

Dusty's spirits plummeted. "Mary, I appreciate the fact that you at least tried. I really do. You must get a lot of nut calls and weirdo requests. I'm not one of those. Do you have children?"

Mary didn't answer right away . . . "Yes, I have a boy and a girl."

Dusty could sense her demeanor was softening. "Well, then, Mary, I'm sure you will understand what I'm about to say. I have become acquainted with a small child, a little girl. She has been traumatized and has asked me to help her. I can't explain why, but I'm the only one who can help her. I think the lady from Seattle knows something that will help me. The lady from Seattle is also trying to help a suffering child. I believe I can help her too. I know I must sound crazy. But please, I'm asking you to forget reason and logic for a moment. Forget rules. Listen to your heart. What if it was your child?" Silence.

"Mr. Burch, I believe you but I can't lose my job over it. I'm really sorry. I have other calls. I've got to let you go."

Dusty was despondent, "I understand Mary. Thank you anyway. I mean it. I appreciate it." Dusty started to lower the phone.

"Mr. Burch," Mary was still on the line.

"Yes?"

"Before I was able to pick up your call, there were two other callers asking for Lana's phone number. They sounded as desperate as you. That's all I can say." Then she hung up.

"Good, God Almighty," Dusty invoked without reverence. "What is going on?"

....

It was after midnight when Dusty got home. He sat in the dark in the living room pondering what it all meant. *How many others share this nightmare?* He had to admit that there were times he'd questioned his sanity. Being crazy made sense, but rarely do those who suffer from delusions ever suspect they suffer from delusions. Now the truth hit him like a devil careening into an arctic lake... a terrifying, but somehow comforting, epiphany: *There were others out there alone in the night, comrades alone and afraid. They are afraid that they are insane. Or worse, that they are not insane...singled out and summoned to the netherworld for some cosmic emergency involving little children.* Dusty found solace in knowing he was not alone. He didn't know their names or faces or anything about them, but he would find them.

He made his way to the bedroom and glimpsed the flicker of the clock as he plopped face down onto the bed. 2:14 am. Dusty kicked his shoes off and started to drift off to sleep. He was too tired to take off his shirt and pants. He could still get a couple hours sleep before she appeared.

The phone was ringing. Dusty slowly pulled himself out of the fog of slumber and looked at the clock. 2:39 a.m. "What the hell?" Dusty picked up the phone.

"Is this Dustin Burch?" The woman sounded hesitant, unsure of herself.

"Yes, this is Dusty. Who's calling?"

"My name is Lana Shelby. I'm calling from Seattle."

Suddenly Dusty was alert. He bolted upright. *Oh, my God, it's her!*

"I'm sorry to call you so late." The voice sounded weak and strained, like she was having to force the words over a lump in her throat. "I received a phone call from someone a few minutes ago . . ." Lana's voice broke. She was fighting back the urge to cry. Dusty felt a small lump begin to develop in his throat. "She didn't give me her name, but she told me that you know something about my dreams."

Dusty was wide-awake and clear-headed. *It must have been Mary at the radio station. She called Lana after she got off work.* The phone was silent again.

"Lana, whatever you do, please don't hang up. I have to talk to you. Are you still there?"

"Yes," came the timid reply.

Dusty's heart quickened, "I have dreams, too. They come every night. A little black girl comes to me every night. She's crying, or suffering. I can't really tell what it's all about. But it is real. I know it's more than a dream. I heard you tell about the little boy who comes to you every night. It's just like my dream." Dusty could hear weeping on the other end. "Lana, do you feel like talking to me about your dream?"

"Yes, I need to talk to someone. I'm desperate. I'm not crazy!" Lana broke down into unrestrained sobs.

Dusty was on the verge of crying, "Lana, just take it easy. You don't know how much this means to me . . . to find somebody else . . ." Lana kept sobbing. "Lana, I know how you feel. Believe me. Please don't hang up. We need to talk."

Lana regained a small grip of composure. "I won't, just give me a second. I'm sorry. It's just that everybody thinks I'm crazy. I've felt so alone. This little boy needs my help and I can't even talk to anyone about it. Lana's speech was broken by small sniffs and sobs. Her voice wavered, "I have been on the brink of an emotional collapse. The only thing that has sustained me is the belief that this little boy is real . . . and he's counting on me. Why? I don't know."

Dusty did not interject. He just kept his eyes closed, silently exhorting. *Thank you, thank you, thank you.*

Lana continued, "I had just about convinced myself that I'm insane and then out of the blue, I get a phone call tonight. The lady gave me your number. Mr. Burch . . . this is not a hoax is it? Please tell me you're for real."

"No! Not at all Lana," Dusty said, "This is real. Something . . . important . . . significant," he searched for the right words, "something terribly urgent is happening to us. I've been hoping for a long time for someone I can talk to... someone I can confide in. As I'm sure you know, this is not something that normal people relate to or understand." There was a long pause. Both people were sizing up the other's legitimacy. "We need to talk. We need to figure this out. And, Lana, I'm certain there are others like us out there." Lana was crying and didn't try to talk. "Lana, I would like to meet with you. I feel like this is more than just a coincidence. I will fly to where you are. Is that okay with you?"

Lana had composed herself somewhat but did not respond.

Dusty continued, "Look, Lana, I know you don't know me from the man on the moon. I'm an attorney in Chicago. I'll give you my website. There's a picture of me and a short bio. You can call any number of people and they will tell you I'm a good man. I'm not a weirdo."

Lana interrupted, "Mr. Burch, I know you're not a weirdo. I feel like this is more than a coincidence as well. I want to meet with you, but you can't come to my house. My husband doesn't understand what I'm going through. I don't even talk to him about it anymore. Don't get me wrong; he's a good man. We have a great marriage. He's just not ready . . . or I'm not ready to . . . you know . . . bother him with it right now."

"I understand, Lana," and Dusty did. He had stopped talking about it to his friends and family months ago, with the exception of Marilyn. "Lana, I'd like to meet with you right away. Even if I fly in and have lunch at the airport and fly home. What would be a good day and time for me to meet you?"

Lana replied, "Any weekday after 10:00. I'm a stay at home housewife. If I go out during the day it's usually late morning. I can meet you at

Seattle International airport. We can talk all day if you want, as long as I'm home by 5:00 p.m. Bill gets home around six."

"Great," said Dusty. He gave her his law office website. "Go to the website and see what I look like. Let's don't use email to communicate. Just call my office tomorrow afternoon and ask for me. I'll let you know when I'm coming in. And by the way, how will I recognize you?"

"I'm 50'ish, brown hair, about five-four." She giggled a little self-consciously. "I'll tell you what, I'll be holding a sign that says 'Mr. Burch.'"

Dusty laughed. The fact that he and Lana were enjoying each other's humor made Dusty more anxious to meet her. He could hardly restrain his enthusiasm. "How about Dusty?"

Lana responded warmly, "Dusty it is. They'll think grandma is there to pick up her little grandson."

"Nah, you aren't that old! Maybe your son. But anyway Lana, I'm very excited about this. I just feel that we are getting ready to . . . I don't know… I just have a feeling what we are experiencing is serious, and if we can figure out what it is, we might be able to help these kids, and maybe other kids around the world."

"I agree." Again, silence. Then Lana's spoke again, her voice was solemn, "Dusty, my little boy will be back tonight. I don't know if he hears me but I'm going to tell him about you."

Dusty replied, "Yeah, so will my little girl. But now at least I have some hope."

"Ok. Well, I'm going to go now, Dusty. I'll call you tomorrow, and thank you so much."

"Thank you, Lana. I can't wait."

A week later, Mary at station KKCR received an envelope without a return address or cover letter. Inside were two tickets for a Bahaman cruise. All she had to do was call and reserve the seven days of her choice.

Chapter 9

Dusty walked out of the gangway into the terminal of SIA. He had first talked to Lana a little less than 36 hours ago, yet he had all the anticipation and news of meeting a long-lost family member. There she was, among the throng of airport humanity, holding a small white poster board with the word DUSTY drawn in bold black marker. Lana must have been a beauty in her younger years. In her 50's she was still very attractive. She had already spotted Dusty. Her whole face was covered with a huge motherly grin.

Lana radiated warmth and sincerity. She impressed Dusty as having the poise and sophistication of a woman who has always been unaware or unimpressed with her own physical beauty. She reminded him of his mother and was fond of her immediately. Dusty approached Lana. He offered his hand to her but she immediately threw her arms around his neck and gave him a long, affectionate hug. It was genuine and spontaneous and just what Dusty needed. He and Lana were going to be a good team.

They ordered coffee at one of the airport restaurants. Dusty paid $4.50 for a small Danish and offered one to Lana but she declined. He could tell by looking at her that she probably didn't eat junk food. Her natural tan and muscles indicated she probably played tennis and golf regularly at the country club.

They traded brief personal histories. It wasn't the typical small talk commonly engaged in by strangers at an airport. Dusty was genuinely fascinated to learn more of his new friend and Lana enthusiastically pursued Dusty for the minor details of his life.

Lana was 52 years old. She was bright, self-assured yet modest and conservative with her views. She and her husband Bill were still madly in love with each other yet his inability to understand her dreams had made her feel somewhat isolated from her family and friends. She had stopped discussing them with anyone, except her personal diary that she had kept religiously for 33 years. Lana had a daughter, Melissa, 24 years old who was a finance major at Stanford. Her son, Dale, 33 years old, was on the fast track at an advertising agency in Seattle. She was fiercely committed to her family and beamed with pride when she talked about them, just like Dusty's mother. Lana's husband was a self-made millionaire who was educated on the GI Bill and owned one of the largest construction firms in the Northwest. Based off the way she spoke of her own children, Dusty knew intuitively that Lana was the type of person to agonize over the thought of another child suffering, especially when she felt helpless to do anything about it. After the getting-to-know-each-other talk was over, Dusty asked her about her visitor.

"He's a young boy, about 5 or 6. He's always dressed the same, like he's dressed for school: jeans, tennis shoes and a blue polo shirt. He has blonde hair and beautiful blue eyes. He comes to me . . ." Lana stopped mid-sentence and for the first time since they'd met, the joyful expression had drained from her face. Her eyes welled a little and Lana grabbed a napkin from the table and patted them dry. "He comes to me in a dream every night just before I wake up. I normally get up around 7:00 to see Bill off. The little boy comes for about an hour and then I wake up just before 7:00. I never have needed an alarm clock, but it's like the little boy knows when I get up and doesn't let me oversleep."

"Yeah, my little girl does the *exact* same thing to me." Lana kept talking like she didn't hear him.

"The weird thing is, I have no idea when he first came to me." Lana's eyes stared off into the distance, fixed but focused on something she was visualizing in her mind. "I remember being aware of a little boy in my thoughts, maybe a year ago. He must have been coming to me in my dreams then but it was vague and not vivid enough to stay in my mind. You know how you will suddenly recall a dream you had the night before? I didn't think too much of it until I started noticing that this same little boy started appearing in my dreams over and over. I couldn't always recall the dream or what it was about, but I started having a clear recollection of a little boy that was troubled. Eventually I started remembering the dreams and over time they became very vivid. It was like he sort of eased into my consciousness over time. I would go to bed at night knowing that he would come. After a few months, the dreams became very disturbing. It changed my thought pattern, my actions, my mood, my thoughts… they became a part of my life. *He* became a part of my life."

Dusty didn't interrupt her. Lana was describing his own dreams almost to a "T" and he wanted to make sure she didn't get distracted as to leave out a detail.

Lana thought for a second, "I yearn to know his name, but there is no way to know because he can't tell me. He can't speak, or at least I can't hear him if he does." Again, her eyes stared off into the distance, just over Dusty's shoulder. He could tell she was imagining the boy. "He's real. I just know he's real, and I… love him. It may sound strange, but I love him as if he were my own child. And I know now, after months and months, that it is more than a dream. I know not only because I feel it, but his visits don't have the abnormal, illogical characteristics that a normal dream does. It feels as if I am *actually visiting* with him in my sleep. The worst part is that now that he comes in focus so clear, I can see that he is in pain. There are times when he appears like he is in excruciating pain… almost as if…" Lana hesitated as if she didn't think Dusty would believe what she had to tell. Her eyes welled up.

Dusty's mind had wandered here before, but he had never wanted to admit the possibility. Seeing that she too had the same fear, he spared her having to utter the words, "Almost as if he were dying?" She slowly nodded her head as tears overflowed her eyelids and ran down her cheek. "Lana, you don't have to worry about if I believe you or not. I *know* it's real."

Lana's tears flowed freely down her cheeks as she sat still. She clinched Dusty's hand across the table, "Dusty, I can't tell you how much it means to hear you say that." She wiped her eyes and sniffled to regain her composure. "It's like a huge weight has been lifted off of my soul… just to know that I'm not imagining this or going crazy."

Dusty cracked a half-hearted smile, "Well, there is the possibility that we are *both* crazy." Dusty's sarcasm was well played and brought a giggle and a smile to Lana's face.

"Yep, yep that absolutely is a possibility. I'd almost rather that be the case." She finished out her unexpected bout of laughter and returned to her serious demeanor.

"No, I'm only kidding. I don't think we are crazy at all. As soon as I heard you on the radio, it became clear to me that this is real. Please, don't worry. There is absolutely nothing you can say to make me judge you."

"Thank you. Thank you, Dusty."

"Is there anything else you want to tell me about him?"

"Well, I used to try and make myself wake up during the dream. But no matter what I tried, I couldn't. He made me stay with him until just seconds before I normally wake up. So, I stopped trying to wake myself out of it. Instead I tried harder and harder to be with him, to console him, to... try and break through. Try to reach him. Like I said I have started recently to see that he is in pain. I can even see him crying. It's like he is gagged and trying to tell me something. It's like there is some invisible demon struggling with him. It appears he is in the grasp of something, or someone. He's trying to get away. After he does this for quite some time, he starts violently rubbing his hands over his sides and abdomen like he has been struck by something or like he is having a horrible appendix attack. Our eyes definitely make contact and then he stops and sort of goes limp like he has resigned himself to the demon. It's almost like he dies right in front of me . . . and then he reenacts the same scene again. The whole sequence lasts about two or three minutes, but he acts it out for me all night long. I plead with him and I ask him what he wants me to do. I try to hold him, but no matter how hard I try, there is a veil between us. I can't touch him or hear him, but I can see him very clearly, and I'm pretty sure he sees me too. He's just a child, though, and if I can't figure out how to communicate with him, how is he going to be able to communicate to me? He's counting on me I feel like, but he doesn't know what to do just as much as I don't. So, he just continues to replay the same scene over, and over, and over. The frustrating part is I can't tell if something terrible *has* happened to him, *is* happening right now, or is about to happen. Whatever it is, he's trying to tell me about it though. And it kills me because if something has happened, then that means he is gone, and I can't bear the thought of that. If it hasn't happened, then I'm lost and become anxious because I have no idea how to keep it from happening." Lana sighed a deep breath, "I try to stay positive. I try to stay sharp so that I can find an answer. In the morning I'm well rested physically—it's not like I lose any sleep—but emotionally I'm drained and depressed. I've never suffered from depression in my life until about the last year or so. Now I don't know what it's like to not be depressed. My family worries about my sanity. I've gone to several shrinks. I've gone through dream therapy. They all look at me as if I'm lost, so I quit telling anyone. They think I have recovered somehow. They wanted to give me drugs for depression or drugs to sleep. I wouldn't let them because I was afraid it would make him go away or keep me from finding out what it is I'm supposed to do. And Dusty, I know I am supposed to do something. I don't know what to do, but I have to find out. He needs me... I know it's real... I just know it. A real child is suffering somewhere. I know that I have a purpose that outweighs all others. That little boy is a burden that God, or whoever, has placed upon me and now I've met someone else who carries the same burden I have. The first time I have had a sliver of hope, any hope at all, was when the lady from the radio station gave me your name." Lana mildly lost her composure she had been fighting to maintain, "Dusty, please, help me figure out what I'm supposed to do. He has chosen me for some reason, and your little girl has chosen you. I can't let him down. *We* can't let them down," Lana paused.

After listening to her account, Dusty knew she was a special person. Right away he felt protective of her. Her story mesmerized him. It was identical to his in almost every detail. Almost. Lana had said that her little boy seemed to be struggling with something unseen. Dusty's did not recall that his little girl acted that way. She was definitely in agony, but he did not recall feeling that she was in the clutches of another presence. And he did not recall her acting as if she had been in physically stricken or in physical trauma. Maybe she was and he just hadn't noticed. One thing was sure, he would see her tonight, and tonight he would pay extra close attention.

"Lana, all I can tell you is that I *promise*, with all my heart, that I will try as hard as humanly possible to help us get through this," Dusty was now fighting not to cry as a lump arose in his throat, "and that I will not give up on you, or me, or the children, even if it kills me."

Lana's face brightened and hope emerged on her face, "I believe you. Now, Dusty, please tell me about your child."

"Well, I have a little black girl that comes to me. My dream is almost exactly like yours and I'm like you, it's to the point where I feel like she is my own daughter now. The worst part for me is I don't know what to do and I'm afraid it's going to start affecting my career. She is trying to tell me something I feel like, but no matter how hard I try, I can't communicate with her either. She is in a lot of pain at times, just like your little boy. It's almost like she needs me to do something to stop her pain, or rescue her, but I'm not sure that I feel like I've ever seen her 'die' in front of me. I just don't know. What you said is true though; it's definitely not a dream. She *visits* me, it just happens to be in my sleep. I really wish I knew who she was, but I have no idea, whatsoever, where I might know her from. I think about it all day long, trying to remember lost memories that she might be hiding in."

Lana's eyes still had tears in them. She could feel Dusty's grief. Her sincerity warmed him, "It's the exact same way for me. It kills me not to know. I hate not being able to refer to him with a name. I guess I will have to wait, but one day I *will* know his name. Until then, he's my little blue-eyed boy." Lana stared into Dusty's eyes with conviction. He returned the gaze and nodded, silently agreeing that he knew she would. Right then, at that moment, she knew she had a true confidant.

Dusty continued for a few more minutes describing to Lana his dreams, but it mostly echoed the details that she gave him. Then he remembered, "Lana, there are others. We're not the only ones." An extremely confused look came across her face. "The lady at the radio station said others had called asking for you. They wouldn't give me any names though. We're just a bunch of kooks who listen and call in to talk radio like everybody else that doesn't have a real life. I even called the next day and tried to get them to let me talk to someone who might help. I gave them my name and number and asked if they would simply give it out to anyone else who called. All I got was 'Sorry, we can't help,' with the typical arrogance and contempt that call in programs have for their own audiences. We're just going to have to find them ourselves."

Lana was excited, "Dusty, maybe they're all over. If they're just like us, then they are going to be looking for others too. All the UFO quacks seem to eventually find each other, right? We need to find our people and meet with them. We need to help each other."

Dusty became serious, "You don't believe in UFO's?"

Lana looked startled like, *oh my God, he really is a nut!*

"Lana, I didn't really want to tell you, but I've also been abducted by aliens for the last four years of my life."

Lana gave a little nervous laugh and a look like, *I think you're pulling my leg, but I'm a little concerned you're not.*

Finally, he burst out laughing, "I'm totally joking. When it comes to that kind of stuff, I'm the most cynical person you'll ever meet. Or at least I was. Now that all this is happening, who knows? Maybe those 'kooks' really aren't so 'kooky' after all."

"Oh my gosh, you kind of had me going for a second! I guess you are right though. Who are we to say that what other people claim to see isn't reality?"

"I know, right? Well, I think the problem is going to be how do we go about finding 'our' people without getting ourselves in the midst of some UFO suicide cult?"

"How do we find them? An ad in the newspaper? If they're all over the country we'd have to place an ad in every newspaper. That could get expensive. And every nut is going to respond to those ads anyway. What if we could get Larry King or Oprah or Dr. Phil to get involved? Maybe they could ask people to call in."

Dusty didn't like those ideas but he didn't want to insult Lana's intelligence. "Lana, do you think they would take us seriously?"

"No, not really. I'm sure they get wacko calls every day. Jerry Springer probably wouldn't even take us seriously . . . unless we're sleeping with our relatives and willing to fight with them on camera. We might be able to get that guy that says he talks to the dead interested. But he is so phony and his audience is no naive and gullible. We may as well pay Dionne Warwick to take up our cause." Lana rolled her eyes dismissively. "But then again, who am I to call anyone naïve? I need to start watching the way I talk about people if I'm going to believe in our cause enough to be able to help it."

Dusty chuckled. Lana was intelligent and witty. He was already feeling sorry that they would have to separate before the afternoon was over.

They fell silent for a moment. The wheels in their brains were turning. Dusty finally spoke, "We've got to assume that the others, the ones who have been chosen by these children, are from all walks of life and various backgrounds and feeling isolated from friends and family. Where would they go to find answers?"

Lana interjected, "I went to the library and read everything I could on dreams. I went to shrinks. I went to the Internet. Finally, I was so desperate I called that idiot on the radio."

Dusty leaned back in his chair and looked at Lana as if he had been struck with a bolt from heaven . . . an epiphany, "The internet, that it's! It's cheap. More and more people are using it every day. We both went there looking for answers, right?"

Lana didn't seem so impressed. "But how? There are more nuts there than anywhere else. How do we reach . . ." she paused and then concocted the term that they would continue to identify themselves with, ". . . The Chosen?"

Dusty grabbed her hands again, "What was it that made you believe I was for real? Why did you trust me?"

"Because your story is identical to mine. It's too much of a coincidence. You couldn't have made it all up."

Dusty was now inspired, "Exactly! We can screen them and look for stories like ours. Lana, I don't know much about the Internet, but I do know there are chat rooms for just about anything under the sun. Yeah, people with nothing better to do gather there with absolutely nothing to say and they'll respond to anything—it's like the CB radio of the new millennium— but what if we get lucky? What if I set up a chat room named 'The Chosen?' and created an email to go along with it? I'd simply state, 'If you dream of a child every night and you need some answers, send me your story.'"

"Shouldn't we be more specific? I mean, that is kind of vague..."

"Well, it'd be like the way the police withhold certain facts from the media to filter out the phony informants from the legit. We don't want to give too much information, because then we wouldn't know if someone was sincere, or just regurgitating our own information. I'm sure we'll get thousands of emails from the perverts and the self-proclaimed psychics, but I'll bet we'll get stories just like ours. Once they email us, we either grant them access to the chat room or deny it. What do you think?"

Lana's eyes brightened, "That's a great idea! I think that could work." Her mind was spinning, "Dusty, let me do it. I need to. I'll email you every day and let you know if we snag anyone. I need this. I have nothing but time on my hands. Please, let me do it." Lana's eyes watered and looked drearily into Dusty's. Even if he had wanted to, he couldn't have told her no. The truth was, he really didn't have enough time to do it and he was relieved that she volunteered on her own.

"Sure, Lana. Absolutely."

Lana was almost in tears again, "Before I can contact or respond to anyone I will e-mail or call you . . . whatever. You and I will decide which ones ring true . . . which ones are The Chosen."

"Sounds like a plan." Dusty smiled. A plan. He liked the sound of that.

It was late in the afternoon. Dusty and Lana embraced affectionately and parted. Dusty checked his phone messages. One caught his attention. It was from Marilyn, "Dusty please call as soon as you get this. It's about the Draper case." Dusty took a seat on the plane. The office could wait until tomorrow. He would be home around midnight. He needed to see his little girl tonight. Would he notice someone or something with her? Would he be able to detect a physical injury that he hadn't perceived before?

It was 2:07 am when Dusty fell into bed. He spent a few minutes going over the day and mentally digested its significance. He eased into slumber . . . and she was there.

Chapter 10

*L*itlkidsRmyThng,   *RoosterZMadman*,   *DesperateSoldier*, *StrangerNneed, Rocketman, Horny2Die4:* All of these were names of users in the chat room labeled "I See Children in My Dreams". While Lana was busy creating a website and chat room, Dusty was doing some research of his own. He couldn't just standby and idle while Lana got things running. She said she had a friend in Seattle who she could trust who knew how to write code good enough to create a simple website. Dusty knew next to nothing about webpage building, plus it was hard for him to help since she lived in Seattle. So while he waited to hear back from her, he thought he would get the ball rolling.

He had stumbled across this chat room in a Google search. He started off by typing: *Seeing children in my dreams.* It wasn't exactly what he was looking for, but he figured he would have to sift through a lot of bullshit to find anything of real merit. This chat room was obviously for perverted pedophiles. Against Dusty's better judgment, he joined in the conversation.

RoosterZMadman: I love it when they scream. I like to slide it in slow as possible, so every inch of me is felt and absorbed to the fullest extent. It makes me tremble with excitement.

Horny2Die4: You naughty little thing you. You probably like 'em young. 7? 8? You sick fuck. My absolute minimum is 10. Then they can actually understand what is happening to them.

DesperateSoldier: I can't stand to hear them, personally. I shove as many articles of clothing as I need to silence them. I'm the one who likes to stay loud… like a silverback. I like letting them know who is in charge. I like to let them know that I could kill them at any moment, but instead I chose to fuck them. I want them to know how lucky they are…

Dusty chimed in as user *Lost soul:* I'm just exploring my desires currently. I'm not sure what I like. But aren't you guys ever afraid of getting caught? Wouldn't letting them live give you more of a chance of getting caught?

Rocketman: We're not murderers man. We just like tight little holes. There are ways around it. You just have to be smart. Gettin' caught is one thing. The electric chair is another. But I'm glad you aren't hiding from your desires.

DesperateSoldier: I agree. We are all human and all humans sin. Who is to judge which sins are worse than others? I can't help my urges. I was made this way. Once I stopped trying to fight it, it was like I was set free. Don't be afraid.

Horny2Die4: Lost soul, you are so brave… so brave!

Dusty wasn't sure how long he could carry on this conversation. He was starting to feel sick. *How could there actually be people out there that talk this way about children? And do these things to them?* His respect for humanity diminished significantly.

He had no idea where to start. He did know that he couldn't read through dozens of sick, perverted chat rooms to find a needle in a haystack. So, he was back to square one. Maybe adding "dead" to the query would change things.

Google: *Seeing dead children in my dreams*

This wasn't much help either, although the search field was much more palatable. Dozens of "dream interpretation" websites populated, giving an explanation for everything imaginable in dreams.

A Bailiff: Seeing a bailiff means you have crossed a certain threshold and feel you must be held accountable for something.

Who the hell has ever seen a bailiff in their dreams?

Most of the information was on average, useless. He found a couple *Yahoo Answers* links. One of them was kind of interesting. Someone had dreams of dead children, but also claimed to experience paranormal occurrences while awake. The children were burning in a house and couldn't be reached. Rain clouds loomed just hundreds of feet away, unleashing a torrential downpour that would've extinguished the fire, but it never came close enough. The most popular evaluation of this dream labeled each aspect of the dream with a psychoanalytic explanation. Everything seemed to mean something, down to the presence of fire and rain in the dream. The person who posted the response claimed to be a dream psychologist and said that fire represents a deep desire in a person, while rain represents guilt and remorse.

Dusty had a hard time believing in the hocus pocus psychology that surrounded dreams, the dead, astrology or fortune tellers, but the article did get him thinking about his dreams in ways he hadn't before. He didn't think this person fit the mold he and Lana were looking for, (mainly because he claimed to experience paranormal activities while awake), but the story did intrigue him. Would he start seeing things during his waking hours? Would she ever come through to him while he was awake? So far, he had only come into contact with her while he was sleeping. He thought that maybe if he could find a way to contact her while he was awake, he could figure out how to help her.

That night he sorted through hundreds of web pages. He read about medieval death rituals and the Salem Witch Trials. He read about ESP and studies on the *sixth sense*. He read blogs of people who claimed to have contacted the dead and blogs that described near-death experiences in detail. Sometimes he just read articles that had nothing to do with what he was experiencing because they were interesting… because it was a nice break from law books and case studies.

He hadn't discovered any solutions, but he had begun the search for answers that would consume his life for nearly three full years. This was the first of many nights of staring at his computer, sorting through documents and anecdotes… trying to fit the puzzle pieces together.

A week later, Lana contacted him and told him the site was up. The link was www.sufferthechildren.com. When he asked her why she chose that name, she simply responded, "Because it was the only name I could think of that didn't sound cryptic or perverted, and it seemed to fit our needs perfectly." That answer was good enough for him.

Chapter 11

D r. Zimmer looked grandfatherly; silver beard, neatly coiffed, and bifocals resting low on the ridge of his nose, looking at the information Dusty had provided on the intake sheet out in the lobby. Dusty had never been to a shrink. He was embarrassed to be sitting across the desk from one now in an expensive leather chair. There actually was a couch on the other side of the room, but the doctor seemed intent on talking to Dusty across the large mahogany desk. Family pictures, a dozen or so diplomas and shelves full of academic looking books lined the walls of the plush, dimly lit office. The shades were drawn and only a lamp behind the doctor's desk, just like in the movies, lighted the office.

Dusty considered looking for other doctors, but the way Zimmer had handled himself as an expert witness for Dusty had him hooked. He was already self-conscious about opening up to a stranger, but he knew that if there was a chance that his dreams were the product of a psychological conflict, Zimmer would discover it. He didn't want to take a chance on one of the many phony psychologists surrounding the Chicago area, the ones that are so desperate for clients that they'll listen to a paranoid schizophrenic for months before telling him that he needs medication. Zimmer charged three hundred and fifty an hour, so he didn't need to draw out a patient's term with him. At this point, Dusty didn't care how much he paid anyway. The high fee actually impressed him.

Dusty jumped right into the heart of his problems. He described his situation to the doctor more thoroughly than he had ever told anyone before. Dr. Zimmer had heard it all, so he wasn't fazed. He offered up about every cliché psychologist explanation ever written, but Dusty was not to be persuaded.

"I've tried everything I can think of to get her to go away, Doctor. Nothing helps. I'm not crazy. I know the girl is real. I just want to know what I'm supposed to do."

Dr. Zimmer waited until Dusty stopped talking. That's what shrinks do. Listen.

"Do you take any medication?" Doc spoke slowly, patronizing, in control.

"You mean, like sleeping pills? Not anymore. They never worked anyway. She doesn't keep me awake. She comes in my sleep every night, whether I'm drugged or not. I've even gotten drunk a couple of times just to see. She needs me for something. She is in some kind of pain. She needs me to figure it out. It's driving me cr . . ." Dusty stopped short.

"Crazy," the doctor said. He had that clichéd look that shrinks in movies always give their patients. The look that says 'The computer in your brain has a stuck key and we've got a lot of therapy ahead of us.'

"Doctor, I'm not crazy. I know you think I am."

"Maybe I could give you a medication to keep you from dreaming."

"It's not a dream! I mean, it happens when I'm sleeping, but your *brain* creates the perceptions in a dream. Something else is creating this perception. Something... outside of me. I can just feel it. I don't want to stop seeing her anyway. I'd rather help her."

Dusty paused to collect his thoughts, "I... I want you to tell me what's happening. How can she come to me every night? Haven't you ever heard of a case like this before? I think it's some kind of ESP. This little girl is real and she is communicating with me from somewhere."

"Has she skipped any nights since she first appeared?"

"No! I'm not sure. You know, I thought she first came to me two months ago, but I've been thinking about that. I think she's been in my dreams for maybe a year now?"

Doc's face didn't betray any emotions as Dusty poured out his soul. Was Dusty convincing him that some psychic phenomenon was at work here? Or was Dusty just another over-worked, run of the mill neurotic, just needing someone to listen to his rants? Dusty had not discussed the little black girl with anyone except Lana. Marilyn really didn't know the extent of it. She just knew Dusty was having just trouble sleeping due to stress.

Doc wrote something on his pad. "You first said she first appeared two months ago. Now you say maybe a year ago. What made you change your recollection?

"I seem to recall that I dreamed about her several times over the last year. It was vague and fleeting, like most dreams are. I didn't bother to think about them the next day."

Doc, still taking notes, "It was the same girl?"

"I know I've had dreams about a black child. They were short, out of focus, but memorable. I think she was learning how to come to me. I think she has made me remember," Dusty's voice trailed off as his thoughts searched for the words like a bloodhound sniffing out a rabbit.

"What?" Doc asked almost impatiently.

". . . that she's been coming to me for more than two months. I'm sure she's been trying to reach me for over a year. I've started to realize that lately. It took her until about two months ago to figure out how to do it. She may yet learn to speak to me."

"I know I've asked this before, but do you recognize this girl? Have you seen her before?"

"I've thought about that possibility. No. I haven't." Deep down Dusty wondered if that answer was really true, but he thought that it was.

"Maybe when you were a little boy?"

"No."

"Maybe you are suppressing a traumatic incident, some sort of guilt relating to this girl."

"No."

"Or any black child?" The Doc was stretching for something to unravel.

Dusty continued shaking his head, "No, she is not a symbol of guilt resurrected from my past. I was never around blacks growing up. I don't know very many now. I don't know any black children."

"Are you afraid of blacks?"

Dusty stopped shaking his head, "That's not it."

Doc saw the break in Dusty's rhythm, "Are you afraid of blacks?"

"No more than anybody else."

"What makes you think everyone's afraid of them?" Doc was now playing.

"They hate us, Doc. They grow up hating whites. Black men commit Ninety percent of the crimes. Every night the local news has one videotape after another, one mug shot after another, of blacks committing robberies, rapes, murders."

"I know a lot of blacks with PhD's; many own their own businesses. Some of my . . ."

"Doc, I know. I guess I just mean blacks in the ghetto. I'm not racist, but no white person is going to be stupid enough to venture into Southeast Chicago after dark. It would be suicide."

"Would you venture into a camp of Hell's Angels, with their lily-white skin covered with leather and tattoos?"

"Doc, this girl is not symbolic of my guilt or fear or anything! She is real and has a name. Something terrible is happening to her and she has come to me for help."

"When did you first have sex?"

"That has nothing to do . . ."

"Just answer, please."

Dusty thought, *it always comes down to sex with guys, doesn't it?* "Okay, eleven years old."

Doc's eyebrows lifted slightly, the only reaction he'd ever betrayed to Dusty. "How often?"

"Just about every day."

Doc stopped scribbling on his pad and looked at Dusty as if he'd had an epiphany. "You're kidding."

Dusty acted confused, "Oh, you mean *with* someone." Dusty grinned. "Sorry. Doc, it's not about sex."

Doc didn't return Dusty's smile. He made some erasures and went back to scribbling. He'd been gotten.

Doc had pursued all the familiar avenues into psychosis: sex, fear, guilt, religion, and Dusty's mother. Dusty knew that Doc was trolling for those deep, hidden psychic wounds that now manifested themselves in the form of a suffering black girl.

Dusty thought several times about cancelling his appointment, but had kept it mainly because, one: he needed to talk to someone in confidence,

73

better yet, a stranger and, two: maybe, just maybe the Doc would become a believer and help him locate the girl. Of course, Dusty could not totally rule out the fact that Doc might end up exorcising some long lost little black girl demon from Dusty's subconscious id, or ego or whatever. For the time being, Doc remained convinced that Dusty was a basket case.

Dusty eventually stopped going to him and sought out other psychiatrists. Maybe one would recall a similar case or be able to explain his phenomena or just believe him! In the end, it was just Dusty and her, playing out some horrible drama. She came to him every night. She was in his thoughts every moment of every day. She was real to him and Dusty knew somehow that she only came to him. But if he was to help her, something had to give. She had become an obsession, eliciting fear, guilt and helplessness every night, and revealing no way to ease her torment and his torment. Dusty was beginning to question his sanity.

Chapter 12

Dusty walked into his apartment, milling over the events of the day. The phone was ringing. It was still early evening, but he just wanted to lie down and maybe call it a day. Whoever was on the phone could wait. He had been on a phone conference close to eight hours already that morning and afternoon. He had tried to get the deposition of the COO of Reston Tobacco moved to Chicago, but it remained at the National Headquarters in Buffalo, NY. He normally would have made an effort to show in person rather than by telephone, but Chad so *courteously* volunteered to go in his place. *Ass Kisser.* Dusty didn't want to go anyway; he knew that the COO had nothing relevant to offer to the case and that the plaintiffs would get nothing from him. It was an *obligatory depo,* as he liked to call it… the ones that have to happen so you can show a jury you minded your P's and Q's, but they have no real impact on the case. He merely listened in to make sure Chad didn't totally fuck it up.

Dusty was already pulling off his tie as he entered the living room. The phone was still ringing. He walked up the stairs and into his bedroom. Still ringing. He threw his coat on the bed and kicked off his shoes. Finally the phone went to his message machine. He reached for his belt buckle, and then heard a familiar, sweet sounding voice play out over the speaker.

"Dusty, this is Lana. They're out there. Just like you said. Please call as soon as you hear this. I can't wait to talk to you." Suddenly he wasn't tired.

Dusty lunged for the phone and grappled with it before he could bring it to his ear. "Lana, I'm here. Don't hang up."

"Dusty, thank God. I've been trying to reach you all day. It's so exciting! I couldn't wait to talk to you. Can you talk?" She was uncharacteristically running at the mouth and it brought a huge, happy grin to Dusty's weary countenance. He giggled.

He was patronizing as he spoke, "Lana, slow down. I'm here. I've got all night. You are the only one I feel like talking to tonight."

Lana could sense the 'I've had a terrible day, somebody put me out of my misery' tone in Dusty's voice. "Are you okay, Dusty? You wanna talk about it?"

Dusty was already getting into a good mood. "No, Mother, I'm fine. Seriously. So tell me what is you are so excited about?"

"Ok. If you say so."

"For real. I'm good."

Lana's speech was now calm and deliberate, "Okay. Well, it's the internet, the chat room."

Dusty could hold back his enthusiasm, "Really? You're kidding."

"No, I can't believe it. I've had twenty or some responses. Most of them are kooky. You know, perverts wanting to discuss little children, but I've had seven messages from people that seem legit."

"What'd they say?"

"Here, let me read them to you."

Dusty could hear the crackling of a piece of paper that Lana must have been holding in her hand already. "This is from someone who signed 'Desperate in Florida.' He, or she, says:

A young girl comes to me in my dreams every night. She can't talk but she is in pain . . . suffering. It's been going on for at least seven months. It's not my imagination. I'm not crazy. She needs my help, yet I can't reach her. I know she sees me. It goes on for several excruciating minutes. She then grabs her face as if she is being struck. I think she is seriously hurt. She then goes through the same routine again. Begging me, pleading with me to help her. It goes on for a couple of hours every night before she leaves me at the same time every night. I am terrified for this child. I have tried therapy. No one understands. Now I am certain the little girl is real and she won't go away until I help her. I found your website online. If you know anything that might help, please write back. I am so desperate. If this is a prank, may you burn in hell.

"That has to be one of us," Dusty exclaimed, "What do the others say?"
"That one was the most descriptive, but here's one that says:

A small child appears in my dreams every night. She is in pain and needs my help. Please tell me what you know. If your details are similar to mine, I will respond.

"That sounds for real," said Dusty.
"I know," Lana continued, "This one says:

I don't know if you are on the level I am. My situation is dead serious. A child is being molested by an unseen attacker in my sleep EVERY NIGHT. It is no dream. If you have information and can verify, I will continue this conversation. I don't do chat rooms. I will know immediately so don't bother if you are a phony. I will set up an e-mail account just for your response. If you give the details that only I know. Dirk (not my real name) in San Luis Obispo, CA.

Lana read the other four messages. Most were very brief and cautious but each contained a specific and alarming piece of information that identified itself with the dreams of Dusty and Lana.

Dusty and Lana analyzed the messages together. There was no doubt, each message contained unmistakable elements of their own dreams. What made them more compelling was the fact that no message introduced new elements or description that deviated from Lana's or Dusty's own story. Each individual account seemed to leave a fingerprint, with its telling lines and grooves, from the same mysterious hand.

"What do we do now, Dusty? We have to contact these people."
"I know, and I'll bet there will be more messages in the days to come." Dusty was sure of it. "We have to be careful. That guy, Dirk, wanting all the details... he could be someone who has molested a child and just wants to find out if someone knows."

"You're right, Dusty. I worried about that before I let you meet me at the airport. But I was desperate. I had to take a chance. But a child molester would not be able to describe the dream. That's how we'll know. They will have to describe our dreams to a 'T.'"

"Right," agreed Dusty. "Do you want to continue on the chat room or do you want me to take over?"

"I want to do it. It gives me a sense of purpose. We have to meet these people, though. Eventually. There is a meaning to all this. I feel as if we are supposed to get together somehow and figure out how we are going to help these children. It's somehow, some way, going to reveal itself to us and when it does, it's going to fall on us, The Chosen, to figure it out, because the children seem dependent on us and are unable to do it themselves, at least not yet."

Dusty and Lana exchanged pleasant, reassuring conversation for a while and decided to talk again tomorrow before they did anything about the chat room messages. Lana would continue to monitor the chat room. They would both think on it. They hung up.

The bedroom was dark except for the red glow of the 11:59 on the bedside clock radio.

The little black girl was pleading again. Crying, reaching. Dusty had witnessed it over a hundred times by now. It was always the same sad, pathetic scene. But tonight he looked harder. More intent. Had he missed something? Was she being assaulted before his eyes? He couldn't detect another presence, but his eyes remained focused, intent, fearful that if he blinked, he would miss something crucial and revealing.

Her importunities always lasted three or four minutes before she was relaxed, then they started over. In this current dream, she was coming to the point where she always relaxed. She was crying violently. For the first time he noticed what looked like her intentionally grabbing her head, like she had been struck. It was so quick and so subtle. It could easily have been mistaken for her thrashing about, but this time he perceived that an outside force might be acting upon her. Dusty had not detected it before. Maybe he had been too distraught himself. It was always so hard for him to look on as she suffered. He always tried to blank it out, but even if he closed his eyes or turned away, she was still right there in front of him, just inches away.

Tonight, his concentration remained fixed. The little girl dropped her arms and began to relax. Her chest stopped heaving and then he saw something else he had not noticed before. She was staring directly at him, her eyes wide and terrified. She saw Dusty and nothing else, but this time, Dusty perceived a slight disconnect. Her eyes had him in their grasp and then, briefly, they let go. They were still open, beautiful and sad as usual, but they were distant...glazed over. She no longer saw anything. This happened only for a second, then she was with him and it started all over again.

When Dusty woke at 5:59, he was sobbing uncontrollably. *Does she die right in front of me? Every night? Inches away*? He knew she wouldn't be coming to him if she didn't need him. If she was alive, then surely she was asking him to rescue her from some unthinkable evil, but if she was dead, what could he do?

Dusty got ready for work. He had to keep his wits. He would be worthless to her if he lost it. He thought of Lana's choice of words. His little girl has *chosen* him, among all others, to be her hero. He looked in the mirror, the dead stare of a child's eye burned into his mind, and swore to himself, and to the little black child, *I will not fail you.*

Chapter 13

Over the next few months, Dusty and Lana sorted through hundreds of email responses. It was just as they expected. Many of the inquiries had come from perverts and pedophiles that were just looking to get their rocks off. The good news is that they were easy to spot. Every email that had an air of genuine sincerity was discussed at length between Dusty and Lana. There were many days that Dusty spent more time on the phone with Lana at work than with actual clients. He didn't care. Getting paid to sort through his personal tribulations by a multi-million-dollar firm was the least of his worries.

After an applicant passed the first step, Lana would send him or her a questionnaire. It had many bogus questions on there that had nothing to do with Dusty or Lana's experiences, but it was a very effective way of further filtering the bullshitters. For instance, if someone answered 'yes' to: *Does your child speak to you in your dreams,* it raised a flag. Up to this point, neither Dusty nor Lana had heard their child speak a word. If that was the only incongruence an applicant might have expressed, they went into a separate 'maybe' group that was to be further filtered once a comprehensive group of 'absolutlies' was established. The absolutlies were given a password to the chat room and were allowed to enter and join in on the conversation.

After three or four months of this process, they had accumulated about 5-dozen absolutlies and another dozen or so maybes. It was April of 2001. The conversations eventually became very heated and philosophical, but at first, the dialogue was very dry and boring: not many details were given; no one gave their real names; only a few told where they were from; and many just watched without participating for a few weeks.

Eventually, more gruesome details began to emerge. Questions began arising about the origins of the dream. There was a big, ongoing debate about whether or not the children were real children, but a majority of the people eventually settled on the belief that the children were real. From that point forward, no one questioned the reality of the situation. The biggest debate after this was whether or not the children were alive or dead. It was a tough subject to discuss, but a user by the name of *SirIsaacBruce* made a compelling point. He posed this question to the group: *Is it more likely that these children have telepathic powers while they are alive, or deceased?* It was a good point. Although telepathy was something new to everyone in the group, most agreed that it would be more likely a phenomenon when expressed by a dead person than a live person. How often do people hear about "ghost" type stories? Very often. Furthermore, *Bruce,* as Dusty referred to him to Lana, made the argument that if the children were all still alive, it was not comprehensible that all of them would miraculously develop telepathic powers that were initiated by abuse, and it was even more unlikely that only children with telepathic powers were being targeted and harmed. This fanned the fire of the group. Nobody wanted to accept the fact that these children were dead, even though that deep down they knew it in their hearts to be a high possibility. Some argued that maybe the dreams were delivered by the Holy Spirit and that the children *were* still alive, being held captive and abused. Dusty was not of this group of thought, and eventually talk died down about it. The conversations almost all assumed that the children had died and now were geared more towards *how* to figure out who they were, what happened and how to help them. A few people even claimed they might have an idea as to who that child actually was, but it was loose and no one could tell 100%.

Many other existential topics were discussed as well. Dusty headed up one conversation in particular. He asked what the others thought about why people had only now started seeing children. He constantly pondered this question. It didn't make sense to him that this phenomenon had only now transpired in the universe. One person, named *Idahotraveler,* suggested that it had been happening for a long time, but that advanced communication had made it possible for people to finally connect. He also said that murder rates and higher population make child murders more prevalent than in the past. These were things Dusty hadn't thought about. He always imagined something cosmic, like Earth's magnetic field had changed, opening up a communication path between the dead and the living. Some members really gravitated towards this line of thinking, preferring the idea that some celestial wormhole had opened. One person was even convinced that it was an early event of an imminent Armageddon, but most people didn't take this line of thinking very seriously.

People in the chat room also did a little digging and found a few anecdotal instances in the past of people claiming to see dead children in their dreams. Not many fit their parameters, but a few cases were pretty close dating back to 1742. Back then though, people weren't taken very seriously and there was no media to propagate the accounts. It would have been next to impossible for people across the country to contact each other and verify that their nightmares were possibly something more. Nothing solid came up, but they all agreed to keep an open eye and look for more clues in the past that might lead to solutions in the future.

Dusty and Lana slowly contacted each new inquiry with very vague and ambiguous responses. They didn't want to make the mistake of jumping the gun or blowing their cover. If there truly was a true "Chosen" group, then whoever or *whatever* chose it, likely meant for it to be esoteric in nature. Dusty and Lana didn't want to give any information to kooks, or worse, killers. If killers knew that people were on to them, they might be more careful, or go on a spree. Whatever approach Dusty, Lana and The Chosen took, it had to be sneaky. A sneak attack with a secret weapon: the souls of the children whose lives were taken… uniting and fighting back against the evil that routed them to a premature afterlife in the first place.

To recruit people, Dusty and Lana would go visit other chat rooms and forums and read about what people were saying. Then they would send them a private email or message if it seemed like a legitimate lead. A lot of people actually found the chat room on search engines and entered that way. Dusty had even done some research on Google and the rising popularity of placing ads on the internet and posted one regarding support groups for night terrors. A few people came to them that way as well.

Chapter 14

It was May. Spring was in full force in Chicago, Dusty's favorite time of the year. He loved the warm air and rain that pattered the green, growing grass. He much preferred it to the snow. Dusty had been working tirelessly to keep up with demands of Reston and all the legal proceedings involved in the Draper case, plus the 4 other cases that had been assigned to him in the past month. All of his spare time was spent talking to Lana, researching, reading emails, or contemplating his situation. He averaged 4 hours of sleep a night, most of which were monopolized by his little girl. His body was starting to break down and he was losing weight. He had come down with a serious sinus infection and stayed home from work on a gloomy, rainy Monday.

He took the opportunity to read through all of the questionnaires to see if he or Lana had missed something. He couldn't find anything after 4 hours that he hadn't seen before. Around noon, he made himself a bologna and cheese sandwich, stuffed with a pickle spear and drank a Pepsi. When he finished, he grabbed a quart of chocolate cookie dough ice cream and plopped on his couch. Thinking.

Dusty and Lana hadn't met or tried to meet any of the people that they had made contact with. At first, Lana had wanted to meet with all of them, but Dusty felt very uneasy doing so without seeing how the chat room played out. Dusty felt it was one thing for him and Lana to meet up and discuss things, but it wasn't feasible or cost effective to fly and meet every person they came into contact with. Plus, they had no idea that The Chosen would reach into the far corners of the world. Lana eventually caved. Up until now, Dusty just wanted to know if there were others out there and maybe get some information that neither of them knew before. He thought maybe they could find a way to deal with it, or solve it, with the help of others. There was no such luck. Each additional member to the chat room provided more questions; none with answers. Lana pressed Dusty on the issue of getting everyone together once more. All the people they found were in the same position as they were. Something had to change.

He picked up the phone and called Lana, "Lana," he didn't give her time to respond, "you are right. We need to call a meeting of The Chosen. I mean, what else are we doing all this for? We need to get us all together and see if we can figure something out. I'm tired of this standstill. We are getting nowhere."

Lana was folding laundry and watching her favorite soap opera. She was still in her pajamas, having a cup of coffee, glancing back and forth at the laptop on the couch beside her with the chat room up, "I'm so glad to hear you say that Dusty!" She had pure joy in her voice. "Now, how are we going to get people from all over the country and all over the world to come to one place?"

"We'll figure it out. So will they, because it's important. It will be our last filter. The true Chosen won't think twice about coming. The chat room has been great, but it can only accomplish so much. Most people aren't telling us much, scared for the same reasons we are. Maybe if we all got together, held a convention… maybe we can get them all to open up. I mean if we are going to solve this thing it's going to take an army of dedicated soldiers." Dusty pulled a pickle spear out of the jar he pulled from his fridge and started munching on it nervously. He didn't have much of a choice for snacks. He hadn't been to the grocery store in two weeks.

There was a silence on the phone for a moment. Dusty knew what he said had struck a nerve and that Lana was thinking. She finished folding her last pair of jeans, "Okay. Let's do it. Let's wait a few months though so we can build up attendance and find new members. Where do you want to hold the convention?"

"I think I have the perfect place," Dusty responded without hesitation.

Chapter 15

July 2001: They came from all over the world to a small resort town in Colorado. Winter Park has an indigenous population of 1,247. It is nestled 12,000 feet above sea level in a geological bowl about 10 miles in circumference, surrounded by the majestic Rocky Mountains. The air is crisp and clear. In the winter it snows almost every day. In the summer, small rain clouds float over the western mountains every afternoon and cleanse the atmosphere with small raindrops as they sweep across the town and disappear over the eastern peaks.

Dusty had been on a family vacation to Winter Park as a kid. He had never forgotten the sheer beauty and celestial atmosphere. He caught his first rainbow trout on a pink powerbait nugget in a stream near the lodge he stayed at, on a fishing pole his dad got him. The stream flowed from the snow-peaked mountaintops and was ice cold to the touch. He loved the piney smell of the evergreen trees and the way they encompassed the landscape. The place became a permanent fixture in his dreams for years to come. He had never forgotten the connection he had first made with nature there and yearned to go back ever since. Now he had a reason, a very good one.

During the peak tourist season—winter, and to a lesser degree, summer—the population may quadruple as vacationers invade the ski slopes, hiking trails and trout streams surrounding the area. Small businesses line the main drag, Highway 88, that runs through the middle of town. Rows of condos are tucked into the evergreen trees at the fringes of the community. Highway 88 winds through the mountains for miles, subjecting travelers to steep inclines, perilous declines and treacherous hairpin curves as it crosses the Continental Divide, a few miles east of Winter Park.

At 12, 400 feet, the highway empties from the high passes directly into the east side of town. The town stretches out for about two miles and ends abruptly on the west side, a bagel shop on the north side of the road and a realty office on the south. Highway 88 then continues about five miles through flat meadowlands dotted with grazing horses and cattle. Small log cabin-style ranch houses are scattered in the distance. At the western end of the Winter Park bowl is Gunnison, a smaller, mirror image of Winter Park. Highway 88 disappears out of the west end of Gunnison back into the mountains.

Five resort hotels and one dude ranch claim various sectors of the Winter Park bowl. About halfway between Winter Park and Gunnison, a two-lane, black top road T's off to the right as you come from Winter Park. The black top stretches for half a mile before winding for another half a mile through evergreens and ending at the entrance of the Winterland Resort, which comprised of 40 acres of condo units, tennis courts and walking trails.

A magnificent stone and brick structure, Winterland Lodge, stands like a fortress in the center of the grounds. The lodge is almost a small town itself, enclosing various restaurants, shopping boutiques and game rooms. The inside resembles a large, open log cabin mall with three levels of eating, shopping and arcades. The upper two stories are rimmed with luxurious apartments for sale or rent by the rich and famous.

Today, a small sign was propped on a wooden easel near the information kiosk inside the main entrance. It read: "The Chosen are meeting in the Roosevelt Ballroom at 9:00 a.m."

Dusty picked the place, but everything else was Lana. She organized the whole thing from bottom to top. Dusty was busy as ever with litigation and Lana eagerly took on the task. She had done a wonderful job.

Dusty stayed with his cousin in Denver the night before and left early for the lodge. He wanted to make sure he was one of the first ones there so he and Lana could be prepared.

He turned off of Highway 88 onto the black top road. He could see the top floor of Winterland Lodge peaking over the trees in the distance.

The sun was up in Denver, but it had not yet cleared the peaks of the Great Divide. The sky was clear and bright blue, but the lodge had still not emerged from the shadow of the mountain. He was listening to a new band he had just heard of called "Explosions in the Sky". The crescendo of the instrumental band's harmonious guitars blended epically with the scenery. Dusty took a deep breath of the cool, fresh mountain air as it whipped through his open window. For the first time in a while, for a brief moment, he felt at peace.

Just then, Dusty noticed an old VW bus had pulled up behind him and was a few feet off his bumper. The guy was weaving left and right impatiently as if Dusty were hogging the road. Dusty eased over to the right and waved the guy on. The beat up white and rust colored van sped past Dusty, contaminating the air with smoke and noise. The passenger side window was missing and had been replaced by clear plastic duct tape. The driver was a longhaired, hippie type who flashed a peace sign and a goofy grin as they exchanged glances. Normally, Dusty would've returned the gesture with the finger and carefully articulated "ASSHOLE." But today, Dusty was in a weird, anxious mood, excited to be there, but a little afraid and apprehensive.

It was a little cooler than normal for this time of the year and he could see his breath as he talked out loud to himself, "Here we go Dusty. You can do this. You are Dusty Fuckin Burch." In his head the dialogue was more something like this: *Is this going to be a freak show of psychics, mediums and paranormal junkies? God, I hope I haven't made a mistake…"*

Chapter 16

The first day, Saturday, was a nine hour scheduled day with a one-hour lunch break. The first half was blocked off for individuals to take the stand and tell the group their story. The second half was left kind of open. Neither Lana nor Dusty could accurately gauge how much time would be taken up for everyone to tell their stories, or if *anyone* would for that matter, so Lana thought it would be a good idea to have a backup plan for after lunch. She devised an individual session that was designed to work like a speed networking luncheon. Each person would sit at long tables facing each other and talk for three minutes apiece. Then, one side of the table would move down the line until everyone had met. Little did they know, 8 hours would barely be enough to get through the anecdotes.

The second day was devoted to group discussions and possibly cataloging The Chosen's children. Dusty had the idea. He thought that eventually, it would be hard to keep the children and their Chosen straight and that a "bible" of sorts would be beneficial to their efforts of solving the mysteries. He and Lana would interview each of the *willing* participants and make detailed notes about their experiences. Whatever time was left over was for fun and fellowship. Lynn also found a local artist that agreed to come and draw sketches of the children derived from the dreamer's description. That was the idea at least, but after conversations with Dusty and putting it out on the chat room, no one seemed to think they could see their child with enough detail yet, especially in the face, to give an accurate description. The artist idea was shelved but both Dusty and Lana thought it might be useful to do in the future.

The morning sun was now bathing the top two floors of the lodge as Dusty entered the huge parking lot at the front of the lodge. People were beginning to gather around the Olympic sized pool that reflected the sunny side of the lodge. It was still too chilly for anyone to venture into the water. The guests were already streaming in and out of the lodge either on their way in to eat or shop, or on their way out for tennis, horse rides, hiking, etc. They all looked pretty normal for the most part. Mostly upper, middle class Caucasian, but sprinkled with people from most races. Dusty surveyed those entering the lodge and tried to envision which ones might be there for the same purpose he was. What do The Chosen look like? Where do they come from? Dusty noticed that he tended to single out odd-looking individuals as potential members of the group he would be spending the weekend with. For the most part, the scene resembled the cross section of humans scurrying in and around a suburban mall.

Dusty entered the large, open doorway into the lodge and immediately saw the sign by the kiosk. Several isolated individuals were standing close to the easel and studying it. Dusty noticed some of them holding a pink colored sheet of paper. Dusty had one in his shirt pocket. It was a schedule of the weekend mailed out by Lana. A nerdy looking little man with black plastic eyeglasses was apparently getting assistance from one of the information employees. Dusty overheard a girl tell the nerd, "The Roosevelt Ballroom is at the far end of the building, beyond the indoor pool, across from the chocolate shop. There's a sign outside the door." The girl was pointing behind her. Dusty noticed that several people in the area took their cue from the girl and headed off across the lodge.

Lana stood behind a rectangle table outside the Roosevelt room. About two-dozen people stood around the table signing registration forms and picking up nametags. Lana was extending both hands to each registrant, clasping a hand, or an arm, or an elbow, welcoming them as she directed them through the open double doors. Her face was radiant. He could see that she was excited and happy to be here. Her presence at the door had a definite calming effect on the arrivals. Everyone was looking at the first indication of anything hokey. Lana's genuine warmth was exactly what they needed.

As Dusty approached Lana, she was shaking hands with a beautiful woman with dark hair. Dusty immediately perked up and scanned the woman's body from head-to-toe. She was a fox. He would have loved to continue his gawking and gather more data with his eyes, but she sauntered on into the ballroom. He had seen enough to know she was worth seeking out to continue his analysis. He made a mental note to look for her when he entered the room. A nasally voice interrupted Dusty's contemplation, "You hear about the e-mails?"

Dusty looked to his side and saw the nerd from the information booth looking at him through pop bottle lenses. His eyes magnified to twice their size. He extended his wiry, freckled hand, "I'm Bruce Crippen. Are you here for The Chosen?"

Bruce wore a short-sleeved white oxford shirt that looked like it had been pulled out of the bottom of the clothesbasket. His light blue polyester pants were too tight and revealed an inch of white sock over Velcro tied tennis shoes. The man stood there blinking at Dusty through those goggles. He looked about thirty-five, had red curly hair, balding and sported a bushy carrot colored mustache. He wasn't wearing a wedding ring.

Oh Joy. Dusty wasn't the type to be straight rude to a person, but he also was really not wanting to befriend someone he might not be able to detach himself from all weekend. *I can be rude and impersonal, or I can roll the dice and be nice to this guy…* Dusty peered into Bruce's soul for a moment and saw such a vulnerable countenance that he couldn't bring himself to be anything but polite, "I'm Dusty Burch," he extended a hand and received a surprisingly firm handshake, "and yeah, I'm kinda here to see what this is all about. Where are you from, Bruce?"

"Grosse Point, Illinois, north of Chicago."

"No Kidding?" Dusty was surprised, "I know where that is actually. I'm from Chicago too. Small world, huh? I live in the city in a loft close to the ballparks off Cranberry." Dusty felt a little bonding take place since they were from the same area, although they definitely did not live in the same world.

"Wow, that's so cool. I travel all these miles and the first person I meet is from my own backyard," Bruce said with a meek smile, unconfident that those were the right words to say to make a good impression.

"What do you do, Bruce?"

"I'm a computer programmer at Bank Midwest downtown."

I never would've guessed. "That's just a few blocks from my building." More people were starting to accumulate as Dusty edged a little closer to the table. Lana hadn't seen him yet.

Bruce's face registered great excitement. "Well, neighbor, what do you do for a living?"

Dusty examined his new "friend." The guy was clearly a dork. Probably lived alone or with his mother, rode the bus to work, had no girlfriend, no guy friends, and generally invisible to the rest of the world. But, for some reason, the little guy was growing on Dusty. For one thing . . . he was one of The Chosen. "I'm an attorney over at . . . ."

"DUSTY!" Lana had spotted him. Dusty turned as Lana came around the table and gave him a long, affectionate embrace. "I'm so glad you're here. We got about fifty people inside the room already and they're still trickling in."

"50?! Wow! I gotta tell ya you've done a great job, Lana. It's great to see you, too." Dusty gave her another hug. "Do you need any help?"

"You could help me at the table here. Everyone has already registered. I'm just checking them off and giving out nametags. If you'll take over, I'd like to go inside and let everyone know we'll be starting a little late. There are extra copies of the schedule on the table if anyone needs one." Lana patted Dusty's hand, "I'll be back in a few minutes. Holler if you need help." She disappeared through the doorway and Dusty circled around behind the table and began to greet people. He saw Bruce just standing there, silent, staring at Dusty. The magnified blue eyes seemed to be pleading, *"Can I hang out with you?"* Several people shuffled nonchalantly in front of Bruce, losing him in the crowd.

Dusty hollered, "Hey, Bruce, I could use some help over here. Do you mind?" Bruce pointed to himself, wondering if there was another Bruce Dusty might be referring to. "Yeah, come on over man." Bruce smiled and walked over to Dusty. *Well, there's no going back now.*

91

Chapter 17

After Dusty and Bruce finished handing out name tags and programs and directing people to their table, they made their way into the room. The Roosevelt Room was about the size of a basketball gymnasium. A small stage was elevated about a foot at the far end. A slender lectern with a microphone stood alone in the middle of the stage. Twenty circular tables were scattered over the red and blue-carpeted floor, with about half of them sitting empty. Primarily large chandeliers, symmetrically placed, hanging from a high ceiling, lit the room evenly with a yellowish spectrum. Each table had enough chairs for six people and was covered by a white tablecloth with coffee and sweet snacks placed in the center. A small folded card had been placed in front of each chair designating which participant would sit there and a stand with a card in the middle of the table represented the table number. The meeting was scheduled to begin about ten minutes ago, but no one seemed to mind. No one knew anyone else in the room, but a light chatter filled the air, as one would expect at a wedding reception. So far, Dusty had not heard anybody talk about their dreams. It was like an unspoken rule. No one was ready or knew each other well enough to talk about such a personal issue. As a result, conversation was to a minimum and most of that was tentative and self-conscious. It appeared that people from all walks of life were there. The sexes were divided about fifty/fifty. There were whites, blacks, Hispanics, Asians...all in about the same proportions as American society. Some appeared to have come from other countries and others spoke little

English. They were blue collar, white collar, old, young, athletic, out of shape and of different sexual orientations.

Dusty was supposed to sit at table one, which was near the front of the room, to the right of the lectern. He walked into the ballroom and stood, casually examining the crowd of people. Dusty and the hippie from the VW bus made eye contact across the room. They exchanged a peace sign and a nod. He began his walk towards the front, aware of his appearance and mannerisms knowing that there was at least one potential suitor in his presence. He didn't look for her intentionally, but his peripheral vision was on overdrive as he tried to locate her coordinates. He tried to walk confidently, making sure his smile to strangers as he walked by was genuine and glowing. He still hadn't spotted the girl he saw out front when he got to his table, but he wasn't done looking. Four other people were at table one and two chairs were empty, one of them being Lana's Dusty assumed.

Before he sat down, Dusty scanned the crowd once more. Before he could find her, he spotted Bruce at a table in the corner at the back of the room. Five other people were making small talk. No one seemed to be acknowledging Bruce. By now Dusty had started feeling protective of Bruce. Dusty smiled at the people at his table and introduced himself, shaking each of their hands, not really paying attention to who they said they were. He was distracted. His hormones were high and now he felt a compelling force telling him to go get Bruce and bring him to table one, but he didn't want him to take Lana's spot. Just then, he spotted Lana sitting on the stage, just off to the right of the lectern and realized she intended to sit there for the session. Dusty excused himself from the table.

As he made his way towards Bruce's table, he finally spotted the dark-haired woman. He felt like he had been punched in the stomach as she was directly in front of him when he saw her. Their eyes met briefly. She smiled politely, not showing any signs of attraction. Her eyes didn't flutter nor did she blush. Her smile was beautiful, but it was a smile Dusty felt could have been smiled at a million strangers. He became self-conscious as he passed-by, smiling back then looking away. *Was I rude? Should I have looked at her longer? Did my smile look stupid?* A hundred thoughts raced through his mind as his gut rolled and flipped. He hadn't had time to regain his composure when he got to Bruce's table, but the stunned look on Bruce's face made the walk worthwhile. Dusty slapped him on the back and said to the table, "Hey, you guys mind if I steal my buddy from you? We got too many empty chairs at our table."

Bruce was up in a flash. "Nice meeting you all. I'll see you around."

Dusty didn't have Bruce follow behind him. Dusty put his hand on Bruce's back and led him, side by side, to Bruce's new designated seat. Dusty might not have noticed the mist in Bruce's eyes, except for those damn glasses.

The lights dimmed and Lana made her way from a table near the middle of the room to the stage. She took a detour by Dusty's table and whispered in Dusty's ear, "Hey, Mr. Attorney, I'm scared to death. If I pass out, will you take over?"

Dusty grinned, "Yeah, Bruce and I got you covered."

Lana went to the lectern. The only sound to be heard was the slight click of the button as Lana turned the mic on. She cleared her throat self-consciously and spoke. She didn't use notes, "Hello, I'm Lana. I'm the one who goes by *SeattleSweetheart* on the chat room. I want to thank everyone for coming. I'm not sure how to start." A catchy little music jingle could barely be heard off to the side of the stage. A man jumped and reached into his jacket. All eyes on him.

"I guess I should start by asking everyone to please turn off cell phones and pagers." This broke the ice a little and caused a collective laugh across the room as many reached for their own cell phones. It was quiet again. "We are all here as a result of your responses to e-mails sent out by myself and Dusty Burch, who is sitting over here." She pointed and asked Dusty to stand. A few people clapped briefly but it was still awkward for anyone to know how to act. Dusty felt an air of importance roll through his body, wondering as a 7th grader would if his current object of attraction was even remotely impressed at his level of importance to the group. As he sat back down, he admonished himself for having such a juvenile thought, then thought to himself that grown men in reality really are no different than a pubescent 7th grader when it comes to women, they just have more hair and the money to go buy one if all else fails.

Lana continued, "Dusty and I met as a result of very disturbing dreams we were having involving young children. Over the last few months, each of you has communicated to us in a way that has convinced us that you share our experiences. Your accounts are nearly identical in every detail—too much for us to pass it off as coincidence. We believe something is occurring around us that is real, that is serious... something that requires us to do something. As you have noticed in our communications, I have referred to us as The Chosen because I believe we all have been chosen to help these precious children who are suffering at the hands of something evil.

"Look around you. We are here to share our stories. Hopefully, through our common experiences, we will discover what our purpose is. I am going to tell you my story first, then Dusty Burch will tell you his. After that the lectern will be open. It is my hope that each one of you will make your way to this stage and share your story with us. I'm not going to establish any particular order. This will be spontaneous. I ask that you line up to my right at the edge of the stage. We're not placing time on you. We want you to say everything you need to say. If everyone speaks for only fifteen minutes, we will be here all day. But that's okay. We have this room for the whole weekend. We will take a fifteen-minute break every two hours and an hour for lunch."

Then Lana then told her story about her little boy in a compelling fashion. Dusty had heard it many times by now. Dusty could see people all over the room nodding as they recognized the particulars of their own stories. Many were in tears. No one talked or gestured to their neighbors. They were all mesmerized, fully attentive, hoping to learn something, thankful to be there. They were complete strangers, but already Dusty could feel a sense of family taking root. Lana finished in fifteen minutes. She received a standing ovation as she left the lectern and returned to her seat, sniffling as she held back the urge to burst into tears.

Dusty took the mic and told about his little girl. His goal was to make it through without crying, which he did, but he came so close a couple times he had to pause for a moment. He was genuine and well spoken. He held none of his sentiments back and talked as if he were explaining his inner tumult to an experienced psychologist, totally free of concern that judgment was being placed on him. He avoided his attorney talk, with big words and unnecessary superlatives, yet still communicated in a graceful and artistic manner. In those moments, he unintentionally set the tone for the group that he was their leader and began his metamorphoses from a single, cocky,

95

slightly self-centered hot shot into an empathetic, compassionate leader who put others before himself. It was supremely therapeutic for his soul. He completed his account in ten minutes. Again, everyone clapped enthusiastically and a few stood. Dusty grabbed a seat and joined Lana on the stage off to the side to give her support.

An excitement was beginning to sweep over the room. A line of about 4 people had formed at the side of the stage and more were coming. It reminded Dusty of the old-time revival meeting that his grandma used to take him to. The high-pitched emotion used to scare Dusty, but this was electrifying. Dusty walked to the edge of the stage and met Bruce, his freckled hand extended for a handshake. Bruce was next. Dusty could see the nervous look in Bruce's eyes and leaned in and whispered into his ear, "Go get 'em buddy. You got this." This made Bruce feel good and empowered and he confidently approached the center of the stage.

Bruce hesitantly took the mic into his hand. His palms were sweaty. His knees were trembling back and forth as he stood at the podium. The dull, yellow tinted lights barely illuminated the crowd. The fact that he couldn't see their faces made him feel a little bit better, but the truth is he had never commanded the attention of this large of an audience by himself. The biggest audience he had addressed was during a family talent show where he played the clarinet as a 12-year-old. This experience was far different. He looked back at Dusty, who gave him an encouraging nod and a smile. His voice quivered as he spoke.

"Hello. I am," he paused and looked around the room, unsure of himself, "I am Bruce Crippen." The way he carried himself and spoke with such emotion captivated the crowd. From the first words that left his mouth, they could sense that he was a very troubled man—a man whose soul was plagued with heart wrenching sorrow, desperate for some answers.

Bruce didn't give as much personal background as the others. He dove straight in, "I am from Chicago. I see a little boy that, that seems to be choking. I feel like I watch him die right before my eyes dozens of times every night. Just when I think I might get some sort of response from him… when I think that for once, he might be seeing me, he begins to cough and squirm, wrestling for his life. I've never had children, but I can only imagine the feeling a parent would feel watching their child die in front of them. I feel as if it is my child. I desperately want to know why this is happening to me. It's been going on for nearly a year that I can remember. It affects my life in every way.

"When I found the website online, I thought it was too good to be true. I was very skeptical. I sat and watched the conversations for a month before I finally decided to join in the chat room conversations. I felt like it was impossible for that many people to be experiencing the exact same thing as I was without it being real, so I took a leap of faith. I'm so glad I did.

"I've never had many friends... I don't have a lot of family. This little child I'm seeing has kind of... taken over all the love in my heart. If there is any way that we are going to get through this, I believe it's together. I will do anything, anything to help this group figure out the solution. I will promise you that. Even if it's the last thing I do."

With that, Bruce walked off the stage. Anyone that felt a prejudice in regards to his dorky appearance immediately felt guilty and like a huge jerk. Bruce had touched everyone. He inspired everyone. He made many who were hesitant to speak all of the sudden feel comfortable. In those moments, Bruce became the unspoken mascot for The Chosen. For what appeared to be a proverbial dork, incapable of arousing emotion from a human being, to suddenly capture the hearts of everyone is such a dramatic fashion, lifted the spirits of the Roosevelt room to a celestial level.

For most that took the platform and told their stories, it was generally the same story being repeated over and over: a child appeared to them in their sleep; the child was unable to verbally communicate, but the child was suffering and in most appeared to be struggling with an unseen presence. The children described all appeared to be pre-pubescent. They seemed to be evenly divided between male and female. The children were of all nationalities and their race, nationality, sex and age did not seem to have any relationship with the person they had "chosen."

Other than the common dream, the members of "The Chosen" did not appear to have any common characteristic or element. The Chosen were white, black, Hispanic, straight, gay, educated, uneducated, young, old, widows, widowers. Almost all were from the United States, however, there were several from foreign nations. There was a professional soccer player from Brazil, a professor from Canada, a retired executive from Japan, and a half dozen other non-Americans. The predominance of Americans, and particularly Americans within the middle states, was probably because of the location of the meeting in Colorado.

The phenomena of "The Chosen" was possibly world-wide and included those who did not have financial resources or opportunity to come to Colorado. Dusty did not remember the names and stories of everyone who spoke. Of course he knew Lana and was developing affection for Bruce, but he would get to know, and love, many more of them. There were several who stood in Dusty's mind for one reason or another:

THE PROSTITUTE

Holly Hedgecorth was a former prostitute from San Luis Obispo, CA, age: 33. She is actually one of the first people who contacted Dusty and Lana through the chat room activity that helped formed The Chosen. "I quit turning tricks and started waiting tables after the little girl started appearing in my dreams. I don't know her name but I love her like my own daughter. I used to be angry and mean spirited. Now I love people. A child needs me . . .she has changed my whole life; she has given me a purpose and I'm bound to find out what it is. The weird thing is, I think I might actually know who the girl is. I can't tell for sure because my dreams are still a little foggy, but a girl in my town went missing several years ago. I remember when it happened it really affected me because I can't have children and I have always wanted one so bad and it affected me so bad because I saw an interview with her parents on the news and I saw how torn apart they were. Their baby was taken from the bus stop. I just always thought I might be having nightmares about that, but it never occurred to me the little girl might *actually* be coming to me until I found y'all. I wonder what could this mean? If I can somehow help this girl and help her parents get closure and especially put the creep behind bars so it never happens again, it would mean so much to me. Maybe it's not the exact same girl I'm seeing, but whoever it is, if she is real, I want to help her."

Dusty was very touched by Holly's account and somewhat jealous that she had even the slightest bit of a lead to go off of. He had always wondered if others might have any clue whatsoever about who the children they were seeing might actually be. He was anxious to hear more.

THE PREACHER

Charles Robertson was a Pentecostal preacher, about 45 years old. He had a congregation of about 4,000 in St. Paul, Minnesota and a live telecast every Sunday morning. He and his wife had five children, ranging from pre-school to high school. "God sends a precious little boy in a vision every night. I believe the Lord has brought us all together to discover his plan for these little innocents. I fear that Satan himself is struggling for their young souls. I can't say I know who this little boy might be like Holly, but I can *feel* him and his struggle. The good lord I believe has bestowed upon me the ability to receive communication from this boy and I believe with enough faith in our father in heaven, he will open up the channels and allow us to help our children. I know not everyone in here may be a Christian, but hopefully you have some belief in a higher power, because I think that is going to be a crucial part in how we go about bringing justice to the evil that we have all become so painfully and intimately aware of."

Dusty took down a note, reminding him to do a little digging into the belief systems of all of the Chosen.

THE TRUCK DRIVER

Dan Blassingame, a truck driver from Orlando, Florida, had been chosen by an Asian girl of about twelve years old. Dan was big and burly like a mountain man. He choked on his words as he described what he believed was the torture of a child by unseen hands. He too was one of the original people who contacted Dusty and Lana through the website. He and Dusty had several early conversations over the phone and got to know each other a little bit. Dusty liked Dan. He seemed like a very genuine, down-to-earth guy who cared about people.

THE BRAZILIAN SOCCER STAR

Pablo, a striking young Hispanic, came all the way from Caracas, Venezuela, where he is a soccer star. He talked in broken English about the little girl in his dreams, who wore a sweatshirt displaying the logo of his team. "Little girl start coming to me after soccer game. I not know who she is. I taught maybe it not real, just bad dream. For some reason, I start feeling like she very real when she not go away. I am believing I need be her angel. Den after two months, I see on paper dat a little girl missing. I

99

keep paper because it… strange. I taught I knew her. Den, I wake up one night after she come to me and I run to paper on table. I see her face clear now. I learn dat I see the girl in the paper." Everyone in the room gasped, some more audible than others, but the room froze. At this moment, there was no turning back. There were no more thoughts in anybody's head that *maybe this isn't real. Maybe there is some reason we are seeing these children other than they are dead.* "I know not what to do. Why she come to me? Can I help her? I want very bad to help, very very bad."

Dusty felt a cold chill run up his spine. *Could it be? Could he really be seeing the same girl?* Dusty wondered why he hadn't seen anything on the news about his girl, but he also hadn't really paid that much attention to the news ever. He tried very hard to picture her face, but couldn't. He realized that until now, he had always had denial running through him regarding the reality of this girl. *Maybe when the denial is completely gone, I'll be able to see her more clearly.*

THE WHIZ KID

Sajid was a 17-year-old whiz kid in quantum physics with a full ride to Stanford. His parents had moved to the United States when he was a baby. A redheaded boy of around nine years old began appearing to Sajid shortly after he started his freshman year at college when he was fifteen. "I never even considered him to be real for the longest time, until I found this group. I started looking because the dreams slowly started to bother me and as I paid more attention to them and gave them more thought, the boy became clearer to me and the dreams were more detailed. I don't have a story like Pablo. I can't say I've ever looked for him in the paper or that it I even pay attention to the news very often because I'm studying so much and the news is so negative it brings me down. Plus, California is so big that unfortunately you hear of kids go missing all the time, so if I had heard about him before I don't remember. But there is no doubt I am going to search now as deep as I need to for clues."

THE DOCTOR

Tom Jeffreys was a distinguished looking black man of about sixty, with close, cropped hair and graying sideburns. "I'm a pediatrician in Boston. My wife of 22 years died about a year ago. Shortly after her death, a young white girl about 5 years old started coming to me in my sleep. She resembles my wife as a little girl. My wife was white. We never had children, but my wife had an abortion 20 years ago because she feared bringing mixed racial blood into our society. She was never able to conceive after that. The little girl has blue eyes but dark curly hair and cocoa colored skin. I believe she is the daughter we aborted and she is in agony."

THE LESBIAN

Kim Lowery was a short lady in her twenties, with short, dark hair and masculine features. She came right out and talked about her sexual preference as if to get it out of the way, "If you can't tell, I'm a lesbian and proud of it, but that's not what we are here to talk about. My child is a beautiful girl of about eight or nine. When she started appearing to me nightly, I thought it was my alter ego. I thought her anguish represented my conflict over sexuality. I came out of the closet shortly after that, but she still appears. You may not approve of who I am but it is obvious to me, after listening to all of you, that our children have chosen us regardless of our race, sex, age, social status or sexual preference." Kim received a standing ovation as she left the platform.

THE NIGERIAN

Chakuma Kwambi was a humanities professor at the University of Arkansas in Monticello, Arkansas. Her child was black and wore sandals and khaki shorts, customary to Nigerian youths. The young boy first appeared to Chakuma about eight months ago, when she was still living in Nigeria. The child followed her in her dreams to Arkansas.

BIKER

Johnny Turner was a middle-aged silver-haired biker with a ponytail and leather chaps. His tough outlaw image was betrayed by the tender, loving anguish with which he described the little toddler who had come to him three months ago. Johnny was certain the boy was being shaken and beaten violently by an unseen devil. Johnny became too emotional to finish his testimony and stood there for several minutes, pursing his lips tightly, but he couldn't close his eyes tight enough to push back the tears.

DL Gleason

MOUNTAIN CLIMBER

A rugged athletic man in his early twenties took the podium. "My name is Nick Hendrix. I'm from a small town called Gilbert, Arizona. I guess I'm what you'd call an adrenaline junkie. I climb mountains all over the world. That's what I live for. When I run out of money, I take a job somewhere and work 'til I have enough to do another climb. I've climbed Everest, K-2, and the Matterhorn. That's where I truly come alive, on the face of a mountain, one misstep away from eternity, or whatever's out there.

"My story isn't any more special or heartbreaking than the rest of yours. I'm convinced the little brown-eyed girl with curly red hair and glasses is real. These children have contacted us all for a purpose. I thought I was going crazy. I made the mistake of telling a few friends and they knew I was crazy... too much thin air. I lost my girlfriend over it." Nick looked like a California surfer boy, blonde, shoulder-length hair, deeply tanned complexion and steel blue eyes. He was the type who found confidence in his own self-discipline and extreme physical conquest. He was insecure and awkward in social situations.

Nick hardly looked up as he spoke. "I'm not afraid at all to climb the vertical face of El Capitan, but talking in front of a group of people terrifies me." The audience embellished a chuckle to offer some reassurance. "I generally avoid crowds and group functions but I had to come here. I was drawn here. My little girl led me to the stage and is holding me up to speak. We have got to find clues in our stories. They're there. They have to be. They want us to get together and share our stories because the answer is there. Each sad story shares common elements. That's how we first recognize each other. But each story is a little different.

"Maybe we need to study the differences. My story is pretty much the same as yours. My little girl comes to me every night. She is pleading for my help. You know, when I'm on mountains, I see bodies of climbers who have fallen or have frozen. Some have been there many years, frozen, unburied. We just leave them there. I have rested right beside them, a few inches from their open eyes. It doesn't faze me. But my little girl breaks my heart every night and she's been coming to me for over a year. In that year, I've spent the night on the top of Everest and other peaks in the Himalayas; I've spent the night on Mont Blanc in the Alps. I was in the

Andes a few weeks ago. No matter where I am in the world, she comes to me every night.

At first, I just wanted to escape her. Now I just want to help her. For the first time in my life, I find that I need to be with people. I hope I get to know every one of you while I'm here. I want to hear about all of your children."

Each story was unique and singularly disturbing, yet each story had the same familiar pattern, a young child in anguish, pleading for help every night. The child always leaves just before The Chosen adults' wake up time. Several people had night jobs and slept during the day. Dan Blassingame, the burly truck driver, had worked three different shifts. In every case the children came to The Chosen when they slept, no matter what time of day. There were no accounts of children coming during naps.

The tears of the speaker and the audience punctuated almost all testimonials. Several unspoken rules of order and protocol evolved that people began to follow voluntarily. No one spoke more than five to ten minutes, except for Lana and Dusty. Orderly lines formed on each side of the stage. As a speaker would finish, the next speaker would come from the right side, the next from the left. Each speaker left the stage to generous and affectionate applause. The audience was riveted by every person's story, even though some of the details were being repeated over and over.

During the middle of the speakers, Dusty had an ill feeling come over him out of the blue. Amidst the accounts of night terrors and suffering children, another child, one that is very alive, came into Dusty's mind. Brian Draper. He tried fighting off the images of the little boy in those tighty-whiteys, standing in front of the room full of lawyers, allowing his molten flesh to be photographed like he was on the cover of some magazine. Dusty didn't want to feel the guilt he was feeling, but it crept up his spine like ice forming on a subzero, Antarctic winter day. He wouldn't allow himself to admit it, but during those moments in that room with The Chosen, his heart was undergoing a transformation, personally and professionally. Brian came to his mind several times throughout the day and to distract himself, Dusty looked across the room at his newfound, female infatuation.

About 20 people had introduced themselves and told their stories before Lana made her way to the podium shortly after noon. They had been going non-stop for over three hours. No one had left the room, except for short restroom excursions. Lana suggested they break for lunch until 1:30 p.m.

Chapter 18

They broke for lunch about 12:30. There were several restaurants and fast food kiosks in the resort mall. Many of The Chosen had gotten to know and become friendly with at least the ones at their table. Many of them went to lunch together, some went off by themselves to each shop, walk around, or call someone. Others were joined by family, friends or mates who had taken the trip with them. No one but The Chosen was allowed in early meetings, however.

Dusty, Bruce, and Lana ended up at a small restaurant. Doris Swiss and Jurgaen Feverstacke joined them. Both had been at table #5. Doris was a widower in her late 60's from Tupelo, Mississippi. She had been too shy to take the podium, but friendly enough to share a little about herself to the rest of the table in between speakers. Doris had a warm, sensitive, grandmotherly appearance. Her brown eyes were still clear and expressive. She had rinsed her hair a honey color rather than go grey. She was a little plump, but healthy looking, maybe 20 pounds heavier than her youthful weight. She wouldn't have been gorgeous as a young housewife, but she would have been pretty.

Jurgaen had not taken the podium either. He barely spoke English. They had seen his name on the name tab this morning when he first sat down, but they had no idea how to pronounce it. He was a 47-year-old pharmaceutical salesman from Rejavick, Iceland, tall, burly and with a full head of curly, dark brown hair. He had introduced himself with a hearty Slavic voice and firm, confident handshake. "Yow pronounce name Fear stack, Jurgaen Fear stack." He didn't talk much after that, other than to punctuate other conversation with an occasional "Yaah!" or "Das iss true" or some other short broken English phrase. He was a successful, self-made businessman whose company of pharmaceutical supplies had expanded to the U.S. a couple of years ago. He now traveled here once a quarter and was learning English.

The group ordered their lunches. Dusty noticed they all ordered water, tea or soft drinks. Dusty would normally have ordered a Bud Lite, but it was as if no one wanted to dull their senses of perception with alcohol.

Lana was genuinely excited and animated, "Isn't this wonderful? All these people here, sharing their experiences... we're not alone. We are becoming a..." Lana struggled for the right description, "not just a support group... a family!"

"Yah! Vamily," Jurgaen understood and agreed enthusiastically.

Lana was right. Dusty looked around the restaurant and recognized many of The Chosen, mostly grouping according to their assigned tables. They hadn't really had an opportunity to get to know anyone else. That would come later.

There were some who were naturally loners or slow to make friends. Some started out sitting by themselves and then eased into a conversation with another of The Chosen. Johnny Turner, the biker, had sat down by himself. The hippie, (or Stone Free as he would come to be known), then came by and offered some kind of male acknowledgement like, "How's it going man" or "Liked your speech Dude." Dusty couldn't really tell, but Stone Free and Johnny were talking like buddies, when Johnny spotted Dan Blassingame, the grizzled truck driver, alone at a booth across the aisle. Johnny hollered something out to Dan, seconded by Stone Free, and Dan picked up his burger, fries and super-sized soft drink and joined them. Dusty noticed that none of them were drinking alcohol.

There were other couplings or groups that seemed to find each other for reasons other than their table number. Pablo, the Brazilian soccer player, was sitting with Sajid, the 17-year- old whiz kid. Dusty imagined they had youth and foreign nationality in common. Nick, the mountain climber, eventually joined them. The people who had gotten up and given their stories found it easier to mingle because others would come up and thank them for their story. That would open the door for the five Ws: What is your name? Where are you from? Why are you here? When did you get here? Who came with you? And so on. Before long, they were sharing their most painful and guarded secrets.

Dusty saw the prostitute, Holly, at a table with two others, a young man and a middle-aged woman from her table. Holly, as one might imagine, seemed to keep the other two entertained with her conversation and gestures. Holly recognized some of The Chosen at a table next to them and in a few minutes, they had scooted their tables together into one group. Again, no alcohol.

Lana looked around the table, "I have been so anxious to talk to you guys. What do you think? Any observations?" The others hesitated. They all had things to say, but instead deferred to Lana's enthusiasm.

Dusty broke the silence, "We're all here because of you, Lana. We want to hear what you have to say."

Lana took a drink of her water more out of self-consciousness than thirst. She paused, collected her thoughts and pushed a square napkin over to Dusty. "You got a pen?" Dusty instinctively knew what she was getting at, but he didn't have a pen.

"Here Dusty." Of course Bruce had a choice black, red and blue bics in his shirt pocket, as well as a mechanical pencil.

Lana continued, "First of all, what's happening is real. We are not under some mass delusion or hypnosis. A child visits everyone here. Does anyone believe these children are figments of our imaginations?" The table corresponded, "No," "Absolutely not," "Dat iss impossible."

Dusty wrote down on the napkin:

1. Everyone here visited by children in dreams
2. The Children are real

Lana was ready to pass the baton, "And what about the children?" She looked at them as if so much was obvious that these were really rhetorical questions.

Dusty spoke, "Jurgaen, Bruce, go ahead. I'm writing."

Jurgaen waved his hand toward Bruce, "You spick." Dusty and Lana glanced at each other and shared a covert grin. In any other context it would have sounded like a racial slur. Bruce didn't notice.

"Well, they are all children. They are both sexes, neither predominant, and none of them are less than three or four or described to be older than the age of fourteen or fifteen. " Bruce looked at Dusty's napkin to see if he was writing it down. Dusty was.

"You're right," said Doris. "As I heard the stories, I couldn't help noticing that. It seems logical that a child less than three might not know how to come to us, but why stop at fifteen or sixteen? Why not seventeen or twenty-five-year olds?"

"Puberty... maybe eet keels zay're powers." Jurgaen had been thinking about this. "All zose hormones dumped in zay'er bodies. Eet steals zay'er innocence."

Lana seemed suddenly convinced, "I think you may be right. Now that I think of it, none of the girls were described being over twelve or thirteen. The oldest boys were described as fourteen or fifteen. Girls go into puberty earlier than boys. Some start menstruating as early as eleven years old."

"Yaah, I haff three girls. Zey all start bleed by twelf. Vat is ze vord... menstruate." Jurgaen added as he scratched his head and looked down at the table. Under no other circumstances would he have shared that information with complete strangers. Bruce was blushing and rubbed a freckle on his arm. He had never said the word "menstruate" and had only heard it spoken about by his 6th grade science teacher and his mother.

After a minute of contemplation by the table, Jurgaen spoke again, "Zey... suffer," Jurgaen added quickly, noticing Bruce squirming in his chair. Everyone paused a second, puzzled and wondering if he was talking about menstruating teenagers. Dusty's eyebrows furrowed a bit and his eyes went to the ceiling in contemplation. As soon as Jurgaen noticed reluctance of the table to agree and before the brutal awkwardness set it, he cleared the air, "Ze Children," he added with his palms in the air. Everyone nodded immediately in agreement.

"And they don't speak," continued Bruce, glad that the subject had changed. Dusty kept writing. He hadn't said anything yet. They were all saying what he'd been thinking.

5. The Children are suffering

Suddenly Dusty was curious. He glanced around the restaurant and was certain he saw several others writing on napkins, menus, vacation brochures and other adapted script. Dusty mused... they were compiling their own lists. Probably mirroring the same observations and questions. According to Lana's schedule, the speeches would finish this afternoon. Open dialogue and group discussion were slated for tomorrow. Dusty realized they would be comparing many similar lists.

"The children are not defined by race or culture;" Doris remarked. "Did you notice that the children are black, white, Hispanic, oriental?"

Bruce added, "And there doesn't seem to be any racial connections to The Chosen adult. Black kids have chosen white adults. But it does seem like The Chosen are only seeing kids from their same country."

"En contraire," Jurgaen interjected.

"We haven't heard about your child," Lana responded to Jurgaen. "Is your child not from Iceland?"

"I do not think so. She is little black girl. Not many black people een Iceland. Not dressed like leetle girls in Iceland. Dress like... how you say... poverty."

Dusty spoke for the first time. "Jurgaen, my little girl is black."

"I know. I hear your story in vroom."

Dusty continued, "Are you pretty sure she's not from Iceland? How do you know?"

Bruce and Lana remained silent. It was obvious where Dusty was going with this.

"I do not know for sure. She duss not spick so I con't hear langvige. I just know eets very leetle I see blacks een Iceland."

Dusty started to press further, but Jurgaen raised his hands halting Dusty.

"Thees haff been troubling me. I haff assume cheeldrin come from same country as adult. I'm sure mine duss not." There was silence around the table as they digested Jurgaen's words, each individual free-associating everything they had heard today—rotating puzzle pieces—hoping they will drop into place.

Dusty was deep in thought—even as he spoke. "Most of The Chosen who have spoken are from America. And we assume that the children are American. No American has perceived their child to be from another country."

"Maybe there's no connection between the nationality or country of The Chosen and the child," Bruce offered, unconvincingly.

Dusty countered, "Bruce, do you believe your child is American?"

109

"I'm sure he is. He is wearing a Hulk Hogan T-shirt." Noticing Jurgaen's confused expression, Bruce clarified, "He's an American wrestling star."

Lana broke in, "Yes, I'm sure my child is American. I don't know why. I can't put my finger on it. I just believe she is. Doris?"

"Oh, without a doubt."

"Pablo, hiss keed from Venezuela—like Pablo."

"That's right," Lana exclaimed, "his little girl wears a sweatshirt with his team logo."

"The Nigerian lady… can't say name…college professor…her child from Nigeria."

The others seemed a little puzzled, Lana spoke, "That's right. Chakuma, she's a professor in Arkansas, but she came here from Nigeria a couple of years ago. She said her child was black and dressed as Nigerian youth do."

"You see contradiction?" Jurgaen had clearly been keying in on this issue all morning. "I live Iceland all life. Never see black girl in dream. Never see black people except T.V."

Bruce, mentally rotating the puzzle piece, "Don't you leave the country for business?"

"I come America first time two years ago—beezness—stay in hotel airport 3 days—go back. Come back next year—same—3 days. But leetle black girl not come to me until 6 months after I come home from America first time. Has been in dream every night since.

Bruce was willing to add another fact to the list. A puzzle piece dropped, but still an awkward fit. "I think we can say there is a geographical connection. It's too much of a coincidence—the soccer player and the Nigerian lady—and Jurgaen has been exposed to American children by coming here—even though briefly."

Dusty concurred, "I agree. It's too coincidental. And Jurgaen has reminded me of something else. The Nigerian lady…"

"Chakuma Kwambi," Lana interrupted.

"Yes, Chakuma, her child came to her just before she moved here about two years ago. Jurgaen's probably-American-child could have contacted him when he first came to America two years ago." Dusty could see they were with him but not quite yet. Everyone's mind was whirring, shifting gears, and trying focusing the lens.

Bruce was the first to see it, "Two years! There are no accounts of children appearing more than two years ago."

"Yah!"

"That's right," Jurgaen and Lana immediately agreed.

Dusty grabbed the pen. Can we write that down? Can anyone think of a story in which the child has been appearing for more than two years?"

They looked at each other for a few moments—checking their memories. Almost in unison they responded nodding from side to side, "No," "Huh uh," "Not yet."

Jurgaen offered a light objection, "But, eef cheeldrin start coming in dreams two years ago, and eef there is geographic tie, why did my girl come een Iceland one and a half years ago, six months after I leave America?"

Jurgaen was having difficulty making his point, but Dusty understood the logistical problem, "If Jurgaen's child made contact in America, why did she wait 6 months to appear to him?"

Lana was ready with an observation, "You know, I have been wondering about the two years. That's just when it started, but kids have started appearing to their chosen as recently as three months ago. Remember the mailman, Charlie Bates? But, no one specifically identified the very date the child came. We all shared the same experience. The children sort of seeped into our consciousness slowly and sporadically over a period of time. Most of the speakers recalled experiencing a vague intuition or hazy image of the child months before the child suddenly emerged into their dreams. Some guessed it was about two to three months. Others as long as nine months."

Dusty was nodding as Lana spoke. He looked at Jurgaen and stated, "The guy from Golden, Colorado said he thought his little boy first flashed through his dreams about six months before he started seeing him on a consistent basis.

"Yah, six months." Jurgaen couldn't remember when his little girl first sparked the synapses in his brain… those little dreams, nighttime thoughts that vanish within seconds of waking. He was willing to bet they started two years ago in America.

Dusty scratched his head, thinking about everything that was just said in regards to a two-year timeline, "Well, let's not make any assumptions that two years has any relevance to this equation yet. We still haven't heard everyone and maybe it's just coincidence. Plus, there's still a lot of people out there that haven't come here to tell their story. Let's keep an eye on it and see if we can find any logic behind it. Honestly, I can't imagine what it would be. I mean, why would people only start seeing children—in the history of humans—two years ago? There would have to be some cosmic, supernatural, coming-of-the-gods explanation that none of us could explain anyway."

Lana offered an explanation, "What if with the coming of the internet and the data age, somehow their spirits were able to connect to ours, like through some sort of…" her eyes flittered towards the sky and her hand made a whirling motion, "radio wormhole? I don't know, it sounds stupid when I say it out loud."

Bruce stepped in and defended her, "No, that's not stupid at all. We have to think outside the box here. At the same time, maybe we'll never know and maybe it's not even important to how we can solve the mystery and help them."

"Thank you, Bruce, you're too sweet," Lana replied as she gently patted his hand. Bruce blushed.

"I agree," Dusty said, "we have to keep an open mind for sure."

Lana looked at her watch. 1:25. "Well, this has been productive, but we've got to get back and get the afternoon session started. Dusty, what do we have on the list?"

Dusty read aloud from the "facts napkin":

1. Everyone here visited by children in dreams
2. The children are real
3. No predominant sex- child or chosen
4. Children are from 3-15 years old
5. The Children are suffering
6. Tied geographically to adult
7. Children do not speak to chosen
8. No predominant race- child or chosen
9. Children and chosen from all over world
10. Children do not clearly emerge into dreams for 3-9 months
11. Timeline? Maybe a two-year common denominator?

"I'm sure we've left some things off, but have you noticed... there are other people in this restaurant looking at lists now?" The others looked around and saw.

"This is going to be an interesting weekend!" Lana could hardly contain her enthusiasm.

"You geet teep. I geet bill," Jurgaen said as he was pulling his American Express out. There would be no challenges. A few minutes later Dusty, Bruce, Jurgaen and Doris were back at their tables waiting for Lana to open the session.

Chapter 19

T he audience's attention remained steadfast throughout the day even though the stories, though gut wrenching, began to sound familiar and predictable. No new clues or insights were offered, only confirmation that they all shared a common, troubling phenomena. They all knew what the speaker was going to say before the story began, but they still listened attentively because they wanted to know each other. They were bonding, coming together, and embracing each other spiritually. In each new speaker, they found a kindred soul who suffered through the mental anguish they all felt. They were "The Chosen," a preternatural fellowship whose nightly transports into the nether world isolated them from the rest of humanity. No one in the room would ever again be without friends; no one would be a stranger.

By late afternoon most of The Chosen had spoken. The same horrible patterns emerged as, one by one, each referred to "my little boy" or "my little girl." No one had named his or her child.

Then Sarah Niedhaus, a painfully shy high school librarian from Lawrence, Kansas startled the audience with her first words:

"I have two children. The first child, a small girl of about seven or eight, began materializing in my dreams about eight months ago. It is so disturbing for me to talk about. All of you have pretty much described my own horror. About three months ago, another girl appeared. She is about four or five."

Sarah stopped to suppress emotions welling up in her. Sarah was twenty years old. She was slender, wore little make-up (if any) and wore her dark brown hair in a pixie cut. Her pink sweater fit loose and modestly. She did not have the looks that turned heads, but her intelligent face and unpretentious mannerisms would easily captivate any man who was willing to contemplate her natural femininity. Sarah continued with soft, measured sentences.

"I don't know how long I can talk about this. I wasn't going to come up here, but none of you have mentioned having more than one child. These two little girls are precious to me. Maybe someone can find a clue in my story. Every night the eight-year-old visits me first. Just like the rest of you she is . . ." Sarah paused a few seconds, ". . . hurting. She always leaves just before my alarm goes off at 6:30 am. Then one night she left earlier than usual. She sort of faded away and everything was black. Then the four-year-old faded into view and began . . ." Sarah stopped, sniffled a couple times and regained composure, "mimicking the other girl. Every night I have the feeling that the eight-year-old deliberately leaves so the four-year-old can take her turn. They are never together but I think they know each other. They don't appear related at all. I just sense they are able to communicate with each other about when it's time to come and go. Another strange thing is that the eight-year-old slowly emerged into my dreams. I don't remember the first time she was there. Just like all of you, I vaguely became aware of a girl in my dreams and the image became clearer and clearer over a period of several weeks, maybe even months before she became vivid and I was conscious of her. But the four-year-old was vivid and animated from the start." Sarah's lips trembled and she paused again. She continued, unable to retain her tears, "I think the eight-year-old brought her to me."

Sarah left the platform. There was no applause as she made her way to her table. Many stopped her along the way to offer hugs and kind words. No one took to the stage for a few minutes. There were murmurs and whispers from every sector of the room. Sarah's piece to the puzzle was the first that had been cut and colored different. She had two children; they seemed to be aware of each other; and, of all the stories, the four-year-old was the only child to have appeared vividly the first time. What clues were hidden there? Did anyone else have more than one child? As the wheels and gears turned about the room, a scraggly-haired man dressed in thrift store apparel shuffled across the stage and tapped the mic self-consciously.

HIPPIE

"Uh, hello, everybody. I'm Daryl Steadman but everybody calls me Stone Free." The man was extending a right-handed peace sign to the audience. Dusty recognized the man as the hippie who had passed him in the VW bus on the highway that morning. Dusty assumed that Stone Free had adopted his moniker from the Jimi Hendrix song of the same name.

"Four boys come to me every night, each of them between ten to thirteen years old. These little dudes are bein' hurt, man. At first, I thought it was, you know, drugs. I drop a little acid now and then and some other stuff, but these little guys kept comin'. You know, just like Sarah said. At first there was just one. Then suddenly this other one started showin' up. Then a few weeks later, the third. About a month ago the last one appeared. They're never together. I think, you know, like Sarah said, I think these little guys knew each other.

"I figured I must be trippin' all the time, man, until I seen this chat room about these children. I mean, I came here sorta 'cause, you know, out of curiosity. But after hearin' all you talk, I'm thinkin', man, this is wild. There's something' freaky going' on here. We gotta figure this out, man. It's like these little kids are wantin' us to be their heroes or somethin'. I may not be an upstanding, normal citizen or overly smart, but I love kids and something ain't right. We gotta like come together man, like John Lennon said, except over *the kids*. Let's make this happen. That's all I gotta say, man." Stone Free extended two peace signs and left the stage to scattered applause. He was weird but he was one of The Chosen. Four children had chosen Stone Free. That gave him a special, eerie aura.

Stone Free's speech sparked a multitude of group discussions and gentle debate around the room. Each table conducted its own little forum on the meaning of it all.

Lana returned to the podium.

"Could I have your attention, please?"

The audience became quiet and attentive.

"You know, it never occurred to me that there might be people who are visited by more than one child. Sarah and . . . Excuse me young man. I'm sorry. What was your name again?"

"Stone Free," the hippie hollered from the back of the room as he raised a peace sign.

Lana returned the peace sign awkwardly, "Right. Stone Free. Anyway, Sarah and Stone Free have experienced some things the rest of us haven't. That could be significant. I'm curious, has anyone else been visited by more than one child?"

Two people on opposite sides of the room raised their hands, a tall, slender, young black man on the left and an elderly Caucasian man to the right.

Lana commented, "I think this is very intriguing."

She pointed to the middle-aged man, "What is your name, sir?

"Tony."

"And how many children come to you?"

"Three," he answered.

Lana asked the elderly gentleman, "What is your name sir?"

A gruff, confident voice bellowed, "Edward Vaughan, and I'm here because I have nine children. All young boys."

There were gasps and mutterings around the room.

Lana glanced at Tony and then back to Mr. Vaughan, "Would you two gentlemen care to come up here and share your stories."

TONY'S THREE

Tony Dennis was twenty-seven years old. He was a pizza deliveryman from Fayetteville, Arkansas. He'd been a star basketball player in Little Rock with a full ride to the University of Arkansas, where he most certainly would have been a starting forward as a freshman. He blew out a knee and lost his scholarship. He dropped out of high school and began selling drugs to other youths in Little Rock's version of the ghetto, the South Side.

He moved on to armed robbery, was caught during a liquor store holdup when the owner shot him in the leg. Tony went to the State Pen in Fayetteville for six years. There he read *The Biography of Malcolm X*, got his GED, read most of the books in the prison library. Psychology and philosophy were his favorite subjects. He kept a copy of Norman Vincent Peale's "The Power of Positive Thinking" and Victor Frankl's "Man's Search for Meaning" by his bedside and marked them like Baptist's do their

Bibles. Victor Frankl's assertion that man can endure any suffering if he can find a purpose in it resonated profoundly within Tony.

Reading had saved Tony's life. He delivered pizzas at night and commuted forty miles to the small town of Monticello four days a week where he was enrolled in an extension of the University of Arkansas. Tony was in his third semester, majoring in education. He wanted to go back to South Little Rock and teach high school after he graduated. Tony's limp was barely detectable as he carried his six-foot nine-inch frame across the stage. He spoke with a thick southern accent, without the Ebonics characteristic most associate with low-income blacks.

"Hi, y'all. My name is Tony Dennis. About a year ago, a little white boy about nine years old became a part of my soul. He came to me just as you have described. I don't have anything new to add to that. Like most of you, I thought I was going crazy at first, and then I realized my child was real and had come to me for help. About six months later, another boy about eight or nine started appearing after the first boy left. The second boy appears Asian, maybe Vietnamese. He, too, is in some kind of pain. Three months ago, a third boy about the same age as the first two started appearing after the first two had left. Just like Sarah and Stone Free, I don't remember exactly when I initially became aware of the first boy. He sort of eased into my dreams over time until he had a definite presence. The other two materialized suddenly. I also believe, like Sarah and Stone Free, that the boys communicate with each other. I love these boys."

Tony's voice became swollen with emotion. "I love them as if they were my own children. I agonize over them every night, as you do. I worry about them throughout the day. I've caused a lot of people a lot of hurt in my life. I'm too ashamed to tell you what kind of person I have been in the past. That's all behind me. But no matter how depraved and pathetic I might have been . . ." There was a long pause as Tony rubbed his eyes with his thumb and index finger as if to blot out certain images, then looked, misty-eyed, across the audience. "...I could never hurt a child . . . my boys need me. They don't know how to tell me what I'm supposed to do, but I promise them every night that they can depend on me to stop their suffering."

Tony left the stage to enthusiastic applause, slightly favoring his right knee.

EDWARD'S NINE

My name is Edward C. Vaughn. I'm 78 years old." Eddie had a full head of silver, white hair, short on top and shaved close on the side. A familiar military style cut. His steel blue eyes scanned the audience with clarity and strength. His lean, sturdy frame was posture perfect. His voice commanded the room, you could tell he was used to it.

"I was infantry private at the 38th Parallel in Korea; a platoon sergeant on Iwo Jima and the Corregidor; I went to Vietnam in '65 where I was captured twice and escaped twice. I have killed and maimed enough human beings to populate a small town. That was my job. It was them, or me. They had the bad sense to be on the wrong fuckin' side.

"I have three purple hearts, a medal of honor and about two and half pounds of lead and shrapnel still embedded in my bones and organs. I retired from the army as a major in 1973 to take care of my wife, Freda, who died in 1975 of breast cancer. We had been married since the day before I left for Korea. We had one child, a son, who died of leukemia while we were in Vietnam. He was five years old. Freda is the only woman I have ever been with. God rest her lovely soul.

"I've seen the worst that man or machine can do to another man. I have never been afraid of anything in my whole Goddamn life. After Freda died, I figured I'd probably be meeting the Almighty myself before too long and I wasn't afraid to tell the son of a bitch that I didn't feel guilt or shame about any of my life. He could let me in or not. I didn't give a shit about being with Him, but... I did miss Freda."

A few in the audience started to chuckle but muffled it quickly. Eddie was not trying to be humorous or clever. In fact he probably didn't give a shit what anyone thought. He had anger and passion in his voice. A man with two and half pounds of lead and shrapnel in him would not have come here unless he had lost faith in his ability to battle this foe alone.

"About six months after Freda died a young black boy about thirteen or fourteen started coming to me. Much as in the way you've already described, my boy appeared to be acting out . . ." Eddie stopped but didn't lose his composure . . . "being raped. As time went on, I sensed that he was acting out . . . there was some Goddamn invisible devil there with him."

119

Dusty lifted his head and did some quick math… *1975? That's almost 30 years ago!* He marked through number 11 on his list from lunch.

Eddie's kick-ass tone had turned to rage. "You already know, from your own experiences, what I witnessed every night. I went to a priest. I went to a shrink. Everyone thought it was related to my combat experiences. 'Did you ever kill a black boy? Did you want to? Did you ever fuck one, Eddie?' I thought I was going crazy… agent-orange, post-traumatic stress . . . I was a basket case! Freda had been the only one I could ever talk to anyway."

Eddie's voice became briefly gentle when he mentioned his wife. "I was living just outside Washington in a townhouse in Rockport. I didn't socialize and was alone most of the time. I thought maybe I needed to get back to work. I had some contacts at the Pentagon and got a desk job doing some low-level intelligence work. The boy kept coming. I even wondered if it had something to do with Freda. For the first time in my life, I was afraid and unsure of myself. A few months passed and then another black boy appeared. Just like you others testified to. This boy was a couple years younger. He was being raped. I quit my job to try and find some answers. A year went by . . . the two boys still came every night . . . then a third boy, about seven or eight."

Eddie looked down, taking his eyes off the audience for the first time. Just above a whisper, "He, too, is being sexually assaulted." Another year and a half and a fourth boy started appearing, the same unseen devil hurting him. A couple of years later, another. About six months ago, the ninth boy, maybe sixteen years old, appeared. They're all black. When I was a young man, I used to call them niggers. I can't believe I ever did that. The boys still appear every night. I love those boys. I know they are counting on me. There's something I'm supposed to do."

Eddie paused and looked up at the ceiling as if he were thinking of something he had wanted to say, but hadn't yet, "One difference I have from many of you though is that my boys appear to me in regular dreams. It seems many of you only see them by themselves, or in a dark void. My children appear in normal dreams. I'll be dreaming about, walking my dog in the neighborhood perhaps, and then bam! They will just appear. It's been so long ago, but maybe at first they didn't. Maybe it was dark, but ever since I can remember them coming, it's been in my actual dreams." He paused once more, as if he was thinking about something, but didn't want to say it. Then he cleared his throat.

"The only fear I have is that I will die before I figure out how to help them. And I have never been so afraid, or felt so helpless, in my life. I'm not really an emotional guy, but when I saw that message on the Internet, I sat there and cried like a baby. Now, every night, I swear to each one of those boys that help is coming. When I was a boy in the mountains of West Virginia, my dad used to say, 'You either eat the bear or it eats you.' Later, when I went to war and found myself on patrol in a jungle somewhere, scared shitless, the enemy hiding somewhere in front of me, I always felt my dad was right there next to me saying, 'Let's go bear huntin.' And that's how I feel right now. It's time for us to go bear hunting and kill that bastard."

The audience stood in unison, as if directed by a conductor, and showered Eddie with applause and various verbal cheers. Like many old warriors, Eddie somehow made profanity, irreverence and a kiss-my-ass-attitude, sweet and endearing. And they loved him.

No one spoke after Eddie.

Chapter 20

B y the end of the day, 43 individuals had taken the stage to tell their stories. That number represented everyone at the conference except for 10 people. Some had been too shy to take the stage; some were too emotional or too troubled to repeat their stories. Many did not feel a need to tell their story, but they needed to hear the stories of the others. If you were in that room, you had a painful story and it didn't matter if you told it or not. You belonged there; you were loved. The Chosen was your new family.

There was never a need to formally adopt the name "The Chosen." Lana had originally used the term and everyone identified with it. It would later be used to address the group in letters, faxes, and e-mails and chat room conversations. The term made everyone feel esoteric in a way, giving even more importance to his or her mission.

Some stories were more troubling than others. Some speakers were more articulate, more vivid than others. There was no posing, no embellishment. They all shed their masks that normally protect them from the world and laid their souls bare, knowing that upon returning home they would be forced to revert back to the mannerisms, social ranks, and contrivances that normally hide and protect their true selves from the scrutiny of others. The experience that weekend influenced most of the group to look at the world with an existential eye, abandoning all pretense and superficiality in their daily lives. The children's suffering, observed on a large scale through the accumulation of anecdotal tragedies, made the daily stressors back home seem trivial and irrelevant.

In that room, on that stage, every word, every gesture, every expression was genuine and could be trusted. Ego and image were nonexistent. The pure spirit of love and compassion embraced The Chosen. They would be as dependent on each other for love, security, nurturing, companionship and purpose as any specie or tribe of humans that had ever evolved on the planet. Their common plight would inspire a certain unspoken code of ethics between the group, eradicating prejudice, deceit, vanity, pettiness, pride and all selfish human indulgences that might deter them from reaching a solution.

Eddie and his nine children had made the most dramatic impression on The Chosen. His tenderness and devotion beamed through his fierce, craggy, angry exterior like a beacon in a moonless night. He was tough, overpowering and intimidating, yet remained immune from the judgments of the others. He had survived war by the most primitive instincts of kill-or-be-killed, do or die, eat or be eaten. He was raw and uncompromised, a true rugged individual. He wasn't the type of "rugged" who frequent bars and music concerts with their tattoos, ponytails, cowboy hats, body piercings and other fictitious perceptions of toughness that run from a fight... Eddie was the real I'll-rip-your-head-off-with-my-bear-hands-and-shit-down-your-neck deal.

As tough as Eddie was, a tiny cavern in his heart had been pried open in the last couple decades and there was nothing but sweetness and empathy inside. He was the only one who had seen children that far back, which was another puzzle piece. Most everyone else fit inside a two-year window. If The Chosen could ever figure out what had to be done, everybody knew Edward C. Vaughan would not hesitate to do it... no matter what it was. Though Eddie wouldn't have given a shit, he seemed to be everybody's favorite.

But somebody else had made a bigger impression on Dusty; someone else had touched him deeper. Her name was Lynn Christopher.

Dusty had first seen her as he was going to get Bruce in the opening minutes of the meeting. Lynn had been sitting at a table near the left side of the room. Bruce had been too stunned to notice that his new friend, Dusty, had taken a long route back to Dusty's table. Bruce had been too misty-eyed to notice that Dusty's gaze had been on a dark-haired, intelligent looking beauty that was totally unaware of their passing a few feet away. Bruce had been so excited to be at Dusty's table, to have a friend to talk to, that he did not notice Dusty's eyes break contact from time to time to admire some object in the distance over Bruce's shoulder.

Dusty was attentive and moved by every speaker. In between speakers, he and Bruce engaged in light, friendly banter with the others at his table, but Dusty could not resist the allure of the beauty at table 13. She looked to be mid-twenties, youthful, yet with an aura of poise and confidence exhibited by one who has found meaning and purpose in life. She had shoulder-length brunette hair, parted down the middle, large sparkling eyes, delicate nose and lips, light olive colored skin, accentuated by dark eyebrows and lashes. She could have been Latin or maybe Italian… except her eyes were as hazel as the Coral Sea. Dusty had been close enough to confirm that.

Do Hispanic or Italian girls have hazel eyes? Dusty fantasized all sorts of character profiles the way anyone does when first looking at an intriguing stranger. He imagined she was single, college educated, grounded in her family and passionate about her work… something that helps others. He also fantasized that she had seen him and was only acting unaware of him as part of that first step of infatuation, when the ones infatuated are afraid to be too obvious. Of course, Dusty's eyes darted away quickly at the first movement of her eyes towards his side of the room. The only problem was that by doing that, he could never confirm if she had ever really looked at him.

Eventually, Dusty did what boys have done since the days of the primordial swamp when smitten by the fairer sex: he confided in his buddy. "Hey Bruce, see that girl over there, behind you, don't look, just kinda turn around." Bruce slowly turned in his seat as if checking out some minor commotion behind him.

"What girl?"

"You're kidding… the girl in the black sweater…don't stare…" At that moment, Lynn looked around the venue and caught Bruce and Dusty staring in her direction. The fries in front of him instantly fascinated Dusty. "For God's sake Bruce, quit staring." Bruce kept looking as if to study the person that had caused Dusty to act like a seventh grader in co-ed gym class. Bruce was never self-conscious looking at girls because he couldn't conceive of a girl ever having any interest in him whatsoever. He didn't even fantasize about girls being attracted to him. He could stare because he was invisible to them. Lynn was engaged in conversation at her table. She may not have even seen them at all. Bruce turned back to Dusty.

"Her name is Lynn. I saw it on her name tag when we were registering."

"Oh my God, she is so incredibly beautiful! I think I am in love."

"She is very pretty, but in love?" Bruce was somewhat amused by the conversation they were having. He never talked much with another guy about girls.

"Pretty's not the word for it. She's incredible." Lynn used her hands moderately to express herself in conversation. Dusty could see a ring on one of her fingers. Could that be a… "Bruce, what finger does a woman wear her wedding ring on?" He was too flustered to trust what his intuition was telling him. He needed a confirmation.

"My mother wears hers on her left hand." Other than that, Bruce had never noticed.

"It's on her right!" Dusty exclaimed, sort of to himself. He could not stop looking at her, profiling the various women she might be. Bruce was surprised that a guy like Dusty could be the least bit vulnerable or self-conscious about women. In the menial profile Bruce had created for his new friend, Dusty loved 'em and left 'em in a tear-dampened trail of conquest and heartbreak.

"Why don't we go introduce ourselves," Bruce suggested. "She seems like a friendly person."

"No!" Dusty bristled. I'm not ready. Not once had Lynn acknowledged him. He caught girls stealing glances at him all the time. Most weren't even bashful about it. There were several women in the venue now that hadn't stopped checking him out since he walked in. Dusty wasn't noticing.

He had been mesmerized by girls' looks before. He had felt immediate sexual attraction to a girl across a room, on the beach, or in a passing car. Everywhere he looked, girls aroused him. It is true. Guys think about sex 95% of the time. Literally. It's instinctive, evolutionary, and genetic. It usually starts with the third-grade teacher and except for the most offensive of the gender; it beams in on every female figure that passes his gaze for the next…maybe forever. And no man has *ever* read Playboy for the articles. Most guys eventually learn that there are things more gratifying than sex; and there is much more to love than sex. Of course Dusty had heard this before. He just hadn't experienced it.

He did not feel the slightest urge to fantasize about her sexually, and that was a remarkable first. The fact that Lynn had not bothered to notice him only made her more sensual and compelling. "Bruce, I have to meet her before the weekend is over! You have to help me. I'm not joking. I think I could marry her right now." Bruce gave a slight uncomprehending smile.

Dusty was looking across the room entranced. His dad had always told the story of meeting Dusty's mom when she was 15 and he was 17:

Your mother's dad worked with my dad and they came over for supper one night. I fell in love with her the minute I saw her. I would have married her on the spot. I can't explain it. Everything about her reached out and put a grip on me that has never let loose. We lived across town and rarely saw each other. She dated a lot of guys. I was kind of shy around girls. I went to Vietnam. She married one of her beaus and divorced him after eight months. Thank God she wasn't pregnant. I took some shrapnel in my leg, was shipped home and saw her coming down the hall of the hospital in her candy stripe outfit. We were married within a month. She was 19 and I was 22. I had never thought about marrying anyone but her.

Dusty knew it had been true for his dad, but he didn't know if it ever happened that way for anyone else. So many of his friends seemed to be married because it was merely the next logical progression in a relationship after moving in together and buying a pet. But Dusty was smitten and the damsel who had delivered the gaping wound was indifferent of his very presence.

"Bruce, I mean it. I need you to help me buddy." Bruce had never been so honored. He would be playing cupid for Dusty effin Burch.

"Anything to help a Casanova in his pursuit of new flesh."

You and me buddy, the dynamic duo." Dusty raised his right hand to strike a high five, but Bruce was a little slow to catch on. He had never been offered a high five by another male. It was his first one and it was a little off target, but it felt good. It was a juvenile, time-honored ritual that marked his acceptance into that universe of jocks, studs and all-around cool guys that had always avoided him.

Throughout the entire rest of the speeches, Dusty glanced every few minutes over at Lynn.

Chapter 21

Lana had brilliantly conducted the first day and Dusty finally felt like he had a thread to hang on to. At the moment, the thread felt like it belonged to a massive wool blanket big enough to cover a city, but it was more than he had before. Dusty felt encouraged.

Almost everyone had left the room after the group discussions, but a few remained chatting quietly. As the caterers cleaned the tables and folded the chairs, Bruce overtly approached Dusty. He leaned up and whispered in his ear, "Are you gonna talk to her or what? There is definitely not a ring on her left hand," Bruce remarked with a childish grin.

Dusty couldn't help but smile. He hadn't seen Bruce go anywhere near her. He wondered to himself how in the hell he could have seen that from across the room, but he didn't ask. He didn't have to.

"When she walked to the bathroom, I followed her," Bruce continued.

"Bruce!" Dusty interrupted.

"Don't worry," he assured, "she didn't see me. Well, I was smooth about it. I waited by the water fountain and when the bathroom door opened, I got a drink," Bruce's face was glowing. He looked like a kid plotting a secret mission to put a whoopee cushion on the teacher's seat, "Perfect position for a clear line to the target as she walked by!"

Dusty laughed out loud at the thought of this. He envisioned Bruce nervously and quickly assuming the "drinking position" to conceal his motive. The outburst was also exaggerated due to an unconscious effort to mask his nervousness. The realization that there was actually a possibility of talking to this woman made his face hot and tingly. Adrenaline flowed through his veins and his heart started audibly beating in his head. A waitress walked by carrying a tray with drinks from the table she had just cleared. Dusty quickly grabbed one and started chugging it.

"Eww," Bruce exclaimed with a disgusted look on his face, "Do you know whose glass that is?" Dusty disregarded Bruce's comment and tilted his head back. He didn't realize he'd just finished a dry martini until it hit his belly.

"Whew!" Dusty gasped as his face contorted and his eyes opened wide. "I wasn't expecting that," he spat out as he hit his chest and coughed.

"Are you okay?" asked Bruce with a worried look on his face.

"Yep. Fantastic! You feel like a drink? I feel like a drink. Let's go get a drink," Dusty suggested.

Bruce thought Dusty was acting strange, "Are you sure you are feeling okay? I don't really drink much. I usually end up pissing my pants. This one time..."

"Perfect!" Dusty said, totally disregarding Bruce's anecdote, "I'll drink for you. Waiter!" he yelled as he raised his hand and turned to find an empty room.

....

Bruce sipped his coke at the resort's bar as Dusty set down his third Bud Lite bottle.

"Dusty, I know I may not be an expert at this, but are you sure you want to be drunk the first time you talk to her?"

"I'm not drunk!" he exclaimed, "maybe just a little tipsy. And of course! The first rule in dating is that you cannot approach a girl when you are stone cold sober."

Incredulous, Bruce responded, "You're lying. I'm not that stupid."

"No, I'm serious. If you're not a little drunk, you inevitably end up looking like a nervous little middle school boy. The hotter the girl, the drunker you have to be. They don't call it liquid courage for nothing, man. Plus, if you fuck it up, you can always blame it on the liquor later," Dusty said with an obnoxious smile as if he had practiced this technique a time or two.

Bruce couldn't believe this might actually work on women, "Dusty, maybe some women. But you really like this one. Don't you think..."

"Bruce," Dusty turned and looked at him sternly in the eye, "I got this. I won't get too drunk. I just need to take a little off the edge. Got it?"

Hesitantly he responded, "Got it. So what is your plan?"

"I have no idea. It'll come. This is about as far as I got."

Observing this ritual fascinated Bruce. He had no idea that even a guy like Dusty could be so insecure when it came to courting women. He always envisioned flowers, a thought-out speech, maybe a rainbow or something. He never would have guessed it could be as easy as getting drunk. He was interested to see how Dusty would pull this off.

"I got it," said Dusty. "Come with me." They walked to the front desk. "Excuse me..." he looked at the woman's nametag, "Eleanor, could you please give me the room number of a Lynn..." he looked at Bruce, realizing he didn't know her last name.

Bruce, quick to catch on, "Christopher. Lynn Christopher."

Suspiciously, Eleanor asked, "And you are?"

"We are acquainted with her through the banquet in the ballroom today. We'd just like to speak with her," replied Dusty.

"Okay," she said, still unsure of what to think of these two. "One moment please." She typed furiously on her keyboard, made a couple clicks of the mouse, then said, "Room 311."

"Thank you so much," Dusty said politely. He directed Bruce toward the elevator. Until now, Bruce had played along. Now inside the elevator, he had to know.

"What are you doing?" he was whispering as if someone else was in there with them.

"WE," emphasizing the *we*, "are collecting contact information for Lana. She lost her drive with everyone's info on it and we are getting it on paper for back up. Bruce let this sink in. It actually sounded like a good idea to him.

"Brilliant! Okay, so what are you going to say?"

"Sometimes you just gotta let it come to you. Over thinking can be bad."

Thinking back to the last hour they had just spent at the bar, Bruce sarcastically remarked, "Really?"

"Shhhhh," Dusty put his finger to Bruce's lips. The elevator dinged and the number above the door turned to three. Dusty walked out first and turned to his left following the sign that read *Rooms 301-324* with an arrow pointing left. The moment he turned he spotted Lynn, standing at her door. She was placing the key in the card reader with her back turned to him. Dusty quickly turned around, pushing a confused Bruce frantically back into the elevator.

"Oh my God! She's right there!" exclaimed Dusty.

"Why did you do that?" Bruce asked, almost offended. "You knocked my glasses off! Those are Lenscrafters!"

"I'm sorry man. I panicked. I turned to walk down the hall and she was at her door, about to go in." The door was closing behind him. Lynn, sure she had heard the elevator door open, curiously looked over her shoulder, wiping her hair from her eyes to get a glimpse down the hallway. Not seeing anything, she shrugged and entered her room.

"Get it together man! It's just a girl!" Bruce encouragingly said to Dusty.

"Yes, yes, stop being a wuss," he said to himself. "Maybe I need to go have another drink," he said as he reached for the 'L' button.

Bruce aggressively answered, "Hell no! Stop making excuses. You can do this. I'll do the talking. Let's just stick to the game plan. Come on." The tables had suddenly changed. Bruce was now coaching Dusty. Dusty hastily followed him out of the elevator.

When they got to her door, Bruce knocked three times. Dusty turned and started walking away, "I can't do this!"

"Coward!" Bruce admonished as he grabbed Dusty's hand and pulled him to the entrance just in time for the door to open. Lynn was in her bathrobe and the shower was running in the background. The two just stood there gawking in awe for a few seconds, looking like the middle school boys they were so desperately trying to avoid being.

"Can I help you gentlemen?"

Bruce spoke first, "Uh, yes. Hello ma'am. My name is Bruce. This is Dusty," Dusty smiled sheepishly, "and Lana had asked us to collect contact information for each of the people that attended today's banquet. You were there, right?"

"Yes I was, and please, call me Lynn."

"Oh right. Well it's very nice to meet you Lynn."

Dusty quietly echoed, "Nice to meet you," as he rose up his hand.

Bruce continued, "I hope we aren't bothering you. We can come back later if you'd like."

"No, it's okay. I was just about ready to hop in the shower," her hazel eyes sparkled as she spoke. Her dark brown hair hung down over her shoulders. She couldn't have looked sexier to Dusty if she tried. He was speechless. She had glanced at Dusty initially, but her gaze was fixed on Bruce as he talked, allowing for Dusty to openly stare to his heart's desire without her noticing, which he did. She continued, "But I thought I emailed all of that to her before the meeting. Did she not get it?"

Dusty, finally courageous enough to speak said, "No she did, but she put everyone's information on a thumb drive and she thinks she lost it. She asked us to go around and collect everyone's info on pen and paper, just in case." His charm was starting to shine through now. He couldn't help but grin at her as he spoke.

Lynn wasn't sure what to think. She was starting to sense a little child's play, so she decided to play with them a bit, "Soooo, why didn't she come get it?" She twirled her hair innocently as she spoke. Dusty looked at Bruce, who looked immediately to the ground. This wasn't quite going as planned.

"Well, uh, we were just helping her out. She's pretty tired from the day and has a lot of stuff to take care of. There were over 60 some people, so we offered to help," Dusty responded confidently.

"And it takes the both of you to get a number?" she continued, cocking her head to the side and shifting her hips. She had them in the palm of her hand. "Are you guys flirting with me?" She looked Bruce square in the eye and smiled the prettiest smile he had ever seen. It broke him.

"Dusty wanted to talk to you. It was all his idea," Bruce explained, "but he was too nervous to do it alone."

Dusty couldn't believe his ears, "Bruce!" he hit him in the shoulder. Every attempt they had made to play it cool was now out the window. Dusty's face turned bright red. He turned to look at Lynn who was still smiling, enjoying this rudimentary form of entertainment.

"Well, is it true?" she asked, unshaken. Dusty didn't say a word. He just nodded his head. "I gotta give you credit," said Lynn. "The wingman approach. Totally original." Now she was just being plain mean.

Ashamed, Dusty apologized, "I'm sorry. I, I just... I wanted to..." Lynn stopped the bleeding.

"It's okay handsome. I'm going to clean up and go to bed. I'm exhausted. You want that info? It's gonna cost you a cup of coffee. Eight o'clock tomorrow morning," she began to close the door. "See you there."

The door shut inches from their faces. Neither of them budged for several moments. They just stared at the closed door. Eventually, unable to speak, they looked at each other and headed for the elevator. Before they got there, Bruce held out a discrete palm offering. Dusty was waiting, ready to accept the low-five victory shake. As the door shut, Bruce couldn't help himself. Before he spoke, his face grew into a full grin and he uttered these two words:

"Mission accomplished." Dusty was so happy he could have kissed Bruce, but he didn't.

Chapter 22

Before his head hit the pillow, Dusty was half asleep already. Not only was he worn out from the day, but alcohol always put him to sleep like a baby. There were many nights in college where he would be the first one to pass out and wake up with permanent marker on his forehead or genitalia of some kind skillfully drawn on his face. One time he went to his business law class with a chunk shaved from the back of his head—unknowingly. He never lived that one down. Needless to say, within minutes he was into a deep slumber.

His girl showed up in normal fashion. It starts with pitch-black darkness. Slowly, a beam of light emerges from the abyss and grows stronger until Dusty almost feels blinded. When the light subsides, she is left standing in the darkness. Lately, Dusty has started to feel that she doesn't seem to be in as much pain as she did when she first arrived to him. He hasn't told this to anyone yet, simply because he is unsure himself. Tonight, however, would leave him without doubt.

At first, his dreams were excruciatingly painful. Watching her, helplessly, was like watching a person being drawn and quartered six feet away. Her agony and distress stuck with him all day. Tonight when she appeared, she crept out of the darkness into a sort of overhead beam of light. This sort of illumination was normal, but now she stood placidly in front of him under the light for what seemed like hours. She just looked at him, calmly. She didn't smile; she didn't frown; she didn't move. As usual, he tried talking to her. He thought maybe this change of pace meant he could get through to her. Still, she never spoke a word.

"Are you okay now? What has happened? Please, say something," he pleaded with her. She never so much as made a sound.

At the end of the dream, she turned and walked away. Slowly, the opaque background dissolved into another scene. At first, Dusty couldn't tell what it was. He recognized some grass, then some trees. Finally, what materialized in front of him was undoubtedly a playground. No one is there though. It reminds him of a scene from *Terminator II, Judgment Day*. The barren ground is mostly dirt and rocks. The equipment is in shambles. Through all of the mess, one thing sticks out above all else: a swing set. The lone swing is detached from one of its chains and it is dangling just above the ground. He doesn't know if this dream is related to his little girl in anyway, but for the moment he doesn't care. Even in his state of lucidity, he is aware that he is dreaming, and more importantly that he is dreaming of something else other than his little girl. He had no idea at the time what it meant, or if it was relevant at all to his cause, but he was dreaming of an object that wasn't a little girl writhing in pain. It made him happy.

Suddenly, a loud, incessant ringing began inundating his brain. The playground vanishes. For a moment, it is darkness and loud ringing. His subconscious slowly recedes until he is left with reality.

When he realizes it is his alarm, he shoots up in panic, "Oh crap!" He searches for his phone and sees that it is 7:53. He is supposed to meet Lynn in seven minutes. Like a madman, he dashes out of bed. His pounding head tells him to reach for the Aleve first. He pops one, brushes his teeth wildly, splashes water on his face and begins to head out the door. He looks down and slowly realizes he is still in the clothes he wore the night before. So he rips his shirt off and grabs a blue polo. He attempts to un-wrinkle his khakis with a few broad strokes down his legs with his hands, but decides being late is worse than a few wrinkles. He sprints down the hall to the elevator, waits a second, and then decides to take the stairs.

At the bottom of the stairs, he collects himself before walking into the lobby adjacent to the dining area. He spots Lynn through the vertical windowpane on the door. He looks at his watch: 8:01. He can feel his diaphragm thumping, so he takes a deep breath and reminds himself, "You can do this. Come on!"

Lynn hears the door open and looks to see Dusty walking through. He is looking around as if to find her, so she pretends she doesn't see him and continues doing her crossword puzzle. The glimpse she caught of him reminds her of how strikingly handsome he was and she too began to feel her pulse in her chest. She looks up when he is a few feet from the table.

"This seat taken Ma'am?" was the first thing that came to his mind.

"I was going to leave at 8:02... you got lucky this time," Lynn responded in a flirtatious tone, yet in a way that left Dusty wondering.

"I guess I did," he said with a smile. "My name is Dusty Burch," he said as he extended his hand, still standing.

"Lynn Christopher," she said as she took his hand. "It's a pleasure to meet you. Where is your friend?"

Dusty saw that one coming and had to laugh, "Yeah, I know. That was pretty lame," he admitted as he sat down across from her. "What Can I say? A pretty girl can make you do some pretty stupid things."

The cheesy line was actually well played and well received by Lynn. His smile and ocean-blue eyes didn't hurt either. It wouldn't have mattered how he justified the instance last night, but his playful tone and modest, humble attitude turned Lynn on right away. She also felt an immediate connection to him, and him to her, because they knew what pangs and toils the other one was going through. It acted as a natural icebreaker, forming an immediate bond that seemed to unite their souls.

"It takes a big man to admit when he's done something lame," she retorted, unable to stop smiling. Neither could he. For the moment, both of them felt as if they had traveled to the end of a rainbow. All of the normal feelings of meeting someone new set in: adrenaline pumping, butterflies, infatuation and instant ecstasy. Dusty was so taken by her natural beauty that he could hardly believe he was sitting in front of her, engaging in conversation with her. For her, it was nothing new for a male suitor to approach her— especially a good-looking one—but Dusty's looks were matched with a distinctly masculine overtone and a confidence that shone brightly, without encompassing him.

"Hah!" he laughed, "I appreciate that. Or it just takes a really ignorant one."

"I have a feeling that is not the case," she assured.

The two fell into a casual and comfortable conversation. She told him about her aspiring dental career in Manhattan, he told her about his law career in Chicago. They talked about all the things they loved: music, movies, family, The Beatles, *Vanilla Sky*, wrestling, soccer, food and travel. They caught up like old friends. With each new fact Dusty learned about her, he became more infatuated. *She is perfect.* He couldn't stop from looking into her beautiful eyes and their gaze hardly ever broke, unlike many first conversations when eye contact is minimized to short, awkward glances.

Eventually, the conversation eased into describing their children to each other. She was seeing a little girl as well. Her girl was around 8 years old and had two blonde pigtails. He told her about his little girl and about the dream he had last night. Together they drank coffee and talked until she looked at the clock.

"Uh oh, we'd better get going. Wasn't our meeting supposed to start at 9 o'clock?" It was 9:13.

"Uhh, yah. We're gonna be a little late to that one." Dusty threw a ten-dollar bill on the table and stood up. "Walk with me?"

"Sure." And together they walked into the Roosevelt room fashionably late. Everyone was already busy talking to one another in the networking line Lana had set up. Lana caught eyes with Dusty and beckoned for him to come sit by her.

"See ya in a little bit. Don't have too much fun," Dusty said as they parted ways. He was still in the mode where he doubted everything he said to her, wondering if it came off idiotically. It was better than saying nothing at all. Her tender smile reassured him.

....

The networking session lasted a few hours. By the end of it, Dusty was exhausted. He took notes about everyone he met. It was one of the most interesting social events he had ever participated in. As each person moved into the seat in front of him, he felt as if he were venturing into another part of the world. A total stranger, with a completely different background, upbringing, core of beliefs and even nationality, would share his or her deepest fears with prodigious sincerity.

The group sessions that took part in the afternoon were mainly brainstorming sessions while people took turns getting interviewed by

Dusty and Lana. Amidst the groups, as well as in the individual interviews, details of the dreams started to be analyzed and scrutinized. Conversations from the chat room were revisited and expounded upon. By the end of it, Lana had assembled a book of web diagrams, outlines, Venn diagrams and scribbled pieces of paper from the groups. Additionally, each participant had his or her own page describing the children in as much detail as could possibly be given.

One of the theories that emerged from many of the groups was what came to be known as the *Proximity Theory*, which was a way of explaining how The Chosen were chosen based off of how close they were to the child either at the time of death or some other crucial moment in time. Since there were so many people and so many variables, nothing could be determined for sure. But it was a good start.

Many groups had lists that were remarkably comparable to the napkin Dusty wrote on in lunch the day before. It didn't appear that people were chosen based off any physical trait whatsoever. The children didn't appear to have any physical traits in common across the board either. These reasons are why *The Proximity Theory* made sense, because Geography doesn't discriminate. But now they just had to find out what clues that could bring, if any.

By the end of the weekend, the members were very comfortable with each other and grasped onto a glimmer of hope. A lot of work had to be done, but they were headed in the right direction. Dusty and Lana had assembled a "Bible" of The Chosen. It had a lot of work to be done to it and was very unorganized, but it served as the single most sacred item that collectively represented the group.

That night, Dusty walked Lynn to her room, where she stood at the doorway, walked in, and wished him goodnight. She made it very clear that he would not be coming in, but she did agree to see him again for coffee in the morning.

This time, Dusty was up an hour early and waiting for her when she came down. He was in Khakis and a blue polo. She was wearing jeans, a black t-shirt that said "Hampton High School Volleyball 1995", and tennis shoes. Her hair was up in a ponytail. She might as well have been on the cover of *Victoria Secret* as far as Dusty was concerned.

Once again, the two talked like old friends for hours, becoming more and more enthralled in each other's presence with every word. Dusty wished the conversation would never end. Her laugh was the sweetest, most pure laugh he had ever heard. She radiated energy and charisma. He had to keep himself from jumping across the table and kissing her, which was all he could think about. He did, however, manage to grasp her hand across the table for a few moments while they were talking. Then, before it got awkward, she casually withdrew to take a drink of coffee. He didn't try again.

She told him about her fondness for horses and how she grew up riding them on her grandparents' farm. Dusty was very impressed when she told him that she was an expert lassoer and helped wrangle up the calves. Once she tried riding in a rodeo competition, but only once. She also told him about her alcoholic father and his lack of involvement in her life. Her mother left him after years of abuse and is now engaged to be remarried.

Dusty told Lynn about his affinity for the outdoors and that his favorite place in the world was Colorado. He told her the story about when he, his father, his uncle and his cousins went on an adventure to fish the wild streams of Colorado for trout. They camped out on a mountainside and were almost swept away by an avalanche. He was sure he was going to die, but his father and uncle dug them all out and led them to safety. He relayed many other outdoor adventures to her and they wildly fascinated her.

And as time passes when two hearts are bonding, before they knew it, it was time to part ways.

"Oh crap, I'd probably better get going. My flight leaves at 12:17," it was 10:34.

"Can I walk you to your room? I can help carry your bags down," Dusty, asked her.

"I actually already checked out. I got my bag right here," she said as she looked down at her feet.

Dusty looked down to see a small coach, "I'm impressed. I expected…more."

"I travel light. I'm not your average girl," she said with a playful smirk that left Dusty smiling and slightly shaking his head.

"I can see that."

"But I'll let you walk me out to the taxi, if you want."

"I'd love to."

As they stood at the entrance of the lodge, waiting for her taxi, Dusty built up the courage to ask her, "So... Lana is still gonna be needing that contact information you know... just in case." His delivery was irresistible to Lynn. She felt very comfortable with his confident, yet almost childish demeanor. He wasn't too cocky, but he knew what to say to get her attention. He wasn't overbearing like a lot of guys, but had more guts than most. She couldn't help but to be attracted to him.

"For Lana?"

"For Lana."

"Okay, but you tell her I said not to bother me unless she has a really good reason. I'm a *very* busy person," she sarcastically remarked as her taxi pulled up to the building.

"Okay, I will. It was really nice meeting you," he said as he grabbed the napkin with her number on it from her.

Lynn smiled and said, "You too, Dusty." She leaned up and kissed him on the cheek. "Just a little something to think about." Then she turned and walked out the door. Dusty couldn't help but to gawk at her the entire time it took for her to climb into the cab. *Damn she looks good in those jeans.* As she shut the door, he stood in the entrance to the resort, holding onto the napkin with her number on it and watched with puppy dog eyes until the taxi disappeared into the mountains.

Chapter 23

Dusty took Monday off work. He needed a day to reset after Winter Park, but reality set in pretty hard on Tuesday when he opened the door to his office and found his desk littered with files, papers, phone messages, pictures, thumb drives, CDs and paper clips. The scenery was drastically different from the majestic mountain ranges of Winter Park. As he set down, he reached into his briefcase and pulled out a postcard that he had bought in the gift shop at the lodge. He put a piece of scotch tape across the top and put it at the base of his computer monitor as a reminder that tranquility does exist in the world.

It was 5:30 am, not unusually early for Dusty, but unusually early for everyone else. He was the only one on the floor, maybe even the whole building, which sat on the corner of 12th and Main Street. He only saw a few cars in the garage, but that could just be the janitors. He liked the feeling of having the entire skyscraper to himself. He felt like he could draw energy from the soul of the universe in placidity. No interruptions, no phone calls, no emails, no colleagues, no... Chad. Just him and his thoughts. He felt like he was losing ground on the Draper case, so after a long, relaxing weekend, an early morning of thinking was exactly what he felt like he needed.

Dusty wasn't the only one up working early. Brian Draper's attorney, Karee, had been at it since 5 a.m. She hadn't taken a day off in six months and worked 16-hour days. Unlike Dusty, she did not have the resources of a large defense firm like SC&R. Her law firm consisted of 10 lawyers. The two owners, Lewis & Fields, had been successful attorneys for close to 20 years in the Chicago area. When they decided to grow their firm a few years ago from six to ten attorneys, they went looking for a sharp, charismatic, courageous and preferably attractive young woman to help represent the firm. They were starting to get a chauvinistic reputation after years of not only not hiring women, but hardly ever representing them. Karee was their public response to eradicate that conception. She worked tirelessly to prove herself in the firm and to maintain an equal status, although she never truly felt as if she was seen as *equal*.

Like Dusty, Karee's main workload revolved around Brian Draper. But unlike Dusty, Karee was very passionate and attached to her client. In a recent conversation with Ron Davis, Ron actually said to Dusty that had Brian burned to death, it would have all been a lot easier. Because now they don't just have to deal with a death, but they have to battle the sympathetic sentiments that a jury will feel toward a burned little boy. Just when Dusty thought he couldn't possibly abhor Ron Davis anymore, Ron found a way. With Dusty's career and reputation at stake, he had to try everything he could to put together a good defense, but deep down inside, he didn't care if Ron Davis was forced to pay every dime he owed to Brian. Dusty was getting paid to represent a man who was trying to keep money away from Brian, while Karee would have gladly given everything she owned to her client just to ease his pain for a few moments.

Dusty and Karee weren't the only ones up at 5:30 either. Brian too, was up. In fact, he could hardly ever sleep for more than an hour at a time due to the nerve damage throughout his body that he had sustained in the fire. His grandparents were also up, for they had to change the dressings on his open wounds every few hours so that they didn't get infected. Although it had been years since the fire, Brian's skin still cracked and bled when it stretched as he moved his body. Sometimes, this alone would wake him up. If for some miraculous reason his body lay just right that his nerves could tolerate the pressure, he would wake in agonizing pain if he made a sudden motion that ripped open a pre-existing fissure.

Across the city, Bruce Crippen was awake as well. He had actually not gone to sleep yet. He had pulled an all-nighter studying the habits of psychopaths, rapists, pedophiles and murderers. Books lay all around him on his desk in his living room and his Internet browser contained 15 open tabs. Many ideas were thrown out at the round tables in Winter Park as to why the children visited them, but the overwhelming majority of the people agreed that they had either been murdered or died in some tragic way. Bruce thought that if he could somehow better understand the people who are hurting the children, maybe he could gain insight into how to catch them. No other scenario sounded more reasonable to Bruce. What else would the children want more than for their killers to be caught to keep them from hurting any more kids? So Bruce decided it would be a good start to get to know the enemy and get to know him well.

Bruce was also busy formulating a comprehensive list of missing children currently in the United States and the rest of the world. Although there was still had no proof the children they saw were real, he and Dusty had talked about the utility in having a list of real, missing children to compare to the descriptions that the members had given. Maybe they would get lucky and find some comparisons. Others from the group may have spent a few minutes Googling missing children in their areas, but no one was as diligent or ardent about the task as Bruce.

If there was a second place, it was Dusty. For the next few hours of his workday, he tried to match up missing children reports with his little girl, but had no luck. Out of the 12 missing children cases in the greater Chicago area in the last three years, not one of them was a little, black girl. When he went back to 10 years, he uncovered 53 reports of missing children, but only five remained unsolved. Of the five, three of the bodies were never found and two were recovered, but no one was ever charged with their murder. One of these children was a black girl, but she was 9 years old, much too old to be his girl. He wondered if somehow any of the unsolved cases were connected...if it was the act of a serial murder. So he further researched the cases of the bodies that were found and discovered that based on the M.O. of the crimes, the detectives did not think the murders were linked.

His next move was to call Bruce. Bruce was also from Chicago and Dusty thought that maybe he could identify with one of the unsolved cases. It was almost noon and Dusty had not done a single minute of office work. As he suspected, Bruce was already a step ahead of him.

When Dusty explained his progress, Bruce responded, "Yeah Dusty, I was already aware of those five cases. In fact, I went back 25 years. It opened up about seven more total unsolved cases in the greater Chicago area. And when I extended the search radius out to 300 miles, I uncovered 27 unsolved cases in the last 25 years. Total cases in the U.S. neared close to 300 unsolved cases, but that's just for children under the age of 16. I'm still working on worldwide."

"Wow Bruce. I'm impressed."

"I have a lot of time on my hands and I don't require a lot of sleep."

"Well, did you recognize any of the cases to be your child?"

"I haven't found pictures for all of them in the U.S. quite yet, but I don't travel much anyway so I doubt it will matter. I say that with the assumption that the proximity theory is indeed correct, but of course that could be a mistake. We haven't quite proved that. I'm exploring other possibilities as well. As far as pictures of children here in Chicago, no. None of them look familiar yet, but I'm still trying to find pictures of a few of them. Maybe no one ever knew our kids were missing."

"But how could that be? I mean how does a kid go missing and no one report it?"

"Well, maybe they were orphans or homeless. Maybe they were accidents that never hit the news. Maybe our children have an unsolved mystery involving their death that they want their parents to know about so they can have some closure; in that case, they never would have been reported missing. There isn't exactly a protocol for how to determine what the dead children in our dreams are trying to tell us. We're going to have to figure it out."

"There's just gotta be something, a missing key. There's must be a way to communicate with them somehow. I just can't believe they would come to us if there weren't a way to help them. I can't believe they would just come to torment us. God damnit! None of this makes any sense! I mean if this is all true, why would they only start coming to people now?"

"Think about it like this Dusty. Maybe there was a breakthrough recently in the spiritual plane that up until now was unprecedented. Maybe there was like a Jesus of the spirit world. Once one of them was able to make a connection, it opened up a pathway for others to enter. Or maybe it *is* just as simple as there is a bigger population now, which means there are greater chances for homicidal maniacs and greater chances for children to be harmed. Maybe God is trying to protect what is most precious in this world.

And let's say one spirit did finally open the door to others, then we could be dealing with afflicted spirits dating back to… who knows?"

"Or maybe the Earth is travelling across an intergalactic highway generated from the gamma rays of an exploding supernova that has opened up telepathic pathways for the dead to communicate with the living."

"Exactly! That could just as well be true! See, we may never know *how* it's happening. I'm not even sure that it will do us any good to look for *how* it is happening, but as long as I live, I will search for the *why* it is happening."

"You and me both buddy. I want to get back to dreams about naked women and mountain streams. Or better yet, naked women in mountain streams!"

"Of course you do," Bruce quickly changed the subject, "and have you ever thought about if there is a serial killer involved? Would that mean that multiple chosen see his multiple victims? I mean, there were several Chosen who reported seeing more than one, but do you think that means they are from the same killer? Or different ones? This thought has perplexed me day and night. I mean does the first victim choose a person, then bring the other victims to him? That would mean, *if* the proximity theory is correct, that the other victims were not subject to its parameters."

"I'm not following."

"Okay. If a person is chosen based off of how close they were to the victim, then that would make sense as to why The Chosen saw the first victim. But as to why they see the second, third, fourth, fifth and so on, like Eddie, it is paradoxical. There is no way Eddie was the closest to each and every one of those victims. Either the first victim made contact and brought the others through to Eddie, or Eddie was chosen for a different reason other than his proximity to the murders. Another possibility is that there are multiple chosen people out there who are seeing the same children. Say each of Eddie's children have a primary Chosen—the one that was closest to them when they died—but can also visit The Chosen of other children that were murdered by the same man… to increase their chances of getting help. To me, it would make sense for the victims of a killer to reach out to as many people as they are able to."

"Okay. I see what you are saying. The proximity theory does present some difficult challenges. Maybe it is only part of the answer. Maybe it has nothing to do with it. What if we are chosen because we have a hidden sixth sense? I mean I've done research on that and there is some evidence that it exists."

"If one were so inclined, he could find evidence that anything exists, and often does. Time will tell, my friend. I've looked through the bible to see if any profiles sound similar, but it's so hard to tell. Even if some of us are seeing the same children, our descriptions are subjective. You and I might describe the same boy and describe him totally different. So there isn't a sure way to tell yet."

"That's true. Some of us *could* be seeing the same children." Dusty thought on this notion a while and let it all settle in. He hadn't ever thought of the situation in this light before and he was glad he had Bruce on his side. "Well, we don't have a whole lot of time, so let's keep in touch Bruce. Don't work yourself too hard. I'm going to actually try and get some work done today."

"Okay Dusty. Thanks for the call. I'll let you find out if I find anything."

"Later Bruce." Dusty hung up the phone.

Just when he was starting to think about work, he reached into his briefcase and pulled out the napkin with Lynn's number on it. His stomach jumped. *Not today. Not today.* As bad as he wanted to sit and daydream about her, he forced the thoughts out of his mind. He put the napkin back in his briefcase in a small little, Velcro fastened pocket. As he started to skim through his emails, Marilyn walked in the door.

She was wearing a black pencil skirt with a white blouse and her mood was unusually uppity, "Hey there stranger! How was your trip?" She came in and set a cup of coffee on his desk and plopped down in the seat across from him.

"Thank you," he said as he looked at the cup of coffee. She smiled. "It was… good. Just what I needed." She could tell that there was a lot more to the story than that.

"Really? Well, I'm glad to hear that. So are you going to tell me what this trip was really about?"

Dusty smiled as if he'd been caught, but maintained a serious tone, "I told you, I went to visit my cousin."

"Your cousin that you hadn't seen in 15 years?" She gave him an incredulous raise of her eyebrow. "You just all the sudden had a hankering to up and see him?"

"What sounds so crazy about that?"

"Dusty, do you think I am a complete idiot? Come on. You've been acting strange. I already know you've been having bad dreams. You even had to go see Dr. Zimmer. Then there was your day trip to Seattle. I've caught you asleep in your office several times in the last couple months. You don't," she paused as if she wasn't sure if she wanted to say it, "talk to me anymore. You seem preoccupied. *WHAT* is going on?"

Dusty sat in contemplation as if he had been caught stealing from the cookie jar. *What the hell? I've got nothing to lose.* "Okay, I'll tell you. But you have to *promise* not to tell *anyone!*"

"Who would I tell? Chad? Stanley? The blonde secretary that can't even remember her own name? If there is anyone in the world you can trust, it is me. I hope you know that."

"Okay. I just didn't want to… burden you. And I didn't want you to think I was crazy. I at least needed to have a little more… proof. If that's what you can call it."

"Why don't you just get it out and stop delaying."

"Fine," Dusty sat back in his chair and put his hands on his knees. "So, the dreams…"

"Yes?"

"They are of a little girl. She comes to me pretty much every night. And in these dreams, she is in pain. A lot of pain. She just sits there in blackness, pleading with her hands, reaching out to me. But I can't hear her. No matter what I say or do, she can't understand me. Or if she does, she can't respond. All she can do is act out what I believe is her final moments on this planet, over and over again. At first, I thought it was just a nightmare. But then it happened every night. I don't dream about anything else. If I do, I don't remember it. And every morning, right before my alarm clock goes off, she vanishes and I wake up." Marilyn continued to sit across from him, seemingly unaffected by Dusty's story so far. She blinked.

"Listen, I know it sounds crazy, I thought I was going crazy, but then I heard another woman from Seattle on the radio explain the same type of thing. I was able to get a hold of her and we met. She was experiencing the exact, same, thing, down to the last detail. But she was seeing a different child. We decided we would stay in touch and try and see if we could find anyone else that was having the same problems. Like, start a support group or something. But then we found a whole bunch of them, or they found us I should say. We created a website and filtered the bogus responses. We only let the people in who described what we were experiencing. From there, it took off. There were daily discussions about people's experiences. Then I had an idea to get us all together. That's what I went to Colorado for. But it wasn't a total lie. I did stay with my cousin." Dusty was making an attempt to mitigate her frustration, but there was no need.

"And why didn't you tell me all this earlier?"

"Like I said, I didn't want you to worry. And I wasn't sure about anything. I'm not sure about much now, but at least I know that there are others like me. This convention… it was incredible. I've never heard so much genuine emotion from total strangers. We are all desperate and all certain that these children are real. Now we just have to figure out what to do."

"Well, I don't think you are crazy. I can't even begin to imagine, but I know you Dusty. I know you wouldn't take something like this lightly. I just hope that you can find a solution. Maybe it isn't real. Maybe it's just a very, strange coincidence."

"Maybe. But I doubt it." The two locked eyes as Marilyn tried to decide if he was actually going crazy or not.

"Okay, well just do whatever you need to do, but you have to keep me in the loop. I can't cover for you if I don't know what's going on."

"Deal." Marilyn stood up and walked around the desk. Dusty stood up and she hugged him.

"Don't try to save the world all by yourself." Dusty didn't say anything. He sat back down as she walked out the door and stared at his computer screen.

"What the hell am I going to do?"

Chapter 24

After his last visit, Dusty had decided he wasn't going back to see Dr. Zimmer because he didn't feel like it was helping him. After going to Winter Park however, he thought he would give it one more stab. He felt like if he told Zimmer that there was an entire group of people claiming to experience the same thing, that maybe he would take him more seriously. In actuality, all it really did was convince him that there was a whole group of psychotic people out there that needed serious help. Dr. Zimmer had seen over 4,000 patients by the time Dusty walked in the door and he had heard it all. Not once was he ever convinced or did he find solid proof that psychic communication with the dead actually existed.

Zimmer was a Harvard graduate and a psychological genius by most accounts. He finished 3rd in his class of 1972 and was a candidate for the Nobel Prize for his work on the parent-child relationship and how parenting—especially in the ages of 6-12 years of age—greatly affects the social status of children. As a result, he relied heavily on empirical data and testable evidence. His dissertation for his doctorate was titled: *Parenting: A Psychosocial Approach to Adolescent Development in Order to Raise Autonomous, Responsible and Successful Children in the Modern Era.* His interest in children was one of the reasons Dusty chose him in the first place, but nowhere in Zimmer's studies did he come across mysterious hauntings of dead children.

After 45 minutes of hearing the same details as previous sessions and giving the same answers to the same questions, Dr. Zimmer became a little annoyed, "Have you ever thought of talking to a psychic?" Zimmer wasn't exactly being serious, but at this point, he thought a psychic might be able to tell Dusty more than he could.

"What?" Dusty retorted incredulously. "A psychic? Are you kidding me? Listen Doc, if you are making fun of me, I can go plenty of places for free and have that done. I don't really appreciate…"

"Calm down Mr. Burch. Calm down. I didn't mean anything by it. I know it sounds crazy, but who knows. Maybe one of them can tell you something. And even if it is hocus-pocus, maybe they can make you think about something you never did before. But," the Doc said while lowering his glasses onto the rim of his nose, "think of it this way. If you say all of this with your little girl *is* real, then why would you have any trouble believing that what a psychic says is real? Both of you are potentially dealing in the same realm. I mean, if there was anyone to give any credit to psychics, I would think it would be you." Dr. Zimmer sat back in his chair with a satisfying look. When he made the initial comment that thought hadn't even occurred to him. It was only in his back pedaling to save face and keep from offending Dusty that he thought of it. He wondered if Dusty caught on or if it appeared that the idea was in his professional approach all along. Dusty was too deep in thought to care or notice.

"Well, I guess you do have a point. I mean if I think psychics are full of shit, then there's no way in my right mind that I could somehow believe this girl I'm seeing is real."

"It might not hurt to try."

"What've I got to lose, right?" Dusty sat up from his chair and put his elbows on his knees. "Well, look, I appreciate you seeing me again. I hope you don't really think I'm crazy, but I guess if I was in your shoes…" Dusty's voice trailed off and he raised his eyebrows. He let Zimmer fill in the blanks.

"Mr. Burch, I don't think you are crazy. I'm just a very black and white person. I need proof before I can believe things. I hope you understand. All I can do is tell you what I think might be going on. It is up to you to decide whether to listen to it or not. I wish you luck."

"Thank you. I'll take it." Dusty got up and shook his hand firmly. The Doctor had a surprisingly strong grip. "Catch ya on the flip side, Doc."

Zimmer wasn't used to being addressed so casually and just smiled awkwardly, "Yes. The flip side."

149

Within the next hour, Dusty had located a psychic in the yellow pages. Before he knew it, he was sitting in a rundown apartment in southwest Chicago being licked by an overweight wiener-dog named Escobar.

Andromeda was the first person to answer the phone that day when Dusty scanned through the yellow pages, so she got the nod. This decision was one of Dusty's "on-tilt" decisions that his college friends always used to make fun of him about when they played poker. As he got older, he had gotten better about making snap decisions based on emotion, but old habits have a funny way of showing themselves when a person is under stress. Under no other circumstances would he be sitting on a green recliner in a cockroach-infested living room, choking on incense fumes, waiting for a Jamaican psychic to read his mind. But here he was.

"Mista Burch, I am ready for you now." Andromeda was a heavy-set Jamaican woman with long dreadlocks almost to her waist. She wore a tie-dyed turban that looked like a giant ice cream cone on her head and wore big, gold-hooped earrings. Her dress was a dark purple and was adorned with beads and sequence. She wore a cumbersome looking black, leather belt that was equipped with a belt buckle in the shape of a triangle. It reminded Dusty of the triangle on the Pink Floyd album *Dark Side of the Moon*. Her feet sported tattered, brown leather sandals that revealed most of her foot. She also wore black lipstick and her eyes had contacts in them that made her look like a snake. She was one of the most interesting characters Dusty had ever seen.

"Thank you. Thank you for seeing me on such short notice. I, I've never done this before, so excuse me if I seem a bit nervous." *Couldn't be the cockroaches*.

"No worries. I make it easy as pie. You are cute, Mista Burch. Very handsome man. I not see many handsome men in my home. A treat it is."

Dusty was so taken back that all he could do was smile. Andromeda pulled back the bead curtains that led to her "office".

"Come. Let's see what you have inside that head of yours." Dusty followed her through the curtain of brown beads into a dimly lit room filled with lava lamps, black lights, incense burners and a small fountain. The lamps gave the room a bluish, purplish hue. In the middle was a glass table with two white metal chairs. Two red candles were lit on the middle of the table and tarot cards lined the edge nearest her seat. Dusty sat down in the seat across from her.

"I don't mean to be rude, but would you mind telling me a little about yourself before we get started?"

Andromeda lit a cigarette before answering, "What do you want to know?" Dusty really liked her strong Jamaican accent.

Dusty scratched his head nervously, "Well, to start with, when did you move to the states?"

"I move here fifteen years ago. I wanted to find a place to," she waved her hand over the cards in front of her, "practice my skills. In Jamaica, I could not make much money. People are too poor and use their money too wisely. Here, well..."

"People blow their money left and right. I get it. So you just left? Your family and everyone?"

"I did not have family. Most people hated me. Thought I was a freak. Here, people love me."

"So you have a lot of friends?"

She hesitated like she didn't want to say what she was thinking. But she did anyway, "Not exactly, but I have had over 100 lovers since I have been here. Sex helps keep my mind clear. Americans are much more free with their sexuality. I have had many men that have sat right where you are. I am very good at... certain things." Andromeda peered eerily at Dusty through the smoke put out by the incense burner.

"Well, that's wonderful. But I'm not here for that." Dusty was so uncomfortable that he almost considered getting up and leaving. He heard a police siren wail outside and dogs barking. He put his hands on the arm of the chair to get up.

She picked up the stack of cards and shuffled them as fast as lighting, "Don't worry Mista Burch. I don't mean it that way. You are not my type, anyway." She continued shuffling.

"Well," Dusty shook his head, "that's a relief." Oddly, he now somehow wondered what was wrong with him that rendered him 'not her type'.

She put the cards down and spread them all around on the tabletop, mixing them all up. Then she picked one of them up, looked at it, and set it back down before Dusty could see what it was. "No offense, you are very handsome. I just prefer a different taste, but I think I can help you. I see you are in much distress. Something bothers you. Something… in your dreams."

Dusty lowered himself back down and stared at her in amazement, "How… How did you know that? How could you possibly know?" He was still a bit creeped out, but his curiosity got the best of him. She stacked the cards in three even piles face down.

"The cards say more than you think. The cards never lie."

He felt as if he was being sucked into an episode of *The Other Side*, but he didn't care, "What do they say?"

She took off a card from the first pile and held it up. On it was a monkey holding two snakes in each hand. His face was a skull and in his mouth was a large beetle of some sort. "This one says your mind is troubled. You possess a power but do not know what to do with it. The snake is powerful to those who know how to use it, but its venom can be deadly to an uneducated master. You don't know if your troubles will harm you, so you hold on to them tightly. The monkey has no face because he is not sure who he is. And the June bug, it represent doubt. You do not know whether to chew it up and swallow it or spit it out. Do you commit to it? Or do you push it away? What to do, Mista Burch?"

He contemplated what she said. *Not Bad.* But perhaps anyone could generalize anyone of those cards to get a person to think it applies to him, just like a horoscope. "How do those work?" He pointed to the cards.

"I do not fully know, but they always tell the truth. I awoke one morning to find them on my kitchen table. I had drawn them in the night. I always knew I had a gift, but never before could I use it to its full potential. I don't know how, but these cards help me express my gift."

Skeptical, but curious, Dusty asked, "What else do they say?"

"Breathe deep Mista Burch; concentrate on her. Close your eyes."

What the fuck am I getting myself into? This lady is nuts!

He didn't even ask how she knew it was a her, he just reluctantly closed his eyes and took a deep breath. He heard her shuffling the cards again and mumbling some tribal song of some sort. His curiosity peaked and he snuck a peek.

"Keep your eyes closed! You must do as I say," Andromeda snapped at him.

How the hell did she know? She wasn't even looking at me?

After a few minutes, Dusty felt a cold air fill the room. Andromeda's shuffling slowed and her chanting diminished. He felt her feet tapping underneath the table. He could smell the scent of the candles. *Lavender?* Suddenly, it was quiet.

"Can I open my eyes now?"

"Yes. Open them. Tell me, what do you see?" Dusty looked down at the cards to see six even piles with three cards face up in every other row. The other rows were face down. He noticed the candles were burning brighter and he could see the cards more clearly. Andromeda sat with her eyes closed and her head tilted up.

"I see a zebra with an elephant on its back in the middle of a pond. It looks like it is spraying water on the zebra. Next I see a knife. It is bloody with a wooden handle and it looks kind of dull. The third one is a bicycle with a flat tire." Dusty's face turned to a scowl as he searched for a possible meaning to any of this. Andromeda sat in silence. After a moment, she spoke.

"Do you want to know the long or the short of all this?"

"Let's go with the short."

She opened her eyes and lowered them to Dusty. She pulled a cigarette from her turban and lit it. She used the incense burner as an ashtray. "The elephant and the zebra: This mean that your burden is heavy and you are trying make sense of it… you can't tell black from white. The water means you are thirsty for an answer. The knife means someone has died. I think you know who this is, but you don't know how? Correct? And finally, the bicycle. You will find your answer with travel, but the flat tire means that you don't know where to go yet. Find that out and you will learn much."

"Okay," Dusty was impressed, "I gotta give it to you. You are pretty good. That pretty much about sums it up. But you are telling me things that I already know. I was hoping to… I don't know. Maybe communicate with her."

"Well, why didn't you say so?"

"I just did." Andromeda took a long drag from her cigarette and exhaled a large plume of smoke. She did so in a very unique fashion, unlike any Dusty had seen before. The smoke seemed to jet from her lips with such force it reminded him of the tail that formed off a jet's wing.

"She is here."

Dusty was bewildered, "She is?" Andromeda sat enjoying the look on Dusty's face for a moment, knowing that he had reached the point of no return and was skeptical no more.

"Yes. She is always near you. Can't you feel her?"

"I don't know," Dusty's face contorted as he struggled to recall any moments where he felt that he could actually *feel* her, "I can't remember. What do you mean *here?"* Dusty's eyes scanned the room frantically as if he would somehow spot her.

Andromeda took a long drag and answered with smoke flowing from her nostrils, "Her spirit. It surrounds you."

"Well can you talk to it? I mean, her?"

"It is not that easy, Mista Burch. It's not like on TV. There has to be a physical mind in front of me for me to read it. I cannot read a spirit's mind."

"Well, what the hell good does that do me?" Dusty pounded a fist harder than he had intended on the glass table and almost knocked off the incense burner. "I'm sorry. I'm very sorry," Andromeda sat unfazed, "I didn't mean to do that so hard."

She moved the incense burner to its original position, "No worries. No worries. You have a troubled mind."

"Well, is there any way? What can I do? Is there anyone who can help me communicate with her? Please, help me. I'm desperate." Dusty grasped her hand across the table.

"Some so-called psychics would charge you more and make something up, but in my opinion, a true spirit talker does not exist. It is a barrier I have tried many times to break, but have failed every time. But let me ask you this: Do you have something of hers? Something that was important to her maybe?"

"No. I do not. I never even knew her. It's almost impossible for me to know where to get something of hers. Why do you ask?"

"Well, I say I can't 'talk' to spirits, but sometimes I can… 'hear' them better than others. It doesn't always work, but a personal belonging of theirs seems to… open doors."

"I see. Well, I'm sorry. I can't help you there. Not today at least."

"It's okay, just thought I'd ask."

Dusty sat and contemplated his options, "So the cards? I mean, what is all this about?" What is all this for then?"

"I'm a fortune teller, Mista Burch. I can see glimpses of things to come and things past. I only get rough sketches, though. You are truly the master of your destiny. The only person who can find the answers you seek is *you*." She took another drag, "Who is this girl?"

Dusty gave her the details in a nutshell. She never even so much as blinked as she listened to his account. When he was finished, she lit another cigarette and pulled a bottle of wine and two cups from under her chair.

"A glass of wine?" she asked him politely.

"Sure. Why not?" She poured a dark red wine a quarter of the way up the glass and handed it to him. The glass was very skinny and tall with a short handle. "Thank you." Dusty took a sip of the wine. "Mind if I bum one of those?" He motioned to her pack of Marlboros.

"Of course." As Dusty lit his cigarette, his mind searched for his next question, but she spoke instead.

"Mista Burch, you need not worry that you are going crazy. This little girl is real, but as I said, I need a mind to read. I cannot see hers. I can feel her presence, but that is it. What she wants you to know, only she can tell you. There is a way, but you have to find it. The answers are in front of you, but you must find the code. Keep searching. She will lead you. Follow your heart. I have heard before that spirits can 'show' their physical counterparts things. I have never seen, but I have heard. There has to be a very strong connection, but I believe it can be done."

"So you think she can 'show' me things?"

"It's possible."

"Like, outside of my dreams?"

"Yes. Conscious visions. Apparitions."

"Like Ebenezer Scrooge and his ghosts?"

"Who?"

"Never mind." Dusty sat speechless across from her, letting the cherry on his cigarette burn half way down before speaking, sipping on his wine. "That's good wine. Damn good." He swallowed the rest of the glass in a giant gulp and set it on the table. "Can you tell me anything else? Do the cards say anything else?"

"Nothing that you want to know, nothing except," she hesitated before pointing to one of the last unturned cards on top.

Dusty understood and immediately flipped the card over to reveal a cryptic drawing of a heart. It was the organ, not the shape, and it was as detailed a drawing of a heart as he had ever seen. Bright red and blue veins and arteries spider webbed around it and it was shaded so realistically that he had to give a triple take before deciding that it was indeed a drawing and not a real picture.

"This one is easy to understand. It means love."

"Love? That's it? Love? What about it?"

"I think you know what this means. Don't fight this one, Mista Burch."

"I don't know what you are talking about…"

"Fine, whatever you say. But you will. There is no denying this one."

Of course Dusty wasn't ready to admit that Lynn's face immediately popped up in his mind when she said the four-letter word, but he wasn't ready to admit that he was in *love* with her. No way. Absolutely no way.

Dusty stood up and put out his cigarette, "Well, thank you so much for your time." He reached into his wallet and pulled out a hundred dollar bill. "Is this enough?"

"More than enough. You take care of yourself. Listen to your instincts. They are the only way you get through this one. Follow your heart. Do not be afraid to do that. You have been afraid to do so before, no?"

Dusty smiled, "You are right again. Thanks. I'll try and remember that." Dust walked out the door and down to his truck. He turned on the radio and immediately *Sunshine of Your Love* by Cream blared through the speakers from the local classic rock station, 101.3. It was one of his all-time favorites.

"No fucking way." He sat and listened through the guitar break as Clapton's fingers melted through the neck of the guitar, smiling as if he'd been struck by lightning, then backed out and peeled away as he headed back to his office to maybe actually get some work done.

Chapter 25

It took Dusty exactly nine days to call Lynn after he last saw her. He didn't mean to be so cliché, but every time he picked up the phone he panicked. When he finally did dial in the digits, he got her voicemail:

Hey Lynn. It's Dusty. The guy from Winter Park. I mean, not from Winter Park, but... you know what I mean. I'm from Chicago. We met in Winter Park. Hopefully you hadn't forgotten my name by now, but just thought I'd clarify. Anyways, I'm just on my lunch break at work and thought I'd give you a call to see how things were. I have a few meetings this afternoon, but I should be free by six. I'd love to talk with you. Have a great day!

He immediately hung up the phone and sat at his desk, stunned at how idiotic he must have come off. "The guy from Winter Park? Really?" He stuffed his cell phone in his pocket and turned back to his computer, which he stared at blankly for five minutes while he imagined all the possible reactions she would have to his message. Most of them ended up with him sitting by his phone all night long until, broken hearted, he fell asleep.

To his surprise, his phone rang at 4:57. He had got done a little earlier than he thought with the motion he was working on and was headed down to his car in the garage. He took his cell phone out of his pocket and flipped it open, "You just couldn't wait until 6:00, could you?"

"What? It's..." Lynn looked at her clock confused, and then realized her mistake, "Oh, don't flatter yourself mister. I forgot you are in a different time zone. But I can call back later if you'd like…" her sharp and quick reply got Dusty's attention. He sometimes misjudged how his sense of humor came off.

"No! No, it's okay. I was just messing with you. I totally forgot about that too. I'm actually just about ready to head out of the office. Perfect timing. Thanks for calling me back." He was a little afraid he had offended her and was trying to make up for it. His heart started racing a little faster as he walked down the ramp under the poorly lit garage lighting. He realized he couldn't remember where he had parked and had been walking aimlessly since he answered his phone. *It was level 3, wasn't it?*

"Well from now on, we are gonna operate on my time zone. Just to keep things simple."

"Hey as long as we are operating, I don't care if we are on Africa's time zone," he had just spotted his car. He opened the door to his black, 4x4 GMC pickup truck and stepped inside. He shut the door and just sat in the darkness, waiting for a reply.

"You're cute." He didn't know her well enough to know if she was just flirting with him, or if she was mocking him. That was one of those sayings that could mean: *You're really an idiot…* or: *I think I like you but I'm not sure yet.* Either way, he wasn't really going for *cute.*

He decided to change the subject, "So how have you been?"

"I've been good. Staying busy. I had class today until about 6:30 after I got off work. I'm about ready to go to the gym, just thought I'd give you a call back. How are you doing?"

"Oh, not bad. Ron Davis is about to drive me crazy, but other than that. I'm okay."

"And he is the…"

"The CEO of the tobacco company I'm representing. The one I told you about."

"Oh yah. That's right. The 'ruthless bastard'."

"Yep. That'd be him. He just keeps on insisting that we try and buy off the plaintiffs for

next-to-nothing. I don't think he understands how much money he could lose if this goes to trial. I know juries aren't supposed to be biased, but even if the facts are 50/50, there's no way anyone with a heart could keep from feeling sympathy for this boy. Any benefit of the doubt will go to him, the boy."

"Sounds like a bad deal."

"Yeah. And every day I work for him, I feel dirtier and dirtier. I've helped a lot of clients before win cases, but never before have I felt so guilty about possibly keeping the plaintiff from collecting damages. It's starting to weigh pretty heavy on me."

"I'm sorry to hear that," she didn't really know what to say. She knew next to nothing about the law.

"Well enough about that. Sorry. I just needed to vent for a second."

"No, it's okay. Vent all you need. Sometimes a person just has to get it all off their chest. It's not good to hold it all in."

"Thanks for understanding. Just with this, and my little girl, I think I need a weekend off." Dusty started his truck.

"Well how would you like to come visit the Big Apple? You said you've never been here, right?"

Dusty couldn't believe his ears, "Are you serious? I wasn't trying to..." he was smiling ear to ear. His last comment wasn't meant to be suggestive.

"Oh I know you weren't. I just thought maybe you could help me start to solve my case. I've been striking out at every turn. Plus, It'd be kind of nice to see you again."

Dusty was smiling so big that his eyes started watering, "I'll take 'kind of nice'. When were you thinking?"

"Just kinda. I'm free this weekend."

"This weekend?" Dusty sounded a little shocked. This was all happening faster than he expected. "Um... yah. I think I can do that." Dusty had told Stanley that he would come in to work on Saturday. *Fuck it. He can't fire me. I'm the best he's got.* "I can book a flight tomorrow. What hotel is close to your place?"

"Well, I was thinking you could stay at my place. If that's okay with you?"

"Are you sure? I don't want to impose. I'd be happy to get a room..."

"Will you stop being such a gentleman already? I'd be offended if you didn't stay with me."

"Okay! Okay. I just didn't want to be presumptuous." Dusty's mind was reeling. This all sounded too good to be true. Here he was, worrying himself to death over this girl, and she's making it easy for him. It never worked out that way for him. He liked it. All his prior flings were game players. Lynn was straight to the point. Aggressive. "So... should I bring an inflatable mattress? Or you have a couch for me?"

"Oh I have a couch. It's pretty comfy. But it's not as comfy as my mattress."

Dusty all the sudden felt himself get an erection. *Is this really happening right now?* "Well now how often do you invite total strangers onto your mattress?" He didn't know what to say. He was trying not to be too forward, but she was taking the reins.

"That wasn't an invitation... I was just stating a fact. Play your cards right and there may be an open spot for you. And you're not a *total* stranger. For instance, I know you need a wingman to pick up girls."

Dusty laughed. "Ouch." He was amused and aroused, but she had turned the tables on him again, "You got me there. I didn't mean anything by that. I'm just not so used to... I'm just the idiot that's always chasing..."

"We're not in high school Dusty."

"Yeah I know." He paused before he said anything else stupid, "I like it. It's great."

"Just don't break my heart. I know people who know people who kill people."

"I'll try to remember that."

"Ok. Well my address is 1214 N. 8th Ave, Apt 214b. I'm sorry I don't have a car or I'd pick you up."

"Oh that's okay. I'll take a cab."

"Train might be easier. Take it to 14th St. and 6th Ave in lower Manhattan. I'm just a couple blocks from there."

"Ok. Well I'll see you then, Lynn."

"See you then. Goodnight."

"Night." Dusty scribbled down the address on an Arby's napkin as he hung up the phone. He backed out of the parking space and started out of the garage... on cloud nine.

The conversation couldn't have gone any better. The weekend was only a couple days away, and now he had a new reason he couldn't sleep at night. He hadn't been able to stop thinking about Lynn since he saw her in Winter Park. Never before had a woman seized his conscious hours like she had done. He realized this was either the start of a very good thing, or a total heartbreak. Now he had a female to occupy his mind whether he was awake or asleep, both of which had about an equal amount of pull.

He didn't call her the next two nights. He didn't want to seem too attached. He figured a little anticipation would be a good thing. He couldn't help himself from sending a perfunctory text message, referencing her favorite movie she had told him about over coffee: *Dirty Dancing*. He happened to see it on TV when he was flipping through the channel. Her response was: "Wish I was there to watch it with you." He left it at that.

He struggled through the next two days of depositions of Unity Insurance employees. He made an objection here or there, but most of the notes he wrote down on his legal pad were ideas of how he could help Lynn start to solve her case. They consisted of: check missing child reports, research news articles for past few years, make a list of everywhere she had been in the last two years, meditate, watch her while she slept in case she talked in her sleep, walk through town to places she visited frequently, make a list of all the children that she knew, write down her most vivid childhood memories, rub her down in hot oils and massage her naked body....

"Mr. Burch!" Karee snapped at him, demanding his attention. "For the third time, do you have the interrogatories that I sent over a few weeks ago for Mr. Lynch?" He scratched the last one off his list before he answered.

"Uh, yah. Got 'em right here..."

Before he knew it, he was on a plane for New York City. His flight left at 5:35 pm on Friday and he flew into a beautiful sun setting over the towering skyline of New York. He didn't eat much on the two-hour flight, just a few bags of peanuts. *It just doesn't feel like a flight without peanuts.* Lynn had texted him just before he left to come hungry because she was going to take him to her favorite restaurant. It was a surprise.

Chapter 26

The AirTran is the fastest and most economical way for people to get to where they want to go from JFK International. Although thousands of people were swarming in the causeways and moving sidewalks, from all parts of the world, finding the way to the train was relatively easy for Dusty. Huge signs direct traffic about every 100 feet in the airport. The engineers expertly designed the giant maze to be navigated by all who were literate. Even if he would have gotten lost, he could have easily asked one of the hundreds of frequent fliers walking through the abyss with their heads stuck in a newspaper or magazine, who obviously knew the place by heart.

The train glided in gracefully to his stop. He was amazed at how little noise the train emitted while bringing itself to a halt. He was looking for the "Lower Manhattan" lights to flash above the doors as they opened, just to be sure. As soon as he saw them, he stepped on board, gelling with the dozens of people around him. The train swallowed up a hundred people in a matter of five seconds and it was off. It made several more stops in the airport before heading out, but Dusty didn't mind. He was enjoying the ride.

Dusty had never been to New York. His parents had carted him around to all corners of the US, but for some reason they never ventured into the Big Apple. He had asked once as a kid to go there, but his dad said it wasn't much different than Chicago, "Big cities are all the same. Why would we take a vacation from Chicago to New York when we can go somewhere like the Grand Canyon?" His dad was right. When he got there, the busy streets, traffic lights, exhaust fumes and crowded sidewalks felt too much like home. The one thing New York had that Chicago didn't however was Lynn.

He stood between a middle-aged, overweight, balding man in a beige leisure suit and a blonde girl who looked to be in her early twenties, wearing black leggings, a pink skirt and a white tank-top with no bra. Her nipples were standing straight on edge. Dusty couldn't help but look every few minutes… she wasn't trying the least bit to conceal it. She smacked her gum loudly and tongued her lip ring while she listened to music. *Oblivious to the world.*

Every few minutes, the computer voice on the intercom announced where they were stopping next. Dusty couldn't help but to think about how he was in *the future*. It never ceased to amaze him how far human technology had come. The transportation was so sophisticated. People just two hundred years ago could never have imagined what was everyday life for Dusty and all those surrounding him. *Planes, trains and automobiles.* In a few hours he had traveled as far as it used to take people a few weeks.

He studied the skyline as the train zipped through the city. His thoughts were of Lynn and somehow everything in the city he associated with her. *I wonder if she ever ate at that restaurant?? Or sat on that bench? Or walked down that street?* The whole city seemed to belong to her and he couldn't wait for her to show him.

The braless gum smacker got off two stops before him. Now his gaze was concentrated on an elderly woman, about 75. She was wearing a tan overcoat. *A little much for this time of year.* In her hands she held a grocery sack filled with fruit, vegetables and a loaf of bread. He couldn't tell for sure, but he thought her eyes were crossed. She was missing teeth and her fingernails were very long. She sat in a vulnerable position, humming. *Homeless?*

The voice on the intercom came on and said, "14th Street and 6th Avenue," the old lady stood up. This was her stop too. Dusty asked her if she needed help with her bag, but she hastily swatted his hands away.

He got off the train into a river of pedestrians. Friday night was a busy time in the city. A lot of people relied on public transportation and it seemed everyone wanted to get somewhere important. He realized quickly that he had better be on guard. People ran into him several times without evening acknowledging it. It was a couple notches less than a mosh pit, but people here were just used to it. *At least in Chicago we say sorry.*

He followed 14th Street west to 8th Avenue and turned left and followed that to 12th Street. He thought it was strange that both sets of cross streets were numbered; one with 'Avenue', one with 'Street'. *How confusing,* he thought. He spotted the red brick building with the sign that read, "Kindlewood Apartments." A violin duo was playing on the corner. It was a song here recognized as "Little Dixie". After all the Civil War battlefields his dad had drug him to on vacations, he could never forget that song. He dropped a five-dollar bill in their jar and headed in the door.

The inside was modern, more modern than the outside of the building portrayed it to be. There were tall, green plants next to the elevator. Shiny, checkered tile lined the floor. Two nice leather couches sat in the waiting area with a 60" flat screen TV that was playing the Mets game. A black, spiral staircase led to the second floor commons area that was visible through the slatted iron bars. It too had a TV, but nothing was playing. He walked to the elevator and hit the up arrow. Then, suddenly he remembered she was on the second floor and opted to take the stairs instead.

I think you can handle one flight of stairs.

When he walked past the elevator, he was reminded of Winter Park, when he and Bruce had gone to meet Lynn. He half expected to see her trying to get in her room when he looked down the hall. Nope. This time he was alone and there was no turning back. When he got to her door, he knocked lightly.

When she opened the door, Dusty was literally shocked by her beauty. She was fully decked out for the evening. Her perfume immediately inundated his nose. *What is that?* She was wearing black slacks and a black tank top lined with silver embroidery. She wore a trio of dangly; shiny necklaces to match and her wrists were ordained with a slew of bracelets. Her lips shone with lip-gloss and her dark eyeliner accentuated her hazel eyes. She wore her hair down, shoulder length, and had curled it so that it was wavy and flowing. Her black high-heels exposed her two front toes that were painted red. He was immediately smitten and consumed with lust. *Holy shit.*

"Wow. You look… amazing."

"It's nice to see you too, handsome," she said as she hugged him around the neck. "Come on in." He followed her through the door. "How was the trip? Oh sorry, you can put your bag over there," she pointed to underneath her staircase, which was also spiral. It led upstairs to a bedroom and a bath. The living room was very open, with a black, leather sofa, a glass coffee table and a 42" plasma TV mounted on the wall adjacent to the door. The staircase was in the back left corner of the room. The floors were hardwood. Stained. The sofa and coffee table were placed on a nice, decorative rug that looked like it could have been from China. The kitchen was behind a bar and looked to be directly underneath the bedroom. It was small, but well furnished. A small dining room table lined the back wall behind the sofa. To the far right was a balcony that looked out over the city with a glass sliding door and white, rectangular draw shades. A tall green plant of some sort was in the corner by the door.

"It was good. I liked the train. It was very… New Yorkish."

"Really? And what's that?" she asked as she sat down on the sofa. Dusty followed suit and sat down beside her.

"I don't know. Big, fast, full, computer voices… there was a girl with no bra. And an old lady swatted at me for offering to help with her groceries, who also might have had no bra."

"Sounds about right. People don't seem to care at all what others think of them. There are so many people here that it's impossible to please them all, so a lot of people just kind of... let themselves go. Is it not like that in Chicago?"

"I don't know… Guess I never really thought about it. I mean there's all kinds of people, but Manhattan kind of seems like its own little planet."

"I like it. It's busy, but busy is good for me. I can't stand to be idle."

There was a bit of silence, then Dusty thought he would test out the waters, "So, how do you let yourself go?"

Lynn laughed, "Well, I'm wearing a bra if that's what you're asking!" Dusty glanced at each of her shoulders with raised eyebrows. "I am! It's strapless!" She punched him in the shoulder.

"Ow! Hey! That was hard!" He wasn't acting. His shoulder throbbed in pain.

"I have an older brother. I'm tougher than most chicks." Dusty rubbed his shoulder and rolled it out.

"I guess. Seems like you've done that a time or two."

"A few," she responded with a cocky smile.

Dusty sat back on the couch and took a deep breath, "Well, I like your place."

"It's not bad. The cost of living is expensive here, so this is as good as a dental assistant in school can do."

"No. It's nice." Dusty peered around the apartment, "You got a punching bag that drops down from the ceiling too?"

"Nope. It's in the bedroom."

"Seriously?"

Lynn nodded her head, "Seriously."

"Wow. I was just joking."

"I mean I know it's a little crazy, but a girl's gotta be able to protect herself in a big city. Plus, it's a good stress reliever."

"I bet."

"What do you do to relieve stress," she asked inquisitively.

Dusty had to pass on the first answer that came to his mind, "Well, I uh, I work I guess. I get stressed when I feel like I'm behind. But as far as physical activity? I have a pull-up bar in my doorway and push up handles. I try to pump some out every night. Every once in a while I'll go for a jog or something. I used to ride a bike a lot, but not so much anymore."

"You ever play racquetball?"

Dusty chuckled and shook his head, "In college once, but I don't know if you can really call it racquetball. This girl I dated thought it'd be a good idea. We had no idea what we were doing."

"Oh my god it's a blast! I used to play with my brother all the time. We have to play sometime!" She was visibly excited.

"Okay. Sounds like fun." Dusty felt his stomach growl. Lynn heard it and looked down with a perplexed look on her face.

"Hungry?"

Dusty nervously chuckled, "How could you tell? So what is this place we are going to dinner at?"

"It's still a surprise. I'll show you. You ready to go?"

"Yes. I'm starving. I've only eaten airplane peanuts since breakfast."

"Good. You're gonna love this place."

Chapter 27

Hot dog stands and musicians lined the streets for seven blocks along their way to the mystery restaurant. Two different times, Dusty was approached and asked if he wanted to buy drugs. The sheer volume of people walking the sidewalks was mind-boggling to Dusty. He had always felt like navigating through downtown Chicago was a pain in the ass, but lower Manhattan was on a different level.

He walked with his right hand protectively covering his back pocket, while Lynn held the other, directing him through traffic. She was expertly maneuvering through the crowd, making decisive moves and fearlessly bumping elbows with strangers.

"Don't you ever get scared living here?" Dusty asked as they passed a group of gangster looking men smoking cigarettes in an alley, bouncing to a boom box.

"I always carry this," she said as she reached into her purse and pulled out a can of pepper spray in a pink canister. "And why do you think I try to stay so fit? When I first moved here, I even took a year of self-defense classes. I've only had to use them once."

"Really?" Dusty said with a surprised look on his face. "What the hell happened?"

Lynn slowed her pace to a leisurely walk as they came to a semi-clear stretch of sidewalk between a jewelry store and an antique store. "I'd rather not talk about it right now, actually. I'm in a good mood."

"No problem. So where'd you move here from?"

"My family is from Hartford, Connecticut. Most of them still live there. I just needed to get out and start on my own. I was kind of going crazy."

A man on a bicycle caught Dusty's eye. He was black, mid 50s and wore a white tank top, holey cargo pants, flip-flops and sunglasses. He was eating an apple, listening to his headphones and singing to himself. He nearly hit Dusty as he passed going the opposite way.

Dusty didn't even have time to say something if he wanted to. He slightly turned and glared back at the bike, but Lynn's arm pulled him forward. "Hey, slow down a bit, will ya?"

She looked at him as if she had been in this situation before, "I'm sorry. It's a habit. I don't do much leisurely walking. Since I don't have a car, I'm just used to walking everywhere I go and guess I only have one gear. Plus I'm starving!"

"You're wearing me out! Some people actually need oxygen when they talk..." Dusty said with a sarcastic smile.

"What's the matter? Big man can't hang? I've even got heels on."

"Oh, I can hang. I ran the mile under five minutes back in the day."

"Impressive," she glanced at him with a smirk and raised her eyebrows, "I could never break 4:40."

"What? No way. You're kidding," Dusty said incredulously.

"Cross my heart," she made an "x" over her chest with her finger, "but I'll slow it down to six flat just for you," she flashed her eyes at him and they locked gazes for a moment. They slowed to a stop at an intersection.

"That's awfully sweet of you," their eyes, still locked, radiating affection. Every minute he spent with her he became more attracted to her. He wanted to kiss her right then, in front of everyone. *Too early. Hold it together man.* The light switched and they began walking across the street. "So how far is this place?"

"We're almost there. It's just about a block away." They passed a laundromat, then a sandwich shop named *Teddy's* that had an old-time barber's pole on the outside of it. Inside it was packed. "They make an awesome Reuben. I go there for lunch sometimes."

"Reuben? Yuck!"

"Hey, don't knock it 'til you try it. I thought the same thing. 'Reubens?' But I was wrong; they are awesome. It's never too late to acquire a taste." Even as they talked about sandwiches, Dusty could not stop admiring her.

She is so positive and happy. And driven and genuine. And... beautiful.

She walked to the end of the sidewalk, "Okay, we cross here." Still holding his hand, she waited for the walking sign to illuminate and started across the street. She led him up a stairwell connected to a building on the corner. "It's kind of hidden from the outside, but everyone knows about it." As they got to the top she told him, "Okay, close your eyes." She opened a big wooden door and led Dusty in. His nostrils were immediately inundated with wonderful smells of cooking meat, spices and rich aromas. He could hear clanking metal and sizzling food on the grill.

He opened his eyes upon her instructions and witnessed 5 or 6 tables with a stove built in to each of them. Cooks were dicing, flipping, burning, spinning and tossing food in all directions. It was a Japanese steakhouse.

"I *love* this place," she said with as much exaggeration as he had ever seen her express. "Every time I go here I leave feeling sick inside and feel like I need to run like 10 miles, but it's sooo good." Dusty had his eyes on a chef lighting a cone of onions stacked on top of each other on fire, flaming from the top like a volcano.

"I've always heard about one of these places, but I've never been to one," he was truly excited and couldn't wait to sit and stuff himself full of shrimp, pasta, soup, salad, sushi, steak... whatever.

"Oh my god, you are going to love it."

The place was called *Teppanyaki*. The inside was dimly lit and oriental paintings lined the walls. Each grill had a bamboo-type, A-frame roof over it and could seat up to eight people. A sushi bar was situated on a lower landing at the back of the restaurant. The workers were all oriental and spoke English, but with heavy accents. A waiter seated them at a table with another family consisting of an older couple with four teenage kids.

As the chicken and mushroom soup was brought out to them, Lynn sparked up the conversation, "So, have you been keeping up with the chat room lately?"

"Not as much as I'd like to. Every time I look it's the same ole song and dance. No one has found *anything*. I mean how can we have this many people and nobody has uncovered even a single clue?" Dusty took a drink of his Saki that Lynn had ordered them.

"Maybe we aren't looking in the right places. Or maybe we just aren't ready."

Dusty tried keeping his voice down as he spoke, "Or maybe we are all just crazy."

"No. No. I don't think so. You know you don't either," Lynn retorted with such conviction that Dusty felt ashamed for saying so.

"Let me ask you something, do you believe in God, Lynn?"

She pondered the question a moment, then answered, "When I was little, I used to go to church every Sunday. I loved dressing up and going to Sunday school and listening to Bible stories, but as I got older, I started becoming more aware of all the contradictions in religion. I didn't understand why challenging the status quo was so taboo. I started wondering if there was a God at all, or if he was like Santa Claus: a fairy tale. I still went to church and read the Bible, but I started reading other books, too. I read a lot of positive thinking books, like "How to Win Friends and Influence People" by Dale Carnegie. Sounds nerdy, I know, but I don't think enough people think about how their attitude affects everything. I even read some of Stephen Hawking as a high schooler. That guy is a genius. It makes it hard to take every word in the Bible literally. I became fascinated with physics and the universe and how it was all created. To me, the fact that all the atoms in our bodies were constructed inside of a star is religion enough for me. I mean how could that be possible and there not be a superior, timeless energy that transcends human comprehension? So, to answer your question, I believe there is a higher power that we are unable to understand, but I don't attach that power to any religion, per se."

The whole time she spoke, Dusty had tingles running down his spine. She spoke so eloquently, yet so confidently. Her view on the universe was very similar to his and he was relieved that he didn't have to worry about being too much of a sinner for her. "I feel the same way, except I never really went to church. I mean I've read the Bible and stuff, but not extensively. I've been around enough religious people to know that religion alone doesn't make you a good person…"

"Exactly! Too many people use it as a shield to hide behind. That's what I realized. That's what kind of drove me away, but ever since my dreams, I've started to revisit my faith a little bit. I've even started praying again."

"Do you think that helps?"

"I don't know. Sometimes. To me it's really more of a meditation. I think they are one in the same. All it really is, is working out the cobwebs in your brain… putting positive energy back into the universe… hoping that it comes back to you someday..." She stared at her spoon that was full of broth for a moment, and then put it back in her bowl.

"Are you okay?" Dusty asked concerned.

"Yah, it's just. Ugh, never mind." Lynn shook her head slightly, as if to shake away the bad thoughts rushing in.

"What? What is it? Is it something I said?"

"No," Lynn was trying to hold back her emotion, "I just… I'm so tired of feeling helpless." Her bottom lip quivered and her eyes inadvertently filled to the rims.

Dusty couldn't stand to see her upset and wished he could just take it all away. He tried offering her some solace, "I know how you feel. We'll get through this, together. I promise. Okay?" Dusty was trying to raise her spirits. The family across the table was starting to look at them a little strange, but they didn't care. They might as well have been in the middle of the Pacific Ocean. Dusty grabbed her hand under the table. "Lynn?"

"Okay. I'm gonna hold you to it though."

"Sounds good." Just then the chef showed up and started his routine.

Chapter 28

Just as Lynn had said, Dusty felt like he could be sick from all the food he ate. For twenty straight minutes, it just kept piling in. With every bite he took, two more were put on his plate. Fried rice, shrimp, steak, noodles, seared veggies, and a delicious yellow hollandaise sauce that he covered everything with. He also ordered a California sushi roll and split it with Lynn. Each roll had a dab of wasabi, a sliver of ginger and a liberal amount of soy sauce. He was filled to the brim. He picked up the tab and she thanked him with a kiss on the cheek.

The walk home was much slower and leisurely than the way there. Lynn clung to Dusty's arm as they walked down the sidewalk. Night had fallen and Dusty noticed that a new demographic was starting to infiltrate the streets. A younger, trendier crowd gathered around bars and clubs. Girls dressed in high-heels and miniskirts emerged from taxis, escorted by men wearing muscle t-shirts and gold necklaces. The beggars, too, were out in full force. Dusty found it fascinating how the rest of the city tolerated the needy, probably homeless, people. They just kind of blended in. No one ignored them, or paid any special attention to them. Every once in a while, a person would give them a hamburger or a five-dollar bill. That's what kept them coming back.

Dusty couldn't get over the feeling of protectiveness for Lynn. The city seemed like a dark hole, waiting to swallow up a beautiful woman like Lynn. He could only imagine the type of creeps and killers that inhabited this place. It wasn't that it was run down and low rent, but that it attracted so many types of people. It was a true melting pot and a person could be anyone they wanted and no one would know otherwise. It would be easy for a predator to hide in the tall grass that was Manhattan and stalk its prey.

The whole way home, Dusty had an eerie feeling. He desperately wanted to know what happened to Lynn that she was so afraid to talk about, but he didn't want to push the bill. Part of him wanted to just sweep her off her feet and get her out of there, but he could tell she felt perfectly competent to take care of herself and he didn't want to be prematurely over-protective. He saw himself quickly getting into trouble at work, spending too much time in New York, trying to help her with her child. He began to worry-second guessing himself-about getting into a relationship. Thoughts of the children they dreamt of creating problems and stress in their relationship began flooding his mind. *Would it be too much?*

Dusty was plagued with a mixture of joy and worry. Her demeanor was glowing, however. He tried to hide his anxiety by engaging in small talk the rest of the way home. He asked her about her job and school. He inquired more about her family and opened up to her about how he has let his relationship with his parents fall by the wayside. He tried pushing all the negative thoughts out of his brain and focus on the present. He zoned out momentarily as they entered the building and walked up the steps. She noticed something was different.

"Dusty, is everything okay?" she turned and asked him as she put the key in the door.

"Yah. Everything's fine. I'm just thinking. My mind has a tendency to race and I forget to talk...," he spoke gently and reassuringly, not wanting to kill her mood.

She left the door closed, almost as if she were waiting to open it until she was sure he wanted to be there, "Good race? Or bad race?" She looked longingly into his eyes, pleading for a positive answer.

"Good race. Very good."

"That's good, because I was thinking of giving you some boxing lessons, but if you're having second thoughts..." she rolled her eyes to the side and raised her eyebrows.

"Absolutely not. I wouldn't miss it for the world." With that, she opened the door and walked through. This time when he closed it and turned around, she was there waiting for him. She wrapped her arms around his neck and started kissing him passionately. Any negative thoughts Dusty had prior to that moment vanished like a mist into thin air and he picked her up and put her against the door. She wrapped her legs around him, still kissing and biting his lip.

She pulled apart for an instant, "About those lessons..." then she returned to his lips.

"Yes?"

"The bag... it's in my room."

"Well I think we probably better go there then, huh?"

"Yah. That's probably a good idea." He lowered her to the ground and she pulled him by his belt buckle, walking backwards to the staircase and started up them.

"You know, I don't usually kiss on the first date."

"Is that so? What makes me the lucky guy?"

"I don't know," she backed further up the stairs, "I guess it's that ever since I saw you at my hotel doorway, I haven't been able to stop thinking about ripping your clothes off."

Dusty smiled, "I can't say I haven't pictured you naked a time or two." She backed into her doorway, kissing him and taking off his shirt.

"You really do have a punching bag in here, don't you."

"We can box later," she said as she pushed him on the bed. Before he knew it, she was standing in front of him in her Victoria's Secret, black laced lingerie. Her body was even sexier than he had imagined. Her legs were muscular, but feminine and her hipbones were visible above her panty line. She had a tone stomach, but not so tone that he could see a six-pack. He didn't like a six-pack on women anyway. Her breasts were perky and bigger than he had expected. But it was her eyes... the passion in her eyes... that aroused him the most.

He had been with many women before, but never had one made him tremble the way his body was trembling. He was falling madly in love with her. As she unbuckled his belt and slid off his slacks, his body quivered. She tenderly kissed the inside of his thighs before pulling down his briefs and passionately massaging his penis with her mouth. He unfastened her bra and revealed her breasts. His world spun and she pleasured him for several minutes with her hands and mouth. She took extra care that he didn't feel any teeth. What turned him on the most was that she seemed to be genuinely enjoying herself. Every few moments, her second hand would cup his testicles and massage them. He rubbed the smooth skin of her back and shoulders with his hands, which seemed to energize her. Halfway through, she reached over to her bedside table and grabbed a hair tie and pulled her hair back so it wouldn't get in the way. She gently moaned, as if she were being pleasured too. Then she sat up and slid off her panties before climbing up his body and mounting him, inserting him into her.

"Oh wow," she exclaimed as she gently lowered herself, "that feels… amazing." She was already moist and ready for him. She lowered her head and kissed his mouth and slowly increased her pace. He caressed her back and buttocks while she rocked back and forth, slowly at first. Dusty reached his head up to kiss her breasts and nipples, which also seemed to arouse her. He could feel her body tightening and her pace increasing. Dusty couldn't lie still any longer. He grabbed her tightly and plunged upward into her, fueled by her moans and cries of pleasure. She took out her hair tie and her hair fell loosely over his face. As she started to climax, she screamed out, "Don't stop… oh my God… don't… stop."

He didn't. It aroused him how quickly she was able to orgasm and he vigorously thrust himself into her until she relaxed on top of him, breathing heavily. He turned her over on her back, never separating from her. "You feel incredible," he whispered in her ear as he started to thrust. She rubbed her feet up and down his legs and moaned encouragingly. As he sped up, she brought them up around his waist. Her fingernails dug into his back and he could feel her start to climax again. He kissed her breasts and caressed her nipples with his tongue, invoking a loud response.

"Oh, Dusty… come on. Come with me. Come baby…" he could feel her getting more wet and decided not to hold back another moment. He rose off of her and grabbed her legs and began thrusting with all his might. "Don't stop… don't. Come inside of me…"

"Are you sure," he said, out of breath and panting?

"Yes. Yes! I'm… on… birth control…please, don't stop" He didn't need any more coercing. With a glorious finale that almost rocked the mattress off the frame, he held her feet behind her head and came inside of her with a storm of ecstasy and emotion engulfing his brain. He had never made love more passionately. As she lay underneath him, out of breath and sweaty, he felt their universal parts joining, forever. Her hands rubbed up and down his back and she moaned soft sounds of lingering pleasure.

He didn't move for several minutes as he caught his breath while still inside of her. She gasped as he rolled off and lay next to her. She was still being stimulated. She immediately laid her head on his chest and started caressing his body with her hand.

"That was the best boxing lesson I've ever had," he said with a smile, still huffing.

"Oh honey, that's only the first round."

As he lay next to her, suddenly his euphoric feelings were replaced with thoughts of suffering children, but he wasn't scared. Her warm body and smooth skin relieved him. He felt that together, they could endure anything. He promised himself right then and there, as the moonlight shone through her bedroom window, illuminating her dreamy eyes, that he would ease her pain. He knew at that moment that he could never let her go, not as long as he had a breath of life in him.

For a while, they laid in silence. She could feel his chest move up and down and could hear his heart beating. Then she broke the silence, "Dusty, I have to tell you something."

"What's that?"

"I just want you to know that…" she struggled to find the words. Dusty gave her time to sort it out. "I don't want you to think that I am… easy. This is not my normal behavior. I know we just met and all, but…"

"Lynn, it's okay. I don't think that at all. For once I like it that a girl I like doesn't play games with me."

"It's been a while for me, since my last boyfriend, over a year ago. I just didn't see any point in dragging it on. It just felt so good to see you," she started to get a little emotional. "It felt good to feel happy again. I just didn't want to hold back something that felt so good."

"I'm glad you didn't hold back. I would have gone crazy until the next time I saw you, and each time after that until it happened. I'm already going crazy enough. I needed it too."

"So you don't think I'm a slut?" she looked up at him with pitiful eyes.

He couldn't help but to laugh a little bit, "No! I know a slut when I see one. And believe me, you are definitely not a slut. I wouldn't have been attracted to you had I thought so. In fact, I thought the opposite."

"What do you mean?"

"I thought you just might be a virgin."

Lynn acted surprised, "Really? Why did you think that?"

"I don't know. You just looked so... I don't know. I think I was more just fantasizing about it," he immediately wished he hadn't gone down that road.

"So now that you know I'm not, are you... less attracted to me?"

He saw that one coming and was ready, "No, absolutely not. Don't get the wrong idea. I could just tell you weren't a slut. Let's put it that way."

"Well, would you believe me if I told you that you were only my second?"

"Second? Huh," Dusty actually was surprised after how good in bed she was. "I guess that makes me one really lucky guy."

"Well, it's true. And yes. You are. I was one of those think-you-are-gonna-marry-your-high-school-sweetheart girls. It didn't work out."

"Well, I'm glad it didn't work out."

Lynn yawned while managing to get out, "Me too."

He began playing with her hair, gently lifting it up and letting it fall. After a couple minutes, he felt her body twitch and could tell she was falling asleep. *I didn't even brush my teeth...* But it felt so good. So right. He didn't want to move. So he fell asleep with her in his arms. Then together, there they were, battling the souls of an angry night. Together.

Chapter 29

As Dusty lay in bed that night, he dreamt of his little girl. For the first time since he started dreaming about her, he was able to see her in an actual real life setting, not just a dark void. The scene flickered in and out of his consciousness, like a bad television signal trying to represent itself on an antique TV. It was faint and fleeting, but Dusty definitely dreamt of her swinging on a swing set. He couldn't make much out around the swing set, but he could see her. She was happy! For the first time, he saw her smile as she swung back and forth, her little feet dangling below her and dragging the ground with each pass. A lump started to forge in Dusty's throat. He felt like he had swallowed a watermelon. It was such a relief to see her in a happy place, safe from any danger. *Why now? What is it that lets you show me more? Before it was just a swing, now it's you on a swing. What comes next, little sweetheart? Will you ever be able to show me what happened to you?*

Dusty was awoken at 7:30 a.m. by a tone going off on his phone that indicated he had received a new text message. Reluctantly, he looked at it, hoping it wasn't Ron Davis bitching about something. Instead, he was in for a surprise.

Dusty,
A new person just emailed about seeing children. I wanted to go over it with you before we let him in the chat room. He sounds like he is legit, but as always, I want to double check with you. He says he is from New York

City. Take a look at the email and let me know what you think. Talk to you soon :)

Lana

New York City? That's weird. What are the chances of Lana emailing me about a new member from New York City while I'm in New York City? The irony of the situation struck a nerve in Dusty. He didn't quite know what to think. Lynn lay next to him, soundly sleeping. She looked so peaceful; he didn't want to wake her and tell her about it. So he got out his laptop from his backpack, typed in the Wi-Fi password to Lynn's network he found on her fridge and laid his head back on the pillow to read the email from the new guy.

To Whom It May Concern:

I found you on the Internet. I'm from New York City. I couldn't believe my eyes when I read that there was a support group for people who see children in their dreams. The description was very vague and I'm not sure why I have to go through an application process, but I will try anything right now. I'm guessing you don't want just any old perverts to be able to gain access to your chat room and pose as one of you. I can assure that you don't have to worry about that with me.

I have been dreaming about children in pain for close to three years now. At first, it started out just as one, but then, I started seeing more. I am currently seeing four children from the ages of 6-12 or so. Two boys and two girls. They act as if they are in excruciating pain, but I can't hear or talk to them. I don't know why they are coming to me, but I fear somebody has hurt them. I have slowly started to think that I was crazy. My shrink thinks I have suppressed childhood memories. My girlfriend left me. I feel as if I might lose my job because can't concentrate. I'm desperate for some help.

If you know of anything that can help me, please tell me. I want to help these children, but I have no idea how to do it. Are they real? Does this sound like something your group experiences? Please respond to me. Please. Thank you for your time.

Sincerely,
Richard Thomas

Dusty wasn't sure what to think. The person sounded legitimate, but something about the timing of the whole situation freaked him out a little bit. Maybe it was the fact that this guy thought he had to say that he wasn't a pervert. He thought that maybe he should meet this guy and check him out for himself since he was in town. Maybe he and Lynn could meet him for lunch and figure him out together.

He lay in bed for another hour thinking about the situation until Lynn finally woke up. She raised her arms above her head and let out a liberating yawn. Then she rolled her back to Dusty and snuggled up her pillow and the comforter, as if to get a little more delight in the comfort of her bed before getting out of it for the day. She curled into a ball and rubbed her face in her pillow, wrapping her legs around the comforter. For the first time, Dusty saw the little girl in Lynn. He came close to her and spooned her from the back. He held her body tightly and kissed her shoulder blade.

"I should probably go brush my teeth. Pretty sure I fell asleep before I could brush 'em last night…"

This made Dusty laugh. She was obviously secure enough around him to speak so freely about something many people are very self-conscious about. "Yah. Me too. I guess we had other things on our mind."

"Yah. Other… so good things." She turned to face him and let out a wide, tight-lipped grin, probably so he wouldn't smell her breath. Suddenly, her eyes grew wide, "Ohhhh my…" she said as she started to sit up. "I didn't bother to clean up something else either. Wow."

Again, Dusty, a little uncomfortable and surprised by her forwardness, chuckled and responded, "You told me to. Not my fault."

"Guess I'll be doing some laundry today as well." She slipped on her robe that hung on a hanger inside her closet door and went into the bathroom. Dusty could hear the water turn on and the back-and-forth motion of her toothbrush. He remained lying on the bed. Relaxing.

He looked around her room and noticed a picture of her and some old friends from High School in a frame on her dresser. She looked just as beautiful and hardly any different. He noticed a CD tower filled to the brim in the corner by her stereo. He immediately recognized the blue spine of a *Nirvana* album—the one that made them big—with a naked baby on the cover. He also recognized a few others: *Enya, The Cranberries, Soundgarden, Pearl Jam, The Smashing Pumpkins, No Doubt, Metallica, 311, Pink Floyd, The Eagles, The Beatles* and *Green Day.* He liked her taste in music.

When she was done, she came out and sat on the end of the bed. "I think I'm going to take a shower. You want to hop in with me?"

"Sure." Dusty didn't know exactly what to say. Here she was again, taking the lead and not playing games. He started wondering if this was moving too fast as he got up and entered the bathroom. She turned on the water, dropped her robe to her feet and stepped in. It was a nice, big shower with a seat and a removable head. The bathroom itself had tiled floors and a row of round light bulbs above the mirror. It was painted a light blue color and was decorated with candles, pictures of outdoor scenery and potpourri. Dusty stepped in behind her.

She immediately put a handful of shampoo in her hand and told him to sit down. He did. She started to wash his hair, tenderly massaging his scalp. She had strong hands, but a gentle touch. It made tingles spread down Dusty's body and he closed his eyes. Her fingernails caressed from the back of his neck, behind his ears, to the top of his head. Then she removed the showerhead and rinsed it out.

"Wow. That felt amazing. You should be a masseuse or something." She pulled him up to her and kissed him.

"I don't want to rub down people I don't know all day long."

"Well, you can rub me down all day long." She kissed him again.

"You're welcome." She began washing herself with a bar of Dove soap.

Dusty suddenly remembered the email he got that morning. "Hey, interesting thing this morning. I got an email from Lana. She said there is someone in New York City who emailed her about getting into our chat room. She forwarded me his email. He sounds for real, but isn't that weird? The same day I get here, we find out there may be another one of us in New York?"

Lynn was washing her arms and torso, "That is weird. Well, maybe he knows something… I wonder if he might somehow be connected to me or my child?"

"I don't know. We don't really know yet if a child only chooses one person. So maybe. Or if there *is* a killer out there that kills more than one, if those children all go to one person or different people. I don't think it would hurt to talk to him. I was thinking maybe we could do lunch with him this weekend since I'm in town. That way you don't have to do it by yourself."

"Aww. Are you looking out for me?"

"Well, I mean, I don't really like the idea of you meeting some strange guy… and since I'm here…"

"Okay. Well see if you can get a hold of him. We can go to the Reuben place."

"Well alright. Sounds good."

The two finished their shower and made love once more before getting dressed for the day. Then Lynn made some scrambled eggs and bacon while Dusty got a hold of Richard through email and explained the situation. He sipped his coffee, watching her work behind the stove in her robe. He just couldn't get over how beautiful she was, and pure. The eggs were great. She put a garlic salt on them that gave them a very unique flavor. Before he finished his plate, he got an email back from Richard and just like that, they were to meet him at *Teddy's*, the place that made good Reubens, at one o'clock.

………..

Sauerkraut hung from the corner of Dusty's mouth as he chewed his food, "You know, this is actually pretty damn good. I have to admit. The only sauerkraut I ever had before was when my roommate tried to make it in college. I put it on my bratwurst and thought I was going to throw up. It tasted like… piss and vinegar. I've never tried it since."

Lynn wiped her mouth with a napkin before she spoke, "Well I'm glad you like it. It's good to step outside your comfort zone every once in a while." She took a drink of her coke and leaned back in her chair. People were all around them at their own high-top tables. Booths lined the walls. The line to get into the restaurant was outside of the door. The wallpaper was made from old newspaper clippings ranging from the 1920s to present day. On the walls hung pictures of old New York. Dusty's favorite so far was the picture of Babe Ruth smoking a cigar in his Yankees uniform. The place had a very historical atmosphere to it. The menu was written on a chalkboard just above the register and the cooks were in plain view behind the bar.

They both enjoyed their sandwiches in silence for a couple minutes. Then Lynn's body perked as she spotted a man who looked like he was looking for someone, "I think that's him." She nodded towards the front door and Dusty turned to look over his shoulder, "Yep. Wearing a Met's ball cap."

Dusty gave a friendly wave and Richard sauntered over to their table. He was a very tall man, about 6' 6" and bolstered a powerful frame. He was in his mid-forties. His head was still full of dark brown hair, but it was starting to grey substantially. His eyes were a cold blue, adorned with black rimmed reading glasses, and his face sported a healthy stubble. He was wearing khakis and a blue collared shirt with loafers. His nose was long and his ears were a little large for his head, but he was overall a handsome looking man.

As Richard approached, Dusty stood up and shook his hand, "It's nice to meet you. I'm Dusty Burch. This is Lynn. I appreciate you coming today."

"Oh, the pleasure is all mine," Richard was still shaking Dusty's hand as he talked. His voice was incongruently soft and mid toned for such a large man. "I know this was very last minute, but thank you so much for fitting me in your schedule. Lana seemed like a very nice person when I talked to her. She said very nice things about you, Dusty."

Dusty pulled out a chair for him and motioned for him to sit, "Yes, Lana is a wonderful lady." Richard sat down and folded his hands on the table.

"So do you guys both live here in Manhattan?"

Lynn spoke up, "I do. Dusty is actually just here visiting."

"Really? From where?"

"Chicago. I'm a lawyer there."

"A lawyer?" Richard acted almost too genuinely interested. "That sounds like a lot of work. Me, I'm just a consultant for a web hosting company here in town. I like it, but rarely do I actually have to talk to anyone. See, they call me a consultant, but really, I'm more like a… oh how do I explain? People send their problems to me and I figure out how to fix them. I get like a hundred emails a day."

"You and me both buddy. But I actually have to go and do a lot of talking, too."

"I bet. I hear that's what lawyers do best. And Lynn, what do you do?" He turned his gaze on Lynn and locked on her eyes.

"I am a dental assistant and I'm going to school to be a dentist. I hate life right now," she added with a sarcastic grin. "I also tend bar a few nights a week at 'The Tavern' over off Sycamore." This was the first time Dusty had heard this and was taken back a little, but it had never really come up. Lynn saw the surprised look on his face, "A Girl's still gotta make a living."

"I understand," Richard took a sip from a glass of water sitting in front of him on the table that had been sitting there long enough to accumulate moisture and dampen the napkin it was sitting on, "My brother was actually a dentist. It seemed like he was in school forever! But at least it will be over soon, right?"

"Well, not soon enough. I still have a couple more years of school. But, it will be worth it."

"Absolutely. Nothing good ever came easy." There was a brief, but awkward, silence as the group had run out of superficial things to say. There was really only one thing on their minds. Dusty struck first.

"Well, let's talk a little bit about why you are here. I read your email, but I'd like to hear in your words what you are experiencing, if you don't mind."

"Absolutely. Well, it started getting really bad about six months ago." Richard looked around to see if anyone around them seemed to be listening. The loud chatter of the restaurant seemed to be masking their conversation, so he continued; "I started seeing a little girl in my dreams every, single night. It got to the point where I couldn't dream about anything else. She would come to me and cry and cry and cry. I couldn't get her to say anything. I tried everything to get rid of the dreams. I went to a shrink to see if they could decipher what she might mean. He told me that it was probably my mind's way of expressing guilt that I don't have a child. I thought that sounded reasonable enough, but when they persisted and grew in intensity, I knew there was something else to it. I began to feel like she was real, like she was in horrifying agony. I tried carrying on normally throughout everyday life, but if she started tightening her grasp on me. I didn't know what I was going to do. Still don't. Then I found out about you guys online."

"Well, you aren't alone. Lynn and I share something very similar to what you are going through. We know how you feel."

Richard started to tear up a little bit, "That makes me feel a whole lot better, just knowing that I'm not the only one. Anyone I tried to tell looked at me like I was crazy, so I just stopped talking about it. I started keeping a journal just to vent out all my emotions."

"You should have been at the convention in Colorado," Lynn said with enthusiasm. "It was like a church revival on steroids. Complete strangers poured out their deepest thoughts and fears to each other. It just felt so good to be a part of something… just to know that you weren't alone."

"What did you guys find? Anything?"

"Well, it kind of left us with more questions. But what it mainly did is give us a fairly positive sense that these children are real and not figments of our imagination. It's hard to deny that these children were harmed in some way and need our help. They have chosen us and it is up to us to find out why and help them." Dusty took a drink of his coke before continuing, "And also, it's given us a team… people that are devoted to finding the answers. We have a resource pool. Hopefully, with the help of everyone, we can figure out whatever it is that we are supposed to do."

"How do you *know* they are real? I mean, couldn't this all be just one huge coincidence?"

Dusty and Lynn started to speak at the same time, but Dusty let her take the lead, "I guess there is no hard evidence yet other than gut feelings, but we just recently discovered that several of the members have found pictures of missing children that very closely resemble the ones they are seeing. Again, that could be a coincidence and there is no telling for sure, but all we can do is follow the bread crumbs."

"Well, I want in. I want to help. Would that be okay?"

"Right now we are in the research stage, more or less," Dusty explained. "We are trying to gather as much information that we possibly can so that we can look for patterns in the data. Right now, we don't know why we are chosen. We have some ideas, but if we can figure that out, I think it will lead us to our answer… reverse engineering. So everyone is compiling lists of places they've been in the last few years, searching for missing children reports, scanning the news, just anything that could give us some clues."

"Well, have you found anything?"

"Not yet. It's still very early in the process, but we have faith. You can join the chat room on the website and stay informed. With everyone being so spread out, it's the easiest way to all stay on the same page."

"Yeah, I can't think of a better way. So, just gather information? Anything specific?"

"Well, we have a feeling that we might be chosen based off proximity. We call it the *proximity theory*. So to test it, we are trying to compile lists of all the places we have been and cross reference them with any missing children reports. Again, it's early in the process, but then again, it might not be that at all. We just have to start somewhere."

"So, like proximity to…?"

"Could be anything. The killer, the murder itself, the child; we don't know."

"Ughh," Richard shook with the chills. "The thought of that is enough to make me cringe."

"Yes. Pretty spooky," Lynn added. Another silence fell upon the table as they each thought about their own child.

Dusty tried to lighten up the subject, "Well, can we buy you a sandwich or something?"

"No. Thank you. I actually need to get going here soon. I have to be back at work."

"No problem. They actually make an awesome Reuben. I've never liked them until today."

"I know. I actually used to eat here quite frequently. My favorite is the meatball sub. Can't beat a good meatball sub."

"I'll have to try that one next," Dusty said.

"Okay, well I hope I'm not prodding or anything, but before I go, I have a question."

"Sure, go ahead," Lynn encouraged.

"When you guys dream about your children, do you see anything else in them? Or is it just them?"

Dusty offered, "Well, so far, just her. And that's pretty much the same story we hear from everyone else."

"Yeah, me too. It's just so weird. I mean, you'd think they would show us something else. Like maybe who hurt them or something," replied Richard.

"Wouldn't that be nice?" Dusty said sarcastically. "I just don't think they are able to. I mean they can't even talk to us. I think they are just on the edge of ESP. They can show themselves and that's it. Unless we find the key."

"Okay, well so far it sounds a lot like the dreams I've been having. I keep looking for something. Anything at all... but so far, nothing." Richard's phone started ringing and he took it out of his pocket and looked at it. "Ah, that's work. I'd probably better get going. But seriously, thanks so much for meeting me. I hope I can help. I'll see you on the forums. Stay in touch."

"Will do," Dusty said as he shook his hand. Richard shook Lynn's hand as well, then weaved his way through the crowd to the door and left.

"Well, what do you think?"

Dusty thought about Lynn's question, "He seemed... okay. Do you think it's weird he just up and left?"

"I don't know. I mean I guess he never said how long he was going to be here. Maybe he just wanted to meet us and only had a few minutes. Who knows? He seemed like a pretty nice guy though."

"Yeah, a little too nice. I don't know. Maybe I'm just being paranoid."

"What do you mean, too nice?"

"I don't know. Just the way he was so... eager to know."

"Well, wouldn't you be? If you found out a whole convention went on without you?"

"I guess so. You are probably right. But the whole thing about me finding out there was another one of us in Manhattan while I am in Manhattan just freaks me out. I mean what are the chances?"

"I don't think we deal in normal statistics anymore. Do you? I mean, what are the chances that you hear Lana on the radio station? Or that you and Bruce are from the same city? Or that I actually called you back?"

"Ha. Ha." Dusty voiced in unamused bursts. "I mean I know what you mean. It's just like, we all shared something there in Winter Park. It's hard to let someone else in. It feels sacred. I guess I just don't want to jeopardize it in any way."

"Come on. I mean there are going to be more. They are going to find us if they are out there, just like I did. We want that. We just have to be careful, that's all."

"Yeah. Careful." Dusty rubbed his index finger around the rim of his glass as he stared at the bubbles fizzing up from the bottom.

"Don't worry so much." Lynn reached into her purse and pulled out her wallet.

"No…"

She cut him off abruptly, "Yes. I am going to get this one. Not negotiating."

Dusty reacted surprised, "Ooooookay boss. Miss I-work-at-a-bar-and-make-a lot-of-money-off-drunk-guys-hitting-on-me."

"Yeah, about that, it just never occurred to me to tell you. It just hadn't come up. I wasn't trying to hide it or anything."

"I know, no worries. I'm sure there are a lot of things I don't know about you still. Well, thank you."

"You are welcome. You just give me a little more of what you did last night, and this morning and we'll call it even. Deal?"

"I think I can do that. Deal." With that, she paid and the two set out to venture downtown Manhattan together looking for clues to solve her mystery.

Chapter 30

Dusty's trip to New York rejuvenated him. He had a newfound happiness—a ball of light shining bright amidst the dense fog that had settled in on his life. Lynn was unlike any woman he had ever met before. During his stay, they had tried to focus on researching and investigating for the children, but they were distracted by the sheer joy they brought to each other. For a couple of days, they forgot about their worries and separated themselves from the world. Both of them desperately needed a release. After the first attempt to find clues ended up with them aimlessly wandering around the city, they realized they had no real direction yet and sort of silently, but mutually, decided to enjoy their time getting to know each other...sans the horribly depressing thoughts.

Once they got back to their normal lives, away from each other, they continued their engagement in the chat room discussions. Most of The Chosen were initially searching for missing children reports, which Dusty and Lynn did as well. Some people were having limited success in finding pictures of children that resembled the ones they were seeing, but many were still hitting dead ends. Bruce suggested in the chat room that people start looking for deaths of any kind as well. He thought that maybe some children weren't showing up in missing persons reports either because their death was never deemed a homicide, or because once the body was found, the alert was lifted.

Thousands of more names and pictures flooded the scene, making the task of sorting through the dead names of children more tedious and depressing than before. Some worked quicker than others, either because their job allowed for it, or because some of the members simply couldn't handle the sheer volume of gruesome details every day. Slowly, more probable matches started popping up in the chat rooms. Bruce and Lynn even found at least one that could possibly be a match to their children, but with only one picture available of each child, it was extremely hard to tell for certain. Dusty still had absolutely nothing. He was starting to worry.

Richard Thomas, the new guy from Manhattan, proved to be a very resourceful addition to the team. Although Dusty was wary of him at first, Richard slowly gained his trust. He was extremely intelligent and seemed devoted to the cause of The Chosen. For whatever reason, Richard raised Lynn's morale as well. Maybe it was because she didn't feel like such an outcast in a city teeming with people… she wasn't quite so alone anymore. Dusty fought off jealousy every time Lynn said she met with Richard to look into the cases, but he trusted Lynn. As hard as it was for him to swallow the thought of Lynn being alone with another man for hours at a time, he was up for anything that raised her spirits.

When Dusty did fly back to Manhattan, the three of them almost always got together to go over new and uncovered information. Dusty wanted to make sure he left an indelible impression on Richard, leaving no doubt that Lynn was his and not to be messed with. Dusty found himself being affectionate towards Lynn in subtle, yet very noticeable ways in front of Richard. A hand on her thigh here, a touch of her face there… he would never admit it, but subconsciously he was marking his territory.

Richard never seemed to notice the slightest bit. Dusty never even caught him staring at Lynn the wrong way. He was about as professional and uninvolved as a man could be. As hard as Dusty tried, he could never find a reason to think that Richard would ever make a move on Lynn. Dusty knew how beautiful she was though and it would take a man being a complete homosexual not to be attracted to her, but as long as Lynn felt comfortable and Richard never crossed the line, things were kosher.

During this time period of the late summer and early Fall of 2001, after the convention, Lynn made her first trip to Chicago to visit Dusty. She helped Dusty search the city for clues for his girl as he still had not even the slightest lead. Their love grew with every minute they spent together. She consoled him through his tumult and became his rock. At times, Dusty became nearly depressed and on the verge of insanity. This "group" he was a part of was reminiscent of a cult in some ways in his mind, especially if what the members all were buying into was all fiction. Dusty struggled with this notion at times because if none of this was real, he was buying into one of the biggest dog and pony shows of all times. He so bad wanted for it to be real, then immediately felt guilty for that thought because of the implications it had. If it *was* real, he wasn't crazy, but children all over the world were being tortured, murdered, raped and worse and he couldn't do anything about it. If it wasn't real, then he was living a lie and allowing his psychotic issues to persuade him into surrounding himself with other… what? Schizos? What does a person even call "The Chosen" and their afflictions and how does one classify their mental state if none of this is real? Through all this fog, Lynn was the one constant that kept Dusty sane. She kept him motivated to find the light at the end of the tunnel, because periodically he felt as if he wasn't even sure if there was a tunnel, let alone a light. During this fall transition where the leaves changed from a bright green to golden yellow and amber, Dusty and Lynn's hearts ignited for each other and transformed themselves. Dusty told her he loved her, which made her body tremble, but she returned the sentiment. Those three words became a part of their daily rhetoric to each other. "Together, crazy or not," he would tell her, "we are going to get through this, and I'm going to love you until the day I die. I just hope it's not soon."

As strong as this love had grown, they both needed a little help. The whole group's morale was low, in fact. There seemed to be a standstill. Something had to happen and it had to happen quickly.

Chapter 31

In February in Tupelo, Mississippi, about six months after Dusty first went to New York, Doris was running late. The Tupelo Ladies Investment Club met every Monday at 10 for brunch in the basement of the Hillside Baptist Church. The club had made a profit of $6,400.00 last year. This year they were up only by $1,700, but there were still three months left in the year to improve their stock picks. There were about 18 die-hard members and you had to be female, 60, a town resident and willing to invest $25.00 per month.

Doris Cone kept the speedometer on 25. She hated being late, but she never broke the law. Doris was running late because she had to stop by Johnson's Rexall Pharmacy to get a refill on her heart pills. She really hadn't taken care of herself in 68 years. She was overweight, diabetic, had varicose veins and heart murmurs. She lived off of her deceased husband's railroad retirement income. It wasn't much, but every month $25 went into the club account religiously.

Doris was this year's treasurer and she would spend the first 10 minutes of the meeting giving her weekly report to the club. After her thoughtfully prepared presentation, the ladies would do what the club was really designed for: talk over cake and coffee. It wasn't really gossip. After all, they were in the church basement. Mainly they would update each other on gall bladder surgeries, arthritis attacks, thyroid problems, diets, medications… and maybe stocks. Dorothy had talked to her friends about the dreams about the little boy. They ooohed and aaaahed, "you poor thing," to be followed by their own stories of weird dreams and premonitions. None of them really believed that little boy was real. Dorothy had stopped telling anyone about him.

Doris was approaching the familiar national landmark on the corner of 4th and Oak. A small, white, one story house, immaculately kept with a sign in the yard that read: "Birthplace of Elvis Presley." Some people, definitely not Tupeloans, were milling around in the yard. A young couple had their heads pressed to a front window, obviously fantasizing about the King riding his tricycle about the front room. Doris slowed to 20 mph as she approached the intersection. Suddenly, something smacked Doris in the chest like a sledgehammer. All of the air left her lungs. She was paralyzed with pain and blacking out. It was happening too fast... the heart attack she had put off for 10 years. Doris's body went into violent death spasms, causing her to smash the accelerator to the floor. She was dead seconds before her car went through the intersection, hit the curb and flipped over twice, coming to rest in the front yard of the birthplace of Elvis Presley.

....

A few days later, a noise pulled Tom Jensen out of his midday nap. He'd been dreaming about riding in a car and the radio kept making a strange sound and then a game show host was suddenly beside him pressing an annoying buzzer on the dash. Weird. But now he was awake. The car and game show host were gone but the buzzer was still going. Tom Jensen couldn't figure out where the noise was coming from. It sounded like the halftime buzzer at the Ole Miss basketball games, except it had been going non-stop for several minutes.

Tom was the apartment manager of a 24-unit complex close to downtown Jackson, Mississippi. The building was run down. Several of the apartments were uninhabitable. The owner was a slumlord that used some of the rent money to bribe various inspectors rather than make improvements. The tenants were mostly transient, impoverished, down-on-their-luckers. Most had criminal records of various sorts and obtained their clothes out of dumpsters or at the Goodwill Store and were normally behind on the rent. Tom got to live there rent-free. He'd been there three years, longer than anyone else there. His job was to collect rent and throw people

193

out if they got too far behind. The building had to be a big tax break for the owner because not much money came in.

The building was four stories tall, six apartments and one community bathroom on each floor. Sixteen tenants lived there now. Most were on welfare, but some had jobs. They all kept pretty much to themselves. None of them socialized together. There were blacks, Hispanics, whites and others of indiscernible nationalities. Some didn't speak English. Each apartment had a front room, bedroom and small kitchen. The community bathroom was at the end of the hall on each floor.

It was an unusually hot October day. Most of the windows in the building were open. Some tenants were lucky enough to have fans. Tom even had a small window air conditioner unit that he banged with his fist on his way out of the door because it had shut off for the fourth time that day. The buzzing continued, like an alarm of some kind. It sounded kind of muffled, definitely not on the first floor. Tom took the stairs to the 2nd floor landing. The elevator had never worked since Tom had been there. The buzzing was higher up. Tom ran to the third floor and heard nothing. An elderly Hispanic man had come out to check on the noise. He was looking up the stairwell, saying something in Spanish.

Willie, a hair-lipped, semi-mentally retarded middle-aged man on Social Security, and Tony, a white, unemployed ex-con, greeted Tom at the top floor. Willie was about the size of a bear and had on his familiar Oshkosh striped overalls, black janitor shoes and no shirt; Tony was white, thirtyish, slender, had on a white "wife beater" shirt and gray gym shorts. They were outside room #41.

"It's coming from in there," Tony said, pointing with his tattoo-covered arm. "We knocked and he don't answer."

"You wan me hack it doww?" Willie offered.

"No, man, I got the key," said Tom as he started knocking on the door. "Hey, Mister Douglas, you in there?" Tom kept pounding. *Mr. Douglas*, it probably wasn't his real name, but it didn't matter, no one was responding.

Tom turned the knob. Locked.

"It sounds like a smoke alarm," Tony said.

Some of the rooms had smoke alarms in the ceilings, going back to the years when the building had been compliant. But none of them had worked for years.

194

"Hey, Douglas, I'm coming in." Lonnie Douglas, or at least the guy living in #41, had moved in about three months ago. His application stated that he was white, 6 feet, 1 inch, 170 pounds, good credit and no criminal record.

Tom had never really talked to him, just small exchanges when he dropped off the check, which was always on time. Douglas was a cigar smoker. He liked Swisher Sweets. He almost always had one in his mouth. He had a glass eye that somehow always teared-up and left a mucousy discharge that never seemed to get wiped from the tear duct. He was clean-shaven with balding dark hair, slicked back like an aging 1950's movie star. He never had any mail or friends. He seemed pleasant enough. The apartment was unkempt. Dirty clothes and dishes were splayed everywhere and old newspapers were scattered about. An old circular wooden table was in the middle of the front room. Tom looked around for the source of the noise and spotted a slender white candle, like those seen at weddings, burning at the center of the table. The flame was sending a thin, black ribbon of smoke upward towards a buzzing smoke detector in the ceiling. Tom stood dumbfounded as he watched the smoke bounce off the cracked, yellow casing of the smoke detectors and without thinking said, "God damn, I didn't think any of those actually worked..." Willie and Tony looked at each other and both shrugged, as if to agree that they couldn't believe it was working either in this shithole of a building to live in. The candle was anchored in a souvenir shot glass from Tupelo, Mississippi, the birthplace of Elvis Presley. Around the bottom of the shot glass were what looked like ashes of some sort of paper, maybe newspaper.

The three gathered around the table staring up at the oddity. Tom blew out the candle, "You gotta be kidding. Has anyone seen Douglas today?"

"I heard him leave for work this morning, 'bout 10, his usual time. He ain't been back. He don't come in 'til after dark," Tony said.

"Did you guys hear anything in his room?" asked Tom.

"No," Tony said, "not until the buzzing started about 10 minutes ago. Willie and I went down the hall trying to get that window open when it went off. We could see the hallway. Nobody came in or out."

Willie gave a toothless grin, "issss loud."

Willie was right. This was a very loud alarm. The windows in the front room and kitchen were open, but covered by tattered screens. There was no fire escape from this room. The drop was four stories straight down.

A rickety wooden chair was a few feet from the table. Tom pulled it up to the table; it wobbled precariously as Tom used it as a stool to step on to the table. The smoke alarm was going loud and strong as ever. Strange, Tom thought, the alarm was fastened to the ceiling by four wood screws. It appeared to have been painted over several times over the years. The old paint still sealed the edge of the alarm to the ceiling. The "X" shaped indentures on the Phillip's head screws were filled with old paint. The alarm had obviously not been tampered with in years.

Tom grabbed the alarm and tried to loosen it from the ceiling, but it wouldn't budge. There was no reset button.

"What's going on up there?" a voice yelled from a lower stairwell.

Tony went to the door, "It's a smoke alarm. We're trying to shut it off."

The same voice spoke, "Alarm? Is there a fire?"

"No! Everything is fine. Just a little… malfunction." Tom looked back down at his companions, "Somebody got a pocket knife? I gotta loosen these screws." Neither Tony nor Willie had one.

"Willie, look in the kitchen. See if this guy's got a knife."

Willie ambled over to the kitchen and pulled open several drawers before coming back to the table, holding a rusty steak knife with a broken tip. "Hee go," handing the converted screwdriver to Tom.

The screws were sealed tight, but eventually came loose. Tom had to rap the side of the alarm to loosen it. Flecks of paint dropped to the table as the alarm cover came loose in Tom's hand. Four Eveready AA batteries were powering the device. Tom pulled the batteries out and the noise stopped. Tom looked at Tony who was gazing at the disarmed device with puzzlement. He glanced down at the residue of old paint scattered about the table.

"Impossible," Tony exclaimed.

Tom inspected the alarm. All the parts were rusty and oxidized. The batteries were old and covered with acid, stuck together. They crumbled in his hands when he tried to remove them. He stepped down to the floor and looked at the candle. Only a quarter inch of wax had been burned. It had been lit just before the alarm went off. Willie, who was in the kitchen giggling idiotically, broke the silence.

Tom went to see what was so amusing. Willie held several Polaroid snapshots in his hand. There were others in the open drawer where Willie had found the knife. The pictures were of a child, a small blonde-headed boy wearing a baseball jersey with the number 14. The boy's mouth was sealed by duct tape. He laid spread eagle on a floor of orange shag carpet. He was naked from the waist down. The little boy stared blankly into space... between eyelids that were partially closed. He was clearly dead.

The Jackson, Mississippi chronicle read: "Child Molester Captured. Police at a local downtown café arrested Ronald Danko, a.k.a. Lonnie Douglas yesterday after pictures of a missing child, Danny Cullota, were found in Danko's apartment by apartment manager, Tom Jensen. Danny Cullota had been missing over a year and a half. He was abducted at City Park here in Jackson when he left his ballgame to go to the public restroom. Danko, an itinerant drifter, led police to a shallow grave outside of town . . ." the story continued.

Chapter 32

D oris's death was not a huge shock to anyone. She was overweight, in her late 60's, and took a cocktail of medication for cholesterol, high blood pressure, sleeping, depression and weight loss. Dusty only had a brief exchange with her during 'speed networking' session at the first meeting and at lunch, but he could tell that she had a heart of gold. The only reason anyone knew about her death was because of Lana. Lana literally was obsessed with keeping tabs with everyone in the group. She wanted to know everyone's well-being, how they were feeling, what they were experiencing and definitely if they were alive or dead. It just so happened that Lana had scheduled a phone call with Doris four days after she had passed because she wanted to learn more about her situation. Doris had not spoken at the convention and Lana knew very little about her. After not being able to get a hold of her, Lana started researching, which is how she came across the news article. She promptly posted to the group of the news as she saw it was appropriate. She also let everyone know the date and time of the funeral and suggested that as a new family, it would be nice for anyone who was able to go and show their respects to Doris.

A handful of people from The Chosen were able to make it. Lana obviously went due to her strong sense of obligation to lead by example; Bruce went because of the whole group, he was the Sherlock Holmes and he wanted to investigate every opportunity he possibly could; Dusty called Lynn who also decided she would make the trip, but really it was just an excuse to visit a new place with Dusty and spend time with him. She did sympathize with Doris's family and thought it was the right thing to do, but she had become so stricken by Dusty at this point that it didn't matter what the event was—she was going.

Doris's family was enormous. She was one of seven kids and had five of her own. Her husband, Donald, was one of six kids. Needless to say, her parent's old farmyard on the south side of Tupelo was full of family members. Two hundred people were crying, laughing, embracing, crying some more, blowing their noses, wiping tears from their puffy eyes and recounting memories of Doris. The grief that filled the air was enough to carry a total stranger to great emotion. *Pathetic.* That was the best word Dusty could come up with to describe the scene as he arrived that afternoon. He had never been surrounded by so much genuine sorrow in one place at one time.

The farm was straight out of a painting. A big, rustic, reddish-brown barn stood 50 yards behind the ranch-style farmhouse. In the space between, a large tent was erected and white folding chairs were set in rows. Doris' body had been so badly damaged that her coffin was closed, but family and friends still formed a long line to say their goodbyes. Although her parents had passed, her brothers still farmed the land and tended to the crops. Seas of golden cornfields surrounded the tent on all sides and the clear blue sky loomed above like a portal for her soul to enter into the kingdom of heaven. No one knew at the time, but Doris would not immediately enter into the afterlife. She had unfinished business. Her death would represent the crucial first step in The Chosen's journey to help their children.

The ceremony was over two hours long, mainly due to the large number of people who spoke about how Doris touched their lives. The open mic session rendered words such as: *compassionate, caring, friend, mother, daughter, sister, cousin, niece, loving, funny, personal, annoyingly talkative*, etc.

Only into the second hour did Dusty find himself wishing it was over. At that point, he proceeded to write love notes to Lynn on the program. She remained unfazed until he wrote: "how about we slip out and head into the cornfield? I think there's enough crying here to drown out any noise…" to this, she rewarded him with a brief smile and a pinch on the inside of his leg. He tried to hide the pain from his face as she lowered her beautiful eyes to him with a stern notion of, "I love you, but grow up and show some respect." He grinned like a lustful teenager. She had grown accustomed to, and mostly endeared, the little boy that would always live inside Dusty.

Dusty and Lynn's relationship had blossomed over the past few months. She had gotten used to his advances and it hardly fazed her anymore. Since his first visit to Manhattan, they had seen each other at least once every other week, sometimes more. Dusty's salary was not exactly hurting and the money was no issue for him. He even bought Lynn's ticket when she flew out to Chicago, but he was the one that usually flew out to see her. Lynn had a strange fear of airplanes and it made her nervous, so Dusty gladly flew. On the days they didn't see each other, they talked on the phone for hours, learning every little detail about each other's childhood, family, fears, passions and desires.

Together they made love, watched movies, drank wine, dined at fine restaurants, went to sporting events, played tennis, and Dusty even took her out on one of his friends boat on lake Michigan to catch walleye—which she thoroughly enjoyed—but mostly they made love. Then, every day for at least an hour, they devoted their attention to their children. They read articles, old and current, they brainstormed the various ways they could possibly help them, they visited places they had been to in the past to look for clues, they watched the news, they participated in ongoing chat room discussions, they even tried being hypnotized… anything and everything that could give them a lead. They had a few ideas, but nothing very impressive. Then, they heard about Doris.

In the following moments after the service, and the awkward phase where everyone is still standing around in groups, afraid to finalize the issue with imminent departure, Bruce quietly pulled Dusty to the edge of the cornfield.

"Dusty, I didn't want to say anything before the service, but I can't hold this in anymore."

"What is it?"

"Okay, well you know how I've been doing all this research on missing child cases around the nation?" Bruce was talking faster the cricket chirps and could barely catch his breath.

"Yeah man… calm down will ya? What's going on?" Dusty said while placing a hand numbers to shoulder.

"Well I found something and I wanted you to be the first to know. I don't know if it means anything, but we need to look into it." Bruce paused, awaiting confirmation to proceed. He didn't realize it, but the events of the day had left Dusty's face emotionless and disconnected. After a few moments of awkward silence, Dusty understood Bruce was looking for some encouragement to keep talking. Bruce thought what he had to say was very important and one of Dusty's full attention.

Dusty's mother had always told him to work on how he presented himself to people, because although he never meant to, he appeared indifferent to what others were saying sometimes. As a teenager and in his early 20s, Dusty would fight to the death every time his mother brought it to its attention. To him, all he was doing was thinking. *What kind of a crime is that?* But as he grew older, he realized the utility of being a good listener and the advantages of making people feel like what they had to say is important, even if it is the furthest thing from his conscious mind. Once he heard his mother's voice in his head, he unfurled his brow, relaxed his cheek muscles, focused his gaze on Bruce's wanting eyes and gave a slight nod of… awareness.

Once assured, Bruce continued, "Okay so Doris died on Monday. Wednesday I came across an article in the *Jackson Daily* online. It's out of Jackson, Mississippi. It said a man had been taken into custody suspected of child molestation. That was weird enough, but authorities released information this morning and said he is also the prime suspect for the murder of a little boy. His name wasn't released, but I saw pictures on the news in my motel room. I need to look through our notes, but I seem to remember Doris seeing a little boy. What are the chances?"

Bruce now had Dusty's undivided attention. His face showed deep contemplation and he didn't speak for a moment. His mind tried to process all the possible scenarios and outcomes that could come of this information. Bruce, anxiously awaiting Dusty's response, batted his eyes and raised his eyebrows, visually sending a signal that he was waiting. Dusty picked up the signal, "Bruce, this could be the break we've been looking for. If this asshole is the killer and we can verify that this is Doris's boy, then we might really be on to something," Dusty was in need of a morale boost. Members of The Chosen had been searching for answers for months, perhaps Dusty more than anyone since he was searching for two. "Let's check the child descriptions and compare hers to the news and see if we can find a match."

"When I get home, I can check the copy of the Bible Lana gave me."

"Yeah, I can too. Unfortunately for Doris, this might be the miracle we need."

Bruce took this in, then his face became filled with concern, "Dusty, what if it *is* a match? Do you know what this could mean?"

Dusty gazed off into the golden cornrows as he pondered the implications. Then, what Bruce was trying to get him to see hit him like a ton of bricks, "No. No, it can't be."

"But what if it is? What if we have to sacrifice ourselves? I mean, if this turns out to be her boy, then either it's the biggest coincidence in the last century, or her death was the reason the murderer was caught."

Dusty's gut flipped and a wave of terror seized him. He didn't think about himself, he was thinking of Lynn. "There has to be another way. That can't be it." Horrible flashes of mass suicides and death cascaded down the waterfall of emotions Dusty felt right now. *This can't be it.*

Bruce was quick to offer a bright side, "Look at it this way, if it is true, then at least we know without a doubt we aren't crazy. We know these kids are real and being hurt, and it will drive us that much harder to find a way to help them. Plus, we would also know that the proximity theory holds true. This would help us narrow our search tremendously. But, we are getting ahead of ourselves. We still have a lot of homework to do. "

"Yeah, like that still doesn't explain *why* she was chosen. I mean, the boy was abducted in Jackson, right? Doris lived in Tupelo. What is that? It's gotta be over 100 miles."

"More like 170, give or take. I mean it's *kinda* close, so it doesn't totally rule out proximity, but 170 miles? That's kind of pushing it. We need to find a link."

Dusty's eyes were still fixed on the beautiful sea of cornfields. The sun was setting on the horizon just beyond, presenting Dusty with timely, peaceful imagery. The pinks, purples, blues and oranges swirled together in a vortex of beauty. "There has to be something we aren't seeing. Maybe we can interview someone in Doris's family. I mean, we don't know a lot about her."

"That would probably be a good idea. In fact, we should probably make up a second questionnaire that everyone should fill out. I mean, what if there is something we all have in common? Something subtle, that wouldn't necessarily jump out at us? Something more… discrete than the general information we asked on the first one."

"What do you mean? Like what?"

"I don't know," Bruce looked back over his shoulder at the tent, wondering if they were taking too long, "like, maybe we all are allergic to peanut butter, or have an affection for ice cream. Who knows. It would just be worth looking at. Plus, it would help us link anything together if anything like this ever happened gain, God forbid."

"Yeah, I like where you are going Bruce. We need every puzzle piece we can get."

"I mean I'm good with data and I'm really good with excel. Maybe there is some type of algorithm here that connects us all. Maybe if we find what that is, we can find whatever it is we have to find to solve these cases without having to…," Bruce's voice trailed off.

"Die."

"Yeah. Die." Bruce's response almost made Dusty feel like Bruce wasn't worried about dying—like he felt he didn't have much to live for, so sacrificing himself didn't seem all that tragic. Maybe it was the way Bruce raised his eyebrows when he said, *die*. Almost sarcastically, yet thoughtful enough that it didn't seem like he thought other people's lives weren't worth living.

"Well, I will start on drafting a questionnaire this week. Can you maybe look into talking to someone in Doris's family? Just see if anything jumps out at you? They seem like nice people, I can't imagine you would have a problem finding someone to talk to. Maybe you could tell them you were in the middle of writing a book about good people dying before their time."

"Ok. I'll think of something." Bruce looked at the ground and sighed, "We should probably keep this to ourselves now, don't' you think? I mean, the whole *dying-is-the-answer-to our-problems* thing?" Bruce asked timidly.

"Yeah, outside of Lynn and Lana, I think that's probably best for now. Is that cool?"

"Cool," Bruce's countenance shifted from serious to excited. "We're like a team… a psychic, secret service squad," he said with a goofy grin.

Dusty couldn't help but chuckle. He put his hand on Bruce's back and guided him back towards the crowd. After a few steps he said, "Indeed we are, Brucipher. Good work."

....

The next day, Sunday morning, Dusty and Lynn sat in their hotel room over two steaming cups of coffee. They stayed at a Holiday Inn just on the edge of town by the airport. The room had two Queen beds, but they shared one and made love until 2:00 am. Her flight for New York was scheduled to leave at 1:00 pm to go back home and his at 2:15. Despite their late bed time, they got up early, around 7:00, to enjoy their time together.

"So what do you think this means? I mean do you really think that the ghost of Doris stuck around to catch this sicko? Does that mean the only thing we can do to help these kids is to die?" Lynn was full of questions and skepticism at Dusty's account of Bruce's findings.

"Honey, we don't *know* anything for sure. But it does seem too strange to be a coincidence. I know that if I were to die tomorrow, the first thing I would do before I walked through those pearly gates is tell St. Peter that I had a little bit of unfinished business—'please hold my spot for a bit'. I know it sounds like hocus pocus, but so does seeing dead children in your dreams! At this point, I'm not ruling out anything. If it *is* a solution to our problem, maybe it's not the only one."

Lynn thought about what Dusty said for a bit and sipped on her coffee. The thought of having to die, that that might be the answer, sent a shudder through her body. *What horrible timing*, she thought. For the first time in her life she was actually considering settling down with a man, maybe starting a family. That would be quite impossible if she were dead. Then, the questions Dusty was afraid would come—the question he most feared because he knew Lynn was the most unselfish person he'd ever met. "If that was the only way… would you do it?"

Dusty knew what she meant, but instead answered, "What? Do what? What are you talking about?"

"Kill yourself. I couldn't live with myself the rest of my life if I knew a killer was on the loose murdering innocent children because I was alive. I mean, think if you were Eddie. I feel horrible for him."

He had thought about it before this moment, but hearing the actual words come from Lynn's lips sent him into momentary paralysis. In an instant he envisioned a thousand scenarios in which she killed herself. Then, in the following misery, he too might follow. Maybe they would do it together, like Romeo and Juliet; their brief love story ending in an epic tragedy for the ages. Then he snapped back.

"Lynn! Babe please don't talk that way. We will find a way, together. I promise. I won't rest until we figure this out." Dusty had to stop speaking briefly. He was feeling his throat swell up and he wasn't quite ready to let Lynn see him cry. Despite his efforts, the rims of his eyes pooled up with tears. He placed his hand on Lynn's. He loved her hands. They were feminine, soft and irresistibly sexy with that shiny crimson nail polish on. As he touched her, his chest began to pound. He could feel his love flowing out of him, through their hands, and he aimed it at the center of her being when he spoke.

"I can't lose you. I would rather die." Then, without thinking, Dusty let his emotions override his actions. This rarely happened to him. He always tried so hard to think rationally, to not be controlled by emotion. He thought it clouded judgment—made people act in ridiculous ways. It was why he became a lawyer. But in this moment, he felt what he would later describe as the *will of the universe,* (what others might call God's Grace), flow through him. This time, instead of fighting it, he embraced it. In his heightened state of ecstasy, he uttered the words, "Marry me."

Lynn's face crinkled and her eyes winced as a smile drew upon her face, "What?"

"Lynn Christopher, please marry me," he got down on one knee. "The way I looked at women changed the moment I saw you. I've never yearned for someone else's company the way I do for yours. I—I need you. And I'm not going to lose you to anything."

Lynn, apparently shocked, started to feel a new sentiment rise inside of her. The bleak existence she envisioned moments ago vanished as a shooting star does in the night sky. Now the Sand Man began to fill her head with thoughts of her own children. They were running and playing safely in a field, laughing as young children do. Amidst all of these emotions, all she could think to say was, "You didn't plan that very well, did you?"

Dusty, appreciating her ability to take the edge off the situation, chuckled and said, "No. As a matter of fact, I did not." He looked down at the floor, ashamed, "I don't even have a ring." She started laughing nervously. He walked across the room and grabbed his briefcase.

"What are you doing now?" she asked, wondering what could possibly be grabbing his attention at this moment.

"Improvising." He opened the briefcase on the other bed with his back to her. She heard rustling for a moment, the silence as he stood there for a couple of minutes.

"Okay, what are you doing? Seriously?"

He turned around and presented a paper clip that was bent into a ring with a somewhat distorted, but semi-impressive heart shape on the top. "This will just have to do for now," he said as he placed it around her finger.

Lynn was dumbstruck. "I didn't know you were so good with metal..."

"Well? I know this is quick, and I'm sorry I didn't plan it out better, but..."

She cut him off, "Of course I will." She spoke with a soft and reassuring tone. "From the moment you walked up to me, all I could think about was how beautiful our babies would be..." She was laughing and starting to cry at the same time. The two embraced wholeheartedly. As they kissed, their chests were beating uncontrollably. The presence that consumed them both would not let go. It was a moment in their lives that most people, if they are lucky, may only get to experience a few times... a moment where it seems that God Himself reaches out of the sky to touch our lives and forever change who we are.

She parted from him after a minute and with a huge smile said, "I love the ring babe, but you are gonna have to do better than that!" Again, thankful for her natural ability to bring humor into a situation, Dusty humbly agreed. They sat there in each other's arms on the floor of their hotel room until their coffee turned cold.

....

Meanwhile, Bruce was busy. He was already on the phone doing his homework on Doris. He picked up and dialed the number he got from Doris's sister. She had agreed to talk with him the next morning, explaining that she was too emotionally spent to do any talking last night.

He heard the phone pick up, "Hello?"

"Hi Bonnie, this is Bruce. I talked to you yesterday. First of all, thanks so much for agreeing to talk to me. It really means a lot. I just had a couple of questions."

"Oh, no problem. Talking about her makes me feel better, actually."

"Sure, I can understand," Bruce said with a soothing voice. "Okay, first of all, can you tell me about Doris's family? Brothers, sisters, Mom, Dad, kids, grandkids?"

"Oh my. Sure. Where do I start..."

Chapter 33

"The Bible". That's what the members of The Chosen called the book of information that contained each member's profile, the child or children they see, a description of the child and any other pertinent information. After the first meeting, Lana spent three weeks compiling the information into an organized, catalogued and alphabetized manuscript for the use of certified members only. She charged a modest fee of $10 to copy and mail the Bible to anyone who requested it. She even took the time to bind the pages together, design a cover and type the information so it was all legible. Dusty had offered to help her, but she again insisted that she needed something to keep her occupied.

The Bible contained a profile of each member who was allowed into the chat room, but the ones who attended the Winter Park convention had more detailed notes and more importantly, a detailed description of each child. There were 11 people who couldn't attend the Winter Park convention and lacked a children's profile page. She had a feeling that some of these were the people that she and Dusty were on the fence about letting in the first place. The acceptance process was difficult, as neither Lana nor Dusty wanted to take light any of the inquiries they got, but they figured they should err on the side of compassion as long as the person didn't pose an obvious and legitimate threat. As a result, she expected for a few to be weeded out naturally.

Two weeks after the meeting though, Lana took the weeding out into her own hands. She sent out a group wide message to the members of the chat room that stated that she would delete anybody's access that did not respond to her in the next 48 hours. Three of the people who didn't attend the convention got back to her and explained that they didn't want to be removed. The remaining eight were booted. It was more or less deduced that they either had no interest in a support group, or that they squeezed through the cracks in the first place. Either way, she did not want to waste time on individuals that weren't interested in contributing to the cause.

Lana was able to obtain descriptions of the children for the other three members who couldn't attend by way of coordinating a phone call with them. Along with the three additions to the initial meeting, plus two more that contacted Lana and were accepted in the following months, (one of which was Richard Thomas of Manhattan), the membership totaled 53. Nine of these were from outside of the US. A bio page for each of the remaining members was created and a phone appointment for everyone was eventually scheduled with the artist Lana had talked to in Winter Park. She decided that even if some of the people couldn't describe their child very accurate, that any sketch was better than nothing. So the phone calls started being scheduled and the sketches started being placed with each person's profile page.

When Dusty called the artist, it was a young lady named Sue who sounded extremely pleasant and beautiful on the phone. She asked a lot of questions about the structure of the face like: "If you had to guess, would you describe the eyes as being far apart, close together, or somewhere in the middle?"; "Would you describe the nose as short and pudgy, long and skinny, or wide and flat? Or any combination of those?"; "Is the mouth and lips full and bubbly, or more flat and skinny?" Dusty found the exercise challenging but interesting. It forced him to really try and visualize his girl and nail down some of the distinct features of her. He felt like that in some strange way, he was now a little more intimate with the situation. When the artist was done, she explained to Dusty that she did not want any payment and that she wanted to contribute to the cause. Lana had explained the situation to her. Dusty asked her for her address anyway under the pretense that he wanted to send a thank you card. A week later, the artist received a check for $1,000 from the Law Firm of SC&R. No one in the accounting department at the law firm questioned the bill labeled "Discovery" made out to Sue in Colorado in the Brian Draper file.

In the end after all the profiles were complete and adorned with sketches of the children, Lana had a comprehensive and elaborate Bible that she was extremely proud of. Each member received one of these about 6 weeks after the convention.

It was this Bible that Bruce turned to when he returned from Tupelo. He decided from that point on he would never leave home without it again. He immediately turned to Doris's page. On his laptop, he pulled up a picture of Danny Cullota—the boy that had been murdered—and immediately he saw a striking resemblance between the description and sketch of Doris's child and the picture on the screen.

"Holy shit." Bruce sat there and stared at the two pictures, making sure that he wasn't making a connection that wasn't there. After ten minutes of barely blinking, his eyes hurt and were watering. There was no mistaking the button nose, the small ears, the brown eyes and the wavy brown hair. He had just discovered the identity of Doris's child.

On the other side of town, Dusty too was studying his Bible. "Holy shit."

When the phone rang, Dusty knew who it was without even looking at the caller ID, "Bruce, are you seeing what I'm seeing?"

"I can't believe it. I mean, is there any way this boy isn't the one Doris was seeing?"

Dusty was still staring at the description behind Doris's page in the Bible. Then he looked at his computer screen with the news article from Tupelo. He did this several times before answering, "I just don't think there is any way that this could be a coincidence." Both of them sat in silence for what would normally have been an awkwardly long pause, but neither of them noticed. "I mean we have a rough sketch, from Doris, that almost perfectly describes a murdered little boy that lived only a couple hours away."

"There's more than that. Her sister told me Doris had a daughter that lived in Jackson."

"No shit?"

"Yeah, and that she went to see her grandkids play baseball at the park whenever she visited," Bruce paused before he spoke anymore, seeing if Dusty could connect the dots himself.

"Baseball... baseball... park..." then it hit him, "Wait! Wasn't Danny Cullotta abducted from a park? Wasn't he playing baseball?"

210

Bruce was staring at the news article as Dusty said the words, "Exactly. They had to have seen each other. She had to have been close by."

"This is incredible. I mean, not that Doris died, of course, but that we finally have a solid lead. We finally have some evidence to actually back up the proximity theory. This can't be a coincidence. No way. We *have* to tell the others."

"Okay. I'm with you. Maybe it will get people to research a little more seriously and try to find a way around the brick walls. I have a feeling that if some of them didn't find their kid on the first page of Google, then they probably stopped looking. It may be a lot more complicated than simply finding a kid on a missing child list somewhere. I'll tell Lana and have her post the info on the forum. I just hope nobody gets the wrong idea and thinks that dying is the only way to help these kids."

"Well, what if it isn't the wrong idea?" Dusty said, immediately wishing he hadn't.

"Well that's even scarier." Bruce pushed his glasses back to the top of his nose and stared again at the article. "If it weren't for the spontaneous eruption of a smoke alarm, Danko might have never been caught…" Bruce's eyes scanned the words for deeper meaning. "You read the part about this smoke alarm, right?"

"Yes. The apartment manager heard it going off. The dumbass left a candle lit."

"I wonder…"

"What buddy? What are you thinking?"

"Hold on a minute, I'm going to try to put us on a three-way with the manager of that apartment building. Just, just don't say anything. Don't let him know you are on the phone. Leave the talking up to me."

"What? Wait, Bruce…" but Bruce had already put Dusty on hold. He had no idea what the hell Bruce was trying to do. *What did this guy have to do with anything?*

After a couple of minutes, Dusty heard a click.

"Hello Mr. Jensen, I'm a reporter from the Jackson Star. I was just wondering if I could ask you a few questions about Mr. Danko. I'm doing a short blurb on how to protect your children form perverts like him and I thought you might be a good person to get some background information from."

Tom Jensen never really felt very important to anyone before and he liked the publicity, even if it was connected to a pedophile murderer. No one from any form of media had ever called him for his opinion prior to this case, so he squeezed every bit of satisfaction that he could from the "opportunity". He pretended he had something very important he was doing, but agreed to "spare" a few minutes to help the cause. In reality, he was sitting on his couch, smoking a cigarette, watching re-runs of *Rosanne*. "So, uh, what do you want to know?"

Dusty still didn't know what Bruce was up to, but listened to him carry on, "Well Mr. Jensen, I was curious about how you found these "pictures" that eventually led to Danko's arrest. I know there was a fire alarm involved, but how come his was going off? Was anyone else's in the building?"

"Well, when we walked in there, there was a candle lit. Son of a bitch could have caught my apartment building on fire."

"A candle… interesting. What kind of candle?"

"It was like one of those, uh, whatchya call it… long skinny white ones."

"Okay, and was this candle in a candle holder?"

"No. Actually, it was in a shot glass."

"A shot glass?" Bruce sounded puzzled. "What kind of a shot glass?"

"I don't know, what do you mean what kind? The kind you take a shot from!" Jensen sounded offended.

"Okay, but was there anything on it? Was it a clear shot glass? Or maybe a souvenir?"

Jensen was starting to wonder why this mattered at all, but he played along, "Actually, there was something written on it, come to think. Hold on. I think I have it still here in my kitchen. I took it and the candle from his room. Threw the candle away but didn't see a reason to waste a perfectly good shot glass. Want me to go check?"

"That would be wonderful. Thank you."

"Okay, wait a minute. I'll go get it." Dusty and Bruce heard the phone bang the table.

"I think you missed your calling, Bruce. Maybe you should have been a reporter."

"Yeah, I know. I'm kind of liking this. I don't think he has a clue. Do you? Does he sound suspicious at all to you?"

"I don't think he cares…" he couldn't get any more words out because Jensen picked up the phone.

"Okay…" he sounded out of breath, "I got it." He reached for the pack of Marlboro Reds on his coffee table and lit one before plopping back down on his couch. "Okay. Looks like it says 'Tupelo, Mississippi, Home Town of Elvis Presley. The King.' It has a picture of Elvis on it." The hair on the back of Dusty's neck stood up. Bruce didn't speak. He sat on the other end of the phone with his mouth open. "Hello?"

"Yes, um, thank you. Thank you Mr. Jensen. You've been a real help," and with that Bruce hung up the phone and clicked back over to Dusty.

Jensen sat smoking his cigarette, puzzled as to why his moment of glory had halted so abruptly, "Hello? Hello? What the fuck?" He stared at the phone as the degrading sound of the dial tone sounded off in his face. "Well fuck you too…" He shrugged his shoulders and sat the shot glass down on the table and poured it full of Jim Beam.

Bruce was still on the other end of the phone, just not with Mr. Jensen,

"Okay," his hands were trembling, "I am freaked out. Are you freaking kidding me?"

"Of all the places… Is there any way this could be a coincidence? I mean let's just say she didn't physically place the shot glass—that it was already in his apartment—then she still chose it. Someone had to have lit that candle. Someone had to have picked that shot glass. It had to be her."

"I agree," Bruce said, as if any other explanation was not even worth considering. "We have to tell the others. We have to. She's trying to tell us something. Maybe we can pose it as the silver lining in the sorrow surrounding Doris's death. I just hope we aren't wrong. I hope this is the right thing to do. I mean what if we *are* right about all this? Just imagine. Do you think people would…"

Dusty was silent for a few seconds before finishing Bruce's thought, "The ultimate sacrifice? I guess if we have to go out, we might as well go out saving children." Bruce didn't respond to this. Dusty tried to perk him up, "I've been thinking about this a lot. Maybe it *is* just a strange coincidence. Maybe she died and Danko was caught on accident and this had nothing to do with her dying."

"Really? The shot glass from Elvis's house? Where Doris was from and where her car came to its final resting place? I don't think so. I don't think we have a choice but to tell the group what we know. I think the most important thing here is that we know that we aren't all going crazy and that we have a place to start looking. We'll just have to figure out what the rest of it means as we go." Dusty couldn't argue.

That night, Dusty emailed Lana informing her of his and Bruce's findings. The next day, this is what he saw on the forums:

Ladies and Gentleman of The Chosen,

We are all aware of the death of Doris. Many of you attended her funeral. But what you may not be aware of is that two days after Doris died, a murderer was caught in Jackson, MS, 190 miles from where Doris died. Pornographic pictures of children were found in his apartment and it was discovered that he was responsible for the death of one, if not more children.

Dusty Burch and Bruce Crippen looked into the matter because they thought it was ironic that only a few days after Doris died, a child murderer was caught unsuspectingly in her home state.

After comparing the picture of the little boy to the profile that Doris had done of her child, Dusty and Bruce were shocked. I have attached her description and sketch of the boy, along with a real picture of the little boy. I think you will all see that there is no mistaking the two. Furthermore, Bruce interviewed Doris's sister and found that Doris had grandchildren in Jackson, where the murderer was from, and frequently visited there. One of the things she loved doing was watching her grandson play baseball at a local park, which happens to be the same park the little boy she was seeing was abducted from. There are just too many dots that connect for this all to be a coincidence.

What does this mean? It means that our children are in fact, without a doubt, real and probably almost undeniably dead. This also means that we have hard evidence as to why our children have chosen us. It seems very likely that Doris was close to this child somewhere around the time he was abducted and/or killed. Maybe Doris was the last person the child saw, or the person closest to him his last moments on this earth. These are still questions to be answered, but I think it gives us a direction to start running.

Some good news is that this also means that if we can figure out a way to catch the killer, that we could possibly save many more lives of innocent children. Now our challenge is to find a way to do so without having to die.

I know this is a lot to take in, but we felt that it was our obligation to inform all of you. Many of us were all but certain that our children were real, but this pretty much erases any shadow of a doubt. We think it would be wise to start a very, thorough search for missing children in your area and beyond and see if you can find a potential match. Bruce Crippen has also formulated another questionnaire that I have attached in this post. We think it is a good idea to start trying to look for similarities in our lifestyles that may play into why we are chosen as well. Maybe we all have something in common with each other that we have never noticed before—and that's one of the reasons we are chosen. And, God forbid anything happens to one of us like it did to Doris, it also might help the group find clues like we found in interviewing Doris's sister that could lead us to an answer.

Please send me the questionnaire when you complete it. Keep searching as well and please keep me updated on what you find.

Good Luck,
Lana

This movement produced some stunning results. Tuesday night, Dusty received an email from Lana that 15 people had already found pictures of missing children that resembled their dream children:

Dusty,
 Several people have posted in the forum already that they had either previously found pictures of missing children that resembled the ones they dreamt about, or found possible matches after hearing about Danny Cullotta. Apparently, other conflicted individuals had already begun the quest for answers, deducing that they were possibly seeing dead children. Few people wanted to talk about it during the convention though, because

they weren't sure and they didn't want to give anyone the wrong idea. I also think that part of it may have been that they didn't want to believe it themselves... if it were in fact true.

Altogether, there are 15 people that are claiming they have come across news articles or some other source that pictures the children they are seeing. There is no way to tell for sure, but after looking at some of the sketches/descriptions we all gave vs. images of the missing children, a few are unmistakably similar.

If this is true, I wonder why more people haven't found matches? I'm not sure if no one was looking before or just not trying very hard, but the news of Danny Cullotta certainly lit a fire under some peoples' asses. Or, maybe because, like Jurgaen, they came into contact with their child outside of their home state? Maybe some children are missing, but not reported? Maybe a person isn't always chosen based on proximity? Maybe some children don't have photos posted... I don't know. There are so many things to think about. I haven't had any luck, personally, but I've only just started my search. This does give me hope, but it also scares me to death. I don't think anyone can deny these children are real and are being hurt. We need to make progress and do it fast.

With Love,
Lana

Upon reading her email, Dusty's heart sank. She was right. It was good news in that now they possibly had more leads and places to start looking, but with every new match found, it further cemented the fact that his little girl was more than likely murdered. He had a gut feeling of this before and somehow, deep inside he knew, but physical evidence somehow made the truth more unbearable.

Lana,
This is good news! I thought we might have some success, but not this quick! Hopefully a few of them pan out. But what do we do with this information? We can't just go to the families and say, 'Hey, I have dreams about your dead child. I'd like to help find the killer'. We are going to have

to be creative in our approach to this. We also had better make sure that these really are accurate matches. I think these people need to be VERY careful about who they tell this information to as well. Start a list of people who think they know who their subject is, and we will go from there. Just remember, we can't do anything about what has already happened; we can only hope to help those that it hasn't already happened to. I believe that together, along with our new friends, we won't fail. WE CAN'T FAIL! Don't work too hard...

With More Love,
Dusty

Two weeks later, all the second questionnaires came back in. This time, Dusty and Lana asked questions based heavily around belief systems and instances that have happened in the lives of the Chosen such as: *Do you believe in God? Are you an atheist? Have you ever had a psychic connection? Do you practice yoga? Have you ever meditated? Do you go to Church? Do you find yourself to be judgmental of other races/religions? Have you ever had a life or death situation or a near death situation?* These questions went much deeper into the psyche of the individuals than the first questionnaire, which was designed to be much more superficial and specific to the dreams the people were having in order to decide if they fit the profile of The Chosen.

As Lana sorted through the responses, something hit her. Just as she had suspected, not one person claimed to be an atheist. Every person had at least some belief in a higher power. She wasn't sure what this meant, but she shot the note to Dusty and Bruce immediately. In her mind, she didn't believe a child would be able to connect with someone who hadn't exercised his or her spiritual channels. This finding too was posted on the chat room and talks erupted about harboring spiritual power and trying to make a deeper connection to God, or Allah, or Shiva, or Transcendent Omnipotent Energy, or whatever a person calls his or her own spiritual guiding light. Not all people were devout to a specific religion. Some were. Some people just dabble and drift through the different denominations. But for certain, no one felt that we came into existence by accident. This was true even before the members started seeing children because another question asked that specifically. Lana called Dusty to talk about this new finding.

"Dusty, what do you think this means? Do you think this is God directly forming a connection between us and the children?"

"I don't know if it's God directly, or just the children and/or our ability to channel Him or whatever energy fields exist out there on the different dimensions that we are unaware of."

"I've been doing some research on that exact thing. I've always been a little weary of other schools of thought, but I've been trying to open up my mind. I was raised a devout Christian and still believe that Christ died on the cross so that we could go to heaven, but I was taught early on not to entertain any other interpretations of God. There's nothing in the Bible about seeing dead children in your dreams, that I know of at least, especially not in this context, so I've been struggling on where to search for answers. I do believe God is playing a role, but if he really wanted the children to be saved, couldn't he just do it himself? This question has vexed me. Why does he need us? I've allowed my mind to open up a bit and stray from my childhood rules of engagement with The Holy Spirit and it's occurred to me that maybe God isn't a separate being from all of us, looking down upon us and watching over us… independent from us. Maybe we all collectively are God, or harbor pieces of him. I mean I always believed we were children of God, but what if literally he exists within our consciousness, or subconscious? I've even been researching a little and found there is what some people call a superconscious. Whatever it is, I think we may be able to 'tap' into it. If so, maybe we can find the answers we are looking for."

Dusty sat and listened intently to what she was saying. She was intriguing him. "I definitely think you may be on to something. You know, I've never been able to really pin down exactly what my beliefs about the afterlife are. I think about all the information out there that's available to us that wasn't available when scriptures of the different religions were written and how they might be written differently if the information was there at the time. For instance, evolution. There is evidence all around our physical world that it exists, yet so many people fight about it. But if there is an omnipotent creator, wouldn't he be smart enough to set evolution into place? To create the matter in the universe and inject the energy into it that sets all creation into place? I mean I know it's hard to wrap your head around, but to me, the fact that every single atom in our bodies, every single electron in our brain that are forming the thoughts and words we are speaking right now, was created inside of a star at the moment it exploded. We are literally made up of stardust. Isn't that enough to believe that there is a higher power? Even if we can't explain still how it all came about or what it looks like to go back to it when our physical bodies leave this plane of existence? I think that some people are just not okay with any gray area in their minds when it comes to God and the afterlife, and that is why dogma exists."

"Dogma? What exactly do you mean by that?"

"Doctrine. That's all that really means; text that cohorts of people adhere to form their belief systems. People usually interpret these texts literally in order to form the base of their belief structure. That's why it's so hard to allow for other schools of thought to be considered, because it literally threatens the very structure in which all their beliefs are based upon."

"Okay, I see what you mean. Geez Dusty, that's all pretty deep stuff. Stardust? I never really knew about that. How can that be?"

"I'm not an expert on it, but basically nuclear fusion exists in stars. Hydrogen atoms bond with other hydrogen atoms and when that happens, energy is released and a helium atom is formed. It's the principle behind atomic bombs. When all the hydrogen runs out then stars continue burning helium into heavier elements. Again I don't remember the exact chain of events, I'm not exactly Michio Kaku…"

"Who?"

"He is a theoretical physicist, but anyway, stars start to expand due to all the pressure from the core and then they contract into dwarf stars and eventually explode into a supernova. At that moment of explosion, it gets so hot for a split second that there is enough energy to form all the rest of the elements in the periodic table. Oxygen, carbon, which we are made of, all of the metals, gold and silver so on. That's why gold and silver are so rare because they are formed near the end of the nuclear fusion process and it's only hot enough to form them for so long that very little of them are made."

"Wow, I never knew you were such a scientist, Dusty," Lana was genuinely impressed.

"Well, I'm not. Trust me, I don't even think I'm explaining in correctly, I just find this stuff interesting and watch a lot of documentaries on it and have read some books. See, to me, knowledge and seeking to understand how the universe works is a 'religion'. It's not that I don't believe in God, it's that literally I don't think I have the capacity to truly understand Him."

"I understand. See, for me, everything you are talking about is interesting, but it's overwhelming. I'm much better off sticking to simple. At least, that's how I've always been."

"And that's okay."

"I do want to learn more though. I am interested in this ability to tap into our inner powers. I've even heard of this school in India that you go to for a month. What if I went there and could learn a thing or two?"

"Really? Like what is it?"

"I'm not sure exactly, but there is a guy who claims he helps people connect to the powers of the other dimensions. He is a swami, which is like a Hindu leader. Maybe it's phony, but what if I just take away one thing that can help us?"

"You never know. I think at this point, with what's at stake, no one could call anyone crazy for trying something."

"We'll see."

"Well, Lana, I just want to say I appreciate you very much and couldn't do this without you. I'm here for you for anything you need."

"I know Dusty. Thank you. I feel the same way. By the way, how is that little girlfriend of yours? Are you guys getting pretty serious?"

"Lynn? She is something special Lana. Something really special. I just hope I don't screw it up."

"You won't. You are a smart man and handsome and charming. Just follow your heart and you can't go wrong."

"Thank you. I hope you are right. Well, I probably better get back to work, but it was nice talking to you. Have a great rest of your day."

"You too Dusty."

....

Three weeks after Doris's funeral, 15 potential child matches turned into 23. Something else very interesting was starting to happen. Members in the chat room were starting to report that their dreams were becoming more detailed. Whereas most people's dreams were initially like Dusty's, void of anything but a dark mass surrounding a distressed child, some were starting to see other images flicker in and out of their dreams. The images were random and had no apparent connection: trees, a house, a road, a lake. The images were vague and fleeting, and mostly scenery.

Discussions started popping up trying to analyze these new images. Most people were in a general agreement that the images were more than likely a result of the children's ability to slowly establish a stronger psychic connection throughout time. However, it was also mentioned that the sudden influx in simultaneous visions was enough to deduce there were other contributing factors. Some people proposed that as The Chosen members broadened their search for their children, the children perhaps "rewarded" them. In other words, as the members narrowed the scope of possibilities, the children began showing them more, as if to say, "Yes. You are on the right track. Keep going".

Others proposed that the ancillary dreams were not a result of the children, but of *The Chosen* members' ability to break the psychic barrier. They thought that their own subconscious' were starting to cope and adjust to the psychic dreams, growing stronger and re-incorporating normal dreams into the child-dreams.

Either way, it was undeniable that as people tried harder to find answers, their dreams started to take on indescribable metamorphoses.

Chapter 34

Dusty had to take some time away from the office to attend Doris' funeral, time that he really did not have. The Draper case was set to go to trial next fall and he still had around 15 depositions he needed to take to round out his discovery. Three of them were very important expert witnesses that would make or break his case. He was able to find and handsomely pay experts to testify that it was a different lighter at the scene, or that the ergonomics of the lighter made it impossible for a child to engage the trigger, or that the lighter had a safety sticker warning parents to keep it away from children. *How could his client possibly be at fault?* But no matter how many people he could find to sell his case, he knew, deep down inside, that the little boy was a victim of ignorant manufacturing and design and should be given justice.

The rest of the deponents were officers that arrived on the scene, eyewitnesses, family members, doctors, economists, therapists, engineers… you name it. When millions of dollars are potentially on the line, neither side cuts any corners. They want the jury to hear every last detail in as biased of a presentation that the law allows. Dusty had an entire room allotted to him on the floor of his office building just to keep paperwork, boxes, exhibits and other miscellaneous items stored safely until trial.

When Dusty had to take Brian's deposition, it was a sad day. He tried to be polite, but there's just no good way to say, "How has being burned over a majority of your body affected your quality of life?" or "Do you remember anything about that day your life was changed forever? Have you found happiness since?" Dusty's job was to make the jury believe, somehow, that Brian wasn't really as bad off as he looked, but Dusty knew that any half-witted jury wasn't going to buy that. So he asked questions about the day of the accident to see if he could pin the blame on someone else. "Now did you specifically remember playing with a lighter? Is there anything else that could have caused the fire? How certain can you be that it wasn't your father's cigarette?"

Dusty felt like scum. And the fact that Ron Davis and his cronies had to be present made him even sicker. *The life of a defense attorney…*

Marilyn started to get worried about Dusty. She frequently checked in on him and sometimes peeked in his door without him noticing just to see if he was sleeping. Sometimes he was. She tried to talk to him more about his problems, but Dusty was increasingly feeling uncomfortable with the fact that she knew.

One afternoon, she caught him sleeping, "Dusty. Dusty, wake up. Hey…" She got no response, so she yelled, "Hey Dusty!" Dusty shot up from his desk and frantically searched for the source of the shout.

"What… What the hell? What's the matter? Marilyn? Is everything okay?" She couldn't help but to chuckle at his reaction.

"I'm sorry, I apologize if I frightened you."

"Well Jesus…" it was as closed to being frustrated with her as he had even been. Marilyn's giggle subsided and she tried to wear a somber face.

"It's just that, you have me worried. Is everything okay? Have you found any information? I'm sorry I just can't take seeing you like this."

"Yes, Marilyn, I'm fine. I'm just a little sleepy, that's all."

"Have you been sleeping at night?"

Dusty rubbed his eyes with both hands and sat up straight, looking at her with confused eyes, "Not exactly." He casually wiped the pool of drool that amassed on the surface of his cherry wood desk with the sleeve of his plum colored button up shirt.

Marilyn was a little hesitant to pursue, but with as much consideration as she could muster, she asked, "Well would you mind if I came in and talked with you for a minute?"

"Sure, Marilyn." His tone made her feel uncomfortable, but she came in and sat in the chair in front of his desk.

"I can't imagine what you are going through, but I want to know if there is any way I can help. Seriously. Dusty, I love you like my own son and it kills me to see you like this. You are miserable." Her brow furrowed the way Dusty's mother's used to when she approached him about cutting too much weight during wrestling season—sincerely concerned that he wasn't treating his body with the healthy habits a growing boy's body needs.

Dusty sat in silence and contemplated how he was going to respond to her. He just spoke the first thing that came to his mind, "I don't like sleeping. I'm tired of seeing her. I feel like I'm wasting time sleeping when I should be trying to figure out what to do about it. So I stay up pretty much all-night and just try to get by with a few catnaps during the day. I don't know what else to do. I haven't been able to match up my girl with anyone yet…"

Softly, Marilyn tried to clarify, "Match? What do you mean?"

"Well, we have all been trying to find missing children cases and see if our child matches up with any of them. Many people at least have an idea of who their child might be. Of course, no one can be 100 percent certain, but some of the descriptions given at the first convention so amazingly resemble some real children it's hard to deny it. I still don't even have a name for my little girl… she just… *is*. She's like a ghost's ghost. I don't understand and it's driving me crazy. I've looked through hundreds and thousands of missing children cases in the last twenty years. With all of them, either the picture I find is nowhere close to her, or the murderer was apprehended and convicted. I'm just afraid I'm never going to figure this out.

"And then Lynn… how in the hell am I supposed to help her if I can't even help myself. She's starting to talk about suicide. I mean, not seriously yet, but enough to make me worry. Ever since Doris died, there's been a lot of chatter about how dying must be the way to solve the case...The Ultimate Sacrifice. Like Jesus or something. I for one think that's a crock of shit, but that doesn't change the fact I know the woman I love would definitely give up her own life for that of a child's—without question. So where does that leave me? It renders me in a heap of emotions during the biggest case of my career with a client who not only wouldn't give his life for a child, but is trying to take everything away from one. So, there. That just about sums it up."

Marilyn had no idea just how deep all of this went and if she was a little worried before, now she was terrified. She didn't betray this to Dusty in the slightest bit, however. She held it inside, knowing that she needed to be strong for Dusty for… whatever it was he was going through. "Dusty, do we need to transfer the case over to someone else? I'm sure we can do that without causing too much of a fuss. It's not worth all this. And I bet I know someone who will gladly take it…"

"Chad? That fucking tool bag? There's absolutely no way I would ever give him the pleasure of taking over one of my cases. Plus, I don't think Stanley would allow it. He knows I'm the best he's got. I can't show any weakness anyway if I'm ever going to be considered as a candidate for partner. That would be grounds for immediate disqualification. Ruth is just waiting for me to fuck up. I got it. I do. I got this."

"Okay, hon, just don't wear yourself down. You need some rest. You have to keep your shark moving; you can't stop swimming or you'll drown," Marilyn gave him a reassuring smile.

"I know. Just keep swimming. I'm going to go get my scuba gear on right now," he gave her two thumbs up and a cheesy smile. "But first, could you please get me a cup of coffee? I will be busy cleaning up this drool puddle on my keyboard."

That tickled Marilyn and she giggled, "Sure hon. Anything you need, but now I know you're in a bad way when you let me get you coffee." The door shut and Dusty leaned back in his chair, once again trying to unwind the unfathomable tangle of obstacles that have accumulated in his brain.

"One thing at a time. Baby steps. Baby steps. Okay, now where did that Engineer's number go?"

....

After a couple weeks of reincorporating sleep back into his routine, Dusty was feeling a little bit better. He figured out that if he could sleep about two hours and 30 minutes at a time, that sometimes she wouldn't come to him. He didn't know why, but he didn't think too much about it. Maybe she was doing it as a favor. He didn't care.

Lana had decided to go to India after all. The whole notion surprised the hell out of Dusty, but he was excited for her. She told Dusty she wouldn't be available for about a month. Lana was a huge support system for Dusty and he hadn't been without her from the beginning, so he was slightly concerned and felt vulnerable. Marilyn was a big help lately, now that she knew what Dusty was going through and Bruce and Lynn were a huge support to Dusty, but something about Lana made him feel safe… at ease. He was very hopeful that Lana would find something on her quest that she could bring back to the group.

One Tuesday evening at about midnight, Dusty's phone rang and an elated Bruce was babbling on the other end, "Dusty! Dusty! Oh my God! I think I may have found my kid! I was looking through a list of accidental deaths in the area and I found a picture of a pair of brothers that drowned in Lake Michigan. I swear one of them is him. He is wearing a Hulk Hogan t-shirt even! His name is Trevor Holmes. The article I read said that he and his brother were out fishing with their step dad on Lake Michigan when they got caught in a storm. It said the boat capsized and Trevor and his brother were thrown out of the boat. The wind carried their stepdad away and the bodies were never found. If this was truly an accident, why would Trevor be coming to me? I have to think there is foul play here. What if his step dad killed him and made it look like an accident?"

Dusty had to process what he just heard Bruce ramble off at 100 miles per hour, "Well, first of all, that's awesome that you think you found him. On the other hand though, maybe you are jumping to some conclusions here about the dad. I mean, if it wasn't an accident, why wouldn't you be seeing his brother, too? Or maybe Trevor is coming to you so you can help find his brother's body and give the family some closure."

"I don't know. That's the one thing that's been puzzling me. Maybe his brother is going to someone else. I'm not positive, but based on the picture he may be a disabled child. Maybe that's why I can't see him. I don't know, but I'm onto something; I can feel it. Even if the dad doesn't kill anyone else, or even if he didn't kill Trevor, I was chosen for a reason. You and I both know that. They don't just come to us for shits and giggles."

"Okay. Well what if it isn't Trevor? Or if it is, how are you going to prove he was killed?"

"I guess that's just the million-dollar question there isn't it, Sherlock?"

Dusty was a little shocked as Brue had never quite been a smartass to him. He smiled on the other end of the phone, proud of Bruce's confidence, "Well, I'll be glad to help. Just let me know what I can do."

"No. You have enough to worry about. I can take care of this. If I need you, I'll let you know. I think I'm going to quit my job. I want to devote everything I can to getting to the bottom of this."

"Quit your job?"

"Dusty, I've got more money than the Sultan of India. Are you kidding me? I've never had any children or a wife to spend it on. My grandparents handed me down a fortune when they died. I was their only grandson. I only work so I don't go crazy. Plus, I've made about a million dollars in the stock market."

"Oh," Dusty figured that being single without kids, he had a lot of money, but he had no idea. "Well, alright then. Guess you can afford to not work for a while."

"I never have to work again if I don't want to. Just take care of your business. I know you have a lot on your plate. You are working on your biggest case, plus you have Lynn. Seriously, don't worry about me."

"Bruce…"

"Dusty, I mean it. I'll call you with updates, but I don't want you spending one second on my case. I will have all the time in the world."

"Okay buddy. You win. Good luck. Don't be a stranger."

"I won't."

"Hey, Bruce…"

"Yeah Dusty?"

"I love you man. I'm really glad I met you. You are one of my favorite people that I have ever met."

Bruce's eyes watered up and his throat swelled, but he held it in, "I love you too, Dusty." Then he hung up the phone.

Chapter 35

As people started finding out more information about their children and who they were, it became discussed whether or not the members should contact the families of the children. Sajid, the precocious Harvard student, was the first to actually contact the parents of the boy he was seeing. His boy had been found hanging in an apple orchard. His intelligence got him into a little trouble. He thought he could persuade the parents to give him clues and that he would be smart enough to solve the case. What he ended up with was being held in jail for two weeks while he was interrogated thoroughly.

Once Sajid had been able to convince the police that he wasn't the killer, he posted his experience in the forums. That was enough to keep everyone else from contacting family members, at least for now. Nobody could do any good for their children if they were in jail. One thing Sajid did discover though through his research was that the FBI had uncovered at least two other orchard hangings, one in Missouri and one in Texas. He searched for other chosen people in those areas, but was unable to find any. Due to the specific M.O. of the crime, it seemed likely the crimes were connected, but the FBI hadn't forensically been able to prove it yet. The fact that these crimes could be connected raised some important questions to the group: *Were there other people out there seeing a single child that was the victim of a serial killer?* If so and if Sajid fell into that category, why wasn't he seeing multiples like Eddie? Was someone else seeing those children? If so, could those people be found and brought in to the group to help solve the cases?

This theory of different people seeing different children of the same killer started fading when Sajid reported seeing a second child, whom he believed to be one of the children of the other orchard hangings. Conversation once again erupted on the forums. Sajid formulated a strong argument that was based on the premise that concentration and meditation on the children deepened the connection and that conviction and belief widens the communication channels which, in his case, allowed space for the other soul to communicate to him. Sajid was from India and came from a Hindu background that believed strongly in the idea of meditation, secret powers of the mind and multi-dimensional planes of existence.

Lana specifically found Sajid's story fascinating. In her recent conversations with Dusty about the Hindu school of enlightenment in India, she hadn't even known about Sajid's experience and belief in meditation. To her this was a sign. She talked with her husband, who was slowly becoming more aware and accepting of Lana's situation, and that's when she booked her 31-day trip to India to learn the art of harnessing this "power" of meditation, manifestation and the power of the universe.

For Lana, going to India was the wildest and craziest thing she had ever done. Her husband was supportive, however he was starting to get a little concerned about the situation. Lana begged and pleaded with him to go and finally he agreed. When Lana returned from India, this is what she shared on the forum with the group:

All,

I just wanted to give you all a brief synopsis of my trip to India. I truly think that through faith, positive energy, God, the power of the mind and a strong will that we can reach a solution to our problems. My mind was opened up tremendously to possibilities I never thought I'd have. I went to a Hindu workshop, essentially, for a month with 80 other people. This place has grown in popularity as people hear about Swamiji. Please keep an open mind as you read my entry:

Every day we took a bus from Bengaluru to Bidadi, which was about an hour south of Bengaluru. Swamiji's adheenam was set on a big property, probably fifty+ acres, sparse with lots of grassland and trees scattered. The main hub had plenty of buildings including modern looking apartment buildings for the people who live and work there, a library, the main hall, a school, a huge temple under-construction, and plenty of other under-construction buildings. His land is expanding to accommodate the increasing amount of people that have been coming to him over the years.

When I got there the first day, I could feel the tangible energy surrounding his property. It was like a frequency, like Wi-Fi, and it took me a few hours to adjust to. I went through some inner turmoil during that time, because it felt so different...so high energy from anything I've ever felt. Once I adjusted, it was wonderful the rest of the month. The first evening we spent there, I saw an eight-year-old move a bronze statuette an inch across the tile floor. Other children that lived there were doing the same thing in their little groups of participants, showing them and teaching them how to connect to God/Shiva/Swamiji to do this. My experience was wild. I didn't move the statue that first day, but I did wiggle it and one of the kids saw it and told me I was doing it. While I was wiggling it, my vision changed quite a bit and it felt like I was channeling something very big, very wild.

We took the same bus ride to the adheenam every morning, usually by 9am. We stayed in Bengaluru, which is a huge city. The people in India were so nice and very willing to help. It was great seeing the citizens of Bengaluru riding their bikes, mopeds, motorcycles, three-wheeled tuktuks, and also plenty of busses and cars. Traffic was unlike anything I've seen in America...even more wild than LA or New England traffic. No one followed the street lines or normal traffic rules. Everyone honked at everyone, but it was only to let them know they were there. Very loud, very chaotic, but it worked. We saw only one traffic accident the entire month we were there, and it was on the side of the highway during a 20-hour bus trip.

We ate a buffet breakfast, lunch, and dinner at the main hall of the adheenam every day, except for the days we were on trips. On those days, we either ate prepared buffet meals at hotels or rented buildings on the road, or we stopped at a restaurant and ate there. The food was satvic vegetarian, with plenty of rice. I don't think I've enjoyed food as much as I enjoyed it while I was there...I still miss it. No meat, no eggs, plenty of paneer (cheese) and dairy Indian dairy desserts. So many sauces...so many flavors!

Swamiji himself was the most intense part of the whole experience. We had darshan (viewing/meditation) of him every day, and many days we had energy darshan, where we came up one-by-one and he would touch our foreheads while he was in a deep state of Shiva. It was crazy intense and I can't explain it with words, besides to say that it felt amazing. He later told us that when he was touching our foreheads, he was injecting Shiva energy, God energy into us, as much as we could handle at that time. We were given bilva leaves coated in honey as we left the stage from this experience. He told us that this was because this energy, which is really what science calls dark energy (related to dark matter), tastes metallic and the honey and the leaf helped with that.

Every day we worked with manifesting powers. Over one hundred of them by the time we left. It was a complete crash-course boot-camp of power manifestation. All day every day was focused on this in some way or another. He has a small group of main leaders and teachers who help with this, the main one named Mahayoga. She was almost as intense as Swamiji, and she was in charge of getting us to manifest these powers. Many of the powers included remote vision, body scanning, healing, answering hidden questions, moving matter, materializing high-energy matter such as gold or diamond, answering length or distance related questions, gaining knowledge on unknown subjects, recalling mass amounts of imagery, etc. All of these used the same technique, with some variance, of connecting with the source of all: Mahadeva, or Sadashiva, with Swamiji acting as a bridge to help.

Every day was like a whirlwind when we were there. We barely slept four to maybe six hours a night. Our physical bodies were put through a lot, and we did SO MUCH every day. One day, probably two or three weeks in, I was having a very rough day emotionally and physically. I kept it to myself, and that day we had an energy darshan. When I approached the Swamiji for my turn, I did as I did the past dozen or so times; I walked up to him who was sitting on his big chair, and I kneeled down so he could touch my forehead. But this time, he put his hand on my head, and almost immediately reached out and grabbed me in a huge hug. He barely did this to anyone, and it really surprised me! I didn't let anyone know that day how down I had been feeling. I even smiled when I kneeled in front of him. After he let me go, he looked at me and said "I am with you" with a huge smile on his face. I nervously said "thank you" and got up and walked back to my seat. That was one incident that I'll never forget. He instantly saw energetically that I was having a really down day and gave me exactly what I needed. A huge hug from the guru himself. What an experience that was.

While in India, I moved a copper bracelet across my seven inch tablet without touching it (with several people watching and oooh-ing) , rolled coconuts, crystals, and water bottles out of peoples' hands and had the same done to me, answered questions about subjects and parts of the world I know nothing about, body scanned people, answered hidden questions, changed the physical size of my Samsung tablet, manifested gold on my hands, and so much more. It felt like a dream, or more accurately made this reality feel like a dream. Quite a trip!

During the time I spent there and in the time I have been back, I have made breakthroughs to my child like I have never had before. I have started to hear her now. We still haven't had full conversations, but she speaks to me and says things like 'hi', or 'don't be sad' or I can hear her giggle. She has been able to allow me to see visions, clues, images... I don't know exactly what they all are yet but I am confident in time I will put the puzzle pieces together. I am extremely confident that my experiences in India and learning how to focus my mind, meditate and manifest powers dormant in my brain have helped me break through to her.

I don't expect you to believe every word I have said. I still cannot believe some of it myself. But I strongly encourage you to study the art of meditation. I know not everyone can go to India, but there are books and yoga classes and many other resources available to you. If you would like to have a conversation with me, I'll be happy to talk to you. Call me, you have my number. I can at least explain the basics and foundations of meditation and channeling energy. We will figure this out, friends. Let's not give up!

Many people took Lana's words seriously and started practicing meditation. Dusty was slightly skeptical of some of her accounts, but he called her and they had a good two-hour talk about the whole experience. Dusty had never heard of these types of occurrences. She told him even more than what she put on the forum. He had seen movies like *The Matrix* and always been intrigued by the idea of living in a world that humans can manipulate, but it was just science-fiction to him. He fantasized about being Neo, and having the power to stop bullets and jump across building tops.

He loved the quote, "There is no spoon", but never had a reason to believe any of it was real, until now. The things Lana told him about children practicing these powers reminded him exactly of the child in the Oracle's apartment building, bending the spoon. He wondered if maybe they were actually living in some sort of Matrixesque reality after all. Either way, Matrix or not, he was going to find a way to help these children.

Chapter 36

It was June, 2002, just under a year after the first meeting of The Chosen. "Can I see your license and registration please?" Officer Wilkins tapped on the window of the grey Econoline Van he had signaled over. Ryker Garage, Tacoma, WA was painted on the sides and back in large white block letters. The stretch of Highway 92 in Eastern Washington state didn't carry much traffic. This was only the third vehicle Wilkins had seen all day.

The driver, a balding heavyset man in his forties with two days' worth of whiskers, was the only one in the vehicle. The van reeked of cigarette smoke. The ashtray overflowed with ashes and butts. An open carton of Camel non-filters rested on the dash. The driver had on a garage mechanic's grease spotted uniform with the name "Gerald" displayed above the shirt pocket.

"Officer, I'm sure I wasn't speeding . . . I'm always careful."

"No, you weren't speeding, sir. Are you aware that you don't have a license plate?"

"That's impossible. I washed the van just before I left Tacoma about noon. I know it was there then."

Wilkins looked at the driver's license and registration. All looked normal. "Do you have your insurance card, Mr. Ryker?"

"Sure do," the driver pulled the card from behind the visor. The van was fully covered; Gerald Ryker the policyholder.

"Well, sir, step out and take a look for yourself," Wilkins moved away from the door. Ryker didn't look threatening but the officer discretely rested his hand on the handle of his Glock pistol.

"Well I'll be. It's gone alright! It looks like someone took the screws off. It musta happened at the gas stop I made about an hour ago. Sorry, officer. I didn't know."

Wilkins believed him. "Well, just take care of it when you get back. Where you headed, anyway?"

"Just makin' a run to pick up parts over in Denton. I got a garage back in Tacoma. Here, take my card. If you ever need anything . . . I guess I owe you one.

Wilkins took the card and gave Ryker back his papers. He opened the door for Ryker. "Maybe I'll do that, Mr. Ryker. I see your van says 25 years experience."

"That was painted on there 3 years ago," Ryker fastened his seatbelt.

Wilkins shut the door, "You take care."

"Have a good one, officer," Ryker started up the van. Just a couple of good ole boys doing their job. A short gust of wind blew Ryker's card out of Wilkins' hand. It fell just under the driver's side of the van. "Oops," Wilkins bent down to retrieve it. His fingers grappled for the card. As he reached for the card, he saw something strange a few inches from his face. That's odd, he thought. How did that happen? A piece of pink cloth stuck out from under the door. It had a dark stain on it. Wilkins didn't remember seeing anything on the floor when he shut the door.

Wilkins stood, "Mr. Ryker, you've got something caught in your door."

"Huh?" Ryker opened the door and the cloth dropped to the road. "What the . . ." Ryker looked genuinely puzzled.

Wilkins started to get that bad feeling. Something was a little off here. He lowered his left hand to grab the cloth. His right hand went back to the gun, this time not so discrete. Ryker didn't move. Sweat bb's were rolling down his temples. It was a pair of cotton shorts, probably a little girl's shorts, pink, with flowered trim at the waist and pockets. They were caked with dark, coagulated blood, and slug trails that looked like dried semen.

Ryker gave a nervous laugh and looked at Wilkins. "Office, I swear . . ." But Ryker was looking down the barrel of the Glock.

Tacoma Times ran the story on the second page: "Local garage owner indicted for rape and murder of missing child." A picture of George Ryker was insensitively positioned next to the picture of Candace Myers. 7 years old. Missing for one year and seven months. Candace had blue eyes, curly blonde hair and a face dotted with freckles. Ryker was also the prime suspect for 7 other cases of pedophilia, molestation and sodomy.

Bruce was the first to catch the news about Gerald Ryker's arrest in Tacoma at about two in the morning while surfing the net. He immediately referred to the Bible to see if anyone was from there in the group. When he didn't find anyone, he was discouraged and a little confused. He thought that maybe not every child chose a person, or maybe not every chosen had found the group. He also thought that maybe the proximity theory only applied to certain people. To test that theory, he tried matching the picture the Tacoma Times posted of Candace Myers to the description she had given. *Blonde hair, blue eyes, freckles…* he flipped through the pages until he landed on Nick Hendrix. "Bingo."

He saw that Nick was from Arizona and immediately started looking for other ways he could possibly be linked to Tacoma, Washington. "Why would Nick be seeing a girl from Washington?" He started looking through the notes that Lana had included on the bio page and saw that Nick was a Mountain climber. Bruce pulled up his browser and Googled "mountains in Washington, Tacoma". Immediately, Mt. Rainier populated the field. Tacoma was just a few miles away. Bruce scratched his head, "Hmm, maybe there is something to this proximity theory after all. I gotta figure out if Nick ever climbed Rainier or a nearby mountain." Bruce knew there was a long shot of any of this being connected; there are millions of blonde-haired, blue-eyed girls in the U.S. He really just wanted to call Nick and find out if he had heard the news or if he had stopped seeing his little girl, but it was two in the morning. He knew he couldn't call Nick at that hour, so he went to sleep for a few hours. He set his alarm for 8 am. He got up, made some coffee and a bagel with strawberry cream cheese, then sat down at his tiny kitchen table to try and call Nick. No one answered.

Okay, it's kinda early… not everyone is up at 8:00. Plus, isn't Arizona an hour earlier? Bruce was very antsy and eager to know if there were any connections. He passed another hour on the net researching Mt. Rainier, then tried Nick again. Again, no one answered. On the bio page, listed under "Emergency Contact Number", was Nick's mother, Hannah Hendrix. "I wonder if ol' Nicks' mom could help me out..." He picked up the phone and dialed the number listed.

On the other end, a sweet, bashful sounding voice answered, "Hello. This is Hannah Hendrix."

"Hello Mrs. Hendrix. My name is Bruce Crippen. I'm a friend of Nick's."

"Oh, hello Bruce. Are you calling about the funeral arrangements? It will be on Friday at 4:30 at the Methodist church in downtown Gilbert." She had obviously been getting a lot of calls.

"I'm sorry, did you say... funeral? Did something happen to Nick?"

Bruce heard a quiet sniffle, "Oh dear, you haven't heard? I'm so sorry, but Nick was killed in a climbing accident last week."

Chapter 37

Bruce's mind was doing circles at light speed. *Dead? Murderer captured? Doris… died then murderer captured… holy shit. What is going on? Ohhh man. Okay, keep it together.*

"I had no idea. Mrs. Hendrix, I'm so sorry to hear that. Is this a good time? Or should I call back?"

"No, it's okay. I actually like talking to Nicky's friends. It makes me feel close to him. I like hearing stories and things I never knew about him. Nick had a lot of friends I never knew about… travelling all over and all."

"Okay, Mrs. Hendrix"

"Oh, please call me Hannah."

"As you wish, Hannah. Are you sure it's okay to talk?"

"Absolutely. Go ahead."

"Okay. Well, first of all, let me just ask you if Nick ever said anything about Winter Park, Colorado." Bruce was trying to figure out how much she knew about The Chosen, if any.

"As a matter of fact, he did. See, Nicky had some psychological issues, and he said he heard of a group that was meeting there that might be able to help him. We were very close, Nicky and I; there wasn't much he didn't tell me. I knew he was seeing a little girl in his dreams. It bothered him to no end. It wasn't like him to go visit a group of strangers, but he was desperate."

"Okay, well I won't go into too much detail about it then. That's not why I called anyway. The reason I'm calling is because we believe these children are real and in trouble. I don't know how much he told you exactly, but we think they were possibly murdered."

"He had mentioned that before."

"Okay, well up until now, we have been having a lot of trouble proving anything: that the children are real, that they are alive or dead, not to mention the fact of why they chose to come to us. But I think I may have found out who the child was that Nick was seeing."

"Oh, my dear. How do you know?"

"Well, I've been on the lookout for any unusual news about children. I heard about a murderer caught in Tacoma, WA and investigated. The girl that was pictured as the victim matches the girl Nick described very closely. We had detailed profiles made of each child to get as close of a picture of what they look like. What I was calling about, to test our theory, is whether or not Nick was ever in Tacoma? We believe that the children might be choosing us based on who is nearest them when they die. I tried calling him first, but obviously..."

"He went there many times, actually. He liked climbing Mt. Rainier. It was one of his favorites." Bruce felt a tingling sensation run up his spine into the base of his brain.

"Would you happen to know the dates?"

"Well, not off the top of my head, but he kept a journal. I don't have any use for it anymore, and if you think it may help you, I'd be happy to send it to you. I'm sure it could tell you."

"Oh, would you? That would be terrific. I promise I'll take good care of it and return it in its original state."

"It's quite alright. If there is any good that can come from Nicky's death, I'm sure he'd want me to help in any way I can. I kind of thought he was going crazy at first—too much thin air—but I know my Nicky and something was wrong with him. If you think you can do something to help these children, by all means..."

"Thank you so much Hannah. From the bottom of my heart. Thank you. And again, I'm so sorry for your loss. He will be dearly missed." Bruce gave Hannah his address and she promised to ship it the next day. Three days later, it arrived in the mail.

Chapter 38

Bruce didn't tell anyone yet about Nick. The only way they would know is if they religiously read the Gilbert, AZ Gazette, or if they called his mom upon the Ryker news, which he found to be highly unlikely. The only one he told was Dusty, his confidant. Dusty couldn't believe his ears at first when Bruce told him about Nick's death and the connection he had with Tacoma, but Dusty needed some hard evidence to back it up. Just like Bruce, he was interested in finding out if any of the dates that Nick climbed Rainier coincided with the dates that Candace Myers was killed.

Bruce knew better than to go through Nick's journal without Dusty, so he called him up on a Wednesday afternoon when he got the package and Dusty left work immediately. He had been on the phone all day trying to line up another expert to back up the theory that the warnings on the lighter were sufficient enough to exonerate Reston from any liability. He hit a brick road every time he got to the client's name… Ron Davis. He was notorious for foul play and well known amongst liability experts. This was not the first case that had ever been brought against Reston and certainly not the last. So Dusty jumped at the opportunity to get away from the office.

The two sat down in Bruce's apartment over a cup of coffee. "Bruce, you have all this money; why do you live in a one-bedroom apartment?"

"What would I do with a big house, Dusty? As if I'm not lonely already."

"I don't know. I mean, you could at least buy yourself a new car, something other than that 1988 Taurus. Something for yourself. I mean, when was the last time you tried to go out and find yourself a woman?"

"Come on, Dusty. Me? I've given up on women. I always thought if I found the right one and settled down and had kids that I would buy a house. Until then, this suits me just fine. I don't need a new car. Sometimes I buy myself an escort… Honestly, I give a lot of money to charity." Bruce blew right past his "escort" comment.

"Really? You gotta be kidding me! How often?" Dusty said, startled.

"Oh, a few times a year. I have a few that I like. I like helping people… mainly cancer research institutions. Both my parents died from cancer."

"No, I mean how often do you buy prostitutes?"

"Oh them? I prefer to call them escorts. I try to find the classier ones. I don't know. A few times a month. I have a few of those I like, too," Bruce gave a sly grin. Dusty was shocked, but kind of impressed. The guy had needs that needed to be fulfilled and had no reason to try and hide anything from Dusty in order to preserve dignity.

"Atta Boy Bruce. Remind me to never touch your junk." They both laughed heartily. "And the charities, how much have you given?"

"I don't know," Bruce said modestly, "a little here and there."

"How much, Bruce?"

Bruce put his hand on his chin and looked at the ceiling, "I've probably given close to two million."

"What?! Oh my god. Are you serious?" Bruce nodded his head in the affirmative. "You are a saint Bruce. A real saint. No wonder that kid chose you. You've got a heart of gold."

"Nah, I don't think that has anything to do with it. I mean, there's a lot of good people in this world."

"Not like you buddy. Not like you. I've never met somebody so selfless. I mean, you could have almost anything you want and you choose to give it all away."

Bruce stayed humble, "Yeah. I guess."

"Okay, well let's see what our buddy Nick left us. Have you looked at it yet?"

"No, I waited for you like I said. It was pretty tough. But hey, I did want to tell you something first. You know Doris, and her situation? Well, the killer confessed! Can you believe it? He confessed. He had killed the little girl in the cornfield behind Doris' family house. Golly. Creep."

"Confessed? Wow. "Dusty's mind served up the beautiful images of the golden sea at Doris' family farm and despite his best efforts to suppress, his painfully creative mind also served up images of horror and evil existing within that golden landscape to desecrate its beauty. He forced the images out with all his mental might.

"Well that makes a pretty damn strong case for *The Proximity theory*. Now we just have to figure it all out. Let's have a look at this journal and see if we can learn anything."

The first entry was dated October 5, 2000. It described Nick's fleeting, recurring dreams of a little blonde girl. It was brief, but he apparently felt the need to start a new journal in honor of her. His initial conjectures were that she was an angel looking out for him, trying to warn him that his dangerous climbing activities were going to catch up with him.

Then entries continued, usually about two or three per week. He started using the journal for more than just his little girl, but she was mentioned in about 80% of the entries. He spoke of very dangerous climbs in which he nearly froze to death. He had to amputate two of his toes on his left foot after he summited Everest. He broke his right pinky and thumb scaling the Grand Canyon after a twenty foot near free-fall retarded only by the friction of his two hands on a rope after his harness broke.

Most of his entries were very short. Some were only a couple sentences. One read:

She came again tonight. It was the worst one yet.

Another:

I found a group on the internet that says they are as crazy as I am. Going to Winter Park to meet them in July. Maybe I'll claim some rock on one of the narly mountains while I'm their. Hopefuly they can help me. Hopefuly she isnt real. Hopefuly they are all figmints of our imagination.

Nick wasn't the best with his communication skills and often misspelled simple words, but there was no doubt that he was a genius when it came to mountain climbing and the outdoors. He talked about people from all over the US who had heard about him and come to him for advice on conquering the world's toughest mountain. He even started a blog and had published a couple of articles.

Eventually, Bruce and Dusty came to a section that was very interesting. Nick started mentioning having dreams about a mountain. This intrigued both of them because not many, if any, of The Chosen had spoken about remembering dreams about anything other than the children. Nick had dreamt many times about mountains, but none that he could remember once his little girl started religiously coming to him. The dreams were brief, but memorable and impactful enough for him to note it dozens of times in the journal. Eventually, he recognized the mountain as what he thought to be Mt. Rainier, his favorite mountain.

Although Bruce and Dusty thought this was strange, they didn't know what to think about it. They tried remembering any other dreams they had. Bruce couldn't remember anything. Dusty seemed to remember briefly dreaming about something else, but it was buried in his subconscious, unable to be summoned at the moment. Whatever the reason Nick dreamt about it, they thought it was a very strange coincidence that Nick climbed Rainier several times; it was where he died and where Candace Myers was found. There had to be a connection. To them, it further proved the proximity theory.

"What if his dream of the mountain is somehow related. Like a clue or something from the girl?" Dusty suggested after a couple minutes of both of them sitting in silence.

"I guess anything is possible at this point. We need to post and see if anyone else is having other dreams that they are remembering. Maybe we all are, but we just don't know it or remember them."

"And what is up with the death thing man? First Doris, now Nick? I mean, come on. Can that really be a coincidence that they die and the murderers of the kid they were seeing are caught? No way. Something creepy is going on here."

"We have to tell the others about all this," Bruce told Dusty.

"Yeah, we have to. I just hope we don't…"

"Set off a domino effect?"

"Yeah. I mean, what if people start… taking the matter into their own hands?"

Bruce knew what Dusty was getting at, "We can't think like that. I think it will just motivate people to try harder, knowing that there is an answer to be found out there. We just have to look hard enough. What about Lana and her trip? I think this meditation stuff might actually help."

"Have you tried it yet?"

"No, not really. Well, a little bit, but it's so hard for me to turn off my mind. I don't know if I can."

"Yeah, I have the same problem. It's definitely tough. But I'm getting better at it. I try to make myself practice at least 10 minutes a day."

"Any luck?"

"No," Dusty rubbed his chin, "not really. I haven't had enough time to master it." Then the buried subconscious image sprang into his memory, "Oh, I remember now! I have been seeing this swing set in my dreams. More and more. This old, dilapidated, rusty swing set."

"Well, maybe that means something."

"Yeah, but what? I can't remember the last time I was on a playground. Probably 20 years ago."

"Well, it has to mean something. We will figure it out, and soon."

"Some people are desperate though Bruce. I mean Eddie? That dude is seeing nine little boys. You don't think he would take a bullet to himself for them? I don't want blood on my hands. And why is he seeing them all? You think *that* guy meditates?"

"No, probably not, but you have to remember he has had a long time for the souls to work on him."

"Yeah. That's true. Gosh, I'm just so scared about what I'm going to find out and what might happen if we tell people what we already know, which at times feels significant and at other times feels like nothing."

"Well, there's nothing we can do but try and find a solution to give them. It would be wrong not to tell them what we've found. The most important piece is that we think most children are connected geographically to their chosen. Doris and Nick all but prove that. Just because they had to die before the killers were caught, doesn't mean that everyone has to."

"I know, I would just feel horrible."

"It's out of our hands."

Dusty sat back on the couch and finished his cup of coffee in one swift gulp, "... Lynn."

"No. Not going to happen. We are going to figure this out. We will. I promise on everything, we will. Nothing is going to happen to her. I promise."

Dusty wanted to believe him. He really wanted to.

Chapter 39

Nick's body was actually recovered by the coast guard after a call from his mother. He had told her where he was going and when she could expect him back. He often returned after he told her he would, but after a week, she contacted the authorities. She also happened to know that he was going to try and conquer the Monroe face. Had she waited any longer, the helicopter would not have spotted the boot sticking up from the snow. He would have been forever buried there for the ages.

Nick Hendrix wasn't the most intellectual person in the world. He always did mediocre in school. It wasn't because he didn't have the capacity, he just didn't apply himself. From the time he was 14 he was climbing mountains. After his Dad died in a horrible car accident, it became his release. He started believing that if such a great man as his dad could be taken without any warning or justice, then life must be a roll of the dice. He began believing that when the universe wanted to take you, you went. So, he started climbing mountains, not to be reckless, but to see just how far he could go. He feared nothing.

Although he wasn't seen as an intellect, he most certainly had his bright moments. He applied himself to searching for his little girl for nine straight months after the first meeting in Winter Park. Once he had a reason to believe he wasn't going crazy, he was determined to help her and get to the bottom of it. He journaled every one of his dreams and experiences. He spent hours a day at the library, searching on the internet and reading newspapers to look for clues. He worked as a caddy at a local Country

Club, so in between rounds, he used the Pro Shop's computer to scan through past Amber Alerts.

After starting to dream of Mt. Rainier several times in the midst of the dreams of his little girl, he started feeling more and more compelled to go back. Not only did he love it, but he thought that maybe, just maybe, he would find some answers. He thought that it wasn't just a coincidence that he kept seeing blips of Mt. Rainier sprinkled throughout his slumber. *Why else would something so majestic be laced into my nightmares?* His last moments, on a stormy May day in Washington, he found himself on a mountain…

"Don't look down," Nick said to himself as he forced his fingers into the pencil wide crevice about arm's length above his head. He hugged the cliff just a few hundred feet from the summit. After 4 days of climbing and 3 short nights of intermittent sleep in sub-zero temperature at high altitude, he was struggling to concentrate. Nick's little girl had come to the mountain with him; the little blond girl in the pinstripe outfit with blue eyes and freckles. He'd hoped that the climb might purge her from his troubled slumbers. He was not so lucky.

She was a mystery to Nick, but so real. He yearned to know why she cried so desperately for him in the night. She had been visiting him for the last 17 months and still he knew nothing about her.

The mountain, too, was real, but Nick knew *plenty* about it. He knew it could kill him quickly, without remorse and with little effort. He knew it could bury him and render him a ghost in a matter of seconds. As he longingly gazed at the summit through the wind and snow—his life on the line—all he could think about was her. Not the mountain. There was no escaping either of them at this point.

Nick was exhausted, hungry, weary, and light-headed from the altitude. This would be the 7th time he would reach the summit of Mt. Rainier, 22,000 feet high, in upper Washington state. Beside from his little girl, his dreams had lately been filled with images of Rainier and he felt compelled to come back. He felt like maybe it would bring him some answers. This was the first time Nick would do it alone though and the first time he would do it by way of the Monroe face, one of the most dangerous ascents in the world. Only Everest had claimed more lives than the Monroe face.

The adrenaline rush more than compensated for the physical beating the mountain had given him over the last few days. Nick had been higher than this. He'd conquered Everest, K-2 and the Matterhorn. Nick had a disdain for those trendy, cyber-climbers who summitted the major peaks of the world assisted by bottles of oxygen, cell phones and their laptops. To him, they were pretenders to the throne, wrapped in a security blanket of techno clothing, space age tools, and satellite positioning. The peaks and valleys of all the great ranges had become littered with their used air canisters, freeze-dried food wrappers, disposable gear and despite all their efforts...frozen bodies. The big mountains don't give up their dead. Their corpses, adorned with fluorescent helmets and body suits, remain as shrines to man's indomitable spirit, or stupidity, depending on how you look at it.

At 22 years old, Nick was a devotee of the "old school." No oxygen, pack your own gear, leave the world and the detritus of pop culture; leave all the Walkman's, plasma TVs, DVD players and Gameboys at the foot of the mountain. One time, Nick got altitude sickness just before reaching the summit of Everest and had to resort to oxygen briefly. This was his only time, but he didn't use it on the descent and he carried his empty container and trash down with him.

The wind screamed across the face of the cliff, trying to peel Nick off like a label on a bottle of Coke. Nick hugged the rock tighter to keep the wind from getting between him and the mountain. This was the toughest part of the climb. He had covered more treacherous ground below, but he had been fresher, stronger and had a clearer head. At this juncture in the climb however, every muscle in Nick's body wanted to take a timeout to cramp. Unfortunately, there are no timeouts in the game of mountain climbing, but Nick was experienced, tough and smart. He had been at this point many times before. As he clung to the side of the mountain, he merely saw it as another ultimate test of endurance. It was these moments that allowed him to sit in a room with other people and know that he was mentally superior, but the high never lasted after the climb. The emptiness returned and he had to keep coming back for another fix. It was what he was born to do.

He kept moving upward, inches at a time. The angle here was not quite vertical, but the rock face was fairly smooth and didn't offer much to hold on to. A mistake here and Nick would slide down the surface about 200 feet. Little granite barbs and shards of ice would rip through his clothing before scraping the flesh away from his bone. He would then jettison into the sky and drop another 2500 feet into a gaping, jagged fissure of ice and stone. His remains would never thaw and they would never be found. But Nick wasn't thinking about falling. He never did. That only made a person tentative, fearful and dead. He had to learn to develop a sense of immortality. Risk it all. He learned to take advantage of all the adrenaline that surged through him that made most people panic.

Nick's fingers walked over the rock above him, exploring for any small fracture or outcrop that would give him brief purchase. The longer he stayed here, gasping the thin air as his muscles and organs screamed out for oxygen, the more lightheaded he became. Every system in his body was on red alert. Funny thing is, nothing made him feel more alive. His hands continued reading the Braille of the mountain. *There!* His left hand found a small knob and he pulled himself up a few inches. His feet were anchored on a thin lip of ice that stuck out about an inch.

It was early afternoon. The sun was now hidden by the top of the mountain. Nick wanted to reach the summit before the sun moved over it. He could then descend on the other side, (a much easier slope), accompanied by the light and relative warmth of the sun. The thought of having to climb in the freezing shadow of the mountain gave Nick a sense of urgency.

The first assault was always on the hands and fingers. They could continue to function below freezing, but only as long as they were busy. Nick's were struggling to stay employed. The cold was already starting to work its way into his extremities, pounding on his nerves and joints like a ball peen hammer. His fingers, toes, feet and hands ached and throbbed mercilessly and were starting to become numb. The freeze would eventually follow the path of the old Negro spiritual, "Dry Bones" . . . the foot bone connected to the ankle bone, the ankle bone connected to the shin bone, etc. until his body seized up, frozen in space and time, and gave up the ghost.

Amazingly, Nick's body was still functioning and he was able to locate the tiniest nodules of support. In some places, there was nothing to hang onto but a small bottle cap of ice. He found the ice was often more stable than the rock. Nick sucked to the wall like a vine. Every square inch of him was trying to hook into some pore in the mountain. His hands and feet each took their respective turns pulling or pushing the rest of his body forward. His feet tried to remember each icy blemish that had earlier supported a hand, but it was becoming increasingly harder.

It was his right hand's turn. Groping around overhead, his fingertips felt only ice. In fact, a huge, frozen curtain of black ice spread out the last 100 feet to the summit. It had its own, unique field of nooks and crannies, much more difficult to navigate than rock. It wasn't impossible. Nick had often traversed black ice, but rock would've been a much more welcoming sight. The one advantage to ice was that it could be chipped and dug out with a pickaxe. Nick's fingers slid back and forth until they found a smooth crater about the size of a golf ball. He pulled on it several times, but his fingers slipped out each time. It gave no hold.

He retrieved the pickaxe that hung from his belt and took several small swipes at the ice. With every swing, his body groaned at the exertion. His feet and left hand were aching for relief. He needed to get his body weight spread out over four appendages again. Nick returned the pick to his belt and reached for the newly created handgrip. Not quite good enough. He reached for the pick again. His bones and muscles were screaming, "hurry up, get it done, you're killing us!" A couple more furious hacks… that should do it. His lungs were screaming and his head was pounding, but he managed to keep balance. The rarified air was beginning to make him woozy. *Just get to the top and you can rest and recover for a couple of hours. Stop being a pussy!*

Nick was able to get his first two knuckles into the ice hole. *Pull hard. Lift your right foot - find the little crag you know is down there. Push up. Now the left foot. Drag it up until you feel that little rail sticking out. Now the left hand. Slide up. There's a nub of rock poking through the ice. Grab it. Now you're going! Fight off the nausea. Ignore the cramping.*

Nick was too intense to feel the fear, but he knew he had better fix the situation quick. His life depended on it. *Okay, need the pick again.* As Nick pulled the pick from his belt, his finger, numbing from the cold, failed to get a sure grip. The pick began to slip. His fingers grappled to hang on, but it slipped out of his hand. He knew it would be disastrous if the pick dropped and miraculously managed to pin the tool between his knee and hand. He put forth all of his concentration, but he could not manage a grip. It was slipping. It fell beyond his fingers and bounced off the top of his boot. Instinctively, Nick loosened himself from the mountain to try and catch it, which caused him to lose his balance and his grip.

The slide lasted about a minute. The mountain flipped, rolled and tossed him over a few times, like a steak, just to make sure and scrape him equally on both sides. By the time Nick reached the bottom of the slope, he had lost a considerable amount of clothing, skin and muscle, but he was still conscious. With one last thud, he was propelled away from the mountain into a sea of clouds and air. Nick began free falling. Blood and small bits of flesh were air blasted from his body and trailed behind him, like the tail of a comet, as he streaked toward the crevice below. In about half a minute the pain would cease, but the thin mountain air had not fully robbed Nick's senses enough to spare him these last gruesome moments. The cold had not deadened his nerves after all. The rock slope had not put him into shock. No, the mountain was careful to ensure that Nick felt every, nick, scrape, bludgeon and bounce before it splattered him like a jar of human jelly off the jagged walls of the mountain's crevice below.

....

Bruce posted on the forum what he and Dusty had discovered about Doris and Nick. The forum blew up over the next couple days with questions, theories, concerns and possible solutions. Everyone seemed to be very devoted to finding an alternative solution to death. The ones that were seeing multiple children were the most concerned. After all, seeing multiples was a pretty fair indicator that a serial killer was involved and could mean more kids were going to die if he wasn't caught. Many that were only seeing singles were still concerned, but not to the same magnitude. It was the multiples that really felt a deep down, depressing, gut wrenching sorrow upon the realization that they might have to sacrifice themselves to help the children, past and future.

As a result of all of this, a major question arose amongst the group: *Would sacrificing themselves, voluntarily, disqualify their souls?* Many were resistant to the notion of suicide, either for religious reasons, or just for the mere fact that Nick and Doris died accidentally; there was no evidence to prove that *suicide* would allow for one's soul to interact with the physical world to catch the killer. Some argued that the deaths of Nick and Doris and the timing of the killers being caught could possibly be a huge coincidence and that it was too early for thoughts of suicide. The thought was running through all of their minds, however... especially Eddie's, whose 9 little boys haunted every conscious and subconscious moment of his life.

Eddie was at a true disadvantage when it came to researching his case. He didn't own a computer, hardly left his house and didn't speak to other human beings unless he absolutely had to. He found The Chosen on a computer in the library that he had to ask for help with the first time, but eventually he learned at least how to turn it on, pull up a browser and find the chat room when he wanted to get in contact. Researching on the Internet was still light-years beyond his capability. He had entertained a couple of phone calls from some of The Chosen to collaborate, however. Dusty, Bruce and Lana were actually allowed a chance for a phone conference with him. He seemed despondent. He placated them, asking them questions about if they were any closer to figuring all of this out, allowing them to poke and prod into his experiences to try and uncover any clues. Deep down though, Eddie was numb. He had experienced the deep, dark depressing torture of his mind for too long and was ready for it to be over. He asked them about Bruce and Doris. He asked a lot of questions about them, actually. He was alone. Lonely. The thought of dying to catch a killer and save more kids was about the happiest thought he'd had in over a couple decades. He tried to cooperate with the digging up of research and making of lists to help identify his connections to his kids and or the murderer, but he just didn't have the resources or the energy to be very effective. The group offered to help, but there just really wasn't much they could do for this old dog. He was flat out done with it all. The only reason he didn't want to commit suicide is because he was afraid that no one would be able to help his kids. So, all the three of them could do was to promise to find a solution as soon as possible. Try they did.

Chapter 40

It wasn't until after Dusty read Nick's journal that he made a real push for people to start paying special attention to anything and everything that they dreamt about. He now truly believed that the children were trying to give The Chosen clues. He kept encouraging everyone in the forum to keep a detailed dream log and to make special note of any images that appeared in their dreams, for they could be possible clues to the murders. After Doris and Nick died and their children's murderers were caught, The Chosen collectively kicked their research efforts into high gear.

It seemed to Dusty and many of the Chosen that the deeper they got into the cases, the more and more the children were being able to express themselves in the dreams. That often meant more intense and uncomfortable dreams. Some nights when Dusty had his nightmares, he convulsed and moaned so wildly that he often woke up Lynn. It terrified her to see him act that way. Lynn loved spending her weekends with Dusty, but seeing him in such pain made her situation worse at times. By this time, she had grown very affectionate towards him. She felt like maybe he had come to her for a reason. She found herself thinking about what he might be doing at any given moment, especially while at work. With every shiny tooth she examined, she could see Dusty's reflection. She loved to imagine what may become of their life together, or if one day they might be able to communicate telepathically. This notion was pondered by many of the members of The Chosen. *Could they possibly be communicating with these children because they possessed some psychic power?* It seemed far-fetched to Lynn, but since she knew so little about why she was seeing her child, nothing was out of the question. She wondered if somehow, through their love, they could expound upon their psychic powers together and communicate via ESP. She hypothesized that perhaps only true soul mates could reach this level of oneness with each other, rendering their relationship one of true cosmic importance: "Dusty and Lynn, the first lovers in the universe to communicate through ESP," she mused to herself. She didn't definitively see herself as having psychic powers, but she couldn't help but wonder. Either way, she didn't have to be a psychic to see that Dusty was quickly becoming attached to her as well. His every action shouted it. He tried very hard to play it cool around her, but Dusty could hardly contain himself in Lynn's company. He shined every second they spent together. This normally might have alarmed Lynn, but with Dusty, it excited her.

Nobody had made her feel like an obsessed schoolgirl in a long time; she liked that. Something about Dusty warmed her heart in the way that the rising sun warms the morning air. Dozens of men had thrown themselves at her in the past. She had been courted in about every way imaginable: roses, baseball games, jewelry, candy, teddy bears… one guy even bought tickets to take her to a super-bowl game. She had been hit on in bars, at church, at work, in school and in the library. She was a tantalizingly beautiful woman with bold natural features, but none of it ever got to her head. In high school, people had even teased her and called her "Belle" after the character in *Beauty and the Beast*. Everyone wanted her, but she seemed oblivious to all the nonsense and carried on in her own, thought-provoking manner. Through all of her courters, no man had ever grasped her attention like Dusty. All of their efforts together never elicited the jittery sensation she felt when she looked into his eyes. He gave her hope that she would get through this.

Dusty was unable to go to Nick's funeral, although he wanted to. The partners assigned another couple of cases to Dusty because his billable hours on the Draper case were starting to decline. One of the cases involved a school bus crash that killed two men and severely injured several children. SC&R was representing the brake manufacturer that supplied the brakes to the bus manufacturer, who was also being sued but represented by another firm. The irony in the situation that Dusty was working on another case involving children on the other side was almost too much for him to bear.

To cope with it, he did what he absolutely had to, nothing more. He conducted the obligatory depositions of the involved parties and researched the facts of the case, but he did not kick his genius into high-gear like he usually does.

Dusty was back to working so hard in fact, he wasn't able to keep up with his routine visits with Lynn. He was back to working as hard as he had before the dreams started happening. They still talked every night and Lynn understood, but she missed him dearly. Instead of every other week or sometimes every week, they hadn't seen each other for six weeks on this current stent. This part was extremely hard for Dusty, especially because he wanted to help Lynn solve *her* case more than anything, not work on the cases defending multi-million dollar asshats that would rather pay more money to defense attorneys than settle with the plaintiffs and pay them for the pain and suffering caused by their own negligence.

Six weeks had passed since Nick's case was solved and there were still no concrete solutions to solving the rest of The Chosen's murder cases. More and more people were discovering the possible identities of the children they were seeing, but no one had "cracked the code" of how to catch the criminals. The Proximity Theory was playing out fairly well, as most of the "finds" did come from within the same city as The Chosen, but knowing that didn't really help solve the case. Knowing their identity and solving the cases were two very different things as well. Dusty knew there had to be something more to the Proximity Theory, he just couldn't quite figure it out; as of this point, he still didn't know the proximity *or* the identity of his "Precious Doe".

Whether they found the identity of their children or not, most of The Chosen carried on their everyday lives like they had prior to the convention, enduring the heartache. Some were better at pushing through the emotional muck than others, but for all of them, knowing that their children were real weighed heavier on them than ever before. It became harder to work, relax, spend time with family, eat, socialize, be intimate, concentrate and sleep. With every day that passed that a solution was not brought to the table, morale diminished. Although some of the members were starting to have a decent idea of who their child was, they had no earthly idea what to do with the information. On top of all of this, several other members reported starting to see multiple children, so the reality that more of these cases probably involved a serial killer ratcheted up the stress and tension of *everyone*. The people that weren't seeing multiples yet wondered constantly *if* they would.

In the midst of the flurry of uncertainty in the group, Lynn became certain she found her girl. She and Richard had run across an article online that described her girl to a "T". Her name was Amber Goldstein and she was eight years old. The article was dated August 21, 1999. Amber had been outside playing with some friends when an ice cream truck pulled up. She ran inside to ask her parents for money and that was the last time they saw her. Police found her sexually assaulted and mutilated body in a dumpster on the northeast side of Manhattan. The only trace evidence was found was a small semen sample, but there were no matches in the criminal database and all leads fell short. The killer was still on the loose.

Richard was becoming a trusted team member and was devoted to getting to the bottom of the mysteries. Lynn needed all the help she could get. They strongly believed that a third perspective would help them narrow the case, so they spent many weeknights together in the library looking for other missing children and trying to find a possible chosen member to match them. Lynn had promised Dusty that she would not go to Richard's house and that he would not come to hers to work. This fact eased Dusty's discomfort, somewhat. Even so, Dusty struggled to fight off the boiling jealousy and insecurities that arose in his heart and mind. She knew Dusty was very busy and hated putting a burden on him to come to New York, but when she found the identity of her child, she called him.

The phone rang in Dusty's office. She had learned to call there in the middle of the day. Dusty recognized her number, "Hey babe!"

"Hey honey. How is your day going?"

"Oh, pretty standard. I had a hearing this morning for the judge to rule on whether or not evidence is permissible in this new bus case. Writing a motion now, you know, exciting stuff. I miss you."

"I miss you too..." Dusty could hear the sadness in her voice.

"Is everything okay, babe?"

"Dusty, I think I found my little girl. You know how lately I've been able to see her more clearly, well..."

Dusty sat up in his chair and felt a little surge of adrenaline rush through his veins, "What? Oh my gosh. How?"

"I found this article," Lynn's voice started quivering. "Her name is Amber." Tears started coming down her cheeks. "Dusty, she..." Lynn sniffled, "She was found in a dumpster." Now she was crying full force.

"Ah, babe..."

"How could anyone do this? This creep posed as an ice-cream man. What the fuck is wrong with this world?"

Dusty's heart broke as he heard Lynn crying and immediately felt guilty that he wasn't there for her. "Honey I'm so sorry I haven't been there for you lately. I'm coming. Today. I'm dropping everything for a while and coming. I don't care if they fire me."

"No, it's okay. I'm okay, I just needed to talk."

"Don't care. I can't go another minute without seeing you anyway. I'm going crazy. I find myself daydreaming about your naked body at least five hours a day."

This made Lynn chuckle a little bit and redirected her emotion, "Only five?"

"Maybe six."

"Okay. Well, I could really use your company right now. Something about knowing her name, who she is... I don't know. I don't know if I'm depressed or anxious or excited. I don't know how to route my emotions."

"Okay. Well, I'll be there tonight if I can find a flight. If not, I'll be there tomorrow morning. I'll text you. I love you babe."

"I love you too, Dusty. Thank you."

"Anything for you. I'm sorry it's taken me so long to get there. See you soon.

"Bye."

Dusty got there the next morning. Lynn picked up him at the airport. When they got in the car, she couldn't resist kissing him. It had been so long since she'd seen him, she was overcome by lust. She started unbuckling his pants then realized they were in a very visible location. She put the car in drive and with one hand in his pants and another on the wheel, drove to a remote part of the underground parking lot. She parked the car and ripped off her clothes and hopped onto the other side of the car. Dusty's hands caressed her entire body, back, butt, legs, feet, breasts, every inch as she kissed his face, lips, neck and ears while gyrating her hips on top of him. They only slowed a couple times as cars crept by. It had been a long time coming and the windows steamed up quickly. It was exactly what they needed from this world. When they were done, they laughed and giggled as they dressed, realizing exactly how close they were to public exposure, but neither of them cared one bit.

Once at her apartment, they started digging in to the case. The problem was that Lynn had run a marathon every year for the past five years, so she had run literally all over the city training. If she was connected to her kid via proximity, then her task of finding that location was monumental. It became a popular belief in the group that if proximity was important to the connection, then finding the spot where the connection was made would help in at least starting to find the trail of bread crumbs. Lynn and Dusty travelled through the city via car, bike, taxi or on foot, but without knowing what they were looking for it was like finding a needle in a haystack. Richard was not having any luck with his child either, who he believed was a little boy named Sam, so they were unable to make any connections that could possibly help each other.

Dusty stayed for three days, and made arrangements for Lynn to come to Chicago the next weekend. He paid for her plane tickets before he left. While he was there, they practiced meditation together. They read books on how to center and calm the mind. It was a very tough practice and they found it extremely difficult to turn the mind off and maintain the position as observers of their thoughts. They slowly made progress. Their dreams incrementally turned into more lucid experiences and their children seemed to be more *aware* of the dreamer, but there was still a veil blocking verbal communication.

They made love, twice a day at least, unable to resist each other's presence.

They mapped out the city and places Lynn had been to so that they could rule out where not to look. This process was laborious but made the task seem a little less overwhelming for Lynn. Overall, it was a productive three days, good for their souls and encouraging more than anything to both of them. However, Dusty became very worried that if Lynn found any evidence that her child was a victim in a string of serial murders, that she would start seriously considering suicide. He knew that if he lost Lynn, then he would go next, whether or not he believed a serial killer had killed his little girl. If a serial killer *was* in the mix, then Dusty figured his death would save more children's lives; if it was a single crime, well then at least the sick fuck would be brought to justice. In either case when Dusty returned home, he worked harder than ever at both of his jobs: being an attorney and a supernatural detective. He worked harder during the days to finish his work so that he could have more time at nights to focus on his little girl. He tried doing both at the same time frequently, but found that the grief of concentrating on both of them at the same time to be overwhelming. So, he tried to separate them as best as he could.

Dusty found himself going on spurts of productivity. He was like a writer that got on a roll only to hit a brick wall, then he would give up for a while and try to resume life until he found another thread to hold onto. If he hit a wall in either case, he would switch to the other one until something clicked.

In this time period after Nick's death, a couple other people claimed to *think* they remembered possibly dreaming about something else except their children. Nobody could say for certain or give exact details, only that they would get flashbacks throughout the day of images they were certain they must have dreamt the night before. Some people were claiming the meditation was helping and causing more images to flow into their brains, others were not having much luck with anything.

One very interesting development came from Sarah, the librarian from Lawrence, KS. She claimed to have heard her child one night when she was out riding her bike. She wasn't certain and couldn't make out what was said, but felt very strongly that she experienced an auditory communication. As a result of this "incident", the term "supercommunication" was coined in the chat room. All this term referred to was the idea that a member of The Chosen was communicated with during conscious hours. This new topic became of interest to most people and soon, everyone was looking to try and experience supercommunication. Some people took the things they heard on the forum as people's attempt to look for answers—experiencing things that weren't there—but everyone had an open mind and took everything they heard into consideration until something came up that either confirmed or denied new evidence.

Throughout this time period, Dusty had neglected to contact Bruce very often. Bruce always assured Dusty he was fine and to keep trying to help Lynn with her case and focus on his work, but Dusty always felt bad, like he should be spending more time with Bruce and giving him more attention. They saw each other a couple of times and each time, they were always brainstorming and philosophizing about the deeper meaning of their experiences. Time spent with Bruce was always therapeutic for Dusty, he just always had a feeling—a protective one—that he needed to be with Bruce more. That feeling never went away.

Chapter 41

Dusty decided it was time to take Lynn down to Kansas City to meet his parents for the first time; their flight left the first weekend in August. He was very excited for his parents to meet her, but he feared that they might not get to meet the real Lynn. He wasn't sure if she could muster up the strength to mask her depression. There were moments when her true personality shown through, but they were brief. It never lasted a whole day, let alone the four days they were going to spend in Kansas City.

Lynn had settled down a little bit after hearing of Nick's death and the case it solved, but Dusty feared she was still dark on the inside—betraying her true emotions around Dusty so he wouldn't worry or put her on suicide watch. He knew that she knew that if he thought she was suicidal; he would stop at nothing to keep her safe. Although Lynn was still extremely distraught, she kept it together around Dusty and never mentioned suicide. He figured if she *was* going to do it, she wouldn't tell Dusty or give him the opportunity to talk her out of it. She would just be gone, forever.

Dusty wanted to bring something nice for his parents before he left, so he took an afternoon and headed to the Miracle Mile. After finding a very nice framed poster of Arrowhead Stadium in the Nike Store for his parents, signed by Priest Holmes, Dusty went for a cup of coffee and a piece of coffee cake at Starbucks. The line was annoyingly long, but he didn't mind. He hadn't talked to Bruce for a few days, so he took the opportunity to call him. The chatter and overhead jazz music were loud enough to camouflage his conversation and he couldn't wait any longer to get this off his chest.

The phone rang once before he picked it up, "Hey buddy!" Bruce sounded happier than ever. I've been wanting to talk to you."

"Bruce, I have to talk to you about something. I have some bad news."

"What is it?"

"Well, I heard Chicago is sold out of the Velcro shoes. Demand was just too high." Bruce chuckled to himself and smiled. Before he met Dusty, he didn't know how to take getting made fun of. It always hurt. Now, he embraced it.

"Well, that's good because I have made a switch."

Playfully, Dusty responded, "Oh yeah? And what's that?"

"Teva sandals. They are quite comfy and affordable."

"Uh, they still have Velcro."

"Well, shit. It just so happens I don't care. Velcro is fucking cool."

"You're right buddy. Anything Bruce Crippen does is cool in my book. How ya been?" Bruce was doing worse than normal. Depression, a condition he struggled with through High School, was starting to creep back into his life. He tried relentlessly to solve his case and help the rest of The Chosen. He wanted so bad to be the hero, the one that could help all of these people feel good again, but he was failing.

"I've never been better."

"Awesome man. Any luck with your kid? Any new clues?" The person in front of him stepped up to the counter and ordered a Grande Vanilla Latte.

"No, no. Not yet, but I'm hopeful! I'm willing to do…" Bruce paused for what seemed like an eternity to Dusty before reluctantly responding, "Whatever it takes." Dusty let these words soak in as he contemplated what all Bruce could mean by, *whatever it takes*. How about you?"

Dusty wanted so bad to believe that he had some sort of influence on the outcome of things, but it felt like a pipe dream sometimes. He was normally very optimistic, but today his pessimism got the best of him, "I'm okay. Been better. Frustrated a little from work and that I don't seem to be making any headway on my case." Dusty looked around him casually. Once confident that no one was paying attention to him, he proceeded quietly, "How can I, one man, possibly do enough to change the outcome of something so, supernatural? So… intergalactic? So… I don't know, Omnipresent?" It was his turn in line. He stepped up and ordered a Grande

Mocha from a 15-year-old, gothic looking girl with a pierced nose, "I just wonder if I'm on the right path. Should I become a monk? Shouldn't I be trying to attain some sort of oneness with the universe or something? I mean how else can I even have a chance?"

"Dusty, what do you think you are doing? Every time you go to sleep and dream, you *are* one with the universe. The supernatural powers that underlie our physical presence and mental cognizance are rendering you one with the universe every time you sleep. They take what is inside your brain and plug it into theirs every night. Or rather, it's more likely *It* is plugging its brain into you. You are the whole reason we are all together and working on this. You cannot discount that. Without you, these kids wouldn't even have a chance. You *are* making a difference. Do not give up faith. Do not give up hope."

This boosted Dusty's morale a little bit, enough to get the back of his head tingling. He collected the change from the cashier and walked to a nearby standing table. He stood and thought for a minute, staring at a mother trying to wrangle her two twin boys while ordering her morning coffee and pastry. "Dusty? Hey I have something to tell you." Bruce made sure he was still there.

"Bruce, do you think I can save Lynn?"

"Are you kidding me? I have no question in my mind. Love never fails. From the first time I met you, I could see the look in your eyes when you looked at her. Love like that always wins. It has to."

"But you don't understand. It's bad. Like, really bad. I had to threaten that if she did it, that I would too. I finally landed on a deal that both of us would do it together if either one of us saw another kid."

"Oh... well. Fuck Dusty. Why would you do that?"

"What the hell else was I supposed to do? I had no choice. Nothing."

"Yeah, but, that's extreme man."

"Yeah, some real Romeo and Juliet shit, huh?"

"You love her that much, huh?"

"Yeah, yeah man. I do."

"Well, then you will figure it out. We will. Together. I promise you, we will."

"I hope you are right Bruce."

"I am. I got your back. Whatever it takes."

"Whatever it takes."

"Keep your head up kid. There's no one better than you. Not a single person on this planet. I love you man."

"Love you too, buddy. Thank you. Thank you for everything."

"Don't mention it. Catch you on the flipside brother."

"Alright Bruce, I'll talk to you soon. I'll call you when I get back in town. Oh, hey, what were you going to tell me?"

"Oh, well, never mind. I'll tell you later."

"Are you sure?"

"Yeah, I'm sure. Take care of that sweet lady of yours."

"Will do bud."

"Ok. Bye Dusty."

"Bye."

Dusty sat alone for a few minutes, nibbling on his coffee cake. Something felt very strange to him, but he didn't know what it was. Something about the whole situation. Lynn, the children, Bruce… He couldn't place his sentiments. Soon, very soon, he would know exactly what it was.

Chapter 42

Bruce lived alone in his North Chicago apartment. His job as a computer programmer provided him with a living, but he had next to no social life. He spent most of his free time developing computer software that he hoped to sell someday. Holidays were insignificant because he was an only child with deceased parents. He was married once, but divorced after two years without having children. As a 37-year-old man, he was lonely and introverted.

His association with The Chosen had given him life. Nobody had ever made him feel as important as Dusty had and he loved him dearly. Recently, his ability to cope with his dreams was diminishing. With every day, he believed more and more that death freed the children from their suffering. After investigating Doris and Nick's death thoroughly with Dusty, Lynn and Lana, he was certain that dying was a sure solution to liberating the children. He had no way of proving it though. Furthermore, there was absolutely no evidence that dying on purpose would solve anything. It was the most heavily disputed topic in the forums and the group was split about 50/50. Finally, he decided there was only one way to find out, especially after he started seeing a second child.

It was a beautiful August Day in Chicago. The sunset was breathtaking as it landed on top of the jagged skyline. Bruce took a look at it over his shoulder as he sat at his desk in his apartment. He took a deep breath and finished the last strokes of his pen, folded the letter and stuck it inside his coat pocket. He sported his best suit. The gun his great, great grandfather had owned was a Colt revolver that supposedly was used by the Army in

Custer's Last Stand. It had been passed all the way down to him and looked to be in near mint condition. It had not been fired since the late 1920s. Bruce figured that if it misfired, then perhaps it was a sign that he was supposed to keep on living. The case held one bullet, which he placed into the revolver. Tears dripped down his face as he placed the long barrel into his mouth. He closed his eyes and thought of Dusty.

When they found the body, the investigator called the number on the outside fold of the letter. Dusty received the phone call while he was in Kansas City visiting his parents with Lynn. An apathetic sergeant explained to Dusty the situation. Dusty stood in awe outside of his parents' house in a light rain, watching his mother talk to Lynn thorough the window. The raindrops landing on his face were as cold as the message coming through his phone's speaker. He heard the first couple of sentences, then the rest became mumbled nonsense. He gazed into the rain hitting the maple tree in his parents' front yard. He remembered climbing to the very top as a kid, exhilarated at the thought of conquering the massive tree. Images of his friendship with Bruce flooded his mind; his glasses, his fuzzy hair, his mousey laugh, his warm heart. He recalled the last conversation he had with Bruce. He remembered how positive and uplifting he was… it must have all been a front for Dusty's sake. Tears started flowing down his cheeks as he heard the officer's last words come through, giving him his contact information. Dusty grimly and mechanically thanked him for the call and hung up the phone. His heart was broken.

He sobbed for 15 minutes outside on the porch. Lynn eventually came out to see what was keeping him so long. He was unable to hide the news or his sorrow from her. What was he going to do now? Dusty relied so heavily on Bruce for morale and collaboration. *How could he do this to me? That asshole!!* Dusty felt as if he would never be the same.

"I failed him, Lynn!" he uttered through his trembling lips as she caressed his head on her shoulder. "I should have been there more for him!"

"Oh, honey. Don't do that to yourself. He loved you. You were the best thing that ever happened to him. This is not on you. You have to know that."

"I couldn't find the answer. I knew something was up with him the last time we talked; I just couldn't figure it out. Something had to happen to him for him to do this."

"His heart was so big babe. He probably couldn't bear not protecting any unknown victims. He was trying to do the right thing, in his mind."

"He was being selfish. A selfish asshole. How could he leave us here alone to deal with this? He took the easy way out…" Dusty felt somewhat ashamed deep down inside for uttering those words, but at the moment that's how he felt and didn't care to apply any filters. Lynn had nothing else to say and decided it was best to leave it alone.

Dusty finished his trip with his family as happily as he could, but he just wasn't the same. His parents absolutely loved Lynn. He couldn't have been prouder of how she took the effort to relate to his somewhat-over-the-top mother. Aside from the horrible news, Dusty's heart was so full upon seeing how his father looked at Lynn. He was enamored as well. His parents had never taken a liking to any of his other girlfriends, at least not like this. It was further evidence she was the one and furthered the tumult he experienced in his brain regarding their children. He had to figure it out. He had to make it work. He wanted this love to live on.

Two days later, once back in Chicago, Dusty picked up a bag at the police station that had been left for him. In it were reams of paper and three ring binders. There was also the letter. He went outside the station and found a bench to sit on. His hands trembled as he opened the letter. Before he could start, he began sobbing again. He tucked his head between his knees and wept for several minutes. When he regained composure, he began to read Bruce's suicide letter:

Dear Dusty,

As you know, the last couple years have been the hardest, most excruciating in my life. I was confused, scared, depressed and thought I was going crazy. When you came into my life, I had no real friends, next to no family and no children of my own. My only hope for a child was crushed when I got divorced. I had considered adopting, but I was terrified that I wouldn't be a good father. When I started seeing a child in my dreams, I thought it represented the guilt deep down inside for never taking the chance. As time went on, I saw how bad Trevor was suffering and I knew it had to be something more. My days were filled with anxiety, fear, depression and I was scared I was going insane. Then I found you.

You gave hope for an answer. The group took me in—accepted me for who I was. They became like family to me. For the first time in a long time, I felt important. My child gave me purpose and I grew to love him as if he was my own. He was my constant companion and I finally knew what it felt like to be a father—to know what it's like to live for someone else. I finally knew what it was like to have a friend, too. My whole life I have been treated like shit by guys like you. After a while, I just stopped trying to make friends, but you renewed my faith in humanity. You made me feel like a real person and the day you asked me to sit at your table was one of the best days of my life. You are such a good person, Dusty. I want you and Lynn to make it out of this alive and happy more than anything in this world. That's one reason why I had to do this.

Trevor is already gone and I can't bring him back. All I can hope to bring is justice, but so far, I have not even been able to do that. You know more than anyone how hard I have tried and although I think that I may succeed if I had more time, unfortunately time is not something we can afford. Every day we waste, more children are in danger. Every day we are alive, we risk stealing from the innocent children of the world who are helpless against the decrepit, evil villains. Nothing in this world is more important than giving those days back, but how can we do that if we don't have answers? Plus, I never had the heart to tell you, but I did start seeing Trevor's brother a couple days ago. I wanted to tell you, but I didn't have the heart to bring you more grief. So now I 100% know that two kids are dead at the hands of some creep, and I don't want to wait to see more. That is why I had to do this. It breaks my heart that you are reading this letter, but hopefully you will understand. If my life catches the bad guy, then we know that if all else fails, we have an ace in the hole to save children—our lives.

After Doris died and the murderer of her child was caught, we knew we were onto something. Then, Nick died and we spent days tracking down that story. We matched a description of his child almost to a 'T'. At that point, we didn't want to believe it, but we knew we had found at least one way to help our kids: dying. The only thing we weren't sure of was if suicide rendered the same results as dying accidentally. If suicide doesn't work because God, or whatever, sends me to hell for trying to save the lives of little children, well then I guess I'll save the lives of any of The Chosen who ever thought about suicide. The way I look at it, I was about to pull the trigger anyway before I found you. I had contemplated suicide dozens of times and was thinking about it almost every day. I was lonely, Dusty. So lonely. And I was hurting so bad inside. My life was black and void of light. You gave my life an extension... a reason to be happy... a chance to live for once. Now is my time to give back. It's what I was always meant to do.

The forum has been talking about whether suicide will catch the killers for months, but nobody wants to take the chance. I don't think anybody WANTS to die, but especially not if they don't even know if their sacrifice will bring justice. That's what I can give to the group. I can at least answer that question. Someone has to, because what if that IS the only way? Then could we live with ourselves knowing that our being alive is possibly putting children in danger? I can't. Not anymore.

In regards to my other child, it was unlike any of the other reports of seeing multiples, so I was never sure. The image was fuzzy—never clear. I think it was a boy, but I'm not sure. He was never in sight for more than a few seconds at a time. I should have told you before this, I'm sorry. But even if what I am seeing isn't another child, the thought that the killer could kill again is sucking every ounce of enjoyment out of my life. I'm not only doing this for the group, but I'm selfishly doing this for me. I realize that if this works, I may set off a chain reaction, but that is why you are so important. It will be up to you to reveal this to the group when and if the time comes. I know you feel close to an answer, but what if it never comes? Then it is our responsibility to tell the group. We can't make that decision for them. Everyone must be given the chance to control their own destiny and we have the responsibility to save these children, WHATEVER the cost. I trust you will pull the plug at the appropriate time, if needed. Hopefully, that's never.

I have been thinking about this for a while, but when Lynn found out who her girl was, that's when I knew it was time for me to act. And who knows, what if I can help you from the other side? What if I am able to be your undercover man? Then maybe I can help you find answers where you couldn't before, or anyone in The Chosen for that matter. We also both know that Lynn is deteriorating and that her heart hurts for her children. You told me she has even talked about sacrificing herself to test the suicide theory. I couldn't sit and watch that happen. I see what you two have and it is rare. You both deserve a chance at love and children more than ANYONE. My chance came and went and I can't change that now. All I can hope to do is try to help make sure that you get your chance. If it works, then at least everyone knows they have it as a last resort. If it doesn't work, then you won't have to worry about Lynn killing herself for no reason. But if it works AND I'm able to help you somehow, then everyone wins.

*If Trevor's murderer is caught soon after my death, then you will not only know without a doubt that our sacrifice can end their suffering, but you will have an abundance of data at your fingertips. Even if I can't come through and give you clues, maybe you can piece my puzzle together by working backwards. Unlike Nick and Doris, you have a lot of data to work with now. I left you all the work I did in testing our theories. All you need to do is connect the dots—find out **how** we can help them on this side of life. My death and the arrest of the killer will give you more answers and clues, I'm sure of it, and if there is anyway while I'm on the other side to help you, I will. Then it will be up to you to figure out a solution before Lynn, or anyone else, takes matters into their own hands. I'm buying you time, Dusty. I know you are smart enough to figure it out. I have faith in you.*

Finally, I just want you to know I died a happy man. As hard as the last years of my life have been, I truly felt joy when I was around you. In the group I found a place; in my child I found purpose; in you I found a true friend. For that, I'm eternally grateful. I love you Dusty. You are the brother, the father, the son and the friend I never had. I hope you and Lynn live a long and happy life with lots of beautiful children! Know I will always be looking down upon you, smiling. Take care my friend and help me give the children the justice they deserve.

Forever with Love,
Bruce

Dusty sat on the bench and wept for five minutes straight with his head between his knees. He had never in his life felt so much grief.

Chapter 43

Dusty walked into the small funeral home located in a run-down commercial district on Chicago's Eastside. Bruce had no known surviving relatives. The city used the place to bury the homeless and indigent. The building shared a wall with a thrift store on one side and a Laundromat on the other. Fluorescent lights flickered above, contributing to the black, depressing atmosphere. Dusty signed the guest book in the small foyer. His was the only signature. An attendant led Dusty into the viewing room, which resembled an inner-city church. There were about ten rows of empty metal folding chairs divided by a center aisle. Gray tile squares, scuffed and chipped from years of wear covered the floor. A preacher's pulpit stood on a raised wooden, platform at the front of the room. Bruce's casket rested on a table between the front row of chairs and the platform. The casket was open from waist up.

Dusty had considered a more elaborate funeral, but given Bruce's minimalist lifestyle and intentional avoidance of pretentious behaviors, Dusty saw this fitting. In fact, in a passing comment Bruce had even said to Dusty he wouldn't mind being buried in the back lot, so Dusty almost felt it would be disrespectful to arrange anything but the most modest of funerals.

Dusty moved slowly to the casket. Bruce looked waxen and pale, except for the bright pink painted lips. Bruce's hair was slicked back. He looked like a slumbering silent movie star. The layers of make-up hardly masked a deep crease, which traveled up the left side of Bruce's face from the jaw to the top of his skull, leaving only half of an ear in its path. And

271

those black, plastic frame pop-bottle glasses magnified Bruce's eyelids grotesquely.

Dusty reached down and stroked his dead friend's forehead. He began sobbing, "I love you, Bruce." The tears dropped onto Bruce's frozen cheek. "I'm proud of you, buddy. You go get that asshole. You get him, Bruce!" Dusty pulled glasses from Bruce's face, folded them and put them in the inner pocket of his own jacket. "You won't need these anymore, buddy."

Dusty heard chairs shuffling behind him and turned to see members of The Chosen filing into the room. Dusty was moved deeply. Bruce had family after all. Lana and Lynn were coming down the center aisle. When they reached Dusty, the three of them embraced tightly and wept. By the end of the service, around 20 people had come, mostly people Bruce had worked with over the years and a few distant relatives. This made Dusty feel better, much better, to know that there were others that cared for Bruce.

A week later, Dusty got a call from a man named Eric from Bank of the Midwest.

"Mr. Burch?"

"Yes, this is him," he replied emotionless, staring at his computer screen. He was sitting in his office preparing a motion to file in the Draper Case concerning the results of some of the testing that had been done on the fire dummies. He was trying to get the evidence repealed.

"I'm just calling to collect your banking information so we can complete a wire transfer from a Mr., uhh… Bruce Crippen."

Dusty's head shot up and his eyebrows furrowed as he responded, "Bruce Crippen? But he's… dead. There must be some kind of mistake."

"Well sir, it looks like this is from a trust. And it also looks like this was ordered upon death. In other words, Mr. Burch, it was in his will. Did you know about this, sir?"

"No. I had no idea," Dusty was in shock and sat in his office, staring at the floor. "How much?"

"Looks like it's just under $4 million, sir." Dusty's head started whirling around in circles. After several more questions, making sure this wasn't a hoax and that the call really was meant for him, he finally gave in and gave Eric the information he needed and quickly ended the conversation so that he could expunge the river of tears and emotion that had been mounting behind his forehead the entire conversation. He sat in his office, alone, for close to an hour and cried. Before this last month, Dusty had not cried in years. Now, he had cried more in the last week than he had in the last five or ten years. He just couldn't get it together. Losing Bruce hit him hard, and this act of generosity, even in death, prolonged Dusty's propensity to shed tears already. It was all just too much for Dusty Burch.

....

For two weeks, Dusty looked through every Chicago newspaper, watched every news channel, read every blog, called every jail—everything he could think of. For two weeks, he found nothing. It seemed to Dusty like it was the most crime free, squeaky clean, uneventful two-week period in the history of Chicago; there wasn't even as much as a kitten being rescued from the trees. Community service projects, high school sports teams, White Sox and Cubs recruiting prospects, Bulls' trading trends, Bears' playoff outlook, used car ads, job postings, stock performances and charity events littered the news—nothing about criminals being caught.

Dusty knew the names of every news anchor on every news station, the names of most of the column writers of the papers and became familiar with many of the funeral home directors in the area. He obsessively called each funeral home to inquire about services being held and read the obituaries until his eyes hurt. The thought of Bruce committing suicide for no reason at all drove Dusty nearly mad. Bruce had become one of the best friends Dusty had ever had and seeing him go was very hard on him. There had to be an answer.

At work, Dusty scanned the internet between calls and meetings. During hearings and depositions, he found himself doodling and daydreaming. He wasn't *inept* at his job, in fact he was very involved, but every minute of every day was influenced by his subconscious urging him to solve Bruce's riddle. He fought off the surging, conscious waves of grief and remorse every minute in order to concentrate on his career, but he was slowly becoming apathetic. He *wanted* to do well and prove himself, but he didn't *need* to anymore. Something much more important was at the forefront of his brain, something much more significant than upgrading his status at SC&R.

Lynn too was very affected by Bruce's death. She was starting to feel despondent. Every time she thought she might have a lead on her case, it fell short. Now that she thought she knew little girl's identity; the scenario became extremely personal and emotionally draining for her. It was as if she had known the little girl; she became attached almost as a mother would be. She scoured the city for signs of Amber's death, visiting hundreds of places looking for signs of supercommunication, many times with Richard's aid, but came up empty at every turn.

Lynn's schooling was starting to suffer. Instead of making straight A's, she let a couple B's and a C's creep in. Dusty was the only thing that kept her sane. She called him every night and talked for up to two hours. It was a challenge for Dusty to keep the conversation casual. He was obsessed with solving Bruce's riddle because he thought that somehow it would help him solve Lynn's. He hoped she would be able to find some signs so when he went back, he had something to work with, but even with Richard's help she had been unsuccessful. So, his phone conversations often were hours of brainstorming places she had been to, people she had met, things she had done. He hated seeing Lynn in such pain, but felt that he couldn't leave Chicago until Bruce's case was closed. She was planning to come back to Chicago in another week.

Dusty also spent a lot of time sorting through the boxes of materials that Bruce had left him. Notebook upon notebook was filled with information on the last ten years of Bruce's life: places he had eaten, places he had driven, bathrooms he had used, gas stations he had refueled at, hotels he had stayed at, stores he shopped at, people he interacted with (a fairly short list)... Bruce pretty much made a comprehensive list of his entire past 10 years. Dusty looked for patterns—any patterns. He tried to pattern Bruce's eating habits and had some success. For instance, Bruce almost always ate Chinese food on Monday. He would also only allow himself fast food, like McDonald's, no more than once a week, usually on a Thursday. Tuesday's and Wednesday's, he ate almost exclusively at a sandwich shop two blocks away from his work. Friday was always pizza. Bruce was an interesting guy and had some very quirky tendencies, but Dusty didn't know which ones, if any, would give him any clues.

Eventually, 18 days after Bruce's death, Dusty saw something on the news during his morning coffee that snagged his interest. It was a brief, 20-

second clip that referred to a strange accident where a water main busted in Grosse Pointe—the town Bruce was from. The strange part of the story was that during the repair, the water company uncovered strange remains while excavating the cement. The construction worker was unsure, but speculated that a dog had fallen in the cement as it was curing, encasing it in a sarcophagus of rock and gravel. Just to be safe, he called the cops to look at it. A forensic team excavated the area with expert tools and immaculate detail. Only a small part of the skull had been uncovered initially, but that evening a forensic team uncovered what appeared to be a human skull. The whole scene flooded with news reporters and cameras as if it were the excavation of King Tut's tomb. Dusty abhorred the media and its attention to gruesome details, but he couldn't help himself. He headed there the next day over lunch.

The drive to Grosse Pointe would have taken longer than a subway and Dusty was pressed for time. He needed to be back by 2:00 for a deposition of Brian's Uncle. Dusty needed him for a character witness to help prove that Brian's dad was a deadbeat. Fortunately for Dusty, Brian's Uncle wasn't too fond of his brother and Dusty thought he could get some good ammunition to reinforce the "deadbeat, drunk dad" theory, taking blame away from Reston and reassigning it to the dad. He hated the subway because of all the homeless and criminals it attracted, but he decided to bite the bullet and save himself about a half hour each way.

Dusty bought a ticket from an African American gal who had a pretty face, but looked like she may have been a recovering drug addict due to the blackish color of a few of her front teeth. The fee was $14.50. He took the change he got and bought a brat loaded with sauerkraut from a greasy looking, overweight cart worker. He left him the extra .50 and thought to himself that the brat guy should use it to invest in some better sauerkraut.

The train was crowded, but not overly crowded, especially for it being lunchtime. He pulled out a book he had been reading called "The Alchemist" and was able to read a few chapters on the ride. The account of the main character's quest to find a lost treasure reminded him so much of his journey and it inspired him to keep the course. It never failed that when in need of inspiration, all he needed to do was read and either by chance or by the grace of God, he would find words that seemed to speak to him directly. It amazed him how the universe often coordinated positive encounters in times of need. It's why he kept reading after college, unlike many of his peers who never picked up a book again.

When he got off the subway, he only had to walk a couple of blocks to the excavation site. He couldn't believe he had actually turned into one of the people he always mocked, filling their daily lives with the drama of other people. He reminded himself that maybe he shouldn't be so judgmental the next time he saw people gawking at a car wreck.

I just have to know if this is one of Bruce's boys. I can't sit in my office all day with this on my mind. Is it just a skull, or a whole body? There's no way this is a coincidence.

The whole time Dusty was there watching the forensic crew, he talked to himself. He felt as if he were in a dream of his own… an episode of the "Twilight Zone". The CSI experts intrigued him. The tools and methods they were using were just like TV. There was crime scene tape around the entire area and cops with badges around their neck. He spotted a tall guy in khakis that he thought was probably the sergeant giving orders to the peons. Assistants were carrying cups of coffee back and forth and talking to the press. The forensic teams were neatly and methodically working to unveil the evidence, taking careful strokes with their scalpels and picks not to damage any evidence.

They had barely uncovered anything new when Dusty looked at his watch and saw that it was 1:15. He was tempted to call Marilyn and have her reschedule the deposition, but this guy had been hard to get a hold of. It took Dusty six months to lock down a date to take the depo. So reluctantly, he walked back to the station, this time buying a large cup of chocolate chip cookie dough Dip 'N Dots before boarding, which he ate so fast on the train that he gave himself a brain freeze.

The next three days he watched the news carefully. On the third day, Dusty saw a story on the news about the cement sarcophagus. A pretty blonde reporter in a red dress spoke fantastically about the remains of a little boy that had finally been removed from the cement. She tried hard to sound remorseful, but she was failing miserably. She stated that the body uncovered was believed to be a boy by the name of Allen DeGerald… That's all he got. He turned it off after the first name he heard wasn't "Trevor" or "Holmes".

Chapter 44

It just didn't make sense to Dusty. None of it. He just knew that *this* story was going to be IT—what he'd been waiting for—proof that Bruce had not died for nothing. Seeing that reporter in her blood red dress, mutter the wrong fucking words sent Dusty into a mad frenzy. It had been almost a month since Bruce's death and there was still no sign of the case being solved. As he sat staring at his computer, Dusty mumbled to himself, "Why? Why can't one thing… one thing be easy?!" He suddenly became enraged and felt a jet of adrenaline pump in his veins and inject itself into his decision-making faculties. He stood up in a fit of anger and unleashed on the first inanimate object he saw, which happened to be his couch. He flipped it over on its back and kicked it several times before his big toe hit a wooden crossbeam on the other side of it. This exacerbated his rage and he tore the cushions off, hurling them across his living room, knocking his framed diplomas off the wall. His coffee table was next, which he lifted above his head and threw across his living room where it smacked his fireplace and broke. Then he stood there, breathing heavily, contemplating what he had just done. "I never liked that fucking table anyway."

Shortly after his unraveling, he started to feel foolish for not listening to the whole news piece. *What if I had heard wrong? Or what if Allen wasn't really his name?* Hope started flooding back into his brain and overtaking his anger as the rising sun melts away an early fall frost. He really couldn't afford to be mad and he knew it. He had to get back on track. He got on the internet and searched for the story, which he quickly found. The news article he read explained that the cement pad had indeed uncovered a little boy's body, identified by dental records. The boy had been missing for two years without a trace, last seen riding his bicycle in his neighborhood. There were currently no suspects yet, but the remains were diligently being scanned for forensic evidence. Dusty pondered to himself. He wasn't prepared for such a twist. He had a strange feeling upon reading this, but could not put his finger on why.

Dusty again became outraged once again, especially at the "No suspects" part. Not only was he disgusted at the thought of a new, different child getting hurt, but it meant that he would have to wait still for Bruce to come through on the other side. The even worse alternative was that Bruce's sacrifice had not rendered itself holy in the eyes of the Great Beholder. This notion was the true genesis of Dusty's rage. If in fact it were true, then how could there be a God so cruel that it would not forgive the sin of suicide even for the act of saving the lives of children? He did not want to live in such a Universe.

In the following hours, Dusty sat on his couch, alone, and drank a six-pack of Miller Lite. He didn't want to talk to anyone or be around anyone, so he turned his phone on silent and turned on some old episodes of *The Three Stooges*. He occasionally faintly chuckled, but mostly sat there staring blankly at the TV, finishing off a beer about every 15 minutes or so. He snacked on a giant bag of Chex Mix and when it was gone and the beer was drunk, he fell asleep on his recliner.

When he woke up the next morning, he heard his phone vibrating on the table beside him. He had woken back up at 5:00 and to pee and decided he had better turn it back on in case Lynn tried to called him. It was Lynn. He looked at the clock and saw 9:15 am. He let the phone ring out so he didn't have to think of a reason why he sounded so groggy at 9:15. He was also supposed to be at work over an hour ago. "Fuck…" He rubbed his eyes and got off the couch. He dragged himself into his room, undressed and got into the shower. As he stood there with the warm water on his face, he tried to remember if he had dreamt of her the night before. He must have drunk enough beer because for the moment, he couldn't recall. He figured even if he had, it was all starting to run together so much that he couldn't remember if he was remembering last night's dream or nights past. His head hurt too much to think about it and he shifted his thoughts to how little water he had drank the day before. He felt like he was in college again and had got too drunk the night before and woke up late for class, except in this case he might have actually cared less. A lot less.

On the way to work he called Lynn back and explained the situation to her. She was a little more than pissed off at him when he told her he put his phone on silent and passed out. Her mind wasn't in the condition to handle such ambiguity. It wasn't like Dusty to not call her or be able to be reached on any given morning and she was worried sick all night. He just sat on the phone while she spewed and vented all her frustrations, calling him everything from a "selfish asshole" to a "fucking ignorant prick". He was strangely entertained since this was the first time, he had ever heard her go off on him so ferociously and impressed at her creative usage of the word "fuck". He decided against telling her this though and sat on the other end of the line instead, smiling.

"Honey, for the last time, I'm sorry. I'm so sorry. I was so upset and so just… discouraged and I… I'm just sorry. It'll never happen again. I promise. I'll never make you worry like that again."

"You better not or I will box the shit out of you! Fucker…"

It was her first sign of relenting, (though she screamed it at the top of her lungs), but even through all the vivacious tones in her voice, he was able to identify the downward slope of her rant. As he walked into work, he told her he would call her at lunchtime and told her he loved her. A quick "Bye," was all he got in return.

Not five minutes after he sat in his office, Marilyn paged him and told him Ron Davis was on the other line, "Tell him I'll call him back. Or actually, tell him I won't… better yet, tell him to go to hell."

"I wish you weren't kidding. I would gladly, but I don't think Clifford and Ruth would be too happy about that." Marilyn detested Davis almost as much as Dusty did. "This is the fourth time he called though; I don't think he is going to stop."

Dusty looked at the postcard of Winter Park on his computer and wished he were there on top of one of those mountains. Reluctantly he answered, "Put him through." Dusty had a hunch Davis was calling about the Judge's ruling on the mannequin burning.

"Burch, I want to know just how in the holy fuck these assholes are going to be allowed to show video of mannequins catching on fire? Being lit by our lighters? You got an answer for me on that one that won't make me think you are a complete idiot?"

Dusty was still staring at the mountaintop, "Ron, I'm not the judge. If you would like an explanation, maybe you can call him. I filed every motion known to man. There is literally nothing else I, Stanley, Ruth the ghost of Clifford, or God could have done to change his mind. Please don't take it out on me, I'm not exactly having the best day." As soon as the words came out of his mouth, he wished he wouldn't have said them.

"*You're* having a bad day? Really? I'm sorry, I didn't realize you were the one who was being sued for millions of dollars. In fact, you are getting paid a ridiculous amount of Goddamn money to see to it that I don't have to pay anyone a fucking dime! How in the hell are we supposed to do that if the jury gets to see those people torch little boy mannequins? Please tell me that."

Dusty might usually have retorted with some profanity of his own, but he was getting cussed out for the second time in an hour and for the second time he was amused, "Yeah, that's definitely not gonna help our case, Ron."

"Is this fucking funny to you?"

"No, not at all," his response didn't quite convince Ron.

"I swear to God Burch if we lose this case, I'll make sure you never practice law at this firm again. If you think I'm joking then you don't know who you're dealing with pal."

"I'll be sure to make a note of that, Davis." Dusty heard a click and then silence. Marilyn walked in a few seconds later.

"How did that go?"

"Wonderful…"

Dusty said this in such a way Marilyn thought he was joking, but couldn't tell for sure, "Really?"

"No. About what you would expect. He is pissed about the mannequins. He cussed me out, degraded me, pointed out my incompetence and threatened my livelihood. Nothing big." Dusty picked up his cup of coffee and took a sip. He realized it was cold, but he didn't care and chugged the last few gulps.

"Yeah, well you should know that you are handling him as well as anyone possibly could."

"It's probably because I don't care."

"Yes, you do. Don't say that," she came and sat down in his clients' chair like she had a thousand times before.

"I'm honestly not sure anymore, Marilyn. It used to be the most important thing in the world to me, now I just feel like it's the exact opposite of my lot in life. I should be trying to figure out a way to help Brian, not hurt him," Dusty put his face in his hands and rested his elbows on the desk

"Just finish out this case. You are already too deep to back out. I mean it's one thing to switch career paths, but another to bail out in the middle of a huge case. It could tarnish your career, forever."

Dusty, half sarcastically, half serious, replied, "Maybe I want it to be tarnished. Maybe I should just go be a trash man. I hear they make good money…"

Marilyn responded in her motherly tone, "Dusty, just because you are down in the dumps doesn't mean you should throw away everything you've worked for. You are good at what you do. Very good. If after this case you want to switch over to the Plaintiff side, then do it. But you have to finish this out, as much as I hate to say it. You are nearing the end. Trial is a month away."

Despondent, Dusty capitulated, "I know. I know." The two sat in silence for a moment before Marilyn changed the subject.

"Well, did you hear about the little boy they found in the cement?"

"Yeah. I did."

"Is he one of your… groups'?"

"Not that I can find yet."

"I feel so bad for the mother. The officials are thinking that it might have been the stepfather. The strange thing is that this guy also had a previous marriage where *two* boys went missing in a supposed boating accident on Lake Michigan. So, I guess once they found this out, he became the prime suspect since he was involved in two marriages where children went missing."

It took a minute for Dusty to process the words. He heard her, but wasn't really listening at first. Then all the sudden the words *Lake Michigan* blew up in his brain, "Boating accident? Like they Drowned in Lake Michigan? Where did you hear that?"

"Well, it's been all over the news this morning. I just happened to turn it on a few minutes ago and they had an update. I hope that guy rots in jail for the rest of his life… and makes a lot of new boyfriends, too. You would think the second wife would have been suspicious, but maybe she didn't know about the other marriage or the other boys missing, or maybe it was just too hard to believe."

Flashbacks of one of Dusty's conversations with Bruce flew through his brain regarding Trevor Holmes and his brother drowning on Lake Michigan. He remembered discussing "foul play" with Bruce and the difficulty of proving it. Dusty became animated, surprising Marilyn, "Marilyn! Oh my God! Do you know what this means? Bruce did it!"

"Did what?"

"He caught the killer!"

"What do you mean? How?"

"He showed them another body! Bruce told me before he died, he thought he found the kid he was seeing. Said it was a case where two boys supposedly drowned on Lake Michigan after the father and them were caught in a storm. The father survived. Then he said he started seeing a second kid in his suicide letter to me. I assumed he was probably just starting to see Trevor's brother, the boy he thought he was seeing, but maybe it could have been this kid that was just found. Or maybe it *was* the brother and he just hadn't started seeing the third one yet, or… oh my God I hope there aren't anymore." Dusty's face tremored at this thought.

"I still don't understand," Marilyn was trying, but this was all a lot to take in.

"Okay, he said he found his boy in the news that he had been dreaming about, Trevor, but that the story said he drowned on the lake in an accident, the storm caught the father off guard and the boys were thrown overboard and he couldn't save them. Bruce wasn't seeing the brother though at first, and we couldn't figure it out. We couldn't figure out why he would be seeing the boy if no murder was involved; something seemed very fishy."

"Why would he see Trevor, but not the brother if there was foul play?"

"That was one of our questions. Well, in Bruce's suicide letter, he told me he was starting to see another kid but that it was blurry. That's the first I heard he was seeing a second kid. I don't think he wanted to give away to me he was planning on committing suicide. When I first heard of the boy in the cement, I was hopeful Bruce had come through on the other side, but skeptical because Bruce's boy or boys had supposedly drowned. My skepticism was strengthened when I heard the boy's name in the cement wasn't Trevor and didn't have the last name Holmes. Yeah it could have been the brother but I thought the likelihood of that was very low without the last names matching. I kind of freaked out in my house and tore up my living room, not thinking about any other possibilities, like this being a third unseen child. But now, I know it had to be Bruce! Bruce had to have done it! If the boys from the lake and the one in the cement are connected, Bruce did what he could to nail the bastard. He showed them another missing body!"

"How could he do that?"

"I don't know for sure. He had to have done something to cause that water main to break. I don't know how all this stuff works yet. I don't know the rules. I mean it seems like he would have to be allowed some serious physical interaction with this plane of existence, but who knows, maybe it was just one bolt he had to get loose."

"Oh my God." Marilyn put her hands in her face and choked back the tears. "So, you think this case is solved and a murderer is caught?"

"I hope so. I mean they are going to have to tag him with more concrete evidence. The fact that he was the stepdad in two marriages where kids went missing isn't enough."

"Well, certainly there is something," Marilyn said hopefully.

"Let's hope. Now I just gotta find out why Trevor chose Bruce, because there is no way Bruce was close to that boat. He hated the water. And from what I could find, he lived nowhere close to those people. What the hell is going on?"

....

Two weeks later, the stepdad, Chuck Smith, confessed to the murder of all three of the boys. As it turns out, he never took the boys fishing. He waited until his wife was out of town and told her he was taking them on a fishing trip. Instead, he tied them up and buried them alive in a pad of cement. Chuck's framing of the accidental drowning was so dramatic that no one even questioned it. He waited for a big storm in the forecast and drove directly into the middle of it the morning after he buried the bodies. The storm was so violent that he was thrown overboard, (or jumped), and had to be rescued by the coast guard by helicopter, made aware by a "mayday" radio transmission Chuck sent just as the storm overtook him. They had to resuscitate him twice and he nearly died. For two weeks authorities searched for the bodies of the boys, but obviously never found them.

Chuck worked for a construction company and drove the cement mixer so he had access to any site and amount of cement he needed at any time. He waited until there was a job that needed one last pour and offered to take care of it himself. This job was a re-pour of a driveway... a driveway that was a few miles away from Bruce's apartment complex. Dusty hadn't figured it out yet, but Bruce must have gotten close to that spot at some point.

As far as the third child, Allen, Chuck masterfully planned his disappearance as well. He conjured up an alibi putting him at work on a poor. He only needed to be away for 15 to 20 minutes to carry out his plan, which his partner didn't notice. This job required two men, and just before Chuck's partner hit the button to dump the load from the truck, Chuck slipped the body in the pit from the trunk of his car which he had strategically positioned to block any view from the street.

Chuck was sentenced to death. Upon hours of interrogation by detectives, it was surmised that Chuck's abusive stepdad had caused tremendous scars to form in his mind, ones that were only worsened when he found out his first wife was cheating on him and felt like he could never get her full love and attention. He attributed this to the two boys and blamed them. It made a killer of him and he methodically planned out his next victim. Thanks to Bruce, it was his last.

Chapter 45

The next weekend Lynn returned to Chicago. Dusty had told her everything that transpired with Bruce's case and she wanted to be there to go over all the facts. At first, Dusty was extremely reluctant to tell her *all* of the details because he didn't want her getting any ideas regarding suicide. He couldn't keep this from her though. Bruce's death ate her alive as well and he had to let her know it wasn't all in vain. The big debate was how to break this news to the rest of the group. Lynn promised Dusty she wasn't giving up yet and wouldn't consider committing suicide, but they both agreed that this information might definitely push some of the others in the group over the edge, especially the ones seeing multiples. They decided to take the weekend to think it over.

Now we are at a point in this story where we return to the beginning. On this terrible night, Lynn sees another child. Dusty has to talk her out of committing suicide, which he does under one condition: the next child that either of them sees, they will both commit suicide together. This Romeo and Juliet type answer drove both of them. They wanted to live together and have children. They did not want to die, but they were both willing to do so to save the lives of the children.

As far as Bruce's death, other than Lana, they kept that secret to themselves for a while. They weren't 100% certain that suicide was the answer and that Bruce's suicide solved his case and they did not want blood on their hands. It was bad enough dealing with the deaths of children, they didn't also want to be burdened with feeling responsible for the deaths of adults as well, especially on false information. After great deliberation,

Dusty, Lynn and Lana decided to wait and if the time came to tell, they would know it. Of course, they risked others finding out, but no one else lived in Chicago nor was tuned into the rest of the group as deep as these three were. And if they found out on their own and took matters into their own hands, then maybe it was meant to happen. For now, as the leaders of the group, that's what they felt was the right thing to do.

Chapter 46

One week later, Dusty and Lynn sat on his couch while revisiting Dusty's "Exhaustive List", (which referred to all the places a person had visited in the past five years, maybe more). Dusty expressed his frustration, "Babe, I'm trying so hard to remember where I could have gone to be around her. I have thought of everything. I have revisited *everywhere!* I still haven't come across any supercommunication and the only thing I can even come close to remember dreaming about is a stupid, fucking broken swing set. I don't even go to playgrounds! It can't just be that we have to kill ourselves! It can't be! I don't think they would come to us if there wasn't a way to help them without killing ourselves…"

Lynn, starting to tear up, "I don't know what to do anymore. Every minute I'm alive I'm scared that some other innocent child is going to die. This is no way to live… I, I just wish we could get a sign. Anything. Just something to let us know we are on the right path. We need a morale boost or we are going to lose everyone."

Suddenly, Dusty became very alert. Something Lynn said triggered a lost memory. "What did you just say?"

"A morale boost, you know, something to…"

Cutting her off, "No, no before that…something about the right path?"

"Oh, well I just meant it would be nice if we could be given a sign to let us know we are on the right path."

Flashbacks and memories raced through his mind. He struggled to connect the dots and make sense of the synaptic explosions. He closed his eyes and thought hard, blocking out every thought and sensory stimulus.

"Wow, okay, I uh," frantic and at a loss for words Dusty tried to explain. "I just remembered something—a place. It wasn't on my list. I gotta go honey."

Taken back, Lynn said, "Where was it?"

"I'm not sure. I'm really not sure. I just remembered getting lost one time on the way home from work. I can't even remember the route I took yet. I… I just gotta go driving… see if it will come to me."

"When will you be back? Do you want me to go with you?"

"No babe, you stay here. Relax… make yourself some popcorn and watch that movie I rented. It won best picture last year. He pointed to 'A Beautiful Mind' on the table. "I'll be back soon," he said as he kissed her on the forehead and walked out the door. Lynn was a little shocked because Dusty never acted that way, but she figured there must be something very important on his mind. Indeed, there was.

Chapter 47

During his drive, Dusty thought about the possibility that this random memory could be the answer. It felt slim, but he wasn't letting anything go. He thought about his little girl. He thought about her race. He wondered if his semi-racist dad ever brushed off onto him subconsciously. Dusty never thought he was prejudiced. He had merely come to believe that all races seek to cultivate and embrace their own common traits, culture and history. This inclination to bond with familiarity is true for the sexes, religions, or any distinct group. Every animal, species, creed, race...whatever, has always preferred to flock with its own. It may not be politically correct, but it's not racism. Racism, sexism, dogma and fanaticism all require the individual to see other groups as contemptible and inferior. It is no more rational than hating a football team simply because it is located in a different geographical location than the home team. He rationalized his way through all of these thoughts on his way to where he thought he was headed. No, he was definitely not racist.

After driving around town for about an hour, listening to Jimi Hendrix and Jim Morrison, Dusty finally found himself at the 71st Street exit off of I-94 heading North, the route he took around two years ago. He remembered it now. He had been coming home from a deposition at a farmer's house in a rural area south of Chicago—about a three-hour drive. He had been on that stretch of highway a hundred times, but he was exhausted and didn't notice he was getting off on 71st Street instead of 90 Highway, which would take him home, until it was too late.

The exit ramp quickly delivered Dusty into the dark, dirty, depressing streets of the ghetto. The digital image on the clock just changed the blue 3 to 4, 12:14 a.m., about the same time he was here last.

Dusty didn't like being here. It scared him, made him feel isolated in a hostile, alien country. As he came down the 71st Street ramp, he recognized the boarded up and abandoned convenience store about half a block ahead on his right. Gang graffiti covered the walls and reminded Dusty of how much human intelligence and creativity is imprisoned it the ghetto.

The street was dark. Streetlights lined both sides of the street, but most were out either by bullets, rocks or lack of maintenance. Dusty could see maybe a half dozen working streetlights for about a mile down the street where a steep hill blocked his view of the rest of the area. It was dark and scary. People, safe in their vehicles, streaked by on the interstate overhead.

He saw a few single-story storefronts on each side of the street. The dim glow of the streetlights barely revealed that most were vacant. A few storefronts did look to be in business, however. He saw a pawnshop that had heavily barred windows and a rundown liquor store. He also saw a gas station about a quarter of a mile down the road that he assumed was in business, but it definitely was not open.

Dusty proceeded slowly down the street into the dark, threatening neighborhood. It gave him the creeps. It literally gave him goose bumps to think about getting out of his car. He couldn't imagine anything more terrifying than spending the night in one of those houses, yet this was the entire universe of some human beings, from birth to death.

Dusty tried remembering the route he took. He couldn't simply get back on the highway before because there was no northbound ramp where he got off. He had driven around, trying to find another way onto the highway. As a result, he zigzagged back and forth, seeing much more of the ghetto than he had cared to.

It was almost impossible to follow his same route, so he just drove around. He saw dozens of small, rundown houses. They were mostly wooden and one story. It was hard to tell which houses were vacant and which had residents. He thought that even the ones that looked vacant probably had druggies and homeless people staking out in them.

The yards were all small, maybe no more than ten to twelve feet from porch to street. Dusty couldn't see grass anywhere, but all sorts of litter, old furniture, broken down cars, bicycles, grocery carts, toys and trash covered most of the lots and the porches. Dusty noticed one house with a lamp glowing through a window. The roof on half of the house was caved in. Ragged bed sheets were weighted down over gaping holes. Dusty wondered if it was for privacy or to keep out water. The screens on all the windows were either shredded or gone. No one was outside.

Is there any happiness or joy in a place like this? The sad part was he knew streets like this covered all parts of the world and that this one wasn't even close to being the most impoverished and decayed. Dusty tried to imagine the suffering, the fear... the dark depression and lethargy breeding like a virus right outside his window. It boggled his mind. He knew there had to be at least some happiness though, somehow, because even though the murder rate is fearsome, it is a well-known fact that suicide in the ghetto is unheard of. He imagined the disparity of living here either produced the most courageous saints on Earth, or the vilest and craven of predators. You were probably one of the two.

Dusty had never considered these matters other than in passing, irrelevant moments. He was for the most part apathetic. Now it was real and swallowing the security of his white-collar life. His loft and law degree meant nothing in this neck of the woods. They were superficial. Insignificant. Those accolades were fading behind him—still on the interstate ramp—refusing to come down. He was just another carbon-based lump of tissue, bones and blood in this urban killing field. To make matter worse, his Mercedes, (one of two cars he owned, the other was a truck), stuck out like a new boy in the prison yard.

As Dusty pondered all of this, he crept slowly through the neighborhood. He stayed at about 20 miles per hour, trying to remember what he had done to get back to the highway the last time he was here. He remembered having to take a five or six block route to get to the ramp leading back on to the interstate. The interstate ramp he came in on was about two blocks behind him.

As he pulled up to a stop sign, he saw the fluorescent reflection of the I-90 sign with an arrow pointing straight ahead. Headed the opposite way was an old model Chevrolet; (he could tell the difference between Chevy's, Ford's and Pontiac's, but never the year or the make). It came to a stop at the opposite stop sign. The car was a four door and had a leather top, which was mostly worn off. He also noticed one headlight was out and the front bumper was held on by duct tape. He couldn't tell if the car was brown or just rusty. The driver's door was dented in by what looked to be a baseball bat or golf club. Christmas lights outlined the rear window and illuminated the five individuals in the car. They were all black and listening to loud rap.

Dusty could barely make out silhouettes, but he could feel them all staring him down. The driver was shirtless and muscle bound. Dusty thought he could make out a plethora of tattoos that covered his body. He also had on a bright yellow bandana. The one on the front passenger side was skinny and had a dark colored ball cap on backwards and wore sunglasses. He couldn't make out any details on the three men that sat in the back, bouncing back and forth to the music.

Dusty felt a sudden rush of fear shoot through his body. He could sense five pairs of angry eyes glaring at him. He knew that blacks and whites didn't particularly mix well in this part of town. Dusty had also grown up believing that black people still resented white people for the unforgivable sin of slavery, so his subconscious was automatically feeling insecure and endangered. He assumed that the five men in that car already hated him, and why not? With what he had seen in the last few minutes? And here he is riding through town in a $50,000 car? He was beginning to believe that their hate might be justified.

They were as astonished as he was at his presence there, only they were not afraid. One of the men in the back seat yelled something, "Honky" or "Whitey". Dusty wasn't sure. He could barely hear it over the heavy bass thump of the music. The others became animated, laughing and pointing at Dusty. Dusty eased past the stop sign and through the intersection. As he passed across the front of the Chevy, they turned their brights on. Both headlights illuminated the inside of his car. Dusty expected a bullet to come crashing through the side window at any moment. He had never been so scared and lonely.

The entire car was now yelling and laughing. Dusty still wasn't exactly sure how to get back to the interstate. With the new distraction, his mind was totally blank. He would have to find his way back to the interstate more than likely with an audience. He knew he was close, but he may as well have been a hundred miles away from the onramp.

All of the sudden, Dusty started thinking about dying. Negative thoughts were starting to creep in his mind. He had started to develop minor bouts of anxiety in his later years and was learning how to curb panic attacks, but it was moments like this that tested his mental fortitude. Usually his panic attacks were onset by perceived, unrealized danger. The perception sent his fight-or-flight response in full gear as it was close to being now, but he had developed ways to ricochet the anxiety before it turned into a full-blown panic attack. As he continued forward slowly, he forced his mind to focus on his actual surroundings, which had presented no *real* threat as of the current moment. Any threat that was present in his mind was a mere perception of danger, which he reminded himself of. No one was actually shooting at him; no one was actually holding a knife to him; no one was chasing him down with a machete. This is the method he had developed in stressful situations to keep him from panicking.

Should I drive slowly as if not afraid? Or race through the streets, ignoring stop signs until I find my way to the ramp? Will that only entice the Chevy to pursue me? Create a frenzy that might not necessarily happen if I stay calm?

His heart was exploding, but his mind was functional. He decided to drive slowly and display some degree of confidence. For all they knew, he had a gun, otherwise he would never have had the balls to come to their turf. Dusty turned left in front of them slowly. The Chevy turned the corner and followed behind, just far back enough so the bright lights lit up the inside of his car and the back of his head.

He tried to concentrate on something other than the car behind him, but it was next to impossible. The D.J. came on the radio and announced a new club opening, which at least represented a thin connection back to the "real world" Dusty lived in. Somehow the familiar D.J.'s voice made him feel not so alone. He reached for his cell phone, just in case. No signal. He reached for the glove box. He noticed a flashlight and pulled it out as if it were a gun. Maybe he could pull a bluff on his followers and at least give them pause. Maybe that was why they had not attempted to stop him...they didn't have a gun. That seemed highly unlikely to Dusty though. He decided against the bluff and put the flashlight back into the glove box.

He switched the dial on the radio. "Free Bird" was pouring from the speakers now. Dusty used to love that song, but constant radio play ruined it. He liked to claim certain songs as his own, even the old ones. He hated it when radio and movies and everybody discovered his songs and mass marketed them to the world. Strange, but it somehow made Dusty feel violated, almost like an invasion of privacy. This classic had been around for a few decades and the radio stations still managed to overplay it, but it was *so* classic and soothing that Dusty still could never manage to change the station when it came on, until this moment.

"And this bird you cannot change..." drifted from the radio and came to Dusty like a lost friend. It was the only companion he had in the world right now. Alien neighborhood, strange car, unfamiliar city... but Ronnie Van Zandt had been there for him since his childhood when his dad used to play the old LP's. It occurred to him that he didn't even know how to work a record player or even how they worked. He had never played anything but cassette tapes and CD's. Thinking of his dad and the image of an old record spinning on the turntable gave Dusty a little comfort though. *What is Dad doing this very moment? Probably reading next to Mom who is watching Frasier reruns.* It made him miss them. He wondered if they could sense by some supernatural phenomenon that he was in danger— terrified, alone, far away, and thinking about them. *"Lord help me, I can't chaaa aaay aaaay aaay aaaay aaaaay aannnngge..."* Then an irrational, paranoid thought hit him, '*Southern band... white southern band... slavery was in the south...what if they can hear my radio? Probably not good*'. He turned the radio off. His mind was on the fringe of frenzy.

Another car was coming from the opposite direction. The car, an old Chevy of some type, rusty and dented, passed Dusty on the driver's side. Two angry looking black youths looked menacingly at Dusty. The young men hollered out to the car following Dusty. They obviously knew each other well, exchanging laughs and insults, but Dusty couldn't hear exactly what they were saying. Dusty's heart was beating like a gong. His shirt was drenched in sweat; he was as scared as he had ever been. Things could get serious, ugly, or even deadly really quick.

The old Chevy moved on and took a right at the corner. The car behind Dusty made a U-turn and followed it. *Maybe they thought I had a gun. Maybe they are going to get one.* Dusty couldn't believe they would just abandon their prize catch, so he decided he had better get home while he still had the chance. He could always come back later.

He drove on further into the gloom and decay, looking for the next sign directing him back to the interstate. Coming here at night was a mistake. A group of blacks were loitering on a corner ahead, smoking, laughing and playing grabass. They all froze and glared at Dusty as he approached. Dusty finally saw a sign directing him to turn right at the next intersection, but he would have to pass right in front of the group on his passenger side. *What if they step in front of the car? Do I stop? Should I run them down and get the hell away?*

Dusty remembered watching Reginald Denny, the innocent truck driver pulled from his vehicle and savagely beaten by blacks on live TV... the Rodney King riots. He had never forgotten that sight. It had made him sick to his stomach. He lost sleep over it for weeks. Dusty had never really seen that kind of blind explosive hatred and all of the sudden he envisioned himself in the same scenario. His anxiety was starting to grab a firm hold on his will to keep cool. He had driven his car deep into the hatred and he had never been so afraid in his life.

He came to the stop sign at the intersection, took a large, deep, controlling breath and drove past the group on the corner. A few racial slurs were hollered. He could only really make out the word, "Honky". One black with a black bandana flicked a cigarette off of the windshield, but this was fortunately the only threatening transgression. If looks could kill though, he would have been deader than a love-crazed buck on the opening day of rifle season. He felt the anger, the angry stares, the you-are-unwelcome-you-are-hated-but-we-will-not-kill-you, stares.

Dusty now remembered the two cars. Where were they? He knew there was no way he was getting out of there without encountering them again. He breathed a short sigh. He could see the interstate over the road about 3 blocks ahead off to the left and so far, no cars. He experienced a slight reprieve from his fear. "I just might make it out of here alive," he whispered as he came to a stop.

Then, there they were. The two cars full of bored, angry, black gangsters turned the corner behind him. He saw them slowing down just enough to exchange some type of communication with the group on the corner, who began gesturing in Dusty's direction. Dusty put the accelerator to the floor. He could outrun them to the interstate.

He came to the sign and the intersection to turn towards the highway in a few seconds. For some weird reason, he turned his left blinker on out of habit, as if he were really concerned about rules of the road right now. He could see the sign to the interstate ramp about two blocks down the unlit street. The fluorescent red, white and blue sign was barely visible off the glow of the one streetlight that hadn't been shot out. Dusty started to turn, but he didn't.

Chapter 48

Every nerve in Dusty's body was screaming at him to flee—to push his foot to the floor and live to see another day. His palms were sweaty and glued to his steering wheel at 10 and 2. He could nearly feel the bass blasting from the car behind him it was so loud. His gut felt like he had swallowed a handful of thumbtacks. For some reason though, as he sat there at the stop sign, he felt compelled to confront his fear. A feeling crept over him and bled into his soul as the tide consumes the shores of a moonlit, sandy beach and suddenly he was not afraid anymore. He laid his head back for a moment, relaxed his death grip on the steering wheel and closed his eyes.

Dusty had been drunk many times in his life. He had even been known in college to smoke a joint once in a while, but the heightened sense of perception that overcame him at that crossroads was unlike any that he had ever felt before. His hands and feet tingled, his hair on his neck and forearms stood on end, his lips trembled, and his scalp felt as if a cool mountain breeze was blowing through it. He felt as if he was floating. Suddenly, with his eyes still closed, something extraordinary happened that he had never before experienced. From behind the shades of his eyelids, a little girl flickered in and out of sight. He had seen her enough by now to know who she was. This had never happened to him in waking moments. Startled, his eyes shot open. As she floated out of his perception, he heard her angelic voice ring through his head as if carried by the wind; it cried, "Here."

This entire experience happened in a matter of five seconds, but to him it felt like several minutes had passed. When he finally came to, he shook his head in disbelief. His eyebrows furrowed and he cocked his head slightly to the side. He blinked a couple times. Then without even thinking, Dusty put his car into park, reached in his wallet, pulled out a hundred-dollar bill and stepped outside. His fear lay dormant in the furthest recess of his subconscious. His courage roared and his confidence soared as adrenaline poured into his veins. He had never in his life taken himself this far outside his comfort zone, but on that night, in the darkest slums of the city, he found himself approaching two carloads of potentially very dangerous black men.

"One hundred dollars!" Dusty screamed out as he waved the bill high in the air. For a moment, the reality of the situation set in and he felt terror creeping up his spine. He thought of his little girl, his dead friends, his potentially suicidal lover, all of the children possibly in danger, and reminded himself why he was there. He took a deep breath and again screams, emphasizing each word, "One, hundred, dollars!" and waved the bill vigorously in the midnight air, careful to leave his other hand in plain view.

The lead car was the car carrying four men. They all were shocked by this crazy white man's gesture. The driver reached over and turned down the radio, holding a black and mild between his fingers as he twisted the fancy knob on the faceplate of the stereo.

"This motha fucka crazy?" exclaimed the rider in the front, looking to the driver with wild eyes and a sense of bewilderment. His name was DeShawn. Out of the whole group, he was the least dangerous looking and was often made fun of for his lack of "gangster skills", but he can twist and distort his face to match the drama of any scene. His teeth protruded from his mouth as he talked. His family could never afford braces.

The driver's name was 8-Ball. He was dark as night and sported a tattoo of a lion on his right deltoid. He had a couple gold teeth, a baldhead adorned with a yellow bandana, and a golden cross around his neck. He appeared as gangster as they come. He didn't respond to his comrade's question. He just looked forward, studying this stranger on his turf, wondering why a guy like him would venture to a place like this at such an hour. He immediately respected him, but that didn't allow him to let his guard down.

"CJ, you strapped?" 8-Ball yelled to the back. His voice was full and commanding.

"Always have, always will be as long as I'm ridin' around wit yo shit startin' ass," replied a muscular man of about 25, wearing a red bandanna and a wife-beater. He was slightly cross-eyed, but refused to wear glasses because he thinks it detracts from his image.

The fourth man was not really a man at all. It was DeShawn's brother, DeJuan, a 17 –year-old who looks as if he's years away from puberty still. He was pudgy, wore a backwards hat and was smoking a cigarette. He took this opportunity to point out the irony of the situation. With a chuckle, he blurted out, "The only dude with a gun in this car can't even see straight!" and immediately braced himself for the open-handed blow that arrived smack dab on the middle of his forehead.

8-Ball, not amused by the comic relief stated, "I got a gun, idiot. I was checking on back up." He took a long drag from his cigar, "Let's see what this white dude wants." All seven men simultaneously got out of both cars, ranging from 17 to 29 years of age. They formed a line in front of the headlights of the lead car. Dusty swallowed the lump in his throat.

"Listen guys," he spoke calm and direct as he slowly walked towards them, "I don't want to cause any trouble. I am willing to give you a hundred dollars if you can help me. That's all I have. You can try stealing my car if you want, but it has GPS theft tracking and would only cause you more trouble. Fair warn-"

8-Ball cut him off, "What the hell are you thinking rolling through these parts at this time of the night white boy? In a Mercedes?" Dusty thought this must be their leader, and that he spoke surprisingly articulate. "Are you trying to pull some shit?"

"No. Not at all. I can explain. Look," Dusty took a few steps forward and lowered his voice, "I am looking for a little girl. I think she might be in trouble. Will you help me?"

8-Ball walked forward and looked Dusty straight in the eye, "What is your name?"

"Dusty. Dusty Burch," he replied confidently. His heart was pounding, but he stayed calm on the outside. 8-Ball grabbed the bill from his hand and examined it in the headlights. He motioned for CJ to come and pat Dusty down.

When 8-Ball was satisfied Dusty was unarmed, he said, "Okay, here's the deal. You obviously got real balls coming up in here like this. You must be crazy or desperate. Either way, I'm a reasonable man, but I'm also really good at smellin' bullshit. So, don't fuck me around. Now please explain to me exactly why it is that you find yourself in our part of town at this hour of the night." The two men stood face-to-face in the middle of the street with no light but the headlights shining on them, silhouetting the rest of the crew. Dusty, relieved at the hospitality, spoke quickly, almost as if he was afraid 8-Ball will change his mind.

"I'm looking for a little black girl. She has cornrows and wears glasses. She has big eyes and she is around 4-6 years old. She..."

DeShawn, the 17-year-old, cut him off, "You mean the little girl that used to live right there?" he said as he pointed to a house across the street. It is the only one that looked somewhat habitable in sight. "She moved away about a year and a half ago, maybe more."

Dusty's heart flew from his chest. "You mean you know her? Does... does she, um, is she about this tall and wear thick glasses?" he stammered as he held his hand about waist high.

"Yah man, I used to see her playin' out in the street all the time when I'd make my runs. One day, they family was just gone. Someone told me they moved or something." Dusty wasn't sure, but thought he had a pretty good idea at what he meant by *"runs"*.

"What do you want with a six-year-old black girl in the Ghetto?" 8-Ball asked suspiciously.

"It's hard to explain." Dusty averted the question and directed his attention back to the pudgy one. "Do you know her name?"

"Nah man. But she used to play out here by herself all day. Sometimes," but he was interrupted.

"Are you some kind of pervert? Cuz I'll cap yo ass right here!" yelled CJ as he retrieved his 9mm Ruger from his belt and held it up sideways. He obviously threatened to shoot a lot of people because one of the men from the other car rolled his eyes, but 8-Ball raised his eyebrows at Dusty as if to ask, *"well?"*

"No! Not at all. I wish I could explain this better. She means a lot to me and I think she could be in danger. Worst of all, I think other children might be in danger. I would never hurt anyone, especially a child! Can you tell me anything else? Do you know where she went?" The despair in his voice was certainly persuasive.

All of the men in the car became more confused the more Dusty talked. One of the others, DeShawn couldn't help but speak up, "What, are you like related to her or something?"

Dusty realized how crazy he was sounding and considered trying to explain the situation, but couldn't bring himself to do it to this group just yet, "No. Well, not exactly. I…" he tried to think of something, anything that might make sense, "I am an attorney. I am working a case involving child abuse and I'm afraid she may be involved. It's a long story, but that's the truth."

All of the men were still contemplating if Dusty could possibly be telling the truth. 8-Ball took a drag and blew it in Dusty's face, "Listen man, it's late. I'm still not real sure about you, but something tells me there may actually be some truth in what you are saying. If we stand here much longer, someone might drive by that's a little less 'friendly', if you know what I mean. Go home. Come back here tomorrow at noon at the park right down the street on South Maple. I'll ask around in the meantime, but for now, keep your Benjamin."

"No, I insist…"

"Shut the fuck up and get in your car white boy," came a rebuttal before he could finish his sentence. Strangely, Dusty felt like it was almost a term of endearment, almost as if 8-Ball were actually looking out for him. In reality, 8-Ball was skeptical that it may be a marked bill. Dusty put the bill back in his pocket and headed to his car.

"What's your name?" Dusty yelled just as he got to his door.

"My friends call me 8-Ball."

…………

As Dusty drove home that night, he couldn't stop thinking about what had just happened. More than anything, he was utterly confused and almost in shock of his conscious perception of his little girl. Although brief, she came through to him like never before. More importantly, he heard her voice ring in his head. He didn't know what this meant. Had he experienced supercommunication? He felt as if he'd reached a breakthrough in his communication with her, but he was left with more questions still. Had he discovered where his little, subconscious companion once lived? Where she died? If so, was he really going to be aided in his quest by a mob of gangsters?

Dusty questioned whether or not he should trust "8-Ball". *What kind of name is that anyway?* But he had started listening more and more to the little voice inside his head, which at this moment was advising him not to judge this seemingly sinister group of strangers. He remembered the book his dad gave him by Dale Carnegie, "How to Win Friends and Influence People" and remembered Carnegie quoting Abraham Lincoln. In regards to the South, Lincoln told his wife not to criticize, as the North might behave the same way under similar circumstances. Dusty had come to believe that blessings came in many forms and prophets in many disguises. Before he got home, he had already decided he would return to the park at the end of S. Maple Street in the ghetto the next day. He couldn't come this far to chicken out. No way! He was Dusty Fuckin' Burch.

When Dusty got home, Lynn was asleep. The TV in the living room was replaying the "Beautiful Mind" DVD menu. She looked beautiful as she slept, on her side, cuddling a pillow. He didn't want to wake her, but he needed to talk to her. He was glad she was here. He didn't want six weeks, or even two weeks to go by again without seeing her. Dusty wanted to keep a close eye on her and couldn't bear the thought of her having to deal with all this alone. She was slowly starting to lose her sense of self and every day seemed to present itself with a mountainous obstacle. Newly acquired friends from The Chosen had already been lost and he was afraid they were going to lose more if the "death solves" theory was true. With every dream she had, she felt her life expectancy being siphoned out of her soul. Dusty saw her fading, down to the absence of humming her favorite song while she brushed her teeth. Every two or three days the tune would change, based on whatever kick she was on: Journey, Queen, Dixie Chicks, Third-Eye Blind, Tim McGraw… now it was nothing.

Dusty's brain had been racing all the way home. He sat next to her for a moment, waiting for her to sense his presence. After a minute, he placed his hand on her knee and softly spoke her name, "Lynn…" She roused slightly. "Lynn, honey." She rolled onto her back and opened her eyes for a moment before closing them again.

He decided it could wait. He covered her with a blanket, covered her with the afghan on the back of the couch, and found his bed and tried to sleep.

Chapter 49

The next morning couldn't have come fast enough for Dusty. He only got about an hour of sleep, in which he didn't remember seeing his little girl. This wasn't unusual. Dusty felt like she best communicated with him in the depths of his slumber, where his consciousness was as far away from the outside world and as close to what he believed to be the "universal consciousness", as possible. Since he started seeing her, he spent hours upon hours thinking about the spiritual implications that came with it. Before, Dusty had always walked the tight wire between the religious dogmatists and the pagans. He never could bring himself to state, without a doubt, what made enough sense for him to claim as his own. What interested him more than anything was the realm of physics and astrology. Nothing anyone could say could humble him or make him feel more spiritual than simply gazing into the cosmos, picturing the atoms inside of his body once as they were, burning inside the flaming hot furnace of a supernova. To him, what more of a miracle does anyone need to believe in a bigger power, one that we simply do not have the capacity to understand? There just wasn't a lot of "black & white" in Dusty's life… until now.

To him it seemed impossible that he and all of The Chosen could be seeing these children without the existence of an afterlife. Where he might have doubted this before, he was certain of it now. Especially after experiencing what he felt, hearing her voice, *feeling* her presence more than ever before—yes, he now had no question that the soul exists on some other plane of being after death. What terrified him now was that if that were true, then is it true that committing suicide condemns your soul to eternal damnation? What about if it were only to save the lives of innocent children? Would God excuse that? Did God Excuse Bruce or is he floating around in purgatory? Dusty could not bear the thought of Lynn's soul, pure as a mountain spring, to spend an eternity in hell. The thought nearly crippled him. He knew that if either of them saw another kid, it was over for them, whether she believed she might go to hell or not. He would not let that happen.

Dusty left for work early, at 5:30. Lynn was still sleeping. He badly wanted to talk to her about what happened to him last night, but he didn't want to wake her up and he'd rather tell her the *whole* story after he went back this morning. Dusty always worked best when the building was empty and quiet. He had learned long ago that being a part of the 6 AM club was one of the best ways to be productive and separate yourself from the rest of the 9-5 crowd.

When Marilyn walked in the office that morning, he asked her to block off his afternoon and reschedule any appointments he had. She begrudgingly agreed. She only required that he view the interrogatories and the answers provided by the plaintiffs for yet another potential expert witness in the Draper case. She needed to know when to schedule the deposition because opposing counsel, namely Karee, kept calling to nail down a date. This particular expert was a Child Psychologist Karee was using to illustrate the immense psychological damage Brian had undertook. Dusty had been putting this off a couple weeks now. He assured her he would and in response to her questioning of his absence, he answered, "To protect the innocent—for once."

It felt like only minutes had passed when Dusty found himself strolling up to the park on S. Maple Street where he was instructed to go. It was an overcast day and the entire sky seemed to take on the same shade of a gloomy gray. It had rained overnight and Duty's expensive black shoes sank into the spongy sod as he approached a loan bench positioned adjacent to a rusty swing set. The chain had broken on one of the seats and it dangled lifelessly, hovering above the ground. Cigarette butts littered the area and only a few spots of grass and an occasional dandelion emerged from the sea of mud. There was a merry-go-round that's brownish color and bits of paint remaining indicated that it was probably red at one point. One metal slide stood erect to the side of the swing that looked as if a strong gust of wind might blow it over any moment. The monkey bars were missing several rungs, and a child would have to have 6 feet arms to get all the way across it. That was it.

Dusty thought to himself that if he had kids, he would never let them play at a place like this. It was a glaring reminder of the socioeconomic differences that exist in the world today. Dusty had been sitting there about five minutes when the Chevy he remembered from last night pulled up. He was never the best with cars, but he thought it was a Monte Carlo and guessed it to be about a 1995, based off the condition it was in. He saw 8-Ball step out of the car. "Alone?" he thought… he couldn't see anyone else in the car. This surprised him, but he figured there were eyes elsewhere not too far out of reach.

8-Ball looked the way Dusty remembered him, only he had on a pair of nicely fitting jeans and a white undershirt on. Stark white. Dusty's eyes scanned the perimeter as 8-Ball approached him, trying to find any signs that others might be watching. Protecting. He saw no one. Not a soul in sight. The house the man last night indicated used to be the little girl's house looked vacant and sat about 150 yards west of the park. The front of the house faced north.

"You come alone?" asked Dusty as 8-Ball sat down right beside him on the bench like he'd known Dusty for years.

"I did. But don't worry, all I gotta do is push a button and black people will just start crawlin' out of the woods by the hundreds," 8-Ball replied in a manner that reminded Dusty of Will Smith. Dusty couldn't help but chuckle, holding back as much of his real laugh as possible. He hadn't meant to, but in the silence afterwards it occurred to him it was probably a defense mechanism. A real laugh offers a glimpse into a person's soul. Dusty thought he must not be ready to share that glimpse with this man quite yet.

Dusty finally spoke, "I wasn't sure if you would come."

"Oh, I knew you would. You looked damn near possessed last night. I knew right away something was troubling you bad. I could see it in your eyes man."

"Is it that obvious?" 8-Ball nodded his head. "You're right. A lot has been on my mind lately." 8-Ball looked Dusty up and down, trying to figure this guy out.

"You gonna be alright… is it…"

"Dusty," Dusty said before 8-Ball even had a chance to spit it out. "And yah. I hope so. I just really hope you can help me. I am desperate."

"Listen Dusty, I asked around about your girl. Turns out, something seems a little fishy. You see, there's a lot of folks that remember that girl, but nobody knows her name. A street over, one lady told me that little girl moved back to her real dad's house and that she lived in that house with her mom and her boyfriend. So, when I went to that house to see for myself, no one was home. I looked in the window and it looked empty. Another old lady down the street told me she saw a moving truck there a year ago, maybe more, but anyway nobody could give me a definite answer. DeShawn, the guy last night who remembered her, said he saw her here at the park a lot, too. Always by herself. He also said that there was one time he rode by and the lady was yelling out the front door at the little girl, telling her to come inside. He said he thought he remembered her yelling the name 'Carrie' or 'Clara' or some "C" name."

"Does DeShawn live around here or something?" Dusty asked, a little skeptical that he was actually getting a legitimate lead. He thought it was too good to be true and that this "DeShawn" guy might genuinely be full of crap. "I mean, how is it he saw her so often?"

"He lives a couple blocks away, but he is always riding his bike through these parts, meetin' clients and shit. You wouldn't think it by looking at him, but DeShawn is pretty sharp. Ain't much get by him."

Dusty continued to sit with his hands clasped together, elbows on his knees, staring at the dangling swing set in front of him, trying to take all this in. He started to wonder if this was all just a wild goose chase. And then as if he were struck by a bolt of lightning, he got up and started walking toward the swing, "No," he said in bewilderment. It can't be." 8-Ball stared in bewilderment as Dusty approached the down swing set.

Memories started flashing through Dusty's mind; memories of past dreams. Half-remembered dreams. Had his little girl been trying to convey something to him? Is this THE swing set she was on in his dreams? *This all can't be a coincidence. No way.* His brain became flooded with possible scenarios. *Why was she able to show me THIS? Why not something else? Is this where she was kidnapped? Is this where she is buried?* Dusty started looking around the ground instinctively, as if he might be able to find some sign of forensic evidence. 8-Ball continued to sit back in utter amazement.

"This white dude really might be crazy," he quietly said to himself as Dusty paced back and forth across the playground. He didn't even bother to ask.

"I'm going to go to the house. I have to see for myself. It's cool if you don't want to come in. I understand. But would you at least just kind of stay around, just in case somebody gets suspicious?"

"You mean of what? Some strange white dude breaking into a house that's been vacant for a while?"

"Yeah, exactly."

8-Ball kind of rolled his eyes, looking up to the sky, "Aight, but don't stay in there too long, ya hear?"

"I hear."

"But before I do, you *have* to tell me what all this is about. Seriously."

Dusty wasn't sure where to start or how much to say, so he put it as bluntly as he could because he figured at this point there was nothing to lose and either 8-Ball would believe him or he wouldn't, "I see this girl in my dreams. It started back a couple years ago almost. She came to me in the night, acting out scenes of torture and anguish. It got to where I couldn't dream about anything else. Just her. I knew someone had hurt her, but I didn't know what to do. Then I found another woman who had the same type of dreams of a different child. I tried shrinks, sleeping pills, booze, everything, but this woman, Lana, helped me the most because it made me feel like I wasn't crazy or alone. Then we created a chat room and started finding people all over the country, even the world. We all got together in Colorado and shared our stories, all eerily similar to each other. Long story short, we all believe these children are real and many have even found instances where the children they are seeing are real murder or missing cases. Since Colorado, a couple of us have died and when they did, we discovered the children's cases they were seeing were solved and the killer was caught." Dusty looked up to see 8-Ball's face in utter disbelief, or maybe it was curiosity. "Deep stuff, huh?"

8-Ball looked at Dusty in amazement, "You couldn't make that shit up if you tried."

"I wish I could."

"So, you think this girl you are seeing lived in that house? And that she is dead?"

"Yes."

"And why did she choose you?"

"We think it has to do with proximity to the body when the soul leaves the earth. A while back I got detoured down here on the way home from work. I didn't even remember or think anything of it until last night, which is why I came back."

"And you think you are going to find some answers in there?"

"I sure hope so."

"Aight, well, then let's go Sherlock." Dusty smiled and nodded.

"Thank you. I know this sounds crazy. But I can't tell you how much I appreciate this."

"Don't mention it. But if you are jerkin my chain, remember I got the black people button. Plus, I know Kung Fu." 8-Ball acted out a Jackie Chan Kung Fu motion with his hands. "Nah, I don't really. But I will fuck you up if you try and pull some weird shit on me man."

"Any weird shit that happens won't be because I made it up, I promise you that."

"Aight, well let's get going."

8-Ball sat in his car and watched Dusty from just down the street, asking himself why in the hell he was letting himself get wrapped up in this white boy's affairs. Something inside of him whispered to his soul that he was doing good, which was something he had been looking for, for quite some time now. Living in the ghetto didn't always provide opportunities to do good. Most of the time it is fight-or-die, so growing up 8-Ball didn't have much of a chance to exhibit the good nature he felt brewing at the depths of his conscience. *This is a chance to make up for lost time,* he thought to himself. He watched Dusty pull up and park on the curb, get out, and wearily approach the front door.

As Dusty walked through the yard, or lack thereof, he noticed paint chipping off the entire exterior of the house. Weeds grew as tall as four feet in just about every direction and the driveway was more covered with grass

309

than concrete. The single car garage was under a bedroom window whose screen was torn and mangled. The garage door had a gaping hole in it, revealing junk from floor to ceiling, consisting of clothing, furniture, lawn mowers, dishes, toys and various other items. To Dusty, it appeared as if someone had left it all behind, possibly in an effort to evacuate the city in a hurry. He paused to observe the condition of the house. Then he thought of his little girl to find the strength to make the ascent to the front door. Before he knew it, he was knocking on the white wooden door. One, two, three times. His heart started beating in his throat in anticipation of what might happen next. What would he say if someone did answer? But he would never know, and almost as if willed by another, he opened the front door and stepped inside.

It became very apparent at this point that no one was living there. Cobwebs dangled in every corner and the musty smell reminded him of the mop water he used to mop his high school wrestling mats with. The house was mainly empty, but it was littered with random household items. Batteries, silverware, socks, food wrappers, hairpins, sheets, picture frames, extension cords… nothing of much value. Dusty stood at the doorway for several minutes, taking it all in before he proceeded. There was no second level. He found two bedrooms down the hallway directly to the left of the entrance and a living area to the right. A basement door stood between the living area and the kitchen on the other side of the wall. Every few minutes he would call out, "Hello? Anybody in here?"

He crept through the house, taking his time, not touching anything except a doll that he imagined belonging to a little girl. It was a "raggedy Ann" doll, blue dress, red curly hair, painted red and fading cheeks, striped socks and black shoes. He found this in a closet in the back room, where it might have laid for eternity, a forgotten love of a child, had he not found it.

After looking at it for several minutes, envisioning a little girl hugging and squeezing it, dragging down the hallway and carrying it to the playground, he became overwhelmed with grief and sank to the floor by the window, leaning his back on the wall. He closed his eyes and leaned his head back, still clutching the doll. At this moment, a sensation came over him, likened only to the night prior, and for an instant the room he was in appeared as if it were in a different time. There was more color, a bed, a dresser and no cobwebs. Startled, Dusty quickly opened his eyes and revealed the same, stark, gloomy room he saw an instant before. He rubbed his eyes vigorously, in disbelief.

Alone, he sat there for a minute with eyes wide open and watering. A tear rolled down his cheek and onto his collar. His rims filled up to a point he couldn't stand any longer and lest he cry, he shut his eyes once again. He began to think about Lana and her meditation tactics. So, although a newbie, Dusty thought he'd give it a try. He took in a deep breath through his nose and released it out his mouth. He did this a few times then began to concentrate on the physical world around him. He felt the carpet underneath him and the weight of his body on the floor. He tried to focus on his breath and block any thoughts from entering his mind. He thought of Lynn and her beautiful smile, but as he practiced, he imagined the thought of her floating away in a balloon. He tried to envision himself as an entity outside of his thoughts, viewing them from afar. He pictured himself sitting on a hill and any thoughts that came by were rolling through in front of him on a railroad track, each thought represented by a train car. He was an observer of his thoughts, whenever they did pop into his mind. He envisioned a placid, calm surface of a pond with willows growing on the edge and a soft, colorful sunrise peaking over its dam. Breathe. He went back to focusing on his breath. Slowly he breathed in and out... in... and out. Once he gained total control over his thoughts, he began to focus on his little girl.

As his eyes remained closed, reality crept away from him and like a growing radio signal, the apparition of the room in a different time began to flicker in and out of his vision once again. It was as if he had traveled through a wormhole back in time, passing through the fabric of space. Once his heartbeat slowed down and he could get a slim grip on the situation, he must have mentally triggered a cosmic switch, relaying his ability to cope with the imminent communication amongst two planes of existence, because there before him stood his little girl. She too was flickering, like a 3D holographic image. For seconds at a time she would appear, then disappear entirely.

Never before had Dusty been able to see her in such detail. Her eyes were more beautiful than he had ever remembered—a light brown hazel with looming streaks of what almost looked to be blue. Her teeth were perfectly straight, in line and pearly white. Her nose was petite and round, almost like a bunny. She wore pink overalls with pink and white pump tennis shoes. Her glasses were round. He found himself trying to remember if he ever saw her in glasses, but trying to remember his dreams about her was like trying to remember long lost childhood memories tucked away in the recesses of his brain. That didn't really matter though. What mattered is that he could *see* her. Not just a far-off apparition, but close and with astonishing detail.

She finally came into view clearly without fading. Dusty was in absolute amazement. He just sat, looking at her, saying nothing. Then he smiled. This version of her was much better than the picture he had to extrapolate from his dreams and reassemble into his conscious brain. Now she stood before him, in the… "flesh?" he thought. He blinked continuously to make sure it wasn't a hallucination.

As he sat there, blinking, she said nothing. A million questions ran through Dusty's head, but instead of asking about how all this could be happening, he said, "Hello. My name is Dusty. I've been waiting to meet you a long time." He spoke softly and slowly with that hint of speech an adult gets when befriending a child. "Do you know who I am?"

The girl stood there staring into his eyes like a hawk, seeing deep down into the house of Dusty's soul. She had a God-like presence about her. He wondered if she would talk, or if she could read his mind and communicate via ESP. Then suddenly the peaceful scene turned into a horror show.

Dusty was blasted with brief, intense images of a man yelling and screaming. Dusty's whole insides were shocked and he began looking for his girl. He began running throughout the house, catching glimpses of her here and there. He saw the girl, hiding in a closet, crying. He saw a woman with a tourniquet on and needles on the floor next to her, with eyes that sunk into her head and deep, dark bags under her eyes that portrayed sadness and depression. He saw cigarettes, smoke, alcohol bottles being thrown against the wall. Every room he went in he saw one depressing site after another.

Then Dusty saw what he thought was a kick to her head, and the girl on the floor… blood. He saw the woman screaming. He *felt* the little girl's pain. Each vision was short… less than a second, so that he couldn't make out many details. He saw the girl lying on the floor. The mother attempted first aid but failed. Then he saw her last breath. Then images of hedge clippers and trash bags. His heart was pounding incessantly. What he thought he was seeing couldn't be true. The swing came into view, then woods, then dirt. They were all mixed together and jumbled, but the feeling he got was that she died and was buried somewhere, nearby. Dusty's eyes were watering and his blood was boiling hot. He had never felt so desperate and afraid before in his life. Then, as quickly as the images had come to him, they disappeared and so did she.

Chapter 50

Dusty sat, waiting for her to come back. After several minutes of nothing, Dusty realized that she wasn't going to flicker back into reality. He began to panic slightly. "Hey, hey! Come back!" He wondered if he did something wrong. He got up and began pacing around the house, looking for her. "No, no, no!" After feeling like he was SO close, like he was about to make a major breakthrough, he was afraid he had lost it and would never get it back. He wanted to see more. He needed more details to be able to know where to go next. He started running through the house, looking for her in every room, closet, corner and shadow he could find. He started to feel like he was on a bad mushroom trip, one that he had been on before only once in his lifetime. Reality spun and his mind melted into his subconscious.

After ten minutes of roaming the house desperately, he finally alleviated his anger and frustration with a mighty blow to one of the living room walls. His fist penetrated the dry wall, blowing a hole in it the size of a bowling ball. It was a clean blow. Afterwards, he stood in the middle of the room, still clinching his fists. His breathing began to slow down and he started trying to collect himself.

"Get it together, Burch," he spoke to himself. His fist was fine and he actually enjoyed the slight throbbing in his knuckles. He had big, strong hands and bony knuckles that protruded from his meaty palms. He had only ever been in a couple fights in his life, but they always ended up with his opponent knocked-out cold. His hands slowly opened and he wiped the tears and snot from his face. "Get it together."

Dusty stood there in disbelief, in awe that he had actually been in contact with his little subconscious companion. She was more perfect than he had ever imagined. For over two years now, he had been searching for answers to the brutalizing scenery of his dreams. He was afraid to sleep, but being awake *terrified* him. Every waking moment that he was not solving this mystery, his "precious doe" was suffering. Had he found a way to end it?

He didn't want to leave the house, for fear that she might return again and he would miss her, but he finally forced himself to walk back out the front door. 8 Ball was waiting for him, smoking a Black and Mild on the curb. By the look on Dusty's face, he didn't know what to say. So, he just said, "Did you find what you were looking for Ace?" He wasn't sure where the Ace thing came from, but it felt right.

"Ace?"

"You know, like Ventura. You white. He's white. You both are like murder detectives and shit."

To Dusty, this actually was hilarious and perfect comedic relief, especially because Ace Ventura, Pet Detective was one of his all-time favorite movies. He was taken off guard and his mind went to a place he didn't expect it to go... happiness. "Oh my God! You have no idea how much I love that movie! Wow. I've never thought of myself that way, but I guess you're right. We *do* have a lot in common. Hey, my girlfriend even kinda looks like Courtney Cox." He chuckled again.

"You don't wear tutus though, do you?" 8-Ball's face contorted into a goofy grin, the first Dusty saw of what would be many.

"Uh no. Not usually at least."

"Ok, cuz that would for sure probably get your ass capped down here in the ghetto."

And as if on cue Dusty hit him with it, "Well, Alllll righty then! I'll have to remember that. Wouldn't wanna get 'capped'. I can catch bullets in my teeth, however.

"No shit?" Dusty smiled. One more Ace reference and he would be pushing it too far, but for now he was right on. "Well, for real. I mean you don't have to tell me if you don't want to, but did you find anything?"

"I'm not sure. I think so. Maybe one day I'll explain it all a little more. I just don't know how to process and explain it all. I don't want to sound crazy."

"Listen man, I've seen crazy. Like for real bat shit crazy. You ain't it. So, if you don't want to tell me that's cool, but if you do… just shoot." 8-Ball took a drag off hit cigar and handed it to Dusty. Dusty had the slight notion to decline, but saw it as a nice gesture and in an odd way an opportunity to bond, plus he hadn't had a Black & Mild since he was a teenager. He took it and took a drag, inhaling just a little bit of the smooth smoke, trying to remember the line that made it burn and sent him coughing.

"Okay," Dusty sat down on the curb and 8-Ball joined him, "well, she came to me. I saw her, which has never happened while I was awake." His demeanor reverted back to the one he wore as he walked out the door. "She showed me things. Awful things." As those words were spoken, Dusty unexpectedly started erupting with emotion and tears. It quickly turned into an awkward sob. "I… I think she's dead man. And the parents did it…" He put his head in his hands and his chest heaved up and down as he let it out. 8-Ball looked around a bit, as if to see if anyone was looking and instinctively put his hand on Dusty's back and consoled him, patting 3 or 4 times.

"Alright. Alright man. Hey, we'll figure this thing out." In his head he thought to himself that figuring it out might include a psychiatrist, but he actually more believed Dusty than not.

Dusty wiped his eyes and got it together.

"I'm sorry man. Didn't mean to do that."

"No worries."

Dusty puffed the cigar again and handed it back. "I appreciate everything man. I probably better be getting back."

"Yeah. No problem man. We'll keep in touch, okay?"

"Sounds good." The two shook hands and Dusty got in his car.

Dusty drove home, bewildered. He turned off the radio and drove in total silence. There was absolutely no way he was going back to work. He called in to Marilyn who argued with him. She explained there was a very important motion that needed to be filed by 5:00. He told her to have one of the new grads finish it. He had been working with one in particular he had in mind. Marilyn wasn't happy but Dusty didn't budge. He was going home. He wanted to see Lynn.

His hands and feet robotically turned the wheel and pushed the pedals as if he had turned on autopilot. The lines on the road melted together with the cars passing by. Images of the little girl and the house filled his consciousness, making him feel sick to his stomach. When he pulled in the driveway, he immediately vomited in his front lawn.

He stammered in his front door and plodded up the staircase to his bedroom. Lynn was studying at the desk in his bedroom. A book named "Dental Anatomy" was open and a cup of coffee set steaming next to it. Lynn lowered her reading glasses that she sometimes wore when her eyes became tired from reading. Dusty loved them.

"Hi honey," she could tell Dusty wasn't quite all there. "Everything okay? You are home early. I tried calling you earlier. What happened last night? Where did you go?" Dusty uncharacteristically started taking off his suit and put the pieces in a pile on his bedroom floor.

"Yeah. I'm okay. Just, I just gotta take a shower. I'll tell you about it in a little bit. Finish up whatever you were doing. Is that okay?"

"Okay, you sure you're okay?"

"Promise." He leaned down and kissed her on the lips. He sauntered into the bathroom and turned on the shower. He opened up his mouthwash and took a gulp, hopeful that it would eradicate the taste of vomit in his mouth. The burning sensation made his eyes water. As he swished the mouthwash violently back and forth, leaning over his sink, he stared at himself in the mirror. He noticed his watering eyes were blood shot and tired looking. It felt as if he were looking at himself in a different realm—a reality that he was not familiar with, nor comfortable with. He took a long, existential look at himself, his face inches from the mirror. *What is going on in my life right now?*

He got in the shower to try and relax. As the warm water ran down his face and body, he tried to fend off his age-old nemesis—anxiety. He had gotten to the point where he had it pretty well in check, but it had taken him years, and every once in a while, in severe stressful moments, he could feel it trying to sneak its way into his life. His thoughts were so powerful that his nervous system was sensing that *he* was in danger, even though he was safe in the warmth of his shower. For years he had been trying to train his mind not to erroneously pose to his subconscious that a threat was present, because he had learned his nervous system couldn't tell the difference between a real and a perceived threat. When he was young, he was afraid of everything that *hadn't* happened, causing his body to send him into a fight-or-flight mode, which eventually lead to panic attacks. Slowly, and with help from his counselor, he had learned how to not send those signals to his subconscious. Even though currently *he* wasn't personally in immediate danger, his subconscious was vicariously signaling to his body that danger was lurking in dark corners of the world he lived in, threatening children of the past, present and future, for he could feel panic starting to set in. He knew once it started, he wouldn't be able to stop it, so he sat down and started his meditation tactic to reroute his thought patterns and reset his nervous system.

He began imaging a scene in the mountains, with a pristine and placid lake mirroring a beautiful sunset on its surface. It had a fresh stream pouring into it, with evergreens lining its banks. He imagined the smell of the pines and the sounds of the birds chirping in stereo. He had a fly rod in his hand and waders on, letting him comfortably trudge through knee-high waters, making skillful casts to likely cover holding his favorite fish—the Brooke Trout. His wrists flicked back and forth, landing a hand-tied fly right on the edge of a rock. He saw the fish boil on it and come up from beneath it, engulfing the fly. He felt the vibration in his hands and saw the fish swimming off. He began reeling furiously and swung the rod back, setting the hook in the fish's mouth. The fish made an impressive run, taking 20 feet of line out of his reel before leaping high into the air and returning to the water like an Olympic diver, barely making a splash. He fought the fish for several minutes before bringing it to his feet and landing it. He held it up against the amber sky, marveling at its beauty, before setting it free back in the water to live the life a fish was intended to live.

Dusty finally calmed his mind enough to concentrate on taking a shower and relaxing in the warm stream of water flowing form the spout. When he was done, he made himself a bowl of canned clam chowder and ate it with saltine crackers. He ate his chowder in total silence, spooning it into his mouth slowly and methodically. He finished it in about twice the time he normally would have, staring at the wall with a blank countenance. He felt like a zombie. He was eating more because he hadn't eaten all day and figured he should, not because he was hungry.

His mind jumped around a bit, from work, to his little girl, to Lynn, to Bruce and The Chosen, to his parents, to his childhood memories of riding his bike through his neighborhood and going to Worlds of Fun in the summers back in Kansas City. As he finished his meal, Lynn came down to the kitchen. "You gonna tell me what's up now?" She put her arms around his neck from behind as he sat at the table. She bent down and kissed the side of his neck.

"I found it Lynn."

"Found what?"

"The place she died…"

Lynn's face became stricken with a mix of terror and excitement, "What? Oh my God! Dusty, are you sure? How, how did you… where did she… Oh my God!"

"I know. When I left last night, it was because I had remembered something from the past. What you said about getting back on the right path, or something to that effect, triggered a memory I had of getting lost one time on the way home from a deposition down south at night. I believe that's what it was from anyway, but that's beside the point. I went driving. Lynn, it was the craziest thing." She was listening intently. She sat down next to him and grabbed his hands and held them. "I found this place off the highway where I got detoured. Well what really happened is I took a wrong exit and got off too early. Anyway, this was like a couple years ago, maybe more, maybe less."

"Honey why didn't you let me go with you?"

"Because, the place I remembered was sketchy. It's straight ghetto. I didn't want to take you with me. I wasn't even sure if it was anything worth investigating and I just didn't feel comfortable taking you when I wasn't sure what I was getting into. And I'm glad I didn't. As soon as I got there, I started getting followed by a car filled with gangsters. I was scared shitless."

"Dustin!" She punched him on the shoulder. "What the hell were you thinking? Going down there at that time of the night in your expensive vehicle. You must have stuck out like a sore thumb!"

"Uh, yah. To say the least. But nothing happened. Well, everything happened, but I wasn't in danger. In fact, they helped me."

"Helped?"

"Yeah, so I felt this presence at a stop sign when they kind of had me cornered. There were two cars at this point. Then it happened. Supercommunication…"

"No way…"

"Yep," Dusty kind of smiled and nodded his head. "I got all fuzzy inside and my mind went kind of numb and I heard her. She said, 'here…' or something like that. I'm pretty sure it was 'here' though."

"Dusty this is amazing! Oh my God! Are you serious? You heard her?" She hugged him around the neck in a joyous outburst. Hope was restored in her at this moment, but the hope, happiness and excitement soon faded as Dusty continued.

"So, I stopped my car, got out, and confronted these guys."

"You did what?!"

"I didn't have a choice. It just came over me. After I heard her, it was like a sign. So, I got out and waved a hundred-dollar bill in the air. It literally just happened. I knew it was the right thing to do. I told them I'd pay them if they could help me. This guy, 8-Ball, he was their leader, confronted me and wanted to know what I was doing in their part of town," he was interrupted by Lynn giggling. "What?"

"I'm sorry, I just can't get over the fact that he's named, 8-Ball," she said with a beautiful, radiant smile. Dusty hadn't seen her smile like this in a while and it sent tingles up his spine."

"I know. I know, just, bear with me here."

"Okay, I'll try. So, you got out of the car, waving a hundred-dollar bill? Wow, they must have thought you were absolutely insane."

"To say the least. So, I walked up to these six or seven black guys who had all gotten out and their leader, 8-Ball and I had a talk. I told him why I was there."

"What did you say? Did they believe you?"

"It was generic enough. I just said I was concerned about the safety of a little girl. I described her. One of his buddies spoke up and pointed to a house across the street."

"That was it, wasn't it?"

"Yes. It was. So, 8-Ball ended up telling me to meet him by the park today at noon. So, I did. He's not that bad. Actually, a nice guy. I really like him. He must have a soft spot. He asked around a little bit and found out the family had moved. The house was vacant so I decided to go in. It looked like someone had just abandoned it. I looked around for a bit and then just kind of became overwhelmed with grief. So, I sat down. I started to meditate like we've been talking about. I tried doing some of the stuff Lana has talked to me about. Then, she came."

"She?"

"My little girl." Dusty's eyes started watering. So did Lynn's. "She showed me fleeting images. She flickered in and out. As long as my eyes were closed it's like I could see into a portal or something. I don't know exactly what happened, but I could see violence. I could feel stress and tension. I saw a man kick her in the head. I saw woods… dirt. Then it's like I lost concentration or connection or something, because the images stopped and she went away. I couldn't get her back."

"Aw honey," she held him close as he stared blankly at the floor, "I know this must be so hard for you. But it's such an amazing thing. You did it. You found her. What you did is going to help everyone. It brings me hope and it will for others too."

"Yeah, but I don't know what to do now."

"We will figure this out babe. We will get these horrible people. We've come too far. I love you babe. I'm so proud of you. That must have been so hard to do by yourself."

"You shoulda seen 8-Ball when I came out of the house."

"He was there?!"

"Yeah, he waited outside for me as a lookout. He seriously must think I'm crazy. But it's weird. He seems so… willing. Like he understands. I don't know. It's like he has some very Robin-Hoodish obligation to protect his realm. I have his number. He said to stay in touch."
"Well, sounds like he could maybe be a good ally."

"I think so. I hope so. We'll see. We'll see."

That night Dusty and Lynn watched a movie together and cuddled on the couch… *Vanilla Sky*, another one of Dusty's favorites. Lynn reminded him of Tom Cruise's girlfriend in a way, except Dusty had more than one day to fall in love with Lynn and he was loving her in reality, not a dream. At least he hoped. During the scene in the movie where Tom Cruise jumps off the skyscraper, back to reality, Dusty pinched himself just to make sure. They ate popcorn, drank wine, and made love on the couch during the credits. Then they went to bed.

It didn't take long before his dreams were up and running the show. This time, something was entirely different though. There was no longer the black void surrounding his little girl like he was so used to. He saw her amidst the very detailed scenery of her house—the one he had just visited. He saw everything in vivid detail, just as it was earlier the day before. Somehow, she was able coexist with his regular dreams or project imagery that she had never been able to do before. Or possibly, his mind had not been able to *receive* it before. She was no longer flickering, as she was when he was actually in the house. For the first time, he actually felt like he existed in the same plane as she did.

The little girl stood there, in her room, staring at Dusty.

"Hello," Dusty said timidly. He got no response. "Can you talk?" Again, no response. Instead, she walked over to him and grabbed his hand. She started leading Dusty to the living room. As he followed her, he noticed the house changing around him. It began to morph back to another time, where things were still cluttered and dirty, but not abandoned looking. She led him to the front door and beckoned for him to follow her out. He did as she pleased.

Upon shutting the door behind them, she looked up at him and smiled. The smile warmed Dusty's heart, but it said something he couldn't put his finger on. *What is she trying to tell me?* It almost felt like she was trying to comfort him. She put his hand on the doorknob and motioned for him to turn it and open the door. When Dusty opened the door, he saw the house was completely transformed. He saw a middle-aged man and a woman. Both of them were sitting on the couch, drinking beer and smoking cigarettes.

Dusty's heart started beating rapidly. He didn't know what he was about to see, but he anxiously awaited what he could only imagine to be disturbing imagery. Then the story began.

She showed him her life, her childhood, her family, her assailant... She showed him how she died; the blow to her temple by an angry boot that left her on the floor for days; the people— her mother and her mother's boyfriend—who did it. He heard the arguments about insurance and outstanding warrants and whether or not to take her to the hospital. He saw the man hit the woman repeatedly when she argued. She showed him the clippers they used to sever her head from her body when she finally died; and she showed him her final resting place in a shallow grave deep in the woods next to the park. Her head and her body were placed in trash bags and disposed of in an attempt to hide the evidence. No one had ever known she was dead because her mother never reported it. The mother never had the guts to stand up to her boyfriend. She didn't want him to go to jail and neither did she. She justified it as a terrible accident—no reason for them both to go to prison for the rest of their lives. She just packed everything up and moved away with him, as if her sweet baby girl never existed.

When Dusty awoke, he was as terrified and emotional as he had ever been in his life. This phenomenon had happened many times over the last year and he wondered when the time would come that he would stop beating his all-time-scared-and-emotional record. He was utterly confused as to how he had been able to see what he had seen. He sat on the edge of his bed, drenched with sadness and aching with pain. He remained in the same position for next to twenty minutes. Had he *really* seen her? Was this all a hallucination precipitated by stress and desperation? Or had she really been able to come and show him the truth. He remained silent and motionless, soaking in what he had just seen. *How am I supposed to fix this? What happened so that all of the sudden she could just, show me?* Then it hit him. He found the place she died.

When Dusty came to this conclusion, elation overwhelmed him. As depressed as he was after seeing the horror, he now had something to cling on to. He had something real that he could share with the group that might actually help. He immediately called Lana and told her everything that had happened in the last couple days. He paced his bedroom back and forth, waking Lynn in the process. She was a little startled by Dusty's frantic voice, but when she realized what he was explaining to Lana, she became alert and excited. Dusty looked at Lynn as he explained the part about the body and where he thought it was. "It was horrible," he stated, "I know I must sound crazy, but I know where she is buried. I *saw* everything. She *showed* me everything. How she died, who did it, how they did it… where they buried her. Those mother fuckers…" Dusty started to tear up, "they… they used hedge clippers to," he tried getting it out but he just couldn't get over the waves of tears and emotion. Lynn once again pulled him into her chest.

"Sweetheart…" she caressed his head and held him tight as he continued to spill it out to Lana.

Dusty finally got out the unbearable statement, "the mom's boyfriend kicked her in the head and just left her there to die. They had warrants out. The mom wanted to take her to the hospital, but her boyfriend, or, whoever, wouldn't let her. She barely put up a fight. They just let her lay there and die. Then they used hedge clippers to cut off her head and they buried her in the woods by a park. That's the swing I saw before. The dreams of the swing—that's why I was seeing it. She was trying to show me something."

Dusty sat on the edge of the bed. Lynn approached him from behind, in his t-shirt. As she heard the words, her heart pounded and her gut tightened. She could feel Dusty's pain as she held her arms around his waist, laying her head on his back. Tears gently rolled down her cheek. With every word Dusty spoke, with every detail he described about the death of his little girl, she cringed. She didn't know exactly what was going on because she had missed part of it, but she had the general idea.

A part of Lynn, a tiny part, wondered why Dusty called Lana first—why he hadn't spoke to her about it. She didn't like hearing this second hand, but then thought to herself that it didn't really matter how she heard it; it wouldn't have made anything better. She knew Dusty's affection for Lana and how close they were and how much they relied on each other for the investigation and analysis in the matters of The Chosen. Dusty found Lana first. All she wanted to do was be there for Dusty. The grief of the situation was just too much. She was tired of hearing Dusty talk on the phone by now. She just wanted him to be done and talk to her, mainly because she had a lot of questions and couldn't hear what Lana was saying very well. The conversation carried on 10, 15, 20 minutes. She finally just laid back down on the bed, staring at the ceiling, wondering about her little girl and what had happened to her, kind of tuning Dusty out.

Dusty and Lana had decided to do a write-up on what happened to Dusty and share it with the chat room. The basic premise was this: always be aware of and continually seek supercommunication, find the place where the child died, if possible have something that belongs to the child, meditate there, attempt to receive any communication and details given in the "conscious breakthrough", then look for the puzzle pieces to be delivered more clearly and vivid during subconscious hours.

Before their conversation ended, Lana had something to tell Dusty, "Dusty, something strange happened to me two days ago. Eddie called me. Vaughan. The…"

"…one who sees 9 kids, I know."

"Well, anyway, he told me he knew Bruce died. Apparently that man is as good of a detective as you and Bruce."

"What? How?" Dusty's stomach dropped. He knew what this could mean. He felt guilty for not having disclosed the information, but fear was the dominating emotion.

"The newspaper. Apparently, he keeps tabs on everyone. After Doris and Nick, he thought a conspiracy might be going on, that we were being killed off, one by one, so he called all the major cities where member of The Chosen lived and requested a copy of their newspaper be mailed to him. He said he wasn't able to get them all, but Chicago…"

"Holy fuck. What did he say?" Lynn by this point was pressing her ear next to the phone to hear what was going on. She couldn't take it anymore and Dusty's face scared her.

"He said he saw that Bruce died and asked me if the boys in the cement were connected. From what he could tell, based off the Bible we sent out, it was a possible match. I… I couldn't lie to him. I had to tell him."

"Yes, you did at that point. Was he upset?"

"No, he was very somber and methodical. He said thank you and that he didn't intend to tell anyone, but I don't know what he plans to do."

"I got one guess."

"Me too. What do we do?"

"I don't think there's anything we can do at this point. It might already be too late. I don't think we break the news yet; I mean I could have a solution!"

"Could have isn't going to be good enough and you know that."

"Give it another week. Give me a little time. Then, maybe we tell the group."

"Okay. Go figure it out. Please call me with updates."

"You know I will. Bye Lana."

"Goodbye Dusty."

Lynn looked at Dusty as he hung up the phone. When he turned, he caught her gaze, "Eddie is going to kill himself, isn't he?"

"I don't know babe. He had dealt with so much grief for so long."

"Why didn't you wake me up to tell me your dream?"

Dusty and Lynn talked it out and he explained to her why he didn't wake her up to tell her first. He said he needed to collaborate immediately before any of his creative momentum dwindled. She seemed to understand, but deep down she still wished she could be Dusty's ultimate "collaborator". He explained to her that she was his anchor, his breath, his life-force… she agreed she'd rather be those things than a mere collaborator.

Before she left town, they researched the area where Dusty saw the girl. They looked at county records and documents, but were not able to find much. After several phone calls and trips to the assessor's, finally someone in one of the city departments, was able to find the last name as "Phelps" as the owners on the house. That was it. Apparently good records didn't exist on houses on that area of town. Taxes hadn't been paid on it the last several years and they also learned, or assumed, there was no mortgage because it didn't appear to be foreclosed on or taken possession of by any institution. They figured it was an old, wholly-owned family heirloom that was abandoned fairly rapidly in order to hide or cover something up, namely the murder of Dusty's little girl.

The two dug and dug but couldn't find anything on any Phelps. Dusty wanted to do something, badly, but knew he needed more incriminating evidence. He wanted to go find her in the woods, but didn't want to blow it. They both agreed that it would be extremely suspicious for him to "randomly" find the little girl in the middle of a wooded plot in the ghetto. So, he remained in Limbo once more until more details could be obtained.

Chapter 51

Lynn flew home on Sunday. The next Tuesday morning Dusty was supposed to go to work, but he wanted to talk to 8-Ball. He felt like he needed to get more information about the area—really pick his brain for... anything. He picked up the phone, then paused for a second, weighing the pros and cons of perpetuating this relationship. He had nothing to lose. He dialed the number and put the phone to his ear.

"This is 8-Ball."

"You know a place to get a good cup of coffee?"

"You just get straight to the point, don't ya?"

"I'm sorry. I just need to talk to you. In person. Some strange things have been happening and I'm kind of at a stand-still and... I just need to talk to you. Can you meet me today?"

"Well, I'm finishing up a couple things, but I can meet you probably around noon. I know a good spot. I'll text you the address."

"Ok, great. I'll see you then. Thank you. I really appreciate it."

....

The burger joint sat on the corner of an intersection of two fairly busy roads in a nicer part of the neighborhood. The place kind of reminded Dusty of a Waffle House, accept it wasn't as nice and it served fried liver and onions instead of waffles. They seated themselves in a booth next to the window. The table smelled like mildew and Dusty noticed the cook forming burgers with his bare hands, not bothering to wear an apron or a hairnet to cover his quite impressive afro.

"Good morning gentleman," spoke a petite, young black girl, "my name is Rena and I'll be your server today. Would you like to try our special? It's a mushroom and onion burger with fries—$5.99"

Dusty glanced back at the cook who was now popping a raw mushroom into his mouth, "No thanks. I'll just take a cup of coffee, black please."

"Same for me," 8-Ball said.

"Alrighty. I'll get that right out for you."

When the waitress walked away, 8-Ball leaned in and whispered to Dusty, "They really prefer if you not use that terminology in here," Dusty wrinkled his brow in confusion. "It's much nicer if you say African American." His face was dead serious and after a moment, Dusty realized he was talking about the coffee he ordered—black. Dusty examined 8-Ball's face for any signs of humor. It remained stoic.

"You want me to order African American coffee?" he finally said to crack the silence. 8-Ball, surprised at Dusty's witty volley, couldn't hold out any longer and burst into laughter.

"That would be a pretty Goddamn good cup of coffee now, wouldn't it?" he shot back, laughing so hard he was almost in tears.

Not to be outdone, "I always said I like my coffee like I like my women," Dusty offered.

"Oh yeah, and how's that?"

"Hot, strong and black!" At that, he had 8-Ball rolling. The two apparently shared a similar sense of humor. It made the situation instantly more comfortable for both of them. Dusty was glad he could get away with that joke without offending him, as mild as it was. It said a lot about his character: strong, secure, gregarious, laidback. Dusty suddenly felt blessed to have found him, like this really might be his opportunity for cracking this case.

When 8-Ball regained composure, the waitress had just returned with a pot of coffee. "I'm glad to see you two are enjoying yourself," she said with a smile. "Here is your coffee." 8-Ball just looked at Dusty and smiled as the steamy coffee filled their cups.

"Okay, let's get back to why you are here."

"Well, she's been showing me what happened to her now, more vividly, in my dreams."

"Like what?"

"Everything," Dusty said as he choked back a lump in his throat. Dusty proceeded to explain the events that he saw happen in his dream to a very attentive and bewildered 8-Ball. He explained the encounter in detail, the visions he was shown and how he believed that his little girl was murdered. He told 8-Ball where he believed the body to be. He opened up to him, fully, about how he came to return to the neighborhood in the first place. He explained about The Chosen and how the group had formed to help the children. He told him about the recent deaths. He told them about Bruce, Lynn, Lana and how they were his support group. He explained Bruce's suicide and the pressure it was putting on him and Lynn. He left no leaf uncovered. He knew if he was to trust 8-Ball, he had to know everything. Several cups of coffee later, Dusty started wrapping up.

"This whole process has been heart-wrenching. I'm tired, I'm desperate and I'm afraid I'm going to start losing people," he took a deep breath. "I'm afraid I'm going to lose Lynn."

"You really love her, don't you?"

"She is wonderful... the most wonderful person I've ever met. And beautiful," Dusty looked out the window into the pale gray sky, "My God she is beautiful. But she is deteriorating through all of this. I have to help her. I can't lose her. It would break me." Dusty tapped his fingers on the table lightly, trapping a wave of emotion in his chest. "So, this is where you come in. Do you think you can help me?"

8-Ball sat back in the booth and folded his hands together. "You might think people call me 8-Ball because I'm... a... a drug dealer or something," he reached into his pocket as he spoke, never taking his eyes away from Dusty's, "but it's actually something quite different. You see, as a kid, I didn't have much to hold on to. My daddy was a thug. He beat my momma, sold drugs out of the house—once I saw him shoot a man in our driveway. I got beat up by bullies daily. One day I asked my momma why God hated us so much. She said, 'Marcellus, you shouldn't bother yourself with asking such questions. He don't hate us. He don't love us. He just let us be to figure it out fo' ourselves, hopin' that he gave us the right stuff to do the right thing. Some people look for that good he put in us, others, they just don't bother lookin'. And every once in a while, if you look real hard, God gives you a sign to see as you will.' The next day, she gave me this."

He held up a children's toy. The Magic 8-Ball. It was the one you ask a question to, shake up, and wait for a response. "I've based many important decisions on this right here. It's kind of like my momma though—I take it for what it's worth. But it has a way of showing you what you *need* to hear at the time. May not be exactly what you end up doing, but it gets your wheels turning in the right direction. You catch my drift?"

"I think I do. I've been doing a lot more looking lately myself."

8-Ball started shaking the 8-Ball, waving it around in circles, "Mr. 8-Ball, should I believe this crazy white boy?"

It read: "*Signs point to yes.*" He showed it to Dusty who just shrugged.

"Mr. 8-Ball, should I stick my neck out to help him?"

It read: "*Without a doubt*"

Dusty asked, "So that's it? It's that simple?"

"Hold on, hold on. Let me finish," he continued shaking. "Mr. 8-Ball, is Dusty going to be giving me that Benjamin he was waving around last night?" After a long moment of youthful anticipation…

It read: "*My sources say no*"

Quickly, as if it didn't happen, he shook it again.

It read: "*Ask again later*"

Dusty started laughing. "I'm liking this technique better all the time!"

8-Ball was humbly dejected, "Did I mention that I only listen to it when it's right?" Dusty was still laughing as 8-Ball whispered, "Stupid fuckin' ball" and put it back into his pocket with a concealed grin on his face.

"I'll tell you what Marcellus,"

"Hey! Only my momma!"

"Okay, okay… 8-Ball, I'll pay for the coffee and tip with this hundred. You keep the rest."

"Nah, I'm just messin' with you man. Wait 'til I come through. I was taught you get what you earn."

"Fair enough. So, you have any ideas?"

"Well, first of all, you can't just go to the cops with info like this without looking suspicious. Luckily for you, I've got friends in high places. I think I could get a plan okayed to expand the park, maybe put in a walking trail. It would be a lot better if someone accidentally found her. Then we can go from there."

"Man, I don't know if I can just sit back and let this be. I mean this is killing me thinking she's in those woods and not knowing. There has to be a way. I need to find her."

"No, you don't. Not right now. I'm telling you. You asked for my help. There is no good that can come of you finding her. You will be the lead suspect! And probably the same for anyone else who goes randomly tramping through those woods without probable cause. I mean, no one even knows she is gone, right?"

Dusty thought for a moment, thought about arguing, then realized how much sense this made, "Okay. You are right. No, no one knows she is gone, that I know of at least." Then, remembering a statement from a moment ago, asked, "What do you mean 'friends in high places'?"

"Well, since we're sharing secrets here…I'm an informant to the Chicago police. My crew and I help keep the streets clean. I got caught selling a bunch of pot a few years ago and they made me a deal. It was the best thing that ever happened to me. I help keep bad guys off the streets and I still get to get high any time I want. I hope that don't change your mind…"

"No. No it doesn't. I've actually, uh, I've been known to *partake* every now and then. I think it should be legal, personally. More money and effort are spent to keep it off the streets when it should be going towards catching murderers, or figuring out how to reduce drunk driving."

"Don't get me started," 8-Ball said, smiling and nodding. "So, you cool? You trust me?" He extended his hand across the table. Dusty looked him right in the eye, peering into his soul. He glimpsed goodness.

"Yes, I do. Let me know what I can do to help," and he shook his hand.

"Well let's go to the park. Show me where you think she is. I'll see to it that area gets excavated. Then we'll see how real you are, Dusty."

"Hey, I have doubts myself, but I feel good about this. Thank you, 8-Ball. Thank you." They shook hands and headed out the door. They each left a $20 bill for Rena. When she got to the table, she picked it up and started to cry. She never left a coffee cup empty again.

....

Dusty went back to work after lunch and got as much done as he could with his limited attention span. He had a few new cases come across his desk that he needed to decline, so he got those out of the way with a few phone calls and asked Marilyn to send them letters. They were all cases that had been referred to him from another law firm, dealing with clients who had taken a new drug that had been on the market to treat blood clotting. His firm did handle product-liability cases, but these referrals were all cases where the clients were old, unhealthy and had a laundry list of conditions wrong with them. This made it hard to pinpoint the drug as the proximate cause for their injuries and/or deaths. Dusty had had Marilyn review the records initially and verify that they had all used the drug, but he needed to do a more thorough analysis and write a letter to the referring attorney to inform him of why they had been declined. He had needed to get to these for a while, so this was a perfect project for his shortened afternoon.

When Dusty got home, he called Lynn and told her about the plan with the park. Lynn was shocked and didn't quite know what to think, but she knew Dusty wouldn't be telling her something like this unless he believed it was legitimate, "Shouldn't you call the cops at this point?"

"No. Not right now at least. I don't want to rush into things and mess it up. I talked to 8-Ball and he said he could help. We talked over coffee this afternoon. Apparently, he's some kind of informant to the cops. He said he has connections."

"Can you trust this guy? What if he is lying? Why can't you make an anonymous call?"

"I have no reason to believe he is lying. I mean, he is trying to help me; what would he gain by bullshitting me? I'm not sure the best way to go about it, but I do know I don't want to act out on emotion. I don't want to make an anonymous call and turn it over without any control. With this plan, I'm going to try and *be* there, like volunteer."

"I don't know how I feel about not calling the cops."

"Honey, what if I call the cops and they think I'm the killer? I don't want to undergo an investigation right now. I just don't want to do something to screw this up. It took me so long to get here. I just want to think it through and do the right thing."

Lynn pondered these statements carefully and realized he had a point, "Okay honey, I trust you. Just, be careful with this 8-Ball guy. You don't know anything about him."

"I don't know why, but I have a good feeling about this guy. His real name is Marcellus, actually."

"Well, I don't really care what his name is, just make sure he's not dangerous. I'm sure there's plenty of black people in the ghetto that would jump at a chance to scam a well-to-do white boy."

Dusty retracted his urge to argue. He paused, taking into perspective her emotional state of mind. Lynn, added after a few seconds, "If it was my little girl, I would do just about anything if I thought it would catch her killer. I still just don't see why you are deciding to trust him instead of taking it to the cops."

Dusty tried to validate her concern, "Listen, you are right. We do need to act fast. I just don't want to tip these people off, whoever they are. I want to catch them. 8-Ball said that going to the cops would make me look suspicious. I mean, why *would* a white boy be roaming around in the woods in the ghetto?"

"Well, why can't he do it?"

"It's just better this way. We think if her body is found by 'accident', it would keep us out of the list of suspects. I can't afford to be under investigation for murder. I could lose my license. And he is helping me. There's no way I could ask him to take that risk. He said he thinks he can get a plan pushed through to restore the park."

"How the hell can he do that?"

"I don't know. Apparently, these 'friends in high places'. Again, I have no reason to believe he would lie to me about something like that. He is a good guy. He tries to keep bad guys off the streets. Yeah, he might smoke pot, but he is interested in keeping his neighborhood safe. And if he knows a little girl was murdered there, he is going to do anything he can to bring justice to rectify the situation. He has a real sense of duty about him. I just don't think he would be jerking me around."

"And you think this will work?"

"I just think if she was found randomly, then it would keep the cops off our back. Neither of us want to be interrogated and seen as suspects. I want it to happen naturally. I want to go about this carefully. Her parents aren't serial killers, this was an accident they are trying to cover up, so I don't think any other kids are in immediate danger."

"Okay, well I trust you baby, I just want this to get over with. I'm starting to think about ways to kill myself... and that really scares me."

"That's not going to happen honey, we will figure this out. Keep thinking of every place you've been in the last few years—bathrooms, grocery stores, gas stations, anything. Write it down. We will narrow it down. The reports of these 'clue dreams' have been talked about quite a bit lately. People have started reporting dreaming about different, random things. They just didn't know what they meant. Remember Nick and his Mountain? He started dreaming about the Mountain, probably because that's where he made contact. I think if people can just get out there and see what their kids saw, they will see what happened and can figure out what to do. We got this babe." She so badly wanted to believe him.

Chapter 52

Eddie looked at the river. It was huge. Boiling. Thunderous. The jagged canyon wall rose five hundred feet, straight up on each side. Somewhere, miles upstream, the Colorado was wide, deep and peaceful, but here it was fifty feet wide and bottlenecked into a torrent of explosive rapids and whirlpools that could devour a river barge.

Eddie had seen tornadoes up close. He was in Galveston when hurricane Carla hit in 1966. He'd flown over volcanoes and felt the ground tremble at 6.2 on the Richter in Japan, but this river was a killer and the scariest beast of nature he'd ever seen; but he was not afraid. He was going to feel the two most amazing rushes a body could ever take: the pure adrenaline shock of jetting down deadly rapids and the agony/ecstasy flash-burn of dying. No fear. No guilt... No coming back. It was his lot in life to do this. He was proud and anxious and excited as hell, but he was not afraid. He would not ask for this cup to pass. He was a Chosen. His death was definitely going to save little souls and send a devil straight to hell.

He looked at the sky. Crystal clear. A hawk, no, it was an eagle, circled lazily overhead. Wouldn't it be neat if the eagle was his guardian angel or something? Who knows? The river made seven steep drops over the next four hundred yards. Each descent was a small Niagara Falls crashing over huge boulders, sending spray and foam thirty feet into the air. A rainbow between the canyon was just above the mist. It was louder than a jet engine. He felt the rumble in his bones. His buddy the eagle still circled above him and it was weird. Over the cannonade that pounded up those canyon walls, Eddie could have sworn that he heard for a brief second the "scree" of the eagle. Eddie waved to his feathered escort and yelled "Showtime."

He fastened his helmet. Sure, he was a goner, but he still wanted to go as far as he could, maybe past the third drop. He only had on his swim trunks though, no life jacket. Eddie stepped into the red kayak that rested just next to the water. The current was raging, powerfully, just a few inches away. Eddie didn't pray. He didn't know if he even believed in God before all this. The only thing he knew he believed in was his "children". What would he pray for? A safe return? He would find out in a few minutes if the Big Guy was waiting for him, anyway. The only thing he hoped for was that he would see those kids one more time, one way or another. Eddie pushed the kayak into the river with his oar. He was off.

The river grabbed the kayak immediately and sucked it toward the middle. A huge boulder stood fast against a wall of water that undulated 15 to 20 feet up the front of the boulder and swirled around to the back of the boulder into a hole, a maelstrom, 10 feet deep and as wide as a camping trailer. The water exploded off the river bottom and rose another 15 feet into the air before it headed towards a group of car-sized jagged chunks of granite about 50 yards downstream. First, he had to get around the big boulder though.

Eddie was an excellent kayaker, but he could not get right. The little vessel turned and dipped, taking him completely under several times as he approached the boulder. No amount of paddling, back paddling, nothing, had any effect on his trajectory. He must have been traveling 45 miles per hour, straight for the boulder. He was about thirty yards from the boulder and the river was showing no signs of mercy; it was having its way with him.

A smaller, angry looking wave, about 6 feet high, now stood between him and the wall of water that blasted the front of the boulder. He went up the wave sideways and saw that the wave went down another 10 feet on the other side and rolled back on itself, creating a pounding backwash current. As Eddie dropped into the hole, the kayak spun around and fell tail first. The front was pointed straight up, like a missile. For a moment, Eddie saw nothing but blue. The sky was beautiful and dominated his field of vision, everything except for a small dark silhouette. His guardian angel was still watching overhead.

Suddenly everything went brown. The suckhole grabbed Eddie like a vise and pulled him under. Way under. The concussion knocked Eddie senseless for a moment. His ears were ringing so loud he could barely hear the roar of the river. He didn't know which way was up. The water Gods were trying to wrench him from his kayak, but he was in it good. He and the kayak were one body, like a unicorn. When was he going to come up? Was he? His lungs were burning. Suddenly, the river delivered him up like a rocket straight into the air. Eddie gasped. The concussion had blurred his vision, but he sensed where he was. He was traveling up the wall of water in front of the boulder. Up he went; there was no use in paddling.

He pulled the paddle up to his chest and bowed forward against the kayak. The river spun the kayak around in a football spiral, maybe 2 or 3 revelations. Then, down he came, just barely over the rock. The back of the kayak clipped the back of the rock causing Eddie to tumble head over heels into the gaping maelstrom behind the rock. Crash! He went under again. Hard. Spinning and whipping around like a rag doll, Eddie held his breath, but it hurt bad.

Three of Eddie's ribs were broken by the whack of the river that greeted him like the highway greets a downed biker. Of course, Eddie only vaguely sensed pain. He wasn't really aware of his broken ribs or the blood that drained from his ears, nose and mouth. Eddie was not going to go easy. He fought to stay conscious. He wasn't *really* coherent, but he still had life and fight in him. He still was not afraid.

Everything from the kayak body on up to the top of his head throbbed, burned and pierced. Any sensation that can assault a nerve and make it react was happening all over his upper body. The river Gods had him now. They were not going to send him back up. They were bouncing him off the bottom, tossing him back and forth between their hands. He would never see the sky again. *Time to check out, fill your lungs with water and get on over to the other side. Breathe in that water, it'll only take a few seconds.*

They say drowning is like the most fantastic, relaxing LSD trip a person can take, but this was not fantastic or relaxing. Suddenly, air. Eddie couldn't really see or think, but his body instinctually gasped for a breath of air in the brief moment his head popped above the water line. He was aware that he was alive and totally defenseless. His body had been designed to endure the beating and live to feel the final, violent mutilation of his body before his soul would give it up.

The kayak stopped turning. It straightened up and headed down stream fast, but steady. Eddie could barely see. There were literally shooting stars bouncing around his cranium. It hurt too much to open his eyes more than a squint. He started to become a little more aware of his body and senses. His hearing was practically gone, but he swore he could still hear the "scree" over the roar of the river, which was incessant. It was deafening. He could now assess that something was wrong with his rib cage. He'd heard something like broken ribs rattling around in his mid-section. He could feel them grinding and grating every time he moved. If this river twisted and turned him again, he would lose consciousness.

He was rising up and down, jetting forward at probably 50 miles per hour. The spray slapped at him, stinging his face like a thousand bees. The kayak had found a seam in the rapids and he was racing down the chute. He couldn't bear to open his eyes to look forward. Every nerve in his skull was misfiring, creating a massive migraine, crushing his will to stay alive. Eddie lost his oar that last time under, (as if it were of use in the first place), so he just hugged the sides, squeezed his eyes shut and went along for the ride.

He suddenly remembered the group of VW sized rocks that were ahead. The ride was going to get really rough again in a few moments. Eddie had not been able to see beyond those rocks; he didn't figure he would need to. There was nothing to see except the rainbow arching between the canyon walls. The river seemed to stop or disappear there.

Eddie's eyes, ears and sense of orientation weren't really working too well at this point, but every nerve in his body was doing what it did best: feel pain. Eddie sensed the rhythm of the water change. It was starting to fight him again. The chute had become clogged. Suddenly he wasn't moving forward. It felt like he was actually moving backward. The power of the millions of gallons of muddy, boiling water lifted him up like a huge tide then suddenly forward and down, down in to a hole. Eddie felt the sudden, violent stop as the river Gods threw the little kayak down on a larger, flat rock, maybe even the river bottom. Every organ in Eddie's body tore from its mooring. Eddie was in shock, hallucinating from the pain. Every bone, muscle and organ became a glob of goo that collapsed into his lower extremities. His brain had no self-awareness, no self-knowledge, no personality. He was a mere organism, suffering the most pain that could be suffered this side of a coma; it was his entire universe.

In his last moments, he had no way of knowing, or caring, but the river Gods had sent him airborne. He floated off the cliff and began a spectacular freefall. Down… down… down. The front half of the kayak was gone. His legs hung limp from the knee out of the gaping hole. He remained untouched by the river until he had fallen seventy feet into the base of the falls. The water raged forming a monstrous cauldron of white, frothing river that engulfed Eddie into the Abyss. He was swallowed with such force that his body didn't resurface until it was found six miles downstream by a fisherman two days later.

. . . .

Before Eddie decided to offer himself up to the river, he left a message to the forum. It read:

You all have been great to me. Getting to know some of you has brought me joy at the end of my life, which is something I haven't felt in a long time. I don't want to let any cats of the bag, but I do want to at least let the cat breathe. Through my own research, and collaboration with our leadership, I have determined Bruce Crippen, one of our own, committed suicide and that as a result of his actions, two boys were found and their murderer brought to Justice. These events happened no less than two weeks apart. After Doris and Nick died, their cases were solved. It left many questions about whether or not taking one's own life would solve the case and I believe we now have that answer.

We all know that the chat room is an open book and that we are here to learn about each other's cases in order to help our own situation. I'm not here to try and convince anyone of anything or to insinuate that Bruce's actions are the final solution, but now that I know that taking my own life is a solution to catch the bastard that has taken the lives of 9 children, whom I dream about every single night and think about every minute of every waking day, I feel as if I have no choice. I wanted to tell you all to be honest with you. I didn't want to hide anything from you. I have a feeling I wasn't he first to know of his death and the results it produced, but that doesn't

339

matter. Maybe Bruce didn't want anyone to know. Maybe he didn't want to be responsible for the lives of others; maybe he was being considerate; maybe the person(s) that knew can't come to terms with telling the rest of us, for he may not want blood on his hands. Whatever the situation may be, it matters not. I am not offended. Hell, what are we supposed to do? This whole thing is a lose-lose scenario. Although I'm not upset that we were not privileged to the events that occurred in Bruce's life and after his life, I feel strongly to make this group privy to the decisions and aftermath from those decisions that I am making.

I am not scared. I am not afraid. If my maker meets me and decides my actions were not just, I am ready to accept that fate. What I will not accept, ANYMORE, is not being able to help these children. I look forward to seeing my wife again. If I have upset you, or if my decisions have caused you inner strife, I do apologize, but none us of should be deprived of any information involving our children. May God be with you.

Eddie posted this message a day before his final journey. When Lana called Dusty, he hadn't read it yet. At first, he felt guilty for not having disclosed Bruce's case to the group. Lana helped relinquish this guilt a bit, but Dusty still felt as if he had somehow betrayed The Chosen. Was Eddie more just? Did he have more decency? Was he braver? Playing these games was not healthy for Dusty. In the end, they both decided it happened and it couldn't have been stopped.

Three days after Eddie died, a man named Jimi Vaughan, Eddie's brother, turned himself into the police. All this time and Eddie had the killer right under his nose. Jimi had purportedly read Eddie's suicide letter, which outlined and detailed Eddie's entire story regarding the children. Eddie left cryptic undertones of his dealings with The Chosen, but didn't give enough information to blow the secrecy of the group or any of its members. What he did outline in detail was the tumult he battled every day. Jimi loved Eddie dearly and although his conscience had not stopped him from taking the lives of nine innocent children, the guilt and responsibility he felt for taking the life of his brother was too much for him to bear. He had always looked up to his older brother. He was a God to Jimi.

Eddie never once suspected Jimi of any sort of heinous crimes. Jimi was a master of deceit and like many serial killers, hid his actions and intent extremely well. Jimi, for a reason only known to God himself, developed an addiction to pedophilia. He led the authorities to the 9 different gravesites he had procured in the last 2 decades. All of these gravesites were five to six feet below ground level under existing parks and playgrounds. All of Jimi's victims were abducted at or near these sites and he felt it was only reasonable to return them when he was done with them. Jimi Vaughan made headlines. Everyone across the country knew his face and became disgusted at the mere site or sound of him. When the court proceedings were all said and done, he was charged with nine counts of first-degree murder and 29 counts of molestation. The state of Colorado sentenced Jimi Vaughan to death.

Bruce's death may have initially slipped by the rest of The Chosen, but everyone was talking about Eddie. For the first time, panic struck the group. Dusty had no idea what was going to happen next, but he could guess. Every morning he woke up expecting a call about another suicide. He figured it would happen any day now. He just knew he had to solve his case fast.

Although Dusty didn't have the final answers, he began explaining his situation to the group. He began slipping clues on the forum and informing the members that he believed finding the spot where a child departed this planet was a key element to breaking the communication threshold. It seemed far-fetched, but some believed him and tried harder than ever to recreate the supercommunication. Some.

Chapter 53

8-Ball was a man of his word. Dusty never asked how, but 8-Ball had successfully persuaded the city of Chicago to implement a park restoration and expansion. *He really must have as much clout as he says.* At this point, he couldn't care less. The two weeks he waited for 8-Ball's answer was torture. He knew he shouldn't go looking for her, but after seeing what she showed him, he couldn't have let her body lay there desecrated any longer. When 8-Ball said the project got approved and would start in October, Dusty was terrified and anxious. *Was she really there? Would they find her?* The thought of real people—total strangers—coming across her body, made him cringe inside. The realization that the world would now see her as a dead, decaying body and not sweet, precious little girl that Dusty knew, was the most heart-breaking notion to ever weave its way through his mind.

Dusty saw her much less during those two weeks, mainly because he hardly slept. He spent long hours contemplating how any human could decapitate her own child, or any child for that matter. *What evil exists in the world that transcends human's innate desire to protect her child at any cost? Rather than send her dirtbag of a boyfriend to jail, the mother covered up his abusive and fatal actions to the extent that she was willing to behead her baby girl and throw her in the woods like trash?* The visions appeared over and over in his head. He couldn't begin to grasp what could bring a person to do such a thing.

Luckily during this time period of waiting, the Draper case was at somewhat of a standstill. The judge was taking an exceedingly long time to rule on the plaintiff's request to do some testing on the lighter that had recently been uncovered by one of Karee's private investigators. They were wanting to show or attempt to show that the facts of the case point to the lighter being the sole cause of the fire and nothing else. They wanted to set fully dressed mannequins on fire and videotape it to show the jury how easily a lighter of this sort could ignite clothing. Dusty had presented enough paperwork and objections to keep the judge busy for a while, but even he had not expected the ruling to take this long. Since the case had such a high profile and SC&R was making a small fortune on billable hours, Stanley had decided to allow for it to be the only case on Dusty's plate. In short, this lull could not have come at a better time for Dusty... he would have been worthless in any important legal proceeding. He was given a few mundane tasks for a couple other cases, but nothing major. His main task was, and always had been, to concoct an impeccable defense for Ron Davis and his multimillion-dollar company, Reston Tobacco.

The "town" that 8-Ball was actually from was called Avondale. Although its population was technically about 250, the area encasing it housed around 2,500 people. This area was deemed the ghetto by most of Chicago, and Avondale lay at the center of it. Often times folks from the city confused the entire 30 blocks from 95th to 125th as Avondale, although it really only took up about three blocks. The rest was just the Chicago metro.

The community of Avondale was extremely excited for the park restoration. It wasn't often that the city showed interest in the ghetto and this small gesture aroused a lot of excitement. They might as well have put in a Disney World. 150 people from the surrounding neighborhoods volunteered to help with the project that second Sunday in October. It was a beautiful day. 8-Ball had told Dusty that he didn't think it was a good idea for him to be there. Not only was he worried about him emotionally, but he thought that a random white man showing up to volunteer for a playground restoration in the ghetto would raise some eyebrows. After much deliberation, 8-Ball promised to try and get Dusty on the construction crew. He had almost succeeded in talking Dusty out of being there, but Dusty was slave to an invisible tide that pulled at his conscience. Something inside of him felt that she couldn't be alone. Although she was already dead, he wanted...needed to be there for her. All 8-Ball had to do was make a phone call to his Chicago PD contact, a greasy, 50-year-old cop named Donnie, and voila. Dusty was in. Donnie knew the right people in the city.

The construction crew superintendent was a man named Bob. Bob was about 100 pounds overweight, wore thick glasses that would give most humans a massive migraine, and talked as a good ol' country-boy would. He didn't ask too many questions about Dusty's presence. In fact, half of his crew were borderline degenerates and he was happy to get all the help he could. New guys were thrown on the Chicago Department of Public Welfare weekly; this was nothing new to Bob.

The crew met up and briefed at City Hall. Before they departed, Bob was required to complete a safety check-off on Dusty, "Here is your hardhat. Make sure you have that there on at all times. A few weeks ago, some numnuts left his off and a goddamn tree fell on his head. Cost the city $42,000 and 'bout lost me my job," Bob recounted the story. "Take your eyes off for one minute and… ahh never mind. Just leave it on. You ever worked construction before?"

Dusty thought for a second about how much actual "construction" work was taking place at the park. There weren't any cranes or bulldozers and only one bobcat was on site. He had a feeling that most of this crew's assignments weren't your typical construction sites—the AAA league of the construction world—but rather than tangle with this man's dignity, he answered, "Absolutely."

"Good then. I'll just save my breath about the rest of the safety mumbo-jumbo I'm required to say. You look like a smart guy. Just don't hesitate to ask any questions. He told Dusty that the existing equipment was to be removed, the ground leveled out and mulched, a walking path cut through the woods that led to a picnic area, and all new equipment erected. This consisted of a three-person swing-set, a merry-go-round, a jungle gym with slides, ropes, a rock-climbing wall, monkey bars… the works, a tetherball pole, a basketball court, (which required extra clearing) and a teeter-totter. The project was scheduled to take a week.

Dusty actually really liked Bob. They talked the whole way from City Hall to the park, about a 25-minute drive south as Dusty rode shotgun. He learned that Bob grew up on a farm in Ohio and that he had four children, all from the same marriage of 31 years. The discussion was one-sided as

Dusty mainly listened, but it helped keep his mind off of the dark issues at hand. *He has no idea what he's about to get into.* Neither did Dusty.

....

8-Ball rolled up to the site with his usual crew: DeShawn, DeJuan, CJ and Tommy. He had showed up at each of their houses and drug them to his car, kicking and screaming, to help with the project. 8-Ball was kind of like their big brother. He had come to know each of them through various happenings in the ghetto. CJ was his childhood friend. 8-Ball was always keeping him out of trouble.

When CJ's mom died, his father became an alcoholic and dabbled in cocaine from time-to-time. There were many times CJ could remember as a boy witnessing his father snorting the mysterious white powder. He was always told it was medicine for his allergies. Had it not been for the cocaine, his dad might have very well let the alcohol take over and beaten him to death. Sad as it was, the powder actually counterbalanced the booze. CJ practically lived at 8-Ball's house from the time he was nine years old. 8-Ball, 14 at the time, had walked by and seen his dad beating the shit out of CJ. 8-Ball stormed into the house, bloodied up his face with a log he found in the front yard and carried CJ out of there. Despite being much younger, 8-Ball was an impressive athlete and at 14 could take on just about anyone in the entire ghetto. Cj's dad from that point on never laid a hand on him. He died five years later from an overdose. CJ now lived in the house alone, although he was hardly ever there.

Years later, 8-Ball and CJ came across Tommy Washington. Tommy took pot smoking to another level and would do anything to move enough product to smoke for free. Sometimes he made a little bit of money, but he could have been damn near rich had he sold even half of what he smoked. Consequently, he was running into the toughest thugs in the city since he was 13 years old. His mom was a single mother of four kids and worked two jobs as a server to make ends meet. He never knew his father. She was too busy to keep a close eye on Tommy, which allowed him to ride his bike all over the city selling drugs to anybody from nine years old to eighty.

Most of the time Tommy was smart about who he met, but one day he had a run-in with the wrong people. Troost St. was the main drag that ran through 8-Ball and CJ's neck of the woods. They lived around 71st St. Tommy had made his way from 65th St. pursuing a new prospect. He never saw it coming. A houseful of gangsters jumped out of the house and nearly beat him to death. They stole $5,000 in cash and nearly a pound of pot. CJ and 8-Ball happened to roll up on the scene. CJ fired his 9mm Reuger in the air to scare them, but that only drew fire back. A two-minute volley took place before the cops showed up.

8-Ball and CJ stayed put, but the rest of the gangsters attempted to flee. Unsuccessfully. The only one that didn't was the one CJ had shot in the leg. The dogs were too fast for the rest of them. As they lay face-down on the concrete in cuffs, 8-Ball scrutinized and cussed CJ for getting him involved.

"You dumb mother fucker. Did you ever think about just hollerin' at em? You oughta know no one in this hood is scared by gunfire. You coulda got us killed!"

CJ acted anything but remorseful. In fact, all he could do was smile and say, "I gots one of em! Did you see? Stupid ass bitch tried hidin' behind a tree. He can't hide from this sharp shootin motha fucka!" As the cops pulled them to their feet, he shouted to the wounded man being ushered to the ambulance, "I'm Wyatt Earp bitches! Don't be startin' shit in my neighborhood. We're protectors of the pea…" he was cut off by the cop door being slammed in his face.

Tommy was barely breathing when he got to the hospital. The two had likely saved his life. After 24 hours in jail and extensive questioning, 8-Ball and CJ were let go. 8-Ball was an exquisite negotiator and knew how to talk to cops. He instructed CJ to keep his mouth shut if he wanted to get out of prison. Among the interrogators was a man named Donnie Proctor. He saw how sharp 8-Ball was and offered him a deal. CJ had in fact shot somebody, but the cops had been after this group called "The Dragons" for years and were grateful to have caught them in the act of a crime, thanks to 8-Ball and CJ. He offered to let them off without any charges if 8-Ball would act as an informant to the police, an underground-ghetto-spy of sorts. He also agreed to let CJ in on the deal. The two were to carry on as normal, buying drugs from dealers and secretly work their way up to the conglomerates.

"You mean we can smoke all we want and turn in the bad guys? I'm in!" was CJ's response upon hearing the news. Aside from all his "gangster" qualities, he actually had a good heart and wanted to keep the streets safer.

They were offered immunity from any crime involving drugs, as long as they agreed to help the cops bring down the ever-growing underground Chicago drug ring. 8-Ball liked the idea of being a vigilante. He was given a private cell phone and was to report weekly. They were given $1,500 a month to buy drugs and for living expenses. The agreement was contracted for five years.

8-Ball and CJ went to visit Tommy in the hospital. He thanked them for saving his life. The dynamic duo added a third musketeer and became inseparable. Tommy became one of 8-Ball's personal informants and soon split an even share of the $1,500. He introduced 8-Ball to DeShawn and DeJuan, his childhood friends, who were working as "interns" at the time they came across Dusty. They all took their jobs very seriously and often put themselves into harm's way to protect innocent people and put thugs into jail. They were true "Ghetto Cowboys", as Tommy liked to say. At first, 8-Ball was wary about taking on the two brothers. He didn't want to be a baby sitter. He decided to test them one day.

Out of all of them, DeShawn and Dejuan came from the least dysfunctional family. Their parents were together and each had jobs. For brothers, they got along very well. Both had graduated from high school and had jobs. DeShawn worked at McDonald's and DeJuan worked at a local hardware store as a janitor. One night they were all hanging out, 8-Ball pretended to plot a crime… "Clockwork Orange" style. He explained to the two that the group was going to break into a house, rape the woman that lived there, kill her husband, and find the loaded cash vault he heard about through the grapevine. He was very persuasive. What happened next surprised him.

"Man Tommy, what the fuck? you said this dude was cool? You go around doin' this sick shit too? I should call the cops," DeShawn spouted furiously. Tommy bad been begging 8-Ball to let them in, unbeknownst to the brothers.

8-Ball persisted, "Chill out man. We can split it evenly. I thought you were cool." He spoke about such heinous acts in a way that was devilishly nonchalant. "Listen, it'd be in your best interest to just help and take the money. Now that you know…" he paused for effect, "it's just be ashamed if I had to hurt people for no good reason."

"Listen man, I don't know who you think we are, or who you are, but I ain't killing nobody! Or raping any woman, you sick fuck! You're the kind of thug that gives respectable black people like me and my brother a bad name and the downtown honkys a reason to call us niggers! Fuck. You. I'm not scared of you either. Threaten us. But in the end, you will be the one who is sorry."

DeShawn spoke with such confidence and vehemence that shivers ran down 8-Ball's spine. *This guy has backbone.* In all the time 8-Ball had been around him, he'd never seen this kind of fire from DeShawn. Before it got out of hand, he nodded to Tommy. Tommy took them aside and explained to them the situation and the nature of the test. It took a while after that for DeShawn to forgive 8-Ball, but he would come to understand. After a while, the crew was a fully-functioning, sophisticated system for fighting crime in the ghetto. They often cruised the streets at night… "gettin' high and fightin' crime," which is how they ran into Dusty.

When they got out of the car at the park, they looked like a bunch of little boys rather than crime fighters. They were scruffy-headed, yawning and couldn't stop rubbing their eyes. Rarely did they have to get up before 10 am. It was 8 o'clock. They all knew Bob as they had worked with him on projects before. As a part of their "gig", they were familiar with many city officials. Consequently, they could just show up and start helping without much explanation.

8-Ball caught eyes with Dusty immediately and smiled with a nod. Dusty wasn't sure, but he was almost positive the look on 8-Ball's face said, 'Nice Boots...'. He was dressed in denim jeans, (the only pair he owned), a holey white t-shirt that read "23rd Annual Holiday Wrestling Invitational- Granite City High School". On the back it read "171 lb. Champion". That was the toughest tournament he had ever won, "The Grind" they called it. 24 teams, three 8-man pools, one champion. Teams from all over the Midwest were invited to the tournament and the bottom two scoring teams weren't invited back. Dusty had upset the number three wrestler in the nation in the semi-finals in overtime. He won in true Rocky fashion, with a black eye, a busted lip and a come-from-behind win. The entire gym was on their feet as they watched Jerrod Jones of Pennsylvania fall off to the number six seed, Dusty Burch. It was a moment he will cherish for the rest of his life; he was never throwing that shirt away. On his feet, he sported a pair of *Little Dickies* steel-toed boots.

He found the boots on sale at Wal-Mart for $35. He figured he had better at least try and look the part of a construction worker, but didn't care enough to spend an exorbitant amount of money. Dusty liked Wal-Mart. Not only was it the best people watching venue in America, but it had almost anything a person could ever need. An economics professor in college once called it the "supreme-getters-of-stuff" and he was exactly right. Dusty didn't even think about going anywhere else, plus he needed some new V-neck undershirts and some detergent. He learned early on in their relationship not to try and take Lynn there. She considered herself of the higher "Target" class and wouldn't subject herself to the lower demographic that was Wal-Mart. 'Wal-Mart doesn't even have a Starbucks. And I feel out of place in there if I'm not wearing sweatpants and a tank top… with flip flops… and no bra.' He didn't even try to argue the subject with her anymore. So, he went by himself.

8-Ball nonchalantly walked over to Dusty, "Killer boots man."

"How did I know you were going to say some sarcastic bullshit?"

"Maybe it's 'cuz you know you out of your element. Lawyer in Little Dickies," 8-Ball chuckled at the sound of that.

"Hey, I gotta play the part. Gimme a break."

"Nah it's cool man. I had a pair of those once. I was in like fourth grade, but…"

"Hey let me ask you something. How much are you getting paid for babysitting today," he looked over at the formidable crime fighting squad.

"Not nearly enough! I can tell you that much."

Dusty looked down at his shoes. His jeans were tucked underneath the tongue so that the tag with 'Little Dickies' was exposed. He quickly reached down and pulled his jeans over the tongue. The wave of self-consciousness that came over him was surprising. He looked around at all the other workers boots: worn, dirty, cut up, sturdy. His were without a mark and the light tan color stood out. He remembered throwing a chair at a kid in third grade for making fun of his turtle-neck; his temper always got him into trouble at school. He imagined one of the other workers telling him that he had a 'little dickie', then kicking him in the shin for the transgression. He felt for a moment like he was back in his third-grade class in that turtleneck, then Bob's commanding voice snapped him back to reality.

"Thank you all for coming today. My name is Bob and I'm the superintendent of this project. I know everyone is excited about the new park, but we have to work together to get the job done. The first thing that needs to be done is trash pickup. Over there by the bench is a roll of trash bags. By the looks of it, this will take up about half of the day. After lunch, we will be cleaning trees for the basketball court and removing the existing equipment. Please ask me if you aren't sure what to do. I'll find a job for ya." He reached into the truck and pulled out a box, "Here's a box of latex gloves to pass around. Let's get to work!"

Most of the people who showed up that day had just wanted to see what all the ruckus was about and if the rumors, (that 8-Ball leaked), were true. 8-Ball wanted a bunch of people there. It meant there was a better chance at finding the little girl. When they saw they were there on trash duty, about half of them left, leaving about 75 volunteers and 15 city workers.

The park had been devoid of any human TLC for almost a decade. There were tires in the woods, furniture, paper bags from various fast food places, thousands of cigarette butts, beer bottles and cans, trash bags, lawn bags full of yard clippings, dirty diapers, condom wrappers, needles... anything imaginable. A large dumpster was deposited on the side of the street for the garbage. It was dark green and about 40 feet long. Within two hours, it was nearly full. Bob decided to call an early lunch, pleasantly surprised at the unexpected volunteers and the quick progress. Bob asked Dusty if he wanted to go eat lunch with the crew, but Dusty respectfully declined, saying he had eaten a large breakfast and wasn't much of a lunch eater.

When the crew was gone and the crowd had departed, Dusty took a seat on the bench facing the swing set. He pulled out a Marlboro Light and sparked it with the book of matches he borrowed from one of the volunteers. On it was printed "Dana's Diner: Avondale's Finest Fried Okra". As he took a drag, he reminisced about eating fried okra at his Grandmother's as a kid. He loved fried okra. She would always get it to have the perfect crispiness, never mushy or burnt, just perfect. He hadn't sat there long when he heard 8-Ball's voice.

"I never knew you smoked." Dusty had been so deep in thought that he hadn't heard him coming. He lifted the cigarette in front of his face and examined it with tired eyes.

"I don't."

"Right, just like you don't wear Little Dickies and you don't see dead people."

Dusty's eyes were still fixed on the cigarette, gazing at the smoke swirls dancing off the cherry.

"My shrink actually suggested I try it. He said that it may help me sleep, something about introducing nicotine and toxins or some bullshit," he paused as he took another drag. "I kinda like it."

8-Ball sat down besides Dusty to his right. "If you're going to smoke anything, you should smoke some of this herbal remedy," he reached into his pocket and pulled out what Dusty recognized to be a joint. "Cigarettes are bad for you. Just plain nasty. You're smoking what they embalm dead people with." He ran the length of the joint under his nose and drew a deep breath, "but this, this is therapeutic. You want to sleep like a baby? Smoke this."

"I can't. What if it changes her... what if it... blocks her? I'm so close. I don't want to mess it up now," 8-Ball listened intently.

"Fair enough. Suit yourself." He sparked up the joint.

"Right here?" Dusty said with amazement.

"Sheeit dude, I own this place. Plus, ain't no one around. And if there was, they'd probably be more suspicious if they was out takin' a stroll and didn't smell the sweet aroma of sensimilla. Someone's always smokin' around here."

The two sat in silence as 8-Ball puffed the joint. He took a deep drag and held it in. Before he exhaled, he started talking, "You know, people freak out over this stuff, but I think there's a lot worse evils out there that we should be focusing on... say child molesters for one. I ain't addicted; I could stop at any time. I just enjoy it, the way some people enjoy a cold beer or a nice stroll around the block." He finally exhaled. "I think crime would actually go down if they legalized it."

"I actually do agree with you on that one. The cops spend so much time trying to track down drug dealers when they should be spending their time on other things. I think if the government taxed it, they'd be out of the hole in less than 10 years. But that'll never happen, at least not in our lifetimes. There are too many right-winged, uptight conservatives in this country to accept a change like that. Granted I don't think we are ready for it, but it sure doesn't make sense that more people die from cigarettes and alcohol than any other substances combined. Crack? Yeah, I think they should shut that down, but weed? Might as well arrest people for getting fat."

8-Ball stared in utter amazement at Dusty's response, "Wow."

"What? You think just because I'm white and an attorney, that I think pot is the devil? Au contraire."

"Well what are you waiting for?" He held the joint up in front of Dusty's face. He looked at it for a second and then changed the subject.

"Do you really think she's in there? This whole thing is just killing me."

"Man, there's only one way to find out. We doin' the right thing. Momma always said when you don't know if what you'd doin' is right, ask yo'self if sittin' and doin' nothin' is better. This whole thing might seem a bit extravagant, but it's the best way I could think of to organize an incognito search party for a girl no one knows is missing… 'cept her piece of shit parents. I for one believe it's going to work."

"So, you believe in me?"

"Yah. I think so. I've seen enough crazy and evil to know what it doesn't look like. I think someone will find her in there." Dusty's gut began rolling and his heart felt heavy. He began to get nauseous. He looked at the burning joint in 8-Ball's hand, "Gimme that." 8-Ball just smiled and handed it over.

"Take 'er easy. That's some strong shit."

"Got it," Dusty replied with confidence, "I've done this before a time or two." He took a long drag and held it in. At once he began to feel it. At first it wasn't so bad, then he began coughing uncontrollably. 8-Ball stared at him, thinking it would pass. Dusty's eyes began watering as he desperately tried to expunge the burning from his lungs.

"I told you…"

"Shhhhhhh!" Dusty spat out as he held up his finger. "I'm O… O… OK. Holy shit!" When he looked up his eyes were bloodshot and tears rolled down his face. "Guess I'm a little outta practice." 8-Ball burst into laughter.

"You flyin' yet?"

"Ha. Ha," Dusty sarcastically verbalized his laughter. He started feeling a little queasy, "I'll be right back." He walked over behind the dumpster and despite his best efforts to hold it in, vomited. He tried being discrete, but 8-Ball was no dummy. His head was spinning and the sky seemed surreal in its opal hue. As he walked back, he peered at the clouds, whose fluffy texture and gentle demeanor at once brought him peace.

8-Ball concealed a grin, "You aight?"

"Right as rain cowboy," he responded with a childish grin foreign to 8-Ball's eyes. He sat back down on the bench. He wasn't sure if he liked what he felt, but it was different and different was good. He sat for several minutes in silence, trying to control his heart rate, before finally saying, "Thank you, 8-Ball. Thanks for being… a friend."

"Don't mention it man. You ain't gonna get all Golden Girls and shit on me now are you?"

Dusty thought for a second about what he meant, and burst out into laughter when he connected the dots, "Man I used to love that show! I watched that with my mom every day. Ah man that takes me back"

"Haha me too! After school, every day. My mom would slap me if I tried to change the channel."

"No way, really?

"Swear to God."

"Wow, that's crazy stuff right there… Golden Girls."

Both of them soaked up feelings of nostalgia for their childhood together on the bench. Dusty stared dreamily at the dangling swing on its chain. Once again, he imagined her. *We're almost there* he thought, almost as if speaking to her. This park pretty much summed up her whole life: abused, forgotten, neglected and treated like trash. He smiled at the thought of her happily swinging on the swing set.

"You sure you wanna go through with this? I can always let you know what happens…"

"I'm sure."

Chapter 54

At noon people started filtering back in. First the city crew, then about half of the volunteers. Bob gave another quick briefing, explaining that the trash pickup was nearly complete and that the next phase was the clearing of the walking path and equipment removal. He introduced Kacy Lane, his right-hand man. He was a young man of about 26, well built, clean shaven and wavy blond hair. He was to head-up the tree removal. He asked everyone that had hedge clippers or shears to retrieve them, as it would speed up the process.

Once again, the area was busy with workers. The jackhammers banged away at the equipment foundation and Kacy was shouting orders diplomatically over the loud noise. A large trailer showed up at 1:00 and the volunteers began loading it with brush. Dusty was part of the disassembly crew. Before the swing set was torn down, he quietly snapped a quick photo with his disposable camera. He wasn't sure why he did it, but he thought it might serve as iconic nostalgia someday… nostalgia not for himself, but for his little girl's happy moments, the few that she had… vicarious nostalgia, so to speak.

Dusty anxiously worked, fearful that at any moment he might hear a scream. By 3:00 it hadn't come yet.

Dusty stopped 8-Ball on his way to the trailer with a load of brush, "That path is pretty narrow. Not covering much ground."

"I know, but how are we going to get everyone to spread out?"

Dusty thought for a moment, "I have an idea. Do you see much trash back there?"

"The deeper we go, the more we are finding. The wind must have blown stuff back there hundreds of feet back there."

"Okay. I'll be right back." Dusty approached Bob and reported that the brush removers were still uncovering lots of trash and that it might be a good idea to sweep the woods before the day's end, while they still had volunteers. Bob was surprised at Dusty's initiative and quickly agreed. He promptly made the announcement.

"Man, you've been working here less than a day and you are calling the shots. Smooth move." 8-Ball was impressed.

"I paid a lot of money for my degree I had better be persuasive every once in a while."

The two headed into the woods along with the other trash bag-yielding workers. Dusty couldn't remember the exact location that she had showed him. It wasn't fluid imagery, more like snapshots, grainy, poorly developed snapshots. He didn't know how close he was and carefully walked through the newly grown underbrush, picking up a piece of trash every now and then. Every snapped stick startled him and his palms were wet with anxiety. Every so often he would feel the hairs on his neck stand up. He lifted every branch carefully and timidly removed each piece of trash, afraid of what it might unveil. He vaguely recalled an image of a tire, but couldn't be sure. He came across a couple tires and cautiously unearthed them before rolling them to the field's edge. Every once in a while, he'd pick a tick off his neck or waistband and throw it on the ground. He tried to control himself, but had literally never felt more anxious in his life. He once again surpassed his prior mark, but this was no time for him to take notice of that.

Then, next to an old fallen elm tree, his foot stepped on something hard under the leaves. He cleared away the leaves with his foot to discover a dirty, stained looking bone. His heart jumped into outer space. He at once began to panic, looking around for any other signs of the remains. He picked up the bone and examined it. It was about ten inches long; about the size he estimated a little girl's femur to be. 8-Ball wasn't far away, maybe 100 yards, and Dusty shouted at him to come over.

"8-Ball, come here. I think I found something!" 8-Ball looked around nervously to see if anyone heard or noticed Dusty, then started walking briskly towards Dusty.

As he got about 15 feet away, he started loudly whispering in a scathing tone, "What are you trying to do? Draw attention to yourself? We don't exactly want people to get the idea that we are *looking* for something. What is it?" Dusty didn't speak, he just held up the bone. 8-ball walked over and took it from him and inspected it closely, "Did you find any more?"

"Not yet."

8-Ball scanned the area quickly and spotted something. He walked over to it and rolled it over with his foot, "Well, I wouldn't get too excited yet."

"Why? What is it?"

"Well, unless you are looking for a dead deer carcass, I think you better keep looking." Dusty walked over to his side and observed what was clearly the skull of a deer. It's oblong shape and muzzle-nose appearance gave it away instantly.

Embarrassed, Dusty defended himself, "Hey, I'm a city boy, what can you expect? Plus, you can't tell me that this doesn't look like it could belong to a little girl," he held up the bone to plead his case.

"Yeah, I guess. I ain't never had a chance to compare little girl bones with a dead deer."

"Well shit," Dusty exclaimed as he threw the bone as far as he could, hearing it smack a tree dead center about 40 yards away.

"Don't get discouraged buddy. We'll find her." But an hour later, still nothing. Dusty was beginning to wonder if he was crazy—if everything was a mad hallucination. He heard Bob call all the workers in on the megaphone, but Dusty didn't want to leave. He kept searching frantically, beginning to run through the timber, kicking over every rock and stump that he could.

Eventually, 8-Ball realized Dusty hadn't come out of the woods. He didn't want anyone to start asking questions, so he went to fetch him. He wasn't hard to spot. He was making all sorts of ruckus as his heavy steel-toed boots plodded down on the dead leaves and sticks. He ran to catch up with him.

"Hey man, we gotta go. We can't do this right now."

Dusty, out of breath, looked at 8-Ball with a crazy eye and shouted, "I *have* to find her. I can't leave until I find her!"

8-Ball, unsure if anyone heard him, tried to subdue him, "Dude, you can't be actin' all crazy like this. Seriously, do you want to fuck up this whole operation? All this hard work I did for you?"

Emotional, Dusty responded without much regard for logic or sanity, "For me? Oh, for me? Yeah, this is all fucking for me 8-Ball. A whole bunch of kids are being killed and you want to think about how much out of the way it is for *you!* Do you understand what we are dealing with here? Don't you get it? More are going to die! More kids, more of us! I'm sick and fucking tired of being afraid. Being afraid of being awake, of being asleep, of whether or not I am going to kill myself, or if Lynn is going to kill herself…"

8-Ball realized quickly how the situation was escalating to out-of-control status, "Ok, I get you. I understand where you are coming from. I *promise* you we will come back. But for real man, we can't do this right here. We gotta go."

"I'm not going anywhere. So, either help me, or fuck off!" Dusty shouted. 8-Ball was getting tired of Dusty's antics and he grabbed Dusty's arm and started to pull him back towards the park.

"Get the fuck off of me man! 8-Ball I mean it." He punched 8-Ball and kicked, hitting him in the face and gut. 8-Ball was scared that someone would come and wonder why this man was acting is such disarray. He didn't want the whole operation to be blown. Dusty was no match for 8-Ball under any circumstance, and finally 8-Ball put an end to it.

"I'm sorry Dusty," he said. Then with one swift motion struck him in the jaw, silencing him immediately. Luckily the crowd was too busy talking amongst themselves to notice much.

8-Ball carried Dusty back to the site, where several workers, including Bob, inquired as to why he was carrying him and what happened. Dusty started coming to his senses about the time 8-Ball sat him down on the bench.

"What the hell happened to him?" asked Bob in astonishment.

"I don't know. I noticed he wasn't here, so I went looking for him. I found him unconscious on the ground next to a tree underneath a pretty big limb. I figured he must have hit his head or something." Dusty looked around and was confused for a second, then realized what had happened and the position he was in. He looked at 8-Ball with glaring eyes.

"I, I guess I must have hit my head on that branch. I was bending over, picking up a piece of trash, and I stood up. That's the last thing I remember. I must have hit my head on an overhanging branch or something," he rubbed his head for theatrics.

"Yeah, when I found you, there was a branch about four feet off the ground hanging over your head. It was a pretty good size one. I bet you just didn't see it and came up too fast and knocked yourself out cold."

Bob, still puzzled, contemptuously accepted the explanation, "I told you to put your damn hat on!" Realizing he was closing the barn door after the horses escaped, he asked, "well, are you ok? Do I need to call an ambulance?"

"No, absolutely not. I'm okay. Seriously."

"Okay, well you better not sue my ass or something like that. You'd be wasting your time; I'm broke."

Dusty, realizing Bob didn't understand that he wouldn't be the defendant in a work-comp lawsuit—that the city would—decided not to explain this nuance and just gave Bob what he wanted to hear, "Of course not! I'm totally okay. Just a small bump." He held up his two fingers on his right hand, "Scout's honor."

"Okay, well folks, I think that's enough work for today. I'll see you back here tomorrow at 8:00 am, sharp. If we move quickly, we should be able to get this done in 4 days. If so, we'll have Friday off. If not, it could be a long weekend."

Minutes later Dusty found himself alone on the bench once again with 8-Ball.

"Well, I don't know what to say. All I can say is I am sorry. I lost my cool."

"Don't worry about it man. If anyone should be sorry it should be me."

"I deserved it. I was out of control. You did what you had to do. And the tree branch thing... nice."

"Yeah, I don't know if he even really bought it, but it was all I could think of."

"I was so confused at first. I almost started rubbing my jaw instead," he chuckled, "that would have totally given it away!"

8-Ball shared in the laughter, "I guess being a lawyer and shit helps you be quick on your feet, huh?"

358

"I was just impressed I could even say anything at all, my head is pounding. I still can't even see straight. You got me good!"

"It was a pretty clean stroke, I gotta admit, but I needed you out like, right then! I didn't want it to be some long, drawn out battle. People would have for sure come running."

"Mission accomplished."

"I'm sorry man, for real."

"Forget about it. I'm really just more upset that we didn't find her. I don't understand. I mean, she *showed* me! I saw everything that happened," Dusty's emotions were starting to take control.

"It's a big forest man, she could be anywhere. Don't get discouraged just yet. We have a few more days. Maybe we'll find her." 8-Ball sparked up another joint. He took a hit and handed it over to Dusty. Without hesitating, Dusty took it.

"For the pain," he remarked sardonically.

"Ha, yeah. For the pain."

....

For three more days the crew worked on clearing the grounds and installing the new park. Each day Dusty and 8-Ball found a reason to make their way to the woods with a trash bag and always volunteered to clean out brush and timber. They never found a body or a trace of evidence. Dusty was more frustrated and upset as he had ever been by the end of the project. He needed this. He needed closure, a morale boost, something to keep him going. His heart hurt and his conscience was heavy. He worked nights at the firm to make up hours. Stanley was breathing down his neck more than ever before, but Dusty didn't care. Marilyn let him know if anything super important came up and covered for him. The partners didn't know most of the time where Dusty was anyway, so skipping out for a few days was only slightly noticeable.

He continued to dream about his girl. Her dreams continued showing the same imagery, but nothing that was ever distinctive. Once she was in the forest, it was all trees and leaves and blurred images. Dusty followed her through the forest for hours in his dreams, trying desperately to see something he hadn't seen before. For two weeks after the project was complete, he went back to the woods and searched after work. He came up empty handed every time.

For the first time in a while, Lynn was starting to be the one offering support. She saw how much Dusty was suffering and it brought her back to reality. She wanted to help him. She wanted him to be okay. Most importantly, she wanted to be there for him.

One beautiful afternoon in late October, Dusty and Lynn were sitting on her balcony that overlooked the city of Manhattan. He had come to visit her for the weekend. The air was crisp and Lynn had a soft, snuggly maroon blanket wrapped around her shoulders, sipping wine, cross legged in her wooden Adirondack chair. Dusty had on a fleece North Face and jeans, also sipping wine. The smell of lasagna cooking in the oven wafted out of the kitchen windows.

Lynn admiringly looked at Dusty with a smile on her face. He was admiring the beautiful Crimson sunset. He caught her eyes, "What?"

"Nothing. You are just so handsome."

"Thanks honey. Not as handsome as you." Lynn smiled.

"What are you thinking about?"

"What I always think about."

"Honey, something will happen. Something will turn up. It's not going to stay in limbo forever. It can't. Too much has happened. You have come *so* far. Just keep your shark moving honey."

Dusty looked into her beautiful eyes, admiring her ability to drown out his worrisome thoughts with little effort. "I love you. I couldn't do this without you. You know that?"

"We found each other for a reason. Together we are going to change the world, babe. Me and you, and the rest of our friends."

"I just hope we don't have to lose any more. I feel like I am so close, and like I can help everyone! But so far all of this means nothing. I still don't even technically know if my visions or dreams are significant."

"Don't put so much pressure on yourself. There isn't any more pressure on you than on any one of us. We *all* have a responsibility."

"I know, but I just feel like I got the whole group together. I am the leader. I have a responsibility to lead. I have a responsibility to you."

Lynn sat and soaked in his words, then began to sing, "Hey Jude, don't make it bad. Take a sad song, and make it better er er. Remember, to let her into your heart, then you can sta- art, to make it better…" She had a beautiful voice—one that could raise the lowest of spirits to emotional bliss. Dusty couldn't help but to be flattered and inspired.

"And any time you feel the pain, Hey Dusty, refrain, don't carry the world, upon, your shoulders. For well you know that it's a fool, who plays it cool, by making the world a little colder… nahhhhhh, nahh, nahh, nah nah nah nah…"

"I don't deserve you," Dusty admitted.

"Of course you don't," she replied without skipping a beat, "but you are good in bed, so…"

"Well at least I got that going for me!"

"Come on, let's go eat dinner. I just heard the timer go off." And the two ate in high spirits, fully enjoying each other's presence, almost as if their life were normal for once.

Chapter 55

Daryl, or "Stone Free", put the porno tape in the VCR. "The Mile-High Club." Hey, it had a concept. It wasn't just humpin' and suckin' and lickin', important as that was. The chicks couldn't get off unless they were doin' it on a fully loaded airplane en route. It had conflict, tension, suspense and some dialogue. He'd seen it many times, but didn't matter.

Daryl, in his own mind, knew he was really only Daryl. He was shallow, superficial and insecure. He had the tattoos, the body piercings, the ponytail and the drug addiction to prove it, all badges of his fierce, rugged individualism. The more people accused him of being a phony, the harder he tried to convince them that he was happy with who he was. But Daryl knew that all those symbols merely shouted, "I just want to be loved and respected." The drugs, the free love and the apathy were all just substitutes for the real things that make one feel alive; family, commitment, purpose and status among peers. He had become comfortable with being weird. Hey, people even believed that Voodoo really would rather wear sandals, a dirty flannel shirt and torn blue jeans rather than penny loafers, a Polo shirt and Dockers. Deep down though, Daryl knew he was the loneliest, emptiest guy in the world. There was no fulfillment in being a rebel, but, hey, if the beautiful people never wanted you anyway, why act like you care?

Daryl was finally complete... content. He had a purpose, a wonderful, compelling purpose. What the world thought of him, what he thought about himself, no longer mattered. He could save children. They are precious and innocent. Only children have accepted him as having anything of value or interest to offer. He was "chosen." Children would live and have a real chance to love and be loved because of his ultimate sacrifice.

The porno was into full throttle. It didn't turn him on this time. It was only a prop to his heretofore empty life. Daryl had his muscle shirt on, sandals and torn jeans. His hair was in a ponytail. He sported some cool, aviator sunglasses and incense was burning on the coffee table next to him. Daryl reached for the most powerful high ball he could concoct. He knew it was gonna feel good. Whatever waited on the other side, it would understand. His existence, here or anywhere in the universe, would be courageous and real. He would never be superficial, phony or meaningless ever again. This was his parting shot to a shitty beginning. Daryl picked up the needle, stuck it in his vein, looked at the two girls grinding in the back of the plane and said to the empty room, "John Belushi, here I come."

Unfortunately, no one found Daryl for a week. One of his regular clients finally tracked him down. Daryl didn't keep great contact with the group either, which meant no one knew about his death, or what may have come from it, for about three weeks. He never had been able to use any of the information the group provided to him to gain any clues about his case, maybe it was the drugs, but in the end, he had enough information to do what he thought he had to do.

Finally, Holly Hedgecorth, the former prostitute who had recently began seeing another child of her own, trolled through the Arizona news and found the story of a man named Terrance Klause who was purportedly drunk driving and taken in. His prints matched those found at a crime scene where a little boy was found in a back alley close to Daryl Steadman's apartment. The killer's attorney had a hay day with a faulty equipment claim. The breathalyzer apparently ran .01 BAC back at the station, but the initial one when he was pulled over ran over the legal limit at .09. The attorney claimed his client was setup and his prints that led to the murder case should never have been acquired and therefore are inadmissible. The judge, after learning that the murder case was connected to three other boys, all found in back allies throughout Gilbert, AZ and surrounding counties, said tough shit. The breathalyzer machine was tested and re-tested and had two cop witnesses that reported a .09 reading at the initial pullover site. The killer obviously reported only having one beer. No one knows how or why that machine read a .09, but in the end no one cared. A sick man had been pulled off the streets, no longer able to hurt innocent children.

Holly worked backwards after hearing this story and eventually found out about Daryl through the obituaries. All the info in the Bible lined up. Another case solved. Another soul sacrificed. She reluctantly reported this to the chat room and contemplated what her next move was going to be.

Dusty plead with the group, begging everyone to give him time. He was so close to solving his case. He stressed the importance of his findings and encouraged the rest of the members to keep pushing on to find clues. Some listened. He spent many hours on the phone consulting people during the time his case was in limbo. He needed to find his little girl to prove his case. He needed some luck on his side and the rest of The Chosen needed to hear it could be done. A lot was riding on Dusty and his ability to come through.

Chapter 56

Marilyn came bursting through Dusty's office door with a newspaper in hand, waving it around excitedly, "Dusty, you are not going to believe this!"

Dusty was busy buzzing through one of his expert's depositions, "What Marilyn? What? For God's sake, you scared me.

"The little girl..." her face beamed with joy, "your little girl... I think they found her!" By now Marilyn knew more than anybody about Dusty's situation, probably even Lynn. Once he opened the floodgates, he just told her everything. So, Marilyn was actually actively looking in newspapers for any signs of reprieve, and here she had found it.

Dusty's face became flush and his heart dropped, "No, are you serious? What does it say? How do you know it's her?"

She plopped the paper down on his desk. The title read: *Decapitated Body of Unidentified Toddler Discovered by Dog.* A picture of the taped off park was positioned under the heading with the boy and his dog in the background, unaware of the photographer. "It's all over the news. A little boy and his dog found a little girl's body in the woods in the ghetto. Apparently, the dog had come from the woods with an old muddy shoe. This peaked the boy's curiosity so he followed the dog to where he had been digging about a quarter-mile past the tree line. He discovered the hole where the dog had been digging, along with the remains of a human foot. He immediately called the cops and within hours they had the whole park taped off and media was swarming. The forensic team uncovered the remains of the body. Dusty, didn't you say in your vision you saw her..."

"Decapitated…" Dusty answered with a dry, monotone voice and a blank stare that indicated the pieces of the puzzle had come together for him. He knew it was her. He thought for another second, then scratched his head, "A quarter-mile? That's it? God how did I never find her? I had to have searched at least a half mile in every direction from that park," Dusty uttered in bewilderment, almost to himself.

"Dusty, there is no way you can beat a dog's nose. Don't beat yourself up. At least she is found and it never would have happened if that park hadn't been restored. You know that."

"Yeah, but what does that mean? What do I do now?"

"Now you MUST tell the others. Everything. Tell them your story. Every, single detail. Maybe you can help them solve their cases!"

"I've been telling them everything that I can, it just hasn't meant much, maybe it will mean more now." Dusty paused, still in shock. "I thought I would be relieved. I don't feel relieved at all. I feel even worse. We have to solve this case now. I just found out another one of us committed suicide. It's starting to get out of hand."

"Oh, my, that's horrible, who was it?"

"His name was Daryl. He intentionally OD'd. The case of four dead little boys was solved, bless his soul. Creep was pulled over and blew over the legal limit, at least that's what the machine said. When he got back to the pen, he was sober. Claimed faulty equipment, but his prints were already in the system and linked to forensic evidence. Daryl had to have somehow tampered with the breathalyzer."

"So, these spirits can just interact with anything they want to?"

"I don't think *anything*, but it sure does seem that either by telepathy, telekinesis or some or some other unknown super power, they can manipulate minor details in the physical world."

"That's amazing. I mean, think of the implications. It basically proves ghosts *are* real. That life after death *is* a thing…"

"Yeah. Something like that. I don't know that it proves there is a God, but it sure doesn't hurt the case."

"This could change the world…"

"I'm not ready to try and prove it to the world. I want to prove it to The Chosen first, then maybe, *maybe,* try to involve the cops, or the FBI, or some other authorities that we can employ to help us solve these cases."

"Well, I'm sure the best detectives are on this case, your case. Whatever the loose ends are, they will get tied up. You have to give hope and morale to your group. If you wait until the murderer is in jail, you may not have a group to tell. You know how long it can take in our legal system to sentence criminals."

"Yes. Yes, I know. Maybe my girl will show me something else. Maybe we will get lucky again."

Chapter 57

The last three weeks had taken its toll on Dusty. He was worn out, physically and emotionally. He never thought it would be possible, but he was seriously considering leaving his firm. When Dusty got home, he called Lynn to tell her about his little girl.

"Oh, honey," Lynn began to cry, "I, I can't believe it worked. Are you okay babe?" Like Dusty, she had extreme mixed emotions. This wasn't a win, confirming without a doubt and having physical, dead, decaying evidence to prove you aren't crazy, but it was a win for the group to have found a solution.

"I'm okay. I just have to tell the others. Like, now. They need to know this."

"I love you Dusty. I'm so sorry. I wish I could be there right now. I know I should have quit school. I feel so awful."

"No, we aren't putting our lives on hold and sacrificing everything. We have to keep living a normal life like we are going to get out of this alive or we don't have a chance. I'm okay honey. I love you too. I will come visit you soon."

"I can't wait to see you again; I feel incomplete without you."

"Babe, that's so sweet. If you feel incomplete, I feel non-existent without you..."

"Just hurry back. Quit that soul-sucking job of yours."

"Yeah, yeah I know. I have trial next month. After that, we'll see. Love you honey."

"Love you."

After eating a quick spaghetti dinner, Dusty ventured into his home office, located at the bottom of the staircase and right inside the front door to the left. It had glass windows and an impressive library. He sat down at his desk with a Miller Lite and a cigarette. He opened the window to the right of him so the smoke could escape without leaving behind too much of a trace. He didn't usually smoke inside. *Fuck it.*

He logged into the website and clicked on the link that took him to the forums. No one was currently online. He left a message. He took in the events of the day with a deep breath. He wrote:

My Dear Friends:

To every mystery there is a key. Our problem is that we have dozens of separate mysteries... but I think I've found a way to unlock our multi-dimensional road maps. I don't understand how it works yet, but for some reason I stumbled upon the answer. At least I believe that it's one of the answers.

First of all, we must believe that our children are real. Some people are skeptical, but to open communication lines, it is imperative to embrace the spirit wholly. NO DENIAL. If we don't believe these children are real, then there is absolutely no hope. We cannot have a single shadow of a doubt, for that blocks the spiritual channels that we need open in order to unlock these mysteries.

I urge all of you to start logging every dream. Write down anything at all that you see. Every detail. Start listening and looking for signs every day. They are trying to come through to us when we are awake, but you have to open up the channels. Eat right, don't drink excessively or do drugs, meditate, even pray. This is a deeply spiritual event.

After you have started cleansing your mind, start trying to lock down where you think you may have come across the child, alive OR dead. Do as much research on missing children in your city and any city or place you have been to. Start with a year, then two years. Travel to these places. Start observing at a high level. Look for "Supercommunication"—an attempt for the child to contact you in conscious, waking hours. If the child is still only appearing in dreams and is unable to show you more, brainstorm back five to ten years, or as far back as you need.

For some time, we have all been talking about finding the spot where our child died, or the "proximity theory". It made sense to us that we would be chosen based on our location to the child when they died. Why else would we be spread over so many different regions? Why else would we have next to no discernible patterns as to the nature of our appearances? Habits? Hobbies? Gender? Or personalities? But we have to be willing to think outside the box. Think bigger. We "Chosen" are a true melting pot of individuals, surely every case is different and has elements to it that can help the others solve their cases. Start with proximity, then branch out. It truly is a matter of applying the scientific method. Only change one variable at a time.

Some of us have experienced these supercommunications. I know when I first did, and it came about because I was trying with all my might to find an answer. I searched my soul relentlessly for any clues that might lead me in the right direction and I pursued every lead. Finally, a memory sparked by Lynn, led me to my solution.

A deep memory lay dormant inside my mind. One night a couple of years ago, I got off at a wrong exit and found myself deep in the ghetto of Chicago. I had trouble finding an exit to get back on the highway, so I ended up driving around for a few minutes. Little did I know, this is the exact moment my child made her connection with me. The event in and of itself was insignificant, which is why I never thought about it again after I left. But when the memory finally came to me, I felt compelled to visit the site.

I drove around for a while, trying to find something. Anything. Then, without warning, my body became tingly and my mind began to "float" in a way. I had no idea what was happening. This is when my supercommunication took place. I very clearly and distinctly heard the word "here" spoken to me from inside of my head. My car was stopped in front of a house, with a car full of what appeared to be gangsters behind me. Something came over me though, and I got out and confronted the men, who had actually been following me around the block. I startled them, for I looked sorely out of place. To make a long story shorter, I was eventually able to persuade one of them to help answer some questions for me the next day.

So, the next day I met up with him and he was able to tell me a little information about the house. He told me the house was abandoned, so I decided to walk in and take a look around. I can't exactly explain what happened in that house, but all I can say is I "felt" her presence. I saw her flickering in and out of existence from the corner of my eye, but I could never really get a good look at her. She was showing me scenes of her death... scenes of the violent events that led to the last moments of her life.

Later that night, she came to me. Through my dream, was able to show me every, single detail. It's almost as if seeing where she died and where the crime took place—with my own eyes—allowed her to show me what she had been wanting to show me all along. I don't believe our children have the power to generate memories from out brain unless our brains have stowed away the sensory data somewhere in the past. My thinking is that their psychic powers are limited. In no way do they have the strength to transmit vivid images and detail on their own. They must wait until the images exist in our subconscious memory independently from them. It's almost as if they combine what is in their memory, with what is in ours. If we share no common memories, then all they are able to show us is themselves... in darkness... in pain.

There was one other image that stuck with me before I found the crime scene. I began to randomly dream of images of a swing, the kind you find at a playground. I had no idea what to think of it. At first, I didn't even know if it was associated with her, but I must have seen that swing on my initial visit to her neighborhood because her body lay in a park very near to that swing, adorned with trash bags and buried beneath the soil. So, pay extremely close attention to ANY detail your children are able to project to you—it could be significant.

Some of you are probably thinking, "Well what do I do once I do know how it happened? How do I catch the killer and bring him to justice?" The answer is, I'm not sure. It will be different for each person. But it is undeniable that being able to see what actually happened will open up clues and doorways that never before had we been fortuned with. At the very least, we will know we have found the 'where'; the dream may even show us the exact 'who'; a news story can tell us the 'when'; and the child can show us the 'what' and the 'how'. We may never know the 'why', but the rest of the clues are surely enough to allow us to formulate a plan. I believe that together we will be able to catch the killers.

Currently, I am in the process of finding the physical evidence to make the case, but at least her precious body is found and can be laid to rest. I was able to find the spot where my child died. I had to be very creative and resourceful and had a little bit of luck, but it couldn't have happened without finding the spot she left this Earth. Make sure you do not spoil the search by making yourself the primary suspect. No one is going to believe that you got information that the police don't have without you being guilty of something.

Although my case is not technically solved yet, it is well on its way. I can only assume that when it is, I will have fulfilled my duty to the girl.

So, in conclusion, I encourage you to keep the shark moving. We will only drown, like the shark, if we stop moving. We have lost some dear to us already, but I plead with you: Never, Never Quit!!!

It might not be the exact same scenario as mine, but try and put as many pieces of the puzzle together as you can. Write down your dreams. Take note of every, single place you have stepped foot since just before you started seeing your child. Visit those places. You are looking for a form of supercommunication—the big hint. It could be different for different people. Once you experience it, that's how you know you are on the right track. Pay attention at every minute of every day. It could come at any time. Let your loved ones guide you. Don't believe in coincidences… EVERYTHING happens for a reason. Follow up on your hunches. Your child is already coming to you, maybe he or she is looking for other ways to alert your consciousness. Maybe God, or the Spirit of the Universe, is helping them. How else could they come to us in the first place?

Maybe it's impossible to get to the place they were killed, so try something else. They will show us as much as they are able to. It may take 5 clues or 5 different supercommunications to lead you to the right place, but you have to keep trying. Summon the creative powers in your soul, for that is what our children are asking of us.

We can't assume that the police, or the FBI, will be willing to help a group of people that claims they can see dead children, or that they will take any information we give them seriously and without suspicion. Much of the information we are able to find can only be known by the killer, so we do not want to incriminate ourselves. Once we find out what happened, we have to be sneaky about how to lead the right people to the evidence. That is where we will all help each other out. We will be here for each other as much as we ever have. We have to be.

You have to <u>BELIEVE</u> your child is out there. Please also believe there is a solution to help them; suicide is not the only answer my friends. When, and I do mean WHEN they come through, it will be in a big way. I believe if you find the spot their spirit left this Earth, you will see the murder itself. It happened to me. Then, it's up to you to be detective. We will help you. You are not alone.

With Love,
Dusty

When he was finished, he pressed "send", went to the kitchen for a bowl of peanut butter blast ice cream and he got ready for bed. Although it wasn't exorbitantly long, it took him nearly three hours to write. He wanted to make sure that he expressed exactly how he felt. Lynn was on his mind. He knew she was probably asleep. He envisioned lying next to her, smelling her hair, rubbing her soft skin with his, rubbing his hands along her buttocks and down her smooth legs. He couldn't wait to get back to her. He was tired of being away from her. He had to fix this.

The story of his little girl made national news. The grotesque manner in which a little girl's body had been treated shocked the nation. Now that he had made so much progress in his case, his dreams of his little girl were noticeably different. Although disturbing still, they were more… peaceful. She seemed to be more at rest. There were times when the murder would replay itself, however, but Dusty was never sure if that was his little girl communicating with him, or his own nightmares plaguing his slumber.

While the case was being cracked, there wasn't much more Dusty could do, so he started visiting Lynn about every weekend, putting all his extra time into her. He felt that he was so close to solving her mystery. The problem was that up until now, she was at his place so often that it was harder for her to be as in touch with her case as he was with his, but she didn't want to be alone without him and he didn't want her to be alone in the mental state she was in, especially with Richard as the only one to console her. Lynn knew Dusty was preparing for trial and on the cusp of solving his little girl's case, so she insisted that she come see him. Every few weeks, Dusty pretty much made her let him go back to New York and do research, but it just wasn't enough. His bosses were already giving him all kinds of hell for the frequent trips to New York, so he couldn't get away any more than he already was. The Draper case was weeks away from trial and Dusty was expected to work day and night, whatever it took, to avert a settlement and deliver a favorable verdict at trial.

Dusty was at a real crossroads in his life. Neglect the biggest case of his life? Or neglect the love of his life?

Chapter 58

The last time Dusty had talked to his Dad was a few months ago. They used to talk more frequently, but ever since Dusty got the job at SCR, calls back home became fewer and fewer. He always thought about it, but just rarely set aside a few minutes to do so. Usually he'd call in random occurrences, like when the Bears beat the Chiefs. Dusty never liked the Chiefs—he wasn't really a huge football fan—but his Dad was a diehard Chiefs fan, so he took full advantage of any opportunity to harass him about it.

They had a good relationship, but they started to drift away when Dusty moved. His dad was a bit heartbroken when Dusty took a job at another law firm seven hours away instead of taking a job with him right at home. It had always been his dream to practice law with Dusty, but he slowly got over the pain. Keeping a relationship with his son was more important than his feelings about the situation. So, Preston didn't bother him. He gave him his space. He gladly welcomed any communication he got from Dusty, even if it was to harass him.

The phone rang for a long time before someone picked it up, "Hello?" Dusty was surprised to hear his dad answer the phone. He never answered unless he was expecting a call.

"Hey Dad!" replied Dusty, excited to hear his voice. Before he could say anything else, his dad spoke again.

"The Chiefs don't play the Bears this season, you know."

Dusty laughed, "Dad, that's not why I'm calling. I don't even like the Bears. You know that."

"Well at least I taught you something right…"

"You taught me everything right, Dad. I'm really sorry I've been out of touch lately. I need to tell you about some things." Preston wasn't used to such heart-felt apologies from his son and it warmed him inside.

"Dusty, you know you can always talk to me about anything. Any time. Anywhere. I'm your father. I don't care how old you get; I will always see you as my little boy."

Dusty really started to feel guilty when he heard the love in his father's voice, even after all the neglect, "I know that Dad. I just don't even know where to start."

"Why don't you start by telling me a little bit about yourself? Ease up to the hard stuff. I'd like to know my little Gerkenfelter again." When Dusty was a toddler, he never thought twice about where the name came from and as he got older, it didn't seem to matter. He just chalked it up to the goofy, strange, unconditional love his father had for him. Dusty had never met another man in all his life who was as brilliant and as idiotic at the same time as his father. His childhood was full of laughter and love. There was never a dull moment. His dad was there whenever and wherever he needed him, even if it meant a good ass whipping. He couldn't imagine his life without him.

Slowly all of these emotions and realizations crept up on him. After a long pause, he tried to speak. The lump had already grown too big and despite his best efforts, he started to weep. His dad just listened. He knew this day would come, when only after giving him space, his little boy would come back to him.

For a straight hour Dusty described the events in the last two years of his life in excruciating detail. He told him all about Brian Draper and the emotional toll the case was taking on him. He explained the situation and painted the picture of a little, helpless boy who was harmed by the people Dusty was defending. He told him about his little girl, the dreams, The Chosen, Lynn, Bruce's death and case, his vision of his little girl, 8-Ball, the park… everything.

At first Preston was in shock. He never interrupted, but he was seriously concerned about the mental state of his son. To his surprise however, the longer he listened, the more it all sounded real to him. The story was such an intricate mixture of emotion, drama, morality, passion and coincidence that for Dusty to make it all up sounded crazier than it actually happening.

After an hour of listening to Dusty, Preston finally spoke, "So let me get this straight. A little girl started coming to you in your dreams. It bothered you and wouldn't stop. You don't remember exactly when you started seeing her. Then you met a young lady with the same problem and together you found a whole group of people across the world that see dead people?" Dusty was prepared to defend himself, but something about that last statement his father made struck him in the gut.

"No Dad. It's not like seeing a ghost. I mean I think they *are* dead, but when I dream about her, she's as alive as you and me."

"Okay, so not ghosts, but what you believe are possibly dead children that need your help," he paused, trying to remember what he heard and regurgitate correctly, "and you feel that upon dying, your spirit is able to find and sabotage the murderer?"

"Exactly."

"And how can you be so sure?"

"It is glaringly obvious. After the first two Chosen died, we weren't sure. Bruce and I uncovered some scary details and worked hundreds of hours trying to put the pieces together. We didn't want to sound any false alarms, so we kept it to ourselves. We were afraid that…"

His father understood, "Afraid that everyone would start killing themselves, for possibly the wrong reason."

"Yes. We weren't ready to have that on our shoulders as well. But we had to do something, and do it fast. "Dusty was choked up again. His father finished for him.

"Bruce knew how much she meant to you. He was afraid that she would sacrifice herself to save her kids and to prove or disprove your suicide theory for sure. So, he did it first."

Dusty was sobbing again. For the rest of his life, he would never be able to think about Bruce without a lump coming to his throat. Bruce had done the most selfless thing of anyone he had ever known. The worst part is that Dusty felt like he could never repay him or say thank you. Not in this life.

"I also think he thought that he could somehow help us out from the other side or that his case would give us the missing clues we needed to solve ours without committing suicide. The amount of documentation he left me was ridiculous. He spent hundreds of hours on top of what he spent with me trying to figure it out. I haven't had any contact with him though and there's no way to tell if he is helping with the several others that have sacrificed themselves since."

"I can't imagine the burden to bear, but sounds like you have found a way out. You aren't thinking about doing that, right?

"I think I have maybe. And no. I don't want to take my life, but I kind of made a deal with Lynn, so…"

"You have to solve her case," his dad intuitively added.

"Yes. I do. I already have enough people's blood on my hands I feel like, helping prove that dying solves the cases. I can't lose her dad. If I do, I don't know what I'll do."

"Dusty, you didn't have a choice but to tell everyone what you found. Listen, if this is all true, it is something way bigger than you are. There is no way you can be responsible for anything. You are not responsible for the decisions of other people."

"I know. It's just the worst part is that it is working. Pedophiles and murderers are being caught because these people have given their lives, voluntarily or not. A guy named Eddie, who has been seeing nine little boys for years, went down a suicidal stretch of rapids on the Colorado River. As soon as he found out about Bruce, that was all he needed. The worst part is that the killer was his own brother. Had Eddie not given his life, his brother would have gone on molesting, torturing and murdering little, innocent boys. He may go down as one of the sickest criminals in American History."

"Jimi Vaughan?"

"Yeah. Guess you've been watching the news. No one would have ever found him. The guy was smart. His MO was different every single time and he waited sometimes years before he struck again so that no one could connect the murders. He even traveled. He would have gone on for who knows how long if Eddie's spirit hadn't found a way to reveal him."

"How did he do it? I mean, how does this stuff happen?"

"It seems like these spirits so far can interact with the physical world; there's just no telling to what extent. With Doris, a smoke alarm went off the in apartment of the murderer when he wasn't there, prompting neighbors and the manager to intervene. That's when they found pictures of the naked children. When Nick died, that murderer was pulled over because his license plate had fallen off. The cop saw bloody clothes in the back seat. And Eddie, well, it was simpler than that. His brother finally turned himself in because of the grief he felt after reading the suicide letter. It explained Eddie's reasoning and apparently, his brother was Jimi's soft spot. It put him over the edge."

"Wow. So, these people's spirits really are intervening to catch these sick bastards?"

"It seems almost impossible to deny. Lynn is pretty much convinced dying is the only way. Or, at least she was until I found my girl, but nothing has turned up. No one knows who she is yet. I'm *still* seeing her. I have to prove that mine wasn't a fluke and help her find hers before it's too late. I have the biggest case of my life on my hands right now though too and I don't know what to do."

Throughout the entire conversation, Preston was on the verge of feeling like he was in an episode of *The Twilight Zone*. Every part of him wanted to reason against Dusty's accounts and tell him to go get help. More help. He kept asking himself if he should treat the situation as if it were real and offer "real" advice, or if that would just make things worse. Finally, he was unable to let himself believe that Dusty could fall victim to such atrocities without there being some trace of truth to it. He knew how smart Dusty was and thought that if after two years he couldn't shake it, and now he was coming to him for advice, he had better not make light of the situation.

"Dusty, ever since you were born, you've been the apple of my eye. From the first time you rolled over to your first word, first step, first pin, you've amazed me. You have never failed to make me proud. I can't imagine what you are going through, but I have no doubt you will find a way. Since you were a boy, I've told you that often the solution to a problem requires extremely hard decisions to be made. Just don't give up hope. If I lost you it would break me. As far as your job... well, you know you always have a place here, with me. Sounds like you need to focus on that lady of yours."

"Yes. I think I do. I won't give up Dad. I promise. Thanks for everything. I guess I didn't scrape the bottom of the barrel when I got you as a father after all."

"You're not so bad either. Love you son."

"Love you too. I'll keep you updated. Go Chiefs!"

"They're gonna need a lot of help this year…"

"Don't they always?" They both chuckled. "Tell Mom I love her."

"Will do."

With that, Dusty knew exactly what he *needed* to do; he just wasn't sure if he had the guts to pull it off.

Chapter 59

A couple weeks had passed after Dusty talked to his father and before he knew it, he was deep in the middle of trial. He had been through a week of jury selection and opening arguments already, plus another two weeks of evidence. Evidence consisted of: eye witnesses, expert testimony from engineers and safety supervisors, doctors' testimony to explain the boy's injuries, economists' testimony to map out the boy's expected loss of income throughout his life, testimony from the family of the boy, (highlighted by his brother who made a very emotional and brilliant witness for the Plaintiff's), expert witness testimony and of course, Ron Davis and anyone important from Reston Tobacco and Unity Insurance. It had been a brutal three weeks thus far. As far as the identity of his little girl, it was still unknown. 8-Ball had found a lead regarding who lived in the house previously, but there was no way to verify it since they were only renters and the information on the owner at the county rendered a phone number that gave a busy signal. Dusty grew more anxious every day she wasn't identified. He just tried to focus on his trial to keep his mind occupied.

Dusty woke up on the day of closing arguments and had his cup of coffee. It was a beautiful December morning with a crisp air, light snow and no wind. The trees were void of any straggler leaves and evenly coated with a pure white layer of snow. Dusty gazed at them through his bedroom window as the sun blazed over their tops, reminding him that there was beauty in this life–a reminder he desperately needed. As he admired the crimson and purple sunrise and the bold amber tones of the horizon, his mental waves became interrupted and bombarded with a hailstorm of reality. He actually envisioned huge balls of ice falling from the heavens, only to be consumed by giant lighters scorching the atmosphere, emitting butane in massive, violent spews like volcanoes. The hail, just before evaporating, transformed and disfigured into gross and hideous figures before vanishing into thin air.

After a brief psychoanalysis, (which he was adequate to a fault at performing,) he realized the inner angst concerning his career was emerging to the surface of his consciousness. The ice figures represented the little boy he worked to deprive of collecting damages—that he deserved—from the huge and violent lighters, Dusty's clients. Prior to this case, Dusty had always been very good at separating his emotions from his law practice, but deep down in his gut, this situation felt horribly different.

Now, the final hour approached for Dusty to face his moral Everest. Today was closing arguments in the trial and the courtroom was filled to the brim with media, lawyers, the public and people involved in the case. After 3 weeks of trial and plenty of attention from the media, this case had piqued local interest.

Dusty had always loved the courtroom setting. He thrived in the anticipation of dissecting his opponent's case and had a natural knack for unveiling the flaws in the logistics of their arguments. He loved the dark cherry wood of the judge's bench and the witness stand. Most of all, he loved being on stage in front of people–real, analytical, blood pumping, unbiased people. The problem was, Karee had been next to flawless, leaving very little room for him to perform his magic, and he believed in his heart that no jury could possibly stay 100% unbiased towards this child. By every calculation he had made, the jurors seemed sympathetic towards Brian. Dusty looked for reactions to pictures and testimony and took note of every mannerism the jury members subconsciously betrayed: a touch to the face, a sigh, a smile, a nod of the head, and most importantly, he didn't remember them ever taking notes when he talked. They seemed to dote on every word that Karee said. These signs worried him. Worst of all, he truly believed that his client's negligence contributed to cause these devastating injuries to this innocent little boy. He could still possibly win though because he had done a masterful job, as always, at exploiting the weaknesses in the plaintiff's case. A good closing argument could be all he needed to push any teetering jurors towards his side.

In any other case, Dusty's beliefs about his client's negligence would not have mattered. He had known his clients were guilty in the past before and either got them off the hook completely, or significantly mitigated the damages. His only shot was to nail this closing argument and convince the jury there was not enough evidence to prove his client guilty. He had learned to never give up no matter what he perceived the sentiment of the jury to be–a philosophy that had won him several cases. His father had always told him that the only guarantee in the courtroom is that there is no guarantee, so he couldn't give up yet. He didn't believe he could win outright, but he thought there was hope for a hung jury. If neither side gets 9 of 12 jurors to deliver a verdict, there would be a mistrial and Dusty would get another chance at getting a better-suited jury for his case.

Dusty was unbeaten in trial so far, a status he was proud of. Now, standing at his platform, moments before his closing arguments were to begin, he took a hard look at the little boy sitting 20 feet from him. He thought of his little girl and all the other children whose lives were stolen from them. He likened them to Brian, whose life was all but stolen from him. Then a notion occurred to him he'd never considered–a notion that shook him to his core. He asked himself: *Am I any different than these killers? I didn't take his life away, but is standing in the way of him trying to get a piece of it back any better? I know Brian can't afford the cosmetic surgeries he needs without a verdict. Who am I to think I should deny him the right to attempt to return his life to some state of normalcy? What would Bruce think of this?*

He took a deep breath and glanced one more time at his notes. He thought about his father back in Kansas City—the man who introduced him to the legal field. He thought about Marilyn, his unconditional advocate, and her subtle gestures that motioned for him to work with his father. Her voice rang in his head, "He would take you in a heartbeat." He thought about Bruce and the sacrifice he had made so that the lives of The Chosen might be spared in order to save the lives of the children. *Bruce died to help children. I'm making a living to do the opposite?*

His closing statement was strong. It pointed out that there were no real eyewitnesses to the lighter creating the fire other than a small boy and reiterated the importance of it to the plaintiff's burden of proof. He spoke confidently and eloquently. He moved on, drawing attention to the drunk and negligent father. He claimed that, although heart breaking, Brian's injuries could have been avoided had the father been paying attention. "Just because the father is deceased," he argued, "doesn't mean there has to be somebody else to blame!"

He was successfully grasping the attention of the jury. His performance was picking up steam. He masterfully addressed every issue the plaintiffs raised and offered impressive counter-evidence. In regards to the absence of a warning, he argued that the butane the company sold to fill the lighter displayed clear and specific warnings and that his company can't be responsible for the irresponsibility of negligent parents. He referenced the deposition of the first responding officer, who found the lighter 50 feet away from the boy. Lastly, he asked if such an important matter can be decided upon by the testimony of a young boy whose recollection of the day was fragmented and unclear.

As he neared the end of his statement, he took a brief pause to collect his thoughts. He had been in the zone previously, successfully blocking out all the lingering external factors in his life. In this brief moment however, they all came flooding back into his mind. It was as if someone simultaneously raised the gates of a Hoover-sized dam nestled between the moral and professional faculties in his brain, allowing for an involuntary mixture of emotion and reason. Flashes of his career entered his mind. Plaintiff after plaintiff's face he had defeated came into view, but none stronger than 'The Look'; the poor elderly African American lady and her daughter that he had denied compensation in his brilliantly conducted directed verdict last year. His gut tightened. He thought about Bruce and the cushion he left for him. *Maybe it was so I didn't have to work and could fix this problem...* He looked at an emotionless Brian, then began to make what would be the boldest move in his career—one that would change the course of his life forever.

"Ladies and gentleman of the jury, although we all agree that Brian's injuries are serious and unfortunate, I must remind you the importance of separating the facts from our emotion. I believe I have clearly and successfully delivered our evidence to the best of my ability and that it speaks for itself. The only thing you have left to decide is…" his voice trailed off. Out of the corner of his eye he could see Brian bury his face in his hands. His heart began to pound in his chest with the force of a galloping cavalry. This was one of those fleeting opportunities a person gets in his life to do something truly great. He was not going to let it slip away. "The only thing you have left to decide is how much money you are going to award this young man!"

As one could imagine, the entire courtroom was baffled and confused at what happened that day. What Dusty had done was unprecedented and consequently he was fired from his law firm and banned from practicing law in the state of Illinois forever. As a result of his actions, the jury awarded Brian Draper 4.3 million dollars—his sacrifice had not been in vain. It was unheard of for an attorney to sabotage his own client and Reston fought to revoke his right to practice law in the entire U.S.—to no avail.

Marilyn could not have been prouder of Dusty; the partners of SC&R could not have been more infuriated or felt more betrayed; Ron Davis wanted to kill Dusty, who eventually had a restraining order put on him; Chad could not have been more delighted to see Dusty leave, for this greatly increased his chances to get promoted; and Dusty… Dusty had never felt more liberated. Luckily Bruce left him a heap of money so he would be fine and he viewed this as a chance to really devote his time to helping Lynn solve her case and the others solve theirs, once and for all.

··········

Lynn couldn't believe what Dusty had done, but she was ecstatic when he told her he was moving to Manhattan. The first night he got back, she had arranged for a night on the town and reserved a room at the fanciest, most expensive hotel in the city. Dusty and Lynn enjoyed a romantic evening together. Their suite had a Jacuzzi bathtub and Dusty bought a couple bottles of Lynn's favorite wine, Relax Riesling. The past few months had not provided many occasions for romance. There had been funerals, Dusty's career (especially the Draper case), and the stress both Lynn and Dusty experienced with their persistent nightmares. They were lucky to find any quality time together, period.

With a full view of the city out their window in an expensive presidential suite, Dusty was not going to let this opportunity pass them by. Coldplay's "The Scientists" quietly filled the background air, accentuating the somber yet ethereal emotions surrounding the circumstances. As they sat face to face in the tub peering over the bubbles, wine glasses in hand, Lynn mused, "Do we ever have to leave here? I mean, look around us. Wine, bubbles, obnoxiously large Jacuzzi's, room service… we'd have to be crazy to go back to our normal lives, wouldn't we?" Dusty, happy to see a glimpse of a woman he fell in love with just smiled. "What? Do you think I'm dumb?" she blurted out defensively.

"No, not at all. I'm just thinking about how beautiful you are," Dusty quickly extinguished that flame, "and that nothing in our lives has been normal lately."

In the momentary silence, the lyrics played: *Nobody said it was eaaaaasy, It's such a shame for us to paaaaarrrrrrrt.*

Dusty, taking in the moment, continued, "Lynn, you know, I don't care where I am as long as I get to be there with you."

Obviously flattered, Lynn went along, "Someone's really trying to get lucky tonight, aren't they?"

"Well, I mean…" grinning and blushing, he was at an unusual loss for words, so he went with honesty, "it's only my most favoritest thing in the world."

"What? Getting lucky? Is that all I'm good for?"

"No, of course not, I just… for me it's just… no one's ever made me feel like…"

Lynn bailed him out, "Oh cut it out I'm just messing with you. I know nobody's ever made love to you like I have. It's impossible. I love that Johnson of yours too much," her eyes beamed with a ferocious sexuality that immediately aroused Dusty. They relished in the time they had together as if they were the only souls left in the universe.

"So, about that getting lucky thing then…"

"Mr. Burch, I'd say your chances are pretty good."

The music was climaxing. The piano played a tune that rang of freedom and human emotion. The guitar harmonized beautifully. To Dusty, it seemed like a soundtrack to his life, like this piece of his puzzle had come together. The candle lights flickered, revealing her perpetual smile. They both continued to soak in the warm water, listening to their soundtrack. After a few moments, Dusty returned to his serious tone.

"You know, I'm serious. I'm not sure how I would have gotten through all of this without you. Lately I've been so scared of losing you. After we lost Bruce and we figured out that dying…" He hesitated at this thought. Lynn rubbed his knee, sensing his struggle. He continued, "When we found out that suicide…"

"You thought I might kill myself? Even after we made our deal?"

The lump in his throat prevented him from speaking, but he nodded his head in affirmation.

"I can't tell you I haven't considered it," she admitted.

"I know that."

"But I'm not going to. You are, no *we* are going to figure this out."

"What if in telling the others, that…what if we have pushed them over the edge? I can't have that on my conscience."

"Awe honey, you can't think that way. We had to tell them. It would be wrong not to. I can understand what you are saying, but everyone is in this together. Even if suicide is the only answer for some of us, that's not a decision you can make for them, and if you didn't tell them about Doris and Nick, someone else would have eventually figured it out. Like Eddie."

"I know. And I know my girl is found, but her case isn't solved yet and what if more people do it?"

"Dusty, remember what we are doing here. Every chosen person is searching for an answer, EVERYONE. You can't take all of this on your own. We are in it together."

"What is it?" Dusty's mind seemed to be in a far-off galaxy. Lynn could see his wheels turning.

"Oh, I was just thinking of Bruce. I'm gonna miss that guy."

Lynn came across the tub, positioning her legs on either side of Dusty in straddling position.

"I miss him too. Let's forget about all of this for a while, okay?" She began to kiss him, setting her glass of wine on the edge of the tub. He followed in suit and brought her closer, caressing her back, relishing at the touch of her smooth, warm skin. They began to passionately make love, freeing their minds from anything but each other. The bathtub, the counter, the bed, the floor, the wall… nothing in that room was safe from their love.

They spent that night as if it were their last night on Earth together, fully immersed into each other's hot, sweaty bodies. Lynn had forgotten to take her birth control and warned Dusty at climax, but he let it go, over and over and over.

Chapter 60

"You're crazy lady!" Sarah smiled at the pilot. She could hardly contain her enthusiasm. She was at peace. The mountains were gorgeous and expansive. They spread out for miles below the plane. The peaks were jagged powdered with pristinely white snow. Sarah doubted if more than five people could be found in the breathtaking and forbidding landscape below. She focused on a prominent peak a few miles ahead. It rose much taller than the surrounding peaks and stood out silently, majestically. *That's the place.*

Sarah moved to the open door. The freezing wind created a vacuum that attempted to suck her out. Sarah grabbed the handles on each side of the door. She could go at any time she wanted, but she chose to wait. She had chosen her peak.

The pilot glanced back. "Lady, you paid well and I promised 'no questions,' but are you sure about this? Do you have someone waiting down there with supplies? You don't have any survival gear, not even a radio. I don't know if I can do this." She looked as if she had no intentions of surviving. She had on a blue jumpsuit and helmet. The parachute pack was bright orange. It had never been used. A CD player, located inside one of the pockets, was sending Wagner's "Lohengrin" into her headphones. It was all surreal, magical and mystical. The mountains... her mission... Wagner.

A sudden burst of turbulence hit the plane and bounced it over invisible rapids in the sky. The pilot turned back to his controls and fought to stabilize the plane. He looked back, "This is pure suicide, lady. Do you even know how to use that chute?"

But Sarah was gone.

She had lost her grip when the turbulence hit. The wind was moving her towards her spot, her landing zone, a mile below and in front of her. She dropped at over a hundred miles per hour, but Sarah felt nothing. She floated gracefully, weightless. A slight pressure from the air that streaked by her caused her ears to pop, but she could still hear Wagner blaring in her headphones. This passage of Lohengrin had always given her the goose bumps. She was getting close enough to her peak to detect that it was barren, jagged and beautiful. It grew larger, nearer. The illusion of weightlessness had given way to the reality that the earth and mountains and rock and snow were moving towards her, faster and faster. Sarah had never known such a place. She spread her arms and legs and absorbed it all. Her eyes started to tear up. Wagner had always put a lump in her throat.

Sarah thought, "Life is incredible." She was certain that no human being had ever rushed to their maker with as much joy and anticipation. She grinned a perfect, happy grin. She knew her eyes must be sparkling. She hit the ground at the pinnacle of her peak and it was all over.

Chapter 61

S arah was a peaceful person, with nothing but love in her heart. She had dreamt of becoming a teacher ever since she was a little girl because she loved helping people and she loved children. Her love for reading led her to become a librarian at a middle school in South Dakota. She loved her job and adored her students, taking care to learn each and every one of their names, as well as the types of books they liked to read. She always had a smile on her face and rarely spoke negative about anyone, or anything. She was not married and did not have children, but her students were her life. She yearned one day to be a mother herself, but she just hadn't found the right partner yet. Children were her life, so when she learned that her life could save the lives of innocent children, she didn't hesitate to make the ultimate sacrifice.

A few members of The Chosen went to her funeral, mainly the ones that she became close with during the meeting, but most were too emotionally spent to attend. Dusty and Lynn didn't go either. It became too depressing to try and keep up with the amounts of funerals occurring in the recent months. Plus, the thought of having to attend unknown amounts in the future lingered in their minds and they didn't want to get into the habit of feeling obliged to attend every one of them. Dusty also didn't want to subject Lynn to anymore grief than absolutely necessary. With every death, her constitution grew weaker. He could feel her starting to slip. Luckily Lynn didn't put up much of a fight when Dusty suggested they just send her family some flowers and a nice card. Cliché? Yes, but he didn't really give a shit about cliché right now.

Although it was becoming extremely hard to muster up the energy to be on the lookout for Sarah's killer reveal, Dusty diligently and religiously scanned the internet for news. He became an expert at sifting through the superfluous websites and identifying reliable sources. He missed Bruce dearly and wished he could pick up the phone and call him. His sorrow was only overshadowed by his will to persevere. The last thing he wanted was for his friend to have died in vain and worse, that many others would fall in the same category.

As luck would have it, two weeks after Sarah's death, Dusty found an article on a South Dakota news website: "Child Rapist and Murderer Arrested at County Fair". He immediately picked up the phone to call Bruce, but then realized his old habit hadn't died with his friend. So, he called Lana. He explained in detail what he had read about with Lynn by his side. He told her how a man was caught attempting to molest a little girl in the woods just adjacent to the county fair. Attention was drawn to the site when the girl's father noticed she was missing. The father ran rampantly through the fairgrounds, searching every tent, booth, building and bleacher. A stranger finally approached him and told him that she had seen a man and a little girl that matched the father's description head towards the woods. She pointed in the direction she had seen them. The father sprinted as fast as he could towards the site just in time to catch the rapist in the act, before he had a chance to kill her. The father beat the rapist within an inch of his life before calling 911. Later, when the father tried to find the stranger to thank her, she was nowhere to be found.

"Do you think the stranger was… her? Do you think that's really possible?" asked Lana in astonishment.

"I don't know. I mean, where are the lines really drawn? Maybe it wasn't her. Maybe she possessed somebody. Either way, this has to be it. After 8 hours of interrogation, the son of a bitch admitted to the murders of several other children."

"Same state, same county, children match the descriptions, I presume?"

"I'm still looking at them, but so far at least one does."

"Son of a bitch. I hope he burns in hell," said Lana, with as much hate in her voice as Dusty had ever heard. "I wish the father would have killed him. I can't take this anymore," Lana started tearing up.

"We're on the cusp of figuring this out, Lana," Dusty's spoke to her in a fatherly manner.

Although people were dying and she hated it, she knew he was right. "I just wish we knew how to stop it before it started, without anyone else having to die! These are good, good people. Why would God, or the Universe, or… whatever, allow the children into our dreams but not let them show us what to do? It's just not fair and it's… it's bullshit!" Dusty just let her vent and didn't speak. She collected her thoughts and regained her composure. "I just hope nobody else has to do this to themselves."

"Me too, Lana. Me too."

Lana calmed down a little bit before saying, "I think I have experienced supercommunication though, Dusty. It happened last week. I had visions, like you did. I think I found where he died. Dusty, I think what you found is our answer, we just have to figure out how to convince authorities to listen to us."

"Oh my God, Lana, that's wonderful! Have you discovered anything?"

"I haven't pinned down the exact details, but I think I know what to do next. My meditations have really helped make the connections. I also did a very strange thing. I found out where my boy lived and broke into the house to get one of his belongings. I don't know if I truly needed it or not, but I took it to the place where I had the supercommunication. I figured I'd try to emulate your experience as much as possible. Now, I think I know where the son of a bitch lives. It's not too far from my work. I must have been close at some point. So, I hired a PI to follow him around while I think of a plan."

"Wow. That's incredible. I can't believe you did that!"

"I had to try something. I thought about approaching the parents, but I just wasn't comfortable. Funny thing is I actually broke back in to put it back. It was a pair of shoes."

"Well, maybe we can keep replicating this method with everybody. Maybe it wasn't just a fluke. If we can get authorities on our side, maybe they can help us obtain belongings if they really do help make the connection. Just be careful Lana. It sounds like you are close, just remember you are dealing with a killer. I'm close to having my killer caught too, I can feel it."

"Well, let's get these guys so the group can know it's more than a pipedream and stop killing themselves. I really liked Sarah. It's just so sad."

"Yeah, me too. All of it is. We got this, Lana. Keep me posted please."

"You too."

"Hey, Lana, you want to know something very interesting?"

"Sure, what you got?"

"Well, I've been sorting through a lot of Bruce's notes and journals. I think he experienced supercommunication and just didn't really know it."

"How could that have been?"

"Well, in his searching, he actually did come very close to where his boy was found in the cement as far as I can tell. He wrote down about three months before he died that he had remembered his dog running away a couple years back. He tried to retrace his steps in finding the dog. He wrote that he had to turn back because he got so sick, like a migraine or something, that he could barely function. He said his vision blurred, his head started pounding and spinning, and that his ears hurt. He didn't say anything about voices, but he did say he was tingly all over his body. And again, based off the description of the notes, I think it was almost exactly where his boy died."

"So, we all react differently possibly?"

"Maybe. Maybe it's a coincidence. Maybe had his mind been a little clearer or had he taken the meditation thing more serious, or had a belonging of the child, or who knows what else... maybe he would have actually experienced it like I did."

"There is just no telling, but that sounds too weird to be a coincidence."

"Yeah, I know. I just feel horrible, like he might have been so close to solving his case and didn't even know. I don't know why he wouldn't have told me something like that, but I guess he just thought he got sick."

"Did he ever have migraines?"

"Apparently he had a history of them in the past, but he said he had not had one in years."

"Well, that's helpful information for everyone still looking. Maybe someone else might be triggered in the same way and now thanks to Bruce, might be able to be clued in."

"Maybe."

"Thanks for telling me. Every little piece of the puzzle helps. Great job."

"No problem. Bye Lana."
"Goodbye Dusty."

Chapter 62

The streets of Avondale were pretty unspectacular this particular evening, but 8-Ball and the crew were diligently making their rounds. *Regulators* blared from the stereo of 8-Ball's "whip", as CJ liked to call it. The bass bumped loudly from the subs that were in the trunk, which made up about half of the car's total value. 8-Ball could feel the compression waves in his chest as his eyes scanned the streets. His comrades passed around a blunt, chonging out the car, laughing and giggling as 8-Ball drove silently through the night. Despite his occasional toke of the blunt, he actually took his role pretty seriously. Every once in a while, something would come up that actually needed attention. A few weeks ago, he came up on a man raping a woman. The crew got out, subdued the creep, beat the shit out of him, called the cops, and put the guy in prison. Many criminals, in fact, were in jail or served time because of the crew's dedication to keeping the streets of the ghetto a safer place.

8-Ball's cell phone rang in his jeans pocket. He pulled it out, recognized Dusty's number, and reached to turn down the stereo. For a brief second, all he heard was Tommy, CJ, DeShawn and DeJuan's voice singing, "Snoop Dogg and Warren G about to regulate…" When they realized the music was off, they all started bitching and moaning, but 8-Ball quieted them immediately, "Hey, shut up y'all, it's Dusty." He flipped open his phone and answered, "What's up?"

Before he could answer, CJ interrupted, "Yo, that my boy Dusty? Nigga put it on speaker phone!" 8-Ball rolled his eyes and knew it would be easier to capitulate now rather than to fight them the whole conversation. He pressed the speaker button and faced the phone towards the back. CJ yelled, "Dustaaaaayyyy! My numba one cracka! Whassssuuuupppppp?"

Dusty laughed and responded, "CJ? Hey man I'm good. How bout you? You boys behaving?"

Tommy shouted, "Only if you call smoking a blizzle in the back seat of my nizzle's car behaving!" The whole car erupted in laughter... everyone but 8-Ball.

"A what?" Dusty's ignorance sparked another eruption of uncontrollable laughter.

DeShawn translated, "You know when you speaking to a white boy, you gotta speak white boy. Dusty, yo, a BLUNT. It's when you take the tobacco out of a cigar and put weed in it, and smoke it..." more laughter ensued from the stoned watchmen.

"Oh. That's cool," he tried to think of something funny really quick, "I always thought they were called cigaweedos." He got the response he was after as the crew took the laughing to a level he didn't think could be reached.

8-Ball cut in, "Alright, alright, enough. Anyone ever tell ya'll that too much weed kills brain cells?" He said this as he took a fat rip off the blunt before throwing it out the window, much to the dismay of the rest of the crew who all yelled at him in unison. "What can I do you for Mr. Burch?"

"How are we doin' on the case? Anyone heard anything about the whereabouts of the parents?"

8-Ball turned the music up just a hair to appease the tapping on the back of the seat that he knew was pleading with him to turn up the jam, "We got a call from a man who claimed to be the little girl's grandfather the other day. He said he heard a story on the news and hadn't been able to get a hold of his daughter or seen his granddaughter for a while. He apparently owns the home his daughter was staying in, the one you... well anyway. He has given the cops permission to search it. Where the hell have you been anyway? I haven't heard from you in like, two weeks? Three?"

"Wait, what? How legit is this guy? Why didn't you tell me?"

"I tried calling you Dusty. Haven't you checked your phone?"

"I've had an interesting month. Basically, I sabotaged my career in an intentional botch at trial and I've moved to New York to help Lynn. I'm sorry I didn't say goodbye. It all kind of happened really fast."

397

"Say what?"

"Yeah, I know. I'm an asshole. I came here so I can help Lynn with her case."

"Okay, so in New York... no job... I'm the one who should be asking you how *your* case is going with Lynn," 8-Ball pulled over at a closed gas station so he could concentrate on the conversation. The crew was now bobbing up and down, rapping to a new song: *Gin & Juice.*

"Well, still no soup. Yet. But we found out something extremely creepy. There was a member of The Chosen, Tyler Dunst, who lived about 100 miles from Manhattan. No one had heard from him for about eight months. He was pretty quiet. I didn't know him well at all. The last thing anyone remembered him talking about in the chat room was a potential supercommunication he had had. Some people think he got into trouble while trying to solve his murder. There was really no telling. The other day his body turned up in the Delaware River. We don't think it was suicide. Pretty fucked up shit, huh?"

"Makes the puzzle a little more complicated, that's for sure."

"I for one think that there's a serial killer around Manhattan. Tyler, Richard and Lynn all see children from this area. I think we're on to him. I think maybe he killed Tyler."

"Well, be careful man. I need you. I've been trying to get the cops on our side, but they say they need proof of all this hocus-pocus. I presented all the evidence you gave me about the other four people and it raised some eyebrows, but in order for them to take what you all say as gospel, they need hard evidence... catch them in the act or something. I mean I'm lucky they are listening to me at all. In order for them to even consider bringing in the FBI, we have to be able to give them hard shit," 8-Ball said with conviction.

"Well, I don't know how they are going to get that. I mean, we don't even know how it happens yet, or when it happens. How are we going to have them there when it does?"

"I don't know. I guess we'll just have to get creative."

"Well, unfortunately I have two other cases you can show them if you need more evidence. Hopefully the more cracked cases associated with our group, the more they will take us seriously. A librarian and a druggie from our group took matters into their own hands as well. It only took about three days in each case for the murderer to be caught."

"No shit?! Wow… how were they caught?"

"Well, one was pulled over at a DUI checkpoint. He was brought in because his BAC read 1.5. Funny thing is, when they brought him in, fingerprinted him and drew his blood, his blood BAC read 0. The breathalyzer seemed to be "malfunctioning" somehow, but it was too late. They ran his prints and it matched prints in the system found at a crime scene linked to one of the children. Busted. I'm pretty sure the criminal was in Daryl's drug circle or a connected circle. There wasn't a lot of news out on this one, so it's hard to tell. The other case a Dad caught a rapist with his daughter in the woods minutes before he might have killed her. He was tipped off by someone at the fair they were at—someone that disappeared afterwards, like a spirit. Maybe it was, maybe it wasn't. Either way, that's two more murderers in the can."

"Okay, get me that info ASAP. In the meantime, you get to cracking on your case and BE CAREFUL! Check in with me every day, please. If we are going to make this happen, I can't have you be going off on two-week sabbaticals any more, got it?"

"Yes mother."

"Good. Well, take care of yourself. We'll get this taken care of, together."

"Okay, good talking with you."

"Always. Oh, and hey, this guy, the grandpa, said his granddaughter's name was Claire. Just thought you might want to know."

"Claire…" Dusty's gut dropped. Something about the reality of it all, finally putting a name to his little girl. "Claire… wow. Thank you. Thank you for everything."

"No problem homie. We are on the homestretch." 8-Ball hung up the phone. He turned to the back seat and said, "Hey, you guys ready for some seriously covert shit? 007 style?"

CJ responded immediately, "Fuck yeah mother fucker! James Bond ain't got shit on me! What you got?"

"Okay, I'll tell you, but you can't tell anyone! I mean ANYONE! Got it?"

In unison, "Yes sir!"

"This is what we gotta do," 8-Ball turned the music down and laid out the super-secret, covert operation for them.

Dusty hung up the phone and sat silently, lucidly dreaming about *Claire*. She was swinging on her swing… she was happy.

Chapter 63

Dusty had actually started to acquire a taste for Reubens. Over the course of the last year, he and Lynn had probably eaten at Teddy's 50 times. It was "their spot", as Dusty liked to tease Lynn. She thought that a "spot" should be a little more romantic and let Dusty know quite often. He knew this, but he liked to tease her about it anyway. He always told her that someday, they would travel off to a far, far place and find a rooftop overlooking the ocean that they could call their *new* spot. But for now, this was their spot, and it was where he was supposed to be meeting her for lunch at noon.

At 12:10, Dusty ordered another cherry coke. He made small talk with Jed, one of the sandwich makers behind the bar that Dusty had gotten to know. They talked about how for the first time in a long time, the Mets were better than the Yankees and actually had a shot at winning the pennant. Dusty was a second-class baseball fan, but living in New York, he didn't have much of a choice. Lynn loved the Yankees and they had been to several games together, so he jumped on the opportunity to opine on the weakness of their bullpen and the strength of the batting lineup. Plus, liking the Yankees gave him another reason to razz his Dad when they beat up on the Royals.

At 12:15, he looked at his phone to see if he had missed any texts. Sometimes, Lynn would get caught up at work helping a dentist and be late to lunch. No texts. So Dusty went ahead and ordered his sandwich. He hadn't eaten breakfast and was starving.

He finished his sandwich at 12:26 and when he still hadn't heard from Lynn, he started to get a little worried. So, he called her. Her phone rang and went to voicemail. He left her a message that told her to call him and that he was starting to get a little worried. He walked outside on the street hoping he would see her outside. He waited there for another five minutes and then finally went back to the apartment. He told Jed to let her know he waited for her if she showed up.

On his walk home, Dusty had to suppress sinister thoughts from creeping into his head, but with every passing minute that he didn't hear from Lynn, they grew stronger and stronger. She wasn't one to skip out on a Reuben from Teddy's, or to not tell Dusty that she would not be coming. She was a very thoughtful person, and usually at the first sign of a change of plans, she let Dusty know immediately. Today, something felt wrong though and Dusty's anxiety was increasing with every step.

He thought that maybe there was a chance she was at the apartment. Maybe she forgot something there and left her phone at the office. Maybe a friend called her with bad news and she needed to console her. Maybe someone at the office had an accident and she had to drive him or her to the ER. Many possibilities ran through his head, but none of them seemed likely when he got to the apartment and he saw that she wasn't there. He called the dentist office and no one had seen her this morning.

At this point, Dusty started to panic a little. He rethought the events of the morning. He remembered seeing her as they ate breakfast. He made her eggs and bacon with toast. She usually got into work about 9:00 and left about 8:40. Dusty headed off to the gym about 8:30 though and gave her a kiss goodbye before walking out the door. Since Dusty wasn't working anymore, he had started exercising regularly. He hadn't missed a workout in two months and this morning was no different.

Come on! Think! What else did you see?

He looked again at his phone to make sure he hadn't missed any texts or calls. Nothing. Then he looked at his email. Again, nothing. He called her close friend, Kristin, whom she saw several times a week. Kristin hadn't heard from her since yesterday.

Dusty's heart began beating rapidly. Lynn hadn't exactly been herself lately, but this was unlike her. She had never done something like this before. Something must be wrong. Sometimes she spent hours in the library and lost track of time, so he tried there. The librarian knew Lynn well, but hadn't seen her this morning.

He started thinking back to the night before. Stir Fry, Yankees on TV, two episodes of *Frasier,* emails… *Emails! She was emailing Richard.* He had been almost obsessively interested in helping Lynn with her children. He seemed to be convinced that they were seeing children of the same killer. He had been very persuasive. Nobody else in The Chosen had claimed they were seeing the same children, but Richard described almost to a 'T' Lynn's children. She was sure that together, they could solve the case.

So Dusty called Richard. Voicemail. He left a message asking him to call him immediately. Dusty didn't like the idea that Lynn might be alone with Richard, but he had come to accept that Lynn was going to do anything she could to find the bastard that killed her children. In all honesty, Dusty was a little insecure about Richard. He wasn't strikingly handsome, but he had a masculine side to him that Dusty could see possibly being attractive to women. Richard was kind of grungy, but he had style and charisma in a redneck type way.

After the third phone call to Richard, Dusty had had enough. He didn't know what other options he had, so he decided to head uptown to Richard's loft. It was a long walk, so he took a cab thirty blocks north to Brandon Ave. The cab driver was the typical middle-eastern, broken English, swindler with a meter on overdrive. Dusty didn't care though; he paid him the $54.70 and got out. He hadn't said one word to him other than telling him the address. The cab driver didn't care. He got his money and started looking for another customer.

Dusty had only been to Richard's once to bring him a copy of his Bible that he had made for him. Most of the time, Dusty and Lynn met Richard at coffee shops or restaurants, so there was never any reason for them to be at his apartment. Plus, whatever insecurities Dusty had about Lynn meeting Richard alone were eased with the thought of them meeting in a public place.

Dusty walked into the elevator and hit button 15. He remembered Richard's room was 15A because Dusty's birthday was on August 15th. *What a coincidence.* Dusty wasn't sure what he was going to say to Richard, but he had to try and get a hold of him.

When he knocked on the door, it opened slightly. It had not been shut all the way. "Richard? Richard, are you in there?" Silence. He could see a dim light coming from what he assumed was the living area. He pushed the door open a little more and again called for him. Again, nothing.

A man and woman got off of the elevator and looked oddly at Dusty. He looked their way and gave them a friendly nod, as if he belonged. They stood there for ten seconds or so, staring at Dusty, and he could hear them whisper something to each other. Dusty looked over again at them, this time with a scowl, and they took off down the hallway.

Dusty's gaze turned back towards the open door in front of him. He yelled Richard's name a little bit louder, but again, no response. Reluctantly, Dusty opened the door and walked into the loft.

The apartment looked clean enough for a bachelor of about 35 years old. There were a few beer cans on the coffee table in the living room and it looked like it had never been dusted, but for the most part it was neat and orderly. To the immediate left was a kitchen area and past that was the living area. There looked to be a bedroom on each side of the apartment. Dusty looked in the sink, still having not moved an inch. In it were bottles of red wine; some opened and some still closed. In the living room was a red reclining chair facing the TV in the corner and a brown couch that looked like it was from the 70s.

Dusty took a step into the apartment. He still had not heard a peep. He slowly looked down the hall to his right. He could see a laptop on a desk in the bedroom at the end of the short hallway. He recognized it to be a 15" MacBook Pro. A screensaver was up that looked like a wormhole travelling through space, changing colors and pulsating rapidly. He called Richard's name one more time and was responded to by silence.

He looked down the left hallway and saw a closed door. He started feeling a little creepy, like he was doing something wrong or breaking and entering, but his desperation to locate Lynn trumped the rest of his emotions. He approached the closed door quietly and slowly, heart beating very rapidly. He tried to push aside the horrible images that were entering his mind. *What if she were in there with him? Naked and wrapped up in the sheets? What if she is dead in there? Oh my God I should have never trusted this asshole!* If any of these scenarios were true, his heart would be broken.

As he got to the door, he reached up and wiped a bead of sweat from his brow. He hesitated before lightly tapping his finger on the door. After a few seconds, he decided to turn the handle and peek inside. In the middle of the floor was Lynn, lying unconscious with rope around her hands and feet and duct tape around her mouth. He didn't notice any blood, but that didn't make him feel any better. He instinctually shoved the door open and headed towards her.

In that moment, Richard stepped out of the closet with a frying pan and whacked Dusty in the back of the head. Dusty became extremely disoriented, but to Richard's surprise, still conscious. Dusty spun around and charged Richard, but Richard was prepared. In his other hand was a syringe full of horse tranquilizers. He shoved it into Dusty's ribs as Dusty tackled him into the drywall. Within seconds, Dusty was unconscious.

Richard pushed Dusty off of him and pulled himself out of the hole in the wall. He stood up, dusted off and smiled at the two bodies lying on the floor in front of him. His plan had been successful.

Two hours later, Dusty woke up tied to a chair in the middle of the bedroom. His mouth was gagged with a couple of old, musty smelling bandannas. He heard strange music playing in the CD player that was on the table in the corner. It sounded like some sort of new age space music mixed with Tibetan monk hymnals. He tried to recall the last moments he was awake and with great difficulty, remembered running to Lynn, then being blasted in the head by something extremely hard, probably a baseball bat or large frying pan. His head was throbbing and piercing his thoughts. He looked around him and tried to gain awareness. He looked for anything that he could possibly use to cut himself free or to alert someone of his whereabouts. The room was almost completely bare besides a coffee table in the corner with the stereo on it and a strobe light in the other corner. His cell phone was not in his pocket.

After two or three minutes of regaining his consciousness, he heard a mumble come from behind him. He hadn't bothered to check before, but upon reaching his hands backwards, he felt another chair. His arms were tied at his elbows and it was extremely difficult for him to bend his arms backwards enough, but with great pain he was able to feel around and eventually came into contact with another person's arm.

"Lynn!" Dusty tried to scream through the bandannas, but it only came out what sounded like a muffled cry for help. He started rocking back and forth to try and wiggle free from the ropes, but they were bound tight and he soon started losing feeling in his arms. He continued to scream for her. She was coming to her senses, but was not aware that the person tied behind her was Dusty. He could hear frequent moans and whimpers, but could do nothing to sooth them.

Dusty became increasingly panicked. Beads of sweat ran into his eyes blurring his vision. Each ankle was strapped to a leg of the chair and he worked on those next. He twisted and turned his ankles until he could feel the rope burning into his skin. Richard was a Boy Scout as a child and his knot tying skills were immaculate. Soon, Dusty realized he wasn't going anywhere. He continued to bounce up and down for a few more minutes, and then became afraid that he would tip both of them over and further injure Lynn. Eventually, he coalesced and sat still, waiting for the feeling to return to his hands so he could at least try to touch Lynn a few more times in what he was sure were the last few moments of his life. As far as he could tell, Richard planned to kill both of them. Why else would they be tied up like this?

As he sat, tsunamis of grief overcame him. *Why had I trusted Richard? Why didn't I trust my first intuition? Who is this mother fucker? Did he know where the children were? Was he the killer? Had he set us up? Did he pose as one of The Chosen to sabotage the operation?* There was no end to the sadness that settled upon him in that barren bedroom. The music that played in the background served as a soundtrack to the sick tragedy that had befallen him and his lover. All he could think about were the years of love and happiness they would miss out on. Where would their bodies end up? In the bottom of the river? In Richard's freezer? In a landfill?

Just as he was working through this issue, the bedroom door opened and in came a person he assumed to be Richard. He couldn't tell because this person was wearing a Ku Klux Klan mask and robe. The man switched on the strobe light in the corner and turned up the music. The song was hitting a verse that blasted what sounded like tubas playing a monotonous note for 5 or 6 seconds before pausing, upon which a keyboard or steel guitar of some sort would fiddle a sinister riff. Heavy gongs kept beat in the background.

Richard began to dance around Lynn and Dusty. His premeditated movements were provocative and evil. He jumped up and down while spinning and slapping his body all over. He came within inches of their faces from time to time, chanting a baleful procession of shouts, growls, roars, mumbles and high-pitched shrieks. It was like a scene from a horror movie, except this was as real as it could be.

Tears streamed out of Lynn's face. She had never been more terrified in her life. She still wasn't certain who the man was behind her, but she could only think of Dusty. Who else would come for her? Who else would be grasping her hand so tightly, caressing the makeshift engagement ring that Dusty hadn't yet replaced? She tried remembering the sequence of events of the day.

Earlier that morning, Dusty had left for his workout. She finished up a load of laundry and sat down for a few minutes drinking her coffee and watching the news before heading out the door for work. Oddly, she remembered a report about a local elementary school gifted program earning second place at a national creative skit competition. Just as she was leaving, she received a text from Richard telling her that he believed he had finally found some concrete evidence regarding the killer.

Of course, Lynn dropped everything she was doing and went straight to Richard's. Lately, she had been deteriorating quickly. Seven people had already either died or committed suicide to catch the killers of their children. With every day Lynn failed to find a clue, suicidal thoughts crept closer and closer. She began frequently talking to Dusty about it, frightening him. He only slept an hour or two at night so he could keep watch on her. In those hours, he couldn't remember seeing his girl, but he didn't know if that was because he had finally come close to solving her case or if he just never slept long enough to enter a deep enough REM cycle.

Lynn remembered entering Richard's apartment after a 20-minute jog. It was 9:00 in Manhattan and a taxi could take way longer than jogging, so she opted for the quicker route. Plus, she had only run five miles the day before, not her usual eight, so she wanted to make up the few miles. She asked him immediately to show her what he had found. He sat her down at the kitchen table in front of some papers. She squinted to read what was written extremely small on a scratch piece of paper and Richard took advantage of her distracted state. He grabbed her around the throat, but he wasn't prepared for the incredible strength and flexibility of Lynn nor the self-defense tactics she was privy to.

She immediately elbowed him in the groin and dug her nails into his forearms until flesh peeled away from it and blood poured out. She twisted free and kicked him in the knee. Richard, although surprised, was not immobilized. He reached for a skillet on the kitchen counter, but Lynn roundhouse kicked him directly in the chest and sent him flying across the room. Struggling for breath, Richard climbed to his knees and discretely reached into his pocket. As she approached his hunched over body, ready to deliver another blow, he reached up and stuck the syringe of tranquilizers in her thigh. She managed to knee him one more time in the face, breaking his nose, before falling to the ground unconscious. Richard had to give it to her. She was one tough bitch.

Richard's dance was starting to dwindle down with the music. At the end of the song, he went over and pressed pause on the CD player. He left the strobe on though and unmasked himself.

"I was wondering how long it would take before you came for your sweet Lynn. How pathetically predictable. You guys make me fucking sick." In a mocking tone, he recited, "'Oh, I've fallen in love with a girl and together we can solve the mysteries of the dark and evil killers of the world', seriously? And who the hell encrypted your website anyway? Any 12-year- old with a computer could have hacked into that piece of shit. This was all too easy. As soon as I saw you fools, I thought it was all bullshit. But then I kept reading. I followed up on the stories. 'Doris's Unfortunate Miracle', 'Nick's *Plunge* of Faith'," he stopped to laugh at his witty comment. "It started looking like you were maybe on to something. So, I had to get in. I had to make sure none of you were on my tail.

"But then there was you, Lynn. It took me a little while to figure out who you were, but soon enough I did. I don't know how you do it, but that little bitch I killed comes to you... and we can't have her be telling any secrets now can we? She started bringing a friend, too? Well that's too bad. I mean, I'm good. No one could ever catch me, but I don't know how to fight psychic freaks. Problem is, sounds like if I kill you, then you win. Huh?"

He got so close to Lynn's face that she could smell the beer on his breath. He apparently liked to get his buzz on before he tortured his victims. He walked around the two trembling in the middle of the room.

"Or do you?" He got in Dusty's face, then licked the side of his cheek. "See, there's no way anyone can catch me. I have no trace evidence in this place. No pictures, no emails, no videos… nothing. There is no way on this earth anyone could ever prove I hurt your little precious children." Richard all the sudden became irritated, "I mean what's the big fucking deal anyway? All throughout the history of humanity, men and women have killed to survive. Killed to protect. Killed to serve. Killed to… enjoy. Ain't no one ever loved me like they did. NO ONE! You should have seen the way they looked at me." Richard began to feign a cry, "It was… beautiful. I didn't want to kill them. Honest. But I couldn't be having them share what we had with no one else! Not ever!"

It was at this moment that Dusty and Lynn realized they were dealing with a true psychopath. *How could he have blended in so easily?*

"I don't know what I'm going to do with you, but whatever it is, I'm going to thoroughly enjoy it." Richard pulled out a knife and ran in across the forehead of Lynn, opening up a small laceration that immediately began spilling blood into her eyes and down her face. Richard began licking up the blood and squeezing her breasts. She could feel him growing hard on her legs as he straddled her. He reached around to Dusty's crotch and began to rub his genitals. "Oh my God you two are just so fucking cute!" He cut a line down Lynn's blouse and ripped off her shirt. Her covered breasts heaved up and down.

Dusty squealed and yelled and tried harder to get out, but he wasn't going anywhere. His wrists and ankles began to bleed and the harder he pulled the ropes on his arms, the tighter it became around Lynn's body.

Richard dismounted Lynn and came to Dusty. He unrobed himself and unveiled his boxers. They were black and covered in skulls. "Now, Dusty, I'm going to take this bandanna off," he pulled his knife close to his face, then went around his head and held it close to Lynn's throat. "If you make one fucking noise, I'm gonna slit your pretty little girlfriends throat and watch her bleed out. Then I'm going to fuck her dead body in front of you. Got it?"

Dusty didn't move.

Richard slapped him in the face, "GOT IT?!" The knife started cutting skin on Lynn and she shrieked. Dusty finally nodded his head.

"Good. Real good. Now, I reckon a big stud like you has never done this, but that don't mean you don't know how it's done." Richard started pulling his penis out of the hole in his boxers.

Just as he got it out, he heard a knock on the bedroom door. "What the…?"

As soon as he got out the words, the door busted down and in came a swat team, fully armed from head to toe. Dusty could not see any of their faces because they were masked, but he could hear the lead man yell at Richard to get on the ground and put his hand behind his back. When Richard refused, the man clubbed him in the back with his stick and knocked him to the ground. Then he walked over to Dusty and cut off his ropes.

"You get one shot, Dusty. You hear? One. That's all I can let you take." Dusty was confused and baffled by what was happening. He just stared blankly at the man. One of the other men switched on the lights and turned off the strobe. Two others stood by Richard to make sure he didn't go anywhere. "Go on. You better make it good." The man took off his mask and revealed himself. To Dusty's surprise, there stood 8-Ball.

"What?! 8… how did you? I don't understand." Dusty struggled to speak as he caught his breath.

"There's no time for explaining now boss. Get up and fuck this mother fucker up before it's too late. The rest of the squad is gonna be here any minute."

Dusty stood to his feet. His head was still pounding. He immediately turned to see a man cutting Lynn out of her ropes. "Lynn! Are you okay? Oh my god, honey? Did he hurt you?" He could see blood covering her face. The amount of blood made the injury look a lot worse than it really was.

As soon as her gag was removed, she sobbed uncontrollably. Dusty kissed her on the cheek and held her. Then in a fit of rage, he stood up and approached Richard. "You sick mother fucker!" Then he took two steps and kicked Richard as hard as he could in the ribs. He heard all the air escape his lungs and immediately went in for another blow. He was able to elbow drop him directly in the middle of his back before 8-Ball pulled him off.

"Hey, I said one! Dusty, that's enough."

"I'm gonna kill him! I'm gonna kill that sick bastard! He killed those kids!" Dusty was kicking and twisting, trying to break free from the two policemen. They were strong though and were able to hold him off. "Let go of me! Let me go! Did you see what he did to Lynn? Did you see what he was going to do to me? Let me fucking go you assholes! I'm gonna kill him!"

"Dusty, calm down. We got him. He ain't going nowhere except the electric chair. He will get what he deserves. But we can't have you going there with him." Dusty was still kicking and averting eye contact. "Hey! You hear me? Calm down, now! We got him! Dusty!"

Dusty finally stopped moving and looked at 8-Ball. Tears were flowing from his eyes, but his mouth remained silent. Right then, six more SWAT team men came into the room and hauled Richard off, followed by paramedics who put Dusty and Lynn on carts and rolled them to the ambulance. Dusty refused initially, but after a couple minutes, he was persuaded by 8-Ball to cooperate. He wanted to ride with Lynn, but of course that was not possible.

Lynn was in shock. She had not said a word. She kept the same blank stare and catatonic position on the stretcher. They checked her vitals and all was well, except for a slightly increased heartbeat. They cleaned the cut on her forehead once she got into the ambulance and bandaged her up. Before they closed the door, Dusty screamed to her that he would see her soon. The ambulances turned on their sirens and roared towards Manhattan Medical. 8-Ball managed to make it into Dusty's ambulance somehow and the conversation that ensued was interesting, to say the least.

Dusty had never been on the inside of an ambulance. He didn't really take any time to observe the contents. He got straight to the point, "8-Ball, would you mind kindly explaining to me exactly what in the FUCK is going on?" Dusty was speaking through his oxygen mask and totally oblivious to the EMTs taking his blood pressure and sticking an IV in his other arm.

8-Ball knew this was coming and he was prepared, "Whoa, Whoa. Calm down. Is this how to treat the guy that just saved your life?"

"Oh, is this funny to you? Is this fucking funny? I'll tell ya, it's Goddamn hilarious to me. I almost choked down a serial killer's cock while he held a knife to my fiancé's neck. Doesn't get much funnier than that, does it?"

"No, Dusty. I do not think it's funny. I just thought you might be a little more glad to see me, that's all."

"Well sorry if I'm not exactly in a friendly mood. Under the circumstance I think you'd understand. Why in the hell did you wait so long anyway? He could have killed us!"

"I had it under control," 8-Ball said in a very calm, monotone voice. "I get it. You are upset, but I'll explain everything. Just try to calm down a little bit. Please. You know how sensitive I am." Dusty sensed the sarcasm in 8-Ball's voice and scowled at him. His silence signified his compliance.

"Well, I'm not sure exactly where to start." 8-Ball took a deep breath and put his hands together in front of his face, as if he were praying. "Let me start by saying that we have been watching you for a while."

"What? Who?" Dusty asked with a wrinkled-up brow and squinted eyes.

"Okay, just let me finish please. Then ask all the questions you want." Dusty still wore the same scowl. "After you found your little girl, the Chicago PD wanted more proof that you and your group were for real. I didn't tell them everything, but I told them there was some weird stuff going on that was hard to explain. I told them after we found the body about meeting you and what you had told me. Of course, at first, they were skeptical, but I've never done anything to varnish their trust, so after some begging and pleading they reluctantly listened. Plus, it didn't hurt that the DNA from the house they searched matched your little girls. Apparently, her grandpa's hunch about his daughter was right. I'm sorry I hadn't told you yet, I needed you to focus here and I didn't want you to know that we were watching you. It would minimize the effectiveness of our plan."

"Wait, so they identified her? Is it Claire?" Dusty's throat tightened and his heart dropped as he waited out the next infinitely long second for 8-Ball's answer.

"Yes. It's over brother. We haven't caught the parents yet, but we think we know where they are. We will have them in the next couple days I'm sure."

With this news, Dusty laid his head back, closed his eyes and breathed a sigh of relief. He hadn't felt this good in years. It was as if immediately all of his worries, fears, anxiety and sadness were lifted from his body. He thought back to the very first time he saw her in his dreams and the sadness he felt. He thought about all the restless sleep and talks with Marilyn and his shrink, the call on the radio where he first heard Lana, his dad, Bruce… wow he missed Bruce. He could almost feel his presence. An image of Bruce's face and those damn thick glasses beamed into Dusty's forebrain. Tears formed in his eyes. He thought about how Claire had brought Lynn into his life, the woman he knew he was meant to be with; he also thought about how Claire reshaped his career and forced him to face the fact that he was never meant to be a defense attorney. He thought about all of his friends who were now gone and the rest who were still living: The Chosen. Lastly, he thought about all the children who had suffered and those who more importantly would not have to suffer. All of these thoughts arose almost simultaneously like Mt. Saint Helen's with the utterance of two words: "It's over." 8-Ball smiled as he sensed the relief and almost felt it lift from Dusty and continued.

"So back to why I'm here. I have to tell you something. I lied to you. I'm not an informant to the police," 8-Ball made a face like he was expecting Dusty to have an emotional reaction, but Dusty remained calm.

"What are you talking about," said Dusty with a smile on his face that said 'what more could possibly surprise me at this point?' 8-Ball made a look with a raised eyebrow that made Dusty feel stupid, like he should have known something. It was the same kind of look that his high school algebra teacher gave him when she called on him in class and he didn't know the answer to the problem that she had clearly shown how to do because he had been busy staring at the cheerleading captain's half-covered tits hanging out of her blouse.

"I am not an informant," said 8-ball, drawing out the word 'informant' and putting quotes up with his fingers. "I *have* informants…" Now it clicked for Dusty.

"You mean you are a cop? You are undercover, aren't you?" 8-Ball smiled an 'atta-boy' smile. "Oh my God I should have known. How did I not know this?" Dusty said incredulously.

"Don't feel bad. I'm a professional at blending in. That's my job. How the hell else do you think I could have pulled all this off?" He smacked Dusty on the inner thigh.

"Holy cow, well I guess it all makes sense. How you knew so much and were able to get so much done always baffled me, but I was so desperate I never questioned it. You just always came through and," Dusty paused, making sure he found the right words, "I felt like I could trust you. I honestly don't know what would have happened if I hadn't met you…"

"You still can trust me, Dusty. I'm sorry I couldn't tell you. I really am, there was just…"

"I get it. I get it. Seriously, you don't have to apologize. I'm just thankful. So thankful." Dusty gave 8-Ball a big hug and squeezed hard. 8-Ball returned the gesture. Dusty pulled back and said, "Go ahead and finish what you were telling me. How did you set all this up?"

"Okay, well Donnie, is actually my boss at the Chicago PD, said that if there was any truth at all to the psychic clues, then they would have to see it in action if they were to even think about bringing it to the FBI's attention. He has worked with the FBI on many occasions and has good friends there. Of course, he was extremely skeptical and I had no idea how I was going to get him the proof he needed, but when you moved to New York to help Lynn, I knew that was my chance. So, I followed you there and kept an eye out, you know, protect my investment. I got clearance from the department under the pretense that it was investigation work on a murder case, which is true.

"I kept my distance. I'm sorry that I didn't tell you, but again I didn't want to jeopardize the operation. If we ever wanted the assistance of the FBI to solve any of these murders, I needed to nail this. So, I wired Lynn's apartment and followed your footsteps. I had to provide hard proof that your actions led to solving the murder mystery. This was the only way. Everyday normal people can't just go up to the police or FBI and say they can solve a case that the FBI has been scratching their heads over without looking like a suspect. You and I both know that. So, we had to get them on our side before there would ever be a chance of them ever listening to any of your 'chosen' friends.

"I started having suspicions about Richard early on, just something about him. Maybe it was the way he was so anxious to help Lynn. I don't know. But I had nothing on him, so I bugged his apartment too. Earlier today I followed you to his house. Donnie told me that I would have a swat team at my disposal because he knew the NYPD's chief of police and that I could call it in at any time if I ever got in trouble. As soon as I heard him crack your head, I made the call.

"I heard him muttering to himself his plans of tying you up and 'having some fun', so I knew he wasn't going to kill you, yet. That's why I didn't bust in earlier. I was listening to everything, as well as recording. If I wanted to get Richard though, I had to make sure I got him talking about the kids. So that's why I waited longer. I'm so sorry I waited so long, but without him admitting to the murders, we had nothing.

"As soon as I could, I ordered the swat team in. Sounds like it was perfect timing, too. Listen man, I'm sorry to put you through all this, but I knew that if it meant getting this asshole and helping Lynn, you would have wanted me to do it. After all you've been through, what was one more wiener in your face?"

This comment actually got Dusty to crack a smile, "One more?"

"You mean that was your first?" 8-Ball feigned confusion.

"Fuck you," Dusty felt satisfied that he didn't need to defend himself anymore and moved on as if to show 8-Ball his vain attempt at an insult didn't do so much as put a dent in his hull. "So, you're saying we have enough evidence for the FBI to use to indict Richard?"

"Well, possibly, and if not, we definitely have enough for a search warrant. They will rip apart every piece of property he owns and if they so much as find a spec of DNA that matches the victims, he is toast. Even if they don't, there is a good chance he will confess. The confession I just recorded should be admissible as it was recorded during another crime, but if not, we can use it to get him to confess again. Sick fucks like this like to be recognized for their work. So, as long as the FBI doesn't screw this up, from now on any bona fide member of The Chosen can and will be used to solve the rest of the open cases. You guys are going to be like the unsung heroes of the United States. Of course, it will never go the public and no one will ever know you guys had anything to do with the investigations."

"But nothing we did brought us the killer. He came to us. I mean, why would they agree to listen to us when we didn't actually solve the case."

8-Ball readjusted his posture on the small stool next to Dusty, "Ahh, but that's where you are wrong. You *did* bring them the killer. This case in particular has had the FBI's attention because of the status of the victim. It was the governor of New York's niece. The family didn't want to go public about the killing. They thought it would bring too much negative attention to the already highly scrutinized public life of the Governor and his family. They didn't need or want reporters banging at their door, so only close friends and family really knew about it. So aside from a couple generic, cryptic articles, there wasn't much the public knew. That's probably why Lynn was never able to find much information on her or the case. See the FBI doesn't care how you brought them Richard. All they will know is that now, thanks to you, he is brought to Justice. And when they find out your other friends were responsible for the capture of several other murderers; I think they just might listen up. Plus, now we have your case too and that was all you buddy."

"Okay, well, I hope you're right. I really do. What if we can show them our Bible now? What if we can show them the descriptions of the children? If they match up with the ones on their list, then they have to believe us, right?" Dusty said as if the thought had hit him and was the epiphany he needed to actually believe the craziness of the situation.

"Well, it's the FBI. I don't know if they *have* to do anything, but my guess is that someone over there is desperate enough to solve cases that he will be willing to try anything. I don't know if the Bible is key here. I mean anyone could find pictures of missing children and put their profiles into a collection. But this is all unprecedented shit. Nothing like this has ever happened before. There are going to be people in the FBI that fight this tooth and nail, but we will just have to persevere. In the end, what we have on our side is that children are involved. They would be stupid not to at least explore the possibilities."

"Well I hope they do. At the very least they can help see to it that we get the resources we need. For me I believe it was about being in my little girl's home, holding something of hers. That's not easy for everyone to do. If the FBI is compliant, they should be able to get us access to more personal items of the victims. I could be wrong, but I just believe that helps make the link. It can't hurt." The Ambulance was starting to approach the hospital at this point. The sirens turned off and Dusty heard the EMTs get out and run around to open the back door.

"There's still a lot of work to be done, but I have faith. You rest up. We are going to need you."

Dusty grabbed 8-Ball's hand, "8-Ball, thank you. Thank you for everything. I can't believe you..."

8-Ball cut him off, "Shhhhh. Call me Marcellus." Dusty squeezed his hand a little harder before letting go. The doors opened and two men and a woman EMT hoisted Dusty out of the ambulance.

"I think I'll stick with 8-Ball. Marcellus makes you sound like a pussy." This comment almost made Dusty feel like he had sufficiently combated 8-Ball's earlier 'wiener' comment.

"Whatever you want boss. All I know is we have one down, about 50 more to go." Dusty nodded in agreement. 8-Ball jumped out of the ambulance behind them and watched the EMTs roll him into the ER right behind Lynn. They were safe and he had done what he came to do.

Chapter 64

Hospitals were always something Dusty tried to avoid. He didn't like the grief, the pain, the… sickness. As a boy, his great Aunt had Tuberculosis and Dusty and his mother visited her on a weekly basis until the day she died. The sight of bloody tissues and the sound of a dying woman's cough was enough to scar any young boy. On top of that, when he was 16, he nearly died and was hospitalized for a month when his appendix burst; It was the most miserable month of his life. Needless to say, hospitals were not his favorite establishment.

As they wheeled him in on the gurney, he began to feel nauseous, "I'm fine. Seriously, I'm fine. I do not need to go in there." The paramedics just ignored him. "Hello?" Dusty raised his voice and sat up from the gurney, "Please stop moving me. I want to get out."

The two men pushing looked at him, then looked at each other. Both of them were about mid-thirties, blond hair (one curly and one wavy) and well built. The man on the left finally spoke up, "I'm sorry, but we've been ordered to take you in for observation. There's nothing we can do about it. You were the victim of a serious crime Mr. Burch. We have to do everything we can to make sure you are not harmed. It's a liability thing more than anything."

Dusty knew this better than most, "Yeah, yeah. I get it. I'm a lawyer. But seriously, I won't tell anyone. Just… wheel me over there to the corner, I'll get up, walk out, and you'll never hear from me again."

"Mr. Burch, I'm sorry. I cannot do that. I'm sure you are okay, but you never know. You could have internal bleeding, or a blood clot, or some other serious problem. It's not worth me losing my job or you losing your life." Dusty knew he wasn't going to win the argument, so he just crossed his arms and shut up as he was wheeled into the elevator and up to his room.

He gawked at several good-looking nurses on the floor before deciding that maybe this wasn't so bad after all. *Maybe I'll get a cute one…*

After the nurse, (not a cute one), performed her assessment and collected his vitals, she hooked him up to an IV. He started to argue, but didn't have any energy left. "Don't worry Mr. Burch, we just want to make sure you are good and hydrated. Let me know if there is anything more I can do to make you comfortable." The nurse was a middle-aged, heavyset woman who had crooked teeth and scaly skin… but she was pleasant.

"Actually, I'd like to see my girlfriend, Lynn."

The nurse, (*Rhonda* was the name Dusty thought he saw on her nametag), smiled and responded, "Okay Mr. Burch, I'll see what I can do about that." Then she turned around and left.

Five minutes later, Dusty was starting to get frustrated. He didn't like the feeling of the line in his arm and didn't see the reason why he was being held against his will. *Just get me the fuck out of here! God damn I want to go home.* His blood was starting to boil a little bit, so he hit the call button. Another minute passed by before Rhonda came in, this time with two men dressed in black suits with slicked back hair. "Who the hell are these guys, Rhonda? I asked to see my girlfriend, not the *Men in Black.* Does it look like there are any aliens in here, gentlemen?" Dusty was not usually this rude or temperamental, but he was over the whole hospital thing.

The two men didn't so much as smirk at Dusty's comment; they showed no reaction whatsoever. The slightly taller one on the left, who still had on his Reybands, spoke, "Mr. Burch, I'm agent Douglas Pine with the FBI. This is Dave Mustane," he gestured with his chin over to the other man.

At least he has his sunglasses off… "Wait. Wait a minute," Dusty interjected incredulously. The officers braced themselves for the same reaction everyone gives them when they tell them they are FBI. "Dave Mustaine? Like as in *The* Dave Mustaine, from Megadeth? Wow, I always pictured you to have a little longer hair." Dave was actually impressed despite Dusty's sarcasm, as most people had no idea who Dave Mustaine was.

419

"It's actually spelled without the 'i'." Dave dimpled his chin, raised his eyebrows and nodded his head slowly in acknowledgement. "You like Megadeth?" Dave asked.

"Like them? I've bought every album they've ever put out. I've seen them in concert a few times too. Holy shit do they put on a show…" Dusty's eyes lit up like a little boy's who had just seen his favorite NFL player signing autographs at training camp.

"Yeah I've seen them a time or two as well. So, I guess it goes without saying that I'm not actually *The* Dave Mustaine. Sorry to burst your bubble. I can't even play the guitar," Dave shrugged his shoulders as if to profess his guilt for never actually picking it up and playing again after his first lesson ended in shame and frustration.

Dusty liked Dave already, too, and sensed the playful sarcasm in his voice. It was the perfect icebreaker, "It's okay. That's probably good for you. I hear he has bad arthritis."

"Really? I…" Dave's face turned red as if he was ashamed for not knowing such sacred things.

Douglas, hardly amused, interrupted and directed the conversation back to the matter at hand, "Mr. Burch, we need to talk some serious business. We have some information that you aided in the capture and arrest of Stanley Memphis."

"Is that his real name?" Dusty said, knowing that answer already, but asking anyway out of, maybe habit, he thought to himself.

"Otherwise known as Richard Thomas," Douglas continued, reminding Dusty of one of those cops you see on CSI with the way he seemed to have satisfaction from knowing such intricate details of the case.

"Okay, yeah. So, what do you want to know about him?"

"Well, a man you know as '8-Ball' has been working closely with us for several months now. He was…"

"Yeah, an undercover cop, I know. I thought he said you guys wouldn't talk to us unless…" Douglas cut him off. This time it didn't really bother Dusty, mainly because Douglas hadn't prematurely ended a conversation regarding one of Metals greatest legends: Dave Mustaine.

"There is a lot you don't know that he couldn't tell you."

"What the hell?" Dusty spoke to himself. He just couldn't wrap his mind around exactly who 8-Ball really was.

"Ok, well anyway, he came to us, through contacts at the Chicago PD, with some bizarre and controversial propositions. He was told to find proof. He gave us you. We equipped him with a small task force to aid him in this special project. I have to admit, at first, we were skeptical, but we were also a little desperate. See, for a couple years now these cases of missing and or dead children have been plaguing us. We have had little success and were open to this… method of… investigation. It seems your stories have panned out and with the capture of Stanley Memphis, we now have confidence in your groups'… abilities. Would you be willing to work with us, Mr. Burch and explain to us exactly how this… supernatural communication is helping you solve crimes? This sort of thing has never been regarded as legitimate by the FBI, but we're dealing with children here. Plus, it's pretty hard to ignore when Marcellus led us right to one of these sick fucks. So, what'dya say?"

"I'd say let's get these fuckers. I can't do it without you and you can't do it without me and my people, at least not as fast as you need to to save lives. When do we begin?"

For the first time, Dusty saw Douglas smile, "Right now. We'll get the discharge orders expedited and get you some comfortable clothes. We'll wait here for you and escort you to our vehicles out front."

"And Lynn?"

"Of course. We already have talked to her and checked the status of her health."

"And….?" Dusty asked desperately.

"Ms. Christopher seems to be doing just fine. A little shook up, but no reason to keep her here. We will take both of you to a local headquarters and begin right away." Douglas was as serious and "FBI"ish as they came and it made Dusty laugh inside.

"That sounds great. Thank you… may I call you Doug?"

"Call me whatever you want, Mr. Burch. As long as we can catch some bad guys, I couldn't care less."

"Doug it is. Now, can we please get this huge piece of plastic out of my veins?"

Once the FBI was certain their key witnesses were unharmed, they told the doctors to release them. Dusty couldn't get dressed quick enough and wanted to see Lynn, but he was nervous to see how she would react to the whole situation with Richard. Images of a psychotic breakdown and fears of their love being swept away by uncontrollable outside forces jettisoned their way into his brain. He tried to squeeze them out; he tried confronting the unpleasant thoughts at the front lines of his consciousness and battling them with a heavy dose of will, but he couldn't keep his brain from turning hazy nor the outside world from becoming surreal. He was in the beginnings of a panic attack, but the difference now from a few years ago was that he recognized the symptoms and could prepare his mind to mitigate the devastating effects. *Chemical warfare of Synaptic Proportions.* He reminded himself that the danger was over and the fear was unrealized.

Lynn was in a room 7 doors down the hallway and was already dressed in her normal clothes by the time Dusty arrived. *That butt in those jeans... God she kills me.* All of the nervous emotions were literally washed away in an instant the moment he laid eyes on Lynn. She stood in her hospital room, freshly changed into a pair of tight-fitting jeans and a form-fitting, long-sleeved pullover that accentuated her breasts and skinny midsection. Her face was beaming. She ran into Dusty's arms and embraced him tightly, "It's all over Dusty..." she began to weep. Dusty had trouble holding back his own tears. "We got that son of a bitch!"

"Honey," Dusty said in a soothing tone as he separated to see her eyes, "are you okay?"

"I couldn't be better. Honestly. I feel like a thousand-pound weight has been lifted off my chest. I'm so glad... so glad I don't have to worry about him hurting anyone else." She continued to sob and re embraced Dusty. "So glad...I just can't tell you..."

"Me too babe. I just have to ask you something. Why did you go there alone? We had talked about that." Dusty said this in as loving of a voice as he possibly could, careful to keep any scolding tones out of the question.

"I thought you were there. He told me to come over because you were there and you guys had made some breakthrough. I didn't even think twice about it. I had no reason to think..."

"Okay, okay, that's enough. I'm sorry I asked, I just had to know. I'm so sorry honey. I should have seen this. I always kind of had a creepy feeling but I never even imagined this!" Dusty truly felt sick inside for letting such a villain get so close to Lynn. His intestines were waging war with the other organs in his body.

"I'm sorry. I should have called you; I was just excited. I can't believe 8-Ball was a cop this whole time. I mean how lucky are we?!"

A voice chimed in from the doorway, "You have no idea." Both Dusty and Lynn turned to look at 8-Ball casually posting his hand in the doorframe.

Surprised, Lynn shouted, "8-Ball?!" He nodded. "Oh my gosh it's so nice to meet you finally. I've heard so much about you!"

"Well, it's a pleasure to meet you too. I'm sorry it had to be under such circumstances." 8-Ball took his hand down and approached the two. Lynn rushed and hugged him.

"Thank you, thank you so much!" Lynn squeezed and started to cry a little. 8-Ball was touched. He hugged back.

"You are welcome sweetheart. Anything for my man Dusty!" Dusty gave him a big smile. 8-Ball looked at him over the top of Lynn's head and winked. Dusty joined the two and wrapped his arms around them. 8-Ball had never felt such a sense of accomplishment. His mother had always told him he was going to grow up different. BE different. She had always said he would be better than the ghetto and he never believed her, until this moment.

Visions of a long, happy life now overshadowed Dusty's fear. A serendipitous rush of emotions swarmed his brain and he could feel Lynn's love flow through her and wrap itself around his soul. *Everything is going to be okay.*

Chapter 65

In the coming months, a lot of work had to be done. Dusty, Lynn and Lana spent many days, hours and weeks strategizing with the FBI. Dusty started by explaining his situation and how he came to find his little girl. 8-Ball, of course, was his main witness and backed him on every detail. Donnie, who was actually 8-Ball's sergeant Dusty learned, not "contact at Chicago PD", backed 8-Ball. They had to do a little convincing to the FBI that none of this was a hoax, but the evidence was astounding.

Dusty's little girl's case, or "Precious Doe" as she had come to be known around the nation, had finally come to a close when her grandfather called in and identified her as Claire Phelps. He had heard the news story when it made its way around the nation and became suspicious of his daughter's recent behavior. He hadn't heard from her in months, let alone get the monthly phone call from his granddaughter he was used to. Raymond Phelps lived in a suburb of Chicago and volunteered to let the FBI search his house for DNA of Claire. He owned the house his daughter lived in. They were able to find a comb that she had used at the house and matched the DNA of that found on the body. With that, Laticia Phelps and Jimmy Cooley became instantly one of America's Most Wanted criminals. Within two days they were located in the town of Yukon, Oklahoma and taken to jail.

It only took about one or two more instances of The Chosen leading the FBI to a crime scene before they were fully invested. Dusty's old friend Jurgaen Feverstacke, the Norwegian member of The Chosen, had done his research and due diligence. He located the child he was seeing in a newspaper article describing the rape and sodomy of a young boy in Boston. With extensive pleading, the FBI agreed to supply Jurgaen with a pair of socks from the little boy in question. Jurgaen couldn't swear to it, but he was convinced the socks helped him in his supercommunication with his child. He had also done some research and found that Iroquois Indian Shamans believed that sleeping with their clients' belongings under their pillows helped connect them to the client so that visitors in dreams could convey messages about the past, future or present. So, he tried it.

Jurgaen's little boy came to him at a pier in Boston when he had been there for business. He had recently dreamt of the pier and visited it with the sock in hand. There he revealed himself to Jurgaen and between that and his bolstered dreams, he was able to discover enough detail for him to lead the FBI to trace evidence and apprehend the suspect. The key piece of evidence was a bloody sandal buried beneath the sand, washed over and over by the rising and falling tides.

Sajid too was able to take the information shared by the group and establish supercommunication with his dream visitors. The orchard hangings were the acts of a serial killer that acted around the nation, and Sajid was able to lead the FBI to a buried "treasure chest" that the killer left in an orchard with trophies from his victims.

Finally, Lana was victorious in her search for justice. She claims her trip to India was her saving grace. Her elevated understanding of the power of the mind and the metaphysical world was enhanced and to her, it brought clarity. Several people found different triggers: Yoga, Massage, Acupuncture, but in the end, Dusty and Lynn figured it was just a deep belief that *something* would work.

Lana led the FBI to a dumpster that had previously been victim to a fire. Three years ago, a woman had bought cold medicine at a nearby drugstore. The woman was attempting to treat her son and ended up giving too much Tylenol and the boy overdosed. The woman dumped his poor little body in a dumpster and lit it on fire with gasoline. The flames burned so hot almost all the remains were destroyed. No one had ever searched the burned remains, as there was no reason to expect a body was in there. This woman was responsible not only for the death of her child, but for kidnapping another child to replace hers, who was the child Lana was seeing first. Lana did eventually start seeing the second child as well. The kidnapped child eventually succumbed to the same fate as the suspect's own child as she forced copious amounts of medicine into the boy's stomach. She picked another dumpster across town for this body. The city had merely put the fires out with a fire hose, drained and dumped it and continued reusing it. Caked at the bottom of the dumpsters, still, three years later, were several teeth and trace evidence. This evidence led to warrants to search all the footage from nearby stores' security archives and audit the transactions, among other things. The FBI was able to pin down the woman that bought the drugs and investigated. The suspect was a single mom who had now another baby's daddy, and another child. She had no family and no one to miss her little boy. Lana had no doubt saved the life of her most recent child. The suspect was sentenced to life in prison without parole.

After that, murderous pedophiles and creeps started falling like flies. The FBI was more than willing to aid in the obtaining of physical evidence for The Chosen to use. An answer was never fully understood as to why the physical belonging of a child was such a crucial role in the supercommunication, but it was assumed that the children needed some sort of physical connection to The Chosen member to complete the circuit and breakthrough. This was not the only factor, however, as the clearness of the mind found through meditation almost always aided in The Chosen's ability to depict clear enough details either in dreams, or conscious visions. A couple tougher cases actually went and visited the same school in India that Lana did and the deep learning about the metaphysical realm and an understanding of the power of the mind aided in the apprehension of those killers as well.

When new "Chosen" members were found, they were taken in, questioned, and either deemed as phonies or ran through the prototypical "Chosen Process". For two years this process occurred until there were virtually no unsolved, child murder cases in the original Chosen group and perpetually worldwide, as children always found a host and the host inevitably found The Chosen or The Chosen found him or her. It took a lot of work for the FBI to get involved in other countries' affairs, but Chakuma Kwambi from Nigeria had helped break the mold and the relations formed between the FBI and Nigerian officials helped set the standard for worldwide cooperation.

Dusty, Lynn and Lana were deemed the Arbiters over a super top-secret group deemed "The Supernaturally Inclined Protectors of America", or SIPA. For two years, the FBI paid them consulting fees, and any Chosen who aided in the arrest of a criminal was awarded $20,000.

National headlines eventually caught on to the success of the FBI in regards to open child cases. "Murderers Beware" became the headlines of the New York Times and many other nationwide syndicates. The FBI was praised for refining their crime-fighting tactics and revolutionizing forensic investigation. Nobody from The Chosen cared that the FBI stole all the glory and they all understood that the world wasn't ready to accept, nor would believe, the notion of "supernatural crime fighters".

No one ever understood why Children were the initial visitors, but many theories were discussed about the pureness of children and how their minds were not distorted with hormones, stress, sin or preconceived notions, which allowed for them to establish initial connections. On the flipside, their minds were not powerful enough to interact with the physical world, which is why they *chose* their hosts. They needed assistance, as their souls and the way they interacted with the physical world were not fully developed.

Eventually the children started bringing more visitors who were adult victims of other serial crimes. What Dusty, Lana, Lynn, Bruce and the rest of The Chosen did for the world's crime fighting syndicate was immeasurable, as almost no criminal could hide from the vengeance of their victims' souls. They, along with their children, paved the way for other souls to serve justice. No one could explain the timing of the phenomenon, whether it be a wormhole that opened up in space that connected spirits, or perhaps the presence of radio, TV and other air waves that are omnipresent in society allow for communication paths to open up between the dead and undead, but no one had to be able to explain it to understand it and utilize the miracle to save lives. In the end, no rational explanation could be offered and there was a general, unspoken agreement, that God, or whatever governing power a person believed in, helped in opening up these connections to stop the vile and heinous crimes that were becoming ever so prevalent in society.

During the busy period of catching criminals, Dusty and Lynn moved to Kansas City where Dusty started practicing law with his Dad as a plaintiff's lawyer. Never in his life had Preston Burch been happier. He now saw his little boy every day. He watched proudly as Dusty married Lynn and they raised their beautiful children together, in peace. The two love birds passed on their crime fighting obligations to willing members of The Chosen who took over as the new arbiters, and still to this day, serial killers are being brought to justice because of the sacrifices of The Chosen.

Chapter 66

One night after their first daughter, Olivia, was born, Lynn put down her magazine and reached for the bedside lamp. Dusty was sleeping peacefully beside her. He had slept peacefully for about year now. At first, it took a while before Dusty could sleep longer than an hour at a time without waking up. He couldn't tell if Claire was actually coming to him, or if he was just dreaming about her coming to him. It confused him, but since the dreams were almost nothing like the nightmares before, he became certain it was his own imagination that was unable to shake the indelible marks Claire had left on it. Eventually, his mind learned to filter out the bad dreams, but he would still see her in random, innocuous dreams from time to time. Although the dreams became less disturbing, (signifying the release of her grip on Dusty's subconscious), he always wondered if she didn't just drop in on him from time to time to see how he was doing. Either way, Dusty and Lynn's sleep at night was restful, soothing and much needed.

Lynn heard a slight rustle in the baby crib at the foot of their bed. She got up and looked in at Olivia, just two months old, sleeping with her thumb in her mouth. She was the most beautiful thing either of them had ever seen and completely melted Dusty's heart to a mushy pulp. Of any people in the world, these two knew how amazing of a blessing their daughter was. She was the purpose they now lived for. She would be loved and cherished with a fierceness and tenacity that few parents could ever understand. Dusty and Lynn had decided to have children immediately after their marriage and hoped to have more. For now though, it was only their precious, little Olivia.

Lynn bent over and kissed Olivia on the cheek and stroked her fine black hair. She then gently covered her with the snuggly, pink blanket that she was brought home from the hospital in. Lynn eased herself back into bed. Dusty's handsome face was relaxed, content and peaceful. She gazed at him with admiring and loving eyes; He was her savior... her soul mate... and she would love and adore him well beyond their corporeal existence. Their love could not be measured in inches, or feet, miles, kilometers, or light years. *Eternity* was the only unit capable of measuring the love that Lynn and Dusty harbored for each other. She kissed him and turned off the lamp. Life couldn't be better.

Amidst Lynn's reflections on life, love and happiness, Dusty was dreaming. The dream carried with it an eerie nostalgia, one he knew all too well. He was in a dark place. The only visible object was a canopy bed, soft and frilly, embroidered like a little girl's bed. It was radiant, as if *someone* had employed a spotlight to cast upon its presence. On the bed he saw Claire in a fetal position lying on her side with her eyes closed. She had on a white cotton nightshirt sprinkled with little yellow ducks. Claire's feet barely stuck out of the bottom of the gown.

Dusty approached the bed and stood next to it, looking down at her still little body. She was beautiful. Her little girl skin was smooth, delicate and dainty. Her dark eyelashes were long and curved. She looked to be peacefully sleeping.

Then Dusty trembled. He could feel his heart racing. He wasn't afraid though. Dusty had come to know and love Claire over the last few years as she came to him in the netherworld of dreams and apparitions. Now, for the first time, he sensed that there was no invisible barrier between them. He could touch her and feel her if he wanted to. He was overcome with love and anticipation about how this dream would end. He reached down slowly and put his hand on her cheek. He brushed back a wisp of hair from her temple. Claire opened her eyes.

Dusty pulled his hand back with a start. The hair on the back of his neck stood up, yet he was not afraid. Claire slowly lifted herself to her knees facing Dusty. Dusty had never seen her so clearly. She smiled at him and never before had a smile lifted Dusty to such an emotional state. A tear fell from his eye. She looked into his eyes, deep into his soul, still smiling. She was such a beautiful child. Though she didn't say it, Dusty could see that she was at peace and suffered no more.

Claire put her arms gently around Dusty's neck and laid her head on his right shoulder. He felt the silky cornrows press against his cheek. Three years of pent up emotion, fear, anxiety, revulsion and love exploded like a dam. Dusty pulled Claire in tightly to his breast, as a parent would do to a missing child. He kissed the side of her head and sobbed, convulsively at first, and then quietly. He couldn't love her anymore if she was his own flesh and blood.

Claire didn't make a sound. She tightened her grasp a little around his neck. Dusty sobbed and lifted her off of the bed, swaying and rocking her gently.

Dusty had been through hell with this little girl. He had seen her murdered right in front of him. He would never forget her tormented screams as he stood by helpless as she was beaten, strangled and butchered by the devils that were raising her. He was even there to see her body buried in a trash bag under the leaves. There wasn't one person on the planet that mourned for her like Dusty did and Dusty was thankful that she chose him. She brought him and Lynn together. She had carved a huge chamber in his heart and taught him that a human's capacity for love is infinite, perfect and miraculous.

Dusty was prepared to stay there embracing Claire until daybreak. He remembered that Claire had always let him wake a few seconds before 6 a.m., but Claire released her grip and pulled back, looking Dusty straight in the eyes. She showed no expression. She didn't blink. Dusty didn't hear her words in his head, but he understood Claire's gentle, loving gaze. It was time for her to go. She looked over his shoulder.

At that moment, another figure came into Dusty's vision. The figure walked up to the side of the bed and grabbed Claire's hand. Dusty looked up to view the figure and to his surprise, there stood his good buddy Bruce. Dusty's heart burst for joy, then sadness, then excitement. He wanted to say so much. He lunged at Bruce and embraced him, squeezing him with great force as if the harder he squeezed, the more Bruce knew how much Dusty missed him, loved and appreciated him. No words were needed. The two separated and Bruce regained Claire's hand. Claire looked up at Bruce and

431

the two locked eyes. She nodded. Dusty watched as the two turned and headed towards a light in the distance. They stopped just before entering and looked back at Dusty. He was filled with content. He waved. Bruce and Claire waved back, and then headed back towards the light, slowly evaporating into an ethereal mist as the light consumed them. Everything faded to black. She was gone and Dusty knew he would never see her again…this side of Heaven.

About the Author

D L (David Lewis) Gleason is the son Dave (David Monroe) Gleason. Dave was an attorney in Kansas City, MO who had his own law practice and raised a family of 5 children with his beautiful wife Carla (Kristi, Karee, Kacy, David, Dustin). He loved his family and was an avid outdoorsman. Dave was also a musician and his favorite instrument was the guitar. His creativity and love for books, movies and history sparked an ambition to start a career in writing. His first book he planned to publish was "Suffer The Children", but was tragically killed in a school bus accident sitting at a stoplight in Liberty, MO. He had many conversations with his eldest son DL regarding this book and although it was largely unfinished, he had written hundreds of pages down on notebook paper. These chapters were disjointed and unorganized as they were the first glimmerings of creativity in the genesis of the book. Many of the chapters were written during trial proceedings or depositions Dave attended where he pretended to be taking legal notes. He paid his daughter Kacy, who worked for him at his law office, to type these chapters. Dave also had a notebook where he learned how to organize his thoughts and create characters, using cutouts of real-life movie stars so he could envision the characters. He learned some of these tactics at a writing convention on the east coast that he visited with his wife Carla. It was one of their last trips together. DL eventually gathered up all the documents and organized them into what he thought was a reasonable timeline, (Dave had written chapters from the beginning all the way to the end). There were a lot of holes and the holes of the mystery were yet to be created. That's where DL stepped in.

DL has a young family of 3 children, (David, Olivia and Hendrix) and a beautiful wife Hannah. He too has a love for the outdoors, music, literature, movies, history, etc. He is a true apple off the tree of Dave Gleason. DL worked through his 20s at the video production business he had started with his Dad and siblings, but eventually had to cease and pursue a career in Insurance to support his family. To finish the book, he worked late at night when the kids went to bed and early in the morning before they awoke. Many times he would go months without writing because it was challenging to connect all the dots. When the family land, Shondalahi, went up for sale where he grew up, he decided he had to finish the book while he could still watch the sunrise levitate over the pond he and his father used to fish in. DL is an amateur author, but a college graduate who has written thousands of pages of journals, personal essays, poems and script ideas. This book is the first book he has ever published and if it goes well, may be the first of many.

For Becca
And our unborn child

"Blowback is what happens when a shortsighted policy comes back to haunt America in ways that are more dangerous than the original threat."

-Sebastian Unger, Fire

"Greater love has no one than this: to lay down one's life for one's friends."

-John 15:13

BOOK I

1

Lake Placid, 1980

A man known by his Soviet superiors as Firebird shrugged his fedora and overcoat dusting the frost off its hems. Another spectator glared at him for a moment, but like the icy conditions outside the field house, he chilled. The stadium's air filled with the shouts of over eight thousand fans, most of whom the man considered to be hostile.

The crowd roared as the American team approached the ice. Not a pro skater among them, the home crowd of the Lake Placid arena was a team of rivals. College kids, some not old enough to order a lager in a New York bar. He smirked as they entered in waves, stalled by security. The Olympic Center walls shook.

"USA!"

"USA!"

"USA!"

The American Olympic Hockey Team circled the ice with pride; white jerseys trimmed in red and blue.

Firebird considered all the American nation faced: assassination, scandal, national protests concerning men and women of color, Vietnam, oil embargo, and the constant threat of nuclear war. Perhaps the nation was due for a miracle, but it would not be tonight. America's hopes rested on the shoulders of kids, kids who were about to take on the juggernaut. The Soviet side. The most exceptional hockey team in history.

Not all Americans had their heads in the clouds. One columnist wrote that the ice must melt to keep the Soviets from obtaining their sixth gold medal in seven Olympic games. President Jimmy Carter bemoaned in a press conference before Christmas that Americans now no longer looked forward to the next generation but rather looked backward at the Greatest Generation as time when America's star shined brightest. He called it a crisis of confidence. Firebird grinned a little broader. Soviet Captain Boris Mikhailov, dressed in all red with white trim, won the face off. One more Soviet victory. Sometimes the Cold War could be physical.

Seconds in and goaltender Jim Craig faced his first test in the clash of titans. Both teams were unbeaten in the Games, but the last time the Yankee boys had met the Soviets it had been a long night for the Boston University keeper. Again, and again the Soviet speed pressed the young man. A slash no call had the Americans in arms while they retained possession of the puck for the first time before losing it.

GOAL!

The Russian had to keep from shouting in his native tongue to refrain from attracting unwanted attention. While millions of Russians and Eastern Europeans had been immigrating to the United States for the last century, a *rezident* must always be mindful of their surroundings. The local FBI were easy to spot in their matching cloaks and fedoras, but a CIA shadow would be much more difficult in so dense a crowd.

More of the Soviet onslaught looked to bury the Americans, but Craig was special. A crushing hit by the American Morrow gave the puck up to their captain, Mike Eruzione. Firebird read at length on the American team and believed the man called 'Rizo to be one of the weakest players. That was why the Soviets were the greater superpower: they believed in true strength and not the underdog. Krutov's punishing blow to Eruzione into the glass proved the point. Coach Brooks withdrew Eruzione, but his replacement hit Krutov so hard the comrade should have stopped to search for his teeth on the ice. The American speed impressed Firebird, and with the crowd behind them, the American team leveled with the Soviet Union.

He sat back in his seat, miffed. The host nation sported a different team than the one who suffered defeat before the Olympics. Everyone began pulling at their hair as the Soviet side responded in haste but once again the body of Craig saved a goal. The *rezident* started to have his cup full of Jim Craig. The man was not supposed to be playing this motivated. Another block, this time a solo stop as three red jerseys sliced the American defense. The Soviet plan of speed, teamwork, and intimidation was not working on the Yankee frat boys. He need not have worried however for the men on the ice in red must have realized the same thing.

Shortly after defending their own goal, the Soviet team settled into a perfect offensive attack. Sharp passes and good coverage mitigated defenders. Skating with intensity, the Reds crossed the ice and scooped the puck around Craig. 2-1!

Firebird swore out loud but covered his jubilant expletives in a wound newspaper. The steamroller has gained its momentum.

Like chess players, the Soviets passed the puck with expert precision after winning another face off. He couldn't control his outburst this time as a long shot by the Soviets was easily deflected. Giving a furtive look around, only a handful of people had heard the Russian and they all dismissed him.

Craig withstood another brutal assault as the period wound down. The Americans responded with their own long-shot goal only to have it swatted away.

A white jersey was skating hard!

He split the defense and scored with one second to play in the period! Tretiak's lousy trash allowed the Americans to draw even with the Soviets once again, 2-2. The *rezident* watched

Coach Tikhonov vehemently argue that time ran out before the goal, but there was nothing any Russian could do.

During the intermission, he searched the crowd for pairs of eyes looking his way for longer than average. As a man of the Moscow underworld, he knew how to find a suspicious tail. He had no incriminating documents on his person and had proper papers for visiting New York from his Washington office. The Olympics were reason enough to travel north in the frigid winter. He didn't bother grabbing a Coke or hotdog. Going to the bathroom also would have gained nothing save for unwanted attention. A suspected rendezvous or drop would be enough to keep CIA attention on him for an extended period. Rather it best to play boring and be taken off of some suit's high priority list.

When the new period opened, Firebird was shocked to see Vladimir Myshkin setting up between the poles. Tikhonov retired the greatest goaltender the world had ever seen. It was too soon to panic, and it was too late to be teaching lessons to a veteran like Vladislav Tretiak.

He sighed a deep breath of relief as Myshkin proved equal to the task, stopping a shot one-on-one. Soviet puck. Perfect passing. He cringed at yet another long shot, but this time the trash was picked up by Maltsev who scored!

3-2 Soviet Union!

A skull-crushing hit on the hero Craig left him slow to get up. As the American crowd booed the Soviet ferocity, the *rezident* silently rejoiced. Craig had to be shut down. He caught himself just in time before he threw his newspaper down when the hearty Irishman rose to his feet. Stars and Stripes flew through the air in salute to the man's resolution. Craig has more guts than Carter, thought the spy.

At the start of the third and final period, the American coach, Herb Brooks, circled his team. Breaking the huddle, Johnson faced off with Mikhailov. The American's attempt fell short. The

Soviet's flew up the ice. A stick save by Craig kept the Americans from being buried. The onslaught continued. Four straight saves and Firebird prayed to a God he didn't believe in that one would not be enough. A senseless slash call gave the American offense their best chance to equalize. He couldn't understand his thoughts, a possibility to deadlock the Soviets.

Possession was the name of the game, and the Americans were up to the challenge of skating with the Soviets. Their passing was fearless and their endurance matched only by their desire. Blocked! The crowd groaned as the Reds cleared the puck. The Americans again went on the attack, but Myshkin was proving why he belonged in Tretiak's net. Silk raced around defenders and paid for it dearly, but a sprinting Johnson picked up the puck.

Goal!

With seconds left on the power play, Johnson scored once again to draw even with the Soviet Union. The *rezident* looked on through his hands as his fears came true. He wagered a whore's annual salary on the game and was beginning to think he may lose his earnings. Born into a brothel, he carried intimate knowledge of the going rate for Moscow women on *Netsky Street.*

Khasatonov's shot went wide allowing the American crowd to soar with joy. Craig made save after save. The Americans had the puck. Coach Brooks subbed in Eruzione. Firebird questioned the move; Eruzione had been quiet most of the night. The captain danced around multiple defenders and buried the puck in the back of the net!

The *resident* buried his face in his hands as thousands of Americans in the arena and millions at home jumped to their feet. The Americans overtook the Soviets.

USA 4 Soviet Union 3.

A beautiful shot by Kharlamov couldn't equalize. The crowd roared.

Shot by Petrov.

No goal.

Kasatonov.

No goal.

Mikhailov controlled the puck. Pass to Petrov.

Shot.

No goal.

Fetisov hit hard by Silk. The Americans changed their lineup. The Soviets backed off the offense. Five minutes left to play. The momentum shifted. The Reds once again moved into their perfect formula. Mikhailov to Kharlamov. Slapshot broken up by Craig. Firebird cursed America. He cursed the players. He even cursed the newspaper. The newspaper had lied saying that the Americans didn't stack up against the Soviet side. Rubbish.

Another change in the American lineup. Coach Brooks growled at his players. With four minutes to play there was still time for the Soviet Union. Krutov moved through the neutral zone skating stronger than anyone had all night.

Shot!

No goal. Krutov and Schneider fought for the puck but Firebird eyed the clock for time was running out.

The American lineup switched again allowing fresh legs once more to challenge the Soviets who were fighting for their Olympic destiny. Coach Tikhonov was in a frenzy while Brooks called for control amongst his players.

Mikhailov played possessed, his red jersey reflecting a demonic hatred and passion. The pass to Petrov was on the mark.

Shot!

Denied!

He once again eyed the clock.

Two minutes or there was no tomorrow.

Another stop! One minute to go. He wondered why Tikhonov had not yelled pulled Myshkin for another offensive player. Shot after shot.

Ten seconds to go.

Five seconds!

Buzzer!

The Americans rioted to the ice. Helmets, flags, and pennants flew through the air. Men hugged. Women kissed. The team of young college boys circled one another as shouts of "USA" clamored to the heavens.

Firebird disguised a glance at the matching FBI shadows. With their attention drawn to the celebration on the ice, he took his cue. The spy turned his coat inside out, the drab brown pattern replaced by solid black. His hat he slipped into the chair in front of him, a gift to the man he dusted with snow before the historic defeat. Being shorter than average, he need not stoop low to disappear behind the crowd of celebrators as he made his way to the exit.

A yellow banner in the entryway read "Get the Puck out of Afghanistan." He couldn't agree more. The Politburo completely reversed the decision not to invade Afghanistan after a civil war erupted from Kabul. He chastised the Soviet leaders, cautioning them to wait and extend a diplomatic hand to the religious zealots running the country; it was they after all who had disposed of American aligned leaders in both the treacherous Afghan mountains and the oil-rich seaports of Iran. Partnership with Afghanistan was vital to success in a place that did not crown victors. Dominion there would allow Soviet access to India unparalleled since the October Revolution. As a result, the Soviet Union could put tremendous pressure on Communist China. In the post-Mao era, the People's Republic was looking more like a rival than an ally. Meanwhile, a strong presence in Iran would allow a more significant foothold and sphere of influence in the oil-rich fields of the Arab empires straddling the

Persian Gulf. The Soviets could dominate access to the Strait of Hormuz before the American aligned Saudi Kingdom could dictate the ports.

With America and her western allies slumping to control the Middle East powder keg, the Soviet Union could retake the world stage in much the same way it had during the early 60s. Securing the ancient lands of Alexander the Great would give his country a distinct advantage in the Great Game. When he telephoned his superiors at the Kremlin, they told him not to worry about the religious zealots or mujahedeen. "It will be easy Yaromir. We have tanks and helicopters while they have horses."

There was one, Soviet Premier Alexei Kosygin, who shared his sentiments. Both men felt it prudent to emphasize the interior of the Middle East. The Ba'ath Party led by Hafez al-Assad in Syria and Saddam Hussein in Iraq held promising futures if the Kremlin would invest in their nations. Both dictators used merely a shade of Islam to control the will of the people, both had vast riches of oil, and both allowed similar rights for women and minorities while maintaining absolute power. With tensions escalating between Iraq and Iran, the time was perfect to pick a side. He grinned a little. Perhaps choose both sides.

Purchasing a commemorative Winter Olympic Games hat, Yaromir brushed through the doors into the cold. The streets were jubilant in the quaint town. He made a point to smile or nod when making eye contact to remain anonymous and not attract suspicion. Ducking behind a newspaper stand, he looked back in time to see the set of FBI agents exit the arena. The men in dark suits and fedoras scoured the crowds for any sight of him. Shrugging at one another they set off in separate directions, each man walking further and further away from their target. Yaromir stayed put a little longer, pretending to read a Chevrolet advertisement to see if any other would be trackers emerged from the arena. After scanning the Comics' page of his paper, he was satisfied with not being followed. He supposed the FBI had won a turf war over the CIA in pursuing the suspected spy. He wondered how the cloak and daggers in Langley would receive another Bureau screw up.

Walking into a café, he ordered black coffee and put on his best smile for the young lady serving him. He didn't have to try hard, letting his eyes linger over the girl's petite frame.

The café felt cozy. The person sitting closest to him elbowed the middle of his back while trying to put on their coat. They muttered their apologies and without making eye contact, took their leave of the café. Yaromir watched as the man pulled his collar up to protect against the brisk night.

When his eyes returned to the table, he noticed the man had left his briefcase sitting under the table by the leg closest to his chair. He registered the drop, slid the satchel under his chair and lingered at the table to finish his coffee. Most Russians preferred tea, yet coffee gave him a more American appearance. A sweet tinge in the air told his nostrils that his counterpart was not so cautious. When he was through, Yaromir wiped his mouth with the back of his hand and picked up the briefcase, making his way to the exit.

Not bothering to check the street for a tail, Yaromir walked into the cold wondering if Afghanistan, with its mountains, was as cold as New York. He wondered how the American college boys had pulled off a miracle on the ice and he wondered how long it would be before America was in need of a new miracle.

2

Estonia, Near Future

Bouncers checked Yuri's body for weapons and paraphernalia. Outside one of Tallinn's hottest clubs, the breeze blew in from the Gulf of Finland carrying with it the scent of salt and fish. Inside, the club's air was thick with smoke, aftershave, sweat, and spilled drinks. The music thumped to a numbing rhythm as the lights flickered to the beat. Scantily clad women danced from polls or many chairs throughout the audience of admirers. For a moment, Yuri wished he could return to the fresh sea air but swallowed his repulsion. The club was a place for his brother, Bogdan. The younger Orlov brother would feel right at home amongst the waves of testosterone and silicone. Despite many protestations, Bogdan had been left to handle the getaway vehicle while Anton lurked in the shadows and Immanuil among the rooftops, each watching Yuri's back.

He eyed his surroundings.

At the center of the dancefloor, he shot a look to the DJ, spinning records from an elevated platform, twelve o'clock. Exits were at his six, eleven and two o'clock positions. Then he spotted his mark, just off the eleven o'clock exit.

Estonia's Foreign Minister Kuril Aponovicius set down his drink to eye some of the women across from his stage in the VIP booth. Despite his gratuitous size and vices, the man had a calculating mind and keen perception. Even as former Soviet satellites such as Ukraine, Czech Republic, and Hungary realigned themselves with Russia and China, the Baltic nations cried out to a disintegrating NATO and fledgling European Union for a more substantial military presence to ward off Russian intimidation.

Thus far, Russian President Vasilyev was able to appease nations like Germany and France from stronger military threats by advocating against stronger alliances and ransoming vast oil resources, the lifeline of European energy. No European country trusted the United States any longer and therefore felt resigned to give in to Russia's demands to promote stabilization on a continent that suffered the brunt of two world wars. But this Aponovicius emulated Cold War trailblazer Ronald Reagan by calling Russia and its recent expansion the Empire of Evil. The Foreign Minister needed silencing before American war hawks listened too well. In Europe, the United Kingdom protested in public against Russian expansionism. The silver lining there lies in 21 Downing Street battling European isolation, even as the EU crumbled to pieces. In the end, no matter how much the NATO partners of the Baltics or Poland cried, it fell on deaf French, German, and Spanish ears.

Yuri moved among the tables, taking care to veer closer to the VIP table. At the foot of the stairs, the music turned from a mindless rhythm to a pulsing beat complete with a revitalized light show. The dancer's frantic movements to the music captured everyone's attention as Yuri ascended the stairs and moved behind the bodyguards towards the exit. When an undressed waitress climbed the stairs with a cadre of drinks, he beckoned her over, replacing a glass with a folded wad of Euros. He smiled though not at her. He smiled at the thought of how worthless the Euro would soon become. Germany and France could not continue to bail out their bankrupt neighbors and call for peace in the former Eastern Bloc. Oh, how they would beg Russia for assistance. Everything had a price. His nation now witnessed a boom in the real estate business.

He lingered by the exit and eased the door open. A faint light from the lamp outside filtered through the gap. Anton placed a needle in Yuri's outstretched hand. Yuri never took his eyes off the club. Plunging the liquid toxin, Polonium -210, into the glass, he waited for another cocktail waitress as the fizz from the poison settled in the glass. When one arrived dressed as a bunny rabbit, he dropped another wad of Euros, this time with specific instructions that came along with the payment. The waitress shrugged and headed for the table. With a gratuitous bow that drew much attention, she placed the drink and few others around the table, collecting more wads of money. She made a show of positioning the folded bills into her fluffy brazier then trudged off; the empty serving tray tucked under her bare arm.

Once Aponovicius took a drink from the glass, Yuri slipped out the exit door and raced across the street to watch the drama unfold from Immanuil's perch. Joining the skinny young sniper, he lit a cigarette, the signal to Anton that he was safe. Anton returned the message with an amber glow from across the street. The motion did not linger but was snuffed out in an instant. None of Yuri's men smoked save himself.

Somebody kicked the steel door open in the street below. Two thick bodyguards rushed into the alleyway. Two more guards followed. One carried the Foreign Minister's legs while the other moved him beneath the armpits. A fifth guard knelt next to the swarthy man and attempted cardiopulmonary resuscitation. The unlucky guard seized his own throat trying to spit out the poison now foaming from the minister's lips. The others looked on helplessly as Aponovicius' body succumbed to the toxin.

Sirens wailed in the distance, but no one heard the five muted shots aimed at each of the minister's guards. Bogdan pulled beside the alleyway. Yuri's massive younger brother slid out of the ambulance and met with Anton. The two men dragged the murdered bodies of the guards by the ankles, throwing them into the back of the meat wagon. Four doors slammed shut as Anton, Immanuil, Bogdan, and Yuri each entered the ambulance in unison leaving the dead body of the Estonian Foreign Minister in the alleyway.

3

White House

Benjamin Hargreaves sighed as the President's secretary asked him to take a seat. He knew by now when his Commander in Chief was stonewalling him. The ancient wooden chair creaked under his weight as he looked into the eyes of Alexander Hamilton. The oil painting was not the actual John Trumbull but rather a replica. Ben couldn't decide if the new President placed the mural outside the Oval Office because the Federalists appealed to the President's politics or if they were fans of the Broadway production. The secretary smiled at him and made a point of returning to her work. Her cold shoulder made him wish all the more that the President see him in.

Perhaps it was a life spent jumping into thin air that made him uncomfortable in the small outer office. Maybe it was the ever-unpopular topic he was trying to raise once more with the nation's leader. He settled his gaze outside into the Rose Garden to run through his mental checklist one last time.

After leaving the Air Force Pararescue Jump Squadron, otherwise known as Guardian Angels, Benjamin Hargreaves followed his father's wishes to enter the political realm. "Movers and shakers walk these halls," his father would tell him.

Putting his extensive skills to work, he joined the National Security Council behind the Baltic desk often working in tandem with the Russian liaisons. With the ear of the Secretary of State, Hargreaves worked hard to convince the blue bloods in

Washington that Russia was a force worth reckoning. Despite pleas from human rights groups, the West remained unaffected by Russia's realigning of influence in the world. Over the years, the ghost of the Soviet Union upended the United Nations, turning instead to growing economies of other BRICS nations for support. Brazil, India, China and South Africa were joining Russia in wrestling power from traditional imperialist states such as Great Britain, France, and even the United States. He was waiting outside the Oval Office to convince the President that the latest assassination of Estonia's Foreign Minister was just another obstacle removed from Russia's endgame of dominating European affairs.

"The President will see you now."

Hargreaves stood, buttoning his suit and nodding at the secretary. She hadn't bothered to wait for his acknowledgment. With one last look at the roses, he opened the oddly shaped door.

"Sorry to keep you waiting, Benjamin, I just finished a high-profile phone call." Hargreaves knew better than to ask who had been on the other line. The only thing that mattered was for President Wallace to give ear to his analysis.

"You're not going to lecture me, are you?"

Hargreaves smiled his most disarming smile. "No ma'am, I certainly hope not."

"I hope not either," she said, her voice rife with malice, "I am not new to the game of international politics after all."

Hargreaves nodded, swallowing hard. President Wallace eyed him for a moment, testing his reaction with arms crossed. Tentatively, she leaned forward and tried to placate him with a smile of her own. "What have you got for me?"

"Ma'am, Estonia's Foreign Minister Kuril Aponovicius has been found murdered in the street days after General Valter's coup in Moldova. I believe this was a plot by Russian insurgents to rid the motherland of NATO's largest whistleblower. Eastern

Europe is outspoken in its agenda to realign with Russia. Hungary, Bulgaria, and Belarus have already pledged allegiance. Several other nations have withdrawn from NATO while we have lost our assets to neo-dictators in Turkey and Greece."

"I don't have to be reminded of what we have lost. It has been my understanding that Aponovicius was not murdered but died from a drug overdose. He was found by a tart in skimpy underwear for crying out loud."

"The police report listed AWOL bodyguards and they still can't decipher the substance that killed him. I can't help but protest that this was a political assassination."

"So, the man gave his guards the slip, probably trying to remain anonymous while he let Euros rain over his women. But you and I agree that Russia is trouble."

Hargreaves' eyes and ears perked up. "Ma'am?"

"You forget your history. My party tried to sound the alarm on Russia after their meddling in the previous election. The phone call I received prior to your entry was from Davoud Isfahan."

He recognized the name of Iran's President.

"Isfahan asked me to open up channels to convince Russia to stop its non-proliferation agenda against the Islamic Republic. I told him that it was my policy to uphold the peaceful agenda of previous administrations to discontinue the use of nuclear weapons. Forty-four did win the Nobel Peace Prize after all."

"What was Isfahan's response?"

"He said that my party predecessor was prematurely given the award as he was responsible for more military action in the Middle East and North Africa than any other American president. That list includes Thomas Jefferson, Bush 41 and Bush 43."

"Did you remind him that the former president also opened the door for his nation's nuclear weapons program?"

"I did, and he reminded me that allowing Iran to have nuclear weapons was part of the deal in allying with his nation to defeat ISIL and prevent another holocaust among Syrian refugees. He also reminded me that 45 pulled the rug right out from under them."

Hargreaves sat back. Trump may have halted both North Korea and Iran's nuclear aims but he feared that too played into the hands of the Russians, just as lessening international sanctions had. North Korea was a non-issue but Iran would argue that there would be no Syrian refugees if their man Assad had remained in power. Not refugees, just victims of an oppressive regime in the same ilk as Saddam Hussein, Pol Pot, or Hitler. "Speaking of a holocaust," he ventured, "how is Israel taking the news?"

"Prime Minister Pavel is questioning our motives. I told him we are seeking balance in the Middle East and no longer supporting just the Jewish State. He says he has reached out to Russia's Prime Minister. The two grew up together in Odessa before Pavel immigrated to the Holy Land using his heritage. They are thick as thieves. Frankly, I don't understand how he can pretend to be peaceful when he is the only one in the region with nuclear launch codes."

Hargreaves shook his head. Iran and Israel were each playing the US and Russia against each other, bargaining for the best deal. He could sense the blowback from the President's policies regarding Iran and Russia. Azerbaijan's military dictator continued to employ the same semblance of democracy so well forged by the late Vladimir Putin while Kazakhstan had long ago returned their capital from Almaty to Astana. As the Great Game evolved, Europe, Asia, and now the Middle East realigned themselves into Russia's sphere of influence. The year might as well have been 1959 or 1979.

"Ma'am, I must insist that the Russian agenda is to isolate the United States. If we don't act soon with full international support, we may lose what bargaining chips we have left."

"Have you ever been to Moscow Mr. Hargreaves?"

"You know of my service to this country, Ma'am."

"Well I've been to Moscow and I've spoken to their youth. The good people of Russia crave stability, they crave transparency, and they crave freedom. If President Vasilyev and the Kremlin were to attempt any more oppression anywhere in the world, I believe they would first have to turn the guns on their people. Kind of sounds like the arc of Russian history don't you think? But then again you were a soldier, not a political scientist."

Hargreaves knew that many administrations laughed and teased about Russia's agenda while at the same time accepting their oppressive regimes with open arms. He knew that he wasn't kidding and neither was Russia. The time for games would soon be up.

Standing, he reached across the Truman desk to shake President Wallace's hand. He smiled at her questioning gaze. "I would like to tender my resignation. It is my understanding that this administration is blind. A polarized Congress is unwilling to see that the clock will soon strike midnight."

President Wallace sighed, but a small smirk played on her face. "Your father will be disgraced by his peers. He will lose his voice, but I'm sure his constituents will keep him afloat. My lone curiosity is what will you decide to do now that you have burned your bridges."

Hargreaves withdrew his hand. "Well ma'am, when bridges burn, and the people hole up inside, it is wise to recruit some brave knights to take the attack to the enemy."

He watched the grin fade from the President's face turning into a deep frown that burrowed in the lines of her face. He turned around and walked out of the Oval Office and into the Rose Garden.

BOOK II

1

Three Years Later

Rowan Wahbeh kept two television sets in her studio apartment. Her male friends loved it and often came over on Saturdays for college football rivaled religion in Atlanta, Georgia. While the exotic, young reporter loved a good party, she cared little for the gridiron.

Raised by well to do Lebanese parents, Rowan studied political science at Georgetown dreaming of sitting at the international news desk at CNN Headquarters in London. The two TV sets were her way of keeping up to date on the news around the world via her station and that of chief rival, the fair and balanced Fox News. She eyed the former as video streamed live from Paris and London. Both heads of state announced their decisions to relinquish their respective nation's nuclear weapons capabilities. The streets in Paris were alive with celebration while the English were, in keeping with their tradition, more subdued.

Russia shocked the world months before Paris or London's decision by citing their South African allies as the purest example of world peace. 'Not only have they overcome apartheid but also pioneered nuclear non-proliferation, surrendering their entire nuclear arsenal," spoke the Russian President Vasilyev. "We of the Russian Federation wish to celebrate that halcyon anniversary by declaring the demise of our nuclear arsenal."

All of a sudden, the world stopped spinning, and the Doomsday Clock was reversed by hours at a time. China soon followed as BRICS nations usurped power from the UN Security Council in broad strokes of diplomacy.

Rowan yearned to be on the front lines of such remarkable news. A Russian-Chinese coalition convinced India and Pakistan their nuclear arsenals were obsolete and both nations signed a treaty ending their status as a nuclear threat as well. Iran, with immense pressure from all corners of their region, capitulated and ceased their atomic weapons program.

That had been last week. Now the world celebrated once more, witnessing as both France and the United Kingdom signed full non-proliferation treaties. That left the United States and Israel as nations in possession of nuclear warheads.

CNN's feed streamed France's President live in Paris. "I call on our oldest, most continuous ally to join the world community in destroying all nuclear weapons. Please, American President, lay down your weapons and be no longer remembered as the nation that gave birth to such a horrible display of power." His speech ended with the cheering of millions surrounding his podium in front of the Arc de Triomphe.

As expected, Fox News broadcasted a taped message of Israel's latest Prime Minister, Miko Ehud, as he fervently argued that peace in the region and his nation, in particular, were guaranteed by the defense of nuclear weapons. "If the world's single Jewish State in existence today were to lay down our arms, we would be overrun by our enemies and pushed into the sea. Our nuclear arsenal is all that keeps lingering enemies in Syria, Iran, and other non-nation state entities from fulfilling their evil will. Our trust in the one true God, the God of Israel, is all that stands between us and a dim future. A future of exile."

Rubbish. Rowan turned off both television sets. Her father had been a prominent Muslim doctor before Israel invaded Lebanon's sovereignty in the 1980s. Thousands died as terror reigned in the streets and innocents could be killed by sniper fire or IDF tanks. Her parent's flight from the war-torn nation inspired her to take up the mantle of journalism and pursue a career at CNN.

The teakettle's whistle disrupted her thoughts. She hurried into the small kitchen. She poured the hot water into a mug of black tea leaves, mint, honey, and sugar. Not quite as good as her mothers, the tea's sweet aroma made her wish she had more time at home.

Her daddy's gift to her upon getting a position at CNN had been a brand-new forest green Toyota Camry. She sat behind the wheel checking her appearance in the visor's vanity mirror. Perfect olivine skin coupled with deep, dark eyes that matched her shoulder-length hair. She was a complete knockout. The network put her in front of the camera grooming her for frontline news. The day's assignment promised to be exciting as she was scheduled to fly in a helicopter reporting on the dangerous work of smokejumpers and to provide aerial coverage of the wildfires scorching much of the American South.

Dubbed the Fire Belt by news media, drought-like conditions in the eastern seaboard and southern states plagued them with fires that engulfed the entire region like a giant snake. One clever anchorman called the fires the Anaconda Plan after General Winfield Scott's plan to seal off the Confederacy during the American Civil War. The war effort displaced millions as the fires razed their homes, schools, businesses, and places of worship. There was hope that as autumn dwindled, rains would soon come as they had in much of the Pacific Northwest.

Stopped at a light in downtown Atlanta, she practiced how she would reveal the devastation and yet look straight into the camera to deliver a ray of hope. "After all," she said to the silent mirror, "winter is coming."

2

Tom Philips' knees tensed as he descended the stairs in his suburban Marietta, Georgia home. Four years playing football for Georgia Tech made Army basic training feel like a breeze but the decades had taken their toll. He breathed deep the smell of fried eggs and sizzling bacon, enough to lift any man's spirits. He pressed on into the kitchen.

Addae, his middle daughter, lived up to her namesake of Morning Sun, being the first of the Philips clan to awaken. The toaster popped and the bright ten-year-old pretended not to notice her father as she plopped two more slices of bread into the machine. Tom shook his head with a smile on his face.

Banging noises from the dining room caught his attention, and he was surprised to find his youngest daughter, four-year-old Kenzie, trying to set the table.

Addae had recruited help.

He gave a start when his wife Portia snuck up behind him wrapping her long, honey-colored fingers across his chest and arms. He felt himself redden at the display of affection in front of the children, but the embarrassment did not register across his ebony skin. She kissed his neck while Kenzie wasn't looking and he let her silk robe run through his fingers as she turned to help Addae finish making breakfast.

His wife was the antithesis of him, a thought that always made Tom smile. While not dumb, he had grown up poor in the bleakest of African-American neighborhoods outside Atlanta while his wife Portia had known a life of privilege and education. His family chastised him for finding the lightest skinned woman he could get away with in his grandfather's historic black congregation. The two were married in that church, jumping over a broomstick just as their ancestors had.

The four gathered around the table and prepared to say grace but just before Tom pounded on the dining table shaking the plates with a wrought iron fist. "Jojo!"

Quick feet padded down the carpeted stairway, and a bleary-eyed thirteen-year-old girl rounded the corner. After breakfast, he knew she would disappear again to wage war against her thick curly hair, a gift from her father's side. Tom shaved his head with a razor every Thursday at Ogletree's Barbershop to tame the wild beast that lived on his dark dome head.

"Jojo, since you were last, you can say grace."

"But I'm always last plus I hate saying grace."

Tom suppressed the urge to bite back at her cheek. Thirteen going twenty-three Portia mouthed. He knew he couldn't be upset. Their oldest daughter took much after his doctoral educated wife. He never won any arguments in this household; even the dog was a female.

"I'll say grace," he said.

Gathering the rest of the empty plates, he joined Portia in the kitchen as the girls readied their backpacks for school. She was doing the dishes, soapsuds floating from the sink and the smell of crispy bacon still lingering over the gas stove. He looked at his watch wishing he had longer to help Portia with the dishes. "I gotta go Sugar."

Portia turned to face him, the front of her apron wet from the dishes. She reached her gymnast-like arms around his neck and pulled him close.

"You call the doctor for me to set up an appointment," he asked. He wasn't getting any younger, and the thought of heart failure or another ailment haunted him as he aged. Leaving his beautiful girls behind terrified him, and he prayed over them every night for their safety.

"I will remember to call if you remember to pick them up from school today. I will be at the office until late." The office for her was on the campus of the Center for Disease Control or CDC in Atlanta. She couldn't even tell him everything that she did, but whatever it was, she earned good money doing it.

Tom nodded. "I will be flying most of the morning, but I will be back in time to get the girls."

"The fires won't reach us here will they daddy," asked Kenzie. Tom earned his living as a helicopter pilot for the Interagency Fire and Rescue in Atlanta. After meeting a CNN anchor covering the fires, the two were to fly to Cleveland, Tennessee where an old friend of his was to tour the anchor around the facility before Tom flew them all to survey the damage done to places like Gatlinburg and Asheville.

"No sweet girl. Men like my buddy Nolan are fighting hard to save as many people and their livelihoods as possible."

"Tell Nolan we said hey," called Portia as Tom slid in for a kiss.

Once outside he turned the Tahoe's engine over with a roar and idled out of the neighborhood. The smell of fresh cut grass and the sound of flags flapping in the wind died away as he pulled into the main thoroughfare.

3

A local church may have donated the long, wooden bench underneath the glass-paned wall. Or someone stole it.

The air smelled of turtle wax and rubber tire outside the aircraft coordinators office in Cleveland, Tennessee. Nolan Hoke sat in the church pew waiting as Dixon Cafferty lambasted another smokejumper for his run-ins with the local authorities.

Cafferty was short, the size of whale, and Texan. The jumper was tall, lean, with long, black Native American hair. Neither man excelled in gaining trust amongst firefighters on account of their short tempers.

Heat reflected back off the windows as light streamed in through the open hangar doors. Nolan watched other smokejumpers play pickup outside against a hotshot crew from California. The hotshot crew was drilling the jumpers, and it made him a little upset. They all called the Interagency Base in Cleveland their home since the beginning of the summer, and each side got along decent despite a long-standing rivalry over who had the tougher job. This debate often got settled during Safety Committee Meetings at the local bar. Both hotshots and smokejumpers were expected to be in peak physical condition resulting in testosterone levels in as high supply as beer or red meat. But beer and rivalry often got men in trouble. Men like the Native American inside the office who were avoided by any veteran for being a mean drunk. Foolish greenhorns messed with him and paid the price. Nolan saw two men sneaking through the hallway with a bucket in their hands but could not see what they carried inside. The duo retreated around the corner and disappeared.

Moments later, after some more shouting by Cafferty, the Native American was dismissed. A loud crash rang through the hallway and bounced off the glass. More yelling ensued as both Cafferty and the smokejumper resumed their tirade. As the man bounded through the hall, Nolan saw that pink fire retardant covered the man's long hair and ran down his back. A faint, Pepto-Bismol trail flowed in his wake. Some real pranksters thought very highly of themselves to mess with that guy. Nolan made a mental note to check all doors before opening them too wide in the future.

"Hoke," called the large Cafferty from his office. The one thing Nolan liked about Cafferty's office was the man's massive St. Bernard named Duke. Nolan loved Duke. It gave him slight pleasure every time he left to see the dog lay flat on his feet and whine. He petted Duke behind the ears and allowed the pooch to slobber on his hand as he stood at ease in front of his superior. Cafferty looked annoyed at this as he peered over a slim file in a manila folder.

"Says here that you requested a transfer to the east," began the superior.

"Yes, sir. I had a few years working experience with Sir and I was eager to follow the Division Coordinator." Sir, a female, had been Nolan's CO in Boise but was given a promotion to front the Atlanta office. Nolan would be close but could not afford to live in the big city. Or maybe he just liked the quiet of the ancient eastern mountains.

"I sure hope you don't think this is a vacation from the west. We work hard out here too."

"Yes, sir." Nolan stood a little straighter.

"It also says here that you're from around these parts." If you called Stuttgart, Arkansas 'these parts.' Nolan figured that being from more of an eastern state qualified him as local. He nodded in response.

Cafferty set down the manila file eyeing Nolan longer than was comfortable. Like a sloth, the large man leaned back and smiled a wide Texan grin. "Well, I'll shoot ya straight. I need somebody to tour around a Clinton News Network spy and some pilot they're sending from headquarters. Now the pilot is one of ours. Sir requested you of course, and I initially said no but then I go to thinking. I go to thinking that you're the new man on the totem pole around here but being that you're not a Westerly like most these fella's you might be a good guide for this communist. Get us some good PR. Good PR means more funding and more funding means more money! Of course, we are the only ones out there praying the fires continue so we can get paid am I right?" Cafferty chuckled at this own joke. Nolan politely smiled. The grim sentiment was accurate. Most smokejumpers and hotshots had secondary jobs in the offseason. Some bartended, others were professional athletes, but most worked at Wal-Mart or Home Depot. Nolan used the time off to travel.

Cafferty sighed after chasing down his chuckle with a little coffee. He seemed to have forgotten the smokejumper was still standing there when he placed down his mug. "Dismissed."

Nolan nodded and heard Duke begin to whimper as he reached for the door. Checking to make sure no pink retardant awaited him he left the glass office and headed for the mess hall to grab a protein and grease infused breakfast.

4

Developed by Robert Edward "Ted" Turner in 1980, CNN became the first twenty-four-hour cable news network. His vision grew to become six lauded networks and make him America's most significant private landowner.

Rowan respected that kind of ambition and power that made CNN the most trusted cable news channel in the world. She efficiently dodged tourists and schoolchildren standing agape at the networks on display HMMWV, a tribute to soldiers of the Iraqi conflicts. The steel behemoth seemed to embody Turner's mission statement that CNN "won't be signing off until the world ends. We'll be on and we'll cover the end of the world, live, and that will be our last event... We'll play 'Nearer My God to Thee' before we sign off."

Once inside the newsroom, the din of a multitude shouting and snapping photos died away replaced with the clicking of computer keys, ringing telephones, and constant chatter. Rowan sat at an unoccupied desk and began reviewing her script drafted by the lead writer's detailing the forest fires overtaking the lower Appalachia, otherwise known as Piedmont. Resources stretched beyond the max with men fighting fires from California to New Mexico, North Carolina to Mississippi. There was even talk of experimenting with artificial clouds; an idea lifted from a previous World Cup.

In the hustle that accompanied every newsroom across the world, Rowan never noticed Tony Fredericks until he sat down on top of her desk. She looked at him through raised eyebrows and caught that award-winning smile. A man full of false charm and full of himself. In his hands were two steaming cups of coffee, the aroma mixing with his aftershave, an aura that served as a force field to some and a spider's web to others. His favorite targets were the impressionable young interns looking for an insider to give them a big break. Tony recently divorced. Rowan felt terrible for his two boys but had to keep her distance whenever they came for a visit.

She wondered if she was supposed to look grateful and neither spoke. Her stalker continued to beam down at her, forcing her to surrender the standoff.

"Good morning Tony."

"Hello, Rowan. How is CNN's most astonishing reporter doing this fine morning?" He held onto the last syllables trying to coax out a southern drawl. Too bad the man was from Ohio or something like that. He wore the same gelled haircut he figured made him look attractive in college.

Tony lowered his eyes to her trying to look serious. "As your producer, I wanted to let you know we'll do two live performances. The first will be over Gatlinburg after you go wheels up then we will beam back out to you just after lunch as you guys hover over Asheville. The city has evacuated most of its population but seems to be holding its own against the fires. Gatlinburg though." He let the implication hang in the air. Here Rowan smiled, both at his attempt at solemnity and to taunt him. "I'm told that I will be spending the whole morning surrounded by a bunch of fire boys."

Tony's smile faded.

"I guess I have you to thank for that." She gave him her most endearing smile.

His jaw set in a firm line.

"Well I should probably get going," she said donning a black leather jacket. "I have to check out a camera and microphone before I meet the pilot." She left Tony Fredericks staring after her.

Tom Philips walked into his usual coffee stop with an air of familiarity. Resting his elbows on the cold counter, he shouted down to his favorite barrister.

"That'll be a black, no sugar," he smiled down the line.

The young man behind the counter flashed a broad smile and extended his hand over the divider. "Good morning Mr. Philips, sir."

"Hey now, my father was Mr. Philips. You know better than that Otha."

The boy smiled some more. "Yes, sir. How are your girls?"

"Doing just fine. How's the elbow today?"

Otha responded by rotating his left arm and mimicking a Heisman pose. Otha Peters led the backfield for the M.H. Jackson Jaguars and on pace for a second two-thousand-yard season. Despite the injury sustained during a game, Otha had yet to fumble all season. Tom's tutelage continued making Otha into a strong back with a near 4.0-grade point average. He hoped the young man would pursue a full ride to Tech but both Michigan and Notre Dame were just as interested in his academics as they were his athleticism.

"Will I be seeing you tonight for supper," asked Tom. Otha was no stranger to any member of his family.

"No sir," said Otha wiping the counter down, working out a new shine. "We're going over to Rome to see Nana. She's giving a lecture tomorrow on Dr. King. We're all going to support her."

Tom had been but a newborn when Dr. Martin Luther King Jr. was calling for reconciliation amongst blacks and whites. Not that he hadn't seen his fair share of violence having grown up in East Point and joining the service. He figured it was as the good book says: violence only begets violence.

"I will see y'all on Sunday though," said Otha, cutting through Tom's thoughts.

"Sounds good O," chuckled Tom tapping the counter with a fist around his coffee cup. "You take care now and don't forget our verse."

"Yes, sir. First Timothy four twelve."

"Amen brother."

Half an hour later Tom touched the Bell helicopter down at CNN Headquarters. He was grateful he drove a helicopter to work and didn't have to commute like the thousands of others trapped under the Atlanta sky.

Without further ado, a tall, slender woman emerged from the complex toting a small messenger bag, leather jacket, and video camera. Despite the sunglasses, Tom deduced the woman was of Arab descent. She was long and beautiful, but he had to hold his cautionary sirens in check. Despite many prayers for forgiveness and to love his neighbor, Tom still froze when first meeting someone who looked off the streets of Fallujah, Mosul or Kandahar. Certainly, atrocities had happened on both sides during the War on Terror; however, he still carried some fears. Fear led to hate. He reminded himself that people always fear what they do not understand.

Crushing his thoughts, he stepped out of the cockpit and offered the young woman a hand with her gear. She took the gesture for a handshake and removed her glasses revealing deep but intelligent eyes.

"If you would please strap yourself in ma'am, we can take off very soon."

"Thank you, Mr. Philips," she said reading his flight suit stitches. He smiled in return.

"Comfortable," he asked, hollering over the din of the whirring engines. Rowan's hair was in her face, but she smiled in the mirror and gave him two thumbs up as the steel machine lifted effortlessly into the air.

On the flight to Cleveland Forward Air Base, they exchanged the regular pleasantries. She couldn't hide a frown when he told her of being in the armed forces, and although he couldn't see it, he felt her hesitation.

"I suppose it is hard to adjust after experiences like that," she offered.

Tom kept his eye on the sky but affirmed her. "Yes, ma'am. I have to say that the sin of man makes murderers of us all. It is as Benjamin Franklin said, 'there has never been a bad peace or a good war." Rowan looked out the window, her thoughts on her parents and now the dark, muscular man who she had just met.

Each retreated to their views remaining silent across the Tennessee border.

5

Nolan ducked below the wash of the rotor blades as the chopper hovered above the helipad at Cleveland Air Base. He cupped his hands around his sunglasses to keep them from being blown away. As the blades came to a halt, he approached the cockpit first. The pilot was just emerging.

"Tom? Tom, what are you doing here?"

"Hey Nolan, they didn't tell you I was the chaperone between your and this pretty young lady?"

Both men were smiling. Whereas most smokejumpers, hot shots, and pilots were from the west, Nolan and Tom were among the few that were native to the South and therefore stuck close to one another when they could. Nolan loved Tom's enthusiastic attitude on life and Tom could see that Nolan had a world of potential at the age of thirty-two.

The two men embraced and then parted so Tom could make the introductions.

"Sebah el hair," said Nolan taking Rowan's hand into a firm grasp. She noticed he put most of his force behind his thumb as opposed to squeezing the hand from the fingers. He also extended one finger along the wrist, lining up their arms.

"You speak *Arabie*?" she asked caught off guard.

"I've traveled a lot," was all he offered. She tried to measure the firefighter up without making too much of a scene. Dark headed with a farmer's tan. He stood at a lanky six foot she guessed and had an easy smile. He did not remove the sunglasses but motioned for the crew to follow him through the large open hanger doors.

As she looked around most of the firefighters were men although there were a few women. They all wore the same light green pants with an assortment of t-shirts and pale-yellow jackets. Some slept on army cots, some read, while others did pushups using a deck of cards to count the reps. She jotted as many notes as possible in her shorthand.

Most appeared tired and dirty like they hadn't showered or washed their clothes in a few weeks. Nolan, their guide, must have shaved before getting this assignment she thought. His pants were in fine enough condition, but his white t-shirt was a muted grey from charcoal stains, grease, and sweat. She chuckled to herself at the thought of experiencing this world of bravado with the likes of Tony Fredericks.

Rowan shook hands with the CO, a sausage-fingered Texan who staged his tablet to lay on his desk with CNN as the open page. He also was not dressed as most of the Forest Service crew but rather a brown business suit paired with a white ten-gallon hat. She almost broke into hysterics. Nolan steered her into another room just off the hanger. The room was a wide-open space with numerous tables half of which looked as though they had tablecloths on them.

"Let me guess," she started, "this is the dining room?"

The smokejumper smiled. "No ma'am, this is the chute room. Like a down sleeping bag, the chutes are stored here until they are ready to be packed which is where the tables come in handy." He swept his hand across the tables. She now noticed several canvas bags dotted the floor of the large, open room. "Every jumper knows how to fold and sew chutes. Everyone is responsible. We must rely on one another. Believe it or not, this is one job the veterans love to do the most. The old salts find the task methodical and decompressing." She ran her hand through the light material thinking it felt similar to a hammock.

"When did the US Forest Service being using smokejumpers to fight fires?"

"The first jumpers were utilized in the state of Washington in the late 1930s. I can't imagine how heavy their gear was back then."

"How much weight do most of you carry?"

"Why don't you come with me to the locker room and I'll show you my pack?"

Rowan looked dubious at first and slowed her feet as they rounded a corner. Nolan removed his sunglasses and opened his arms. "Come on," he said, "it won't be like what you think."

It turned out he was neither wrong nor right. It was cleaner than Rowan had expected, but the stench of body odor and humidity still hung in the air making her want to grab her sides for protection. When they got to his locker, she noticed his yellow jacket hanging with another pair of sturdy boots, a blue backpack, a canvas backpack, and two pictures taped to the mesh wall. The first picture was an old headshot of a man with the same black hair and brown eyes as Nolan. The second photo was a more recent one of Nolan and a woman who despite appearing youthful had to be his mother. Rowan was startled to see that the woman had fine blonde hair and sky-blue eyes. She looked little like her son, but there was the hint of a firmer jawline and higher cheekbones that the mother passed along to her son.

Nolan cleared his throat and began removing the smaller, blue pack. "The other pack is for your chute and jumpsuit, but this pack is a huge lifeline out there. While smokejumpers always jump in pairs, you can be isolated in a hurry and solely responsible for holding your line. Many pilots like our Tom are very daring, but they are not always cleared to get us out of the bush once the sun goes down or visibility becomes impossible.

We are more or less left to our own devices until we get picked up or hike our way out of there."

"Isn't that dangerous?"

Nolan smiled patiently. "Well ma'am, to be honest, that's why we like a long fire season, the overtime and hazard pay make it worthwhile to most fellas."

"And what do you do with your hazard pay?"

"I told you. I travel a lot. Anyway, inside this pack will be MREs, our MyMedic supplies, extra water, a sleeping bag, some tools, rope, and our iconic tool, the Pulaski." He pulled the Pulaski out of the locker. To Rowan, it appeared to be a combination ax with a spike on the end for busting rock and digging trenches.

Nearing the end of the tour, they entered the mudroom where immense vats of pink fire retardant, or mud, were stored before being pumped into the planes. "This is why we use airstrips for our forward operating bases," explained Nolan. "We have to load the mud onto big tankers, usually a helicopter but occasionally a military plane. Since we are so close to North Carolina, a lot of our planes are on loan with pilots from the National Guard. They don't stick around base though. Guardsmen and professional firefighters don't always mix well." Rowan snorted, slapping him on the arm.

"Hey, what's your tattoo," she asked pointing to his shoulder.

"Oh that," he shrugged trying to pull the sleeve down. "That was a mistake."

"Well, mister, what is it?" She thought it looked like Humpty Dumpty or a football.

"It's a rugby ball with a UM stencil. I played rugby for Ole Miss, that is the University of Mississippi."

"I've heard of rugby. Rough sport. Do you have any other tattoos?"

Nolan scratched the back of his head. "Yeah, well, I have another one on my other arm." He lifted his sleeve to reveal an intricate weave of sharp lines.

"Is that one of those barbed wire things I see all the boys in the gym wear?"

"No, not exactly. It's supposed to represent a crown of thorns with the Ichthus, or fish, and the Greek symbol for Christ woven in there. Mom didn't approve, but I guess there are worse things to do in college. Where did you go?"

"I studied poly-sci at Georgetown. We didn't call it a party unless it went down on a yacht."

Nolan laughed. "Oxford is known for its share of Southern Aristocracy."

After the tour, Nolan helped Rowan into the helicopter. While her back was turned getting into the seat, Tom flashed Nolan a conspiratorial smile. Nolan would have flipped him the bird but knew Tom would have disapproved. Tom deserved that kind of respect.

Nolan set his Epperson Mountaineering pack on the deck and strapped it to the steel seat. Even though he wasn't in the field, no jumper or hotshot left base without his pack. They all donned black headphones that helped drown out the rotor wash and allowed them to speak to one another.

The Bell helicopter had been gutted for practical use and held little creature comforts. Still, Rowan was in high spirits and her company proved to be as uplifting as the method of transportation itself. She clamped her hands over the headphones for clarity as Tom cleared them for takeoff.

"Center, this is Spartacus, do you read?"

"Five by five," came the reply, this time the southern drawl sounded genuine.

"Center, we are in route to Gatlinburg, over."

"Copy that Sparty. Y'all be careful out there. Center out."

Nolan knew that the trip to Gatlinburg from Cleveland would not take long. "What's the itinerary today?"

Rowan smiled. "The usual. We swoop over Gatlinburg to show the destruction. I throw a few statistics while you hold the camera. I make mention of how the fires are still raging and could push south if winter doesn't save us."

She watched Nolan's face drop. "Why would you say the fires are pushing south and that we have to be saved by winter?"

Rowan tried to keep her encouraging smile but she could tell he was wounded. "Shots fired. I'm sorry. To be honest, it's meant to instill a sense of urgency. Americans have a crazy pension for danger, the closer to home the better."

"It's too bad all these fires, this was always one of my favorite parts of the country," said Nolan peering out the side of the helicopter into the forests below. They hovered over tides of green and brown, but large plumes of grey and black loomed closer. There were lots of cars on the road as mass evacuations took place from significant population centers. He wondered if it could get so severe as to reach Atlanta. In reality, he knew better. The weather was turning, and the Indian Summer was coming to a close. More and more resources were being pulled to put an end to the wildfires and the so-called Fire Belt. Rumors of artificial clouds made him smile to himself.

Rowan eyed him with curiosity. "Where all have you traveled? Do smokejumpers get frequent flier miles or do you depart too early?"

Nolan resumed his seat in the steel chair, the wind no longer washing over his face. "My mom was surprised that I wanted to become a firefighter. I didn't know what to do with my life, and so she suggested I travel. I think she wanted me to give back in a way and join World Vision or something. Now in the offseason, I just pick a place and go to it."

"You just go to it?"

Nolan smiled wider this time. "Yeah."

Doesn't leave much time for a woman she didn't add.

Rowan helped Nolan get the camera set up as they soared above the mountains of Tennessee. "As you can see below me, Gatlinburg is absolutely devastated. It is essentially a ghost town." Rowan relayed her message via live stream back to Ed Callahan in Atlanta. Nolan had strapped Rowan to a harness with sturdy rope to keep to her upright. Tom was a fine pilot, but the winds created by fire could take on a life of their own. Nolan held onto the camera while Rowan held her gaze. She hoped the lighting was good enough to reflect off her eyes. "Looking below, acres upon acres are scorched. The southern winds are colliding with winter's approach bringing cooler winds from the north. These winds could potentially twist and turn and swirl together to create what firefighters call a firestorm. Scary business, Ed."

Nolan stopped himself short of laughing out loud. Sure, what the pretty reporter was saying was entirely possible but all the same, it sounded theatrical. He could only imagine the images he was helping to broadcast in homes across the United States. Rowan was holding her hand to her ear listening to the network headquarters. He imagined the man on the other end of the mouthpiece. "What is that you say, Rowan? What is the probability that the fires could reach us here in Atlanta pretty lady?"

He couldn't stop chuckling to himself. The camera began to shake, and Rowan cut him to the quick. "Ed," she began but paused as Nolan centered the camera on her deep brown eyes, "the likeliness of a firestorm will become greater and greater the longer firefighters work to subdue the blaze. There is the legitimate fear amongst the population of Atlanta that the fire could reach them if not stopped now."

Right, thought Nolan. Rowan gave him another look then she spun her head letting her hair flow in the violent wind. "This. This is what captivating news looks like."

"Firefighters are however optimistic that they can stop the fires as the blaze runs south exiting the Chattahoochee National Forest. I spoke with Cleveland Forest Service Base Operator Dixon Cafferty, and he assured me that the flames would die considerably as the blaze consumes the forest, essentially running out of fuel."

Nolan made an effort not to drop the camera. When and where did she get that information?

"Chief Cafferty informed me that he is coordinating firefighters from Georgia, Tennessee, and even as far away as California or Boise. Their mission here is to ensure the tranquility of these forests and bring an end to this devastation."

Rowan touched her ear as she heard Ed talking. "We certainly do appreciate the brave work those men and women are doing. Men like Chief Cafferty and so many others. Just catastrophic these fires. That was Rowan Wahbeh; I'm Ed Callahan from the front desk of news, CNN."

After the successful broadcast over Gatlinburg, Tom veered the helicopter to the east, opening up the Rolls Royce engines.

"That was captivating news," said Nolan stowing the camera beneath his seat. "I didn't notice when you got that quote from Cafferty." His eyes watched her, waiting for an explanation.

Rowan gave him a placating smile. "I saw the map on the wall and improvised a little bit. I figured that Chief Cafferty wouldn't mind the news spot."

Nolan ran his hand through his short-cropped hair. "I suppose that is the truth."

"The Air Attack Officer has informed me that a Hercules will be intersecting our path to Asheville." Tom's deep voice carried loud and clear over the wind and roar of the rotors. "It will be using I-40 as a guide in an attempt to split the Nero Fire into two smaller parts. I thought that might be something you would be interested in filming."

Rowan looked confused. "That sounds awesome but what is a Hercules?"

Without turning around, Tom spoke through the headphones to inform her. "A Hercules is a C-130 Tanker and one of which the National Guard pilots utilize to aid civilian efforts. The huge cargo bays are capable of dropping eighteen thousand gallons worth of fire suppressor in one pass."

"Surely with that much stuff it will split the fire, right," asked Rowan.

"I'm willing to bet it will open a corridor but the situation will remain extremely delicate. Fires tend to create their disastrous weather, and sometimes the wind and heat are too much for firefighters to make much headway."

True to Tom's word as they hovered closer to Asheville, the sky grew darker. The winds picked up, pulling the helicopter through the wind stream. Tom was an experienced pilot, but he had to work hard to keep the chopper level for the young reporter.

Rowan could see the devastation on the ground below. Ripped up forest, strewn debris, and torched earth. Dropping lower, she began to feel the intense heat as trees lit up underneath a darkening canopy. The wind roared, and streaks of light blazed through the clouds. Waves of green and yellow cascaded below. Despite the turbulence, she was glad to be high in the air away from the inferno.

"Look alive," said Tom. "The tanker should be visible in another few minutes."

Nolan strapped Rowan back into the harness and grabbed the camera. For the time being she held onto another strap leaning towards the window searching through the smoky haze for the tanker.

Massive propellers cleared through the smoke as a flat green plane made its way towards I-40. Tom had taken the helicopter lower to be level with the low-flying tanker as it made its pass.

Rowan could make out the neon orange painted numbers along the side: 211BC.

A piercing noise shot through the air followed by a terrific thunderclap. The thunder rolled, but it was not Mother Nature that caused the cacophony. Rowan stared in horror as the Hercules burst into flame and began to list. The plane was headed straight for the ground.

Suddenly she felt a knot in her stomach as the helicopter lurched upward. Tom called the emergency into the headphones. "Guard Tanker 2-1-1-Beta Charlie is down. I repeat..." Rowan heard no more as she threw off the headgear. She spun as Nolan's hand reached her shoulder to pull her from the open bay door.

Another piercing shriek and this time the impact sent tremors through her body as some unseen force struck the helicopter. Tom called into the radio. His voice registered a higher octave but in control; clear as he issued a mayday back to headquarters. Despite his best efforts, the helicopter continued to spin out of control. Rowan felt her stomach lift. The world was a blur of steel, bark, and fire.

Nolan blinked in disbelief as the body of the CNN reporter disappeared. One moment he was reaching for her the next moment she was gone, vanished into thin air.

The helicopter descended into a death spiral with Tom fighting for control. Nolan strapped in with multiple belts onto one of the steel-framed seats and held onto the struts with a white-knuckled death grip. The helicopter's siren blared. Tom held back on the stick but to little avail. They were going to crash.

"The Lord be your shepherd, Nolan!"

The helicopter hit the forest canopy. All went black.

BOOK III

1

Pierce Hoke creaked the door open to his son's room. The hallway light's soft glow ebbed its way across the floor and onto the bed. The boy was sound asleep, his face hidden under a bent arm.

Pierce waited patiently as the young boy struggled to awaken. The snoring receded. The bed springs snapped as he rose. Looking out his open window, he said, "It's not even light yet."

"The night is darkest just before the dawn, son," said the boy's father. "Hurry and brush your teeth so we can hug momma before we leave."

The wood-burning stove heated the large living room that doubled as a dining room and kitchen. The scent of pinewood hovered in the air. Marjorie Hoke hugged her son and her husband inside the door handing them each a sack lunch. The sack contained two sandwiches, a sour green apple, dried venison strips, and a tin of cherry pie. Pierce lingered for a half step to plant a kiss on Marjorie's lips and forehead. The screen door slammed shut. Pierce met his son on the wooden porch.

It was a frosty start to the day. The boy Nolan threw a stick into the yard as Samson chased after it. Pierce made the beagle shake off his dew-wet coat before climbing into the cab.

In spite of the cold, Pierce drove with the windows down. "Works better than coffee" he always said. The Classic Bronco's throaty V8 thundered down the grass-ridden path away from the Hoke homestead. The air felt invigorating as the morning fog hung low, holding the rising sun to a colorless orb.

The fog dissipated over the drive and the sun sparkled as if God were a great blacksmith hammering His anvil. Samson cuddled into Nolan's lap, and the boy covered him in his arms using the small dog as a pillow.

Too soon he felt the bumpy gravel road and heard the rub as the tires passed over a cattle guard jolting him from his nap. Pierce eased the Ford, named Lee after Lee Iacocca, with trailer in tow into Newton Anderson's front lawn as the man and his two sons came out to meet them. Mr. Anderson reached through Pierce's open window, and the two fathers shook hands.

"I got a fallen tree in the field. You're welcome to any wood you can fit on the trailer. We'd love to stay back and help, but we got a long drive to Oxford ahead of us."

As the two men spoke, Nolan held Samson, and Newton Jr. pulled himself into the passenger window. Newt had been Nolan's best friend since diapers. The same age, the two friends were separated by school districts but teamed up during summer league. Newt, a large farm boy, was a menacing presence behind the plate while lanky Nolan made a habit of chasing down long balls in the outfield. Nolan got his physical stature from his father who was also tall but had muscular calves and sinewy arm muscles that were good enough to have pitched for the Memphis Redbirds before being married and having a boy. Now his father was a senior member of the fire department and one of the most respected men in the rural community.

"How do you think the Cardinals will do this season," asked Newt.

"Dad says it will be awhile before we see a red October," sighed Nolan.

Newt laughed, a scar around his mouth turning his cheerful face at an awkward angle. "I agree. October is nearly a year away."

Both boys laughed as Mr. Anderson once again shook hands with Pierce and threw his arm around Wes, the youngest. "Just be sure to close the gate when you leave," he hollered after the Hoke boys.

"Will do, thanks again Newton." Pierce once again fired up the Ford shifting into four-wheel drive before pulling into the open fields.

Minutes later Samson soared out the door and darted for the fallen tree, struck by lightning in a recent storm. His dog tag jingled as the short-legged Beagle hopped through the taller grass. Nolan was thankful for his leather boots but soon shed his flannel jacket as the sun began to beam through a cloudless sky.

"Wish it was a bit cooler don't you," said Pierce. Nolan played fetch with Samson while his father cranked up the Stihl chainsaw. The two companions wandered through the forest to avoid the chainsaw's whine as it chewed through the timber. Nolan loathed the sound the same way his father detested the din of a vacuum, and his mother hated buzzing insects. Blessedly, a shrill whistle signaled the end of the sawing of logs.

"Let the work begin," Nolan told the dog who looked up and wagged its tail. "Sure pal, you get off easy." The dog rolled over and gave Nolan his most sorry face.

When they reached the clearing, Nolan saw that his father had already assembled the logs into rows ready to be split. A solid wood-handled ax was merely an extension of Pierce Hoke's arm. Nolan watched as his father created a deep schism on the first blow. He saw the tall man bring the ax over his head and before the swing, his right hand would collapse atop the left in a mighty blow cracking the wood with a great snapping sound. The forest shuddered, hacked into smaller sections for throwing into the furnace. Wasting no more time, Nolan squared up behind his row of logs and began to work thinking of the ax as his bat and the wooden center as a baseball ready to be liberated from the confines of Busch Stadium.

After a few hours, Nolan no longer had the same strength he once possessed. His biceps felt like tennis balls lodged inside of them, but that paled in comparison to the tightness in his quads and rear end.

Chopping wood could often be a time of contemplation. Nolan spent most of the morning thinking about the Anderson boys and family. His father no longer spoke but churned along pumping his arms like that of a locomotive. Nolan dropped his ax and took a drink of fresh water.

"Dad," he said, "how come I never had any brothers or sisters?" Pierce lifted his ax but stopped partway as if he had struck an invisible barrier. The blade struck the earth next to his boot. "Like the Andersons," pressed the boy.

Pierce walked to the Bronco's tailgate resting the ax against it. He stroked the stubble on his cheeks and seemed to be searching for the right words.

"Well son, your momma and I tried for more kids over the years," he said stooping on the tailgate next to Nolan. "I guess the good Lord knew that a young man such as yourself was all that we would be able to handle." Nolan smiled. His father responded in kind. "Your momma was a pageant star; her beautiful blonde hair and blue eyes made her the envy of every man. I think she would have loved to have had a girl but we just never were pregnant again. After some time, we just figured that we had gotten lucky with you."

"I would have liked a little brother," said Nolan. "Somebody to play with like Newt has in Wes."

Pierce hung his head a little and nodded in understanding. "I know son. It is good for children to grow up with siblings. But your momma and I are mighty proud of you. It takes a village to raise a child. You and the Anderson boys have many villages behind y'all."

"Kinda like a big family?"

"Yeah."

Pierce turned to continue chopping the wood but stopped and sized Nolan up. "You know, you got me to thinking. Your grandfather used to say that the world was changing. He said it ain't no place to be raisin' kids anymore." Pierce stopped to see that he had Nolan's attention. He did so he continued. "There were times before when people would stop having kids because they feared the future that their children faced. Life is a hard but precious thing, Nolan. Every day is a gift and a responsibility."

"Manhood is just around the corner for you and the older you get, the more responsible you will have to become. I guess folks like your grandfather were just scared. They were scared of the way people are behaving and scared of the responsibility it would take to set the world right."

Nolan stood stock still as his father spoke. He never knew his father to be a hard man, but he knew better than to interrupt. Folks of all ages stopped to listen when his father took the time to express his thoughts. Maybe it was his work in the fire department or perhaps it was something else but Nolan, like everyone, paid close attention to what the man had to say.

"We wanted another child, but we first wanted you, Nolan. We wanted you to grow up knowing what love is. Now we are excited to watch you grow in independence and strength. We pray you grow up to be the kind of man this world needs. You're much too young to understand everything now, but someday you will meet the love of your life; the two of you can be partners, finding the light in this world and spreading hope. That was our hope for you son and our promise to God in raising you as our boy. I pray that you will not be selfish with your life but selfless just as God our Father was with His Own Son. God did not send His Son to earth to rule with a mighty hand but to save the world through sacrifice. That is compelling love. That is the way that your mother and I love you. I pray you too will be compelled by love to serve others." Pierce picked up his ax and marched to the next sawn stump. "A man plans his course, but the Lord establishes his steps."

Nolan watched his father once more. With perfect form, the man resumed chopping wood.

Thump. Thump. Thump.

2

Drip. Drip. Drip.

Water and jet fuel fell onto Nolan Hoke's forehead mixing with blood and pooled into his eyes, ears, and nostrils. He awoke with a snort lying crumpled on the backside of the pilot's chair. He could smell the fuel and leaped to his feet grabbing ahold of the bolted-in seats to lift himself up. His head pounded. When he brought his hand down, his fingertips were red with blood. Pain in his knee caused him to stumble back onto the rear of the pilot's chair.

That's when he realized the helicopter crashed. Tree limbs jutted through the structure and the cockpit's shattered glass. With fear in his voice, he called out Tom's name.

Branches snapped, causing the helicopter to sway as Nolan pivoted his weight to reach around the seat to Tom's body. He looked around the fuselage; the female reporter was nowhere to be found. Summoning the courage, Nolan reached a hand to Tom's neck checking for a pulse. He found none.

Inching further, he tried to get a look at his friend. It was clear the cockpit had taken the brunt of the crash, probably saving Nolan's life but taking Tom's with it. He wondered if the mighty man had maneuvered the helicopter this way on purpose and hung his head in regret. The entire bubble had collapsed around Tom although he appeared to have no entry wounds. He thought it must have been the sheer force of the crash. Death caused by blunt force trauma. Even the man's watch had shattered, a pilot's Ventus Caspian.

Hot tears stung Nolan's eyes. Tom's final moments had been not to save his own life but to save Nolan. To live, his friend had to die.

Tears flowed faster now. Nolan reached under Tom's olive drab shirt and yanked on the dog tags strapped around the neck. O Positive. Protestant. Nolan vowed to find his family, his wife and three daughters. Like his father, their father had died a hero. He tucked the dog tags into his pocket.

Blood still flowed freely from the capillaries in his forehead. Nolan reached above him to detach the lime green med kit from its place on the bulkhead. As he unzipped the flap, his eyes caught movement through the open bay door. A light flickered in the distance.

Acting by reflex, he dropped the med kit, the contents spilling to the forest floor below. With precious time running out he unstrapped his pack from the seat legs and began a desperate search for a length of rope.

He could now feel the heat as the forest withered under an intense blaze. There was no time to lose as fire in a tree canopy could cover ground like lightning, leaping from branch to branch igniting the treetops. If the forest fire was jumping, then it could reach the helicopter and ignite the jet fuel spewing from the tanks.

Finding a coil of rope, Nolan furiously began weaving a makeshift harness around his waist. The fire grew closer, the heat wave propelling him out the open window. He attached the other end of the rope to the fuselage as the wind picked up causing the helicopter shell to groan against the trees. He pulled on a pair of gloves with his teeth and fastened his pack.

He hated leaving Tom's body, but it was impossible to free the man's muscular frame from under the crushed fuselage. With one final look, he leaped off the helicopter using his boots and gloves to create friction on the rope to keep him from smashing into the ground. While it was insanity to try and outrun a fire, Nolan had to get away before the blaze reached the chopper and blew the fuel tank. Smoke filled his lungs as the forest took on an ashy grey color mixed with a sulfurous yellow glow. Flames crawling along the ground caught a dead pine shooting fire like a tower in the sky.

Fighting to stay upright as the blaze sucked the oxygen out of forest creating a wind tunnel, Nolan kept his ears tuned to the forest around him. The trees began to pitch and sway catching one another on fire. He needed a place safe enough to deploy his fire blanket. It alone stood between him walking away and being turned to ash. He navigated the forest floor in search of a dry river bed to dive into. Unstrapping his rucksack, he pulled out the collapsible fire shelter and let the wind fill it. Then he cradled the pack, his lifeline, in the fetal position cinching the fire shelter around him. He hoped the dry ditch would allow the firestorm to pass over him and he was thankful to have worn his thick forest service clothing to keep from getting his skin burned. Staggering hot temperatures sometimes made the shelters a death trap, melting the occupant inside.

An explosion rocked the trees as the tempest grew. Nolan wished he had thought to grab a helmet before jumping from the helicopter. Carefully, he fiddled with his pack to withdraw his radio and water bottle. He tried in vain to reach headquarters. The storm generated by the fire or perhaps his trench interfered with the signal. Smoke prowled under the edges of the shelter making him fight the urge to throw the blanket off in search of cleaner air.

Instead, he clung close to the earth to fill his lungs with the purest oxygen from the forest floor.

Sweating profusely, he let the radio slip to the dirt through his fingers and drank from the Lexan bottle. Hydration was critical as the temperatures outside the shelter reached well over the boiling point. At these temperatures, rocks could fly through the air like missiles before exploding.

Hail fell from the sky peppering Nolan with debris. He tucked his head close to his knees curling his pack into his chest. The gale of the firestorm threatened to wrench the makeshift shelter from his grasp. As the fire neared, the only thing denser than the heat was the blast of the gale. It sounded like being at the bottom of a waterfall.

Nolan writhed fighting to stay beneath the raging fire as it consumed the forest around him. "Mayday. Mayday. This is Hoke. I'm stuck in the storm. Does anybody read me?"

Another explosion. This time a tree cracked and fell to the ground shattering upon impact. Next time he would grab a hard hat.

Images of his father and mother, both deceased, crossed his mind. Would he see them soon? Would his lack of belief get him to where he would see his father or his mother again? He thought about Tom, another man of faith. Would he ever see Tom in the next life? His breathing became more rapid, forcing Nolan to fight for control of his rising panic. Desperately searching for air, he pushed his lungs to expand and exhale slowly.

3

After what felt like an eternity, the winds died. Nolan's shelter ceased its violent rippling. Cramping in his right knee caused him to wince in pain as he struggled to straighten the leg. His exasperated panting was the only sound. He threw back the film of the shelter gasping for better air. Trying to stand he was racked by a coughing fit as his lungs flooded with soot and smoke. Soaked with sweat, his clothes were filthy rags, but his head wound had ceased bleeding.

Taking in his surroundings, Nolan was grateful to be alive. Several trees lay on the ground or barely stood, their hull's broken. Everything in sight took on a charcoal color. The forest declared a scorched earth policy. Foliage crunched under his boots into black dust.

Still not raising anyone on the radio, he stowed it in his pack and plotted a course for higher ground while maintaining his distance from the direction in which the wind carried the firestorm. Smoke rose from the forest floor allowing heat to permeate his rubber soles.

He fought to keep his thoughts clear of Tom and Rowan. He did not remember the reporter's last name, but he figured he could contact CNN to inform them of her catastrophic death. Coming to terms with Tom's death would be much more difficult. Nolan knew his wife and daughters personally although he was not close to the family. He would tell them of Tom's uplifting presence whenever the large man was on duty.

Somehow try to explain Tom's decision to pitch into the forest nose down in an attempt to save Nolan's life. He would pay the respect he held for the man.

A clearing appeared in the distance through dense pines still standing downwind of the fires. It seemed the inferno was still having an indirect effect on them as the seasonal green points swayed, tinged with a deadening brown color. Perhaps it was just a sign of early winter.

Nolan was somewhat surprised when the clearing turned out to be a paved road. More surprising was the intense light and heat emitted from the hill above the road. While the forest was dark and grey, the slope was alight with flames glowing and flashing. The road seemed to serve as a defense, shielding Nolan from the cascading flames. The clearing allowed him to see the orange painted smoke rising high into the open sky washing out the sun.

The smoldering fire put on a harrowing display but he knew a hotshot crew could dig an entrenchment and begin setting the fire down. Undaunted he figured he could keep an eye on the hill while holding out that someone would be utilizing the road to penetrate the brush. He climbed higher, the brisk air refreshing his body and mind. Static emissions sent him tearing into his backpack.

"Hello! Hello. This is Nolan Hoke, smokejumper with the Cleveland Air Base. Is anybody there?"

The static haze remained until a muffled voice emerged.

"Is anybody there? I am smokejumper Nolan Hoke of Cleveland. I survived a helicopter crash that killed two others. Does anybody read me?" He gripped the transmitter, willing somebody to hear him.

First static then the muffled voice became more discernible. "...Operation Road's End... at Appian Way..."

None of this made any sense to Nolan. The gibberish message broadcasted on the emergency wavelength. If pranksters were holding down the channel during a nationwide state of emergency they could be held behind bars. Confusion clouded his judgment. Despite modern technology, he never carried a smartphone or device. The ancient flip phone he preferred to take vanished, another item lost in the crash.

"...President speaking... prepare... Appian Way."

The President? Could it be them on the channel? He could not make heads or tails of it. He did hear the crackling fire bed approaching, prompting him to pick up the pace.

After treading the fire for an hour or so, the road descended again alerting Nolan there would be little chance of picking up a signal. His brain churned over the meaning of the brief message. A faint buzzing sound broke him from his reverie. Lost in thought, he failed to notice the road opening into a large space complete with rusted vehicles and buildings roofed with sheet metal. Looking behind him, he saw a dense forest with the roughshod winding lane. To his right stood a lot decorated with abandoned vehicles. Organized by size the lot displayed weathered lawnmowers before a line of sedans. Behind the cars were a few vans with the large windows shattered and rotted pickups. Backed into the wood were three paled school buses. One was painted white with blue trim advertising a Pentecostal Church.

Looking at the dreary shops and rusted cars, the tune of Bob Dylan's *Ballad of Hollis Brown* played in his head. The buzzing grew louder through the opening in the trees, trees whose dull leaves matched the nature of the town. The place captured the heart of Appalachia.

Coming around the bend, the vibration he heard was an electric plant, fenced with barbed wire but still pumping watts of power. The tune in Nolan's head ceased. He became hyper-aware of his surroundings.

Something appeared wrong with the town. Despite the electric current the whole area seemed abandoned. Nolan wished he had more than a pocketknife for protection. If something or someone were to leap out at him, he was not sure he would even have the energy left to run for his life. For just a moment he hoped the town was as abandoned as it appeared.

Several buildings were boarded up, but pickups weighted down by toolboxes, compressors, generators and mud-terrain tires sat idle outside other shops where recent activity seemed to have taken place. At a crossroads stood a small gas station with a few vehicles parked outside. The area was a stone building topped with a red tin roof complete with four pumps. He figured the shack was as right a place as any to get information.

The doorbell jingled when he walked in breaking the silence of the town. Nothing moved, so Nolan sidled into the walkway. His nose was assaulted by the smell of Pine Sol overlapped with the sweet tinge of tobacco residue and more than a handful of mold. Lining the rest of the store was the typical shelves of snacks, motor oil, and souvenirs. Towards the wall stood iceboxes still humming with electricity.

Mountain Dew!

He greedily gulped down two ice-cold cans.

A click sounded somewhere behind him while he gorged on the caffeine. The click was not a single click, but a small series of light clicks followed by a louder locking mechanism. Growing up around guns and Hollywood movies, the sound was unmistakable. Somebody had a revolver trained on his back.

Nolan stood motionless save for his hand that gripped the now crushed aluminum can.

"You gonna pay for that sonny?"

Nolan turned. The man standing before him had leather skin and looked about as ancient as the rusted vehicles left vacant throughout the town. He dressed in a plaid flannel under a down vest with sturdy pants. The clothes were old as though he had worn the same garb for decades. Only the chrome-plated revolver in his weathered hand appeared to be in proper working condition. Lucky me, thought Nolan.

"Yes, sir. I have money. I'm sorry. I was so thirsty and in need of caffeine."

The senior man eyed Nolan, keeping him in limbo without replacing the hammer on the revolver. "Your uniform fits that of the Forest Service. You a fireman?"

Nolan eyed the pistol while answering. "Yes, sir. I'm a smokejumper. My friend flew a reporter covering the fire when we crashed."

The revolver did not move. "You crashed? What is the capital of Illinois?"

"What?" Nolan couldn't understand this guy. "Look I can pay for the drinks."

"Answer the question."

"Springfield."

"Where is the guard placed on a line of scrimmage?"

No pistol movement. Nolan had to play ball. "Between the center and tackle."

"Who is the present husband of Betty Grable?"

Now he knew the old man had to be crazy. He had no idea who Betty Grable was. "I have no idea. What is this? Where is everyone in this town?"

The old man scratched his white goatee with the empty hand. At last, he cocked the hammer and let it rest harmlessly against the barrel. Nolan tried to remain calm.

The man smiled. "You're too young to understand Betty Grable or even Rita Haworth for that matter. How old are you? Twenty-eight? Thirty?"

"Thereabouts. The name is Nolan Hoke. Like I said I'm a smokejumper with the Forest Service out of Cleveland. Where am I?"

"I don't see how it matters where you are," said the senior lowering the gun. "It's my town seeing as how I'm the last one left. Everyone else done flew the coop. I reckon you have something to do with that. Folks used to call me Cato when they were around. You say you fell out of a helicopter?"

"Yes, sir. The reporter fell out of the chopper. The pilot, well he died upon impact."

"Friend of yours you said."

"Yes, sir."

The man turned and motioned for Nolan to follow. The two sat across from one another at a built-in table in a row of built-in tables. The man crossed long, skinny legs before taking out a pocketknife. He tested the blade, cutting a few strands of hair on his arm. After a moment's silence, he nodded towards Nolan.

"It seems the world has done you a turn Fastball. Folks in this town all knew each other. A hard-working town where everyone took care of the other. There were some bloody fights, but then again you knew those folks too and kept your distance. This place," he said motioning all around him "was a bit of gathering joint. Kids come here for a bottle of Coke and whatnot. You can consider yourself a friend here. Feel free to take what you like."

Nolan figured this was as close to an apology he might get for having a gun pulled on him. Looking out the window he could see a storm front coming on, the clouds darkening and the wind whistling over the ground.

The old man, Cato, excused himself and returned a moment later with a steaming bowl of oatmeal and pushed it towards Nolan. Nolan's stomach churned at the smell of apples and cinnamon. Perhaps the extra stress of near-death added to one's appetite.

"My father was a veteran of the Pacific Theater," began Cato sitting once more across from Nolan while the firefighter wolfed down the oats. "People said they were the Greatest Generation, but my father came back all kinds of sideways. Had these horrible nightmares."

"When I was born, in 1951, I was just another mouth for the poor broken man to feed. We never had any money. I dropped out of school at thirteen going down into the mines of West Virginia as the model American flaunted their newfound wealth at the birth of consumerism. Big swooping cars with V8s, modern steel appliances, and competitive marketing urging Americans to buy what they did not have. Yes, sir, it was the American Dream. Even the outdoors was looking to be tamed which is how I ended up here in due time."

"The year was 1969. I was eighteen years old. It was a wonderful time to be eighteen. I left the mines and Vietnam War protests for the sanctity of the open road. I tramped rides from West Virginia to New York to San Francisco, listening to the Stones, *Gimme Shelter* seemed to sum up much of our fears back then, like the world was dying. I let my hair grow long and slept with women of all ages. I once met Douglas Thompkins at a climb near the El Cap."

Like the question about Betty Grable, Nolan didn't know who Douglas Thompkins was but decided to let it go. What he needed was to see if Cato had a serviceable phone.

"I returned to West Virginia in 1976 for my daddy's funeral. My brothers were there. My sister had married off in Canada vowing never to return. My daddy took his own life. The telegram from my sister simply read, 'At Last.' That peanut farmer from Georgia was president with America trying to grow up but making all the same mistakes in its two-hundredth anniversary. Hostages in Iran and this god-forsaken music called Disco. Then in 1980, the unexpected happened. I was in a honky-tonk when a couple of college boys beat the crap out of the Soviet Union in a game of hockey. It was the nearest thing I'd seen to anything good happening since I was born. Filled with a little hope and a lot of warm Jack I walked out of that bar and didn't stop walking 'til I got here."

Nolan couldn't believe it. "You walked here?"

"Yep. Just the clothes on my back and this here friend." Cato reached into his back pocket and pulled out a silver flask. He spun the container on the table with a familiar hand. There was etching on one side, but Nolan couldn't make sense of what the little words said. Cato popped the cork and flipped the flask over his mouth, taking a sip.

"All right Fastball," said Cato handing over the flask full of hooch. "Why don't you open up a little bit?"

Rain pelted the windows and pinged off the tin roof as if nails fell from the heavens. Thunder rumbled overhead long and slow like an oxen team pulling a laden cart over a cobblestone road. Growing up in the south, Nolan knew the weather would appear to be heinous but never did stick around for long. He was thankful for the rain. The heavens that held back for so long decisively opened up and stood a chance of aiding firefighters in giving the Appalachian region a reprieve from the forest fires.

After reminiscing with Cato, the business proprietor showed him into the Manager Closet to use the hardline. Trying several times without success Nolan gave up. Cato tossed him a woolen Anasazi blanket from a cot and said he was free to make a pallet on the floor.

"I'd offer you the cot," Cato said, "but I'm over seventy." Nolan smiled and gratefully took the blanket into the open floor.

Lying on the ground, Nolan began to think about Tom. He missed the big pilot with a bigger smile. The man was a rock and kept a positive attitude no matter the circumstances. Nolan figured he could use some of that optimism right now. He knew to be thankful. Here he lay, alive, fed and sheltered in the mountains as a stormy night continued beyond the walls.

He felt guilty too. Tears stung behind his eyes as he recollected seeing a crumpled picture held in place by the pilot's console before Tom's lifeless body. In the photograph was Tom with his wife and three young daughters. He curled further into the blanket trying to seek comfort.

"I'm alive," he cursed the still air. "I survived."

He tried to be more objective. He wondered if anyone in Cleveland or Asheville knew the helicopter and water tanker fell out of the sky. He wondered if Tom had time to radio a mayday or perhaps someone on the consumed C-130 had been able to. Maybe the firestorm was also responsible for scrambling radio signals making it impossible to communicate. He tried to put himself in either Cleveland or Asheville imagining the scene at headquarters. Perhaps someone at CNN in Atlanta realized the young Arab reporter had not checked in or reported for her afternoon spot while high in the sky.

Nolan felt the moonshine stirring in his head, the woolen blanket decompressing the stress of the day from his body. Blissfully, a drunken sleep overtook him. Nothing disturbed him, not even dreams.

The next morning, he awoke and slogged into the men's bathroom eying himself in the mirror for the first time since lifting off Cleveland Air Base. Grime saturated his jet-black hair and his face. Standing out the most were his eyes. Deep brown irises swam in a pool of opaque yellow, the blood vessels more prominent. He recognized the oxygen-depleted look of victims that had succumbed to too much smoke. Rubbing his eyes, he blindly turned on the shuddering faucet and splashed his face with cold water.

Emerging from the bathroom, he slipped on fresh wool socks and his leather boots. They were his favorite pair, all brown with mesh for breathability. He added red laces emulating Robert Redford's character in the movie *Up Close and Personal*. The figure wore the boots on dangerous assignments. Something Nolan identified with.

Cato stood behind the counter packing an external frame pack with snacks and coffee powder. "Morning Fastball. I already packed a duffel and laid it next to your pack. Left you a few Mountain Dews as well."

"What's going on?"

"I've got a niece in Knoxville, or so I'm told. She may be the last family member I got left. I understand you have a base or something to return to. You are welcome to any car in the parking lot."

"Okay."

Cato stopped packing his duffel and came out from behind the counter. The old man extended a hand Nolan's way. "Say," said Nolan. "Why do you call me Fastball?"

The old man grinned, his white whiskers expanding to reveal a toothy smile. "Don't tell me you ain't never heard of Nolan Ryan, the Ryan Express?"

"Of course. I would know of Nolan Ryan, even if we were raised on the St. Louis Cardinals. I didn't take you for a baseball fan."

"Hey," said Cato spreading his arms, "It's America's past time. If there is one thing I know a lot about, it is passing the time." The old man pressed his hand into Nolan's with a firm shake. With his other hand, he gave Nolan a steaming cup of coffee. "This will get the blood flowing."

The old man eyed Nolan. "You've got a new lease on life son and in so doing you have given me one as well. Now I never was religious. The way I figure, if God were a Father like the father I knew of then His children would have already left Him. But I do hope you can move forward. Life is a hard but precious thing."

Nolan stood still, struck as if by brick upon hearing his father's own words muttered by a man who was a complete stranger not more than twenty-four hours ago. He absent-mindedly shook Cato's hand. The old man smiled and nodded before heading out the door. He heard the engine turn over and the tires grind on the gravel parking lot before Cato motored away.

Working in a daze, or perhaps a hangover, Nolan grabbed his Epperson pack and the brown duffel and walked into the morning light. Parked outside was a rusted Chevy pickup that would forever embody the unknown town. The other vehicle took him by surprise. A brand-new hybrid.

Realizing he left the keys to any transportation hanging back inside the gas station he dropped the bags and began searching for a key rack. He knew he would never consider the Chevy truck. No Ford person would be caught dead behind the wheel of a General Motors product. The hybrid would be bad enough, but without knowing where in the world he was, he figured gas mileage would be a premium. That triggered another thought. He grabbed a road map from the spinning wire display before reaching for the door. The last thing he saw in the dark gas station was the wall clock. The analog clock read 8:15. Nolan kicked the door open with his toe and stepped out. He didn't realize the clock ceased moving since the day before.

Outside the sky was a particular myriad of colors. The sun rose in the east sending a burst of color over a field of dandelions. Yellows, oranges, and reds mixed with brown hills and fall leaves. To the west, banked at the shores of majestic purple mountains were the remnants of the waning storm. The dark cumulonimbus clouds contrasted the bright sunrise with such intensity they appeared as two great beings waging an empyrean war. Flashes of lightning burst out of the shadows striking against the bright beams of light emitted from Helios' chariot.

Throwing the two bags into the rear seat he nearly slammed the door shut when he caught movement across the empty road. He had seen a flash and then nothing.

The hairs on the back of his neck stood on end. He could feel eyes watching him. Becoming unnerved, he edged beyond the hood of the car to get a better look.

Leaping into the road, a great cat emerged from the thicket. She prowled down the middle of the open tarmac. Her sleek, muscled coat shimmered gold in the morning light. The puma eyed Nolan, as he remained frozen not just in fear but curiosity as well. The cat's eyes burned hazel with flecks of amber. The longer the two stood before each other, the less Nolan felt afraid.

Too soon the panther dropped her head and padded away. He watched her disappear into the distance wishing he could have remained frozen in that moment forever.

Considered two hundred million years old, millennia of erosion, climate change, and flooding of biblical proportions rendered the sloping Appalachian Mountains into some of the most beloved country he had ever seen. Rain once again tapped on the windshield as he sped his way south to connect with I-40 East.

Thunder rumbled as the rain fell in sheets pounding the glass and obscuring the road. Despite being tuned to an emergency channel, the car's radio remained silent. Crossing the state border into North Carolina, the sun shone through a cloudy sky gleaming off the wet glass to give Nolan the sense of being in a heavenly place. Everything sparkled and shined.

His mind drifted amidst the beauty. He remembered being afraid of storms as a child, leaping out of bed and skirting to his parent's room without ever touching the floor. One day, when still a boy, he and his father were riding in the Bronco when he asked what made storms so terrifying.

Pierce Hoke smiled to himself and said, "I often rejoice in the storms and the rain."

Young Nolan sat bewildered. Pierce's smile never wavered as he flicked on the radio. Turning the volume dial louder, the boy recognized the heavy guitar riffs and pounding drums of the hit song *Everlong* by the Foo Fighters. The music blared loud enough to rattle the windows of the steel 4x4. He clapped enthusiastically and drummed the dash. When the song ended, his father dialed back the radio as a new song began.

"You see, you and I like to play the music loud right," asked his father.

The boy nodded.

"The way I see it, storms are awesome. Thunder, lightning, rain, it's all pretty exciting like God's hard rock."

The boy sat back trying to imagine liking a massive thunderstorm.

"Your grandfather used to count on the rain back when he was your age. He was the only son on his daddy's cotton farm. They needed the rain to make the crop grow, but it took hard work. They had to harvest all the cotton before the rains came. The cotton would get wet, and everyone would have to wait for the sun to dry it up."

"I would work hard if I lived on a cotton farm," piped up Nolan.

His father chuckled. "I know, son. I remember as a boy sitting on dad's porch listening to Paul Eels call the Razorback games. We'd go out there and listen to the rain bounce off the tin roof and sometimes when it was cooler we'd sleep out there. There is no better sleeping than during a rain shower."

Nolan saw his father's face looking back at him through the rearview mirror. Though still younger than his father had been at his premature death the characteristics were visible. Nolan had Pierce's black hair and brown eyes shaped like those of a cat. The pointed nose, sharp features, and darker complexion resembled his father who contrasted immensely from his Nordic mother.

Dusk fell over Smoky Mountain National Forest bathing the fall leaves in a glimmer of golden light followed by deep oranges and a blood red. Nolan had chosen well as the hybrid registered more than enough gas to reach his destination. Rather than return to base in Cleveland, he felt it prudent to contact Asheville as directed by the original flight plan. Somebody there may have been expecting the reporter and her entourage and would have some answers as to why there was no communication since the crash. He also wondered how in the world two aircraft, both the helicopter and the water tanker, were downed by the firestorm.

The cold air outside brought with the night prompted him to turn on the cars climate control as he rubbed his hands on his knees in anticipation of reaching civilization. He had not seen a soul since departing from Cato.

4

Flying thirty thousand feet above ground, Captain Yuri Orlov sat with his eyes closed to ignore the whine of the plane's massive engines. Someone nudged him with their boot. Annoyed, Yuri looked across the aircraft at the painted faces of his men. They each stared back at him stone-faced. Solemn and ruthless, his men embodied the Siberian taiga for which their homeland was infamous.

Dressed in full Kevlar battle gear, Yuri was the consummate warrior. Named for the fabled knight Saint George, legend had it he saved a king's daughter from being sacrificed to a menacing dragon and baptized the entire kingdom. Yuri followed more in his father's military footsteps preferring a baptism by fire.

A graduate of the demanding Khabarovsk Commanders Training Academy, he excelled in leadership, physical training, and tactical awareness. Afterward, he received Special Forces training and given a commission in the 14th Brigade of the Eastern Military District. Two years in Spetsnaz, Yuri was awarded the coveted Maroon Beret by competing against fellow soldiers to determine who excelled at the highest level. Soldiers fought in a variety of tests to evaluate their resiliency and competency even under extreme mental and physical duress.

Sitting across from Captain Orlov in the Ilyushin Midas was his younger, but much larger, brother Bogdan. The men called Bogdan "the Bear" for his imposing stature and preference towards hand-to-hand combat. The Bear was an expert in both the Israeli Krav Maga art and Samba developed by Cossacks in the tenth century. Samba influenced a punishing form of combat known as *Systema Spetsnaz*.

Bogdan's hulking frame coupled well with his full, jet-black beard kept under a bronzed but bald dome.

Next to the giant was the squad's designated sniper, Immanuil Popov. Like Yuri, Immanuil bore a more religious name denoting the bygone wishes of a peaceful mother. He never developed the habit of a pious Orthodox priest. The tall, thin youth proved much more adept at taking lives than saving them. He honed his art of marksmanship hunting elk and black bear along the shores of Lake Baikal, the oldest, deepest freshwater lake in the world. Yuri often reflected that some of the lake's purity had embedded itself in Immanuil's spirit for he loved the boy the most. He doted on the young soldier much more than he did his actual brother. He knew Bogdan didn't mind; the whole squad was protective of Immanuil.

Last on the bench opposite Yuri sat the team's point man, Anton Kozlov. The five-foot ten sinewy sleuth was a remarkable athlete. A former cross-country skier, fierce and fearless, Anton made the perfect addition rounding out the shock troopers.

He looked at the dossiers in his lap given to him by a man at a desk in Dyagilevo. Inside the top-secret folders were details of the Carthaginian Solution: Russia's colossal attempt to overwhelm American defenses by air, land, and sea.

Operation Mercury. The least extensive of a three-pronged battlefront, Operation Mercury referred to Russia's naval blockade and overwatch of critical ocean routes to cut off American shorelines from future allied support. Maintaining the element of surprise, Russian submarines dared not venture beyond the Arctic Circle or the eastern Pacific Rim to curtail any Japanese vessels. These warships would encroach upon American shores once the nation appeared subdued. Russia's intervention in North Korea and China's increased activity in the

South China Sea further allowed both the Japanese Fleet and American 3rd and 7th Fleets to remain on full alert but with their attention diverted. Over sixty-percent of American military assets were thwarted. If Yuri's father had still been alive, the former Soviet Naval Officer would have loved to see the American Navy circumvented by such byzantine maneuvers it so masterfully employed during the Cold War.

The second dossier applied to him. At least for the time being.

Operation Gomorrah referenced Russia's colossal air raid attempt. Commencing from ports like Vladivostok, Magadan, Ust-Kamchatsk, and Anadyr, Russian aircraft carriers transported short and long-range aircraft like the Midas he rode in to bombard American airspace. To win this new war, the Kremlin employed Machiavelli's tactics that injury must be done and ought to be of such a kind that the offender does not stand in fear of revenge. The attack would make Pearl Harbor look like a turkey shoot.

Every pilot knew it was a suicide mission. The Americans were put on high alert and scrambled thousands of jets to protect their airspace. The American fighter pilots were slaughtered. Yuri knew it was the slow knife that penetrates the deepest. After years of Russian flybys, the Americans fell into a stupor. American reaction time had been adequate but being adequate and being prepared were two different things.

As he watched the painted deserts turn into grasslands and later into forests, he knew with greater certainty that America's defenses had acted too late. Los Angeles, San Francisco, Salt Lake City, Denver. All gone within the first few hours of the attack.

After the firebombing ended, Operation Cannae would commence resulting in the seizure of vital American infrastructure. Given America's vast resources, the Kremlin deemed that the nation not suffer destruction but instead looted and pillaged. With such endless depths of oil and natural gas between the two lands, Russia could render the Middle East obsolete, undercutting their temporary Iranian allies. That kind of power could hold the world hostage ensuring profits for the next millennia. In the meantime, Russia's dealings with Turkey, Iran, and Syria allowed the coalition to detain both American 5th and 6th Fleets in the Mediterranean and Red Seas respectively.

A soft red hue doused the cargo bay extinguishing Yuri's reading light. The gears of the bay door began rotating, cold air rushing in making both Immanuil and Anton shiver. Five minutes to drop.

The pilot could not allow the aircraft to slow down for long allowing it to be picked up on radar and blown out of the sky by remaining American defenses before completing its objective. All that was needed was a lucky strike, and the entire mission of securing the Eastern seaboard would be over.

Yuri and his men would be jumping from thirty thousand feet in a high-altitude, low opening drop, better known as a HALO jump. The target lay sprawled in the forested mountains of Oak Ridge, Tennessee. The site was chosen during World War II by General Leslie Groves as a classified facility for atomic bomb research. Only illiterates were allowed to collect the trash and could not have a funeral home due to the absolute secrecy of the experiment. Tucked away in the mountains of eastern Tennessee, Yuri and his precision jumpers were to descend on the quiet town and secure the facility as part of a valued target under Operation Cannae codenamed Operation Harborage.

In a post-nuclear Russia, the ability to prevent an American counterstrike was critical to ensuring victory. Everything had led up to this Yuri knew as he tucked his briefings into his Kevlar jumpsuit. The flybys, the aggression in Europe, the dealings with Iran and the capitulation of most of the Western world to surrender their nuclear arsenals, all had been part of a grand scheme by President Vasilyev to make a decisive stroke in the quest for world domination. Just as the world watched Hitler through the process of appeasement, just as American Congressmen paid off the Barbary Pirates or Roman Senators paid tribute to Carthage, the whole world was responsible for allowing the Russian Federation get this far. He couldn't help but smile. Now came the hammer, shrouded behind a veil of peace.

The other soldiers affixed their breathing apparatuses to their helmets and inspected one another's gear for the high-altitude jump. Each man would leap into thin air with over sixty pounds. Starting with the headgear, they equipped themselves with NVGs, a Skull communications device, body armor, a parachute and a reserve chute. Of course, being Spetsnaz, each soldier carried an array of weapons.

Minding his step, Yuri approached the mouth of the Midas tanker feeling the pull of the outside air urging him to slip over the edge. Night had fallen during the flight prompting him to lower the NVGs but it was impossible to see through the cloud cover below. Included in each man's equipment was a canister of red dye that would emit a trail allowing each member to perceive one another in the vague conditions over the course of the jump.

Turning to face his men, he first caught the eyes of his shadow, Anton. Yuri knew the daredevil would open his chute last. It was natural for the point man to be the first on the ground. Immanuil would jump last allowing the aircraft to float above more of the denser forest before leaping to the earth. Equipped for long-range reconnaissance, the young sniper would provide cover and relate enemy positions from his hide while the team infiltrated the facility. He nodded in silence to the group and each soldier raised a fist. They were ready.

Captain Yuri Orlov turned once more to face the swirling dark abyss below.

5

Diving was the moment he loved the most in the entire world. All anyone who ever jumped out of a perfectly good airplane could hear was the rush of the wind, the roar. Yuri heard nothing. He cultivated the complete silence over more than twenty-five years as a Spetsnaz operative jumping into hot zones worldwide.

Enveloped in the silence and darkness, he never felt freer. His childhood with an abusive father and a broken mother ceased to be a part of his past. Intense physical and mental demands of life in the military fell away. After a lifetime of war, Yuri wondered if moments like these were the closest he would ever come to having peace.

Below, he could just make out the red mist floating through the clouds denoting Anton's location. The fearless athlete looked like a specter hovering above its prey.

Breaking cloud cover and dipping into a cobalt sky, Yuri dove into the formation to join Anton and Bogdan as they descended upon Oak Ridge. Built on a college campus blueprint, the facility snaked through the dense forest helping to prevent unwanted eyes from getting too close to the sensitive area.

While Russian cyberattacks knocked out all but the lowest wave communications throughout the United States, Yuri knew American soldiers would be on the highest alert after going full dark.

After deploying his chute, Yuri shouldered his silenced Kalashnikov and peered through the enhanced infrared optics to take out any sentries on the perimeter.

The small Spetsnaz squad landed without incident in the tall pines triangulating their position around a Quonset hut. Smoke cover had long since dissipated. Each Russian operative stowed their dark chutes. Yuri approached the hut reaching the south side just as Anton and Bogdan reached the north and east ends respectively.

Yuri's men tossed gas grenades through the air ventilation. When two guards emerged, coughing and covering their mouths they were strafed at once with suppressed weapons fire to their backs. Bogdan and Anton slung both soldiers back into the hut. Now instead of wishing for silence, Yuri strained his ears listening for any sign of detection.

"GRU was right about one thing," whispered Anton using the Skull communicator attached to his neck, "our approach was not all that difficult." Bogdan swore in agreement prompting a shove from Yuri. GRU stood for Russian Military Intelligence and employed more spies abroad than any other national spy agency. Their word was bond. Their word was ruthless.

"The wildfires raging in this part of the nation are working in our favor to reduce the population but do not bed Mother Nature for she is a fickle mistress," said the Captain. "Immanuil, check in."

Immanuil tapped his bone mike twice to signal his preparation was complete.

Yuri turned to the two before him pointing to the two dead guards bleeding on the floor. "Be on watch. This facility will not fall as easily into our hands." Both men nodded and readied their weapons. Bogdan carried the larger Ustinov Personnel Gunner while Anton led the way with his subcompact of the same make while Yuri raised the gate.

Bogdan cursed under his breath sweeping for American soldiers. "We should have taken this place with a full airborne division. They could be anywhere."

As if on cue two American soldiers emerged around a building. The look of shock barely registered before they too were cut down. Silenced weapons are discreet but not silent. The Russian warriors double-timed to the next building. Moving from laboratory to laboratory, they placed remote charges on each structure before they reached their objective: Experimental Materials Lab.

In the far distance, Immanuil's long-range rifle cracked to life. He carried his favorite hunting rifle, a Steyr SM12 and Swarovski X5 Scope. "The Marines must be zeroing on our location," said Yuri as they approached the coded entrance. "Setting the charges to fifteen minutes."

Anton began cracking the door safe as Bogdan swept the perimeter with his powerful machine gun. When the door buzzed open, Anton wasted no time plunging inside, neutralizing three guards.

"Eleven minutes," said Yuri donning his NVGs as Anton cut the power to the facility.

Dozens of men and women dressed in white lab coats ran in a frenzy. Several died in the crossfire between Yuri and his men combatting Marine guards. Somewhere an alarm was tripped, the repeating klaxon adding to the chaos and distress. Papers littered the floor, many splotched with blood.

Never stopping, Yuri, Bogdan, and Anton cleared room after room. There was no time to waste. Upon reaching the control room, the trio relaxed their pace. Inside, the room locked on closed-circuit CPUs, was information on America's nuclear arsenal. While the data itself was impossible to crack into, Yuri wasn't interested in deciphering. The only purpose necessary was destruction.

Yuri nodded to Anton who began spraying explosive gelatin over the door. Despite still wearing helmets and NVGs, each man knew the other's stature and mannerisms. Trained elite warriors whose practiced maneuvers took little thinking.

Bogdan fired once more, a deafening array of power as more American soldiers slumped in a lifeless heap. Anton lit the fuse and ducked around the corner. A thudded boom signified the blown door. "Five minutes," said Yuri.

Without breaking stride, Bogdan popped three incendiary grenades into the room. A hiss. A pop. An explosion. "Objective complete. Topside now." Anton led the way with his subcompact. Speed was of the essence now as the remote charges ticked away to imminent demolition.

Rounding the last corner, Yuri threw off his goggles and could see the light beneath the door. A loud blast assaulted his ears as flashes of gunfire erupted. Anton fell back, his chest peppered with rounds from the enemy's assault. Yuri had no time to bring his weapon to bear. Two more American soldiers emerged from the darkness.

"Put your weapons down," shouted one soldier.

Yuri threw down his assault rifle, but the American's head snapped at an awkward angle. In a flash, Yuri wondered if Immanuil had shot him but dismissed the thought. They were still indoors.

Caught by surprise, the other two Americans spun on their heels, dropping like sacks of potatoes, one after the other.

Blinding light emitted with the klaxon reflected off a white lab coat. Striding with confidence, pistol in hand, was a tall blonde woman. Yuri reached for his weapon, but a shot at his feet waved him off. Confusion reigned inside Yuri's mind. His temper was building and his internal clock screamed that time was up.

When the female assailant got close enough, he could make out a smile on her face. "*Zdravstvuyte*," she said addressing the men in Russian. "My name is Cicero. You will take me to Commander Yaromir."

Yuri had no idea who Cicero was, why she spoke to them in Russian or what she was doing in the Oak Ridge Experimental Materials Lab.

"Yuri," hastened Bogdan. "There's no time."

The woman lowered her handgun prompting Yuri to take her by the arm. Bogdan threw an unconscious but alive Anton over his shoulder as Yuri kicked the door open.

Using his NVGs, Yuri's eyes settled on the slow but robust M939 Personnel Carrier. Squeezing into the cab, he started the big rig and hammered the accelerator. The engine lurched, pouring black exhaust into the night sky, as they roared down the pavement looking for an exit. Small arms fire ricocheted off the armor-plated truck and cracked off the thick-paned glass.

"Yuri, watch out!" Bogdan pounded the dash in panic as two Marines entered the road; one sighting a Javelin missile system while the other loaded the grenade. The lightweight weapon would turn them into scrap.

He didn't hear the crack of rifle fire, but he did see the missile operator slump forward as if shoved from behind by his partner. The soldier's partner soon followed him into the pavement.

Immanuil. The young sniper played the role of guardian angel well. Bogdan let out a whoop as the five-ton behemoth crashed through the security fence. As soon as the giant truck gashed through the obstacle, they spotted a red flare.

"We've got wounded," said Yuri into the bone mike.

"I've secured a helicopter," came Immanuil's response.

With no time to lose, Yuri swung near the landing pad. Disembarking from the truck, Yuri set a grenade with the pin removed under the seat. Any shift would cause the mechanism to spring and the shell to explode. Bogdan once again hefted Anton while Immanuil brought a stretcher to meet him. Anton was the team's best driver and pilot, but Immanuil would have to do. Bogdan tended to a still unconscious Anton pulling apart the body armor and assessing the warrior's damage.

"He's still breathing. He'll pull through. I would suggest painkillers for the next month. Probably has crushed ribs." Yuri hated being callous in regards to one of his men, but Bogdan would have to save it. "*Da*. Immanuil, you've got to get us in the air."

The sniper responded by hastily flicking switches and pulling back on the reticle while the blades lifted the bird off the ground. No sooner had they gained flight that the nuclear weapons facility, begun in the latter days of World War II, burst into flames.

Now, assured of their relative safety, Yuri popped a Camel from the cigarette pack stowed in his breast pocket. Accustomed to the flurry aboard a helicopter, he put a protective hand over the flame of the lighter and flicked it shut. Sitting back and taking a long pull he eyed the tall but slim woman who had gotten the drop on the Marine guard and saved their lives.

Despite having no armor save for her lab coat flapping in the wind, a woman, three decades his junior, appeared to be neither apprehensive nor afraid. A professional. She was used to such situations as this.

"So," he said in Russian, "You appear to me to be a spy."

No response. No bat of the eyes, no widening of the irises.

He took another pull. "Tell me, what is your name?"

6

Amidst dark skies and sprinkling rain, Nolan pulled into Asheville, too dark to make out much of the damage caused by the Fire Belt. He saw no vehicles entering or exiting the city but followed the city's lights from many miles out. He knew from charts adorning the walls at Cleveland Air Base that a good portion of the town sustained damage. The governor of North Carolina and the mayor of Asheville had each called for states of emergency. They also had to get in line.

Upon reaching the French Broad River, his lights shone on a few faces. Those faces looked back at him in a mixed manner of curiosity and apprehension. Nolan coasted, circling a logjam of debris. A lumberjack looking man stood in the middle of the bridge holding a full palm in the air for him to stop.

Nolan put the hybrid in park and opened the door to get out. The lone sounds on the bridge were the wind and rain. Due to arrive in the city the day before, he couldn't help but think that something enormous had taken place. The manner of the city folk made his hair stand on end, evidenced by the large man bearing down him.

The lumberjack looked the part. Woolen long sleeve shirt, durable tin cloth pants, and sturdy boots. His beard reached a broad chest, and one forearm bore the tattoo of military insignia that Nolan did not recognize.

"Delta," said the lumberjack. His dark eyes remained unseen but evidently took note of Nolan's assessing gaze. "What's your name friend?"

The man offered no hand but stood to wait for an explanation.

"My name's Nolan Hoke. I'm a firefighter, a smokejumper."

"Impressive." The Delta warrior crossed his arms. Behind him, other men of similar build began to assemble forming a V-shape behind their leader. The wind blew a chill through Nolan. None of the others appeared affected. The Appalachian hills were their home turf.

Nolan's single thought was that he had made a mistake. He should have gone back to Cleveland and reported everything to the base.

"You have a unit," asked Delta.

Nolan nodded before answering. "I was due here yesterday via helicopter with a reporter wanting to cover the damage to your city. We flew out of nearby Tennessee but crashed. The crash killed the pilot and reporter."

"That is to say your bird fell out of the sky."

Nolan nodded. The wind blew hard again, its strength invisible in the dark, bringing an icy sting of rain from the mountaintops.

The thickset Delta warrior threw a bearded chin over his left shoulder. "Titus was with Force Recon in Aleppo. Lots of birds went down."

"Oorah," said Titus, a younger man with straw-colored hair. Nolan could see baby blue eyes reflected by the hybrid's lights. The man wore a blue t-shirt with a white skull emblazoned over the heart and the words Swift, Silent, Deadly italicized across the shoulder.

Delta took a few steps towards Nolan dropping his arms but keeping them loose. Nolan had no doubt those arms could strangle him in seconds. "Your accent is right, but you ain't hill folk," said the soldier.

"I'm originally from Arkansas. My father fought fire before a fire killed him. I guess being this close to it gets me closer to him."

"Good." The large soldier stepped closer this time extending a rough hand. "The name's Tiberius. Titus and these here boys are some of my kinfolks. We're not related exactly, but you might know what I mean." Tiberius assessed Nolan, still holding his hand in a crushing shake. "Then again you don't stand like military."

"No, sir. Just a dude who fights fires."

"You need to be at the hospital. Grab your gear; I'll take you."

Nolan saddled up with Tiberius and his men inside the soldier's blacked-out Ram 2500. Titus slid in the back next to Nolan, his mouth smacking on chewing gum. Another former soldier who appeared to be of Hispanic descent took shotgun. He couldn't help but notice the man firmly plant a Benelli 12guage between his feet.

Everything about Tiberius, his friends, and his truck screamed *Don't Tread on Me*. These men were elite warriors; the last thing Nolan wanted to do was be on their wrong side. He had no idea why they deemed it necessary to ditch his car and go to the hospital, but he was in little position to negotiate. They drove past City Hall, the unique Art Deco building that reminded Nolan a bit of Batman. He absent-mindedly scanned the skies for the Caped Crusader.

"Do any of you guys have a cell phone," ventured Nolan. "I haven't been able to reach anybody since the crash."

"Negative, we have been in the dark since 0800," answered Titus still keeping his blues on the road.

"Why do you think we were watching the bridge," piped up Tiberius from the seat in front of Nolan. "We've been awaiting the government or someone to show up with answers."

"And?"

"So far nothing but you."

Nolan sat back in his chair. In his head were more questions than ever.

Soon the lights of Asheville Mission Hospital greeted the approaching Ram as Tiberius pulled into the ER Entrance.

"This is your stop."

Nolan opened his door and leaped onto the pavement. Titus tossed him his Epperson pack and the brown duffel. Tiberius leaned out the window, his black eyes seeming to absorb all light. Nolan noticed for the first time how unusually large they were. "You will find your fallen brothers in there," continued the former soldier. "If the need arises you will find friends on the outside as well."

"How will I find you?"

The large man smiled. "Don't worry, we'll find you."

Inside the hospital was pure bedlam. Nurses carried patients, supplies, and papers in every direction. The other thing Nolan noticed confirmed Tiberius' words. His brothers were here. Most of the patients waiting to be seen or being ushered by a nurse bore some form of firefighting crest. Ladder crews, hotshots, and smokejumpers were each labeled by t-shirts, coats or helmets.

He saw a pretty nurse with soft brown hair struggling under the weight of an overweight man holding a bandage to his face and cringing in pain. Nolan scanned the room for a free gurney. None were in sight. He hustled to the nurse and her quarry gingerly placing his head under the man's armpit and supporting the lower back much like locking down a rugby scrum.

"I love you," breathed the nurse, relieved to have assistance with the heavyset patient. Despite the seriousness of the moment Nolan couldn't help but smile. Compared to meeting Tiberius and his boys Nolan was pretty sure she had rescued him.

Swinging into an open room, Nolan helped lay the patient on a clean bed. The nurse busied herself checking vital signs and writing them down on a clipboard. As soon as she pulled back on the bandage covering the man's face, he howled and cursed, throwing his arms and nearly knocking the woman into a beeping machine. Nolan reacted fast, seizing the man's meaty arms and holding them down to his sides lying over the man's body to keep him from reaching out again.

The nurse took a deep breath, collecting herself. "You good," she asked without looking at Nolan.

"Yeah. You?"

"Yeah."

Peeling back the gauze once more the man winced forcing Nolan to strain to keep his bonds. She wrote down more notes. He watched as she fed the burned man morphine through an IV. Shouting from the hallway distracted Nolan as he lifted his arms from the doped firefighter. Moving to the doorway, he saw a frenzied man with small eyes dressing down a petite nurse.

"I don't give two horse craps what standard procedure is," yelled the old chief. "This hospital is bleeding life as badly as my men. I need a sterilized room now!"

Nolan now saw a woman with the look of a professional brazenly approach the chief from behind and tap him on the shoulder. The boss whirled on one foot, but the woman stood her ground. She was tall with short dark hair and perfect nails. Nolan took her for a lawyer or business proprietor.

Rather than addressing the irate old man, she first gave a consoling look to the petrified nurse. "Jane that will be fine. Why don't you go check for an empty bed in there?" The polished woman pointed over Nolan's shoulder. She gave him a surprised look as he stood in the doorway but recovered quickly turning on the fire chief. This time it was he who turned mum.

"Chief Seneca," continued the woman. She commanded all attention as if all the chaos ground to a halt. "Asheville Mission Hospital is the last remaining hospital capable of the kind of care your men need. Most of the staff and other patients have been evacuated further west away from their families, homes, and personal caregivers. I strongly suggest you let my professionals work or you will cease to be one."

The small fire chief swallowed hard. Nolan watched him blink and close his eyes. Then he walked away. The roar of the hospital resurged as staffers and patients resumed their business.

"You." The stern woman pointed at Nolan, still standing in the doorway. "Come with me." Nolan gave a pleading look to the pretty nurse he assisted. She merely shrugged.

So much for the love, he thought.

Nolan followed the well-dressed woman back out the lobby and into the street, her heels clicking on the pavement. He welcomed the late autumn peace as few cars went by while the two stood outside the large hospital.

"Tiberius sent me after you. Said he caught a hog, whatever that means." The woman smiled to herself. Nolan didn't respond so she stuck out her hand. "My name is Sheila Townsend. I am the Mayor of Asheville."

The pair walked into the parking lot. The temperature dropped considerably, and the woman breathed warm air into her cupped hands before speaking. "I understand you're a fireman. There's a friend of mine that teaches at the university whose home has taken a lot of damage. Do you think you could help him clear some debris? It would be a personal favor to me." She gave a big smile. Despite her age, the woman was quite attractive. "I never forget a friend."

Nolan laughed. "Save it. I'd be glad to help, but you've gotta explain to Tiberius why I'm not at the hospital."

Shelia patted Nolan on the shoulder. "Don't you worry. I've been handling the likes of Tiberius for a long time." Her face took on a severe look that Nolan thought looked a little like longing.

Mayor Townsend led Nolan to her vehicle. He couldn't help but double-take at her choice of transportation.

"Surprised," she teased, hopping into the open driver side. She put on a full parka to fight the bitter wind.

"A little," said Nolan throwing his pack through the open cab and climbing into the opposite seat. The duffel he decided to leave to those in greater need at the hospital. Shelia put the old Jeep into gear and backed out of the parking lot.

"I'm a Democrat. This old Jeep helps with some of the last remaining vestiges of red bloods in our progressive town." She gave a wink and rocketed the war wagon onto the street dodging traffic barricades and emergency vehicles. "We vacated most of the city due to the fires and extended the students fall break. It has cost us a ton of business revenue not to mention many families will return to burned out lots instead of homes."

Nolan sat back in the seat. The cold night air stung as the mayor accelerated. "I can't help but think you and Tiberius have history," he said over the hum of the engine.

Sheila briefly took her eyes off the road to look at the smokejumper. "We were sweethearts in college. I wanted to get married; he wanted to be a Green Beret. I didn't see him or talk to him for years after that. Occasionally I would get a letter from Germany or Japan. They were always months out of date. He never talked about himself, just asked about me. I was in grad school, and I too had left North Carolina."

"Where did you go?"

"Berkeley. I got as far away from here as possible. After that I had nowhere else to go, so I came back, ready to change everything." She laughed and tightened her grip on the wheel. "It was another decade later when one day I saw him in the grocery store. He told me he was at Bragg, training jumpers. He made full captain, a hometown hero."

"How did he get back to Asheville?"

Sheila wiped a tear from her eye. "My momma told me he blew his knees while leading some rookies. The Army suggested he retire, so he returned home and visited the VA. Many of the older folks still remember us together, but it's been over twenty years."

"I'm sorry."

Sheila patted his knee with a long slender hand. It was a mother's touch, but Mayor Townsend was striking enough for Nolan to regret not having showered in a few days. If not for the fresh air he knew the cabin would be quite malodorous.

The Jeep ground to a halt. Nolan caught the smoky aroma of burning wood and took a deep breath. The fire blackened many brick buildings and shattered most of the windows.

A man dressed in blue jeans and leather jacket carrying a Filson briefcase exited the building and made his way over. "I thought I recognized your Jeep Ms. Mayor," said the man. Nolan noticed that he was much older up close than he appeared from further away. He took the man to be in his eighties, but he still stood average height with a full head of red hair and intelligent blue eyes.

"Yes, professor, I want you to meet a new friend of mine," said the mayor. The man looked into the Jeep and took Nolan in.

"Student?"

"No, he's a firefighter. Ty found him. I kinda like him so I was hoping he could stay at your place."

The man nodded. "Yeah, fine by me. You say he was found by Tiberius huh?" The man looked at Nolan. "I see you faired alright. Come on. I'm just grabbing a few boxes from my office before they demolish the place."

Nolan looked to Mayor Townsend. "I leave you in good hands," she said with a smile. He stepped out of the Jeep, grabbed his pack and began following the professor into the hall. "Rachel is a fine nurse," called the mayor. Nolan turned. Even in the night, he could make out her flashing white smile.

He didn't have time to think about what the mayor meant before running to catch up with the professor. The entire building brought back scents that were all too familiar to a fireman like Nolan. They wove their way through boxes, swivel chairs, and filing cabinets.

"The sprinkler system ruined much more than the fire seemed to," complained the professor. "I hired several grad students to blow dry my books and manuscripts."

"Anything I can do," asked Nolan.

"Oh, just help me carry a final box or two but what I would love is some help tomorrow taking down some trees. They fell over and caught my shed on fire. After that, of course, the mower caught fire and the old gardening magazines. You get the idea. You help me do that I will provide you with three hots and a cot. Sound good?"

"Sounds good if you ask me."

The professor extended his hand; the shake was firm. "They call me Gruff."

"Nolan Hoke, nice to meet you."

"Nice to meet you."

Grabbing a box each from Gruff's office, they made for the professors loaded down Land Cruiser. "An 80 series," said Nolan admiring the off-road rig, "very cool."

"Nobody makes them like they used to. Let's get you cleaned up before we grab a bite to eat."

After a shower and a fresh set of clothes, Nolan felt much better. Surprisingly the professor wore close to the same size clothing. He threw on a pair of jeans, a flannel-patterned shirt under a waxed canvas jacket and a spare ball cap. Nolan kept to his hazard-proof boots. While waiting for the professor, he strolled the parlor taking in the collection of manuscripts and tomes. Volumes written in Latin, Greek, Hebrew, and Arabic, filled the shelves. He made out the names of Livy, Silenus, Josephus, and Tacitus. He reached for a prominently displayed piece titled *L'Africa* from off the walnut bookcase.

"He didn't win because he could not get the rest of the Republic to fight with him," said the professor from the kitchen. "The entire peninsula was loyal to the motherland. He couldn't turn them against Rome."

Nolan turned. "Who?"

The professor shrugged and gave a knowing smile. The man was in his element. "You asked the question so let's see if you can find the answer."

Nolan thought hard. Steel blue eyes stared back at him awaiting a response. Who couldn't turn Rome against itself? "Julius Caesar was loved by the people, ushering in the reforms needed to save the Republic."

The professor grinned wider and nodded encouragement.

"He was even known to forgive his enemies, forgiving Brutus on more than one occasion. So, the answer would be his rival, Pompey."

The professor's smile faded little as he looked down to the stained concrete floor. "Your recollection of Shakespeare is good," he said with a shrug. "But I am afraid that Rome's greatest *inimicus* was not its eventual dictator or his defeated rival. No, the man I am referring to is the subject of that book. Hannibal Barca, son of Hamilcar. The great general from Spain laid siege to Rome for fifteen years and yet he could not turn the Italians against the Eternal City. *Unitas*. Rome grew whereas Hannibal was recalled to Carthage to save it from destruction. *Unitas*. Unity gives strength."

Gruff let the words linger in the air. Nolan started laughing. "You would have loved my dad. He was a big history buff like you and Irish to the core."

"Well, I'm from California. Come on."

In the Land Cruiser, Gruff asked Nolan how he got to Asheville. Nolan explained the doomed helicopter flight, the reporter, Cato, and Tom.

"I'm sorry about your friend," said Gruff. "You say that both the National Guard tanker and your helicopter fell out of the air?"

"Yeah. That's what I saw."

Gruff held the wheel not looking at Nolan. After a moment, he said, "That's very strange."

7

The slender woman before him pulled the cigarette from his darkened lips. After taking a good drag herself, she breathed into his face. With a husky, Russian accent that had all but disappeared earlier, she answered Yuri's question. "My name is Marta Bunin."

Yuri frowned at being toyed with by the young woman. From the cockpit, Immanuil yelled, "Captain Orlov, this Blackhawk we stole is low on fuel. I request we land in the nearest city to refuel or find alternative transportation."

"Affirm- "

"Set a course for Knoxville," interrupted Marta. "Commander Yaromir has never been far since my arrival in the United States some fifteen years. He was the Kremlin's contact when I studied at Washington State University and has been my handler ever since. He will be in Knoxville."

Yuri sat back surprised. "You speak of Commander Sergei Yaromir?"

"Yes. You know of Yaromir?'

Yuri chuckled, but his face darkened. "Yes, I know the man. He has the Russian sickness; a spook."

Before becoming a commander in the Federal Security Bureau, the successor of the KGB, Sergei Yaromir had been a naval officer working alongside Yuri and Bogdan's father. The man personified a parasite sucking the life out of all those near him claiming the power for himself like cancer.

"What makes you think he's still alive," asked Yuri.

"Trust me; he'll be there."

"And what about you? Are you like Yaromir, a kleptomaniac crony?"

Marta's jaw became taut. Yuri thought he struck a nerve. "I came to the States for college. My father, we don't talk, but he is an attaché to President Vasilyev. When I got to Wazzu, there was a flood of messages for me from him through the mail from Lubyanka Square. I was being recruited to join the Committee."

She referred to the KGB. So, she too was a spook; that much he already knew. "How did they get your mail from Lubyanka," asked Yuri.

"The forwarding address came from the Children's World, the old toy store."

Yuri wanted to know more about her connection to the squalid Yaromir, but at that moment Anton woke up. "Ah, Anton, just in time. We will be entering the city known as Knoxville very soon."

"I thought our objective was the CDC in Atlanta," questioned the operative. "*Da*, we will secure the disease control facility in good time. Immanuil-"

"*Da*, Captain."

"What is the ETA?"

"We have to double back a little. We should be there in five minutes according to the map."

Yuri sat back in the jump seat surmising the damage of the United States of America. Flames brightened the night's sky casting a dull orange glow over the bombed-out cityscape. Immanuil descended to follow the meandering Tennessee River into the heart of the city. The smell of the river mixed with the intense sting of cordite. Yuri pictured Mikoyan Mig35s dropping their payloads of ZAB-500 fuel explosive bombs. Bombs so powerful they were capable of absorbing the air's oxygen, burning hotter and longer, evaporating breath right out of human lungs. First, one exhaled their last breath. Then, they inhaled scorched poison searing their airways. Yuri surmised it far better to be killed by the bomb's blast than by outlying effects.

At 2130 hours, Immanuil dropped the Blackhawk in the parking lot of a massive football stadium. Everyone including Marta pointed at the destruction of the massive sports complex. It was a shell of its former self, blown from the inside out.

"Look at that place, it must have taken a direct hit," said Bogdan.

"Weapons ready," hollered Yuri. "Anton, Bogdan. Secure us some wheels. Manny, when they get back, you're with Anton. Marta, you're with Bogdan and me. Make it fast comrades."

Yuri occupied the passenger seat of an SUV that reminded him of the ancient Ladas back home. "Mercedes Benz AMG G65," said Bogdan as he revved the potent V8 and plunged into the burned-out city with enough power to coerce Yuri's mouth to crack into a grin. Marta gave a whoop from the back seat. Anton, back to his old self, pulled abreast of the Captain and crew. Immanuil flashed a subcompact Vityaz-SN. The machine gun varied from his usual sniper rifle but allowed the young operative to fire rounds from the tight space of a vehicle window and more importantly, shot in a hurry.

Despite the destruction of the metropolitan area, the two vehicles raced through the night. The air was crisp giving Yuri such merriment he felt like a boy again. Bogdan played with the radio, but only static issued out of the speakers.

"It appears as though we are under violet skies, brother," said the bear-sized warrior.

Yuri turned in the seat to face Marta. "Where will we find your handler?"

Marta bristled. "I am not Yaromir's lap dog." Yuri ignored her, so she moved on. "He lives off the university campus to the east." She leaned forward to address Bogdan.

"Watch out!"

Bogdan turned the wheel narrowly missing the lead vehicle. Their bodies illuminated by red brake lights, Yuri rolled down his window and heard battering rams pounding the ground below. It sounded as though a thousand hammers were pummeling the earth driven by a chain gang army.

"What is it," asked Marta pulling on Yuri as he slid through the passenger window. He put down a hand commanding her to remain silent. Immanuil emerged through the lead vehicle window but ducked back inside as a rush of animals swept both vehicles. All manner of gazelles, zebras, and diminutive hogs fanned around the cars like a roaring river. The hammer of hooves shook the ground. Yuri heard a not so distant roar above the din.

Each Russian soldier clung to the roof of the vehicles now as a pride of lions pursued the frantic feast. Yuri counted four males and five females although it was hard to tell with accuracy given their speed. Immanuil made quick hand gestures from in front. Saluting the sniper, the duo spun their vehicle around peeling after the wild chase scene. Yuri pictured the young man brandishing his prized Tokarev semi-automatic rifle. The ancient infantry rifle carried the young man's flair for the dramatic with a wooden stock and modified optics, but it was as reliable and versatile as the famed American M1 Garand of World War II lore. He wished his soldiers happy hunting.

The first man he, his brother and Marta encountered looked familiar enough in any large city throughout the world. Dressed in denim from head to foot, an aged man of color pushed a shopping cart and carried a sack in his left hand as though it were some limp appendage. Yuri took the man for a despondent veteran. Bogdan tapped his shoulder and nodded towards the vagabond. Pushing his foot to the floor, the SUV rocketed forward. The old man threw up his arms in defense, blinded by the bright halogen bulbs bearing down upon him. At the last moment, Bogdan turned the wheel careening the powerful vehicle sidewise and swiping the man's basket and missing him by mere inches. The basket bounced across the dark street littering it with all the man's worldly possessions.

"Why not just kill the man," asked a disgusted Marta.

"He had no life left in him," answered the Bear.

The trio sped into a suburban sprawl complete with craftsman houses and gated communities. Yuri felt like General Zaroff having tired of animal game instead trapped and hunted the most dangerous game of all. Man.

He couldn't believe how utterly unprepared the prosperous nation had been to deal with the Russian blitzkrieg. Even Japanese pilots commented upon their return to their aircraft carriers how responsive American servicemen and women had been during the attack at Pearl Harbor. Years of complacency made America weak. Cities now lay in ruin from Seattle to Washington DC. He knew pockets of resistance would rise and persist to the very end. He was the tip of the spear, seeking out surviving population centers and gave the command to either annihilate or enslave those they encountered.

He thought of his father's words concerning *mujahedeen*: "They hide deep in the mountains, buried underground." Vodka always slurred his father's words; the once proud officer brought low following the death of Yuri and Bogdan's mother. "They lie in the ground for days, eating snakes or rats for food, waiting for our tanks to drive overhead before unleashing the bomb strapped to their chest, or sometimes the chest of a woman or child."

His father spat the name Afghanistan like swatting at a mosquito. "Syria, Iraq, Iran, all great nations with great leaders," his father said referring to Assad, Hussein or even the Ayatollah Khomeini, "But Afghanistan, there is no leader in Afghanistan, just the scourge that God hath wrought."

Early calculations estimated that American coastal cities, in particular, those in the west would fall in rapid succession due to their proximity. The interior states with less dense populations were deemed less threatening, yet Yuri grew up watching Westerns and knew well that many of the more rural states like those in the south were home to a more patriotic bunch more likely to be armed and dangerous. As evidenced by the American Civil War, those living in the south were far more lethal with a rifle, running in the wild far more than those softened by life in the city. Yuri hoped the fighting American patriots protecting their families outside their front door would not impede total victory.

The damage done to the cities and homes had forced neighbors into the streets seeking consolation from each other in the open air lest brick and mortar should fall without warning. When the haggled residents of the southern suburban community saw headlights approaching, they waved their arms believing the beams belonged to police or rescue.

Little did they know they welcomed their demise.

8

Nolan reached for his seventh slice of pizza. A local joint called Lucullus' Diner had been the professor's suggestion. It did not disappoint. The pizza had been cooked very thin like a chip with sun-dried tomatoes and green peppers. Nolan also requested grilled chicken to top his portion.

"The pizza," informed Professor Gruff, "is baked using the traditional Italian method. It's much less fattening so eat up because tomorrow I'm sure I can find some work for us."

"Where did they get the name for this place," Nolan asked taking a sip of the establishment's brew called Pliny the Elder. Asheville was known for promoting the local brew scene.

Gruff smiled wiping his mouth with a napkin. "I had a small hand in that" Nolan leaned in to hear the details of the story in the lively atmosphere. The restaurant was small and made of stone making sounds reverberate off the walls. "I had a student several years ago, a bright young lady who went to Tuscany to study architecture but wound up falling in love with the cuisine instead. After studying over there for a while, she came back to start this bistro. See the name Lucullus is in honor of Lucius Licinius Lucullus."

"You lost me at Linus."

Gruff smiled broadly. "Lucullus was famous as a giver of such grand banquets that the proverb 'Dining with Lucullus' is derived from him. The chef believed in this idea of an Italian party but with keeping tradition having the whole family gather together for a big meal." As Nolan looked around, he noticed the long, broad construction of each table. Few families in town remained. But that did not stop the bistro from being stacked to the rafters adorning the walls and vaulted ceiling.

"To Lucullus!" Gruff shouted raising his glass. The entire restaurant rang in unison raising their glasses and responding to the call. Peering at the many faces, Nolan picked Tiberius out of the crowd and gave the man a raised glass salute. With a silent nod, Tiberius returned the favor in kind.

Another face beamed back at him but only for a moment before resuming conversation with others at the table. The smiling eyes and easy laugh belonged to the nurse he had met when restraining the burned firefighter in the hospital. Her long brown hair fell in waves well beyond her shoulders and naturally curled towards the end. She was fair skinned and not the sort of caliber a former rugby player got used to carousing around with, but Nolan found her pure nature hard to take his eyes away. "

"Ah, Rachel is a fine young lady," said Gruff following Nolan's gaze and interrupting his thoughts. "She took my survey of the Old Testament the one year that I taught it. Very bright student, I know that many are fond of her," he added with a conspiratorial smile.

Nolan's mind replayed the half-second smile allowing his gaze to drop to the table. He had to change the subject. "Tell me, is Gruff your actual name or something far more sinister?"

The professor sat up straight and grinned. Whether he had guessed correctly or if the professor knew this was an attempt to drop the subject at hand, Nolan could not tell.

"Funny you should use that word, Nolan if that is your real name. You see I am a true sinistra or left-hander. It's a shame the negative connotations derived because the left is indeed not always right. For instance, did you know that when bats take flight from the underground, they always veer to the left?"

"I had no idea."

Gruff smiled. "Well is it any wonder then that one associates bats with vampires and the word sinister with a certain level of rancor?"

"I think I hit a nerve."

Gruff opened his hands to show he meant no harm, his smile never wavering. Deliberately, he offered his hand. His right hand. "The name is Gareth Evans. I'm sure there is a doctorate in there somewhere." Nolan shook the offered hand laughing.

"So where does the legend come from?"

The professor set down his dark brew after taking a sip. "It's my voice. Rather harsh with no shrill, even in a large survey class. Hence the nickname."

Sitting back, Nolan liked this man who appeared much younger and fit than men half his age. "I bet you have students eating out of your hand." Where this man led, many followed. Then it clicked. In his mind's eye, Nolan remembered the olive drab box, folded flag and Mameluke sword hanging over the mantle. His mind flashed to the tattoos on Titus' arms, the man who guarded the bridge into Asheville. "You too were a Marine."

Gruff smiled. "No better friend, no worse enemy. That's the motto of 1st Division Marines taken from the Roman general Sulla. The draft came before any college plans and my chosen career path. I was a young kid from outside Los Angeles, a surfer brat when one day I got a notice that I had been drafted to fight in a war. I threw the first one away. I had heard a little about the war in some jungle country, but I knew they couldn't tunnel their way to the shores of Long Beach. Lo, and behold, the war did find me when a man in a uniform showed up at my mama's door and demanded I report to the nearest recruiting station. My family history includes some stints in the Navy, so I was assigned there. With my last dose of freedom, I chose to join the Marine Corps. From there my freedom to choose anything was suspended. I served the Corps.

"As it turned out I wasn't too bad with a rifle, something my superiors in the Corps took notice of when it came time for MOS. I held the distinction of joining the Scout and Sniper team orchestrated by Jim Land and Carlos Hathcock."

"I've heard of Hathcock," interjected Nolan. "He's from Arkansas like me. My father introduced to me to one of his pallbearers when I was a kid."

Gruff's eyes glazed over in memoriam. This time his voice caught and no longer sounded so gravelly. "He was more than human. The Vietcong called him White Feather and sent their best to hunt him down, but he got them in the end; shot an assassin right through the scope, through and through."

Nolan's blood cooled. A sniper saw the face of his victim before pulling the trigger. They saw the contour of the face, the color of the eyes, the pink mist.

Gruff took another sip then continued, "My life changed so much because of the Corps. I learned to be dependable, to have sound judgment, and that life was no longer about me but about we; something a surfer bum certainly tried to avoid." He laughed, the guttural tone returning. "I went to school on the GI Bill, met my Rebecca who gave me fifty years of boundless love."

The two sat in silence finishing their drafts. Despite all that had happened Nolan couldn't help but feel content. The professor opened up to him, showed him kindness, and touched his soul as no man had done since his father. Feeling an urge for fresh air, Nolan excused himself from the table and made his way onto the concrete steps outside. A deep velvet sky blanketed the hills over Asheville. He inhaled deeply, the cold mountain air pouring down his throat reinvigorating his body. He pulled the canvas jacket tighter around his chest. Condensation already began to set on various windows in the silent night foreshadowing a frost by morning. He breathed deeply again. Peace.

The porch door swung open and clattered shut. Light footsteps padded on the concrete. When the footfalls did not reach the steps, Nolan turned around wondering who was standing behind him. His company was not the professor as he had suspected but the nurse from earlier, Rachel.

"Sheila said you would be out here," she said. Nolan saw for the first time that her eyes shone an icy sort of blue, the greying effect pronounced by her grey heather sweater. She mistook Nolan's startled face to assume he did not recognize the name, Sheila.

"Sorry," she went on. "Mayor Townsend I mean; she is like a member of the family to me."

Of course, she is, he thought. The professor's words about the pretty nurse being a fond member of the community rang in his ears.

She took a step forward extending her hand. "I'm Rachel Brown." Nolan choked down the words forming in his mouth that he already knew her name and concealed it by awkwardly blowing warm air into his hands before taking hers.

"Nolan Hoke." She returned his shake in a firm grip, a sign he knew his father would approve. "What brings you out here away from your friends?"

"I wanted to thank you for helping me earlier today. A woman needs to challenge herself every day but I don't think I could have restrained that pained man without help. I saw you get up and I had to say something before you left."

He smiled. In a whirlwind, he was falling for the nurse, hook, line, and sinker. "I just wanted to get some air. The professor promised the mayor to provide me with food and shelter for services rendered."

She sidled in closer, resting on the iron rails beside Nolan. "Would those services be offered because you are a fireman yourself?" Taken aback, she seemed to know more about Nolan than just his name. He wondered how much Mayor Townsend had divulged. It all began to feel like a setup. Not that he felt like complaining. "Sheila also said you were very charming and easy to talk to," she said beaming but not looking at him.

A lump began ascending his throat lodging itself behind his Adam's apple and made it difficult to breathe. "Is something the matter," she mocked. Nolan knew he needed to regroup. Girls were so hard to read, a major the reason why he never bothered. "Rome wasn't built in a day," his father would remind an impatient son.

"Nothing the matter," he said grinning. "I'm trying to deduce what you know about me versus what I already know about you."

Rachel crossed her arms in anticipation. "Do tell."

He rubbed his hands together giving her an appraising eye. "So far you have given me your full name. I know your occupation. But what you are not aware of is that I happen to know you are twenty-eight years old, own a dog, drive an ancient Mitsubishi, and you hide your high maintenance through a tough veneer, but your independence proves that you are still single and prefer it that way."

She did not respond but stood bemused, the color draining from her face. She could almost be a ghost and Nolan chastised himself for going too far.

She looked down for a half second pulling at the sweater around the shoulders. Nolan felt crestfallen. He knew he blew it.

"Well, you sure know how to make an impression, Sherlock." She looked up at him, a slow smile forming, and her confidence was returning. "How did you deduce all that?"

"You had no purse at the table save a wallet and a pair of keys belonging to the only Mitsubishi out here. I took notice of your Montero since that was my first set of wheels as a kid. The dog hunch came from the whistle on the keychain."

"And what of my age and the other secrets a girl keeps?"

"Forget I mentioned it. I took the challenge too seriously. I was a big fan of Sherlock's adventures as a boy. Read all the books." His deprecating demeanor disarmed the nurse as she smiled.

"Is this how you meet all the new girls?"

He scratched his head. "No, not exactly. Sorry."

"Strike one. I don't have a dog. The whistle is for getting lost in the woods. Asheville is so beautiful, so many places to hike. I turned my ankle hiking late one night. This little siren saved the day. Strike two, I am not twenty-eight, but I do appreciate the attempt to shoot low on a girl's age."

"Strike three?"

"Strike three. You haven't let me have my turn yet."

He smiled, this time opening his arms for closer observation. He leaned against the rail and awaited his assessment. "Alright."

She made a show of calculating his dimensions and personality, circling him and making clicking noises with her tongue in disapproval. He almost shook with laughter. "You're just a little older than me, or around the same age. You either don't eat a lot or haven't eaten very much lately. You are resourceful but used to having things done your way. My conclusion is that you are a stubborn boy but you are genuine, and everybody likes you anyway."

Nolan clapped his hands. "A fair assessment. I am thirty-two, and the diet of a fireman like me consists of high protein bars and MREs. Besides, I'm told that I hide food well anyway. I am an introvert, yet your words do me a kindness."

"Aunt Sheila hasn't stopped talking about you since coming back to the hospital to find me. She likes you. I like you." Her greying eyes and beaming smile lit up the dark porch.

He stuck his hands in his pockets, the heat from embarrassment rising to his cheeks. "Well aren't we a pair, I like you too."

"Walk me to my car?" He offered her his arm as the two descended the steps together, crunching on the icy ground.

9

Thirteen pairs of eyes reflected off the high-intensity bulbs shining from the Mercedes, shielding Yuri, Bogdan, and their weapons as they disembarked. One of the displaced citizens ventured from the pack, his hands cupping his face to see past the blinding lights.

"Hello? Police?"

Yuri took the man for a white-collar professional. Despite the burned-out city, the man was still attired in a suit, the jacket of which lay across the shoulders of a middle-aged woman wearing pearls and a white blouse. They portrayed the perfect power couple.

"Hello," repeated the man trying to coax some authority into his shaking voice. Neither Yuri nor Bogdan moved from behind the lights of the SUV.

When the salt and pepper haired man took another step forward, Bogdan stopped him dead in his tracks with the sound of an AK-12 assault rifle cocked and ready to fire.

"Gangs," said the man faltering in his steps. "You're in a gang. Look, we don't want any trouble." He panned his arms in a circle to draw attention to the state of the neighborhood. "We have nothing left to offer."

Each American recoiled as the report of a hunting rifle cracked in the distance. Yuri stepped forward, blocking a headlight to come into full view. "You are wrong American. You and your nation have so much to offer. You have resources, people, food, technology, and safety. You have these in abundance. You lie to my face."

The businessman noticed Yuri's thick accent but couldn't place it beyond a few action movies. "Who are you?"

"I am Captain Yuri Orlov. I must subdue the American nation and its people in the name of Mother Russia. We have greatly enjoyed bringing you and your countrymen to your knees."

"Russians," questioned the woman in the blouse. "I thought you were our friends. Didn't we defeat Hitler together or something?"

Yuri's body shook with laughter. He shot the woman in the torso, the bullet carrying through the ribs and lodging inside her left-side lung. The man who addressed Yuri dove in time to catch her withering body. He held the dying woman as she struggled to find her breath, the blood pooling inside her perforated lung. Bogdan opened fire with his assault rifle cutting down the remaining civilians like wheat struck by the scythe.

Inside the vehicle once more, Marta suggested the brothers stop the killing spree and carry out the order to find Commander Yaromir. Yuri bit his tongue as Bogdan hit the throttle. Taking orders from the much younger woman burned him, but he knew he could not put off meeting the loathsome troll born of the Russian underground.

In the road ahead, a lone dark figure emerged from out of the flickering shadows. Light glinted off something shiny rising in the closing distance. Too late Yuri recognized the object and its design.

"Bogdan! Move!"

The shot rang out like a clap of thunder. In a heartbeat, the windshield shattered followed by a roar of pain from Bogdan. The massive man's right arm slumped, causing him to lose control of the wheel. The powerful SUV lurched across the road plummeting into an embankment of debris and toppled over.

Yuri felt more than heard Marta's shrieks melting into grinding steel as they slid several feet.

When the wreckage came to a stop, Yuri pounded the passenger door with his feet in an attempt to force it open. Fighting the pain, Bogdan rolled through the broken windshield and squeezed off three well-placed rounds in the man's torso. Despite the pain in his brother's shoulder, Yuri watched the Bear get to his feet and kick the large firearm away from the homeless man's outstretched arm. Each Russian surveyed the man's body. Yellow, dead eyes, tar black smoker's fingers giving way to dark skin that hung off the man's bones, and a sizeable beaked nose that poked from underneath a worn Husqvarna cap.

Bogdan winced in pain bringing them back to the matter at hand. The gunshot entry had no exit wound. Though large, Bogdan could not bleed out forever. Yuri searched for suitable transportation while Marta began dressing the wound and stabilizing his brother's arm.

He searched, but most of the vehicles along the street were in various states of disrepair. Being a wealthy suburb, most of the cars sat in the garage. The problem was that most garages had collapsed, crushing their occupants. Other vehicles were blackened shells, or the tires had melted right off the aluminum rims leaving a sticky wet mess along the pavement.

Thinking of his brother bleeding in the mysterious spy's hands brought on a distant memory. Yuri no longer saw the cars as he searched for a decent ride amidst visions from the past.

Ten-year-old Bogdan was already large for his age, the size of baby Grizzly. Pushing him down the hill in the sled took all the strength a much older but smaller Yuri could handle. Once moving, however, the aluminum saucer they rode in was all but impossible to stop, a verifiable freight train sliding down a frozen gorge. As the wooden thicket came closer and closer, the wiser Yuri swiftly tucked and rolled away to safety. The denser

Bogdan was not quite so graceful, or lucky. The young boy collided with the tall, mighty trees wrecking his body and separating his shoulder. Once Yuri dragged his delirious brother home, their father laid the boy across an ironing board. Two swigs from a sweating crystal-clear bottle and the former naval officer drove his knee into the boy's back to reset the shoulder. Bogdan didn't dare so much as cry out or even whimper. He sat there biting down on his lip until it bled to hold back the tears.

Wiping his mouth, their father locked eyes on Yuri and asked how the incident occurred. Like a panther, the old man prowled around his older son waiting for the truth. Yuri watched his father remove the belt from his darkened, sweat-stained pants and knew that he would pay the price for choosing to save himself and leave his brother.

At last, he found a nondescript mobile van large enough to accommodate Marta as she tended to Bogdan. He changed a flat tire and hotwired the engine to start.

When the trio rendezvoused with Anton and Immanuil, the pair was eager to regal them with their hunting tales, but all hands went to digging the slug out of Bogdan's shoulder. "I need alcohol, gauze, and some tweezers," commanded Marta. Each man complied with her requests as Bogdan bit down on his webbed belt. Yuri drove, keeping his eyes wary to the sides of the streets as he navigated towards the hotel Yaromir had taken over since the siege to establish as his headquarters for the southeastern portion of Operation Cannae and the subjugation of the entire American nation.

10

After bidding Rachel goodnight, Nolan sat down once more with Professor Gruff who said nothing but kept a permanent grin on his face. The professor paid the bill nodding his head adieu to Tiberius and his boys who each lifted a glass in return. The large man fixed Nolan with a gaze that felt something akin to acceptance.

In the car, it was hard to determine the damage caused by fire and Nolan began to think of what it would be like to call Asheville home. The blackness of night would give way to a new dawn, a new sunrise and a fresh start. He felt pain in his heart at the loss of Tom, but he also thought of Cato, the mayor, Tiberius and the professor. He thought of Rachel.

The two men retired to their respective rooms. Nolan felt a surge of love for the older man as Gruff doused the light but kept his door ajar in an almost paternal sense. Smiling to himself, Nolan eased into the bed of the richly decorated guest room.

The quiet contributed to Nolan's pensive mood as he ruminated on the future. Thinking of Gruff, he missed his father.

There would be no better person to share this new beginning with than his dad. He felt an urge to pray as he did when he was a child but thought instead of Cato's words regarding God; God, who was known to many as a Father.

"If God were a Father like the father I knew of," said Cato while dining at the gas station in the abandoned town, "then His children would have already left Him." Nolan knew the opposite to be true. As his thoughts drifted into sleep, he knew that if God were anything like his father, then God had already left His child.

That night the air surrounding Nolan was thick and hot causing him to perspire. Tom angled the helicopter higher to escape the rising flames of the inferno below. The fire reached higher with every pass, stretching towards them with long, harrowing fingers.

Rowan, the reporter, stood smiling with perfect teeth and perfect skin. She looked ready for her close up, but Nolan knew something was wrong. "You shouldn't be here," he said to her. He couldn't utter the words he knew to be true: *You're dead*.

A loud shriek tore his stunned attention away from her. When he turned back, she vanished, like a wisp of smoke. Tom's admonitions were incoherent from the cockpit. Nolan felt his insides churn as the helicopter plummeted to the flames below. He pressed his hands against the bulkhead. The steel wall was remarkably cool to the touch.

He looked down towards his boots where the deck of the helicopter should have been, but instead, he stood on the faded pink tile. The steel bulkhead gave way to a dark faux wooden door. Without thinking he recognized the room as his nana and papa's kitchen. It was a room he had not been in for over fifteen years, but the memory remained as though he visited yesterday.

Sitting at a large octagonal table of the same dark shade as the door, was his mother, collapsed in a faded yellow chair. Inconsolable.

Uncle Declyn and Aunt Bixby stood solemnly by, his uncle's eyes locked on the floor while his aunt whispered to nothing but space. Nana moved towards him with her arms open for a hug, but Nolan stood still crippled by grief. This was his father's family, attended by each member of that family save the one that connected them all. Another man appeared in the open doorway. Nolan recognized him as Deputy Ernest Shaw, an older man but a close friend of his fathers. White-hot tears stung the back his eyes once the lawman began speaking.

"Declyn," acknowledged the deputy.

"Shaw," replied his uncle in greeting.

The lawman looked down at his fingers, spinning a wide brim hat before speaking. "I am aware that you all know a few of the circumstances surrounding today's tragedy." He nodded in Uncle Declyn's direction. "But as much as it pains me, I wish to give you the details regarding Pierce before it comes out in the papers." Here he looked at Nolan. "Your father died a hero son."

Nolan's body rocked. He found one of the empty chairs at the table, all wind stolen from his sails.

"I just finished my report with Deputy Gordon and Deputy Matheson. Lafayette County Dispatch put out an APB shortly after two-thirty this afternoon calling for all available emergency responders to report to the Jiffy Lube on 8th and A." Nolan saw his uncle leave the room without a word. His uncle worked for the tire and lube shop and had been present during the explosion. "As you all know the Jiffy Lube is in the industrial sector with lots of buildings in disrepair. Fire Chief Walton determined the cause of the explosion at the auto shop was due to a nearby gas leak that went undetected. An open flame resulted in a catastrophic explosion. We determined that two people died in the initial blast. The concrete building managed to withstand the immediate damage, but flammable materials continued to add fuel to the flames.

"Rescue teams responded immediately finding and securing half a dozen citizens from the surrounding area as the inferno spread from building to building. Before giving the all-clear, a grief-stricken mother cried out that her young daughter was unaccounted for." Deputy Shaw paused before continuing, taking a deep breath. "Pierce was the first to react, sprinting into the growing flames the engine crew tried to extinguish. Declyn, brave fool, followed his brother's footsteps before being tackled by firemen in protective clothing. Rookie firefighter Nelson Bridges instead followed Pierce into the building on the brink of collapse.

"Visibility in the strip mall had to be next to nil. Smoke from burning tires enveloped the area making it hard to breath; we had to force everyone back. We could hear through radio transmission that the men were calling for the young girl. Must have been terrified, the poor thing. The ceiling, engulfed by fire, began to bend. Nelson called in that they spotted a long pink sock protruding from underneath a desk. The rookie said the girl fought off Pierce's aid at first, but he managed to pull the fifty-pound girl from under the counter just before that portion of the ceiling caved, crushing her hiding place.

"The rest of the ceiling had withstood all it could muster. Nelson said he could just make out Pierce's mask through the smoke and though the two couldn't make eye contact, he knew what the man was thinking. Nelson threw up his arms in protestation at the same time Pierce threw the young girl into the rookie's arms. He caught the screaming child and fell back into the hallway. The clearance was just enough to save their lives, but Piece was- the collapse entombed him."

The deputy turned to leave.

Nolan ran after the deputy, catching him in the driveway. Not very big but of even height with Ernest Shaw, Nolan spun the man grabbing him by the lapels. Rather than fight back the older man just held the boy's arms still, a disarming smile on his face. When Nolan relented, Shaw kept hold of him in a tight hug. "I lost my father when I was younger too," he began his voice deep and thick as a jar of molasses. "I was older than you, sure, but I never went to no college. I was just a rookie on the force. It was shaping time in my life, and many times I wanted to quit.

"But my old man was a fighter. Survived smallpox and an abusive father himself. A soldier after that, he taught me how to take a hit; taught me what it meant to be tough. The hard thing was that he was all that I had. See my folks had divorced which was not something folks did back then, so he turned to drinking. I guess his past horrors had come back to haunt him.

"My daddy was not a man like your father but he did have a deep sense of right and wrong. He was killed outside a bar in Fort Smith late one night when he saw a man beating the daylights out of some woman. Witnesses say that he caught the wife beater's arm before taking another swing. I remember what a cold cock from my old man felt like and I do not envy the man at the bar that night. What he did not see was the woman, the one he was trying to defend, reach into her purse. He died that night in the alley. He wasn't a good man, but it does something to you, losing your father.

"Pierce was a good man, one of the best men I have ever known. Good God in heaven, he loved you. I know the last thing he thought of while he was rescuing that girl was of you. He couldn't dare let someone, another parent, lose his or her child."

"But what about losing him," raged Nolan grabbing tighter around Shaw's back. "Did he think about me losing my dad?"

Shaw patted the boy on the back. "He lived a life of sacrifice and did a lot of good for people in this poor town. I reckon the good Lord decided He needed your daddy."

Marjorie Hoke took her sobbing son from the deputy. He watched the tall, skinny-legged man stalk through the grass before his figured rolled into flames.

11

As Bogdan lie in recovery, Yuri walked the resort where Yaromir made his headquarters. Other soldiers paced the grounds in silence. Looking into their faces, Yuri observed a coalition of nations that had thrown off the façade of NATO member state status and instead aligned themselves once again with the world's most emergent superpower. Mercenaries. Hungarians, Czechs, Kazaks, and Azeris mixed with Russian born soldiers keeping watch over the most forward operating base of Operation Cannae.

Wars with NATO-affiliated nations were an expensive but rewarding investment. What little the Captain could see in the darkened grounds came the silhouetted shapes of helicopters and armored personnel carriers. To reach further into the American South, warships rode on barges bound for the Tennessee River. He thought of the Polish-made RPG-20 Grenade Launcher strapped inside one of the nearby helicopters. The powerful yet portable launcher was capable of propelling six grenades in rapid succession via a rotating cylindrical magazine based on similar South African concepts. One of Yuri's prized possessions was the MSG90 A2 Sniper System manufactured by the venerable German company Heckler and Koch. Years ago, he used the rifle to fire a 7.62 NATO round accurately under eight hundred meters. He used the weapon to shoot from outside a secure perimeter to assassinate a leading Ukrainian general on diplomatic tour asking Western European nations for military aid. After the assassination in the German capital using a German military rifle, relations broke down isolating east from west and dooming the sovereignty of Ukraine. He knew taking down the American nation would prove a much more difficult test, but the shot placement would remain the same.

Right through the heart.

He pulled out a cigarette and breathed the plume of smoke deeply. The sweet smell of tobacco momentarily covered the stench of burned out vehicles, homes, businesses, and patrons that used to dot the eastern Tennessee landscape. Staunching the cigarette, he made his way back to the lobby. He caught furtive glances of the hotel's waitstaff held prisoner by the armed sentries surrounding the building.

Bogdan sat up on the improvised operating table near the large kitchen. Lying next to him was the disassembled Grach pistol he used to kill his attacker. "What are the odds some bum gets a round off and puts me out of the fight for good?"

Yuri frowned. "He's dead. You're not."

Bogdan grinned. "Five terrorists, twenty hostages. Twenty-five body bags. This is Spetsnaz."

"How is the shoulder?"

Bogdan pulled back the olive drab shirt to reveal pink, freshly sewn stitches. "Stiff. Have you seen Yaromir?"

Yuri hung his head knowing a meeting with the kleptomaniac was unavoidable. "*Nyet*. He evades us until he wants to be seen."

"What of the American President? Any word on their whereabouts?"

"I suspect that if this nation's former leader never made it to their mountain hideout."

"A kingdom without a crown."

Yuri looked once more towards his brother's wounded shoulder. "You swore oaths worse than father while Marta dug out the slug. I was impressed."

"And like father, Yuri, I saved the best material for you."

"You always were the most colorful interview after hockey matches. Too bad you were such a waste of talent." Bogdan's hulking frame made him a crushing blue-liner for the Academy's varsity squad. Recruited worldwide, he was little interested in fame or fortune. For Bogdan, hockey was a youthful excuse to hurt another person and leave his mark on a more personal level. Once able, younger joined older as an elite member of Spetsnaz.

Marta walked in closing the door behind her. "I was hoping to catch you both. Your rooms are ready. Commander Yaromir, of course, had the very best picked out for each of you. The spoils of war he called it." Neither brother responded leaving an awkward silence hanging.

"You are *bogatyye*," said Yuri.

Marta's eyes grew large then venomous. "*Nyet*. I am not politically connected. My father was a naval officer same as yours." Her accent became thick in the flush of emotion.

"You are from Odessa."

This time she was taken aback. "Yes. *Babushka* was Jewish, a survivor of the Prague Ghetto. Father and mother moved to Moscow after the fall of the Soviet Union. He said he wanted to be near the seat of the new power. I was just a child. After many years, we moved to Brighton Beach here in America. I grew up speaking Russian and English, but I guess we never lost our Odessan accents."

"So long as we are on the same team," began Yuri. "Bogdan and I have much in the way of history with your handler. We will not hesitate to harm you if you get in the way of our objectives."

"*Da*, I understand. No love lost between Commander Yaromir and myself, but I too have objectives, and I will see them full to the hilt." With that, she turned and padded out the door.

Bogdan met Yuri's eyes with eyebrows raised. They both found Marta Bunin to be a bit of an enigma. "Come, brother," said Yuri. "Let's get some supper."

12

Nolan awoke to the sound of sizzling bacon and the smell of pancake mix. Still in a daze, he glanced around the bedroom wondering where he was. He lay in crisp, fresh sheets underneath a down comforter all working against his will to get out of bed. Ibuprofen and a note lay next to him on the nightstand:

I put your clothes in the laundry and laid fresh ones outside the door. Breakfast will be ready when you are. –Gruff

He opened the door to find a pair of blue jeans, a grey V-neck, and soft flannel long sleeve. Placing the clothes on the bed, he instead ran downstairs for the meal. Levity filled the scene downstairs. The professor mixed pancakes in a large yellow bowl complete with apron and chef's hat.

"Oh good, you're awake. Go ahead and have a seat while I finish the last of the batch. Bacon and OJ are already on the table."

Orange juice wasn't the only thing on the table. Raspberries, blueberries, whipped topping, sausage, scrambled eggs and most of the pancakes lie in wait. The soiree looked too much for just two men to consume. "Have to get our carbs up today," said the professor reading his bewildered look. "Dig in, please." Precisely as he sat down the doorbell rang.

"Don't move," instructed Gruff. "I'll see what we have." Laughter drifted in from the entryway. Nolan turned to see the mayor walk in followed by Rachel Brown. The nurse looked ready for work, her hair pulled tight and clad in light green scrubs, but she bore the most genuine if not embarrassed smile he ever saw. He shook hands amicably with Mayor Townsend and with Rachel while the professor set two more plates on the table.

Well into the meal Nolan looked around the table and thought how much he enjoyed the company of each person seated. The thought of leaving them behind filled him with deep regret.

"You know I haven't checked in with the base in Cleveland since I got here. I wonder if anyone even knows where I am," he said looking in the mayor's direction. "I promised Gruff I would stay to help and believe me the last thing I want to do is leave, but I at least need to call in. Are the cell phones working yet?"

The table fell silent. The mayor wiped her mouth and set her napkin in her lap. "I'm sure they will allow me to stay down here," he added. "I was on my way here before the crash anyway." He looked around the table staring at each member's blank face. "What?"

The mayor spoke up first. "I suppose Tiberius told you about the cellular grid going down. Did he also mention that some authorities closed down our regional airport? Or that we requested government aid?"

"He said some of that. He said that was why he, Titus, and the boys were on overwatch."

"It seems the problem has continued," said Mayor Townsend. "Black Mountain is concerned. They are in desperate need of aid, and there is no television, Internet, or anything."

"Seriously? What's going on?"

"We wish we knew. Asheville gets the rap for being a bit granola, but even we rely on international news and the World Wide Web."

"I'm sure they're working on it," piped up Rachel. "At least all the systems are still working at the hospital. Speaking of, I need to be going." She placed a hand on Nolan's shoulder and saw herself out. The solid oak door hammered shut to keep out the cold.

"She gets off work at seven," said Mayor Townsend. Nolan sat there for a moment before her message gave him an epiphany. Rising from the table, he chased after Rachel into the cold.

He burst through the door just as the engine to her Montero Sport turned over. A pale sun shone through hazy, smoke-ridden clouds. She rolled down the window smiling through the furry hood of her down jacket. "What are you doing? You need to get back inside before I see you as a patient."

For the first time, he realized he ran into the cold without much more than his nightshirt and a pair of shorts. He started dancing to keep his bare feet from cementing into the ground. Rachel couldn't stop herself from laughing.

Nolan was panting, his cheeks already beginning to turn pink. "I was wondering. I don't know what Cleveland will want if I get into contact with them. I was wondering if I could take you to dinner."

Rachel's smile turned into an outright beam. "We should probably do dinner soon. I mean, you don't know when your boss will summon you back right?"

He rubbed his hands together and then rubbed his sides looking something like a rooster. "Yeah. How does seven thirty sound?"

"Tonight?"

"Tonight."

"That barely gives a girl time to prepare."

"No need to prepare. I like you so much already."

Rachel blushed, her eyes swimming. "Seven thirty then Nolan Hoke. Now please at least put on some pants." Nolan could see the wave of embarrassment hit her after the words left her mouth, her face going a deep cardinal red.

"Whatever the nurse orders."

With that, she pulled from the drive and meandered through the smoldering neighborhood.

After Mayor Townsend said her goodbyes, Nolan finished getting dressed including throwing on a flannel-lined waxed jacket. The morning temperatures in the mountains threatened to drop around freezing.

13

Yuri awoke at dawn. No alarm clock, no rooster, just the seasoned habit of a soldier. Outside his room on a platter were a glass of orange juice, a slice of toasted Russian black bread, and his pack of cigarettes. Standing over the small breakfast was a sight he recognized from childhood folklore.

Despite being raised by a pious Orthodox mother; all Russian children grow up hearing the old Kievan Rus stories that originated from the first Russian civilization. Next to the food stood a wooden carving of Mokosh, protector of women and childbirth.

Rage filled Yuri's lungs. It was a joke of Yaromir's to carve the goddess and give her as gifts. The irony of the present came from Yaromir's upbringing. Men of Yaromir's ilk were born from sin, dumped into streets of Moscow's red-light district. They survived by preying on the weak that no doubt resulted in Yaromir creeping his way into the darkened alleys of the KGB. Yuri knelt down and grabbed the small token throwing it across the room striking a vast crystal mirror.

The sound of shattering glass brought both Bogdan and Anton charging into the plush hotel master suite. Anton brandished a silenced Makarov pistol. Yuri put up his arms in mock surrender.

"*Dobroye utro,* Captain," said Anton. He tentatively lowered his sidearm. "We were just on our way up. Commander Yaromir has requested our presence in this hotel's restaurant."

Yuri stood before the window looking out among the destruction of Knoxville. Smoke blackened out the morning sun. He peered far to the south as the forests of Sevierville, Pigeon Forge and Gatlinburg lay smoldering. Wildfires combined with thermobaric carpet-bombing devastated the city. If not for the rains, he was sure the entire town would have been wiped out. He thought of Rilke. *Before us, great Death stands. Our fate held close within his quiet hands.*

Yuri and his men stood with arms spread as a Mafioso type checked each soldier for weapons. Two searched while two others kept assault rifles trained. Yuri wanted to wipe the grin right off their mouths. They all matched. Formal attire, shaved heads, thick necks, and sunglasses. Satisfied the henchmen opened the double doors revealing a long cherry table. At the head of the table sat a small, sniveling man. His bald head exposed age spots and his pointed beak of a nose diminished soul-less black eyes. His was a world of deception and intrigue; Yuri's was the battlefield.

A thundering roar caused Yaromir's other guest to spill her glass. Each soldier whipped around to find himself within swiping distance of a Siberian Tiger. They eased a step back as the tiger paced her new lair testing the iron chains.

"I call her Sasha," said the old spy clapping his withered hands. The echo made a hollow sound as though his hands were without bones. "Please, Captain Orlov. You and your men may have a seat."

Yuri glared at Marta who busied herself by wiping her spilled water with a dinner towel. Following their commander, his men assembled their plates after he reached for a fresh slice of black bread.

"Yuri," laughed the old man, "your men respond like Pavlov's dogs." The comment lingered in silence. The padded feet of the tiger and the clinking of dinnerware were the only sounds.

After a few minutes of eating Yaromir continued. "You have a remarkable record Yuri, much like your father. My memory tells me though that you look much more like your mother. You have the best. You should be thankful." Both Yuri and Bogdan bristled at the old man's mention of their mother. The man had no shame when it came to women, something as apparent now as it was then. Marta dressed in a fashion to Yaromir's liking, the tight Garbage girl outfit accentuating the dirty blonde's long legs rather than her sharp green eyes. As Yaromir wanted, she looked like an item up for sale along Moscow's crude streets. Yuri felt a tinge of pity for the young lady.

"Marta is a treasure, is she not," asked the old man petting his young spy. "Comrade President Vasilyev and the Kremlin are proud of the success we have achieved. America is devastated; her leaders are dead or in hiding while you and your men represent the tip of the spear, ready to deliver the final blow. As was foreseen by myself and others, pockets of resistance have emerged. The Americans are not ready to give up the fight. The 7th Fleet has joined with the Japanese in a virtual suicide mission to break apart our supply chains. Resources are stretched thin."

"What of movement in the North Atlantic," asked Anton.

"No movement yet. The Norwegians are keeping a close eye on our movements, but everything is very mum. Gentlemen, the important threat is the one before our very eyes." The elderly Yaromir eyed each soldier before speaking further. "The history of the American people is a strong one. They have spent centuries subduing this land. They will fight to keep it and may I remind each of you that you are behind enemy lines. If we fail to put down insurgents, then we risk exposing Russia to failure. The Kremlin will not accept failure. I will not accept failure and neither will you." The aged spy paused to take a sip of Chamomile tea. "Your mission is one of search and destroy. Find enemy strongholds and extinguish them before our objectives go up in smoke."

"You want us to tour the countryside looking for trouble? On whose authority?" Yuri growled.

Commander Yaromir gave a rueful smile. "Soon this will all be under your authority."

Yuri sat back, confused.

The spy smiled, revealing tea darkened teeth. "Your orders come straight from President Vasilyev. You are making the rank of Major and given the title of Commander of the Eastern Seaboard. You will command forty men from this location. Let me be the first to congratulate you," he said standing. "Your father would be proud were he still alive."

Yuri openly winced while Bogdan and the others marched out without preamble. The toughs surrounding Yaromir tensed, but he waved them off, still clinging to Yuri's hand.

"As the commanding Major, would it not be prudent to take our resources now and ensure our larger objectives to the south? What about Operation Pastorious?"

"Operation Pastorius is taking some time, chiefly in the South. If you are referring to Atlanta, I should let you know that air support would be insufficient and surveillance of the region is imperative hence the reason for your new mission. Like the hound, you are to sniff out the enemy and root them from their foxholes."

"What will you do?"

"I am to meet up with forces to the north and converge on Washington DC. The American capital is vacated. Russian occupation of the city will send a literal and symbolic message across the globe that we are in control. Also, FSB operatives require further assistance in finding a man known to us as Mary."

"What makes him so important?"

"Americans ignored him when he played herald regarding the Motherland's intentions. I suspect that this shadow operative pieced together with other like-minded warriors and may pose our biggest threat to securing this burning nation's chief city."

"With whom shall I communicate with once we are ready for new orders?"

"Don't worry," said Yaromir with a pat. "I will find you. Now, go catch for us the foxes."

Moments later Yuri, Bogdan, Anton, and Immanuil stood hunched over a map of the continental United States. Dozens of soldiers stood around them and assorted Russian armored vehicles known as Tigrs. Russia's answer to the venerable but outdated Humvee, the Tigr was equipped with a supreme off-road capability and wrapped in olive drab ballistic armor for protection. Each behemoth was loaded down with extra fuel and entrenching tools strapped to the roof to navigate the unknown distances and rural terrain in route to American hideouts.

"Stay aware men. Treat everyone you see as hostile. The American South will be harder to navigate than the northern cities set in grid patterns. The populations are sparse and known for being close to their land. They will know their way around a weapon and will not hesitate to use it. Their ancestors held every advantage in the Civil War save a large population. Gentlemen, this time they will not be encumbered by this. Look around. We only have each other.

"Furthermore, we are fully enveloped in the fog of war. The Kremlin has sanctioned our hunt, but we are on our own until told otherwise. As your commanding officer, I will maintain strict military discipline during the daytime." Here Yuri smiled. "But comrades, I realize that we are all men far from home and our women. Many of you are mercenaries, and like great generals of the past, I will see you paid handsomely."

A round of cheers rose in the cold air echoing off burned and bombed out buildings. "Remember your training and put rounds on target."

Each man retired to his respective vehicle. Yuri paused at the lead Tigr, one outfitted with a debris-clearing grenade launcher. He was pleased to find the scout rig manned by an all Spetsnaz crew. Leaning in to talk through the window he pointed at the map and said to the driver, "set course for Asheville."

14

Armed with a Victor Ax, a shovel and a sledgehammer, Nolan and Professor Gruff set to work clearing the debris of the old man's burned out garage away from the house. Nolan could see the telltale line the firefighters took to save the house. One patch of ground still clung to deadening grass while just beyond lay a grey blanket of ash. The winds once again shifted bringing hazy ash clouds back in the atmosphere. Same above, as below.

"The firefighters saved what they could," said Gruff from behind a pile of rubble. He was shoveling piles of ash away from the garage. "We fared far better here in North Carolina than they did in Tennessee as I'm sure you're well apprised of."

Nolan nodded. "Gatlinburg sure took a beating but so did your college," came his reply. Gruff snorted in return while Nolan swung the sledge on the opposite end of the rubble to dislodge fallen beams. Once loose from the nail, the boards fell with a clatter.

The scratching of tires sliding on gravel caught their attention. Nolan turned around, stunned to see Tiberius and his boys disembarking from the Ram, making their way across the dead grass. He shook hands with Nolan first then the professor. Nolan noticed Titus hanging back scanning the area. He wondered how much PTSD the former Force Recon Marine carried.

"Gentlemen, I'm sorry to bother you in the midst of your work, but I wanted to make you aware of a situation."

"What sort of situation is that," asked Gruff pulling off his gloves.

"My rig is full otherwise I'd offer you a ride," pressed on the former Delta leader. "Follow us to Biltmore. I hope to find answers there." The professor merely nodded then made to put away their tools.

Once at Biltmore Manor, the most significant manor in the United States, Nolan spotted Mayor Townsend's jeep. What he also noticed were half a dozen Humvees parked in a semicircle following the estate's long driveway. It didn't make any sense. The tan colored vehicles looked more suited for Nasiriyah than the foothills of the Smoky Mountains. Young men in battle dress uniform carried armfuls of supplies into the hallways of the manor. They looked as though they were setting up a command center.

Tiberius' rig screeched to a halt before a makeshift checkpoint. Nolan and Gruff rolled down the windows to hear the ensuing argument. After a moment of heated discussion, the sentry spoke into a shoulder-mounted radio. Ultimately, the guard vigorously nodded and lowered his rifle letting it hang at his side. No words; the camouflaged man waved both trucks through.

Coming around the drive of the venerable mansion Nolan saw a man running down the steps. He was a tall man in a crisp uniform that didn't quite fit right. To Nolan, the man appeared more at home on a motorcycle with slicked-back hair, a lean jaw, and cold blue eyes. Fast on his heels was Mayor Townsend. Nolan and Gruff followed Tiberius and his men as they sprinted up the steps to meet the newcomer.

"What is the meaning of all this," called the cold soldier. He swung on Mayor Townsend. "Do you have anything to do with this?"

"Tiberius has been keeping watch on our community since the grid went down," explained the disheveled mayor.

"US Army Captain Tiberius Wilson, Retired," said the lead with a salute.

"Lieutenant Colonel Ray Tryst, unretired," came the reply sans salute. "Now I need to know pronto why you and your gang are interfering with a military operation."

"Military operation? Just what on earth is going on?"

"All in due time Captain, your hospitable mayor has assured me..." began the Lt. Colonel. Nolan scanned the Humvees watching dozens of uniformed soldiers remove supplies. He caught one remove a yellow backpacker's rucksack that struck a familiar chord. Walking towards the soldier decked in standard-issue Oakleys, the sun reflected off a metallic object that fell out of the bag. Before the soldier could stoop to pick it up, Nolan swiped the silver flask from off the ground.

"Hey that's mine, give it back," ordered the soldier, but Nolan had already turned his back to the man, shielding the flask while he read the inscription: *Though like the wanderer, the sun gone down, Darkness be over me, my rest a stone. In my dreams, I'd be nearer, my God to Thee.*

He closed his hands around the cold silver flask knowing it belonged to Cato.

The soldier's furor garnered the attention of others, and dozens of armed men surrounded Nolan. The offended soldier made a move to take the flask back. Nolan once again shouldered the man aside prompting his comrades to press their rifles closer.

"Stop! Lower your weapons," yelled Gruff running into the foray between Nolan and the tensed soldiers.

"Tell him to give that back," said Oakleys. "I found it first."

"We are not children," hissed the Lt. Colonel pushing his way through. "Everyone stand down."

Nolan glimpsed Tiberius and his men ease their hands away from the small of their backs. He wondered if each of the Asheville men had been willing to draw their sidearms on the US Army for his sake.

Tryst turned on Nolan. "I suggest you get out of here before we place you in the brig."

"Where did you find this," he said in return holding up the flask. "I know who this belongs to."

Tryst calmly reached and took the flask from Nolan's hand before giving it back to his trooper. "Clear out," he said with a deadly glare. The soldiers snapped to and went about their business. Tryst turned back towards Mayor Townsend and Tiberius. "We are placing your town under Marshall Law. Everyone available will be expected to meet on this lawn tomorrow morning at 0700 hours. Am I understood?"

"Will we finally know what is going on," pleaded Sheila.

"Am I understood," repeated the martinet.

"Crystal," spoke Tiberius with an equally cold stare. He rounded his finger in the air signaling his men to load up. Taking Sheila by the arm, Tiberius helped her inside the truck. Standing in the door, he flicked a two-fingered salute to the Lieutenant Colonel before driving off. Gruff and Nolan followed suit.

"What do you think is going on?" asked Nolan inside the confines of the Land Cruiser.

Professor Gruff rubbed his chin before answering. "I think we may have larger problems than just our communications being down. What it is I cannot quite put my finger on. Those soldiers were extremely on edge."

"Well you can't just declare yourself dictator of a town right," cried Nolan.

"We have few answers right now. We can hope that by tomorrow morning we will get down to the bottom of this. It has been a weird few days, first the fires, then the telecommunications go down and now this. It would be helpful to know what the rest of the country is doing."

"Yeah," said Nolan half-heartedly. He was beginning to wonder if the helicopter crash was not somehow part of a more comprehensive scheme. He looked to the sky as if another helicopter would materialize out of thin air bringing news and relief to the town but all he saw instead was a dismal sky.

15

Yuri sat outraged. Debris fields made the major highways all but impossible to navigate. Unable to take any more idleness he threw his door open and fought the wind gusts to the lead vehicle. Pounding on the reinforced door, he ordered the driver to step out. "What is taking so long?"

"Major, there is so much debris. If we are clearing each car out of the way then we have to stop each time and maneuver around the rest of the convoy," said the orderly, his accent placed him from the Caucasus, his eyes giving way to slight oriental slant. Yuri scanned the horizon. Steel cages that used to be cars carrying people during their morning commute littered the road. If not for the strong gusts of wind and the brisk temperatures, the smell would have rendered any battle-hardened soldier nauseous.

Reaching inside the Tigr, he grabbed the shortwave radio. "Attention all units. Due to extreme difficulty in clearing the roads we are going to rotate the scout vehicle." He paused to make sure the message got through. Several clicks responded in the affirmative. "Each time a lead comes up to an impassible obstacle, they will clear the obstacle for the remainder of the group and rejoin us at the end of the line."

Yuri's plan involved rotation. Once the debris was cleared using a ten-thousand-pound winch, that vehicle moved aside and rejoined the convoy as the rear guard. The effect would be a circuit and therefore save time.

"Keep your eyes peeled. Over and out."

Over two hours later the convoy stopped once more inside the Pisgah National Forest. The journey thus far had taken double the standard time, yet Yuri thought the chain gang approach was working smoothly. Dense forest darkened the road as the convoy paraded down the highway. The radio squawked to life, breaking radio silence for the first time since Yuri's address. They had not seen a living thing during the entire trip.

"Major, this is lead, over."

"We read you, what is your sit-rep?"

"There is debris in the road, but it strikes me as peculiar," said the soldier. "You said to make you aware of anything out of the ordinary." The soldier seemed to save the last bit as validation.

"*Da*, what do you have?"

"Two vehicles placed perpendicular to the road. They are not difficult to move, but their placement is intentional. How do we proceed?"

Yuri thought it prudent to be cautious. Should American soldiers be running the dense woods, they could have planted improvised IEDs around the obstacle. "I'll be there in one minute."

The intentionality of the cars' positioning was not the lone warning sign. Graffiti ran along the broadside of the crumpled vehicles reading: *Danger! Murder Inc.*

Stamped across the tinted windows was an image Yuri recognized from his time fighting Islamic State terrorists alongside American Special Forces. Painted in white was a narrow human skull with an over-imposed red target sighting on the left eye. Many Americans battling radical Islamists in the Middle East adopted mascots to boost morale and increase a feeling of invincibility. It created an ethos to blanket the Americans from their enemies; us versus them mentality. The team concept perpetuated in American sports made it easier to motivate young soldiers to give everything in service for their country.

Whistles shot from around the woods, a signal from scouts in the area. Yuri caught sight of ill camouflaged targets readying themselves in the wooded thicket. Soon pop shots were taken. Just as a medic assesses wounds on the battlefield, Yuri took stock of the danger the threat posed. While he knew each of his men were ready to level the trees, he raised his right arm high in the air to steady them.

"We've got you surrounded. Kindly evacuate your stations with your hands in the air."

Yuri breathed the crisp mountain air. Exhaling slowly, he watched his breath mix with the overcast sky. "This is commanding officer Major Yuri Orlov, to whom am I speaking?"

"Major, you are speaking to a people tired of government bureaucracy. On account of the grid being down, we declare ourselves a new nation. Now surrender your weapons and supplies."

"What joy," said Yuri. "For you are not looking upon an instrument of your government's suppression of rights but rather we are brothers in arms. You could even consider us liberators."

There was a pause before the bullhorn sounded again. "Who are you?"

Yuri took a step forward. "As I mentioned, I am the commanding officer, to whom am I speaking?"

"I'm coming out. Remember, we have you surrounded." Yuri suppressed a smile.

The speaker was a weathered man dressed to more adequately blend into the thick forests of the American South than the uniforms of Yuri's soldiers. Yuri stepped forward to meet the old timer with an outstretched hand. The man wiped his hands off on his pant legs before shaking.

"Y'all say you're a bunch of liberators? Just what on earth is going on?"

"Sorry," said Yuri, "I still didn't catch your name."

The man looked up at Yuri and down the line of Tigr armored vehicles. "Where is it you said you was from?"

"My men and I represent the tip of the spear. We have subdued your nation and will soon make use of American resources. My and I are here at the accord of the President of Russia."

The man's eyes rose in bewilderment. "Russia?" He moved to draw his sidearm. Yuri proved faster. In a flash, the Russian withdrew his Grach pistol and separated the old man's cerebrum from his brain stem. The man's body crumpled to the asphalt. A fury of hail fire erupted from the cavalry unit decimating everything in their path.

When Yuri waved his arm calling for a cease-fire, the forests, momentarily ringing with gunfire and screams, fell silent once more. Anton approached keeping his eyes on the wood. "Sir, should we check for signs of life?"

"*Nyet*. We should press on if we are to meet our objective by sundown. If our encounter here is any indication, then fighting in major population centers in the mountains may prove tiresome. I want to establish a line in the sand before I unveil my plan to take the CDC before Commander Yaromir."

"He has the ear of the Kremlin."

"Yes, and our success in these ranges is imperative."

"*Da*. I will see that we make all haste."

Yuri clapped Anton on the back. The soldier's steady hand and leadership were second to none. Soon the giant Cummins diesel engines were fired up; the obstruction towed aside allowed the Russian cavalry to once more parade south.

16

At the professor's house, Nolan stood over an ax chopping salvageable trees into logs for the wood burning stove. The whine of a chainsaw buzzed as Tiberius took a turn felling trees. Titus, the youngest of the bunch, helped the professor lift the charred remains of a door from the garage rubble. A second member of Tiberius' crew, a Hispanic man named Azarola, sawed limbs off the downed trees surrounding the lot.

Shortly after noon, a small sedan approached the workers, grinding to a halt before the driveway. Looking up Nolan saw a woman he did not recognize. She was rotund and jovial as she opened the trunk to her car. The other men approached the woman having placed their tools aside.

Despite the cold, most of the men stood around the car stripped of their jackets. Azarola, his chest heaving from splitting wood for the last hour, stood shirtless as steam lifted off his tanned frame. A modern-day John Henry.

"Don't y'all just look delicious," said the heavyset woman with a smile. Her thick red hair bobbed as she moved.

"What do you have for us, Mrs. Toops," said Professor Gruff.

"Well I just thought y'all might like some lunch," she said, her long North Carolina drawl lingering in the sunshine. She lowered the tailgate to Tiberius' Ram and began laying out roast beef sandwiches. "These sandwiches are my recipe, lathered in peppercorn with melted cheese on homemade buns." Nolan's stomach growled. Mrs. Toops emerged once more from behind the trunk carrying a glass pitcher so large it took her two hands to carry it. "I used my mother's favorite sweet tea recipe."

"Mrs. Toops, you are a delight," said the professor.

"*Gracias, amiga,*" said Azarola leaning in to kiss the woman on the cheek. She was old enough to be his mom, but Nolan caught her eyes lingering on the man's chiseled chest and taut shoulders. Nolan felt a pull in his chest and thought of Rachel. He had traveled so much since his mother's death, a chance to lose himself in the suffering of those less fortunate than himself. Now Nolan couldn't help but long for the community he saw around him, good men and women who had welcomed him without reservation. He began to wonder if he had at long last found himself a home.

Pounding away at a new log, Nolan thought more and more of his former family. A slow rage began to build, fanned by memory and regret. His father, killed in the line of duty. His mother, succumbing to cancer.

He saw their faces, their smiles. He saw the old farmhouse, the rural road in Arkansas, the tall pines.

He saw the pines in flames below, the ground running beneath the helicopter.

Bringing the hammer down, Nolan blasted another log. The National Guardsmen plane explodes before his eyes. Another hit, another split. The helicopter piloted by Tom swerves in the air. Another swing, the reporter falls out of the sky. Lifting the ax above his head, the helicopter slams into the tree line.

He pounded harder and harder until a knot threw the handle back at him swinging his body around. His legs were too weak to control the spiral causing him to fall to his knees in the dirt. A strong-gloved hand grabbed him by the shoulder causing Nolan to look up into the deep eyes of Tiberius Wilson.

"The thief comes to steal, kill, and destroy. But I have come so they may have life and have it in full." The former soldier stepped away from Nolan giving him space. Professor Gruff looked on, concern etched across his face. Titus and Azarola gazed into the forest with keen interest to avoid being nosy.

Embarrassed, Nolan propped himself up keeping a hand on the ax's wooden handle. Taking a deep breath, he acknowledged the quote, "John 10:10."

"My father was a Baptist preacher from Paducah, Kentucky. When we moved here, I was still known as Pastor Wilson's boy. It was only after I joined the military and lost good men that I learned to appreciate my father's favorite verse. Before each mission, I feared failure. I felt the need to control everything, a tension so coiled up I wanted to burst. After returning home, the only thoughts I carried were the memories. I lived in the past, second-guessing every decision.

"The brass thought I made an excellent tactician, considering every outcome. They promoted me to Captain and put soldiers under my command. The men who didn't come home were sacrifices upon the altar of freedom. But I didn't worship freedom. I worshipped duty. Each man I lost I had to justify my decision that ultimately cost them their lives. I recognized the thousand-yard stare of veterans in the street, and I identified with them. I couldn't face a future of hope, of joy, and of love." Here he dropped his head before looking into the distance. Nolan thought the warrior could see Sheila Townsend's face through the hazy, smoke-filled sky.

"Then, like so few that are fortunate enough, my father called from the hospital. He told me this, his favorite verse, and told me to get to work. He said that the thief was stealing the life out of me, but there was hope in the One who gave all of Himself for others. We cried together. The next day I checked into the VA and met Titus. That same thousand-yard stare already dooming his youth. I could see the walls closing in, and I wanted to help him. Azarola, Julius, and Marcus ventured in. We committed ourselves to helping others and helping the community. We chose to continue to live. Trips to the Florida Keys hunting shark didn't hurt either," he added with a smile.

"What I'm saying is, I know you've dedicated your life, but you are a slave. You carry the past. I hope that when the time is right, you can accept the joy promised to you and live life to the full."

"He better start soon," interrupted Gruff, releasing an armful of debris. "A young lady is expecting him."

Nolan glanced at the sinking sun and realized the afternoon had slipped away. He looked to the professor for help. Shrugging the professor said, "I promised you all the amenities of bed and breakfast. Might I recommend the hot shower."

17

Dusk fell in the mountains, the tall pines casting long shadows across the roadways. Clouds made the pale sun illusive. The roads darkened. There was little time to lose as Yuri hoped to be in Asheville, a major mountain hub, before nightfall. The large town lay just beyond the Pisgah.

He hoped to be able to circumvent the larger city by pressing through the Pisgah National Forest and take Asheville from the southeast towards the airport. Trouble followed the Russian coalition, however, as it passed through the dense woods beginning with the separatist ambush and, as now, halted by obstruction. As the convoy tried moving along the bank of a muddy river, one Corporal Popov failed to see a jagged crevice. As his Tigr slipped several feet, the front right tire smashed into the outcrop and crippled the wheel assembly. Yuri reacted without hesitation, ordering the occupants of the permanently cemented behemoth to grab as much gear as possible and disperse themselves amongst the remaining rigs. He knew better than to waste time digging the damaged Tigr out of the earth, and he was eager to get going. Corporal Popov, a fellow Russian, apologized profusely for the lack of judgment but Yuri waved him off.

"What matters most is that we reach our objective before more precious time is lost. We must establish reconnaissance, ready our weapons and each man must get some rest. I order you to pass the word that any man not responsible for driving is to sleep. Those who are driving will be exempt from recon duty."

"*Da*, Major. It will be done." Popov hurried off to carry the message.

Yuri sat back as the Tigr lurched forward to complete the short trip out of the national forest. He held no doubt the regional airport would be guarded as part of the American President's cover decree to destroy all serviceable airstrips. Priority number one would be to subdue the airport, rest and feed his troops before checking weapons and besieging the city. Winter's approach meant he could play with the optimal time of striking just before dawn's early light around five in the morning.

Despite the top condition of his men, most of them were Eastern European mercenaries whose morale could shift like the wind. He knew to keep them eager with the promise of American riches ahead. Other worries concerned him greater. He did not understand the condition of the people of the American South. The city survived the Russian Air Force having been nestled in the forest further from the reach of most bombers and still had a sizable population despite recent wildfires. Sun Tzu's *Art of War* taught *If we know that our men are in a condition to attack but are unaware that the enemy is not open to attack we have gone only halfway towards victory.* History was a great teacher not to underestimate one's enemy on their territory. He thought of General George Armstrong Custer, who with two-hundred and fifty famished, exhausted men, led a charge against Crazy Horse in the Battle of Little Big Horn, one of America's greatest military blunders. He vowed not to repeat any such mistake. Using a red hue flashlight, he poured over topographic maps of the area visualizing the battle ahead.

"Sir." Anton, one of a handful designated to approach Yuri without preamble. "The Asheville Regional Airport is just beyond the thicket. May we begin to send out a scouting party?"

Yuri nodded in agreement with his right-hand man's recommendation. "*Da*, this mission is important to our success in the region. I need you to be my eyes and ears."

"Of course. May I request bringing Manny, and a second sharpshooter-scout team?"

"It will be as you have requested."

"We will have eyes on target within the hour. After a sweep, I will report to you before midnight."

"Make sure you rest Anton; the future of Russia is counting on you."

"*Da*, Major." "

"Good." Yuri glanced back at his map, once more calculating the timetable to take the city. There was much to do before sunrise.

18

Emerging from the steaming shower, butterflies enveloped Nolan's stomach. He gripped the sink tightly while shaving to steady himself. In the shower, he thought long and hard about Tiberius' speech on letting go of his past. Now, with a cute nurse waiting for him at a local bistro known as Mae's, he thought of the future, in particular, the next few hours.

Fighting fire is a cake walk compared to this. Dressing in a pair of navy chinos, a dress blue oxford, grey sneakers, and a tan Seneca blazer, he felt far removed from the olive drab pants and Big Bird jacket of a smokejumper.

He ran down the stairs and reached for the kitchen door when Gruff called out to him, "Aren't you forgetting something." Nolan spun around in time to catch the keys to the Land Cruiser.

"Thanks."

"One more thing," said the professor holding up his hand. Nolan screeched to a halt once more.

"Where's your watch? A gentleman has to show responsibility on the first date. You've got to wear a watch."

"I don't have a watch," said Nolan letting his hand drop from the doorknob. The stool slid back on the tile floor. Gruff approached Nolan lifting his left arm and unfastened the leather band. He took Nolan's arm and placed the watch there instead.

"I can't borrow your watch," stammered Nolan. The watch was a classic Seiko dive watch with a navy face and red bezel.

"I want you to have this, Nolan." He pumped the old man's roughened hand as a gesture of thanks, his eyes beginning to pool.

"Take these too," said the professor pulling a handful of roses from a vase on the windowsill. "Girls like flowers."

Mae's perfectly complimented the quaint town. An old, white painted house outlined by a white picket fence. A powder blue sign by the French doors boasted home baked goods. Nolan breathed in deep the smell of fresh bread as he passed through a small gift shop.

Heading into the dining area, he spotted Rachel sitting on the far side of the room, a single lit candle set in the middle of a table for two. He smiled, admiring her pure beauty. Her wavy brown hair cascaded down small shoulders wrapped in a warm grey sweater, her legs folded in bold yellow pants.

He swung left, sweeping the restaurant and brought the roses to her nose from behind. Startled at first, she recovered with a deep breath. "Yellow roses, my favorite," she said as Nolan sat down across from her. "They are both so beautiful and yet sad," she said with a frown. Nolan did not know what to make of the comment. Rachel seemed to say things that came to her mind without much forethought and yet he couldn't help but be awestruck by her sincerity. "Sorry, I meant that in the military, they are given in love by a service member who is about to leave."

Her comment made Nolan think of Cleveland, the fire base, and, most of all, Tom.

"I hope I didn't say something wrong. Already." She sat up straight as if the create distance between herself and her thoughts, or her and Nolan.

"No, no, no. Nothing like that. Did I ever get to tell you how I got to Asheville?"

"Sheila mentioned that you were a firefighter so I assumed you were here to help us clear the debris."

"Well, that's partly true." He paused, then chuckled to himself. Tiberius' words about not letting a thief steal what remaining life he had left rung in his ears.

"What's so funny?"

He looked at her eyes and at first saw nothing but Tom staring back at him. Swallowing hard, he forced himself to focus on her grey, blue eyes.

"Something I heard today. It doesn't matter right now how I got to Asheville. What matters is that my stomach is grumbling and I have no idea what is good to eat here."

"Mae's is family style, so there's no menu. You're just gonna have wait and see."

As if on cue, a waitress brought a basket of rolls and bowls of potato soup. "Can I get y'all anything to drink?"

"Just water for me please," said Rachel.

"I'll have a Coke please, ma'am," said Nolan.

After she left, Nolan tried to bring the conversation to more familiar territory. "You know in baseball games when the home team is up to bat they play that player's warm-up song?" Rachel nodded wondering where he was going. "Well, I want to know what your song would be if you were at the plate. What would you want to play to get you pumped up, ready to hit a home run?"

He dived into his soup while she ruminated on her answer. After he finished it off, she answered. "*Tiny Dancer*."

"Seriously? You would listen to Elton John to hit a home run?"

"What," she giggled. "I used to take ballet and loved that song about a dancer."

He shook his head. "Okay. Still, you wouldn't listen to anything with a bit more pop in it?"

"I thought Elton John was pop?"

Nolan almost fell out of his chair. For all her brains, he had to remind himself that girls didn't speak to each other in baseball statistics, historical facts, or pop culture references.

"You asked the question," she continued. "Why don't you explain what a fireman listens to."

"I haven't played ball in a while. In high school, I stepped into the batter's box to a lot of Switchfoot. Now I would probably choose something a little older, something my dad may have listened to."

"Like *Tiny Dancer*," Rachel teased.

"Hardly. I think something more like *State Trooper* by Bruce Springsteen. I love that part where he whoops and hollers partway through the song. Plus, my dad was always speeding so I think he carried it like a theme song."

"I shall give it a listen sometime. Would you pass me a roll?" Nolan passed the roll and took off his blazer, hanging it off the chair. "What made you want to become a nurse," he asked.

She dabbed her hands on her napkin and smiled. "That's one of my favorite things. When I was a girl, my father took me to see the movie *I Dreamed of Africa*. I became fascinated with the idea of life in the wild. My senior year of high school I spent spring break in South Africa. I toured numerous hospitals assisting victims of AIDS and their families. They coordinated with orphanages funded by UNICEF. It was so sad. Many of the mothers that were infected had been so because of rape. I think I cried every night.

"After college, I looked into organizations like Doctors Without Borders and the Teach for America, but when my mom got sick, I put that on pause for my dad. My brother took up running as an obsession and began entering marathons all over the nation. He dropped out of college to join a professional racing team, so I stayed here. Sheila was great, making an extra effort to check on our family during her busy schedule. She became like an older sister." She fell silent.

Nolan dropped his fists from his chin. "My mom got sick too. My dad went first, in an accident. He was a firefighter. My mother had been a missionary in her younger years. I guess that's why I travel so much when I'm not fighting a fire."

Rachel reached her hand across the table to rest lightly on Nolan's. "Where do you like to go?"

"I love everywhere. The open American road, Rome, Jerusalem, Cape Town. Prague is one of my favorites. I always harbored thoughts of being a war correspondent and traveling the world."

"Not great for relationships but I understand. Once you travel, you get hooked. I love taking photographs of people and the landscapes they inhabit. My brother and I convinced dad to climb Machu Pichu with us last year. They both beat me up the mountain."

"I'm sure you did just fine," he smiled. The waitress brought large crockpot jars full of mashed potatoes, green beans, pot roast, gravy, and other comfort foods.

Rachel speared fried okra with her fork and pointed it at Nolan. "You're easy to talk to." She plopped the okra in her mouth. He smiled before dipping back into the golden waves of mashed potatoes. There was enough butter on them to sail a ship.

After the meal, Nolan helped Rachel into her coat, and the two stepped into the frosty night. Rachel took off without warning, crossing the street to a small house with a dimly lit porch. She squealed with laughter as he gave chase.

A tiny bell chimed inside the door. Nolan's nose wrinkled at the assault of smells saturating his brain. The shopkeeper caught his eye before returning to her novel, a worn copy of *A Tale of Two Cities*. "I love candles," said Rachel sweeping one off the long, wood-stained shelves. She raised it to her nose and breathed deep. "Mmmm… fresh baked cookies."

"No way," said Nolan. "Let me try." The aroma of warm dough and rich chocolate rising from the candle jar transported him back to his mother's table.

"Now you find a candle and I'll find one then we'll see if we can guess each other's smell."

He smiled. "You're unique; you know that?" Rachel grinned, spinning on her heel and walked across the shop. Nolan looked around catching the amused look of the shopkeeper's upraised brow. Perusing the open shelves, he drifted from scents of baked goods to prank candles. Sulfur, Poopy Diaper, and Road Kill sat dormant under large glass lids. He thought about purchasing one and sending it to Cleveland as a gag for Dixon Cafferty. He would send it with a note declaring his retirement from the Cleveland station.

He fell in love with Asheville. Sheila's hospitality, Tiberius' support, Gruff's adoption, and, deepest of all, Rachel's heart. Looking across the shop, he watched her select a candle. He could hardly explain the reasons to himself, but he knew he felt love. He had no idea what he would do. He promised himself that his future would be in Asheville.

"You better hurry!" Rachel spied him, hiding her face behind her covered candle. He made a last second selection. At last, he found one that, in his mind, symbolized the new beginning Asheville had given him.

"Ok," said Rachel. "You guess first." She unscrewed the lid. Nolan inhaled the candle's scent in dramatic fashion. "Ugh, you're such a boy," she laughed slapping him on the arm. "What is it? What is it?" She practically bounced up and down. Never one with keen senses, his grandfather could read the fine print on a tax form without aid, but Nolan took after his less fortunate parents.

He did, however, have a keen memory. He recalled smelling the candle's scent walking the gated communities of Bethlehem. White-washed iron fencing surrounded each white stone house, protecting citrus trees from casual looters. The smell Nolan now inhaled brought back green vines and white-pink flowers adorning the gates.

"Jasmine."

"That's right!" Rachel cried jumping with enthusiasm. "Okay, my turn." She mimicked his dramatic intake of aroma. "Oooh. This candle makes me thirsty. It's like I've been wandering through a vibrant forest and have come upon a waterfall."

He liked the way she put thoughts together, like a never-ending stream or brook.

"Am I smelling rain?"

He smiled. "Well done. It's called Cascade. I thought it fitted that the rains saved Asheville and other places from more fire damage."

"A new beginning, like a baptism."

"Uh-huh." He didn't quite know what to say. He had grown used to religious references by virtue of faithful parents and livelihood in the South. As of late, the words struck a deeper chord. Tom. Tiberius. Rachel.

"Hello? You okay in there?" She stood before him, a little concerned.

He shook his head, clearing the cobwebs. "Yeah, what do you say we swap candles and hold onto them for one another?"

She blushed, hiding behind the Cascade candle. "What a sweet idea."

Back outside, the evening's twilight hue was giving way to the darkness of night. The couple rounded Rachel's car, she hugging herself against the cold, he rubbing her arms to keep the blood flowing. "Nolan, I had a wonderful time with you tonight. You are every bit the gentleman I hoped that you were."

"I appreciate that." He fixed her with a look. "Listen, I like it here. I've been doing a lot of thinking. So much has happened and I would like to make a habit out of being here. Asheville isn't too different from southeast Tennessee."

"Are you saying you're thinking of moving here?" Her voice registered another octave higher. He nodded, smiling.

"What do you think?"

She sidled closer to him her face close to resting on his chest. "I think that would be grand." Her grey eyes sparkled like opals in the night air.

"Well I will let you get some rest, I know you're busy at the hospital."

"You'll be glad to know the gentleman we restrained made a full recovery. I work tomorrow. Perhaps you can find me after?"

"I'll see if Gruff can release me."

"Goodnight Nolan," she said laying a hand on his arm before turning to get behind the wheel of her Montero.

"Sleep sweet Rachel."

Nolan pounded a fist in the air behind the wheel of the professor's Land Cruiser. What an excellent time, he thought turning over the ignition. Reflecting on the week's events as he drove, dull yellow beams lighting up dark roads hiding along the blackened, burned forests. He dodged open bed trailers weighed down by recovered debris and fallen timbers. All along the streets leading to Asheville, burned or sunk wood lay strewn in piles awaiting pickup by tractor trailers in route to the nearest mill.

The front door to the professor's house opened without needing a key. Nolan crept up the stairs to his bedroom. He hung his clothes on hangers before sliding under the sheets. Rubbing his eyes and pinching the bridge of his nose he was overcome with remorse for the lives of Tom and the reporter who had died in the crash. He thought of the town meeting at the steps of Biltmore Manor in the morning. He wanted to hear the briefing and get answers as to the military presence. Despite the first impression he may have made with the soldiers, he vowed to utilize their communications to get in touch with Cleveland and inform them of Tom Philips' sudden death.

As his eyes at last shut with sleep, he and the inhabitants of Asheville had no idea they rested while a conquering army looked on preparing to lay siege.

19

"**M**ajor Orlov, the airport is deserted."
Yuri ruminated on Anton's report, scratching his face and lighting a cigarette. "There is no guard at the airport. What is the status of the runway?"

"The job appears hasty, but enough pockmarks were made to render the strip useless. We would require much more equipment to utilize it for landing craft. Visibility is also impossible with all this haze."

Yuri blew smoke into the cold night air. "For once we have good news. We need only concern ourselves with the city now. Anton, you should get some rest; you have worked very hard."

"Sir," the point man paused. "Yuri, we have another problem. Upon our return, we found Corporal Popov shot between the eyes from close range."

"What are you talking about." His blood was up. Flicking his cigarette to the ground, he confronted his most trusted man. "Who could have done this?" He implored Anton to say the man had wandered and been discovered by Americans but his instincts told him that scenario was impossible. The hit had been an inside job.

"Immanuil is tracking the murderer now."

Yuri hurried into camp, followed closely by Anton. "Bogdan," barked Yuri.

The large man turned his eyes up slowly from his MRE. "Where is Immanuil? A man has been found dead." Bogdan raised to his feet in an instant. The three set off to find the young sniper.

"He crossed my path not five minutes ago," said Bogdan tramping over the foliage in the dark. "He seemed to be heading this direction." He pointed away from the airport further to the southeast.

Even the forest was quiet, devoid of animal life in preparation for winter. The silence and darkness made Yuri more conscious of his steps while tracking Immanuil. Emerging from the thicket into a burned clearing the men found their companion bound at the wrist, both hands behind his back. His face revealed deep bruising, and blood ran down his nose without restraint. "Who did this to you," demanded Yuri grabbing the young man by the lapels and pulling him to his feet. With a flick of the wrist, Anton severed the knots that bound him.

"Never send a boy to do a man's job, Yuri."

Each man spun to face the voice. A man of average build stepped from behind a blackened tree, pistol in hand. Anton and Bogdan raised their AK-9 Assault Rifles in unison covering the man.

"Ah, ah, ah," he said waving a forefinger. "I pull the trigger at this range, and I'm bound to hit one of you." The soldiers saw that he was right and lowered their weapons.

"Identify yourself," commanded Yuri. "What do you want?"

"I went on patrol, securing your perimeter, and testing the American strength. Apparently, this town possesses a military presence. I liberated these from previous bearers." The man tossed two sets of dog tags at Yuri's chest. He skimmed the descriptions. Rosenblatt: US Army; O Positive; No verse. Young: US Army; B Positive; No verse.

Yuri spat on the ground. "I will have you thrown before a firing squad! Tell me, on whose authority did you engage the enemy?"

"I need no authority. Popov impeded the mission by his negligence, costing us precious time, so I eliminated him." He turned the pistol from side to side. "Go. Take your young scout and leave. I will be watching you tomorrow, and you will not want to disappoint me."

"This is rubbish," hissed Bogdan once Yuri and the men returned to camp.

"He said he would be watching. What does that mean?" asked Anton

"He came out of nowhere," explained Immanuil, "I knew I was close to finding him, but he got me from behind me with a knife to my throat." Yuri sat in silence trying to explain the man's presence to himself. "I heard some men talking in my search," continued the young sniper. "They were discussing a man who grew impatient as the journey wore on. They said he didn't even bother shooting at the men and women in the forest, just scoffed."

"I should have screened all Yaromir's men before we departed," said Yuri. "Now we have this to deal with before we lay siege to an American city."

"He rode in the Tigr behind Popov's. The Hungarian driver said a man tried to pass himself off as a Ukrainian separatist, but they knew he was lying."

"How?"

"They never trust a separatist with more than a rifle. They heard this man blabbering about someone called Firebird and how the invasion was sluggish now that the initial surge was over. They called him very impatient."

"You mentioned that." The pieces fell into place for Yuri. He was being watched. Indeed, someone had been with him since the beginning of the invasion, reporting back to the man he despised the most. "Firebird is a call sign for Yaromir. First, Marta. Now this man. They are spying on us."

"My hatred of the man grows deeper still," sighed Bogdan.

"Yes," answered the older brother. "You're lucky to be alive Manny. Now we know two important things: our movements will all be analyzed and reported to the highest offices of the Kremlin and second, that the city of Asheville does have a military presence. I order all men to get some good shut-eye and to avoid this spy. Give everyone his description."

"I doubt it will matter little," said Immanuil from his crouched position on the ground. "He will have disappeared by now."

20

Nolan sauntered out of bed. He stretched first his back then his leg muscles to iron out the previous day's work. He showered to clear his sinuses and breathe life back into shoulders. He dressed in simple tin cloth pants, a grey henley, the waxed trucker jacket and his sturdy boots. The sun's auburn rays shone through the windows promising a warmer day of work. He hoped the meeting with the soldiers would clear some of the cobwebs and allow him to get in touch with Cleveland.

"Gotta get our protein in today," said Gruff as Nolan broke into the kitchen. Laid out on the table were eggs, Greek yogurt, sausage, berries, and chocolate milk.

Sitting down, Gruff busied himself with his fork. "I haven't prayed to God since the day my Becca died. She was the stronger of the two of us, and I just couldn't face the Almighty with her gone." He spoke slow, measuring his words with his thoughts. "I feel strongly about praying now if you will permit me."

Nolan looked down at his plate but kept his eyes open. Gruff began speaking to God but rather than listen Nolan thought more about the man's hesitance to talk to God since his wife died. Gruff's lament resonated with him. Both his parents had been firm believers in Christ and lived as though each day had a purpose. He too carried their belief during his childhood years, but the deaths of his parents had shattered any notion that God was a God of love. With both of them gone he began to think that perhaps their calling to a higher way of living was from a bygone era, outdated and useless. It did not spare his father from a burning building or his mother from cancer.

When he looked up, Professor Gruff was staring out the window, the bright light shining upon his weathered face. He pictured the professor looking much like his father may have looked in old age. Face tanned with deep lines of experience and wisdom. Hands rough, not withholding them from productive labor. Voice calming and fathomless. His father would have retained a honey drip drawl that poured slowly as molasses.

He smiled at the thought.

"Rachel is at the hospital," broke in Nolan as the two ate.

"Last night was good?" asked the professor wolfing down a plate of eggs. The man ate like he was back in basic training.

Nolan nodded his head. "I like it here. I like her. I told her I was thinking of staying in Asheville."

Professor Gruff's eyes drifted from his plate to Nolan. The man broke into a smile so broad eggs began to fall from his mouth. Nolan laughed, clapping the older man on the back. "Come on Gruff. We got work to do."

Hundreds of Asheville's citizens joined Professor Gruff and Nolan on Biltmore Manor's grounds to hear the military address. The professor pulled the Land Cruiser behind the multitude; the large mansion shimmered gold in the rising sun as they pulled within range. Nolan remarked to himself how lucky the estate was to have survived the devastating fires if only to be given quarter to a strange and somewhat unwelcome occupation. He and Gruff found Tiberius' truck parked precariously close to an erected podium fashioned from the rear of an open bed M939.

The morning carried an early winter chill. Several in the crowd shivered as they awaited the Lieutenant Colonel's address. At last, the cold man emerged atop the podium, his face shaven and his uniform pressed. He seemed to be stealing himself; his chest erect as if to give a rallying speech to stir the troops. Mayor Townsend joined him, smiling nervously at her townspeople. Nolan heard Titus chuckle. Tryst tapped his finger twice on a bullhorn to call for attention. The multitude fell silent. Like Nolan, they too awaited news from the outside world, craving contact with friends and loved ones. Lifting the amplifier to his mouth, Tryst began to speak.

21

"The United States has been suddenly and deliberately attacked. Russian Federation airships have destroyed much of America's infrastructure and taken control of our remaining resources. What has descended upon us is an elite fighting force, one that has proven itself capable of rendering the United States a third-world country in a matter of days."

Dissention spread like wildfire throughout the crowd. Somebody swore and kicked at the dirt. Shouts raised in fear, anger, and panic.

"Sounds like a nightmare!"

"What was the level of their success?"

"If the Russians are working with the Iranians, it's no wonder we were caught without warning."

"How could this happen? What about NATO?"

"What about the United Nations?"

Tryst held up his hands calling for peace.

A shot rang out, the blast echoing across the valley.

Hit in the chest, Tryst's lifeless body crashed to the wooden platform. Blood pooled from underneath his body staining the maple wood a deep crimson. The mayor screamed a horrid scream, her white blouse speckled with blood and organic matter. Panic ensued, soldiers and citizens alike ran for cover. Nolan watched Tiberius bound up the podium steps tackling the mayor as sniper fire peppered the scene. Ducking low, he grabbed Gruff and pulled the man to safety behind a parked HMMWV.

"We were at a training exercise in Texas, on our way to Quantico," yelled a bewildered soldier, cradling his M4 Carbine. Nolan recognized the soldier as the one who held Cato's flask. "The devastation in Knoxville was outrageous. They're all gone. Boston. DC. Chicago. New York." The man began to sob, and Nolan could tell he was having a hard time focusing. Large armored vehicles poured from all sides canvassing the lawn and closing in on trapped Americans. Nolan saw several fleeing civilians shot in the back as the tank-like cars swarmed upon the helpless. A thwacking sound near his head brought his attention back behind the HMMWV as the soldier's body crumpled to the ground. A silver glint reflected in the sunlight. Nolan bent over and saw the flask tucked inside the soldier's chest pocket. He pulled it out, pocketing Cato's trusted sidekick.

"We've got to get to the Ram," hollered Titus. Nolan was relieved to see the young Marine, Azarola, Julius and Marcus making their way towards him and the professor. Bullets pinged off the steel bulkheads of the HMMWVs. Titus picked up the killed soldier's M4 and began covering their retreat. With Titus behind the weapon, Azarola threw open the tailgate to reveal a truck vault with sliding rail system. He issued primary carbines and secondary pistols. Nolan caught his .45 and chambered a round. Like many who grow up in rural Arkansas, he knew his way around a firearm. The sidearm, he noticed, had a small grey anchor along the chamber.

"Sig Sauer P226 SEAL," said Azarola. Despite the din of war closing around them, he saw the Hispanic soldier hand Gruff a genuinely lethal instrument: an M14 Carbine paired with a high-powered scope.

"The hospital!" Nolan was near frantic with worry about Rachel. He hoped there was still time to get to her. Azarola nodded, putting the 4x4 in drive. Julius and Marcus rode in the bed, rifles pointed in every direction.

Breaking into the open highway, they were appalled at what they saw. Carnage littered the roads. Azarola veered left and right, tires screeching, as explosions rocked the highway. Rocket-propelled grenades punched holes into retreating vehicles before exploding into great balls of flame. The smell of cordite, tar, and burning rubber stung their nostrils as they raced down the street. Nolan had a sinking feeling the Russians were funneling them into the road. A trap.

"We got company!" Julius yelled as a behemoth Russian Tigr roared from the trees and strove to catch the fleeing group. Now all faces were marked with panic as the chase led into a residential area nearing the north end of town.

"Incoming!" Azarola veered hard to the left. The sound of an RPG hiss soon filled their ears before the explosion launched the vehicle into the air. Fire enveloped the wreckage as it came down on its side.

22

For the first time since leaving the Oak Ridge Facility, Yuri felt pleased. The initial assault on the small mountain town had been a success. Putting Yaromir's spy from his mind, Yuri used the darkness of the previous night to best plan his siege.

As the spy alluded to, Asheville carried a military presence but no defensive positions or fortifications. What more, the military convoy seemed to be holed up in one central location. The lawn offered decent view should there be an attack but Yuri knew that a surprise hit would send the majority into a panic. He planned to turn a strength into a weakness. Men circumvented the large manor in a classic pincer movement, trapping all the American forces.

Indeed, the scene before Yuri as he, Bogdan, and twenty men made their way across the lawn was apocalyptic in scale. Explosions rocked the skyline. "Some are still alive," called Bogdan pointing atop the podium attached to the M939 Carrier. Several soldiers fanned out, surrounding the rostrum as a handful of Americans took cover from behind. Wood chips hurled through the air as Russian assault rifle fire ripped through the makeshift platform. Bogdan bounded up the steps, Yuri sprinting after him. Cornered below were six huddled Americans, a woman, and an armed man among them.

Yuri instantly leveled his assault rifle at the armed combatant, but a bear-like paw came crashing down on the barrel. Dropping the gun into his sling, he drew his Makarov bringing it right underneath the throat of his attacker.

"Bogdan! What are you doing?" Yuri demanded.

"That man," the younger brother said, pointing at the armed American, "I want to fight him."

"As you wish." Yuri stepped aside, holstering his sidearm. Spetsnaz disarmed the man with the weapon, binding each captive and bringing them onto the platform. The lone woman begged for mercy. Yuri thought about shooting her much the way he had the woman in Knoxville.

Bogdan had bigger things in mind. The man stood his ground. He looked much like Bogdan. Clipped hair, broad chest, bearded face. "You were a Navy SEAL."

"Delta." Still, the man did not move. "I fight your man. You let these people go."

"This man is my younger brother. You fight him, and he will kill you. Then we will kill your people."

"You let the people go now. I will give you your sport." The man moved closer to the steps, almost spoiling for a fight. The woman reached out to the man, but he brushed her off. Never taking his eyes off Bogdan, the man ascended the steps.

"The woman stays, the rest may go."

"No!" The man went to the woman. Soldiers strong-armed both into the center of the podium. Yuri let the remaining four Americans go free. They wouldn't make it far.

He righted three chairs and indicated the woman to sit. He and Anton occupied the other empty chairs. Sitting back, he clapped his hands. The woman sobbed, "Ty, please don't." The man put a hand to her, placating her. Yuri noticed the blood smeared across her blouse. She would have been close to Immanuil's shot.

"Even if I die, the woman must live. Those are my terms."

"You have my word as a warrior," answered Bogdan. "When you die, no harm will come to her."

Another explosion rocked the air, the sound vibrating for miles. The fight began. Yuri measured the two men as evenly matched. Bogdan held a slight size advantage but judging by the American's footwork; he was the faster of the two.

The heavyweights circled one another, gauging for weaknesses. Tiberius landed consecutive hits to Bogdan's solar plexus, shorting the man of breath. Yuri frowned. Undeterred, the Bear moved in. He blocked the next round of blows, throwing a haymaker. The American lowered his head in time for the hammer to come down on his shoulder. Still, the power of the blast threw the man to the ground. The woman shrieked, making Yuri smile.

On the ground, Tiberius saw an advantage. Staying low, he feigned a pounce. When the massive Russian made for a grab, he swooped underneath, sending his fist through the knee's connective tissue.

The Bear roared in rage. Fighting blind, he fended off the American. Yuri watched his brother's movements become telegraphic. Standing, Yuri moved to help his brother, to protect him.

Heaving loudly, Bogdan eyed his brother, drawing focus. Tiberius charged, going high. Bogdan parried a kick and pounded the eye. Tiberius staggered back, his eye shutting of its own accord. The American was not down for long, however, once again maneuvering inside Bogdan's fists to land another wave of punches. Fighting for his life and the lives of many others, the Delta warrior abandoned all sense of self. He followed two crossovers with a blinding uppercut. The blow snapped the Russian's jaw shut, shattering his molars. He stumbled backward, causing Yuri once more to leap to his feet. Everyone stood, closing around the fighters. Bogdan's face erupted in blood. He spat a collection of teeth and tissue. Tiberius once again charged. Spetsnaz training taught a warrior not just how to endure the utmost pain. It also showed an elite fighter how to fall.

Bogdan absorbed Tiberius' bull rush. Ignoring the pain in his knee, he managed to wrap his legs around the American's torso. The man gasped in agony. One bone-crushing blow was all it took to disorient the brave soldier. Bogdan sat up, cradling Tiberius in his arms like a child. The dark-haired woman screamed, clutching her throat, as despair consumed her. Bogdan placed a massive paw on Tiberius' forehead. He whispered his thanks to the man for an honorable fight.

Then it was over.

23

"Is everybody alright?" Nolan called out. He hoped someone would answer. The smell of smoke and burnt rubber thickened the air. He threw his head back against the headrest and coughed, barely able to open his eyes. Beams of light filtered through broken glass and twisted metal. The ringing in his ears almost made him feel at peace, insulated from the world. He dared not look around the cabin, afraid to find himself back in the helicopter, everyone dead. Steeling himself, he forced his eyes open. The Ram sat with seats facing skyward, each occupant strapped in like astronauts awaiting launch.

A voice.

"Az, don't move your body. Are you hurt? Don't move lest you have back or neck injuries." Nolan undid his restraints and leaned forward to reach Azarola, the truck's driver. A hand grasped his shoulder, rooting him in place. Turning, he saw Professor Gruff undoing his restraints.

"Gruff," panted Nolan. "You're alive." Turning his attention once more to Azarola, Nolan climbed into the center. Placing a hand on the center console, he slipped. His stomach lurched at the familiar feeling of something hot, wet, and sticky.

Blood.

Azarola lay in the driver seat, saliva mixed with blood covering his chin. "Got to move," he said. "Leave me here." Nolan looked down Azarola's torso to assess the man's wounds.

The diagnosis wasn't good, without an immediate ER, he wasn't going to make it. Nolan figured the RPG blast sent shrapnel through the driver side door, shredding it and embedding itself in the man lying before him. Azarola's eyes locked on his, the man's abrupt grasp strong as he pulled Nolan in close. "Take Titus. Get him out of here. Prop me against the rig with my pack."

Nolan reached for the ex-Marine's pack and noticed it was full of enough C4 to level Times Square.

"It's *adios amigos* for these murdering thugs," grinned Azarola. Blood continued to sprinkle his face and neck.

"Az."

"Go!"

Gruff popped open his door and began evacuating Titus, still unconscious, from the carnage. Nolan cradled the younger Marine's head and neck to stabilize him.

"Time's running out," panted Gruff. Nolan looked around. "Maybe we can hide him in the neighborhood." No place seemed safe, not even-

The hospital!

Everything seemed to slow down. Nolan walked in a daze as he and Gruff carried Titus down an empty avenue. Minutes felt like hours as they made their way without cover in the besieged city. He heard a pounding noise and became aware of his body making a slow descent into darkness. As his body followed a familiar voice deeper, there came a glow. The glow burned brighter. Nolan felt hands reaching for him, supporting him. He wondered if he were alive or dead. A clap boomed in his right ear, bringing his focus back.

"Nolan. Nolan snap out of it!" The darkness gave way to light. Details emerged. Several pairs of eyes looked back at him, eyes rimmed in gold from the glow of the ceiling lamp. Half a dozen men and women had sought shelter in what was an underground cellar. The extra hands took hold of Titus and lay him down on the solid concrete floor. A young woman stooped low to check Titus' vital signs. Nolan retreated to a solid wall to prop himself up. He feared the worst.

"This man is alive," said the woman.

Gruff stood, hands on his hips. "We've got to move. Ty is still out there, and we've got to beat the Russians to the hospital."

Once outside, the sky blackened with smoke from destructive fires. Nolan and Gruff moved in earnest, neither one slowing down the other, as they made their way north towards Asheville Mission. Block after block passed as they evaded Spetsnaz patrols. Running onto a tree-lined boulevard, the hospital lay just a little further. Nolan could tell the professor was beginning to tire, but the old man pressed on. Nearby screams brought both men grinding to a halt. Gruff unslung his long-range rifle, eyeballing the telescopic scope, panning to the east. Nolan looked through the haze, waiting.

"Spetsnaz are marching down the street. It looks like they've hit upon a denser populated area. They will aim to seek and destroy." Gruff lowered the rifle, his eyes asking Nolan what he wanted to do.

"We need to move. Those people could use our help."

The professor nodded. They advanced down the street, keeping close to the walls of houses for cover. Nolan hoped they would still reach the hospital in time.

24

Major Yuri Orlov's success was undeniable. Hundreds, maybe thousands of Americans were slaughtered in moments. He thwarted potential threats, insurgents, and rebels from one of the nation's last remaining population centers. The large Tigr rolled through decimated city streets, it's lugged rubber treads stamping the pavement. With him were Bogdan and Anton. Bound in the rear compartment sat a distraught Mayor Sheila Townsend, her sobs muffled by the gag in her mouth.

Despite their military presence, Yuri's forces had caught the American city by complete surprise. Bridges remained intact, a tactical disadvantage for the town. Anton turned the wheel to cross the French Broad River into the core of the city. A flash of color caught Yuri's attention as another Tigr passed them. He recognized the driver's sneer as belonging to Yaromir's spy. Loathing filled Yuri's heart, but he replaced it with battle-hardened experience, a heightened awareness bordering on paranoia.

"Stop!" he commanded Anton. Without hesitation, the Tigr ground to a halt. American small arms fire peppered the tank, ignored by Yuri and his men. The other Tigr was now midway over the bridge when a series of explosions severed the connection over the river. One intelligent soldier had rigged the deck to blow following the Russian attack, it was a lucky play for them, but Yuri knew his instincts had just saved the lives of him and his men. The weight of the other Tigr now worked in tandem with gravity to pull the behemoth down. He winced as the rebar steel gave way and four Russian souls plunged into the water below.

Enemy fire now concentrated on taking out the remaining Tigr, shots popping off the reinforced windows prompting Yuri to take control of the situation. A small portion of the bridge had succumbed to the blast. The rest looked just enough to risk an attempt to cross. He hoped the venerable Cummins engine was as robust as advertised.

"Now Anton," he barked. "Let's cross that bridge!"

"*Da*, Major," came the reply. The point man reversed and lined up his approach. Putting his foot to the floor, the Tigr lurched forward, hurling towards the gap in the bridge. Filled with adrenaline, Bogdan and Anton hollered as the truck launched into the air.

A sickening crunch and squealing of tires greeted them on the other side. "We made it," yelled an excited Anton. The younger soldier grinned from ear to ear, oblivious to American soldiers now emerging from positions along the river bank.

"Anton, you are a magician," called Yuri. He could just make out the muffled screams of the mayor in the back. In such a high-stress environment, she was bound to pass out soon from lack of oxygen.

"Time to unleash the beast," bellowed Bogdan. Opening the hatch to the Tigr's menacing turret gun, he was greeted with a hail of bullets but refused to back down. Fanning the belt in his left hand, Bogdan guided the turret gun, round after devastating round, into the soldiers along the riverbank. Anton powered the tank-like vehicle down the river bank as the assault on the Americans continued. The well-placed returning fire forced Bogdan to duck back inside the safe confines of the armored carrier. Skidding to a stop, all three men exited at the same time, weapons at the ready. Anton, the sharpest shot, dropped three American soldiers in rapid succession.

Seeing the Russians in the open, some of the American fighters saw a chance to gain control of the tank. Their gamble proved fatal however as Bogdan and Yuri fired from right to left, strafing four more soldiers. Yuri felt rather than heard the whoosh of air as bullets whizzed by his skull. Dropping to his stomach, he lined his sights in the direction of the attack. Squeezing the trigger, he placed a tight three-round burst of return fire. The human head was an incredibly difficult target to hit, but all three rounds struck home, killing his would-be assassin before the body hit the ground.

Anton waved the all-clear, the sound of gunfire now replaced by ringing in the ears. "You are like a cat, Yuri," laughed Bogdan, clapping his older brother on the back. "You have nine lives."

"I wouldn't be so sure of that," said a man stepping from behind the vacant armored vehicle. He leveled his Makarov pistol at Yuri and his men.

"You!" Yuri brought his assault rifle to his shoulder, mirrored by Bogdan and Anton. Yaromir's spy now stood before them, covered with mud from head to toe. Despite the damage on the bridge, it appeared the man had survived without a scratch.

"Give me one reason why I shouldn't blow your head off," seethed Bogdan.

"Heel your dog, Yuri," said the spy, not lowering his firearm. "I want what you want, but first I must commandeer your vehicle. Join me or walk but comprehend this: I am in control."

Yuri looked at Anton hoping his point man still carried the keys to the Tigr. His hope was in vain as the spy produced the keys, dangling them from his open hand. Yuri balled his fists. "No more wasting time! You drive. We find Immanuil, and we burn what remains of this city."

The spy smiled like a Cheshire cat. "I wouldn't have it any other way. Where to?"

"Asheville Mission Hospital."

25

Rocket fire whistled through the air. Explosions set fire to homes that had escaped the wildfires. Heaping piles of rubble followed in the wake of the small Spetsnaz patrol. Nolan and Professor Gruff leapfrogged their way towards the special-trained warriors, bent on protecting the innocent families still trapped inside their burning homes. Setting up shop behind a wood stack, the professor unfurled the rifle's sling and began tracking the destructive patrol.

"We will have to move fast. I will cover you as you search the homes. I will get one shot. One shot, one kill. Then I will move, always advancing in a crossing pattern so be sure not shoot me in the back." The professor was instructing Nolan on how their counter assault would go down. Nolan listened attentively but couldn't keep his hands from shaking.

"Stay low," continued the professor. "Your job today is no different than any other day. You are to enter a burning building, rescue any survivors, and get them to safety."

"What about the hospital?"

"As I advance on the Russians, make sure you are too, never staying in one place too long. If they get a fix on you, it's over. Keep in front of any walls to cover your back. As you advance, we will get rid of the threat then rendezvous at the end of the street to carry out our main objective."

Nolan could tell the man was no longer a professor but had slipped back into the psyche of a professional Marine sniper. He stole himself for bravery to complete the task ahead. He imagined the gunfire and rockets as giant engines soaring high above a blazing forest. He was ready to jump.

Gruff, lying in a prone position to minimize movement and maximize concealment, eyed the telescopic scope's crosshairs. Rather than bothering to check for insignia, pulling the trigger on the highest ranking first, the former Marine chose instead to assess the soldiers that posed the most significant threat. Finding his target in the second row, Gruff timed his shot to take out the grenadier before he had time to squeeze off another rocket.

His heart stopped beating, his breath measured. He timed the steps of the soldiers, marching three abreast down the street. Exhaling gradually, the old Marine squeezed the trigger. The recoil took the veteran by surprise as he let loose a perfect shot. The supersonic round found its residence in the enemy's heart.

"Go, go go," yelled the professor. The Spetsnaz, recovering from the shocking death of their fellow soldier, began fanning out to sides of the road, weapons raised in search of their new enemy.

Sprinting through the yard, Nolan reached his first house, crashing through the door. Through the large living room windows, he watched another soldier stoop to pick up his comrade's RPG. Pink mist painted the air around him as Gruff dropped the soldier with another flawless shot.

This guy is driving nails, thought Nolan as he searched around the home for occupants. "Hello?" he yelled running from room to room. "Hello!"

As a fireman, he knew that many civilians, children mainly, were afraid in such dire situations and more times than not found a small place to hide. Such actions were discouraged to children from an early age, but an annual drill seldom competed with hardwired instinct. Still, Nolan had precious little time to spare and trusted his gut that the house was indeed vacant.

Exiting the house, he looked across the yard at the next one. The Spetsnaz had continued advancing as well and were no more than forty yards across from him. Machine gun fire erupted, chipping the side of the house and sending Nolan ducking for cover. It had been over fifteen years since Nolan had shot a firearm. Having done so often as a youth the sensation felt familiar but distant. Returning fire, Nolan let loose six errant shots to shield his route to the next house. Turning the corner, he lined up the front and rear sights before squeezing the trigger. He aimed for center mass, but the round sank, shattering a soldier's pelvis. The man dropped kicking and flailing in pain.

An immediate risk neutralized, Nolan tried to take in the cacophony of the battlefield. In his mind's eye, he watched another Russian Special Forces shoulder his assault rifle, lining up a shot. Frozen in place, he had no time to take cover. Everything happened in slow motion. The soldier smiled, his finger reaching for the trigger. Nolan turned away in a futile attempt to protect himself.

He never heard the shot. Never felt the bullet.

26

The soldier's head exploded. The nearly decapitated body slumped forward and fell to the ground. Nolan squinted then checked himself for entry wounds. He was clean. Gruff had saved his life.

"Somebody help! Help! My boy!"

Nolan's attention was drawn across the street as a woman charged from her blue and white house. Her hysterical outburst gained the attention of the soldiers as a hail fire of bullets erupted at her feet and through the air around her.

"What are you doing," yelled Nolan, coming across the yard towards her. "Get back! Get back!" The woman slipped in the grass, but by some miracle escaped certain death as she half ran, half crawled back to her front door. Dozens of rounds splintered the wooden threshold where the woman had stood just a breath before.

Obscured amongst the thicket of trees lining the neighborhood was a boy about five years old wearing a green polo and khaki shorts. He was crying and frozen by fear. Hoping the professor was still in the guardian angel business, Nolan took off sprinting towards the boy, firing his pistol as he went.

The boy stood stock still between two houses. Nolan scrambled over a drainage ditch as automatic fire sent dirt, rock, and metal into the air around him. Without losing stride, Nolan scooped the little boy into his arms making a mad dash for the neighboring house for shelter. A piercing whistle drove Nolan and the boy to the ground. Using his broader body to shield the boy from the grenade blast, Nolan collapsed covering his ears from the explosion. At such close range, the grenade sounded immense. The brown siding house exploded into a shower of debris mixing wood with dirt, stone, and glass.

Grabbing the boy by the arm, Nolan ran into the house. Entering through the kitchen, Nolan reached for the Sig Sauer but realized he must have dropped it after the explosion. He needed to come up with something fast. Defenseless, he and the boy slid under the thick marble island as Spetsnaz breached the front door.

The boy's small chest rose and fell rapidly. His eyes remained fixed on the blown-out doorway connecting the kitchen to the utility closet. Inside the doorjamb lay a solid oak Louisville Slugger. Nolan motioned for the boy to remain still while he wrapped his hands around the wooden bat.

Harsh voices echoed off the walls, one of them getting closer to the kitchen. When the soldier's boot stepped onto the tile, Nolan let loose with a swing worthy of Stan Musial or Mark McGwire. Despite superior armor, the Spetsnaz soldier doubled over in pain giving Nolan a chance to gain the upper hand. Riding the soldier to the ground, Nolan wheeled on his comrades, firing armor piercing rounds through the sheetrock as both men fought for possession of the assault rifle. The barrage mowed down three Spetsnaz, their bodies crashing hard on the wood flooring.

Not deterred, the remaining soldier wrestled with Nolan, trying to regain control of his weapon. As a firefighter, Nolan was active, but the soldier seemed impervious to pain as multiple blows to the abdomen had little effect. Growing tired, Nolan could feel his edge slipping. The soldier flipped the American on his back, putting pressure on his neck. At six feet, Nolan had considerable arm reach and tried to punch the soldier in the face, but yet again the attacker was unfazed.

Precious air evacuated from Nolan's lungs. He knew he would not be able to draw another breath. Flailing with his arms, he grasped in thin air. A grating noise filled his ears as something metallic skidded across the tile. Reaching out, his hands grabbed hold of the boy. The soldier's eyes had been focused on his own and were not aware of the item in Nolan's hand. The boy had given Nolan a knife.

Closing his eyes, Nolan plunged the sharp blade into the soldier's collar, burying it in the man's soft tissue above the bone. Clutching his neck, the soldier released Nolan and fell over backward. The boy was crying again as Nolan once more pulled him by the arm, heading outside. This time he was armed with an assault rifle.

"Silas!" The boy's mother cried, taking the kindergartner from Nolan. She stroked the boy's light blonde hair as the trio retreated behind the house.

"Go through the woods to the south," instructed Nolan. "Maybe half a mile to Biltmore Village. There is a house there like yours. It has a cellar visible from the street. Survivors are hiding out there. They will help you, but you must go now." The woman nodded and turned to her son to seek shelter.

Rounding the house, Nolan now caught the Spetsnaz from behind. The longer barrel of the assault rifle improved his accuracy as he fired upon the soldiers. He stopped shooting just long enough to take cover behind a car, advancing on the soldiers. He was getting close to Gruff now. Nolan peered from behind the car frame, the street devoid of the same fighting force they encountered moments before.

"Rally on me!" The retired Marine sniper turned history professor was waving him on. Nolan dived into a sprint.

Their eyes met. The professor jerked backward, hit by an unseen force. The old man's grey eyes never left Nolan's even as life itself did.

Nolan slid the last remaining feet, reaching for Professor Gruff. He cradled the old man in his arms. "Don't give up the ship," he whispered. The chest no longer rose, a hole penetrating the heart.

Since all surrounding Spetsnaz had been cut down, Nolan deduced the shot had come from afar. Another sniper had gotten the warm-hearted Marine. Ignoring personal danger, Nolan held the man's body close and wept. He could feel the enemy sniper's eye upon him, zeroing in on his face before pulling the trigger.

An enormous explosion sent concussion waves through the mountain air, blasting the trees. Even hundreds of yards away, Nolan could feel the heat of the blast. Smoke billowed in the breeze from the south. Something in his mind told him to get moving. Only someone tampering with Azarola's body could have caused the explosion of such magnitude. The ensuing shockwave covered Nolan as he searched for transportation to the hospital. Running north, he tried to keep his mind from despair. Rather than thinking Rachel could already be dead he placed all his thoughts and efforts thinking about her, her body, her face, her smile. He pushed harder and harder focused on reaching her before it was too late. Entering the road Nolan was a man possessed.

A black Chevrolet Tahoe appeared intact, save the windshield cracked in a million pieces. Nolan hated himself as he slid the dead occupant onto the ground. The cabin reeked of blood and death, the gas meter running low but the hospital was not far away. Nolan reversed from the pile up before throwing the mighty V8 into gear and rocketing for Asheville Mission.

27

"Charges are ready sir." Anton stood before Yuri passing the remote detonator to his commanding officer. "All the doors are sealed, nobody gets in or out." Yuri took the remote device from the point man's gloved hands. His eyes traveled up the walls into the windows as numerous citizens looked on in despair, pounding the glass. There were no uniformed personnel among them. Yuri was quite confident that every American soldier had been wiped out before reaching the hospital. As for the hospital patrons, they stood no chance. Many had surrendered. Their bodies were piled high by a firing squad waiting on the front steps. He had no idea how many men he had lost. More critical was the extinction of the American people and their way of life, their *rebellious* way of life.

"Are you going to do it Yuri or do would you rather I murder these people in cold blood?"

Yuri did not have to turn to recognize the voice of the spy. He toyed with the idea of seizing Yaromir's rat and throwing him into the hospital. Bogdan was undoubtedly capable of strong-arming the man. When Commander Yaromir asked the inevitable about the fate of his spy, Yuri could shrug his shoulders.

Another voice called out to Yuri, one carrying youth and joy that warmed Yuri's stone-cold heart. Immanuil came running.

"Ah, Immanuil," Yuri said clapping the young man on the shoulders. "How goes the West?"

Immanuil peeled off his ghillie suit making him look much thinner. "The West is crumbling sir."

Yuri smiled. "Good. It is good to see you." He was trying to cheer the young sniper, but he could tell something was on the soldiers' mind. "Speak Manny. What is it?"

"It's nothing, sir. We have killed the enemy, and our objective is nearing completion, but I fear for this war, sir."

Each man took a step closer. Bogdan, Anton and the spy each closed on Immanuil to hear the sniper's observations. Yuri nodded for Immanuil to continue.

"Major Orlov, I fear the resolve of this nation. When in battle I shot an old man through the chest. He died in an instant, but he did so in peace. I saw his eyes just before he died. He was a tested warrior, one worthy of the title. The old man was a sniper like me and despite his age managed to kill nearly a dozen Spetsnaz before I stopped him. I fear Russia's success should we inherit a nation of men like this one."

It was the spy who spoke first, clapping Immanuil on the shoulder. "Do not worry young Popov. America is no longer a nation of warriors. They have traded their warrior's code for retirement plans and health benefits. They are soft in the hands, forgetting the feel of the rifle and the plow. We will swat them like flies." Immanuil looked down at the ground but nodded his understanding.

Yuri hated the spy, but even he had to give the man credit. America was long removed from their famed Greatest Generation that volunteered everything to defeat Nazi aggression. Yuri smiled at the thought for it was the suffering Soviets who reached Hitler's compound first surrounding the deposed dictator. History would often wonder if surrounded by compassionate Americans, Hitler may not have committed suicide, but anything was better than falling into Soviet hands. "*Da*, good speech. Immanuil is here. It's time to go."

"Don't forget about the charge Yuri," muttered Bogdan as the men once more mounted the Tigr, this time with Immanuil in tow. Yuri waited until the tank reached a safe distance and he could no longer hear the pounds and pleas for help before depressing the switch igniting hundreds of pounds of C4. The massive explosion shook the atmosphere for miles.

28

Nolan saw the white flash just before he heard the explosion. Seconds later his Tahoe broke through the brush and skidded across the hospital parking lot. Gripping the wheel, he tried to find the emergency entrance, but no such thing continued to exist. The entire complex was on fire.

Exiting the SUV, his body recoiled at the heat of the flames. Leaving the assault rifle in the cab, he grabbed a merino wool scarf from the passenger seat, spinning it around his head to act as a smoke filter. Without a second thought, the trained firefighter, like his father before him, plunged into the fire and darkness.

The first thing he saw was the remains of a reception desk. A large crater had opened pulling everything down into it in a massive pile of rubble. Flames licked the walls and rooms above exploded as oxygen tanks ignited shooting funnels of fire down dark hallways.

"Rachel!" He yelled again and again, dropping the scarf each time to call her name. Tears pooled in his eyes as grief, and the intense heat took a heavy toll on his body. At these temperatures, he knew the water from the sprinkler system would be searing hot. He had to hurry.

He searched every room on the ground floor hoping Rachel would be where she was when they first met. He could not believe that such a beautiful beginning would have such a devastating end. Another explosion rocked the building as more oxygen tanks ignited from above. A terrible groaning sound warned Nolan's trained ears that the roof was about to collapse. Back in the lobby, the ceiling above the reception desk crater began to bow, turning brown like sugar melting into caramel.

"Rachel! Rachel!"

No answer.

He was out of time.

Charging for the exit, he had mere seconds before the interior of the structure came down upon him. Leaping over scorching debris, he pushed his oxygen-deprived lungs harder while the roof came crashing down around him.

The door burst open covering him in sunlight. Exhausted, he fell to his knees and doubled over in tears. "I'm sorry. I'm so sorry. I wasn't there..."

He pounded the asphalt. Pound, pound, pound. Sobs racked his body. Blood fell from his hands, cut by glass and debris. Rolling to his knees, he looked into the ash-grey sky.

"Why God? Why?" His throat closed and he could no longer speak, just breath. *I was ready to forgive You. I was prepared to start again. Now, this? So much death? Why?*

A sound like rain beginning to fall approached closer and closer. Letting his face fall to the source he saw a large armored vehicle bearing down upon him. Unarmed, he had no way of deterring their determination to run him over. The pitter patter of the Russian beast grew louder when another piercing sound erupted from the other side of the parking lot. Barreling towards him was another massive vehicle.

The door to a Bulldog 4x4 Fire Engine burst open. A young woman with jet-black hair reached out her hand towards Nolan.

"Quick! Get in!"

BOOK IV

1

Nolan slammed the door shut on the large Fire Engine just as machine gun fire hammered the sides. The mysterious female let off the brake and pumped the gas with such ferocity that Nolan's head whipped back in the headrest. He twisted in the seat for a final look at Asheville Mission Hospital. Machine gun rounds continued to pound but the vehicle's sheer size kept Nolan and his rescuer safe.

A hard turn to the right threw Nolan into the driver's lap.

"Do you know what you're doing," he asked above the roar of the engine.

"No idea," she answered turning the wheel like a maniac.

"Give me the wheel," he commanded. While not an engine driver himself, he knew enough about the Bulldog to appreciate its venerable size and speed. At the rate his rescuer was going, the Russians need not give pursuit. Rather than switching seats, the young woman, maybe a student at the university, shifted to the rear compartment where she had hidden away an AK-74 assault rifle.

"Where did you get that," asked Nolan, doing a double-take.

"Found it," came the terse reply.

He shrugged, turning his attention back to the road. The Russian Tigr bearing down on them was respectable in its own right, and he knew a plan was needed fast to avoid capture or death. A maelstrom of gunfire erupted on the passenger side as the Tigr pulled even with the fire engine, positioning itself to overtake the fleeing occupants.

He hammered the accelerator, the large tires easily finding purchase on the country road as he led the chase out of town. A loud exchange rang in his ear rendering him deaf as the woman, lying across the back, fired the assault rifle on full auto through the window at the Russians. The smell of cordite filled his nostrils, but the sudden violence took the Russians by surprise as they ceased firing, ducking for cover.

The road grew rugged putting both the Bulldog and Tigr on their home turf. Their engines roared as more power surged to the giant tires gripping the dug out fire lanes through the scorched forest. Nolan hoped that their large escape vehicle would be able to navigate the narrowing country roads. Making matters worse, large stacks of felled timber lay along larger spaces in the path creating a dangerous hazard at such high speeds.

"I'm out," yelled the woman from the back seat. "You have to find us a way out of here!" She slid back into the front passenger seat, leaving the assault rifle smoking in the rear.

"You didn't grab another magazine?"

"I'm not a soldier! And don't yell at me!"

With her seatbelt fastened, Nolan now went on the offensive, allowing the smaller armored vehicle to come abreast of the Bulldog. His goal was to use its greater size to try and run the Russians off the road. The driver was skilled, however, and the nimbler Tigr evaded Nolan's attempts.

Knowing a boarding attempt from the rear would be suicide, Nolan calculated they would need to make another effort to come abreast. Sure enough, the Tigr thundered back, the Russian faces set in determination. Nolan weaved away from the Tigr, hoping one more attempt to ram the attackers would achieve the desired effect. Biting his tongue, he turned the wheel into the Russian vehicle.

Crunch! The sound of twisted metal rang in his ears as the steel guards of both behemoths became intertwined.

Once hooked, Nolan pressed the accelerator, dragging the smaller vehicle. He took the next bend in the road in a full arc. Just as he hoped, a large stack of lumber lay at the end. Row upon row of long timbers sat in the road bank.

"What are you doing," pleaded the woman. "You're going to get us killed." She recoiled in her seat, turning away from the stack of lumber.

She screamed.

At the last moment, Nolan pulled the wheel, missing the pile by the narrowest of margins.

BOOM!

The Russian Tigr hooked on suffered a far worse fate. Anchored by the massive fire engine, it took the lumber stack full speed. It struck the logs, weighing tons apiece, so hard that they began to roll down the hillside in a bone-crushing avalanche. Tires, glass, wood, and metal burst apart in a cringing explosion. Nolan's last-second maneuver had not given the Russian driver enough time to correct his trajectory as they plunged into the wood.

Nolan drove on. His hands, broken to bits by the asphalt, bled freely to the floor. The woman let her hands fall from her face, her black hair a sharp contrast as her face drained of all color.

2

Part of the deal in manufacturing the GAZ Tigr armored personnel carrier was that it had to be better in every way than the American HMMWV. That meant it had to be faster, stronger, and even by Russian standards, safer. Yuri also conceded that he had to thank the Americans in a small manner for hand building the robust Cummins diesel engine. Although the engine block could be seen through the hood and resembled a chewed meatball on a stick, the bulletproof fabrication had saved his life. Being so close to Sweden, the Russian military also borrowed five-point harness specs from the automaker Volvo. Yuri felt glued to his seat from the moment of impact. Looking to his left, in the driver seat, he saw that Yaromir's spy had survived as well. Not even so much as a broken wrist, the excuse for a man had wisely withdrawn his hands from the wheel at the last moment before the torque wrenched it from his grip.

"That hit hurt me worse than their Delta soldier, brother."

Yuri smiled at his brother's joke. Undoing his harness, he began checking the status of his men. Bogdan was already trying to shoulder his door open, the frame compacted from both sides after the collision. Anton was coming to. The point man's olive drab bandana did little protect his skull after slamming against the ballistic glass knocking him unconscious.

Yuri smiled at him too. "Welcome to your finest headache, Anton." The man groaned in return and held up a hand begging Bogdan to stop rocking their rig back and forth.

"I'm trying to help us escape," said the giant man.

"Try the turret your wild boar," whispered the athletic soldier. Bogdan grinned in return until he caught Yuri's eye.

"What is it, brother?" Everyone sat in rapt attention as they all turned to face the Major.

Yuri swallowed hard. "Immanuil. He wasn't." His throat tightened. "He wasn't strapped in."

Bogdan threw his entire weight behind a bear-like fist, propping the turret hatch open. A cold grey sky filtered through the opening. Yuri exited first, leaping off the armored vehicle and wrenching the rear hatch open. Both arms fell limp at his side. The rest circled their commanding officer. No one dared touch the prone forms of Immanuil and the woman in the open compartment. Yuri leaned forward placing his hands on the sniper's young face. A touch on the neck confirmed his greatest fear. There was no wound and there no pulse. The boy had died of a broken neck. Yuri hung his head.

Anton reached in to check the woman captive's vital signs. She had lost consciousness repeatedly during the chase. Her flaccid body survived the crash, much like a drunken driver's body, and though stricken, she was alive. He placed her body to the side, forgotten for the time being.

Yuri backed away from the wreckage never taking his eyes off the young man's body. His fists clenched as rage overtook him, building steam like a locomotive. He would burn America to the ground for this! But first, he would start with the men directly responsible for Immanuil's death. One had escaped. The other stood right before him.

"You did this," Yuri spit out, eyes boring into the spy. "You killed Manny!"

The spy looked around in terror for anything to appease the outraged commander. Neither Bogdan nor Anton took a step in the condemned man's defense. "Please," the man stammered. "The American... Yuri, think!"

Yuri charged the spy bringing his knee deep into the man's abdomen, doubling him over. He then pushed the rest of the man's weight down, forcing him to his knees. The spy brought his arms up, shielding himself from another strike. Instead of moving in for another blow, however, Yuri backed away. Bringing up his Makarov, the spies' eyes widened. "Yuri *nyet*! *Nyet*!"

"*Duskbedanya*," said Yuri. He fired three shots into the man's torso. Standing over the man, he watched the chest rise and fall with much difficulty. Then he put another round between the eyes.

Without a look at either of his men, the Major began a slow walk back towards the burning town, his boots grinding along the rocks in the road.

Anton stood over the dead spy and spat in an open eye, "*Vyshara Mera*." He placed Immanuil's dead body on a makeshift gurney and dragged the metal sled behind him, scraping along the road.

Without ceremony of his own, Bogdan grabbed the unconscious woman, still dressed in her business attire, and slung her over his shoulder. The American and his rescuer had gotten away, but Bogdan knew they would make the nation pay. He contemplated how he would kill much more as he followed the other two, his footsteps falling flat with the extra burden.

Many miles later, the late autumn sun neared its apex coaxing heat from the earth. The only sound came from the scrunching of boots on rocks and the occasional grunt. Bogdan and Anton lagged behind Yuri, burdened still by the weight of another body yet neither man dared to pull Yuri from his isolation. Yuri had doted on Immanuil like a son. Indeed, their small unit was closer than family. It was he who had first spotted the young sniper's potential and he who had promised and cashed in on favors to have the prodigy transferred under his tutelage. Immanuil Popov managed to be both a lethal weapon and an innocent youth. Yuri thought he now should have convinced the handsome nineteen-year-old to choose another profession if not for the incredible skill and God-given talent! His heart burned within him. He had no outlet for such grief. What was it his mother always wailed before his father as he beat her? *Those who live by the sword, die by the sword*. America, he promised, would kneel beneath his sword.

He turned back to look at his remaining men. Eying stalwart Bogdan, the man sweated but showed no signs of fatigue while carrying the woman. Anton, the smallest, was the purest athlete of the bunch. His chest heaved, and his head did not rise as he dragged thin but tall Immanuil on the sled. The short but sturdy legs churned and Yuri thought of the mighty tugboat tucking low while pushing the great liners out to sea.

At last, he came upon a small red truck that lay abandoned in the road. Americans were too trusting he thought as the driver side door popped open, keys dangling from the ignition. When the engine turned over, Yuri crept the dusty Ford back down the road. Bogdan laid the woman in the bed of the pickup before grabbing the other end of Immanuil's stretcher to be loaded beside her. The woman stirred a little, but her eyes remained closed. All three men ignored her as they slid into the bench seat.

Nothing, save steel reinforcements, remained of Asheville Mission Hospital. Less than half of the mission appointed Spetsnaz troopers remained alive. They gathered in the parking lot flanked by serviceable Tigr armored vehicles awaiting Major Yuri Orlov's orders. Some ate, some slept, but no man played games or carried out a charade. They too had lost comrades in the fight against the Americans. A somber mood carried them into the afternoon. Of the forty-three men under Yuri's command, just fourteen had survived. Yuri recounted the number of dead. Immanuil was dead. The sniper previously confirmed the death of eight soldiers. Four more bodies, in various pieces, were discovered. They died instantly after a massive explosion by a booby trap. He atoned for the spy. *That leaves sixteen dead and missing. Sixteen unknowns for the cause.*

"Yuri," Bogdan called. "The men are wondering what we are to do for our fallen comrades. One of them is religious and believes that someone should at least say a word." Bogdan let his words hang in the air. Yuri knew he was being asked to speak over each of their fallen comrades. It was his duty as commanding officer. He looked down at his feet. Beneath his boots, hidden under blown bits of the hospital were the charred remains of an American flag. It was perforated with burn holes but still recognizable. Yuri ignored the flag seeing the face of Immanuil instead. Like Yuri, he too was predestined for the priesthood if fate had given them religious fathers instead of fighters. Without looking up, Yuri acquiesced. They would take some time to remember their dead.

3

Driving north along Interstate Highway 26, Nolan didn't stop until he and the mysterious woman reached Madison County. He hoped that by sticking to the major highway, they might find survivors. He had no idea just how wrong he was.

The streets leading to the Tennessee border were unlike anything he had ever seen. It soon became apparent that the large Bulldog 4x4 was much too large to navigate the littered streets of debris and wreckage. Cars lay strewn, decimated by automatic machine gun fire launched from Russian aircraft.

When he leaped out of the fire engine, he came around the front to find the woman with her head between her knees. She coughed a dry, ugly cough as though she were choking. He moved towards her, but she put an arm up to stop him. "It's okay," he said, "I'm a fireman."

"And I'm a grad student," said the woman. "Please, I just need some space." For the first time, Nolan took notice of his rescuer. She was tall, almost as tall as he, dressed in black slacks, a white V-neck, and a simple jacket. Her black hair was cut short, falling just above her shoulders. Her face was sharp with light brown eyes that held flecks of gold.

"I've never seen anyone die before." Her voice rose just above a whisper. That was all it took for his knees to buckle. He put an arm out, throwing his weight onto the brush guard before he fell. "I fired a gun at those men who were," she stumbled, grabbing her knees once more, "who were going to kill us. I've killed a man and shot a machine gun at others. I had no idea I was capable of that."

Nolan looked at her. He wanted to comfort her. He knew what death looked like. His father. His mother. Friends who fought fire. Victims of fire. Tom. Gruff. Rachel.

"You don't look so good. Your poor hands."

The woman took Nolan by the shoulder led him to sit on the Bulldog's steel bumper. She poured water on his hands and offered to let him drink the rest. He gratefully accepted.

"I've seen death," he rasped. "Too much death but I've never taken a life. The destruction. The city. Gruff. Rachel." He broke out in a sweat as if his brain couldn't accept what he knew the truth to be, that his friends were dead and that he had killed in return.

She looked away and began assessing the vehicle. "We need to get moving," she said looking to the north. "I'm Lauren Bostwick, by the way," the college student said. Nolan looked up to meet her gaze.

"Nolan Hoke. Thank you for saving my life."

Taking him by the shoulders, she led them to another vehicle more suitable for a long journey. Given his nauseous state, Lauren chose to drive. He lay down across the back seat, holding his hands close, motionless, watching the trees float past.

Three hours passed without another human being in sight. He hadn't slept but stayed in a perpetual state of wariness, eyes open, but never seeing. The drive took them from the mountain forests into the bleak landscape of coal country.

"What are you studying," asked Nolan, sliding into the passenger seat.

"I chose Finance before a random Psychology course shifted my attention towards the Humanities. It took longer, but I thought Occupational Therapy sounded more like me. Now I'm working on my Masters, at least I was before the fires shut down the campus. I don't even know after this. What do you think happens now?"

"I have no idea," answered Nolan. "We were hardly given any answers." His mind reflected back on the helicopter crash, the way in which the helo sustained impact, and how the Hercules C-130 exploded. All along, he thought it was some accident. Now he realized that it was no accident. Whether mistaken for military or not, both the C-130 and Tom's helicopter were *targeted*.

"Do you think that what happened here has happened all over the country?"

Nolan thought for a moment. "Given that we know the Russians are involved, I can only imagine that they came from the west. If that is the case, then we fared far better, and perhaps survived longer, than many Americans."

Lauren merely nodded in return. Checking the fuel gauge, she said, "We're running low."

4

Fresh earth filled Yuri's nostrils as he packed the dirt atop Immanuil's grave mound. Several other identical mounds flanked the young sniper's final resting place spread out in a V-shaped pattern with his cresting the top. The fourteen remaining Spetsnaz including Bogdan and Anton had gathered around Yuri who spoke words of thanksgiving over the dead, words of encouragement over the living, and words of warning over the United States.

Now all was quiet save for the smoldering remains of Asheville Mission Hospital, left alone to burn to the final ember. Smoke billowed high, a signal over the air akin to that employed by Native Americans.

Yuri wiped his brow of sweat, his battle helmet replaced by a field cap denoting the rank of Major. Looking high into the mid-day sun, he was blinded by its bright rays that masked the year's late chill. With the wind came a repeating but muffled noise from the east. He whistled to Bogdan, nearby, to follow his gaze. The sizeable Russian warrior lifted both hands to fight the sun's glare and peered into the distance. Ninety seconds later three Kamov KA-60 helicopters touched ground in the open field where the fallen Spetsnaz and coalition soldiers had been laid. Each soldier kept their weapons at the low-ready position. Yuri waved them off as a lone figure emerged in Russian dress uniform denoting the rank of Naval Commander. The large, bulbous nose and small beady eyes were immediately recognizable. Yuri stepped forward and formally saluted Commander Sergei Yaromir.

After returning the salute, Yaromir surveyed the vast destruction giving a mild clap, slapping his fingers into the opposite palm. He strode with pride to each fighter, addressing them in their native tongue: Russian, Hungarian, Czech, Belarussian, and the last Ukrainian member left alive.

"Well done Major Orlov, your conquest of this enemy outpost is absolute." He surveyed the area some more. "Walk with me please, Yuri." The two men distanced themselves from the stone-faced soldiers, walking to the south. "I have news Yuri, but first, I wonder, what became of my spy." As the ultimate spy, Yaromir could read the micro-expressions, or tells, that gave away when a person was lying to them.

"Many of my men have been killed. I was not aware I needed to keep tabs on the man you sent to spy on me."

"And yet, you know how he died."

Yuri paused. "I killed your spy myself. He was an arrogant fool whose actions cost me the life of Corporal Immanuil Popov."

"Your beloved sniper."

Yuri hung his head. "*Da.*" To his surprise, the Commander clapped him on the back.

"We have lost much more than your boy, Yuri." Yaromir looked back at the burning hospital. "It seems as though America was able to launch multiple nuclear warheads from ancient Polaris submarines off the White Sea, north of St. Petersburg."

Yuri stood incredulous. "To what result?"

"I am afraid the results, though much is still unclear, are terrifying. Our President and the Kremlin are no more. Our political, economic, and cultural seats of power are destroyed. The two targets were Moscow and St. Petersburg. With force much greater than that which dropped on Hiroshima, I am afraid the devastation is immense."

"That's impossible! My team secured nuclear facilities and others before any American retaliation was possible."

Yaromir shook his head. "No, not just Americans. At least it was not they who launched the submarines." The old man coughed, bringing a handkerchief to his lips.

"Who then," Yuri demanded.

"We were deceived by an enemy who has never trusted us and in turn should have never been trusted by us. Reports are vague about how the subs were provided the warheads. We do know that it was the British, operating under friendly terms in our waters, that launched the attacks."

Yuri could have fallen over under the weight of history. No other nation besides America had ever launched nuclear weapons against another nation. That was the wisdom behind President Vasilyev leading the way for non-proliferation.

"*Dovorey no provorey*," continued Yaromir, growling like a junkyard dog. Trust but verify. "They lied to us. I tried to warn the Kremlin, but those great imbecils wouldn't listen. The French I knew were trustworthy, having been our oldest ally since the Treaty of Tilsit but the British have always manipulated our efforts. From Mansfield Cumming's plotted assassination of Rasputin to his thwarting the Soviet cause in India, to Winston Churchill proclaiming the Iron Curtain during the Cold War, it would have proven wise to pay attention to history!"

"It doesn't matter now. We have reduced America to rubble, and for what?" Yuri was beside himself. His whole life given in the service of his nation to have it swept under his feet while on the cusp of bringing the world's greatest superpower to its knees.

"It gets worse. I just received word that NATO is staging its troops to establish a western front. Their first goal will be Prague, followed by Warsaw and the Baltic nations." The old man, looking feebler by the second, hung his head and placed a hand on Yuri's shoulder. This time Yuri did not pull away.

"What do we do now," he asked as he scanned the plain back towards the awaiting soldiers. Dusk was coming and the temperature continued to drop. Yuri shivered, but he did not know whether or not it was from the cold.

Yaromir withdrew his arm and began to walk back towards the remaining conquerors. "For now, we return to Washington DC. We gather more information. What remains of the Kremlin will demand our return to prepare for the inevitable NATO invasion. But," he said turning back to Yuri with steel in his eyes, "if it were me I would make sure every inch of *this* nation burns to ground before we accept that we have made an error in being here."

5

Dusk fell faster now as winter approached. Nolan was afraid to use the car's headlights. Lauren reasoned that the low fog lights might be okay. Signs in the distance announced that they were approaching Pikeville, Kentucky. The town resembled an oxbow, winding its way through sloping hills of coal. They crawled through the city at a snail's pace. The small mountain town reminded Nolan of the one in Tennessee he wandered into after the helicopter crash. He brushed Cato's flask still tucked in his pocket. A lifetime seemed to have passed since he left Cleveland.

They parked outside a gas station. The pumps were still operable, but they were going to have to enter the deserted building to turn the right one on. Inside, the place was a bit more modern than the one Nolan had crashed in with Cato. There was a full coffee bar complete with stainless steel appliances and a computerized Coke machine offering a medley of flavors at the touch of a button. A dining area fenced with a soggy buffet to the side of an elevated clerk desk that sat in the center of the large station.

Without a word, Lauren attacked the coffee bar, the whirring sound of the machine filling the deserted place. After a quick sweep, Nolan shuttered all the windows and dead-bolted each entrance. He gratefully took a steaming cup of instant coffee from Lauren and filled his nostrils with the aroma. Anything to cover the lingering smell of old food hovering from the buffet.

"I found more good news," said Lauren, returning to fill her cup.

"What's that? Did you find anybody?"

"No, but I did find some showers."

Nolan felt his body tense with anticipation. "Showers?"

"Yep."

"Would you like to go first?"

"I would love to, but if anybody here needs a shower, it's you."

"What do you mean?"

She recoiled away from him in mock disgust. "You reek a disgusting cocktail of sweat, mud, smoke, and testosterone. If you don't take a shower this instant, then I'm going to find a new gas station."

Stripping off his dirty clothes, he tried to pat the dirt and sweat off of them, starting with his pants. The shower's hot water took some coaxing out of the rusted spigot, but it felt amazing. He cowered under the hot spray as it helped numb his mind, shedding both grime and memories of the last several hours. He tried to pray knowing that his father often used such private opportunities to cast his cares upon God but no words came to Nolan. The silence suited him just fine as he let go of his troubles.

In the mirror, he doctored his hands. He pulled the shards of glass and rock out his knuckles, rinsing them with cool water and wrapping them with paper towels. Four aspirin and a good night's rest would do him good.

Lauren couldn't help from raising an eyebrow when Nolan emerged from the steaming roam dressed in a towel. He slid his waxed trucker's jacket back across his shoulders as the cold night bit at his exposed skin. Large meals and physical labor had done his body some good to stay in firefighter shape. Nolan could feel her eyes on him as he walked through the dining area to grab another cup of coffee. He nodded, not turning away from the machine, as she called out saying she would take her shower. "I hope you left some hot water," she said over her shoulder.

When she left, he looked outside the windows checking for movement or any lights in the distance. The sky darkened to a deep purple, the mountains and trees falling black in the backdrop. He lit a few candles, careful to keep them away from the windows. His stomach churned, urging him to grab a handful of protein bars and satiate his hunger.

"I'll take first watch," said Lauren emerging from the shower half an hour later.

"You sure?"

"Please," she said lifting her coffee cup. "I'm covered." He needed no further prodding as he found an open bench in which to lay. Covering his head with his arm, he fell asleep.

Minutes later it seemed, he was being prompted awake.

Sensing a dark figure move over him, he awoke with a start. The figure brought a candle over to reveal their strong but feminine face.

"You were having a nightmare," said Lauren. He sat up, eyes adjusting to the dim light. He rubbed his forehead, a mop of sweat coming off. "Go on," she prompted. "I took Psychology, remember? Tell me about the dream. I love dreams."

Nolan pulled his knees close. Lauren sat in the bench across from him, her features glowing in the candle light. "Well, as you said, it was a nightmare."

"Sounds mysterious."

He took a moment more to refresh the images in his mind. "I was alone. It was colder than it is now; snow fell to the ground, and the wind cut through me like I was wearing a sheet. Everything was dead, like after a fire. I was also lost. I know that I was lost because in the dream I knew that I was supposed to be following people. But I couldn't find them. The frozen forest had left me all alone."

"Scary."

"It gets worse. In the snow, there was no path, and I fell into a large hole. The dirt was black and full of rocks. I remember feeling pain in my ankle." He reached for his ankle, his mind still feeling the pain.

"Getting off the ground I heard a twig snap, loud as a gunshot in the desolation. I could feel the hairs on my neck stand on end, a sort of electrical current in the air. I exhaled, but the breath came out in a growl. I turned in the pit. A pack of wolves held the high ground, their lips and teeth red from a recent kill. Then it dawned that I was in their den. They encircled me but kept their distance. I was too scared to move. I willed my hands to feel for a weapon."

"How many were there? Numbers can be important when interpreting dreams," Lauren interjected.

He shook his head, "I don't know. Maybe eight or nine. I remember I was supposed to be in a group, but I got lost."

"Eight can be important. For many, when they dream about an octopus, it means that they have too much on their hands and feel excessive stress to accomplish all their tasks, like a mother of several children."

"I don't know how many tasks I have to accomplish. There certainly has been plenty of stress in life as of late," offered Nolan.

"What happened next?"

"They made a semicircle around me. One, a brown one, leaped into the pit with me. My hands found a stone. I knew it wouldn't be much use so I thought I would try to strike it near the eyes and then spring on it, hoping for the best. I had my plan made up then the she-wolf backed away."

"She was a distraction see," continued Nolan, his eyes empty, focused on the memory. "The pack's gaze hovered over me. As I turned, I saw the largest, blackest, most terrifying monster heaving over me. I barely twitched a muscle before he was on me, pinning my sides with arms made of iron. I could feel his hot breath on my neck. His eyes were red, but darkness grew in the center. His gaze locked on my mine and I knew it was over. The jaws clamped on my neck and I woke up."

"Let me get you a glass of water," she said. When she returned, Nolan drank to quench his dry throat.

"I'll take watch now," he said. "I feel wide awake. You try to get some rest." Lauren stood up, patting him on the shoulder before lying a few feet away. He stood and stretched. Rubbing his eyes, he walked towards the window wondering if a dream meant a warning.

6

Yuri took little notice of the green grass sea flowing beneath him as the helicopters soared to the dark ruins of Washington DC. When they touched down in the vicinity known as Georgetown, he and the remaining soldiers silently filled out and found their way to new sleeping quarters. Commander Yaromir made a show of wanting to have a word, but one glare from the battle-weary Major rendered the point mute.

Yuri had to thank the old spy for saving him the best suite. A beautiful penthouse renovated from the old foundry. As Yuri shrugged off his gear, he walked into the ornate bathroom turning the water to near scalding. Grabbing a solid mahogany chair from the dining room, the warrior carried it into the shower with him. Placing his head in his hands, he calculated the cost of the past twenty-four hours.

Immanuil. Moscow. St. Petersburg. All were gone. He felt foolish for believing the audacious plan of Operation Cannae could succeed. He contemplated the strength of American resistance from this point forward. The fools in Blacksburg hadn't known what they were dealing with, but they were organized and eager to resist authority. Asheville itself had proven a costly victory, at least for him and his men. While American Imperialism had stretched the nation's resources, he couldn't help but wonder if his own President's ambition had been too grand. Were Russian troops now spread too thin across the American continent to subdue it? He knew from lessons learned in Afghanistan, Syria, and Eastern Europe that the answer was yes. He felt that the entire playing table swept anew. For Russia's objective to be completed, they had to seize America's infrastructure. To seize infrastructure, they had to eradicate resistance. To quell opposition, they needed reinforcements. Reinforcements were going to be hard to come by now that the heart of Russia smoldered under rubble.

Sun Tzu's words drifted into his skull catapulting his doubt over the abyss. *"Confront them with annihilation and they will survive. Plunge them into a deadly situation and they will live. When people fall into danger, they are then able to strive for victory."*

Wiping condensation from the hotel mirror, he took his time toweling off and eyed himself in the mirror. Brilliant blue eyes under black, military cropped hair reminded him he was more fortunate than his brother, already bald. He popped tablets of ibuprofen chased down with a glass of water. Setting the glass on the marble sink he heard the unmistakable sound of breaking glass followed by what his experienced ears told him was a muffled gunshot. Bolting from the bathroom, he dressed in a flash, grabbing a smaller Vityaz-SN submachine gun. Without a second thought, he hit the hallway.

7

"**H**ush!" hissed Trevor Johnston. The twenty-one-year-olds adrenaline was shooting through the roof. Nothing was going according to plan. "Quiet! They will be coming any minute now!" His words placated the female chef holding the Russian made pistol.

It had taken over half an hour for everyone to agree to the plan. Trevor, himself a young intern at the Georgetown hotel, had been planning a course of action since the ancient Russian assumed the place as their base of operations. The others took much more convincing. Trevor gulped as he caught the eye of his most significant detractor. Melvin. Melvin was the curator of the hotel, a bald man with a thin neck and thick circular glasses. Due to some sick, misguided allegiance bordering on levels narrated in a Hernando Tellez novella, the older man contested Trevor's plan. Trevor had the temptation to tell the man, *Just Lather, That's All*.

"We have a duty to our guests, no matter their race, creed, or nationality," Melvin cried upon hearing Trevor's plea for action.

"They have a female prisoner! What about her guest treatment," Trevor challenged. He, Melvin, the female chef, and a young waitress were huddled together before the changing of the guard, the exact moment when Trevor wanted to spring his surprise. He noticed the black-clad soldiers had brought back an older but attractive female prisoner. One girl, the young waitress he tried all semester to seduce, told Trevor that if his plan succeeded in rescuing all of them he would be a hero. Trevor gravely nodded in silent assent. The plan shattered the moment the gun went off.

The chef dropped a wine glass to distract their guard long enough for Trevor to come from behind with the chef's knife. He sliced the guard's carotid artery and deftly lowered the dying man to the stainless-steel floor. It was then that Trevor made a mistake. Passing the soldier's Makarov pistol to the chef, he trusted the woman to have enough sense to keep it from going off. Instead, she let loose with a round when the dying soldier grabbed her ankle as they prepared to make their escape. A single shot fired, and now everything was blown. Trevor knew he had to remain calm if they still had any chances of living. Even Melvin seemed willing to follow Trevor's lead. It also didn't hurt that he was one holding the soldier's assault rifle.

Everyone fell silent as they followed him from the kitchen into the hall.

He took a moment to wipe his sweating palms along his pant leg. Shouts and the pounding of boots echoed from above. Trevor gulped down his fear. The time was now or never.

Each member followed Trevor as he sprinted across the bricked dining room. They covered the distance in seconds. Reaching for the door, he hesitated. An avid diver, he realized his breath bordered that of hyperventilation. Breathing deep, he wrenched the doorknob and spun into the hallway. Gunfire erupted from behind the walls in the hallway, shattering the glass windows walling off the foundry inspired area. A metallic ringing lingered in the air. Trevor felt a sudden impact slam into him but saw nothing in front of him. Arms pulled him back into the dining room before the group retreated into the recesses of the brick walls.

The female chef, armed with the Makarov, covered the group as Melvin ran back to the kitchen. Trevor slumped against the wall, sliding to the ground as the egg-headed curator beat a hasty retreat. Trevor swore under his breath at the man's cowardice. How could they possibly hope to escape if they didn't fight?

To his surprise, Melvin returned, this time armed with a first-aid kit. First, he looked at the old man in confusion and then fear realizing it he was he who needed the first aid. Melvin placed a hand on his shoulder. "You're going to be alright, son."

Looking down his side, he saw the cause for Melvin's concern. Blood soaked his powder blue tailored shirt. He reached for Melvin, grasping the man's lapels in his tightest hold possible. Sweat beaded at the break in his hairline. Nothing was going according to plan.

More automatic gunfire assaulted their position, too close for comfort. Trevor grimaced in pain as Melvin worked frantically to patch him up. The chef returned fire with the assault rifle. She screamed in a wild, terror-filled rage as she fired round after round at the Russian Special Forces. Trevor realized his foolishness. They were going to be overrun, and he would be responsible for costing Melvin, the chef, and the young waitress their lives. Not to mention his own. Looking past Melvin into the stainless-steel kitchen his eyes fell on the many gas stoves. His grimace gave way to a smile. Trevor Johnston had another idea.

8

Anton and the other members of the assault on Asheville met Yuri in the hallway. The men reached the bottom of the stairs and began clearing rooms, frog hopping one another on the way to the kitchen. Another staccato of gunfire erupted as the men joined Yaromir's Mafioso bodyguards, already pumping lead into the dining room with their Uzis. Glass and brick exploded as the small group of Americans retreated into the kitchen prep area.

Yuri succumbed to rage. The armament of the Americans meant they managed to overwhelm their guard. He promised he would find the one responsible and make them watch while murdering their accomplices.

As the shooting subsided, the thick-necked, tuxedoed Mafioso entered the shattered room, their weapons held high. Harsh Muscovite voices barked at one another as to who was going to be the first to breach the kitchen. Not wanting to miss out on the action, a handful of Russian Special Forces shadowed the thugs. Yuri motioned for Anton and Bogdan not to follow suit, pressing his open palms to the floor to ask them for patience. Both men ceased their assault and waited. Seconds later a massive fireball erupted, shooting through the old structure and out the remaining windows into the frosty night. The heat was intense, but Yuri's instincts once again saved he and his men from a gruesome death.

Allowing Anton to take point, Yuri scanned the blown-out area. Using a tactical light at the end of his Vityaz, he sifted through the smoke, avoiding large chunks of flesh. The cold night air blowing from a large hole in the factory was all that kept him from succumbing to waves of nausea. The stench of burnt hair and charred brick would haunt him the rest of his life.

9

Trevor Johnston was still in pain, but he trusted Melvin's assessment that the ricochet nicked his side missing any vital organs. A pressure patch now rested underneath his shirt to staunch the bleeding. The improvised bomb had been a success, yet nobody celebrated as they tried to escape the enormous hotel. They all shivered against the cold but rather than flee for safety, they each resolved to find the woman captive.

"Melvin, you know this place better than anybody. Where do you think they would hold a hostage?"

"The original design of this building was to cast metal works before being converted to our immaculate hotel. There must still be dozens of unused ventilation ducts that lead to the cellars below where the hotel stores wine for prominent guests. I'd bet all Solomon's treasure that the Russians have her placed down there."

"We've got to move quickly. That explosion won't do more than slow the soldiers down."

Melvin rubbed his glasses against his shirt. Looking into the clear, starlit sky to test them he said, "Follow me."

The chef covered Trevor, Melvin, and the waitress as they worked the exterior vent off the air duct. "These should lead straight into the cellar," informed Melvin. "Once you drop down there, it will be very dark, but the tunnels are clean."

"I've still got my phone," said Trevor pulling himself into the duct. "I can use the flashlight on it."

"Right, good luck."

"Don't forget this," said the waitress handing Trevor the Makarov pistol. He tucked it into the small of his back and prepared to let go. Looking back the at the young waitress, Trevor took her chin in his hands and pressed his face against hers in a desperate kiss. Their eyes held each other for a brief second.

Trevor let go.

He landed hard in the brick cellar. Three quick coughs consumed him as dust swarmed in his lungs. He cursed himself for picking up the habit of smoking while joining a fraternity. Pulling out his smartphone, he shone the light down the narrow passage and up into the duct. The glow couldn't penetrate the darkness of the air duct but did illuminate his path. He pulled the pistol from his waistband, holding it in his dominant hand while the other held his single source of light. The tunnel appeared endless like something out of *The Twilight Zone*. Trevor twisted his nerves into operation telling himself how Melvin and others frequented the dark cellars to bring prestigious guests the hallowed wine from their vaults. Feeling along the wall, Trevor paused ever so often for any hint of noise. He hoped to hear voices of the captured woman's guards or maybe even her breathing to tell him where she might be hiding. Realizing his phone's light may alert someone to his presence, he toned the illumination down and held it just above his knee. A far-off trickle of water dripped, the sound echoing through the tunnel.

After what felt like an eternity, he came upon an arched entryway. The sound of dripping water had become greater as did the smell of wood. He figured he was getting closer to the wine barrels. He hoped the woman was close. He had no idea how Melvin and the others were fairing above ground.

A scratching noise brought his attention back to the tunnel. Dead ahead of him, something was making a sound in the dark. His breath quickened, and his hands began to shake. Inching forward, Trevor shone the light along the floor ahead of him.

Though blindfolded with a cloth, the movement of light caught the woman's attention. He found her! She jerked her head in his direction. He could tell she was afraid. She tried to push away from his light, using her legs to shuffle her body across the room.

Placing a comforting hand on her shoulder, Trevor whispered, "Don't be afraid. I've come to get you."

10

A nton proved once more what a magician the operative could be. Yuri was worried about his right-hand man following the aftermath of the battle in Asheville. The excitable and self-proclaimed adrenaline junky had not uttered one word since spitting on the corpse of Yaromir's spy. The Major could feel it in his bones that Anton blamed himself for young Immanuil's death. The spy had gotten the better of Anton, stealing the keys and driving the armored personnel carrier that ended Manny's life.

His worries were extinguished however as he watched Anton Kozlov deftly evade the machine gun fire emitted from behind the old brick façade of the five-star hotel. Circumventing the enemy wide enough not to draw attention, Anton separated himself from the other soldiers pinned down by the chef's barrage. Yuri watched his man advance via a night vision monocle, visualizing him aim at the enemy with his silenced submachine gun. Anton's weapon emitted three-bursts of light followed by little sound.

The female chef spun a full three-hundred and sixty degrees after taking a round in both the arm and shoulder. The third round missed the woman's head by some fortune. With their gunner down, Yuri called an immediate cease-fire as Anton charged the enemy position, taking them by complete surprise. All three raised their hands in surrender as the dark-clad soldier kept his machine gun shouldered and ready to fire.

Securing his submachine gun, Yuri withdrew his pistol as he sprinted around the corner. Several other soldiers followed, surrounding the small group. Yuri placed the pistol's muzzle into the temple of the unwounded female. She was a young woman and burst into tears, convulsing with terror in the face of death. He left her alone. The other woman, dressed in a cook's attire, appeared to be losing a lot of blood, so he stepped over her as well. That left an older bespeckled man as skinny as a yardstick. Crouching low next to the man he aimed his pistol dead center of his forehead. "How many others are with you?"

"I have no idea what you're talking about," the desperate man cried. He clung to the lapels of his shirt as a sort of safety blanket. Even as he closed his eyes away from the gun, Yuri could tell the man was lying. The terror was genuine, but he lied all the same.

Not taking his eyes off the old twig he ordered the young woman brought over to him. The woman screamed and writhed, trying to break away from the Russian's grasp but she was no match for the soldiers who were trained to feel no pain. Still looking at the old man, Yuri placed the gun in front of the young woman's face. He asked again, "How many are with you?"

Tears streamed down the girl's face as she cried. In the wake of such fear, the man quaked. "Just one more. A man."

"Where is he now?"

"He's trying to rescue the hostage you brought back with you."

Yuri spun his finger in the air. Five men spread out around the hotel in unison, creating a moving perimeter sweeping for the rogue saboteur. "Is he the one who created the bomb?"

"It wasn't a bomb. Trevor let the gas in the stoves burn in the air, waiting for a spark."

"Reckless. You could have all died in the blast," said Yuri putting his sidearm down. All eyes followed the pistol. He looked at the young waitress, her porcelain skin, and bright blue eyes. He pitied her. To kill her would be no different than any American and yet here she was, so close. So personal. To let her live would prove a more heinous crime once Yaromir got his hands on her. It was a matter of time. As far as Yuri was concerned, the man would always be a pimp. He took a step away from the group. Closing his eyes, he gripped the pistol and shot the young waitress in the head. The chef screamed, a guttural, primal scream before she too was silenced. The old man, despite his feeble and gangly appearance, managed to roll to his feet and scamper in the direction of the Potomac River. One soldier, shouldering his rifle, waited for the right moment before dispatching the man with a clean shot.

Yaromir rounded the corner, chest heaving, his belly protruding from under his nightshirt. Yuri holstered his weapon. Looking at the young woman, Yaromir's eyes asked the question. *Why?*

You know why, Yuri answered back with a deadly stare.

11

Gunshots echoed through the brick tunnels. "This is a stupid idea," said the female captive. "You're going to get yourself killed."

Trevor was now sure the woman used her looks more than her brains to get what she wanted. Didn't she realize he had rescued her! He never encountered drama like this in the frat house. After paying his dues freshman year, everything came to *him*. Rounding the corner of the tunnel, he checked his grip on the pistol for a better hold. They had also found a carbon knife for popping champagne bottles that the woman now carried. He put up a closed fist to stop the woman's forward progress much as he had seen in too many action movies. She must have seen the same film because she grounded to a halt.

"See something," she asked in a whisper.

"We've got to be close to an exit," he responded. "Let me go take a look."

"Be careful."

Once again Trevor could feel the sweat and shakes returning as he crept along the cold, dark corridor hoping to see the light at the end of the tunnel. He looked down at the light emitted by his smartphone and steadied himself. Turning off the phone, his eyes adjusted to the darkness around him. In the distance, he could make out stairs leading to a dimly lit hallway. Flashing his phone in the woman's direction, Trevor signaled the all clear. Looking back at the light Trevor could feel his pulse relax, and his hands grow steady. Pupils expanding, Trevor caught three flashes of light from outside the tunnel.

As Sheila Townsend rushed in her stocking feet to meet Trevor, his lifeless body fell to the ground. Her screams were caught in her mouth by hands reaching from the shadows. Thrashing against her captors, she sank her manicured nails into the closest man she could find leaving three deep gashes in his neck. Another soldier rewarded her with a crack in the skull by the blunt end of a rifle.

A ricochet could prove fatal in the dense entryway. Seeing one hostage secure and another down, Yuri whistled a cease-fire, the sound streaming down the tunnels. Turning to see Yaromir ascend the steps back to his room, he wondered if the ancient spy had any more cards yet to play.

12

"**N**olan, wake up!"

He rose in an instant. Rubbing his eyes, he asked for the time.

"It's almost dawn," Lauren hissed. "I think I saw movement outside."

Now he stood wide awake. "Do you have the machine gun," he asked, sliding out of the wooden bench. Lauren darted across the room, bringing the assault rifle back for him to hold. The empty weapon felt useless but he hoped it would make someone think twice about approaching the station.

Looking out the windows, the pitch blackness rendered visibility to a few feet. The notion that they were fighting blind left him with a deep sense of vulnerability. He knew most military units and nocturnal animals could all utilize night vision to hunt their prey. He could hear Lauren's labored breathing behind him. His pulse quickened. He shivered, it was going to be a cold day. "Stay out of sight," he whispered to Lauren.

"Is it them," she asked, unmoving.

"I don't know. It's best if we aren't both seen. Perhaps they'll think I'm alone."

Not far from the window sat the car they found abandoned during their flight from Asheville. Through the darkness, he could just make out the gunmetal frame of the vehicle and the nearest gas pump. He watched as a dark mass seemed to hover behind the rear wheel well, a black hole that appeared to be growing larger. At first, it had no shape but coming into focus; it began to form. It was a man!

Nolan tightened his grip on the assault rifle, not knowing if the form represented friend or foe.

Lauren gasped from the corner, the sound drawing his attention away from the body in the window. He spun in her direction but suffered a blow on the head. Flashes of light burst behind his eyes. Chased by a splitting headache, his legs collapsed underneath him.

Rough, practiced hands grabbed him by the torso, lowering him to the ground. Still unable to see his assailant, he felt his hands pulled behind him secured by flex cuffs. His feet too were bound and his head covered in a blackout mask. He tried to fight, but a shot to the solar plexus snuffed out his will to resist. Without a sound, his body was lifted and carried.

"Lauren!"

The only response was another shot to the abdomen, making him gasp. One swing and his body slid along something long and smooth. Then two large doors slammed shut. Within moments, he heard the engine turn over. He tried pulling his hands from behind his back, but a boot in his chest prevented any further movement.

"What do you want? We're Americans. We fled for our lives."

Still no answer. An image of being under the blanket after the crash in the firestorm came to his mind. He remembered not to panic. Despite being abducted he focused on the fact that he was not dead and if he wasn't dead then there may still be a way out.

The ride was bumpy but surprisingly short. Nolan got the sense that his captors had taken them off the beaten path but resided close enough to town that whoever they were, they could have been watching for a long time.

When the van came to a stop, two doors opened, allowing him a glimpse of light filtering underneath the mask. Whoever had put the cover on his face did not tie it off, sparing him greater claustrophobia. Four hands grasped his clothing, and a metallic clanging noise pounded down a tunnel as he once again plunged into darkness. Jostled against other bodies, he descended a flight of stairs. The sensation reminded him of the cellar used for survivors in Asheville. Another metal door ground open as the floor leveled out. Rough hands threw him upright in a cold, steel chair. To his relief, his captives cut the bindings loose and removed the hood.

Still, he could not see. A great light shone on his face, the intensity causing him to turn away. Turning left, then right he could just make out featureless figures lurking in the shadows in both directions. Heat from the lamp's glare caused sweat to begin beading on his forehead and pool into his eyes. He rubbed the sweat from his eyes and tried to clear his vision. As more details emerged, he noticed another dark figure just beyond the lamp. He knew the form was a man but could make out anything futher. The figure waved a blurry hand in front of the light, the motion taking no longer than a blink. Instinctively, Nolan followed the man's movement.

"Are you afraid," asked the voice.

Nolan blinked sweat from his eyes. "Yes."

"Are you aware of the calamity facing the nation?"

Nolan thought of the numerous dead. Close friends and millions of strangers he would never meet. Dead. He blinked twice. "Yes."

"Do you know why you are still alive?"

"No. Is Lauren still alive? Did you take her too?"

"How long have you two known each other?"

"Is she alive? I will answer your questions if you can tell me if she is alive or not."

"You are in no position to negotiate. The woman is unharmed, but we are focusing on you. We know who you are and what you do. What we do not know is how you ended up in Kentucky."

"We fled. The girl saved my life and we fled together, heading north to get away."

"From where did you flee? Your base in Tennessee?"

Nolan ducked away from the light's blaze. "No. I was on assignment with a man and a woman in route to Asheville. We crash landed. I guess now I know that we were shot down. I was the only survivor. After meeting a man named Cato, I made my way to Asheville where I fell in with the locals. The military showed up, but just when we heard the news about the invasion, we were attacked. I tried to get to the hospital." His throat constricted. His mouth moved, but no words came out.

"And so, you fled Asheville and now you are here?"

Nolan nodded.

"How many jumps did you make as a fireman," continued the voice after some moments pause.

"What do you mean?"

"Perhaps I am a pilot. Perhaps I am a fireman. How many jumps have you logged?"

"Three hundred and eight. Five to pass, the rest in the field."

"What is your favorite part of controlled falling?"

Nolan smiled, he couldn't help it. Not only was jumping a passion of his but something in the interrogator's voice hinted at amusement, a shared comradery that he found both noninvasive and affirming.

Lights flickered on, dimming the lamp's glare and revealing a room of solid concrete where almost a dozen men and women, all clad in tactical gear, and well-armed held him in an icy stare. Focused but impassionate. The interrogator himself leaned forward, his face set with deep brown eyes and a trim black beard with flecks of white. He had a look of high intelligence, but the eyes gave him an air of compassion. Perhaps the man was a counselor or a teacher. Nolan thought he looked American enough and had not detected any hint of an accent.

"Please forgive the charade Nolan but we had to make sure we could trust you. I know you may have wished for better methods but rest assured our measures are taken to ensure the security and safety of this facility."

"Who are you? Where am I?"

"Sorry," said the man standing up and prompting Nolan to do likewise. "My name is Benjamin Hargreaves. Welcome to my facility. These are my operators. Here you will find survivors of the doom that has befallen our nation. We are not mere bystanders though. As you can see, I have assembled a crack team that I hope soon we will able to launch an insurgency to restore the United States."

Nolan didn't know what to think of the man. He appeared harmless enough, but what little he knew of history, he knew there were those whose charming appearance served to hide a crazed despot.

"I was in the Air Force," said the man. "I was once what you call a Pararescue Jumper or PJ. Jumping was one of my favorite things to do, and I loved helping people. That was why I joined the State Department after a knee injury clipped my wings."

Nolan now understood the reason for the question about parachuting. Air Force PJs were legendary. He had known a few over the years that later jumped to fight a fire. They were like Clara Barton but on steroids and carried the latest in American weaponry. "Life in the shadow of the White House, I am afraid, wasn't kind to my nerves and it came close to destroying my conscience. Funny how dropping into war zones from a C-130 seemed like a walk in the park compared to those shark-infested waters. As a soldier, I traveled the world offering aid and serving America's interests. As a student of history, I saw the writing on the wall, connecting the dots allowed me to see the die cast. No matter who the leader was, it was evident that our day in the sun was coming to an end and with that, there would be those who would seek to wipe America off the mantle. I tried to blow the whistle on colonization and several world movements that I knew would culminate in an attack. Nobody believed an attack of this magnitude was possible. Nobody thought the Russians had the capability but pretended to do so with bluster. They forgot it was bluster that kept Americans in fear for half a century.

First one audience would point me down the hall, then the other would. At last, I found like-minded folks on both sides of the aisle and we began searching for international support. Through a very wealthy senator, we established this compound off the books and began to assemble a strike team." Hargreaves took a deep sigh. "An order slowly executed is an advantage lost. Sadly, we were still too small and too ill-equipped to deal with something this large. Our best hope is that an underground movement, like a spark, will ignite the firestorm that will repel our enemies."

Nolan followed the man around the room dumbfounded. The eyes of the soldiers never left Hargreaves or himself. When they came up to the first soldier, the man neither moved nor blinked. "Nolan, please allow me to introduce you to some of my favorite people." None of the soldiers spoke as Hargreaves introduced both male and female operatives from all parts of the world. Most, Nolan assumed, were American but he counted at least one Israeli, one South Korean, and a female from a Latin nation. The final two men looked by far the most imposing. The closest of the duo, introduced as Mason Grey, did nothing to acknowledge him save for a tightening of a stalwart jaw. Nolan judged him at six-three, the man's grey eyes boring right through him. Hargreaves made no attempt to force any pleasantries from any of his operators.

"Our final man has been a partner of mine for some years now," smiled his tour guide. "This is Rasputin." The stalwart had been tall, but this man was a mountain. Nolan now recognized the man who had stood outside the window beside the car. He had probably been disabling the vehicle before standing in the window. The man was a downright imposing wall of muscle.

"Rasputin huh? That's an unfortunate name."

The mountain man chuckled from deep within his belly. A smile of perfectly straight teeth shone through a dark, coarse beard. "That it is friend. That it is."

"South African," said Nolan. It was not a question, more a statement of fact. The man's proper lilt with a heavy twang was a dead giveaway to a traveled man like Nolan. The man clapped Nolan hard on the back, nearly breaking his ribcage.

"Our new friend is not such a *domkop* is he, Ben? Well, well," said Rasputin, smiling even broader.

"Each man and woman you see here Nolan is a personal friend of mine. They are committed to exterminating our unwanted visitors. I think you could be of great help to us as well, but we can discuss that at a later time. For now, I want you to relax, look around, and make yourself at home."

"I appreciate all this but what about Lauren? Is she okay?"

"She was hard to reassure that she was in good hands but I have it on good authority that she has been properly fed and is now awaiting your release from my company."

Nolan was eager to get away from the four solid walls and new acquaintances with weapons, but he had one final question. "Where am I?"

Hargreaves opened a red, heavy door, swinging it outward into a grey-coated hallway with white flooring. "You are in a secure underground facility established by the government during the 1950s as a station of command and control should nuclear fallout threaten our nation's top leaders. The senator who privately purchased this property from the government has a similar facility in her home state of Minnesota. We have limited contact with them given the distance, but she and her people remain committed to freeing the United States."

"Nolan!" The scream echoed down the corridor drawing much attention. Lauren leaped into Nolan's arms hugging his shoulders tightly. "This place is amazing," she said sucking something sticky off her thumb. "They have running water, a cafeteria, and a radio room."

Hargreaves lifted his arms in an open gesture. "Nolan, I hope you forgive my first impression. I am glad you two are here. Please, feel free to find sleeping quarters and check with our registrar to get outfitted." Looking at Nolan, he added, "I will call on you soon." Without an answer, Nolan turned with Lauren and walked into the foray of American survivors and rebels.

13

Yuri Orlov stood on the balcony of his Georgetown suite overlooking the Potomac River. Day seven since the invasion. One week. Yuri spat over the railing in disgust. Casting his gaze across the river, he should have been seeing Ropucha landing ships unloading helicopters and soldiers. Instead, America's byzantine dealings with Great Britain had gotten the best of Russia, annihilating the heart of his homeland.

There was no second wave of Russian aerial attacks, decimating outlying communities. That job had been left to Yuri and his men for mop-up duty, ending in catastrophe. Advanced American technology, medicine, and weapons should have been loaded and shipped, bound for Anadyr, Magadan, and Vladivostok.

Bogdan slid open the door behind him, the only person besides Anton allowed to encroach upon his privacy. "How are our preparations coming along?"

"The facility we have nearby is perfect but has there been much success in the other centers?"

Yuri nodded in understanding. Earlier that morning he sent Bogdan to nearby Andrews Air Force Base, to the east of the smoldering remains of the White House. Following the launch of Operation Cannae, Operation Pastorius began, green-lighting Russian moles like Yaromir throughout what was left of the United States to round up American survivors posing as federal aid camps. Its success was slow, but after a week, large population centers such as Los Angeles, Denver, Chicago, Philadelphia, and New York were being rounded up and guided to indoctrination camps run by Russian apologists. The facility he commandeered for such a cause was Andrews Air Force Base. Sheila Townsend, like thousands of other Americans, now sat incarcerated behind heavy steel doors. Bogdan made good on his promise to the American warrior.

"I have contacted Konstantin in Chicago and Josef in New York. They are doing well, but our resources are stretched thin, especially in the South. I fear a riot in many places would release our hold of that area and may spread to others. Dallas, San Antonio, Atlanta."

"You have a right to be worried," said the older brother, "but do not forget that the South is still very sectionalized and we have made it near impossible to communicate. I have plans for Atlanta. Let this city serve as a litmus test. America is on its knees."

Both brothers looked over the balcony into the horizon. November was nearing its end, a suitable period ushering in winter, a season when things die. Dark cumulonimbus clouds hung low threatening to unleash icy sleet or snow at any moment. "Was it worth it," asked Bogdan.

Yuri choked. "At the cost of St. Petersburg and Moscow. True, our homeland has burned to ashes, but you can't call it a fair fight."

"Still, we have destroyed their cities, murdered their people and what have we gained?"

Yuri looked harder into the distance as he contemplated an answer. "Russia, brother, is not dead. The backs of her people are still straight and strong. America is dead, her people enslaved. Russia may not be making off like Titus with the Temple gold, but we have opened its resources to the world.

Perhaps her former allies will not come to her aid after all in light of the vast riches."

"With America out of the way," picked up Bogdan, "our Iranian allies will be free to sweep the Zionists into the Sea. An Arab coalition will be free to redraw the map according to their ancient tribal lands."

"If one can ever get them to agree. I fear the Persians will try to dictate as much as possible to the weaker Arab nations. Without America, the Jordanian and Saudi regimes are history if they are not already. I hope there are some Russian Jews smart enough to return to the Motherland. We could use their expertise now," said Yuri thinking of Moscow's destruction.

"Will the same happen to us now that the Moscow's leadership is a glorified ashtray?" Bogdan asked rubbing his tanned baldhead before stroking his thick black beard. "Our strong leadership that drew nations from their NATO and European Union treaties was vaporized."

"You are more correct in your thinking that you know little brother. Yaromir explained to me that America's allies were regrouping. The fight will not be over in the Balkans, the Baltic or the Persian Gulf for quite some time."

Moments later Anton met the Orlov brothers in the lobby, his rifle still slung behind his back, but in a relaxed dress without any body armor making the athlete look as though he could grow wings and fly at any moment. "Major Orlov, I report good news and bad news."

Yuri betrayed no emotion. "Bad news."

Anton, not as phlegmatic as his commanding officer, dropped his head and stared at the thick red Persian rugs adorning the hotel's grand entryway. "Sir, the American patriots have rooted out the mole in Dallas. He was hung this morning during the early dawn hours. The city's militia is rapidly expanding its influence and creating a buffer zone in the heart of the nation reaching parts of Louisiana, Arkansas, and Oklahoma. My hunch is if this resistance continues then the American Midwest or Breadbasket may not succumb to our forces."

Bogdan raised an eyebrow to Yuri as if to say he had been right to be worried after all.

Yuri seethed inwardly. Without the destruction of Moscow and St. Petersburg, reinforcements could have been counted on to secure the grain fields and starve out American resistance. "Any other bad news?"

"If the American Midwest and American South can connect and organize their resources, they may be able open a front line capable of securing their borders from Denver to our backyard. The Mississippi River allows them great transportation north and south with minimal detection. They could go underground. St. Louis and Chicago could be turned over if they are not careful. That is, however, where the good news comes in."

"Go on Anton!" barked Bogdan throwing up his hands.

"Cartel floods the southwest opening Dallas' underbelly to a new enemy. Meanwhile, moles in Austin have severed Dallas aid to San Antonio rendering the city surrounded."

"For once I do not envy Americans," put in Bogdan. Yuri had to agree. The Cartel was rumored to be as ruthless as ISIS whom he and his men had battled protecting Russian and Iranian interests in Syria.

"Suffice it to say," said Yuri grabbing the brief from Anton's hand, "the west coast and east coast are within our grasp, what lies ahead is to press deeper into the interior."

"What do we do now," asked Bogdan.

"Now," said Yuri looking his men in the eye, "we press on our objectives. Torch everything."

14

Despite their initiation to the underground facility, Nolan had to give Hargreaves and his people a ton of credit. The bunker was impressive. Compartmentalized managers oversaw the daily operations of things like utilities, security, transportation, personnel, communications, and even education. The mess hall, shaped like an octagon, served as the central hub. From the center, long hallways fanned out in each direction leading to the different sectors. In the southwest corner, deep in the mountains, lay the housing section. Nolan and Lauren were each given a bunk complete with clean, crisp sheets, two pillows, a towel, a washcloth, and bar of soap. Nolan thought about making a joke about prison, but considering the vast resources available, he considered himself grateful to be there. Bathrooms, dubbed the Roman Bathhouses, were community style and separated by gender with private bathroom options given to families. He learned that few whole families had managed to arrive together at the bunker. The invasion rivalled the scenes after a major natural disaster. Everybody had lost a loved one.

Nighttime became the worst for Nolan. Each night he relived the horrors of Asheville in his nightmares. It took a few nights before his bunkmate, a refugee from Louisville, requested a new room. He knew Lauren would want to hear about them and each morning she looked at him with interest, but he decided to keep his dreams of the dead to himself. She too, and everyone around him, had already suffered so much, he didn't want to add to their grief.

It was getting late one night when another nightmare woke him from his sleep. Looking at Gruff's dive watch, the hands said the hour had not yet even passed midnight. Feeling restless Nolan decided to throw back the covers and wander the compound. Dressed in a pair of sweats and a hoodie, the cement floor felt cold to his feet but drove the sleep from his body.

Slinking into the mess hall, Nolan couldn't help but find the deserted place a little eerie. During the day, the mess hall was teeming with refugees and cooks, children and soldiers. The smell of the night's meal, chicken spaghetti, wafted from the scullery. Through the dark hallway, Nolan could make out a dim light emanating from underneath a distant door.

The cramped space many first encountered when first finding shelter in the underground was affectionately known as Radio Shack because it was the communications closet helping to transmit messages over the airwaves, encouraging any listening Americans. The MC of the underground radio was a former Air Force engineer and retired carpenter named Donald Hugh. Don, as he was known, had worked on various military projects such as the Global Positioning System, self-guided smart bombs, and the Reaper drone program before retiring.

Light spilled into the dark hallway as Nolan inched the door open. Peering in, he found the small room deserted. A desk lamp revealed the ancient radio booth aglow with red and green lights and a wall map of the United States pinned with thumbtacks of various colors. He had no idea what the various colors and lines on the map meant, but they reminded him of TICC meetings at the Cleveland Air Base in Tennessee. The TICC served the larger agencies such as the SACC in Atlanta and the National Interagency Fire Center in Boise, Idaho. It felt like forever ago since he last stepped foot in the TICC. He could still smell the rich aroma of coffee hanging in the air.

"Can I help you, son?"

He jumped out of his skin. Behind him stood Don Hugh, holding a fresh cup of coffee. "Did you come all this way for a cup of coffee," asked Don noticing Nolan's stare.

"No, sir. I couldn't sleep. When I saw the light on, curiosity just led me to it."

Don settled him with a long look before shrugging it off. "Well come on. It isn't very often that get company while I'm on the airwaves. I promised not to play any of the heavy stuff," Don laughed.

"What kind of things do you usually play," asked Nolan taking a seat in a swivel chair. Before him was an array of knobs, switches, lights, a microphone and the soft hum of electricity.

"I play what Hargreaves wants me to play," said Don throwing up his hands in mock surrender. "Hymnals mostly with the occasional Ozark Mountain Daredevils. I did tell him the best way to motivate fighters and simultaneously annoy the stuffing out of the enemy was some good ole-fashioned Metallica. We used to lower boom boxes down into their bunkers during the Gulf War, cranking it up to eleven. Black Sabbath had Hussein's Guard begging for mercy. Came out of their holes unarmed with their hands up." Don took a sip of his coffee and looked at the clock. "Oh hey, it's midnight. Time to light her up!"

For the next half hour, Nolan sat back as Don reported news and made pop culture references to traditional American values encouraging those who may be listening to reflect on their lives and loved ones. He threw in songs by Jeff Buckley, U2, and James Taylor.

"That concludes our broadcast for tonight folks. Remember to hold your loved ones close and pray the sun will rise on a better day. For those of you in the trenches, a word of encouragement: our friends have sent their care package. *Lucky*

Strike has gone to war. I repeat, *Lucky Strike has gone to war.* That's all folks. Thanks for tuning into 207AM the Underground. May God bless America."

The soft hum of electricity clicked off as Don leaned back in his chair raising the cup once more to his lips. Turning to Nolan, he asked, "Did you learn anything new tonight?"

"What did you mean by that last bit," asked Nolan. "It sounded very cloak and dagger."

Don fixed him with a conspiratorial smile. "We hit them back!"

"Who?"

"The Russians. We got those suckers back. The British, somehow, got ahold of two of our submarines. Cables reached our ears that they launched warheads at Moscow and St. Petersburg. The nukes incinerated the Kremlin and the Russian Federation is reeling while our NATO allies are regrouping after being duped for so long. The Russian threat may be coming to a close." The man was so excited, he could hardly contain himself. Part of Nolan couldn't help but feel for the innocents lost in Russia and angry as to why both nations had to suffer for the decisions made by small groups of people. He didn't know much about politics, but he did know that at least a democratic government was responsible to their people for power, he doubted there was very much democracy in mind when Russia launched the attacks against the United States.

"Say, you haven't noticed anyone snooping around here have you?"

Nolan's mind flashed to the grim SAS operative of Hargreaves'. The cold eyed operative he met the first day standing next to Rasputin always stared and never spoke, giving Noland the creeps. "No," he let out slowly. "Why do you ask?"

"Well at first I thought it was nothing but I always leave my ciphered messages in a locked safe. I won't tell you where the safe is unless you already know. What were you doing out so late by my office?"

"I told you, I couldn't sleep. Look, I just followed the last light left on in the building. Looking for company I guess. Why don't you ask that Grey character? The Brit seems shrouded in mystery if you ask me."

"I can vouch for Mason Grey," said a deep voice from behind the two men. Startled, both turned to find Benjamin Hargreaves, looking a little worse for wear, standing in the doorway.

"Ben, you scared the devil out of me," choked Don, a fit of wheezing overcoming the overweight man.

"That was a fine broadcast, Don. *Joshua Tree* was always one of my favorite albums growing up. Why don't you get some sleep?"

"Ah, sure thing Ben. I'm sure I just misplaced my book. Getting to be so that I hardly keep track of my mind."

"You're the tip of the spear," said Hargreaves patting the old man on the shoulders. Then he looked to Nolan. "A word with me please," he said. The underground leader turned and walked out. Don sighed audibly fixing Nolan with a pair of raised eyebrows. Nolan shrugged in return, following Benjamin.

In the dark hallway, Hargreaves paced with his hands clasped behind him, his back arched forward like a professor in a great hall. "I met Mason Grey as part of Britain's promise of friendship to France following the numerous acts of terror in the previous decade. One of the lesser known coordinators for the multiple attacks was a talented University of Paris student named Indira Mukhtar. She held infinite intelligence and stunning beauty."

The men rounded the corner heading in the direction of Hargreaves' private quarters. "As foreign leaders and diplomats flooded Paris, security resources were stretched to the breaking point. The biggest fears permitted the theory that the attacks were a trap to draw so many of the world's leaders from Jordan to South Korea to the Pope into the open. The Strategic Air Services got a tip on the location of Indira's base of operations. We had to act fast. I joined Mason's SAS unit as a medic to put a hit on her place with the objective to take her captive."

"At the apartment, the point man placed explosive glue on the door and we all took cover should anything inside be rigged to blow. The men tossed flashbangs and stormed the apartment. Each man spread out clearing rooms for Indira but she wasn't there. I entered as the commander was calling it in. Once the cordite cleared, I smelled something stronger like rotten eggs. Since I was standing by the door, I grabbed the closest man I could by the collar and threw him into the hallway."

"What happened next," asked Nolan. Hargreaves unlocked the door to his study and led the way inside. It was warmer in the room than in the hallway and both relaxed in leather office chairs.

"Indira Mukhtar was a clever witch. The sprinkler system ignited showering the men in acid. I covered Grey's ears so he wouldn't hear his brother burn."

"What about you? How did you cope with the sounds of the dying?"

"As a PJ, you see all kinds of stuff. You're used to the adrenaline, the death, and the smell of death. You get so used to it that you build a foxhole deep within your soul to lock back the memories. You do that so you can go to sleep at night and wake up the next day ready to do it again. *So that others may live*. That's the PJ motto. Whatever we see and do is for that cause, even for the enemy when possible."

Hargreaves leaned back in his leather chair taking a sip from a glass of filtered water. Despite the late hour and his haggard appearance Nolan thought the man seemed to have endless energy. "When I joined the State Department, I did so because I didn't know what else to do. My father had been in government. After several knee surgeries, I knew I was going to have to hang up my wings. It didn't take long for me to see that other nations were amassing against the United States be it through intimidation like the Russians or economic withdrawal like India or South Africa. The rise of the rest. Using my contacts, and a like-minded senator, I began amassing a task force."

"But, as you said before, you ran out of time."

"Precisely. Which is why we're all here."

"Surely you don't expect to hide out here and wait for the end, do you?" Nolan thought he had read Hargreaves better than that. What was all the bluster about the Pararescue Jumpers if he abandoned it during America's greatest time of need. Hargreaves set his glass down and leaned across the desk. Fixing Nolan with a hard stare, he said, "You've seen this army up close. A plan is in place. There's a spot for you if you're interested?"

Nolan looked back, wondering what was behind the man's brown eyes. Eyes that had met with heads of state, generals, and enemies of peace. "What makes you think I'm your guy?"

Hargreaves couldn't help but look crestfallen. "My soldiers are elite, but I need someone with firsthand experience of what these invading forces can do. Furthermore, your work as search and rescue can prove vital to Park and Dr. LeFevour in offering aid to any friend or foe you come across." Hargreaves paused. "It is a lot to ask of a person."

He didn't know what to think. "Are you recruiting me?"

"We believe they are capturing refugees under the guise of federal aid. If this is true, we need to liberate those camps and get it on the wire to warn Americans of a trap. The mission is voluntary. I will allow you to join the briefing. Then you decide."

"I understand."

"Good. The meeting is at 1200 hours tomorrow. I expect you to bring a doctor's physical."

Feeling less like a refugee and more like a soldier, Nolan took that as his dismissal. He eased out of the chair. "Goodnight, sir."

"Goodnight."

Once more in the hallway, Nolan wondered what the good doctor would determine. No, he was not sleeping. Yes, he had nightmares. Yes, he saw her face every night. Yes, he saw the bullets riddle the professor over and over again. No, he never got there in time.

For anyone.

15

War is violence.

Union General William Tecumseh Sherman spoke those words and acted on them in the summer months of 1864. Once called The Storm, General Sherman blazed a trail of death and total war deep in the heart of the South burning Atlanta to the ground on his way to the sea. Novelists printed the scene before it was reproduced again by Hollywood's *Gone with the Wind*.

When the television went out over a week ago, Owen Drover knew Atlanta's days were once again numbered. A consummate bachelor, he searched for the TV remote finding it under his fiftieth birthday present to himself. Her undergarments were made of lace and wire making it easy for him to spot the remote lying next to her drunken body on the floor. Clicking channel after channel, the results came back all the same: blank screens and snowy images.

Pouring himself a few fingers of 12-year-old King's Ransom, the slightly rotund pharmaceutical tycoon looked over his leather and mahogany penthouse. Peering through the empty glass, he decided the end had come.

Reaching into the bureau, he pulled out an HK .45. The woman did not stir. He laid a few bills next to her. She would wisely be gone before he returned. He punched the button for the ground floor and rode the elevator to the garage where his maroon Jaguar XKR-S awaited.

Atlanta quaked in pandemonium. Most had taken to the streets after all telecommunications ceased to be operable. Drover tried calling clients, then the mayor, a golfing buddy, before deciding to raise the governor on his smartphone. Each ring flat lined in his ear, confirming all towers were down. Cruising past all the markets, he knew that Walmart promised to deliver the number of goods he would need to hole up.

Downshifting, he pulled into the busy parking lot and joined the queue for space. After stepping out of the car, he wished he had brought a jacket to keep back the harsh wind. "Wow," said a dark-skinned homeless man. "Nice ride." Drover pulled his silk shirt up to reveal the .45 in his waistband to discourage any trouble. The old man backed away with his hands up. Inside, the store looked much like the outside. People ran everywhere, convinced like Owen that something was wrong. Ramen noodles, meat, and milk were all gone from the shelves. He knew baby formula and toilet paper would be next. Already, young men were ignoring blue-vested staff and looting flat-screen TVs and Apple products. He piled his cart full of canned goods and spices. If the four horsemen of the apocalypse were descending upon Atlanta, then commodities like salt and sugar would soon be worth their weight in gold. He also shopped for buckets of chlorine. Living and working in the world's premier disease research facility, he knew chlorine was essential is protecting against deadly pathogens. With one cart full and another well on the way Owen realized he would never fit all of his groceries in the Jag. Still, his ancestors hadn't driven sheep and cattle across the dangerous mountain borderlands of Ireland and Scotland for him to give up now. Once settled in America, they took on their livelihood as Drover for a namesake, establishing a determined line of Scot-Irish blood.

Nearing the checkout line, Owen saw his opportunity for a new set of wheels. Most the law-abiding patrons buying supplies were attempting to do so by credit card, only to be denied by the cashier. One young man, wearing atrocious but expensive clothing was waving his arms, screaming at the scared cashier. The man wheeled around when Owen tapped him on the shoulder from behind. The offender was much taller, but Owen outweighed him by one-hundred and fifty pounds.

"Were you the one with the chrome Escalade parked out front, homie?"

"It's an H2, why do you ask," spat the tall, young man.

Owen's eyes flashed. "I'd be willing to buy your groceries in exchange for your keys." He made no mention of the Jaguar sitting in the parking lot. He would come back for it later.

"You're crazy, old man," said the kid but without any real conviction. Doubt clouded his eyes, but dozens of other patrons began pulling at their keys willing Owen to offer the deal to them instead. They pleaded on behalf of their children, but Owen wasn't interested in dealing with others. He would only do business with someone like him. The young man's pregnant girlfriend began begging him to take the deal. Then, just like Esau selling his birthright for a cup of soup, the young man handed over his keys. Drover paid for both sets of groceries and set out to find his new ride.

Hartsfield-Jackson International Airport closed later that day. Hospitals fell overrun. The National Guard moved in to protect the Center for Disease Control. After a week, reports of a Russian invasion came over the radio waves. The news jolted Owen Drover into action. His employer, Blue Pharmaceuticals, had an office in the CDC. Drover knew the facility carried much more than innovative insulin products. Inside secured containers were some of the world's most potent viruses and diseases.

Greek legend records that Zeus' ally against Cronos, a Titan named Prometheus, was very fond of his creation, the Bronze Race or humankind. Teaming with Zeus' wise daughter Athena, Prometheus stole fire from Zeus' palace as a gift to the humans as a means of cooking and tool making to cultivate the land. Drover considered this the Greek rendering of the Agricultural Revolution. But Zeus was angry with Prometheus for giving the humans fire, punishing the Titan severely for centuries.

Zeus, having been tricked by Prometheus, sought to deceive humanity in return. He asked Hephaestus, the forge god, to manifest a feminine figure. Zeus breathed life into the character and presented her with a jar, but strictly forbade her from opening the gift.

The god-head awarded the woman and her jar to Prometheus' brother Epimetheus. Epimetheus saw the woman's great beauty and called her Pandora. Zeus waited for Pandora's curiosity of her jar to get the better of her.

According to myth, Pandora opened the jar for the briefest of moments but in doing so unleashed Zeus' punishment on all humanity. Disease, betrayal, malice, strife, and death emerged from the jar, plaguing human history for the remainder of time. By some accounts the last remaining item to escape the jar was Hope, helping humanity to cope with the result of Zeus' reckoning and the first mortal woman's everlasting error. If the Russians were to gain access to the Center for Disease Control, they could pour out Pandora's Jar and unleash an untold plague upon the United States.

16

Yuri Orlov went through his mental checklist over and over. His men's faces were once again indistinguishable inside the KA-60R scout helicopter, smothered in grease black and washed by the red glow of the chopper's cargo hold lamp. He ripped off his Kevlar helmet and ran his hands through his hair prompting a nudge by his brother. *If God does not bring it, the earth will not give it,* their father would often say. The Orlov patriarch however never confessed a belief in any god and Yuri was not the same fatalistic soldier that his brother was.

Determined to learn from the mistakes of Asheville, the first move he made was to operate beyond Yaromir's purview. Acquiring twenty gunships, NATO designated Havoc and Alligator attack helicopters, for the siege Yuri laid out key targets.

As noticed in Asheville, populations gathered in times of struggle. Like the days of old when a city under siege would draw its bridges, so it was in the modern age. Unlike Asheville, Yuri came prepared with bridge busters armed with the likes of infrared missiles and Gatling guns capable of firing with such velocity they left an exit wound the size of a bowling ball.

The first targets would be universities and sports arenas just as the initial invasion had been for much of the United States. The gunships would expend most of their payload on the very heart of Atlanta, strafing Georgia Tech, the Dome, and other various high priority targets within the Five Points.

His helicopter and those of six others slowed to a silent still above North Druid Hills overlooking the Center for Disease Control. Fast roping onto the field Yuri could make out the National Guard garrisoned at Emory University. Many of the elite soldiers chosen for the mission were veterans of the battle in Asheville, eager for another go at the enemy in their territory. He looked at the sniper to his left, the black-clad soldier breathing through his mouth and out his nose. He had trusted Immanuil implicitly and missed the young sniper's presence now more than ever. Through red-tinted binoculars, Yuri could make out three Abrams tanks flanking the west, east, and southern corners of the CDC. They were blind from behind entrusting the hills to the north to protect them; precisely where Yuri and his team of Spetsnaz now waited in silence for the Russian gunships to light up the Atlanta skyline.

The National Guardsmen ran in wild disarray as the night erupted in flame to the southwest. Captains and Lieutenants commanded in vain for their men to remain at their posts. Several screamed that their wives and children had been interred at the Dome, now a large cement coffin.

Much to Yuri's chagrin, the three Abrams tanks and their crewman remained at their posts, guarding the various contagions held within the CDC's chambers. Yuri's men checked their weapons one last time then he gave the order to move out.

Descending the hill, the Spetsnaz moved swiftly and silently. Only once panicking guardsmen operating spotlights overthrew their cover of darkness did the Russian assassins open fire.

Taking the weekend warriors by complete surprise, those on the outskirts of the barricades fell in rapid succession. Each soldier threw flashbangs in unison to disorient the guards. Upon igniting, several of the American soldiers fired towards the light and sound, killing their brethren in friendly fire on the southeastern end of campus. Yuri gave a fleeting glance at the sky in that direction to calculate the progress of Havoc and Alligator helicopters decimating downtown Atlanta.

Red and green tracer rounds shot across the sky, lighting their surroundings like Christmas. The sounds of shouting and diesel engine exhaust filled the air, but there was little rifle fire as the Spetsnaz cut down the American defense. Forty-five well-armed, highly trained soldiers descended upon the Americans. The first sign of casualty initially took Yuri by surprise as a loud concussion boomed from the east. The tank's blast sent a fissure into the ground knocking several Russian coalition soldiers to the ground and killing four.

Yuri tasted blood as a young soldier rounded the cement barricade meeting the steel tip of his fixed blade across the throat. Soviet history from the Battle of Stalingrad taught the elite warriors to approach close-quarter combat without remorse. Kill or be killed, it didn't matter how.

Another blast from the eastern flank caused Yuri to yell curses upon his men for not silencing the nearest tank. He needn't have used bothered however for it was Anton who placed demolition charges on the cannon turret, rendering it useless. The fifty-caliber nest atop the tank also sat idle as sniper fire took out the gunner.

Fire fell from the sky as a Russian escort gunship fired upon the Abrams guarding the southern end of campus. With little armament left, the remaining guardsmen began fleeing their posts, most taking to the streets that led downtown. Others, being overrun, tried to surrender but were given no quarter.

"I want the other tank!" Yuri yelled sprinting to the west where the final Abrams remained. "Bogdan," he called after his brother, "secure the armor!"

Bogdan, never questioning his brother, sprinted for the western barricade, mowing down the tank's defenders without breaking stride. Their shots were erratic while Yuri's soldiers were calm under pressure, wasting nothing.

Smoke now hung low in the air, making breathing and visibility difficult. Fear took hold of him as he watched a Havoc bank west. Its target was the Abrams tank. The attack chopper's Gatling rotors were heating up, ready to fire.

17

The grandfather clock chimed eleven pm while Owen Drover sipped the amber whiskey of his forefathers. The large windows that usually revealed the Atlanta Botanical Gardens were dark from his Morningside penthouse. From the comfort of his leather-backed sofa, Drover's eyes caught sharp flashes of light. The following concussion wave shattered his windows sending shards of glass cascading to ground below. The cold winter air whipped at Owen's soft grey hair.

Uninjured by the blast, Owen Drover leaped to his feet and raced to the open air that used to be his windows. Shielding his eyes, he watched in horror as a mushroom cloud of fire erupted from downtown. Hundreds if not thousands were being slaughtered right before him. More flashes of light were emitted from the sky as if God's reckoning had descended upon Atlanta. Sirens wailed and plumes of smoke billowed in the air looking like great ghosts stretching across the dark skyline.

Owen Drover assessed his penthouse and prepared his mind for the path he was forging. Like the Confederate garrison overwhelmed by Sherman's March to the Sea, so too would be an American soldier. Drover thought of his Scot-Irish ancestors as he donned his hunting tweed and high-kneed boots. Grabbing an assortment of weapons, Drover reflected upon his belongings. The hardwood furniture, the English leather, and elegant bedroom. All bought with his mounted wealth to craft an image of power that no longer mattered. Owen Drover knew he was outmanned and outgunned. He knew that his choice to defend the Center for Disease Control would be one of suicide but he also knew he had one tactical advantage over the Russian enemy: he knew the terrain.

Before closing the door to his life's work, he looked upon the Dover family crest. A stag with great horns stood over a scroll written in type to mimic the ancient Gaelic texts. A non-religious man, the psalmist yet struck a chord with Owen's will to throw off America's oppressors. The scroll read: *"Blessed be the Lord my strength, which teacheth my hands to war, and my fingers to fight."*

Never staying in the same place twice, Owen Drover continued to take pot shots at the Russian soldiers. Winded and covered in dirt, Drover breathed deep to fill his lungs not just with oxygen but also with life. He felt more alive than he had ever felt before. Not even defending his company in high court held a candle to the thrill of stalking another man. General Zaroff may not have been so crazy after all, if only the name didn't sound Russian.

Armed with a silenced SPEC-OPS M4 Carbine with ACOG scope and laser pointer, Drover spared no expense. He looked ridiculous in his sportsmen tweed wielding the expensive weapon, but style points counted little as he knocked off enemy invaders. Besides, he could go for style points later. Before the end.

Making his way north, he continued to fire upon the black-clad soldiers, disappearing within the panicked masses as he moved. Some were smart enough to arm themselves, but in the panic, many innocents got caught in the crossfire or trampled. Thousands followed the railroad track while he pressed on, into the fray.

What he saw once he got to the CDC made him stop in his tracks. All the resistance was gone. The Russians had taken the facility. But he hadn't come this far to succumb now. Finding a parked car, he threw a rock into the driver's side window igniting the alarm. The shrill siren fought against the sounds of a blazing city, distracting a small number of Russian guards.

Running as hard as he could, Drover crouched behind a much more substantial SUV, this time trying his best to open the locked door and kill the car alarm without raising suspicion. Turning the engine over, he aimed the 4x4 in the general direction he wanted then took a small tube and locked it in place atop the gas pedal.

Soldiers placed well-aimed shots through the windshield but could not bring the SUV to a stop as it crashed through the army barricade and sent the Russians sprawling. No strangers to IEDs, the elite Russian soldiers approached the vehicle with caution to determine if it were rigged to blow.

Huffing out of breath, he dropped the heavy carbine, gripping his pride and joy in both hands, eyeing the entrance to the Center for Disease Control. Satisfied he was ready to add his blood to the family's history, Owen Drover began to charge.

18

Yuri screamed and fired his assault rifle into the air but the armored helicopter paid no heed as it soared over the CDC headquarters. Tossing his weapon aside, Yuri sprinted through the bullets and haze, covering his mouth so as not to breathe in the smoke and death.

He watched in horror as the Havoc lined up its approach, ready to fire. Searing hot pain shot through his calf, knocking him to ground. Hobbling to support his weight against a barricade, Yuri didn't want to look towards the east; afraid the helicopter had fired its kill shot, vaporizing the last tank and his younger brother.

Looking first towards the sky, he watched the Havoc circle back west, back towards the fleet.

"Bogdan!" he yelled. Running as best he could from the shot leg, Yuri hobbled towards the wreckage.

Instead, Yuri found Bogdan and several other Russian soldiers standing proudly atop the captured Abrams waving their arms and pumping their fists in the air. He would have been unhinged with such a display of hubris in the middle of battle if he were not so relieved to see his brother alive. He was also glad to see Bogdan reach from underneath his black Kevlar and produce the White, Blue and Red bars of the Russian national flag. The soldiers draped the flag over the tan American tank.

Laughter began to fill the air, as the Spetsnaz soldiers tasted victory. Many of them clapped Yuri on the back, congratulating him on the acquisition of both the Abrams tank and the Center for Disease Control. Major Orlov reminded each man to remain vigil. "We are not finished subduing Atlanta," he rebuked. Pointing to the southwest, he reminded them to all look at the intense air war. "Atlanta held together even at the end of her country. Thousands will soon come pouring down these streets. Be ready." Then, he smiled and slapped the tank's turret, drawing a loud cheer from the men.

Surveying the damage, he watched a strangely dressed man, roughly his age, bull rush a side entrance carrying a powerful weapon. The man posed a dangerous threat. If he were to sabotage anything, it would mean failure to Yuri. He dispatched twelve men to pursue the intruder. For once, Yuri was worried about his fellow soldiers. Spetsnaz were not known for finesse and in close quarters combat with deadly contagion all around. He worried one false move would prove fatal.

19

Safely inside the CDC, Owen Drover checked his Holland & Holland side-by-side 12 gauge to ensure both slugs were loaded then slapped the walnut stock back in place. He moved in haste, disabling security measures and resetting them to slow down the Russian force. His heart raced. He threw off the oppressive tweed shooting jacket despite the colder temperatures outside the building. While most the laboratories and research kiosks were off-limits to visitors, Drover held inside information as a significant pharmaceutical lobbyist. To many, the CDC was the premier pathogen research facility in the world, but to men like Drover, it was like all things, a business. Businesses were in the business of making money. That is what Drover was good at and got paid a lot of that money in return for services rendered.

Passing through vaulted doors, he warned a skeleton crew of uniformed researchers, scientists, and doctors to secure lethal pathogens from the Russians. Some tried to hold Drover up, but one look at the engraved double barrel shotgun sent them looking elsewhere.

Gunshots and screams echoed throughout the halls as the Russian soldiers neared. Needing to buy time, he looked at the ceiling. Taking out his lighter, he waved the flame under a sheaf of papers, watching them until they caught the desk on fire. Sheets of water poured from the sprinkler system, but Drover ensured the inferno continued to spread. He placed an O2 tank outside the office and ran down the hall. Taking careful aim with his Holland & Holland, Drover waited for the Russians to emerge into the hallway. He fired both barrels into the growing blaze, igniting the oxygen tank at the feet of the soldiers. Light flashed in an explosion so intense it sent a fireball into the night's sky. He popped the slugs out and reloaded, firing once more down the hall. Flames continued rising, covering his exit. Throwing open the fire door, Drover slipped into the concrete stairway.

20

Yuri barked orders, driving himself hoarse. Using a bullhorn, he coordinated his foot soldiers into four groups. A veteran of the Asheville invasion led the central assault team, responsible for routing out those inside the CDC while Anton maneuvered the second assault team to catch survivors in a crossfire. Bogdan spearheaded a group of soldiers converted into firefighters to follow the heels of the leading force in an attempt to salvage sensitive materials. Yuri himself led fire crews responsible for extinguishing the growing flames from overtaking the building. The Spetsnaz commandeered fire engines and water hoses as a way of assaulting the fires with a torrent of water. Explosions rocked the west wing sending orange balls of flame into the sky; charred with smoke. Over the roar, Yuri heard helicopter rotors spinning upon the scene, the burning CDC drawing the Russian pilots like moths to a flame.

With no radio contact, Yuri took of sprinting back upon the northern hills reminding his snipers to be mindful of insurgents or even ambush. The snipers complained that a commanding view was impossible given the size of the complex. Ash began falling in tiny grey flakes while the western quadrant burned.

Soon another soldier came running to the ladder truck where Yuri presided over the fire's containment. "Sir," addressed the soldier. "The fire is contained to the western quadrant of the building. The outside fire crews have ensured it cannot spread while the interior crews report they will need more men to keep more from burning."

"What of Bogdan," questioned Yuri looking down at the soldier feet below.

"The commander's brother has forsaken the western quadrant to the flames, splitting his team further to search the remaining quads in his immediate vicinity," informed the soldier.

Yuri nodded. "We must trust his instincts. Good, now what of the insurgent who began the fire?"

The soldier gulped down his fear. "Sir, I regret to inform you that we have not yet apprehended the saboteur who has fired upon on soldiers though we believe him to be working alone."

Yuri's mind flashed to the tweed dressed man he saw enter the building. A degree of admiration played across his lips. Still, the man was a threat to be eliminated. "You are a well-informed soldier. What is your name?"

"Private Sergei Litvinenko, sir."

"I will make that Corporal Litvinenko. Now I want you to get these men inside to repel the flames."

"*Da*, commander!"

"And Sergei, one more thing. Extinguish the American."

21

The darkened stairway felt gritty and damp under Drover's extended hand as he passed down the steps. Cradling the shotgun while holding himself upright, he could feel his heart pounding in his chest, in his ears, and throat as well. Hurrying down the steps down towards the basement level, he did not know whether or not the Russians had managed to follow him. Nearing the bottom of the stairwell Drover heard a soft noise separating itself from the dripping of condensation.

Armed with his Holland and Holland 12-gauge and imposing frame, he rounded the steps and cornered four sets of small white eyes. The whimpering grew into sobbing as he drew nearer. Crouching on the ground floor were three scared girls and their mother, each of African-American descent. Rage flashed in Drover's eyes. He tightened his grip on the buttstock.

"No, please," pleaded the woman. She was afraid, but her eyes betrayed more than that. Distrust. She could sense his hate, a discernment woven into the very fabric of their being since the Middle Passage. Drover noticed that she wore a white lab coat belonging to a CDC doctor or research scientist. "Please don't kill us. These are my daughters." Her eyes shone with intelligence despite her fear.

Drover swung the shotgun, its double barrel pointing at each one in turn. Typical, he thought, no man to speak of. His thoughts were interrupted by a blast above and the immediate surge of heat brought on by flames licking the cemented ceiling several feet high. Shots rang out followed by indistinguishable shouts in the harsh Russian tongue. Drover glanced at the cowering girls and with a jerk of his head motioned them ahead into the basement level.

Running as fast as they could, the five sprinted away from the stairwell door as another explosion shook the walls and threw the steel door off its hinges. He knew the soldiers would soon follow. He hoped they were too late to suppress the exploding labs.

Trying desperately to outrun their attackers, the youngest girl fell to her knees. The woman screamed drawing Drover's attention. He noticed the one that had fallen proved to have the darkest skin of them all. She lay on the ground sobbing and holding her right knee, a glint of blood shining in the dim light off her midnight skin.

Drover brought the Holland and Holland Royal to bear coupled with the emergence of Spetsnaz soldiers exiting the stairwell. The shotgun blasts reverberated throughout the concrete cellar as two black-clad soldiers fell to the ground unmoving. A dark streak of movement surprised Drover while he attempted to reload the gun. The mother had run to her child and using powerful biceps had cradled the girl in her arms. More soldiers poured from the doorway as Drover slapped the stock into place. Sidestepping the retreating figures, Owen fired first one shot then another in rapid succession, aiming for the center mass of two separate soldiers. They doubled over each other forming a small pile of limbs, the blood pooling beneath them.

Drawing two more slugs, Drover turned to face the woman and her children. "Go. Now. Follow the ventilation pipes to the ground and make your escape."

"What about you," asked the woman putting her lithe arms around her girls.

"Somebody has to ensure you make it to cover," responded Drover. A sharp pain stabbed at his back causing him to stumble. The woman took a step towards him, but he threw up his hand. Sliding to a pillar for cover, he drew his precious 1900 Webley revolver and checked the cylinders. Ensuring the gun was in proper condition, he lined up his final shot, spraying the Russians with one last round of buckshot. Dropping the powerful shotgun, Owen went on the offensive. Catching a soldier by surprise the Russian's armor managed to stop most of the Webley's bullets but the rounds had buttoned him up from groin to sternum. The masked soldier fell to his knees clutching his chest as the remaining soldiers responded with suppressing fire.

Owen Drover's body fell to the ground, his hand still clutching the small revolver in the direction of the enemy.

22

They brought their Major the saboteur's Webley and a finely crafted double-barrel shotgun. Yuri admired the walnut stock and hand carved engraving of the scattershot and thanked his men for the gifts. "Each one of you is to be commended," he told the soldiers.

"Now many of us must be getting back but some of you will stay behind to guard this treasure box for the future of the Russian Federation." He looked around at each soldier, singling out Corporal Litvinenko. "I am placing Sergei in charge. With the dead and wounded aside I can spare twelve men to stay with Litvinenko."

Twelve hands shot through the air. Yuri nodded in return. "Good, now where is Anton?"

It had not dawned on any of the soldiers that their commander's right-hand man was not present.

"I am here Major Orlov," said the athletic point man rounding the lone remaining American tank. He ushered three small girls and their mother, each of African descent. The woman had a healthy appearance about her, her arms wrapped around her children.

"Take them as prisoners," ordered Yuri.

Ninety minutes later, the helicopters lifted into the night's sky. Soaring above ground, Yuri looked over the charred remains of the west end, the Center for Disease Control, the armored tank, and the dispatched Kamov helicopter left in the care of

Corporal Litvinenko and his men. Running over the Holland and Holland shotgun with his hands, he could not help but feel the mission was a resounding success. He gave the order for complete silence amongst all personnel while gliding back north, enjoying the victory.

23

When Nolan awoke, he ambled into the mess hall for the late bird special, oatmeal. He had little reason to complain however as he mixed the instant oats with water, butter, and protein powder. The secret to excellent tasting oatmeal was the butter. Nolan took three packets from the condiment table in the center. Washing the full meal down with milk, he placed the bowl on the stainless-steel counter that opened to the dishwasher. After a shower and shave, he dressed in blue jeans and a grey long sleeve shirt.

Walking down the corridor, his boots squeaking on the mopped linoleum floor, Nolan made his way to Doctor Hendricks' office for his physical and psyche evalutation. The doctor occupied an ample space next to many classrooms. As Nolan got closer, he heard the beautiful notes of a piano.

Curiously, he eased the classroom door open and slid in behind the piano player who effortlessly tapped out Beethoven's *Für Elise*. To his surprise, the pianist dressed in all-black fatigues. The figure was short and slender, like a female. As he approached, he noticed that the soldier was no female at all but rather the South Korean soldier Nolan met the first day he arrived at the underground.

Park.

"Who goes there," called the Korean, not bothering to turn around. Nolan eyed the collapsible M4 in the corner but the soldier did not attempt to do anything except to stroke the keys.

"Um, it's Nolan. We met the other day."

"I remember who you are. What can I do for you, Mr. Hoke?" The Asian's voice sounded like rolling thunder.

"I didn't mean to disturb you. I was on my way to the doctor when curiosity got the best of me."

Park spun on the pew without sound, a hard feat considering his polished black leather boots. "Dr. Hendricks is a good physician, but I do not see that you are injured."

"I'm not," said Nolan, laughing at himself. "Well, not that anyone can see at least."

"Ah. You are a broken man," the South Korean growled. Nolan turned to go, but the Korean soldier continued. "My mother played the piano. We were a very fortunate family, for a time."

Instead of leaving, Nolan pulled up a chair nodding for the man to continue.

"My American name is Samuel Park, that is what my passport and military records say. But I was born and raised in North Korea. My father was a wealthy man, by those standards. He operated numerous factories in a far northern province. He employed only women and apart from the occasional military inspection, left to his own devices. We were fortunate that we had enough money that my older sister and I didn't go straight to labor camps and learned to play from our mother."

"The other reason this proved providential was that my father pirated Christian radio transmissions from Seoul. He would piece together different messages we caught to form a sermon that he taught to his employees. My mother would then play music as the congregation bowed their heads in worship. We had to be very careful about spies. I was sworn to secrecy before I even learned to speak. Instructors taught me in school that our Beloved Leader was perfect and he alone knew true government and justice. As a student, I was taught to spy on my parents and friends should they ever speak ill of the Beloved Leader of the state. In my heart, I did not love the Beloved Leader, so I kept the family secret. We were Christians. We followed the Lord, Jesus Christ."

Park leaned back on the piano bench, lifting his chin. "Sometimes when I close my eyes, I can still feel her hair tickle my face and breathe in the smell of the oaken piano."

"When I was seven or eight, I was sitting on my mother's lap while she practiced. My father burst through the front door, a bandage atop his balding head. He yelled for my mother to hide and protect my sister. I was terrified. He charged at me, his eyes wide with terror. He grabbed me and placed me inside the piano, atop the strings."

"We may have been wealthy, but this was still North Korea. Our diet consisted of rice, and so I was a tiny child. Many times since then I dream I am at the supper table with my family eating rice. No sooner had my father shut the piano lid that the door exploded. My father rushed the soldiers who opened fire with their assault rifles. I opened the lid just a crack to see half a dozen men dressed in all black spread out in an alluvial fan, each man a member of the secret police wearing a monocle flashlight over one eye."

The Korean paused, a lump forming in his throat. His voice was hoarser than ever. "I never saw my family again. Eventually, a woman from the factory wandered in and found me after searching the house. She said she was my aunt, but I knew this to be a lie. I couldn't be sure if she were the same person who turned my father in or was there to help. She took out a piece of bread and emptied soup from a thermos to coax me into trusting her. I had not eaten in days and was very hungry. She fed me for three days. We did not leave my family's house; she never left the window except to cook or use the latrine. Her clothes smelled a mixture of cabbage and feces."

"One day, a man came to visit with a black hat and black sunglasses so that you could not see his face. He carried a worn briefcase, but he never opened it. The woman said this man was going to give me a future and that I would now be going with him. I asked her where I was going. She just smiled. He smiled too, but I did not trust this man. Too many children disappeared without a trace from Korean communities. I was fortunate, he said, God had smiled on me. I was still scared, but it did not matter because they took me away. My first ever car ride. We drove over the frozen mountains and upon seeing civilization again, he slowed the car to a stop. A man emerged from a frozen forest and told me to get out of the car. While I stood outside, the two men cut away the bottom of the backseat and told me to hide underneath the cushions. The bottom of the car was a snug fit. Both doors slammed shut, and we headed for the town's checkpoint. Lying under the seat, I could hear the rocks scraping the undercarriage; my body bounced each time we hit a pothole. At last, we would stop at one checkpoint and then another checkpoint. Every checkpoint on our way to the DMZ that bordered South Korea."

"It took more than three weeks before I crossed the DMZ in a shopping crate bound for the airport in Seoul. I have since learned that the man with dark sunglasses I feared is called the Angel of Pyongyang in South Korea. He is a man who works for the state government and yet is a secret believer who uses his position to rescue children from slavery through bribes, intimidation, and deception. A modern-day Harriet Tubman."

"Officials in South Korea determined that I was too uneducated to be sent to the United States. They needed refugees who were able to share their story for publicity and raise awareness for charitable donations from the West. Instead, the officials sent me to an orphanage where I was given my name, Samuel, after the Biblical judge of the Old Testament. It turns out that the diet in South Korea was much better than that of my native country and I took a particular liking to chicken. I grew strong and learned to fight because the South Korean kids were always bigger than I was and picked on me. When I turned eighteen, the Army conscripted me into service. Ironically, I showed great aptitude for Intelligence. After two years in the Army, your CIA approached me offering me a college education at the Naval Academy in Annapolis, Maryland. I studied Medicine and American History with the intention of becoming a Corpsman, at least officially."

"It was while studying medicine that I met my wife. She was beautiful, not the kind of woman you would think would be at all interested in a man like me. Blonde hair, sea blue eyes, and the fairest skin of any person I have ever met. She was completely different from Koreans. We were introduced at a bible study attended by students of medicine, be they civilian or paramilitary. A few missionaries on furlough led the Bible study. I think I went because my parents died for their faith but in truth, I had no real faith of my own."

The last remark sent a ripple effect through Nolan's brain. "You were angry at God. He took the people who meant the most to you and tossed the rocks that anchored your life," he said to nobody in particular. Park read his thoughts for he nodded in understanding.

"I went to that Bible study a cynic, a man who depended only upon himself despite my whole life being beyond my control. I visibly shook as the old missionary spoke of God's grace and His victory on the cross of cavalry. He said that there was no one who was righteous, none who can ascend the hill based on his merit. God so loved the world that He found a way to connect to humankind by offering His self in human form, sacrificing His Son, Jesus, so that none would perish but have everlasting life."

"I became a dead man that night. All that I had held up inside me, the control I sought in earnest, I realized had been for nothing. I was nothing. Rather than feel worthless, I felt free. I began weeping so loud that others soon took notice and began giving me a wide berth. All save for my beautiful wife. She knelt down beside me, taking my hand and she softly cried on my shoulder. She told me that God loved me and had a plan for my life. She said that I had to acknowledge His sacrifice and His true atonement for my sins for His saving grace. I surrendered to the Lord and He did a great work in me to give me a new life. I placed my faith in Jesus and surrendered my control to the Lord that night. I knew then, for the first time in my life, that I was truly free."

Nolan leaned forward in his chair as his shoulders tensed. Park's faith was the faith of his parents, long buried deep in the dark recesses of his heart. Now that faith seemed to be hammering its way back into the light. Park allowed him a few moments to wrestle with his demons.

"We lived a life of bliss. Three years, I lived with the most peaceful, beautiful, God-fearing woman to ever walk this planet. I thought life was perfect. I was a crack government operative with a beauty queen at home. Then I was on an assignment in a non-disclosed state when I got the call. There was an accident involving a drunk driver on the Arlington Memorial Bridge. Her father, an admiral, had some pull and got me home that very night."

Tears streamed down Nolan's face, dropping onto the slate floor. "My dad," he started just above a whisper. "He died saving another. My mom carried her faith, strong even after his loss, but I merely went through the motions out of respect for her. I stopped being a pretender when she died. I've spent so much time wondering why?" He looked in Park's eyes. "Why did God do this? Why would He take my dad? Why would He allow a faithful man and father of three like my friend Tom Philips to die while I lived?"

Park's voice matched Nolan's whisper as he leaned into the firefighter. "Jesus says 'the thief comes to steal, kill, and destroy but I have come so they may have life and hit it in full.' I know you blame God, Nolan. But God does not need your forgiveness. He does not need anything, but instead, He gives. He gave His self to us. If He gave up everything, then He is worthy of the same."

"I've had enough of this group therapy session," cut in a voice from the back.

Mason Grey.

Nolan was so fascinated he never saw the SAS operative had joined them from the door. "We've all sacrificed things we can never have back in this world, so what? I've got work to do." With that Grey pounded the door with a balled fist as he made his exit.

"What happens next? What happens when I say that I irrevocably believe," asked Nolan.

Samuel Park stood, looking over Nolan. "Do you state your belief now Mr. Hoke? Do you believe that God is sovereign and has a plan? Do you believe that part of His plan was to send His Son as the ultimate price for your salvation and that of all of us?"

"I do! I do," Nolan cried. "I realize now that my parents were ready to die. I know they loved me, and they showed me every day, but I know that God was their first love. I remember that. They lived their lives as though it did not belong to them."

"I must warn you," said Park. His voice was so course he could have scared the dead. "You already know that life does not get any easier. Given the state of things, those living in America will die in the coming months from war or disease. Should you live through it, you will find yourself among the few. But you can rest assured that you belong to God's family, considered a friend, for His salvation has come to you. You are to set your mind on His plan and consider His grace in your daily life."

"I'm ready," said Nolan, standing to join Park. The two men grasped shoulders. "How do I stop blaming God and join in the faith of my parents?"

"First you must confess with your mouth that Jesus is Lord and admit your need for a savior."

"Then?"

"When Philip met the Ethiopian, he interpreted the Scriptures as given to us by Isaiah. The newborn believer wasted no time in making his conversion public through Jesus' example of baptism. You too can take this step."

"I remember being baptized as a kid."

"Yes, but your faith is now your own Mr. Hoke. If you are ready, you can make your public confession to follow the Lord. You may take some time to reflect on this."

"No, no more wasting time. Let's roll."

Park smiled, a rare occurrence indeed. "Good. Let's bow our heads."

24

The morning after the raid on Atlanta, Yuri ordered Anton to see the transfer of all prisoners to Andrews Air Force Base. After a quick breakfast of eggs, bacon, black bread, and tea, Yuri joined his brother for grappling practice, *Systema Spetsnaz*. The hour session ended with him resetting his trigger finger. Bogdan smiled, having beaten his older brother once more. Yuri had to admit that Bogdan was a world-class wrestler.

Anton met him in his room after a shower and shave. "Ah, you're back. Everything goes well," he asked, toweling off.

"*Da,* Major. Sir, Commander Yaromir requests your presence."

Yuri turned back to the bedroom and began dressing. Instead of his preferred battle-gear, he chose instead to take a higher approach. Dressing in a tailored suit, he thought he would catch the retired pimp off guard. "Thank you, Anton Kozlov. You have served me well and you have served Russia well. Now, please get some rest. I can handle Commander Yaromir myself."

"Of course, Yuri," said the man, bowing out of the immaculate suite.

Descending the brick staircase with care, his leg still tender, he went to meet the ancient spy. His aching progress was halted by two thick-necked bodyguards. The tailored Mafioso could have been clones of their foolhardy brethren that charged the kitchen and went up in smoke. Upon closer inspection, he could see the younger of the two thugs was missing some fingers and wore a flesh-colored eyepatch. Yuri stopped short of the men forcing them to approach him. The younger of the two grimaced with each short step.

"Major Orlov, you are requested to bring your arms to your sides while we check you for weapons," said the older of the two henchmen. Finding him clear, the suits allowed him to pass to the second flight of bricked foundry stairs.

Commander Yaromir sat alone at a large oval table. Sasha roared from her heavy chain, pacing back and forth in her alcove. Yuri couldn't help but look at her enormous size, the rippling leg muscles, and vicious, yellow teeth. He saw nothing but bloodlust in her black eyes.

Looking at Yaromir, the ancient man's neck fat rolled out of his neck collar. "Do not worry Yuri," said the spy lifting his arm to Sasha. "She cannot get you from here." He smiled his most disarming smile. Yuri seethed in return.

"I believe congratulations are in order Major Orlov," the old man continued, his smile still plastered across his face. "I have, of course, been well briefed of your excursion and sweeping victory. It seems Corporal Litvinenko is now in charge of Russia's newest medical research facility. I have been in contact with the Kremlin since this morning, detailing your courage, expertise, and ability to overwhelm the enemy."

"You have contact with the Kremlin," interjected Yuri.

"Yes, Major Orlov. While we lost the President and many others, key comrades in the Motherland form a chord of leadership that still plays on. Based on your recent acts of heroism, they believe you are the perfect candidate to defend our nation's sovereignty."

"I am being called back to Russia?"

"Oh, come now. I told you this would happen, didn't I? After the devastating nuclear strikes, those fledging peasant countries that comprise NATO believe they can overcome the greatest empire since the Cold War."

"So, you are sending me away. What will become of the work here?"

"American has fallen. With your defending of Russia's borders, the Kremlin can send new waves of soldiers, eager to pillage this former nation. With so much land, it will be a peasant's paradise." The old pimp's eyes gleamed. He believed the garbage he was trying to sell. "You will be like the great Russian's of old, defending our nation against the likes of modern Napoleons and Hitlers."

"I am assuming that I will be promoted."

"Of course," said the man with a wave. "You will be Supreme Commander, answerable to no one. Not even the Soviet would dare touch you."

"What if I refuse?"

Yaromir pounded the table, clanging silverware and china. "Our enemies are amassing outside our mother's door. Do you let her children starve and be led to slaughter in this nuclear winter? Everybody sees *us* as the weaker state. The situation is dire Yuri!"

Yuri was incensed. Something didn't smell right to him, so he pressed the issue. "Just say it! You want me gone! Despite outpacing you at every turn, you have always kept your eye on me. You cannot handle that an Orlov is going to subdue this land, not you!"

"Is that why you killed my spy," asked Yaromir, grabbing a silver knife. His rage caused his red face to look blotchy.

"Your spy was insolent and vain. He undermined my command and got Immanuil killed! I found his actions worthy of treason and delivered the penalty for his impotence."

"For revenge!"

The spy lunged at Yuri, but Yuri was quicker. Leaping to his feet, he caught the old man's outstretched arm and turned him around. Crashing into the wall, Yaromir wheezed but kept hold of the knife. Yuri grabbed a red silk tablecloth.

Yaromir tried running but was cut off. The tiger roared in the background. The feline paced faster and faster, sensing prey. Terrified, Yaromir called out for this guards.

Trapped, Firebird lunged once more with the knife. Yuri dodged, landing a hammer fist deep in the solar plexus. The blade clanged to the floor. Yuri rushed, plunging the silk cloth deep into his enemy's throat.

For revenge.

Shots echoed through the cellar. Yuri felt a sharp pain as he threw Yaromir behind the table, clutching Yaromir's throat in his hands. Using the table as cover, he held Yaromir down with his knees as the man's body thrashed, the eyes bursting in the vessels. He thought of his father and mother. His father maligned by Yaromir's swindling and lying tactics. His mother abused by the snake now dying by his hand.

For revenge.

Another roar. Sasha smelled blood. Yuri turned just enough to see the majestic Siberian Tiger perched atop a crumbling dumbwaiter. She pounced, claws glinting in the light as bullets flew and shards of wood hissed through the air.

Yuri turned at the last moment, using Yaromir's body as cover as the tiger gorged on the fat old man's corpse. Scared for his life, Yuri made his body as small as possible as claws and bullets ripped through clay, wood, brick, bone, and mass. He never heard the grenades drop.

With a resounding, apocalyptic boom, the concussion blasts enveloped the small cellar causing the stairs to cave in, burying Yuri, Yaromir, his henchmen, and the tiger.

When the ringing in his ears subsided, he could detect muffled cries, and the sound one hears when breaking the ocean's surface after a dive. Opening his eyes, all was black. He couldn't feel his right hand. He couldn't move his body. Afraid, he wiggled his toes, cursing himself for not wearing his combat boots. Closing his eyes, he gave silent thanks that he escaped paralyzation. Opening his eyes once more, a small light shone in his right eye. The cries grew louder, and the pressure on his body lessened. He felt hands along his legs and torso checking for wounds. The white linen shirt he had been wearing was cut away; it's color soaked in red. Pressure on his leg caused hot, sticky blood to wash over the hands of his helper.

"Bogdan, I've got bleeding from the thigh and possibly two gunshot wounds to the abdomen." He recognized the voice. Anton. "He needs a doctor now!" Anton moved away. He couldn't see around him, but he knew that they had cleared all the debris from his body. Looking into his brother's eyes, Yuri summoned the strength to speak.

"Grenade."

Bogdan smiled.

"You could have buried me."

"That is Spetsnaz, big brother."

Yuri smiled too. "For revenge."

25

Nolan spent the rest of the morning searching the compound for Lauren. He wanted to tell her that he may be leaving but he couldn't find her. One of the younger women she shared a dorm with informed him that she was buried in paperwork. Lauren had become something of a secretary to one of the underground's personnel operators and he never saw her except at breakfast. He was glad she was getting on.

Checking his watch, he realized it was almost time for Hargreaves' briefing, so he made his way to the private study chambers. Knocking twice, the door opened. Already assembled were many of the foreign covert operatives he met upon first entering the underground. Park gave no signal that he had helped Nolan see God's higher purpose. Only Hargreaves and Rasputin seemed pleased to see Nolan join the clandestine meeting.

"Ah, Nolan. Now our team is complete," said Ben Hargreaves. Nolan approached the oaken desk where the operatives poured over a handful of topographic maps. Each soldier wore moss green fatigues for winter, save a helmet and a weapon.

"Speculation points us to a concentration camp outside our nation's capital," continued the underground leader. "Once you enter DC, it shouldn't be hard to pick up any enemy activity. I can personally attest to the significant damage the Russians manufactured there." He paused to look each man and woman in the eyes. "I hope to draw a line in the sand. The Russian homeland is in ruins. Our allies are mounting a counter-offensive to make sure freedom endures, but it's up to us to rise from the ashes. We have to gather our people, restore hope, and make sure this great country is not wiped off the map."

The man spoke with such fervor, each soldier's back stiffened. Looking around, Hargreaves smiled, comprehending his chosen warrior's resolve. Turning to Rasputin, he ushered the floor to the South African. The large man placed both hands on the table. "We will travel in two groups, changing transportation as it avails itself on the way to our objective. We will travel under cover of darkness. Our mission is to observe these camps, liberate them if possible and offer assistance to anyone we can."

"What if we encounter refugees on the road," piped up Doctor LeFevour.

"Our timetable and objective do not allow them to come with us, but all Americans deserve our help. We will offer them the best we can and help them find better means for surviving this war. I don't have to remind anyone here that the smaller our group remains, the faster we will move. The lead vehicle will be Grey, myself, Pope and the doc. The rear vehicle will be Gutierrez, Breckenridge, Hoke, and Park."

"Why the civilian," asked Grey.

"He's seen these soldiers up close," answered Hargreaves. "He knows what they are capable of. And he volunteered for the mission same as you."

"When do we move out," asked Park.

Rasputin clapped his hands together. "Right now. From this point on we call ourselves Kukris One and Kukris Two."

"What's a Kukris," asked the Latina soldier. Gutierrez.

"It's ancient Nepalese blade bused by the Royal British Gurkha soldiers. Legend says that once the blade is drawn, it must take blood to be sheathed again."

"Great."

"Well, I think we've covered it, ladies and gentlemen," said Hargreaves calling the meeting to a close. "Take charge and carry out the plan of the day."

Rasputin helped outfit Nolan with the gear he would need for the mission. As it turned out, the equipment was not all that dissimilar from a smokejumper. A medium weight rucksack toted a digital camera, sleeping bag, and food. Other essential gear was a Kevlar helmet, flak jacket, and matching solid moss green Moleskin uniforms. He was allowed to keep his boots. The armorer issued him a collapsible M4 Carbine complete with an ACOG Scope, flashlight, suppressor and laser sight. For a secondary weapon, each soldier carried a suppressed HK 9mm. The reduction in stopping power offset the elite soldier's excellent marksmanship. The need for stealth outweighed the need for brute force.

Fully outfitted, Nolan joined the men and women around two non-descript SUVs. Most of the operators busied themselves with the stowing of gear.

Rasputin clapped him on the back. "You look like a warrior."

"I feel like a fake," Nolan admitted.

"You have fought flames to save the lives of others. You do not fear death. That is the warrior ethos. I heard about your piano lesson, though I prefer Tchaikovsky myself. I am proud to call you a brother." Nolan thanked him.

"We are all named and we are all known," said Park, coming around the Range Rover. We need not fear what lies beyond, but I pray that while there is breath in our lungs, we will be used for His glory and the restoring of a people." Rasputin and Nolan nodded in unison. Park brought his right hand up, facing Nolan with a solid salute. Park held the pose until he self-consciously returned the gesture. Nolan caught Grey looking over the Korean's shoulder. Making eye contact, the Brit gave an almost imperceptive nod.

When Hargreaves descended the concrete steps for a final inspection, all activity ceased. Each of the eight volunteers approached a solid navy line, eyeing their leader. "At ease."

Rasputin approached. "Sir, the Kukris are ready to begin." Hargreaves clasped the warrior's hand, the sound reverberating in the cavernous hall.

Hargreaves paced the line, looking at each volunteer. Coming to the end, he held Nolan's gaze for a brief second more. "I don't have long. This mission must make haste or my absence will be noted." He paused but for a moment and glimpsed at the ceiling above. "The only souls who know of this recon mission are all present. There is no hurrah for clandestine work, no fanfare for those operating like the French Resistance of World War II, in occupied territory. Should you succeed in gathering information and rescuing prisoners, our nation may yet survive. Should you fail, then I fear the clock will strike midnight for the American way of life. Nations themselves are not worth living and dying for. I served this country and saluted the flag, but I do not pledge allegiance to dirt."

"I swore to defend my nation, as a soldier and as a diplomat, against any foe, foreign or domestic, should they seek to ruin my neighbors' way of life. I am willing to sacrifice you, my closest and most trusted friends, for the betterment of the American people. Should you accept this mission, should you allow yourselves to be sent like lambs to slaughter so that more may be saved, please step forward."

As one unit, eight pairs of legs crossed the Rubicon. Hargreaves shook each soldiers hand in turn before they about-faced and mounted their rigs for the ride to Washington DC.

26

The drive carried on in silence for hours, making few stops. Breckenridge drove the rear car while Nolan sat next to a statue silent Gutierrez in the backseat. No signal given, nor any lights used; each driver navigated using night-vision goggles. The choreography reminded Nolan of playing rugby. While communication remained an essential part of the game, it was trust in one's teammate that moved the ball most efficiently. Beautiful switches or scissor maneuvers were made possible at a moment's notice slashing through a team's defensive line thanks to precision and team chemistry. Implicit trust was evident amongst the operatives.

By early evening the dark had already descended as winter crept in. Dusk orange skies had given way to midnight blue. The mountainous landscape looked grey, like a ghostlike eeriness as they entered the dark forests of the Appalachians. The sliver of an ivory moon made a glimmer through the trees.

The trip was slow, with occasional bursts of speed as the open road cleared. Nolan ached for some music, but his ancient iPod did not survive the intense flames following the helicopter crash. Breck had tried the SUV's radio, but it broadcasted white noise. The quiet had a pensive effect on his mind. He tried his best to picture Rachel as she was on their date. Changing his thoughts, he reflected on his training as a smokejumper. It had felt like Navy SEAL training at the time. Log hauls, marathon runs, endless drills all culminated in Hell Week where the dwindling class of those looking to "make the jump" would be chopped in half. He spent two years as a Hot Shot or ground pounder in the Cascades before being given a chance to be considered for Jump School.

While hours spent amongst fire could be exhilarating, he figured one of his favorite things about being a smokejumper was the tedious task of folding parachutes. The systematic almost mindless process allowed him to decompress. A fan on 90s rock, he sometimes hummed along to the Foo Fighters, Third Eye Blind, Goo Goo Dolls and the Cranberries. Other times he would speak audibly to himself rehearsing decisions, mistakes, the behavior of the fire and even conversations while fighting the fire, lips moving while his hands, on their own accord, packed parachutes. Without knowing it, his lips and hands moved as he drifted to sleep.

"Hey, wake up and shut up!"

Nolan jerked awake after someone tapped his knee with a sharpened point. A train of drool hung from his chin and darkened wet spots spattered his chest. In a groggy haze, his saw Gutierrez glaring back at him. He figured her sour attitude came from not being assigned the same car as Grey. He had noticed the short but pretty Latina soldier shadowing Grey most mornings and evenings in the mess hall. To his knowledge, Grey never so much as smiled at her. The other female, Doctor Bianca LeFevour, was much more pleasant to be around and one of the few underground survivors that he felt he had developed an acquaintance. Blonde haired and sparkle-eyed, Dr. LeFevour was a French-Canadian who first traveled the world volunteering in the Peace Corps and later saw action with *Médecins sans Frontières*. With her native French tongue, she worked many theaters in West Africa, combatting Malaria and the Ebola outbreaks long after international outcry ceased.

Screeching tires brought the Explorer to a halt throwing Nolan into the driver's headrest. Gutierrez swore. "What are you doing Breck?"

"Look to the west," said Breckenridge. Everyone looked through the windows seeing nothing but pitch-black sky. Nolan's breathe condensed on the windows. He tried looking for the moon, but the orb lost its opulence. A knock at the window caused them all to jump. Gutierrez swore again.

Breckenridge rolled the window down, taking off his night-vision goggles. Park lit a red-lensed flashlight so everyone could see. Nolan recognized Rasputin's bushy beard and could just make out his coal black eyes. "Good evening all. Did you notice that we are not alone in the forests?"

"I did," answered Breck. Nolan thought Breckenridge may have been a SEAL but couldn't remember.

"Their presence means we can't stop here and may have to proceed with caution," continued Rasputin checking over his shoulder. Nolan could hear the idle of both engines, ready to move if necessary.

"It's getting late," said Breck.

"Then again someone could need our help."

"It's getting late," Breck repeated.

"Our boat has an even count, two to two."

"As to what, I don't like sitting here. We need to move and bed down before dawn."

"So Breck votes to move on, what do the rest of you say," asked Rasputin.

Nolan couldn't help but wonder why it was up for debate. Rasputin was the leader; his decisions should be followed without hesitation.

"Now hold on," said Breckenridge. "I heard Hargreaves' speech. I didn't cross the blue line to leave Americans stranded, besides I can't let the Ranger take all the glory for never leaving a man behind."

Gutierrez crossed her arms, but a faint smile played on her lips.

"I say we check it out," said Park as he leaned across the middle console.

"Gutierrez," posed Rasputin.

"Hooah," came the reply.

Rasputin's dark eyes came through to Nolan.

"Let's go check it out."

Plunging through the dark forest Nolan fought hard to tell the professional soldiers from the foliage. The thickness of the woods, not touched by wildfire, shrouded everything in sight. Even Doctor LeFevour adopted the dark. Covered in mud, carrying a weapon, he just wanted to lie down, go to sleep and wake up to a new, brighter, warmer world.

Three sharp whistles pierced the air due west of his path. The bursts signaled the situation was under control and there was no threat. Coming into a clearing, the soldiers snapped together a perimeter. He saw LeFevour, sans helmet, crouched over a body that was lying flat on its back. Various articles of camping gear littered the clearing, and so too, were more bodies.

"Nolan, help me triage the victims," instructed the doc. He searched the ground for the nearest body. Coming alongside a balding man, he noticed the man was unconscious, propped against a canvas rucksack. The man's face bronzed from long hours in the sun, his arms folded across an M16 from a bygone era. Touching the man's body, Nolan felt nothing but ice. The man's open arms revealed a mass of purple skin, yellow pus, and the red of infection.

"How long have you been here," said Nolan to the man. Checking for a pulse in both the wrist and neck, he was sure he could feel a faint heartbeat. It was no good, however. With Sepsis, the man was as good as dead. To be unconscious and slip into an eternal sleep was now the best the man could hope for.

He diagnosed three other bodies. Two, he believed would live, but the third had already died. Turning back to the second, Rasputin came and kneeled next to him. Both men looked at a woman who blinked back at them but did not move a muscle. "Can you tell us your name, ma'am," asked Nolan shining a penlight in her eyes as Rasputin filtered her water through a straw. The pupils responded to the beam and her eyes followed the movement of his wrist. Still, she did not move.

He was about to ask the question again when she swallowed and looked at Rasputin. The large man took that as a cue for more water. She drank of her own power and nodded she had had her fill. After a deep breath, she said, "My name is Audrey. We took shelter with a group of people following the attacks. A man named Dan Haskins blamed the damage from the attacks on a weak, liberal government and he warned that more attacks would soon be coming. Many were hesitant at first, but he pressed on saying that gangs would soon be heading to more remote areas once they conquered the cities. He said Blacksburg would be doomed if we didn't follow his lead." She took another sip of water and wet her hands to clear dirt from her face. Nolan thanked the Lord for His provision since the helicopter crash. This woman, though young and once pretty, looked like she had aged decades in just a week's time.

"He said that he and his men felt prepared and we would live if we followed his every order. But we couldn't ever be prepared, not for them. His goons were typical misogynists. A woman could only speak when spoken to." Her eyes welled with tears. "That was one of his rules. He said the rules would protect us." Her eyes were harder now. "But the rules didn't protect us. Those big soldiers drove through with their big tanks; we thought they must be Americans. We thought rescue had come! But Haskins said he wasn't giving in to another liberal stooge doing the bidding of a politician. He said he was going to march up there and give them a piece of his mind. A real McCoy that one. He walked into the road to meet their leader. I couldn't see very well, so I moved a few feet away from my boyfriend. I crouched down behind a log when the large man blasted Haskins away. After that," she paused, remembering. "After that, they started shooting all at once. It was like a rain of fire. My boyfriend died instantly. If I had been next to him, I would have been killed too."

"What are you doing here," asked Grey. The SAS operative stood above the trio, his M4 cradled in his arms. Rasputin fixed the Brit with a hard stare but reset his gaze on the girl. It was a legitimate question.

"There were rumors of aid camps set up by that same government Haskins hated. He hated it so much he even blamed it for his wife's abandonment. After some debate, those of us who could still move decided to try and find help."

"You left others behind," asked Gutierrez, now joining in the discussion.

"Are they still alive," piped up Nolan.

Audrey shook her head. "We left four days ago. I guess no one believed we would ever turn back."

Nolan watched Breckenridge turn and spit in the dirt. Grey swore, murmuring under his breath in a distinctively higher lilt. Dr. LeFevour pulled Rasputin away from the group. The good doctor's movements spread in a circle as if to envelop the marooned Americans. Rasputin shook his head but his weathered face registered that he was pensive rather than stoic.

Driving further into the night, the team bedded down in a grocery store on the outskirts of Roanoke, Virginia. In the end, the stranded Americans still breathing were allowed to accompany the Kukris as far as the grocery store and were left to their own devices.

At dawn, a pale morning sun rose into the pink, newborn sky casting a deadeye on the smoke and destruction of the eastern seaboard. The scene was one of genocide. After switching vehicles found in the parking lot, it was on the move once more, bound for a concentration camp outside DC. Nolan thought of Asheville and the battle he survived there. He thought of the professor, the mayor, and the soldiers, but mostly he thought of Rachel. He wished he could cover his face with her thick brown hair. The convoy coasted along I-66 just north of Manassas, the battleground for two Civil War engagements. The extent of damage done to the outskirts of the nation's capital was unlike anything anyone had ever seen. It became evident to Nolan that eight men and women were woefully unprepared to infiltrate a city in the midst of utter annihilation. His hands began to shake with fear. Traps and spies could lie anywhere. There was no intelligence on how many Russians occupied the capital. How were they supposed to evacuate refugees without being caught?

Scanning the incinerated, gaunt landscape, Nolan asked no one in particular, "Where is everybody?"

27

Screeching tires and sparks interrupted everyone's thoughts as the lead car blew all four tires thanks to a hidden trap or spikes. Gutierrez cut the wheel of their ride to avoid falling victim, but it was too late. The SUV slid across the strips, popping the tires. The momentum carried the large vehicle over sending it onto the driver's side. Nolan ducked as a spray of glass entered the cabin, the steel uprights grinding along the asphalt.

After the sliding stopped, Nolan heard loud clinks of metal on metal sounding all around him. Sensing that time was short he unbuckled himself and crawled around the backseat. He could make out a few muffled groans over the din of machine gun fire as he searched the cargo for his weapon. The 9mm was already on his hip, so he slapped a magazine into his customized M4 carbine. Without a look back, he ducked through the blown rear window and into the street.

Adrenalized blood pumped into his ears while the airway constricted, tunneling his vision. The lead vehicle was upright but immobile as Nolan stumbled around the wreckage of his ride. Grey was the first to emerge from the other SUV, his M4 shouldered, lining up shots as he rounded the SUV's dark hood.

Shielded at present by abandoned vehicles along the road, Nolan waved and yelled for Grey to find cover. The SAS operative continued firing prompting Nolan to shoulder his weapon to lay down suppressing fire. Leaning around an 18-

wheeler, he gave the Russians five successive three-round bursts. Grey continued to seek and destroy the enemy from his perch, but as Nolan chanced a glimpse of the Brit, a bullet found Grey's lower torso doubling the tall soldier over. Racing towards his companion, the enemy fire stopped him short as bullets peppered Grey's chest. Nolan watched in horror as Grey slumped against the passenger side of the dark SUV and fell beneath the undercarriage.

Bullets ripped past Nolan's head forcing him to cower behind the big rig's engine block. Rapid gunshot fire also erupted behind him as Rasputin emerged from Nolan's six. Nolan frantically waved the soldier towards the wreckage. The South African spun and began to pull on Gutierrez's feet while Breckenridge gingerly slipped the Latina's torso through the vehicle's open window.

"She's not moving," Breckenridge shouted over the cacophony of gunfire.

"Nolan," said Rasputin slapping the firefighter on the shoulder, "you've got to buy us some time."

As if in response, more assault rifle fire erupted from around them as Park, Dr. Lefevour and the final operative, Okafor, began to fan out, drawing enemy attention away from the wreckage while laying down suppressive fire. Nolan followed their example, shuffling to his right, keeping the M4 shouldered and steady.

Across the plain, Yuri commanded his shock troops to ensnare the American insurgents in a pincer maneuver. The Spetsnaz contingent was small, but Cicero's message accounted for under a dozen soldiers. He adjusted his optics to get a better view of the enemy position. The Americans fired wild, pinned down, and in distress. Yuri mused that they did not realize their peril. His troops cast a wide net. Once the firing commenced, the constriction process had begun.

Visibility was sparse from his hideout in the thicket, so Yuri stepped onto the plain. Pain jolted from his legs through his back, ramifications of the dust-up with Yaromir's henchmen. Anton diagnosed him with two gunshot wounds to the abdomen and a laceration via tiger claw to the upper thigh.

Smoke rose from the wreckage as hot gasses of machine gun fire were emitted into the cold atmosphere. Yuri hoped his sniper tandem was faring better than he was at viewing the Americans. They were given an explicit instruction not to engage unless they identified a target. Cicero's message also informed them that individual soldiers were considered valuable targets of intelligence. He panned the battleground for a soldier described as having a generous black beard; in essence looking for a man built similar to Bogdan. That shouldn't be too hard, he thought. The Americans fanned out from their defended position, making a harder target but also exposing themselves.

"Commander Orlov." Yuri turned to the speaker and invited him out onto the plain. The speaker was reluctant but did not want to appear weak in front of his commanding officer. "Sir, Sniper Two reports that the package has moved away from the wreckage and can be isolated."

"Bogdan," Yuri roared, "See to it that any Americans pinned down use their blood to make the grass grow." Bogdan sneered in reply. Seconds later the scream and smoke plume of a rocket-propelled grenade blasted through the trees. The rocket detonated upon impact, striking the asphalt just below the overturned enemy vehicle, a devastating blow.

Nolan heard the bomb's high-pitched whistle. He witnessed the warhead exploding beneath the stranded vehicle. He tried to scream in warning, but the shockwave sucked the air from his lungs while the blast threw his body into the ditch along the highway. The impact threatened to knock him unconscious. Writhing in pain, Nolan was unable to dodge falling debris as bits and pieces of car, asphalt, and utility lines came down around him.

Pinned down, the battle waged on. He tried to move, but a massive beam across his chest made it impossible. He thought about trying to dig at the ground to roll under the severed pole.

The pain in his chest began to lessen. Nolan looked to his left to find Rasputin straining under the weight of the wooden beam. The sun was rising behind Rasputin's silhouette, but Nolan could still make out the hulking figure, red-faced and veins bulging. The broken beam must have weighed hundreds of pounds. Soon as he could move his arms, Nolan tried to help to push but felt feeble.

Still, the beam rose. Rasputin's face was set in fury as he chanted in soft Afrikaans. First Nolan heard the words as a whisper, but as the pole rose, so too did Rasputin's incantation.

At last, the heavy timber was high enough for Nolan to slide out from underneath. Rasputin blew a succession of short, screeching whistles. Even in the cold, winter air, his fatigues were soaked with sweat. Chest heaving, he offered Nolan a hand. Forgetting all around him, Nolan smiled at the gesture.

That's when two shots cut the air.

"*Nyet! Nyet!*" Yuri fumed in rage. Drawing his Grach pistol, he ran past the soldier who had shot the target. Without stopping to aim, Yuri fired blind, killing the offending Russian. The body dropped like a sack of potatoes.

Anton hurried to catch the dying insurgent before it too slumped to the ground. The massive soldier had been the one Cicero warned to take alive as having the most intimate knowledge of the underground and the ultimate target, a mastermind codenamed Mary. The intelligence locked in the man's brain, Yuri knew, could hold the key to defeating American resistance cells.

Climbing up the berm, it was too late. The large soldier was dead.

Behind him, another soldier, American, screamed in a mixture of rage and horror. As his eyes met the soldier's, a flash of recognition passed between them. With a wave of his hand, Yuri ordered his men to take the American captive. Once the soldier could stand, Yuri marched towards him. Arching back, he landed a solid right cross through the man's jaw. The man was right-sized, just over two meters tall but Yuri was thicker. The man stumbled to the ground.

Trying to stand, the man grimaced in pain and fell once more. Pressing his boot on the man's chest, Yuri caused the American to howl. "Look at me," Yuri commanded. The soldier's brown eyes met his own and Yuri knew. He detected fear but also a shred of rage. Yuri knew this man was the one from the chase in the mountain town. He too was responsible for the death of Immanuil. "What is your name?"

"Nolan Hoke."

BOOK V

1

A metallic door clanged shut, the sound echoing off solid walls. Heavy boots thudded down a concrete floor. Rough hands supported Nolan under his arms. Harsh Russian passed back and forth between his captors then the black shroud was pulled back off his head. He eyed his captors in a placid daze, but no one returned his stare.

They dragged him through a narrow corridor, boots squeaking on the wet surface. White tiled walls reflected the soldier's flashlights casting a dim glow throughout the hall.

He felt for sure that either the fallen telephone beam or the Russians themselves had broken several of his ribs. More agonizing was the anguish knowing he had lost more friends in battle. He wondered how much more loss he could endure. He sang to himself the words of a hymn he could remember his mother singing in the kitchen, so many years ago. He pictured the warm sun beaming through the window and his mother's golden hair shining with radiance. Clouds moved in, hiding the sun but moving on at regular intervals to reveal it's light once more.

A swift kick interrupted his reverie. The clouds and intermittent sunlight disappeared replaced by fog colored walls and a jade incandescent glow emitted from portholes fastened to steel bulkhead doors. A dull thudding noise thumped from behind the closed doors. Nolan knew they were being sounded by fellow prisoners. Fellow Americans.

The guard not bearing Nolan's weight knocked his tubular nightstick on a steel door. The deep boom carried down the forlorn hallway. The door ground open sounding like a locomotive steaming along iron rails. Two other guards raised him to his feet before shoving him in the back. Stumbling, he fell face down on the hard, cold floor. Unable to lift his head, Nolan heard the heavy door grind back into place. A screeching lock slammed with finality.

Unlike what he had seen going down the hall, there was no window to his cell. The only light was emitted from the dead-still bulb that hung from the ceiling. The only sound came as water dripped and circled the drain making a gurgling noise next to his ear. The flat grey ceiling mirrored the drab concrete he lay on. As above, so below.

It could have been hours. It could have been days when they awoke him with a start sliding back the metal latch that locked him in his chamber. Water pooled around his mouth, filling his nostrils and choking him. He awoke with a snorting cough and rolled to his back. Raising his arms, he tried to shield himself from the soldiers and their weapons. One of the soldiers laid a tin tray of meager food in the corner of the cell where the water dripped from its source. The water slid onto his sandwich, soaking the bread. The soldier then started to lay down a cup of water next to the tray but paused as if to taunt Nolan. Smiling in malevolence, the soldier pitched the cup at him, splattering the uniform he was captured wearing. A word of Russian passed between the two soldiers and they were gone. The lock slammed shut.

Nolan sprang upon the meal. He couldn't remember the last time he had eaten. The bread tasted like a wet sponge, and although Nolan hated bologna all his life, he savored the food. Carrots and peas also adorned the tray. He wondered what meal this constituted as. Was it lunch or supper? Did they bother changing the meal variety at all? He also questioned how many meals he could hope to look forward to eating.

As he ate, he took in more of his surroundings. The wall remained bare save for a few graffiti marks not much higher than ground level. The first was a crude drawing of half circles with a long drop over a horizontal line. At first Nolan thought it a horizon but upon inspection it looked like a man's face peeking over a fence line. Two bulging eyes spied at him while the nose hung low over the line like a long, droopy tube. An inscription below the figure read: Kilroy was Here. A second message under that read: What is your name?

The second brand was a roughly etched but detailed eye. Nolan could make out the eyelids, iris, and pupil. The inscription warned: OPEN YOUR EYES.

He sat back away from the wall. Like most Americans, he never imagined he would land in prison without some due process. He tried not to despair but couldn't help wondering if he would ever see the sun again.

2

Fourteen miles away Yuri Orlov sat alone in his new Georgetown study listening to *Scheherazade*. Composed by the famous Nikolai Rimsky-Korsakov, *Scheherazade* was more relaxing than the furious *Flight of the Bumblebee*. Korsakov's talent was rumored to be by divine appointment, writing his first symphony with no formal training. Yuri further admired the man for having been trained first as a naval officer, like many in the Orlov clan. The liberal Korsakov even participated in the Revolution of 1905, this time as a Professor of Composition at the Saint Petersburg Conservatory.

A sworn teetotaler, Yuri took a long pull straight from the Stolichnaya bottle. Russians never drank vodka without reason, and they never drank alone. Drinking vodka was a social activity meant for celebration or commiseration. Raising his glass container in the air, he saluted his men's apprehension of the American Special Forces unit and undermining of their forward operating base. Similar hideouts would soon be routed as Cicero's intelligence reports filtered through the airwaves. He also lamented the loss of his nation's great cultural cities, Moscow and St. Petersburg. The most significant capital in all of Europe had been obliterated. Looking at the woodblock map on the wall, Yuri couldn't help but chuckle to himself. The entire United States lay in ruins around him. Millions were dead. For him, the war had cost the life of one enemy and one member of his family. He lifted the glass bottle to his lips twice more, celebrating the death of Yaromir and commiserating the death of Immanuil.

He set the glass on a mahogany nightstand, standing and wiping his mouth. A knock sounded at the door. Anton's voice carried through the heavy oaken door. Cicero had returned to interrogate the American captive.

Eyeing the vodka glass, he left it sweating on the table. Victory had yet to be toasted.

3

The latch retracted. The metalized door ground open at a sloth's pace. A colossal Russian nodded appreciatively at the cell's dreary décor. Nolan lay in the corner by the door, slumped over with fatigue and loss. A smile crept across the Russian's lips.

"*Da*," said the Russian clapping his hands together. "You are Nolan Hoke and I am Bogdan Orlov, your escort for this evening's entertainment." The smile grew tighter, like a shark before consuming its prey. Nolan looked up, confused to find that the Russian knew his name. The Special Forces carried no identifying marks, save for an American flag stitched into the shoulder.

"Come, Nolan, get up."

Roaming like a monkey, Bogdan picked him up with care. Almost at the door, the giant Russian shook him from head to foot. "No funny business, ok?"

In the white-tiled hallway, Nolan tried to sneak glances through other portals, but the man known as Bogdan kept redirecting his jaw. Bogdan was his single escort. Nolan inferred the gargantuan Russian thought he would be plenty of enough muscle to manage the American though he appeared unarmed. Nolan knew the Russian had figured correctly.

"Where are you taking me," ventured Nolan.

"You have special meeting, a reunion, you Americans call it." Nolan knew he had recognized the cold steel eyes of the Russian commander who killed Rasputin and took him captive. Those eyes had been the same ones he had stared down in a fit of rage during the burning of Asheville. Nolan held the man responsible for the death of so many he had come to love. Rather than feel apprehensive about seeing the Russian commander again, he welcomed a chance to confront the man after all.

At the end of the hall stood a door. A door with a massive V stenciled at head level. Bogdan pounded three consecutive times on the windowless door resembling that of Nolan's cell. The booms echoed throughout the prison. Inside was a narrow room taken up by an aluminum table with a light chair on each side. He occupied the chair opposite a great mirror. Bogdan posted himself against the door, the room's only exit, with his arms crossed. The same grin played on his face as when he had entered Nolan's cell. Another guard, already in the room, walked around Nolan and stood at ease on the other side of the room. He made no other movements and made no noise. Nolan sat unrestrained.

Three consecutive booms gave a dull thud from the outside. As Bogdan reached to open the heavy door, Nolan began to rise, his rage having built courage within him to strangle the Russian commander responsible for so much death and destruction. What he saw though stopped him dead in his tracks. Like a deer caught in the headlights, he ceased all motion and stared. Instead of a steely-eyed Russian elite soldier, a startling attractive feminine figure with a look of high intelligence walked in. Though her hair color was a dirty blonde, a somewhat more natural look with her prominent cheekbones, the doe-eyed woman was unmistakable.

Each man watched her as she sat in the vacant chair across from Nolan. Overcome with shock; he resumed his seat. Smiling demurely at his astonished gaze, she waited for him first.

Not able to utter more than a whisper, Nolan cried, "Lauren."

4

"Hello, Nolan. One should know better than to trust Greeks when they come bearing gifts," she chastised. "My real name is Marta Bunin. I am a *rezident* agent of the Federal Security Bureau. I-"

"You are a mole."

Marta sat back in the chair. Beaming she said, "You must consider yourself extremely lucky to be alive."

Nolan felt as if his insides burned with acid. He didn't feel lucky. Leaning over the table, he thought he was going to be sick. So wounding was her betrayal. "What did you do," he stammered.

She continued to eye him in an amatory manner. "Don died of sudden cardiac arrest. Peanut allergy. Who knew? His throat swelled, nobody heard his attempts to scream. I left the radio room playing clips of the old man in the whorehouse explaining America's imminent demise to Captain Nately on repeat." Nolan recognized lines from Joseph Heller's novel *Catch-22*. Required reading in high school, he remembered a debate ensued as to whether America would indeed one day face destruction. The thought that the day they discussed had come to pass filled him with grief.

Marta started laughing. "You were so brave in Asheville. You drove us to safety from the men in this room." Nolan looked first at Bogdan then at the other, slimmer man in the corner. "Why didn't you leave me to die?"

"Simple. The Russian invasion was no longer a surprise. It's a matter of time before more Americans run into their foxholes arming themselves to fight back. I needed a host to vouch for my fabricated backstory. You were a wonderful accomplice. As the perfect gentleman, you saved my life from my countrymen and sold a lie to get us admitted to the underground."

She relaxed a bit, sitting back in her chair, crossing her long legs. "Once in the underground, I was on the hunt for a man codenamed Mary. He masterminded resistance movements over the airwaves."

"Hargreaves."

"Correct. I watched the leader's movements and gathered information. He kept the mission of your Kukris so close to the chest that I didn't know of it until hours after it launched. After several key members of his entourage went missing and you were not at the breakfast table with your oatmeal, I knew something was up. I interrogated Don and killed him. I sent a message that you were on your way. I asked for Rasputin to be left alive. Instead, I got you!"

Nolan couldn't take any more. Leaning away from the table, he placed his hands on his knees and emptied his stomach. Marta's metallic chair screeched across the floor as she stood and came around the table. Her eyes looked darker, more menacing.

"Where is Benjamin Hargreaves," she demanded. For good measure, she slapped him across the face.

The blow stung but something more released inside him. He had no way of knowing if she were telling the truth but if Hargreaves were alive, then there was still hope. He resolved then that the Russians would not get anything. Though Nolan held no sensitive information, he promised himself that he would resist and make her task as difficult as possible. Perhaps he could buy time. Another smack in the face from Marta brought his eyes back to hers.

"Where is Hargreaves hiding," she cried. "Where are other underground networks? Where did you plan on taking the refugees? Answer me!"

Nolan kept his head down, absorbing more of Marta's barrage. A sudden pain burst atop his head followed by a pounding blow into the table. If his nose had met the table first instead of his forehead, it would have been crushed. Yanked by his hair, Bogdan brought a serrated edge to the nape of his neck.

"She's too easy on you American," breathed the large Russian. "I will not."

Bogdan's bushy cheek brushed against Nolan's as he eyed the sharp knife. A high-pitched whine gashed the tension. Heavy boots shuffled across the room. Nolan opened his eyes as another Russian crashed into his chair forcing both he and Bogdan to the ground, into the vomit. Bogdan was up first. The two men began arguing. Nolan looked at the newcomer, recognizing the man's face. He was not a friend but foe.

Rolling to the balls of his feet while maintaining a crouched position, Nolan got a head full of steam before planting his shoulder into his adversary. The rugby style tackle was flawless as he grabbed the man underneath the buttocks and drove him into the air before dropping the Russian to back to earth, *hard*.

The man went limp but did not blackout. Nolan detected a previous injury as the man winced in pain. All other thoughts were cast asunder as a blunt hammer came down on his skull.

First, he saw stars. Then he saw nothing.

5

That night after the encounter with the captured American Yuri soaked his wounds in an ice bath. The swift tackle he endured had opened a fair share of stitches from the fight with Yaromir's henchmen. A knock sounded at the door. He remained in the tub.

Marta entered followed by Bogdan. Yuri let his chin fall to his chest. "Speak."

No one did.

"Speak," he commanded. A sharp pain raced up his spine. The cigarette he had been nursing fell into the bath. Both Marta and Bogdan shuffled their feet. It was Bogdan who spoke first.

"Commander Orlov," he began with contrition. "Agent Bunin and I have different methods of interrogation for this American captive. The agent's methods are not just useless against his detachment, but I find them childish. He knows that she has betrayed him and he will not answer her questions. More drastic measures are necessary."

Yuri nodded. Marta paled. She moved to speak. Yuri raised a frosted hand silencing her. "Brother, did you think it such a good idea to play bad cop during such an enlightening interrogation? We gleaned much from Marta's session with the American." Bogdan opened his mouth to protest, thought better of it, and took a half step back. The color returned to Marta's cheeks. Yuri looked at his brother for a brief moment more as if cementing his place in the ground.

Fixing Marta with an unsettling gaze, he said, "Tell me, Miss Bunin. How long have you lived in America?"

Her reaction made it clear she was confused by the question. "My family moved to America when I was sixteen. I have lived here most of my life. I told you that. My grandmother was from Odessa. We moved to Brooklyn Heights to be among fellow Ukrainians and Jews. The FSB recruited me because I was born Russian but grew up American. What is this about?"

Yuri twisted the water faucet back on. This time steam rose as scalding hot water poured out melting the ice cubes. His face became distorted behind the sheet of steam making him look ethereal. "Why did you move to America?"

She began to shake. Her eyes shone wet with tears. "I felt as though this had always been my purpose, to be an agent for Mother Russia. I hated America. My friends and I would pour over magazines of the beautiful women in the West. Their perfect hair and nails were greeting Mr. Right at the door to their home with all the latest appliances. In Moscow, they spoke as though this were a reality for all Russians, but it was not true. Not for me."

"Why did you double cross your country," asked Yuri.

She swallowed hard as tears fell of their own free will.

"One October I saved up all my money to see my friend play the bass at the theater. It was *Nord-Ost*. He was much older than I, but my best friend and I adored him. Being that *Nord-Ost* was a love story, I had my head filled with fantasies that night. I bought a new scarf and was excited to pretend to be a famous actress going to a premiere."

Deep breathe.

"Chechen terrorists held the theater for three days before Spetsnaz besieged it using opiate gas and their guns. My best friend died days later in a hospital for consuming too much of the gas. I convinced her to steal from her parents to have the money to come with me. I felt a ton of guilt at her death. I hated

Putin for his cavalier tactics. When I expressed my anger to my musician friend who lived, he put me in touch with Anna Politkovskaya, an outspoken critic of Putin's. They both said that life for a survivor of *Nord-Osti* was complicated. My friend faced death every day."

"Politkovskaya was from New York and put me in touch with another Yankee journalist, Paul Klebnikov. I moved to America. One year later Klebnikov was murdered in Moscow. Thousands of Ukrainians and Russians from Brooklyn Heights to Brighton Beach decried Putin again using Politkovskaya's words that the Russian President and his lackeys as the 'Stalin of our times.' They murdered her in an elevator like an offering to Herod's niece on Putin's fifty-fourth birthday. Her daughter, a former romantic rival of mine, was pregnant at the time. I still harbored an ill will towards America, but I had a new desire to seek the end of Putin and his criminal schemes." Marta tried to fix her face with an air of self-righteousness, having defended her actions.

Yuri eased out of the draining tub and sat atop the tile, a towel draped across his lap. "I will admit, you never raised my suspicions. Not even after you said your handler was Yaromir did I suspect you of anything. But then he flew down after we destroyed the town in the mountains and informed me of the nuclear strikes on our two greatest cities. Despite my hatred for the man I knew he was innocent. Knowing the British were involved was my first clue. I knew they could not have activated the American submarines without help. I knew there was a betrayer in our midst."

Marta quivered, turning her head from side to side. Yuri continued. "During World War II they operated a double agent operation known as the Twenty Committee or XX. I guess it was they who got to you before the FSB did."

Marta fell to her knees unable to stand any longer. Her face was in her hands as she sobbed uncontrollably.

"You hung your own rope during your interrogation of the American. You managed to kill the radioman and sabotage their whole operation to stay above suspicion, but you failed to assassinate the greatest target and left it to us to pump more information from a captive who is not even a soldier." He reached under his towel, his hands finding the pistol's cold frame.

"Please," she pleaded. "I can explain."

He shot her between the eyes.

Bogdan stood at the door, his face devoid of arrogance or malice. Yuri detected a hint of fear in his brother's countenance. He waved the big man off. "I do not blame you for anything brother." The Bear stepped from the door and picked the dead woman's body off the ground without prompt.

"The American, this Nolan Hoke, may not know much but he does appear to be a close confidant of the man we are after. How do you suggest we go about getting him to speak?"

Yuri looked into the tub. The last vestiges of water circled the drain.

"I think I know the solution."

6

Nolan watched the fly as it drew close to his dinner plate. The insect approached the tin pan but reversed course in midair to avoid the stench of the forgotten food. He calculated it had been over a day since he last ate. His stomach churned, but most of the pain resided in the goose egg that lay on the back of his head.

Apart from the blow to his occipital lobe, he felt absolute betrayal at the hands of Lauren, a friend, who turned out to be a Russian spy named Marta Bunin. The Russians had also confiscated his boots. They were his favorite pair of boots.

He began to wonder how much longer he could get a grip on all the madness. All the untold death. He cried out in despair, an arm reaching out for unseen support. "God," he moaned, "I can't go on."

He had thought he could fight the good fight, as his father had. He had hoped he had the will to defy death and accept sacrifice but the pain was real, and he was all too alive to feel it.

Scarcely two weeks ago his worst fear was of being grounded by the ogre Dixon Cafferty. Since then he kept survival, hardship, and heartbreak as his companions. Marta's chilling words haunted him: "You must consider yourself very lucky to be alive."

Feeling prompted by utter hopelessness, Nolan began to cry and then he started to pray. He bowed his head into his knees implored the God of the universe to help him understand. As he prayed with eyes closed, with his back against the wall, his body became rested. As his body rested, he slept.

The mud slipped from underneath his boots. Sweat rolled into his eyes and down his back while the strong smell of cedar filled his nostrils. Ahead of him in line, a man of African-American descent shouldered his portion of the logs dense weight over a massive shoulder. The man looked carved of granite, but he grunted all the same.

"You're almost there Hoke," said the familiar voice from the man in front of him. "Can't give up now."

Nolan couldn't place the voice, but he was emboldened and shrugged his shoulder deeper into the bristles of the felled timber's bark. Soon there came a clearing and the trees opened up to a river. Nolan and five others laid the log on the river's bank.

"Well now, see there Hoke. That wasn't so bad, was it?" The tall, ox-built man began to turn around, extending his hand as he did so. Nolan reflexively shook the proffered hand then looked into the man's eyes.

The man was Tom Philips.

"Tom?"

"Hey Nolan," the man beamed, his teeth as white as a wedding gown.

"What- what are you doing here?"

"I do what the Father tells me," Tom said, still smiling. "He tells me that I got to go now though. Been real nice seeing you again son."

Nolan grabbed Tom's shoulder as the man turned away. "You can't leave. Please don't leave."

Tom laughed. "Trust me, son, you're gonna like what's next." Tom turned letting Nolan's arm fall limp and began to walk down the river. The others carrying the log had all disappeared. Several paces away Tom turned his charcoal face back over his shoulder. "Take care of my girls Hoke," he called. Then he set his face to the sun and walked into it.

The strength in Nolan's knees weakened and he fell to the beach. Drawing his legs to his chest, he continued to watch where Tom had gone. So many questions raced through his mind and yet he felt strangely at peace. Tom often had that effect on people, which is why Nolan liked him so much. And missed him so much.

A tap on his shoulder brought him to his feet. Spinning around he could not see for a myriad of color shone in his face. The colors gleam burst around him. He thought at first that he had stepped into an opal or a rainbow. No one shade was very distinct. He saw blues that swirled to reds to oranges and yellows. They were warm yet they refreshed him like a glass of water.

As his eyes adjusted a face began to emerge from the blast, a face so pure it took considerable effort for him to discern it. A form began to take shape from the bursting rays. Both figures watched as the kaleidoscope of color left them, shimmering across the sky.

Still watching, he felt a warm hand slip into his. Turning to face the newcomer, Nolan's eyes were stung by the driving force of tears.

"It's you."

Rachel nodded, a grin playing on her face. Nolan's pulse quickened, his fist tightening around her clasped hand. He looked back up the beach where Tom had disappeared. "But you, you can't be here. Tom can't be, can he? Where are we?"

"Relax Nolan." Rachel's voice carried a note that floated in the air. She smiled, her gaze more brilliant than that of a thousand suns. "Would you like to dance?"

Dressed in an all-white sleeveless gown, she moved to take Nolan's arms as the two began to sway on the silted shores of the riverbank. The gurgle of the river's path and splashing tide provided a natural symphony as if the rocks themselves were crying out in a chorus of one song. Nolan gulped down the courage to ask the question. "Am I dead?"

Rachel giggled and covered her mouth with a white-gloved hand. "Sorry. I had hoped not to laugh when you asked that question."

Nolan hoped his eyes did not betray his urgency.

"No Nolan. You are not dead. You are still a prisoner locked in a cell, but you are no longer dead in your transgressions."

Nolan remembered the words of his father, truths uttered so many years ago. "I think I understand this. Does that mean that God has accepted me?"

"The sacrifice of His Son Jesus has chosen you. You have been given eternal life. There was much rejoicing in the halls of the saints the day that you repented. Christ the carpenter is fulfilling His promise to build a place for you." Her smile never wavered.

"How do you know all this? Are you dead?"

"I am in the image of the invisible God."

Nolan shook his head. "These things all sound so familiar. If you are dead then how is this possible? How was I able to see Tom?"

Rachel's smile continued, but her voice took on that of teacher reaching out to a pupil. "You are being allowed to see. Tom and I are at the will of the Father, and that is all."

"But you came to see me, does that mean you still love me?"

"I am *in* love."

Nolan shook his head unable to fully comprehend her meaning. "I am in love with you," he said after a moment. "When I die, will I get to be with you?"

"We are neither married nor given in marriage."

He couldn't help but feel frustrated with her cryptic answers that hovered beyond his grasp, but her gaze and her smile held him in their sincerity. She was more beautiful than he could ever remember. They danced to the music without tiring. A magical moment.

Too soon, her steel blue eyes were flecked with a dazzling opal just as when she first appeared. Grasping his shoulder, she grew very serious. The swaying of their dance stopped. "Nolan my time is short. You must persevere in the faith. None but God knows what He has in store for you. Do not shrink back lest you be destroyed but hold fast to hope. Continue to let the Lord's goodness shine in you."

Nolan's eyes clouded as he realized he would have to say goodbye to Rachel, possibly for the rest of his life. He didn't want to bear being without her again. As the colorful multitude returned, enveloping both, Nolan felt a sincere warmth and a reassurance stirring within his heart. Rachel, seeming to understand his feelings gave an encouraging smile, radiance yet unmatched to anything he had ever seen on earth.

"You are not alone," she said as if placing last second instructions. "In your life, you will be tested, but you will always have Him."

He swallowed his grief and all too soon he could feel Rachel slipping through his grasp, the colors swirling around her legs, torso, and arms as if sweeping her away.

"Wait!" he said pulling her close to him in a last ditched effort. Her face showed longing, but he could not tell if it were for him or to return. Holding her gaze and memorizing her features he said, "I love you. Please tell my mom and my- my dad hello."

The colors swirled in a torrid gale. Rachel laughed as she rode the whirlwind of light.

Then she was gone.

7

D amage to the occipital lobe, Nolan knew, could cause severe trauma to the visual cortex and induce hallucinations. He doubted delusions had quite the healing affect his encounter with Tom and Rachel had been. Bolstered by the vision, he felt a quiet strength building within.

The next time Nolan was drug from his cell he and Bogdan were shadowed by the smaller, athletic built soldier. Whereas Bogdan Orlov still carried no visible weapon, the nameless sentry carried a silenced submachine gun across his chest and a holstered sidearm. Nolan recognized him from the previous interrogation. He had yet ever to hear the man speak. Bogdan nudged him forward, putting a massive bear paw in the middle of his shoulder blades. He began to pray against the fear creeping into his heart about the uncertainty of his future.

The three men followed the same path Nolan had taken to the interrogation chamber. Each time he tried to get a glimpse into some of the windowed cells Bogdan would shove him forward. He gazed into the jade hues of the cell windows and the captives contained therein. Most did not meet his eyes, but when an old man with a white mustache met his gaze and smiled at him, Nolan instinctively smiled back. Captivity had not beaten that man and Nolan continued to pray that neither would be defeated in the days ahead.

At last, they entered the door to the interrogation chamber except for this time the silent soldier gave way, not to a table and chairs but a small stepladder and a barrel of water. Nolan once again was shoved in the back pitching him into the room. As he stumbled, the muscle-bound Bogdan grabbed a handful of black hair and marched Nolan towards the tank.

Nearing the stepladder, Nolan fought back kicking the ladder from under his feet. The ladder clattered to the ground but not without bruising his unprotected feet. Bogdan rammed a knee into Nolan's chest driving the breath from his lungs. Then the two Russians hoisted him over the lip of the tank, his feet now flailing in the air searching for purchase.

Together the soldiers dunked Nolan's torso into the tank again and again. In between gasps, he cursed himself for being so stupid. The pounding he received courtesy of Bogdan had given him no breath before being plunged into the water. Now he thrashed for air to refill his lungs as his face surfaced.

Soon the questions started.

"Where is the man who sent you?"

"How many were sent to spy on this location?"

"What was the next stage of your plan?"

The questions came so rapidly the Nolan had little time to hear them before being launched back into the water.

Opening his mouth to speak they dropped him again, the icy water flooding his airways. The need for life-giving oxygen was so great, Nolan's whole body wracked itself in a coughing fit. The two Russians dropped him to the ground. His body rejected the water he had swallowed, throwing it up all over the concrete floor. His vision blurred, dark circles closing in.

"You are not a soldier. Why were you with the American insurgents?"

He shook his head. Bogdan gave him a swift kick to the abdomen. Nolan rolled over. The lone light bulb dangled from its wire. He thought of the colors that had surrounded Rachel.

Nolan smiled.

Bogdan smiled. "Are you ready to talk?"

Nolan shook his head.

Without assistance, Bogdan grabbed him by the lapels of his soaked jacket and threw him back into the water basin. Further, into the dark pit, he went. His nose connected with the bottom of the deep pool. Blood polluting the water in crimson. With one swift yank Nolan crashed back to the concrete floor. He gasped for air as the pain from his ribs was excruciating and made it hard to breathe. He knew he was going to die.

"Talk American," said Bogdan. He appeared in no rush to save Nolan's life as he flipped the cuffs of his jacket. The massive forearms tightened threatening to bust the jacket at the seams. Another swift kick to his abdomen and Nolan doubled over in the fetal position. Boots leading away and a screeching sound told Nolan that someone had opened the heavy door and left. He and Bogdan were alone.

"Come on Nolan. You can tell Uncle Bogdan. I'll even let others live if you tell me."

"Others," stammered Nolan. "I told you. I don't know anything." His plea earned a chortle but no kick. Bogdan helped Nolan get to his feet, his arm around him like an old friend.

"You believe in hope. I can tell. The tough ones always do and to tell you the truth American; they live the longest. It used to make me sad watching them die. They tried so hard to live, by prayer or by defiance. Whatever suited them. Now I'm not into that sick stuff but my friend Anton, he is cold. He's like a brother to me, but even I have nightmares about him."

Three hard knocks boomed into the dense room causing the water in the tank to ripple. Whatever resolve Nolan carried was fading fast. The waterboarding had broken him; the feeling of drowning almost enveloped him before ejection from the drum. He began to pray for further protection. When the door opened, two men entered, both dressed as soldiers. Nolan knew he was not prepared for what would come next.

8

When Mason Grey entered the room with the soldier called Anton, Nolan didn't know what to think. He nearly asked out loud whether Mason was there to betray him as well.

The Russians placed a thin, metallic chair in the center of the room. Anton bound Grey to the chair with a heavy black cord around his wrist and ankles.

Realizing they were going to torture Grey to get information from him, Nolan tried to move forward, but he was held by Bogdan. Anton stood in silence just behind the SAS operative.

Bogdan whispered, "You will now begin talking. Anything. Everything. If you don't begin talking, my friend Anton begins pumping lead into your captured colleague."

Nolan felt cold sweat splash down his spinal cord.

Mason Grey began thrashing, trying to loosen his bonds. He tried standing on the balls of his feet but having been spaced too far apart the soldier lost his balance and crashed to the ground. Anton clenched the neck of Grey's jacket and up righted his seating position. Now standing opposite of where he was before, Anton withdrew a Makarov pistol. The two Russian soldiers did not indicate being rushed. They were having fun.

"Speak Nolan."

"I told you already. I don't know anything!"

"Speak, or Anton puts a bullet in him!"

"Hargreaves tried to warn our leaders about Russia's power grab and what it could mean for the United States, but nobody would listen. He started finding people who agreed with him and brought them together. That's all he told me."

"How did he know to warn people about the sleeper cells?"

"He must- "

"Shut up Nolan! Don't give them anything! Ah-" Grey's warning was silenced as a shot rang out. The British veteran clamped his teeth down hard and tried to endure the pain. Nolan saw the round had punctured his right forearm, a through and through. Rather than keep quiet, he now desperately wanted to give them as much information as possible to save Grey more pain.

"He must have known. He would have been watching for signs of Russia's insurgency. Y'all were not very subtle when dealing with NATO or performing fly-bys. He must have known your nation was waiting for a weak spot to emerge to strike our entire nation."

He watched Anton replace the pistol across his chest and breathed a little more comfortable.

"How many underground cells is this Hargreaves in charge of operating? Whom have you made contact with?"

Nolan began to panic anew. "I- I don't know."

Another shot rang out. This time Grey could not stow it. Letting out a manacled scream, his cry sounded a bit like a bark inside the underground concrete walls. Blood seeped from under Grey's left foot. The commando tried desperately to reach his leg to stop the bleeding but to no avail. His bonds held tight.

"Please," Nolan begged. "I'm trying to help! The man didn't tell me anything. He didn't have to!"

Bogdan seethed with anger. "You're lying! You know something so speak!" Anton began to raise the gun again, slower this time, eyeing Nolan as he did so. He leveled the weapon off at Grey's head. Tears fell from Nolan's cheeks as he silently pleaded Grey's forgiveness.

Grey whistled through his teeth, his eyes locking on Nolan's. "No greater love than this, for one to give up his life for his friends. Nolan*, don't give up the ship*."

The shot rang out and Nolan feared the worst. This time, however, Grey let out such a high-pitched scream it didn't sound human. Great hands pulled Nolan past the bleeding soldier and out the door. "You appear to be telling the truth American. Since you are of no use to us, you will die a long, slow death in your cell. Think of it like being buried alive. As for your comrade, he too will die slowly and alone where no one can hear him scream."

Back in his cell, he worried about Mason Grey's fate. He lay on the floor for hours thinking about the Russian's cruelty and whether or not Grey was still alive or tortured further. Nolan knew that Grey was much more familiar with Hargreaves than himself. Grey was *Sine metu*. He possessed no fear, prepared to die rather than surrender to the enemy.

Nolan wished he were so steadfast. He wondered if now, at the greatest time of need, where God was. Nolan remembered praying, and the vision he received. He believed that as a sign he was going to be protected. That was before they dragged him out of his cell to be tortured and watch another man on the brink of losing his life. He felt abandoned by God. After all, he thought, *was not Jesus abandoned on the cross after praying in Gethsemane*?

9

"The American knows nothing." Bogdan shut the door and sat next to his brother. Yuri turned to look at the younger Orlov. The hulking warrior started to show fatigue but not from lack of rest. It was beginning to dawn on each soldier under Yuri's command that despite a near total annihilation of the United States, the soldiers themselves were alone, trapped in enemy territory. There were no more reinforcements. The Russian Air Force had nothing more to bomb, and the moles had failed in their mission to deceive the American people. Underground radio messages prompted survivors to turn against *rezidents* and fifth columnists posing as federal aid administrators. Now at the doorstep of American power they had also failed to cut the head off the snake. America's allies were guarding the seas. While Russia might rebuild after the terrible loss of government and culture, the United States too would rebuild.

Three days later Anton entered the small office. Although naturally melancholy, something in the operative's expression told Yuri that something was wrong. "Anton, what is it?"

"One of the mercenaries in section eight has failed to check in. Hungarian. Trustworthy."

Yuri reflected on what Anton was saying. Many of the mercenaries were prone to wander, unleashing their own precious form of torture on captured or stranded Americans. Persians were the most lethal. The Shi'a warriors imposed their will upon inhabitants of the once Great Satan. Like Gaul or Celtic warriors of the ancient world, the torture methods and tales of despair the Muslim mercenaries carried out were enough to make Yuri blanch. Mercenaries from former Eastern Bloc nations were much more stable and counted upon to retain professional discretion.

Looking up at Anton's dark eyes he asked if Anton had seen to the gap in security personally. The answer was negative. "Go see to it. If we need to raise the alarm, then notify me that instant."

Then the lights went out.

"Anton, see to the breach. Bogdan, find the American. He must be involved somehow." Both men nodded and rushed to carry out their orders. Anton cradled his submachine gun expecting heavy fire when he found the hole in their security. Bogdan withdrew both a Makarov pistol and tactical knife almost of their own volition, his Spetsnaz training operational without even needing to consult the brain for movement.

After covering each other down the short hallway, the two soldiers split as a Klaxon began to sound overhead. The sound was almost blinding in the dense halls, but it served to disorient the intruders. The two lifelong friends looked down their respective hallways towards one another and nodded a final goodbye. Bogdan raised two fingers first to his lips then saluted Anton's back as the smaller athletic soldier disappeared around the corner.

10

Anton felt more than heard the bullets whiz by his head. *Compressed weapons. Tight pattern. Professional.* He returned fire and retreated to the recesses of the building to draw his attacker into the open. He expected the incoming flashbang, closing his eyes and opening his mouth to release pressure from the shockwave. What he did not expect was for more compressed weapons fire to immediately follow the stun grenade's blast. He just managed to escape another barrage. Firing blind, he wondered how it was possible for the intruder not to be affected whatsoever by his grenade. It was impossible.

He slapped another magazine home and laid down suppressing fire to cover his retreat. Despite Olympic athleticism, Anton found himself breathing hard and sweating profusely. He knew the smell that emanated from his sweat and tried to choke down the implications. He was being hunted, and his body reeked the smell of fear.

The hunter was patient, waiting for Anton to make a mistake. He knew he had to turn the tables or suffer the consequences. Since he was close to the outside perimeter, he searched for the warehouse's loading bay. Bullets followed him down the corridor. Just before opening the bay's entrance Anton caught sight of his hunter. The figure dressed in all black including a black mask with red lenses.

Both men fired at each other. Retreating into the open room, Anton withdrew his secondary weapon. He doused the auxiliary lights, plunging the room into darkness. Turning to his right, he found a built-in ladder and climbed onto the scaffolding. The space stored numerous wooden crates and a pulley operated crane. Standing in the dark, he waited for his predator turned prey to enter.

The clicking of steel echoed through the room. Anton was ready for another flash. What happened instead was a red cloaking gas hissed through pores in the grenade, expanding throughout the dark room. Moving forward, he fired six successive bullets into the scarlet haze hoping to catch the hunter as he entered under the gas. To his great surprise, shots peppered the air and ricocheted off the metal around him as the hunter fired his semi-automatic.

Peering through the dissipating mist, Anton saw the eye sights of the hunter's mask glow a milky white. A heartbeat sensor! He ducked just in time as well-placed shots splintered the crates where his head had just been. This time he did not return fire. Still holding the high ground, Anton waited to make the most of his opportunity.

11

When his light went out, Nolan could not see the bulkhead door slide open, but he heard it. He threw his arms up expecting to be grabbed by the large Russian. Evidently, they were trying a new tactic on him. They were going to throw him into darkness, disorient him, and beat him. Perhaps they were going to push him down a flight of stairs.

Instead, no hands took hold of him. Sitting up, he saw several dark, human-like forms running past his cell. In the dim light, he could make out a multitude of prisoners as they ran from their cells.

When he emerged into the dark hall, he chose not to run in the direction of fleeing captives but instead pushed against the tide. He had to find Mason Grey.

Racing for the room used for interrogations, he rounded a corner as emergency strobe lights flashed. The corridor was empty. He knew he was getting closer. Turning another corner, flying debris struck him in the face.

He hadn't heard the gunshot. Peering around the whitewashed corner, Nolan saw the familiar figure blocking a set of doors that read: INFIRMARY. The giant Russian took up the entire entrance.

Bogdan.

Nolan hit the stairwell hoping to put distance between himself and his armed pursuer. Bolting up the steps, he crashed through the door, but a tool he was very familiar with caught his eye. Chancing for extra time, he broke the glass shield with his elbow and pulled the ax from its resting place. Shots rang through the narrow stairway as Bogdan charged in.

In the hallway, Nolan knew his weapon was still a far cry from a pistol, so he set about looking for a place to spring a trap. Turning to the nearest door, he entered a large classroom. In it was the perfect diversion.

Grabbing a marker, he sketched a human form on the projection screen and attached it to an easel. Easing his way to the door, his heart stopped as he heard the unmistakable metallic cinch of loading a fresh magazine. Bogdan was close.

Stealing himself for courage, Nolan kicked the door open and pushed the easel into the hallway. The wheels rolled with ease. Four shots rang out from close range. Knowing Bogdan would advance, Nolan escaped around a wall, waiting for him to enter.

12

Anton wondered where the other Spetsnaz and mercenaries were whose duty it was to patrol the perimeter of the facility. Being that he was in a loading bay, he figured the place should be flooded with men. He worried that the American response to their countrymen being captured was so overwhelming that there was no chance any Russian had of making it out alive.

His thoughts grew deeper as semi-automatic fire erupted from the other side of the room from the entrance. His hunter had circumvented the place and was now coming from behind him. One the one hand, he could sprint for the ladder and try to run out the only exit, but it would risk time and exposure. His hunter would waste no time putting a bullet through his head on the ladder. No, the only choice was to take the hunter on. Checking his magazine, he counted five rounds. Breathing deep, he thought of Immanuil. See you soon, brother.

Anton somersaulted into the open walkway firing as he did so. Hitting the ground running he rushed the hunter. The soldier emerged from behind a container. Anton hit the inside of his arm in time to send the bullet wide. He then shouldered the hunter into a shipping container and placed both hands on the remaining pistol.

In the darkness, twenty feet above the ground, the two warriors wrestled for control. Anton kicked the back of the hunter's knee causing the man to loosen his grip. Seizing the pistol, Anton tried to turn it on the man, but the hunter managed to release the clip. The slim magazine slipped through the metal scaffolding and clacked to the ground. With one bullet remaining in the chamber, the hunter squeezed Anton's finger, depressing the trigger and sending it harmlessly into a wooden crate.

One warrior equaled the other in size. Anton's body was harder, his training more ruthless. He twisted the pistol and swung it across the hunter's face, displacing the mask. The hunter was not down for the count yet however as he responded with two uppercuts into Anton's solar plexus causing the Russian to stumble backward.

Achieving separation, the hunter stepped away from Anton and assumed a loose fighting stance. Removing the broken mask, the hunter revealed a shock of black hair, thin, narrow eyes and a bulbous chin. Anton couldn't help but be confused.

"You're North Korean," stammered the Russian. "I thought you were with us."

"I escaped as a child from the oppressive regime that killed my family. Since then my name has been Samuel Park."

Anton pulled out a tactical knife and Park did the same drawing from behind his back and holding the handle in an underhand position.

Park waited for Anton to attack.

Throwing a faint, Anton made to rush Park, but as he pulled back, he released the knife with a flick of his wrist. The run-away Korean brought his right arm across his body to spin away from the darting blade but not in time. The blade sunk into the Korean hunter.

Not wanting to lose momentum Anton seized the knife buried in Park's shoulder but then howled in pain as the opponent's knife came down and struck home inside his thigh. Red-hot blood poured down his trousers as Park pulled up on the dagger, widening the wound. The two separated briefly to assess their damage and that of their enemy.

Each had a gaping wound punctuated by a knife in their tissue. Park seemed reluctant to pull the blade from his shoulder whereas Anton found he was losing the ability to stand. Neither man spoke.

Park marched on Anton. Despite the raging fire in his leg, Anton managed to fend off the Korean. He tried desperately to pry the knife from the man's back. With so much blood loss, he knew his clock was rapidly approaching midnight. Blocking another punch, Anton grabbed Park's wrist and head-butted him.

The Korean receded as if attacked by bees, a royal shiner already forming under his slanted right eye. The eyes themselves flashed in rage. Park bull rushed the Russian smashing him into the rail.

Seeing his last chance, Anton grabbed the knife and began to yank it from the muscle tissue. Park howled in pain as both stood up in unison, clinging to one another for support. Seeing his chance, Park reached inside Anton's arms and unleashed with the fury of a hurricane. Anton's hand closed on the knife handle but had no strength to withdraw it from the Korean's back as no less than twenty-five successive blows connected with his torso tenderizing him like meat.

Park stepped away from Anton as his body slumped once more. But then the Korean rushed again, smashing him against the rail.

Anton struggled to stand, blood flowing from his mouth. Wiping his chin, he knew one more blow would do it before the end came. He smiled at the darkness, his body beaten so severely he knew of little else to do.

When the Korean moved in, he moved so fast Anton was defenseless. He took a crushing blow to the chest as both boots hammered his body sending him over the rail.

Twenty feet below Anton tried to raise his head but found that he could not move. His legs and arms felt as if they were no longer a part of his body but rather just a memory. He heard the Korean's boots slide closer to where his body lay and felt the hunter's presence grow nearer. At last, his eyes found Park's. The man showed no sign of pain save a glint of blood running down his arm.

Park nodded to Anton, but Anton could not return the gesture. Then he left.

13

Bogdan hammered his way into the classroom but checked his fire. Keeping the pistol in front of him, he strafed to the open portion of the room on his right. Nothing in the place moved and yet he could feel the presence of another. He knew it was the American that he gave chase. He also knew the American didn't have time to run further. He was in the room.

The room was dark, but lights from the outside shone through the large windows casting everything in shadow. Bogdan wished he had brought a flashlight with him. Or a submachine gun. With a thirty-round burst, he could obliterate all the hiding places in the room. Instead, he was limited to shot choice.

Nolan could hear the massive Russian's footfalls as he cleared the room. Hiding, he knew it was a matter of time before the door opened. He stood away from the door with the ax raised high, ready to swing.

Bogdan inched towards the broom cupboard. The door was shut. He figured the space too narrow for the American to maneuver around much inside. Still, in a pinch, the closet would have made a desperate hiding place to an untrained civilian. He took careful aim in the dark and squeezed off four rounds forming a diamond shape in the closet door.

Nolan heard the booms of the pistol's discharge as the noise reverberated off the walls. Instinctively he cowered lower in his stance but tried not to make any sound.

The Russian kicked open the closet door, the wood splintering. To his chagrin, no American body lay dead at his feet. Turning on the balls of his feet, he felt a surging rage build inside him. Despite his training, pure genetics took over. Bogdan cursed the American aloud, picked up the closest desk and threw it across the room. The desk struck an overhead projector, shattering the glass lamps. Approaching the next one, he turned it over. Kicking more as he made his way across the room, he lost all control. Seeing red, he threw open the double exit doors and stopped dead in his tracks.

Nolan's father loved baseball. He admired the Arkansas Razorbacks and St. Louis Cardinals. Most evenings when weather permitted Pierce Hoke would drag his young son into the yard to play catch. Often, Marjorie Hoke had to ring the bell several times to signal time for supper. Though tall, Nolan was lean like his father and neither Hoke boy could swing the bat like a major leaguer.

As Bogdan stormed across the empty classroom, Nolan choked up on the ax handle and positioned his feet to swing. Closing his eyes, he relived every evening of catch and batting practice in nothing more than a heartbeat. When the Russian crashed through the double doors, he swung the ax with the force of each memory. Turning from the hip, the ax blade buried itself deep in the hulking man's chest. Nolan released the ax handle, his hands still clenched as Bogdan collapsed straight backward like a domino. The Russian never moved again.

More doors burst open. Shouts rang throughout the hall. Caught by surprise, Nolan had no chance of escape as men in black fatigues poured from both sides of the corridor.

"Cease fire! Cease fire!"

Flashlights mounted on special weapons systems covered him from head to toe, but no one pulled the trigger. One black-clad soldier lowered his weapon and tore the Velcro off his shoulder. The shoulder sewn flag beneath the patch was the stars and stripes of the United States. The cavalry had come.

"Nolan," said a familiar voice. "We've come to get you and everyone else home." The soldier stepped into the light and removed his mask. Hargreaves.

Nolan filled with tons of questions as he followed the soldiers back down the stone steps to the ground level. Someone had even found his boots and a pair of socks. Stringing the laces up just the way he liked, he saw Samuel Park approaching him through the crowd. "Did you find Grey," he asked.

Park smiled at first, seeing his friend but grief soon replaced it. The Korean hung his head. "We will give him a soldier's burial." The rest was best if left unsaid.

Park reached down to pull Nolan from the Infirmary steps. A young, curly-haired girl with ebony skin ran out the hospital door. "Mama! Mama!" she cried. Nolan tracked the little girl as she ran to a tall, intelligent looking woman pushing against the multitude. She wore a lab coat with an even younger child on her hip. Nolan assumed the woman had been helping in the Infirmary. So many had entered captivity wounded and were only now getting proper treatment. With the facility in safe hands, everyone rushed for freedom.

"Addae Philips! What am I going to do with you?" admonished the mother. Something about the small family, another daughter stood nearby, pulled at Nolan and he started making his way to them.

"Can I help you, ma'am?" asked Nolan. He was already taking the middle girl's hand in his own.

"Thank you. Lord have mercy, thank you. Please, will you help me get my daughters out of here?"

"Yes, ma'am."

"Oh, I wish Tom were here."

The comment gave Nolan a new heart rhythm. He peered at the woman, recognition dawning on him. "You what ma'am?"

"My husband, Tom. Tom Philips. He would know what to do."

Nolan recalled the vision where he saw Tom and Rachel on the beach. What was it Tom had said? *Watch over my girls?*

"If y'all follow me, ma'am, the soldiers will help us get to safety." He took Addae in his arms. She cradled her own around his neck. "Stay close."

As the multitude escaped the prison, he could feel the fresh, euphoric air against his face. Soldiers lined the corridors, guarding the exodus. They followed hundreds, scaling the Capitoline Hill as dawn awakened. Below, a blackened city rested. Above, bursts of reds, oranges, and yellows streaked across the sky.

In the distance, he saw the pockmarked walls of the White House and perched high above, the nation's flag.

Every face, brightened by the rising sun, turned and *in the dawn's early light, that Star Spangled Banner did yet wave.*

EPILOGUE

1

The lectern beckoned, but he was not yet ready to address the resurrected nation. A soft drizzle fell from slate grey heavens. The hallowed ground of Arlington National Cemetery shone green against the bleak backdrop of a damaged city, a ruined country. Below the podium, dozens of dignitaries, soldiers, and politicians, all mourners, sat on collapsible chairs beneath a black canopy of dripping umbrellas.

Reluctantly, Benjamin Hargreaves approached the rostrum. A faint light glowed over a now dampened speech draft. Microphones from the key networks fought like weeds to broadcast his speech over the radio waves to millions across the land and millions more across the globe. He gripped the wooden stand with both hands before eyeing the somber crowd.

"Love your neighbor as yourself. God in human form spoke these words of kindness more than two millennia ago to instruct His followers and guide them when they felt wronged. Before we say goodbye to my friend Mason Grey, I would like to take a moment to talk about another man who when the forces of Hitler's tyranny threatened our sovereign ally, Great Britain, he answered the global call to love his neighbor as himself."

"William M. Fiske III is not buried here although he was an American fighter pilot. After an Olympic career, he was the first American to join the Royal Air Force, died in the service of the British on August 16, 1940, before the United States had entered what we now know as World War II. Inscribed in St.

Paul's Cathedral, his plaque reads, 'An American who died so that England might live.' Love your neighbor as yourself."

"Today we Americans are still called Americans and gather to honor Mason Grey who in many ways resembled William Fiske. When I met Mason, he was part of a counterinsurgency team hoping to give the world a light to follow in the shadow of fear cast by international terrorism. He lost many great friends and sacrificed much so that others may live, a creed I lived by during my time as a Pararescue of the United States Air Force. After our meeting, Mason became a deep friend of mine and somebody I knew I could rely on when the forces of oppression once again looked to wrap their fingers around global freedom and brotherhood. Today we bury my friend, an English citizen who died so that America might live, as a reminder of the ultimate sacrifice given to love one's neighbor as himself."

Hargreaves paused to look down the podium as the color guard fired a military twenty-one-gun salute while pallbearers spread a heavy woven Union Jack across Grey's coffin as his coffin lowered into the watery sod grave. When the band of bagpipers had finished, America's newest leader gazed into the faces of the crowd. Some were somber, but many more stood sat resolute.

"Love your neighbor as yourself. As former President Ronald Reagan said about the forces of tyranny, 'Regimes planted by bayonets do not take root.' When a coalition of military forces under the leadership of the former Russian Federation sought to murder and subdue our great nation, they found their objective impossible to complete. This too is reminiscent of warfare, in a time of antiquity, when the gates of a young Roman Republic were under siege by a superior enemy. Hannibal Barca, one of history's greatest commanders, did the unthinkable by crossing the Alps with a fighting force made up of war elephants surprising Roman generals who were woefully unprepared to meet such superior force and intellect. His army of mercenaries and professional warriors ransacked the nation whose destiny was to rule the known world. Hannibal's forces pillaged city after city, but one thing they failed to do was break the resolve of the Roman people."

"Through great sacrifice and untold loss of life, Roman citizens all over the Italian peninsula refused to concede defeat and greater still, refused to turn against one another. Love your neighbor as yourself. Centuries later, Romans would carry this tradition as they swore allegiance to the Empire, a tradition that Americans would later model when we pledge allegiance to the flag, indivisible! The American people did not abandon one another but stood strong in the face of adversity and overwhelming odds against a superior enemy. When we stand together, neither deception nor force can overcome us. When we stand united, we stand as a nation of liberty and justice for all. Love your neighbor as yourself."

The wind lapped at his notes and umbrellas swayed. Every eye remained fixed on him. He could not tell from the distance, but many of the men and women in attendance sat straighter, their jaws forming hard lines to round out their faces. Many cheeks glistened with tears.

"I stand here, as the second appointed President in our nation's continued history, a precedent not invoked since our nation's birth. Like George Washington, I too will promise to step down after a four-year term." Hargreaves looked down at his notes surmising his first official state of the union address.

"During these next four years, a lot will be asked of you, the American people, and the international community. We must rebuild. Though burned, we must produce food to feed not only ourselves but also those in hunger. Though broken, we must forge products that ensure the daily lives of citizens preserve a high quality of life. Though bleeding, we must administer aid and medicine to the global community to give hope to future generations that will inherit the earth. The United States of

America must once again be a beacon as our global partners, and we, seek to rise from the ashes."

Taking a drink of water, he caught Nolan's eye in the front row before Grey's open grave. Seeing him here brought him back to the final stages of the Russian prison operation. After securing the great soldier Bogdan, he and Nolan had parted ways. Leading a team back into the depths of the prison, they encountered Commander Yuri Orlov. With the team standing outside the bulkhead with a flashbang at the ready there came the unmistakable sound of a gunshot. He had entered first.

The Russian leader lay on the cold concrete floor, a Makarov in his hand, bleeding from a self-inflicted wound in the stomach. As the dying man lay in Hargreaves' arms, he said, "At last my Scipio has come."

Then he died.

A quick glance at Sheila Townsend, his handpicked Vice President, gave Hargreaves the confidence to press on with the hardest part of the meticulously prepared speech.

"Last of all, I ask that we adhere to another of Christ's principle in regards to our enemy. Growing up in a shame-based society, when one is struck, the honorable response is to strike back harder, to defend one's good name. But Christ said to His disciples to turn the other cheek. As our nation rebuilds, I will ask the American people to love their neighbors as themselves and forgive the Russian people and her allies across the globe that sought an evil decree against us and freedom everywhere."

As predicted, the crowd began to stir. Some who were sitting stood up. Some who were standing shook their hands or raised a fist in anger. Some who were on the fringes began to look for a sub rosa retreat. President Hargreaves held up a firm hand to silence the crowd. With some hesitation, those in attendance began to regain composure allowing him to continue his address.

"Love your neighbor as yourself. Our nation has carried a dark legacy and will continue to do so as the only nation to authorize the launch of nuclear warheads that were manufactured by our scientists on another sovereign nation. The cities of Moscow and St. Petersburg, with populations the size of many of our states, are no more. Centers of government and culture have forever vanished off the map. Articles and relics of history are lost. As an officer in the Air Force, I had the opportunity to spend time with men and women who had lived on the International Space Station. Apart from living in close quarters with several different nationalities, they had the unique opportunity to look outside themselves and see the world as a whole. I remember one of the members saying to me once, 'You know when I see the earth from that distance I realize just how small it is. In the right spot, I can almost see every ocean at once with all those peoples in between. Egypt, India, Mongolia. Nations great and small have no borders, no individualities, just all humans living on the same small planet.' Ladies and gentlemen, the United States has a responsibility to take part in the international community. To quote Emma Lazarus' *The New Colossus* which adorns our now bullet-ridden Statue of Liberty, the United States of America is still the Mother of Exiles. *Give us your tired, your poor, Your huddled masses yearning to breathe free.* We have one planet and one chance. Love your neighbor as yourself. Thank you and may God bless us all."

President Hargreaves turned and descended from the lectern into the dark tunnel. The final sounds came from the echo of his footsteps, the light smattering of rain and the voice of a small girl who began to sing *Nearer My God to Thee.*

2

Registers pinged, change dropped, and paper bags crinkled. In Asheville, North Carolina semblances of consumerism and a market economy grew just as they were all across the United States. Many of the older patrons often wondered if the day's society resembled life as it had much in the 1960s, a time only remembered in history class. Shiny new cars gleamed in the vast parking lot revealed by full, clean windows. Smiling faces greeted neighbors pushing shopping carts, holding children, or sitting along one of the wooden benches. Everything ran a little slower in the forty-five years hence America's near collapse. There were no credit card machines, no self-checkouts, and not as many people to run daily operations.

Rafe Hollander walked at a brisk pace through the throng of patrons. His wife diagnosed herself with morning sickness. He had rushed out of the house to get medicine while using the time to clear his head. The linoleum floor squeaked under rubber-soled shoes as he spun around the aisle narrowly avoiding an elderly couple. The old woman gasped and dropped their ice cream, but her husband caught it. The older generations seemed to be made of stronger reflexes and were a little more conservative than those of Rafe's age. Theirs was a generation that had known life before the invasion and had forged a new nation out of the rubble. He had been but a boy from Bristol yet he too still had nightmares of explosions from time to time.

With milk, cereal, and medicine cradled in his arms, Rafe made for the cash registers guarding the exit. Each checkout was the same. Some teenager stood at the register with a matured bagger to organize the purchased items. The shortest line was the one closest to the exit and Rafe hurried to be next. When the cheery girl behind the register bent over to grab spilled quarters, he groaned to himself. He now noticed the reason why her line was the shortest was that the other patrons had sensibly avoided the girl's bagging partner. Despite his tall, broad stature, the old man had such rounded shoulders it looked as if Atlas had set the world down to weigh upon him; the weight of time and memory. His movements were slow. Methodical. Rafe thought he saw the old man's mouth moving as though talking to himself. The lady in line grabbed her bags, thanked the young girl and pushed her cart through the double doors.

"Rafe, I don't remember seeing y'all in church yesterdee." He turned around to see his friend and card-playing buddy. The man was also the manager of the grocery store.

"Oh, hey there. Nah, Veronica is sick." He lowered his voice. "She may be pregnant."

The manager smiled wide. "We knew it! Mallory mentioned it to me after y'all left the other night. She had already figured out that Veronica may be expecting."

Rafe smiled too. "I guess women just seem to know a lot faster than men do."

"Ain't that the truth?"

The two men stood in silence for a while, the line still stagnant. "Say," ventured Rafe. "That old man bagging the groceries. What's his story?"

The manager followed Rafe's gaze. "Oh, you mean old man Hoke?" Then the manager went quiet for a while. The next person in line moved. The two men automatically shuffled forward. Rafe would be next, so the manager lowered his voice. "Nolan is a war hero. He's not from here, but he fought when our town was under siege. He saved a lot of people's lives. I don't know how many living now still remember. Some of the older folks still stand up to shake his hand when he walks by, but we were just kids then you know?"

"Does he have any family here?"

The manager swallowed a little. "He could have, but she died. He never loved another. Some say that's why he talks. He's talking to her. Her and God."

"You don't think he's crazy," Rafe asked.

The manager smiled, a small gleam forming in his young eyes. "I think we all owe him a debt of gratitude. Keeping him on board is just my small contribution." He clapped Rafe on the back. "Looks like your next. Give Veronica our best and congratulations on the baby."

Rafe smiled, joy infusing his body at the thought of a newborn baby. Would it be a boy or a girl? What would they name it? "Alright, you take care now Silas."

When his shift was over, the old man Hoke shook hands with the elderly folks as was their custom. The automated glass doors opened allowing the sun's rays to shine down on him as he waddled across the pavement.

Hewn from local timber, the house he built was taking a long time for him to paint it. Coming onto the porch, his hounds, Grey and Gruff, raised their noses to greet him. Nolan petted each in kind along the snout and behind the ears. The old dogs didn't roll over as much anymore.

Once inside, he lowered the leather straps that helped him tote his groceries onto the farmhouse table. The opened windows allowed the breeze to blow the curtains and tablecloth. He put the milk in the icebox then shuffled past the bedroom to the spare room where he kept his books. Most he confiscated after the war from Professor Gruff's study and others gathered over the decades. Still trying to make sense of Livy and even Gibbon, he enjoyed the works of Hemingway, Faulkner or London.

The wooden floorboards creaked underfoot while he selected a leather-backed novel and made his way back onto the porch. The screen door slammed shut as he settled into the rocking chair. A faded flag blew in the soft breeze over a wheatgrass yard before a color-filled sunset.

Giving Back

Just as the fictional Hargreaves told his operators that he served more than just a nation, I believe that America is temporary. While our nation is great, it is not destined for eternity.

That being said, since I was a boy, I have always been enthralled with the service and sacrifice of our nation's heroes. In my mind, "the service" is the most appropriate term for men and women who are trained, dedicated warriors, both near and far, to serve and protect our nation and its people.

Just as the fictional Tiberius found a wounded Titus in the veteran's hospital, I wanted to find a way to give back to those who have given, and been wounded, in service to our nation.

10% of every copy sold will be donated directly to Disabled American Veterans.org. DAV is dedicated to empowering veterans to lead high-quality lives with respect and dignity. This non-profit provides a lifetime of support for veterans of all generations and their families.

For more information on Disabled American Veterans visit: www.dav.org

Acknowledgements

My first attempt at writing a novel would not have been possible without continued encouragement from various family members over the years. My wife Becca who would allow me use of our one computer when she could. She got the first read and always encouraged me to "keep going." To my parents, Lance and Tracy, and Becca's parents, Jon and Lori, for putting up with stories of my ideas and helping me continue this pursuit. To BB and Papa for bestowing me with the tools of this trade. To my brothers, sisters, and grandparents for being so excited to have a copy in their hands. To the Saunders family, Prudes, Whites, Hills, Williamsons, Rice family and the Clark clan for all your support in my writing.

Author's Note

The inspiration for this book began shortly after my wife and I were married in late 2013. I taught high school history at a private Christian school in Bethlehem. Being surrounded with so much history, both ancient and current, was truly humbling.

The idea that I could try my hand at writing began with many friends and family back home telling me how much they enjoyed our monthly updates. The seed was planted to start writing for fun. I have always enjoyed survival, dystopian, or post-apocalyptic tales.

The latest trend seemed to be the Fall of America via a rogue EMP, or electro-magnetic pulse to shut down the grid. While plausible and dangerous, the characters in many stories inevitably commandeered the situation with their preparation and foremost knowledge. I began to envision ways around this common plot.

Following the headlines surrounding ISIS, Russian annexation, and tension in Ukraine, I developed a plot that I hoped would be original, albeit fantastic. Four years later, the plot is not as original as I intended but I do hope readers follow the trials of the characters as they rely on one another and react to play the hand they are dealt rather than overcoming via advanced tactics and preparation.

For my own enjoyment, and hopefully the readers as well, I included multiple references to Ancient Rome and World War II. Two eras of history rich with personal and collective impact but especially in how they continue to forge the United States. If you are interested in a full bibliography or a list of references, please check out my Facebook page.

If you enjoyed any of the themes in this story, then please consider adding your thoughts and a positive review via the book's page on Amazon.

For future works, please visit me on Facebook @lathamchamberswriter or drop me a line at lathamchamberswriter@gmail.com

May the God of hope fill you with all joy and peace as you believe in Him, so that you may overflow with hope by the power of the Holy Spirit.
    -Romans 15:13

Made in the USA
Lexington, KY
13 August 2018